YOUTH
IN
REVOLT

AIVIA
PRESS 223A9

YOUTH
IN
REVOLT

The Journals of Nick Twisp
Volumes I, II, III
(Youth in Revolt • Youth in Bondage • Youth in Exile)

C.D. Payne

AIVIA Press • Sebastopol, California

Manufactured in the United States of America.

FIRST EDITION

10 9 8 7 6 5 4 3 2

An Otis Knickerbocker book

Cover art by C.D. Payne

Library of Congress Cataloging-in-Publication Data
Payne, C.D. (C. Douglas), 1949-
     Youth in revolt: the journals of Nick Twisp / C.D. Payne. -- 1st ed.
        p.   cm.
     Contents: v. 1. Youth in revolt -- v. 2. Youth in bondage -- v. 3. Youth in exile.
     ISBN 1-882647-00-9 : $24.95
     1. Title
     PS3566.A9358Y68 1993
     813' .54--dc20   92-41439
                    CIP

To Joy

BOOK I

YOUTH IN REVOLT

JULY

WEDNESDAY, July 19 — My name is Nick. Someday, if I grow up to become a gangster, perhaps I will be known as Nick the Prick. This may cause some embarrassment for my family, but when your don gives you your mafia sobriquet you don't ask questions.

I am 14 years old (nearly) and live in Oakland, a large torpid city across the bay from San Francisco. I am writing this in the tenuous privacy of my bedroom on my annoyingly obsolete AT clone. My friend Lefty gave me a bootleg copy of WordPerfect, so I'm doing some writing to try and learn the command codes. My ambition is someday to be able to move entire paragraphs in a single bound.

My last name, which I loathe, is Twisp. Even John Wayne on a horse would look effeminate pronouncing that name. As soon as I turn 21 I'm going to jettison it for something a bit more macho. Right now, I'm leaning toward Dillinger. "Nick Dillinger." I think that strikes just the right note of hirsute virility.

I am an only child except for my big sister Joanie, who has left the bosom of her family to live in Los Angeles and sling hash at 35,000 feet.

The next thing you should know about me is that I am obsessed with sex. When I close my eyes, ranks of creamy thighs slowly part like some X-rated Busby Berkeley extravaganza. Lately I have become morbidly aware of my penis. Once a remote region accessed indifferently for businesslike micturition, it has developed—seemingly overnight—into a gaudy Las Vegas of the body, complete with pulsing neon, star-studded floor shows, exotic animal acts, and throngs of drunken conventioneers perpetually on the prowl for depraved thrills. I walk about in a state of obsessive expectancy, ever conscious of an urgent clamor rising from my tumescent loins. Any stimulus can trigger the show—a rhythmic rumble from the radiator, the word "titular" in a newspaper editorial, even the smell of the old vinyl in Mr. Ferguson's Toyota.

As much as I think about sex, I can only with extreme difficulty conceive of myself actually performing the act. And here's another thing I wonder about. How could you ever look a girl in the eye after you've had your winkie up her wendell? I mean, doesn't that render normal social conversation impossible? Apparently not.

THURSDAY, July 20 — My mother just left for work. She gives people driver's tests at the Department of Motor Vehicles. As you might expect, she is extremely well informed on all the arcane rules of the road (like who has to back up when two cars meet on a one-lane mountain road). She used to keep Dad up-to-date as he drove along on all the motor statutes he was violating. That's one of the reasons they got divorced.

I'm not speaking to her right now. Last Monday I came back from two miserable days in my dad's custody to find she had painted my bedroom a ghastly pink. She said she had read this color was widely used in hospitals to calm mental patients. I told her I wasn't mentally ill, I was just a teenager. Meanwhile, I am now embarrassed to invite my friends over. When you're a slight, unathletic teen who reads a lot and likes Frank Sinatra, you really don't want the word to get around that you wank your winkie in a room that looks like Dolly Parton's boudoir.

FRIDAY, July 21 — I got a headache from reading, so I thought I'd try typing for a while. I'm still using the F3 (help) key a lot. Too bad life doesn't have an F3 key. I'd press it and tell them to send over two chicks—sixteen years old and more than usually horny.

This summer I'm reading Charles Dickens. I've read *David Coppertone, Great Expectorations, Little Dorrito,* and now I'm deep into *A Tale of Two Townies.* Sidney Carton is so cool. If he were alive today I believe he would be endorsing fine scotch on the backs of magazines. I like Chuck a lot, but let's face it, you could read him for years and never come to a dirty part.

I am boning up (you'll pardon the expression) on Dickens in anticipation of taking Miss Satron's English Literature class next term. I'm going be in the ninth grade at St. Vitus Academy. This, they tell the parents, is the most elite and rigorous prep school in the entire East Bay. Only 40 scholarly wankers are admitted each year from literally dozens of applications.

Ravishing Miss Satron has wonderful bone structure and wears tight sweaters. She is also said to be extremely well read. Needless to say, she looms like a titan in my masturbatory fantasies.

I am back to talking to my mother (my birthday is coming up soon). She says she will buy new paint for my bedroom, but I have to apply it myself. (Personally, I'd prefer a tasteful decoupage of *Hustler* outtakes.) She's suggesting off-white this time, but I'm insisting on manly khaki.

SUNDAY, July 23 — Dad was supposed to pick me up at 10 a.m. for some father-son bonding experiences. At 11:15 Mom called his rented bachelor's bungalow and found him still in bed. (Doubtless with his latest bimbette.) Mom give him one of her canned high-volume diatribes. At 12:10 he screeched into the driveway, blasting the horn.

The drive over to Marin went about as I expected. First, you should know Dad pilots a leased BMW 318i (the cheap one). He would dearly love to move up to a more prestigious model, but—as he often reminds me—he is burdened with crippling child-support payments. In the journey of 16 miles he changed lanes 82 times, honked the horn seven times, and flipped the bird to four drivers (mostly confused old ladies). Dad is more cautious with men now after he was chased for 15 miles on the Nimitz freeway by a carfull of Iranians swinging lead pipes out the windows.

In between the scary moments, I tried to make conversation with Lacey, Dad's latest bimbette. She is 19, a newly minted alumna of Stanfort (with a "t") Institute of Cosmetology, and voluptuous in the extreme. Since I am frighteningly inarticulate around girls, I force myself to practice with Dad's bimbettes. Lacey, however, seemed more interested in laughing like a maniac and urging my father to "step on it, honey! Make that turbo scream!"

When we got to Kentfield, I learned that not only did Dad not have any activities planned, he wanted me to mow his damn lawn. For free! "Why?" said Dad, "because, pal, I'd like to have something to show for my $583 a month in child support besides a cancelled check." How about a loving relationship with your only son, you creep!

Finally, I agreed to do it for $5, pointing out that a gardener would charge at least $50. "Yeah," said Dad, "but you're not Japanese."

While I was gassing up the mower, Lacey came out on the patio in a weensy bikini for some al fresco power tanning. You didn't have to be a geologist to see that her body has more dramatic outcroppings than the coastline of Albania. Later, Dad came out and invited Lacey in for a "nap." Like all of Dad's bimbettes, she didn't have to be asked twice. As they were going in, arm-in-arm, I detected what looked to me like a smug glance in my direction from Dad. What a competitive asshole! Perhaps that's why I'm so uncompetitive. I've curbed my aggressiveness in reaction to his relentless excesses. Fortunately, I am writing all these revelations down in a notebook for use someday when I go into analysis. They should prove a real timesaver.

I just remembered. I never got my five bucks!

MONDAY, July 24 — Today I finished *A Tale of Two Sissies*. What a noble and moving sacrifice. Could I ever perform such a deed for the woman I love? Probably not.

Since my pile of reading material had dwindled dangerously, I went to the library. I arrived to find the building full of unwashed people talking to themselves. Why do the homeless take such a keen interest in literature? Will this be my destiny someday? Reading Turgenev while residing in the back seat of a '72 Dodge Polara?

One particularly repellent fellow asked me for a quarter. I gave him my standard reply: "I hear McDanold's is hiring." Not very compassionate, but what do you expect from the spoiled offspring of two would-be yuppies?

The atmosphere was so dreary, I came back without a book. I'd go to the bookstores in Berkeley, but Dad is late (as usual) with my allowance—penurious as it is. I have 63 cents to my name.

TUESDAY, July 25 — Nothing in the house to read except *California Farmer* magazine. We get this because Dad is a copywriter for an obscure ad agency in

Marin that handles agricultural accounts. Were he free of familial responsibilities, Dad would be in Paris, penning a Lasting Work of Important Fiction. Instead, he goads bug-fearing farmers into despoiling the earth (and their Mexican farmworkers) with mega-death herbicides. I was fooling around in Dad's office one day and discovered his thesaurus fell open naturally to entry 360: "Death — noun."

I wrote this poem about his plight:

A writer of promise named Dad
Is quite literarily mad;
His kids are so grasping
They've made him a has been.
Now the hack bends his muse to an ad.

What a congenial form of poesy is the limerick. I believe it is the only form that is certain to endure.

Noting I was bored, Mom suggested I go over to the park and find a pick-up game of basketball. She is, of course, completely out of her mind. Short honkie teens do not play basketball on the public courts of Oakland.

WEDNESDAY, July 26 — One more week to my birthday. Mom finally asked me what I wanted. "A 386 motherboard," I replied firmly and decisively. Most of the members of Byte Backers (St. V's computer club) have already upgraded. Some even have 586s!

She looked doubtful. "That sounds like something else for your computer. You spend too much time at that machine. You should get outside in the fresh air. Have some fun."

"Doing what?" I asked. "Stealing rebounds from future NBA stars?"

She told me to watch my smart mouth. I've heard that line before.

FRIDAY, July 28 — My friend Lefty called up to say he was back from his vacation in Nice. (I'll be lucky if we go to Modesto for ours.) I invited him over, but cautioned him that if word got out I had a pink bedroom, I would be forced to tell Millie Filbert (who he's had a crush on for years) why he's called Lefty even though he is right-handed.

In case you haven't heard, Lefty's erect member takes a sudden and dramatic turn to the east about midway up the shaft. Although this worries him a lot, he's never been able to bring it up (so to speak) with his parents.

"It would kill them to know I even get hard-ons," Lefty says. He worries this abnormality will lead to targeting errors when he gets older. "What if I shove it up the wrong hole?" Lefty's grasp of female anatomy is somewhat tenuous; he imagines there are orifices galore down there.

Meanwhile, he pursues a treatment of his own devising. Every night before going to bed he tapes his dick to his right leg. Then, lying in bed, he mentally undresses Millie—thus putting counter-rotational tension on the shaft. So far, this has not straightened out the bow.

After telling me about his trip (strange food, unintelligible natives, cute girls without tops arrayed like cordwood on sunny beaches), he got to the real news: he has found his older sister Martha's diary. And a real page-turner it is. She writes she "went all the way" with Carlo, an Italian waiter at their hotel in France. And did a few other semi-kinky things with him as well. Now all she can do is "think about sweet fat cock." Under this sizzling confession, Lefty has pencilled in: "For a good time, call Nick Twisp," followed by my phone number.

I'm ready if she calls. My Conduit Of Carnal Knowledge may not be particularly "fat," but it probably qualifies under a broad definition of "sweet." And I'm sure I'm better read than that guy Carlo.

AUGUST

TUESDAY, August 1 — Tomorrow I will be 14. A milestone in any man's life. Time for some serious stock taking. The issue can no longer be ignored: I am still a virgin. To be honest I have never even kissed a woman to whom I was not related by blood or marriage. In fact, I have never even held a girl's hand. Nor do I have any immediate prospects for finding myself digitally, oscularly, or genitally linked.

Since my last birthday I have gained a total of three and one-quarter inches—two and one-half inches in height and three-quarter inch in erect penis length. If it were all the same to my DNA, I'd just as soon those figures were reversed. I am still struggling to reach six inches, while Lefty has already sprouted past seven inches. To be sure, less of his growth effort is being devoted to mental development. Still, if I am not destined to be tall or good-looking, it's only fair that I be granted some compensatory phallic elongation. At the very least, I should be spared the ravages of adolescent acne. (My face is beginning to resemble a pepperoni and eyeballs pizza.) I think they should take some of the billions they're throwing away on dandruff cures and cancer research, and apply it to really important matters—like wiping out the scourge of acne.

WEDNESDAY, August 2 — Happy birthday to me. Thirteen was a crummy age; let's hope 14 is an improvement. So far it's been a real scrotum squeezer.

Mom gave me $20 this morning to get my hair cut. She likes me to get it professionally styled in a salon where they play loud rock music. That way I can come out looking like a successful real estate agent, junior division. Instead, I go to the $9 places and pocket the change. (I feel I am still too young to tip.) So I'm sitting there, minding my own business, when the barber says, "By the way, did anyone ever tell you you're going to be bald by the age of 30?"

What! Yes, it seems all signs point to a clear diagnosis of incipient male-pattern baldness. But, I protest, my dad still has all (well most) of his hair. "No matter," replies the learned barber, "baldness is inherited through the mother's side." Terror paralyzes me as I remember Uncle Al's acres of clear-cut scalp. Apparently, I am going to grow up to be a short, pock-marked bald guy. My only hope for enjoying any intimate female companionship at all is to obtain great wealth—as quickly as possible. That's it for literature. It's get-rich-quick books for me from now on.

All this was so depressing, I had to go to Rasputin Records and buy two Frank Sinatra albums (both from the '60s when he could still sing). The clerks are so condescending when you're not buying the latest output of the Moist

Panties, Puking Libidos, or other such heroin-addicted, heavy metal group. So I always tell them my purchase is a gift for my aunt in Cleveland. Personally, I feel the world would be a much better place if every radio station played Frank's version of "My One and Only Love" at least once an hour. Fat chance!

Then, after dinner Mom brought out this gaily wrapped package that was precisely the right size and shape to contain a 386 motherboard. Eagerly, I tore off the wrapping, ripped open the box, and stared in stunned disbelief. An official Rodney "Butch" Bolicweigski first baseman's glove! Thanks, Mom. Just what I always wanted. Another mitt for my closet. I now have enough gear to equip a triple-A ball team.

Mom persists in believing I will someday bring glory to the family on the playing fields of a grateful nation. Have I confessed to her that I'm always the last guy picked when they choose up sides? Yes. Have I abased my manhood by admitting to my mother that I throw like a girl? Yes. Does she listen? No! Just keep giving me mitts and someday I'll turn into Rollie Fingers. What I can't understand, if she wanted to breed jocks, why did she mate with a dork like Dad? He needs professional coaching just to pull a jockstrap on straight.

11:50 p.m. My birthday is almost over. No call or card from Dad. I am squeezing a zit on my chin the size of metropolitan Fresno.

THURSDAY, August 3 — Our neighbor, Mr. Ferguson, brought over three birthday cards for me that had been delivered to his house by mistake. The postman for this neighborhood shuffles through his route in a drug-induced haze. I suspect he even snorts his dog repellent.

Card Number One, from a prominent Marin advertising man, contained a check for $15 (no doubt an impressive sum back when he was a troubled teen). Card Number Two, from a voluptuous Marin hairdresser, contained a full-frontal Polaroid of the sender in her most revealing swim togs. I have seldom been so deeply moved. Timidly, I allow myself to fantasize that she may possibly be attracted to younger men. Card Number Three, from a globe-trotting flight attendant (my sister Joanie), contained a crisp new $100 bill. Not a bad haul!

Here's the message in Dad's card: "Happy birthday, kid. The birthday I'm really going to celebrate is your 18th! Ha-ha. Just kidding. Yours sincerely, Dad." It would serve that miser right if the state extended the cut-off age for child-support—say to 35.

I am rich! Gripped by the fever of materialism, I wander happily for hours through the great shopping mall of the mind. "Spend, spend! Acquire, acquire!" whispers the sweet subliminal music.

FRIDAY, August 4 — My bankroll is down to $87. All I have to show for it is a headache, a stomach ache, sore feet, an I'M SINGLE, LET'S MINGLE tee-shirt, a tube of industrial strength zit salve, and a paperback book: *How I Made One Million Dollars in High School and Was Accepted by Yale* by Herbert Roland

Pennypacker.

Why are people so suspicious when a 14-year-old youth pulls out a $100 bill? OK, maybe I could be a crack dealer. What's it to them! I wonder if teen millionaire Herbert Roland Pennypacker has this problem?

SATURDAY, August 5 — I came back from the library to find Mom cuddling on the couch with Jerry, her repulsive boyfriend. They immediately leapt apart and pretended to be fascinated by the wallpaper. I can't imagine why my mother wishes me to believe her relationship with Jerry is platonic. Anyway you slice it, I've got her beat for celibacy champ in this family.

Jerry is a long-distance truck driver, which fortunately keeps him out of town a lot. His ultimate ambition is to go on permanent state disability. (Every man needs a dream!) He files claim after claim (for a different incapacitating debility each time), but the stuffy bureaucrats in Sacramento continue to insist on solid x-ray evidence of degeneration. (He should send them a scan of his skull.) Jerry says if he were African-American he would be "pulling down a big state check, no questions asked."

After 12 years with Dad, Mom apparently decided she needed a less intellectual consort. Not that Dad's non-stop cultural one-upmanship qualifies him as a deep thinker. His mind ranges widely: from arid to vapid, with stops at banal, insipid, and shallow. But Jerry's gray matter doesn't even register on the gauge. The needle sits there at Cretin and doesn't budge.

Physically Jerry is also a curiosity. He is completely devoid of an ass. I suppose he must sit on his spine. His pants hang perfectly flat, while out front his angry red beer gut balloons out like the front end of a '51 Studebaker. As long as Mom's known Jerry, I've been struggling to think of a commendable thing to say about him. No luck. He may be God's perfect asshole.

11:30 p.m. Woke up to the sounds of a woman screaming. It was Mom. I'd scream too if Jerry were making love to me. Improbably, the dolt seems to have some talent in this area. Mom did a lot of hollering with Dad, but never that I can recall out of pleasure. Do all women scream at the moment of ecstasy? Why don't they have 800 numbers where teens can call up with questions like these?

SUNDAY, August 6 — Another typical East Bay summer morning: foggy, gray, and bitterly cold. I began this cheery day by sharing the breakfast table with Jerry. After ten minutes of listening to him slurp his Cheerios, I was ready to go for the meat cleaver. Pouring his coffee, Mom said, "Isn't it nice of Jerry to drop by so early?"

The woman takes me for a complete idiot.

After breakfast Mom turned on the furnace and we sat around reading the Sunday paper. Jerry read the sports pages and all the used car ads. He believes a man should never keep a car longer than two months. That way, he says, "you always have the thrill of owning a new car."

However stimulating his current vehicle, Jerry always keeps a big FOR SALE sign taped in the back window—so as not to miss any passing impulse buyers. So far he's had only tepid interest in his present car—a battered '76 Chevy Nova, painted (by Jerry) in camouflage colors.

I started reading *How I Made One Million Dollars in High School and Was Accepted by Yale*. For being a successful millionaire Yalie, Herbert Roland Pennypacker is a pretty turgid writer. I'm having trouble getting past the introduction.

Lefty dropped by and we wanked off to my *Penthouse* collection. He has marked all of his favorite spreads (so to speak), but usually selects the Pet who resembles a mature Millie Filbert. After wiping up, he informed me his sister found his addendum to her diary and is now on the warpath. Because of the journal's inflammatory contents, she can't rat on Lefty to their parents. But she has promised to make his life "a living hell." We both agreed it is not wise to cross a sexually frustrated woman. I was disappointed in her reaction as I half expected her to call.

Dad was supposed to take me out for a belated birthday dinner, but he never showed. So I had take-out pizza with Mom and Jerry. The latter drank an entire six-pack of Colt 45. Even his loving girlfriend looked appalled.

MONDAY, August 7 — I painted my bedroom! The ghastly pink is no more. What a lot of tedious work. I'm glad I'm an intellectual and so do not have to look forward to a lifetime of such menial drudgery. I'd much rather sit in front of a computer terminal and get my brain irradiated all day by an electron beam.

The khaki was rolling on too brown, so I mixed in some green I found out in the garage. Turns out when you combine latex and oil-based paints, the colors tend to separate on the walls. After a period of extreme indecision, I decided I liked the mottled effect.

When Mom got home from work, she let out a scream and said it looked just like the prison cells of IRA detainees in Ulster. These unhappy chaps do something to their walls you won't find in *Better Homes and Gardens*. I told her not to worry, that faux wall treatments were all the rage now and that a decorator would have charged thousands to produce the same effect.

She said she would never step foot in my room again. Best news I've heard in months!

Lefty just called in a panic. His sister told him that she saw Millie at the mall holding hands with some college guy. I told him not to worry, that it was just part of Martha's campaign of psychological warfare. Lefty is naturally feeling vulnerable as he has not seen Millie all summer. He desperately wants to phone her, but is too chicken. He says this separation anxiety "is almost enough to make a guy look forward to going back to school." Coming from Lefty, that is a remarkable statement.

TUESDAY, August 8 — Dad called from his office to apologize for missing our dinner engagement. Someone broke into his Beamer and stole Lacey's purse.

Since it contained both her address and door key, Dad had to stay all night at her apartment to protect her and her valuables until she got the locks changed. A good story, but he must have forgotten he'd used the same one on me about six months before. Only the bimbette had changed.

I asked Dad if he was giving much thought to my back-to-school wardrobe. He asked me if I was giving any thought to a summer job. With the conversation thus at an impasse, we hung up.

Lefty came over in a blue funk. His sister heard on the grapevine about his penile eccentricity and told his parents. Naturally his mother got hysterical and wanted to see it, but Lefty fought her off like a wild man. He has a doctor's appointment tomorrow morning at 10 a.m. "If I don't kill myself first," he says.

To cheer him up I suggested we call Millie to see how she was doing. Lefty was dubious, but finally his curiosity won him over to the idea. I dialed the number while Lefty listened in on the extension. After many rings, Millie's mother wheezed a dispirited "Hello."

"May I speak to Millie, please?" I asked politely.

"Who is this?" sniffled the voice.

"Uh, a school friend," I said.

"Not that monster Willis, is it?" she demanded.

"No, it's Nick. Nick Twisp."

"I'm sorry, Nick," said Mrs. Filbert. "Millie is indisposed. And will be for about the next seven-and-a-half months." *Click.*

This put Lefty in an even darker mood. It's not easy to hear your childhood sweetheart may be expecting another man's child. Especially when the status of your own manhood is in question.

"My life is a living hell," said Lefty as he departed.

WEDNESDAY, August 9 — I counted 39 hairs in the shower drain this morning and 27 more on my comb. The long emasculating march toward disfiguring baldness has begun!

I also squeezed 17 engorged pustules on my face and seven erubescent carbuncles on my neck. It will be a miracle if I don't get blood poisoning. Yet, though I look like a medieval plague victim, the world expects me to go on being a happy, busy teen. I despair, knowing every fresh eruption places another oozing wall between me and the soft, yielding warmth of feminine flesh. Or, to put it more succinctly: pimples postpone pussy. Perhaps I should give up fried food.

Lefty may have to get an operation! He has something called Peyronie's disease. In three months if vitamins don't straighten him out, surgeons will be chasing him with machetes. He is feeling totally humiliated. The doctor injected him with something that gave him a killer hard-on, then he had to lie there and have his erection professionally examined. At first his mother insisted on being in the room, but Lefty refused to unzip until she split. Most embarrassing of all, the doctor was a woman! And kind of a cute young one too.

"The first time a woman touched my dick," said Lefty, "and I didn't enjoy it at all. I sure hope I'm not gay."

Good news. Jerry is off on the road again. I hope he's hauling cucumbers to Bolivia. He sold his Chevy to a sailor at the Alameda Naval Air Station. The camouflage should fit right in on the base. At least one car in the parking lot will be fooling our enemies (whoever they may be).

I asked Mom at dinner if she really liked Jerry. Her reply: "That's none of your damn business!" After five minutes of angry silence, she went on: "Jerry is OK. You should try to be nicer to him. How many men do you think there are who'd be interested in a 41-year-old woman with two kids, no money, and stretch marks? He's no Cary Grant, but he's better than nothing."

Mom is a realist about everything except her age. She's 43.

THURSDAY, August 10 — Lefty and I went for a hike up in the hills above the UC campus. This is not like me, but even my body requires some exercise occasionally. Lefty wanted to get out of the house. He made the mistake of telling Martha he disliked her Joe Cocker album, and now she plays it incessantly.

It was sunny and mild, with a few fleecy white clouds floating like becalmed zeppelins above the azure bay. (I may save that sentence for recycling in a future novel.) Rounding Inspiration Point, we were startled to spy in a secluded clearing down the ravine a naked couple making love. Naturally, we crept closer for a better look. Finally, those Cub Scout forest skills were starting to pay off! If only I'd thought to bring my binoculars. They looked like Cal students—a cute Asian coed and her honkie jock boyfriend, happily humping away in the brown grass. They climaxed, rested for a bit, then hopped to it again—while Lefty and I looked on in breathless silence.

After the show, we lurched off to find our own secluded spot for some manual hydraulic relief. My explosive discharge felled a mature eucalyptus grove. Lefty's dislodged a dozen three-ton boulders. Yet afterwards, we both agreed crazed teen horniness locked us ever tighter in its torrid embrace. My body is broadcasting a desperate signal: It needs it bad. Very bad.

SUNDAY, August 12 — Another fun-filled Sunday in Marin with Dad and Lacey. One of the tragic consequences of divorce is that the kids are legally obligated by the courts to spend a fixed amount of time with their dads. In normal families, dads and children happily ignore each other.

It was a killer hot day. Even though the air conditioning in Dad's Beamer was on the fritz, he made us ride over with the windows up so the other motorists wouldn't think he didn't have any. The only compensation was an outrageously sexy bead of sweat the stifling heat brought out on Lacey's upper lip. I longed to daub it off—with my tongue.

Once in Kentfield, Dad said he would take me to buy some school clothes if I washed his car. I agreed and got totally fried by the sun while de-griming the fine German steel. Dad watched me like a hawk lest I drop the sponge and pick up some paint-marring grit. (We both suffer from extreme blemish anxiety.)

After lunch (at McDanold's) we went clothes shopping in the shiny Beamer—to the Sebastopol Flea Market! I got three shirts, two pairs of pants, a jacket, and a belt—for a miserly total of $8.65. Dad was prepared to spend more, but I drew the line at previously owned shoes. This fall I shall be going to school dressed in the height of fashion—for the year 1973.

Lacey had on a groin-swelling yellow polka-dot sunsuit and alien invader's sunglasses. She flirted with all the bikers selling motorcycle parts and even knew two of the most criminal-looking by name. Dad was extremely jealous and did a lot of inward seething. He looks like heart attack material to me; I just hope he's adequately insured.

Dad sprang for hotdogs at the flea market, so he didn't feel dinner was called for later. I took my hunger and new wardrobe back to Oakland. (But I am not going to let him weasel out of the promised birthday dinner!)

While I was cooking up some frozen French fries (I feel the link between fried foods and acne has not yet been positively established), the sailor dropped by with two of his buddies looking for Jerry. It seems the Chevy went only 17 miles before the engine blew up. They also found evidence of a banana in the transmission. When I told them Jerry was out of town, they looked quite crestfallen and promised to return. They also left the dead Chevy in the driveway. Across the camouflaged hood someone had spray-painted, "Pay up or die!"

MONDAY, August 13 — Millie Filbert is getting married! To Willis, the alleged father of her alleged child. She's 15 and he's 20. Martha heard about it on the grapevine and woke up Lefty this morning with the news. He exclaimed, "This is a day that will live in infamy!" Just kidding. Actually, his precise words were "Great fucking balls ache!"

Lefty came over immediately for some peer counseling. I told him Millie was a cheap tart and he was well rid of her. He agreed and said he hoped she had a long and difficult marriage to an inveterate wife-beater. He said if he'd known she was such an easy lay, he definitely would have gotten up the nerve to ask her out. Instead, he wasted all those years worshipping her from afar. Then, for emotional closure, I had him tear up the *Penthouse* Millie-look-alike Pet. Lefty said he was feeling better, so we had a morale-boosting whack-off session. Even though he has been sneaking extra doses of his vitamins, he still looks as crooked as ever. Millie will never know what she missed.

I think the sunburn helped my acne. So I am trying to spend more time outdoors. Even if I die of melanoma in 20 years, I feel it will have been worth it. I asked Mom for some money to buy sunglasses, but instead she gave me her old pair. It took me 45 minutes to chisel out the rhinestones. That accomplished, they still don't look like a style Tom Cruise would wear.

Like an early-morning erection, the sailor came back. (I am trying to introduce more similes into my prose.) This time Mom had the pleasure of chatting with him. The sailor demanded she write him a check! She explained that was impossible, but said she would try to contact Jerry. While the sailor waited, seething nautically, she called Jerry's dispatcher, who gave her the number of a motel in Iowa City. When she called the motel and asked for Jerry's room, a woman answered! The woman said Jerry was in the shower and could she take a message? Mom turned red, hung up, and told the sailor she would get him his $900. Even if it was the last thing she ever did.

TUESDAY, August 14 — Mom found my Polaroid of Lacey! She claimed she discovered it "while putting away some clean socks." Yeah, like I always keep my argyles hidden in the back of my bottom desk drawer. With the parental Gestapo on patrol around here, privacy stops at the bathroom door. And even that sanctuary is hardly inviolate.

Mom really hit the roof when I told her the well-proportioned semi-nudist was Dad's latest girlfriend. She stared in horror at the photo, her face contorted by revulsion and envy. Then I got a 25-minute grilling about Lacey. Mom takes a morbid interest in Dad's love life (don't we all?), so I don't mind inventing a few details here and there to watch her boil. To cope with my torrid revelations, Mom chain-smoked throughout the interrogation.

I told her no Lacey did not appear to live with Dad, but she did hang her bra and panties in his bathroom. I said I didn't know if it was serious, but they spent a lot of time in the bedroom taking naps. I revealed that Lacey liked to sit on Dad's lap during "Masterpiece Theatre" and blow into his ear. (I made that up.) I said she called him "Thunder Rod" and he called her "Sugar Puss." (True, believe it or not.) I told her Lacey liked fast cars, knew bikers by their first names, and carried a small flask of brandy in her décolletage. (All true.) I said she came from a prominent San Francisco family, graduated from Stanford at 19, had an IQ of 163, and did secret work for the government involving hair. (More or less lacking a factual basis.) Finally, I said Lacey was fun to be with, had a good sense of humor despite being such an intellectual, and had a mature outlook on the beauty and wholesomeness of the human body. Therefore, I wanted her photo back.

Mom snorted, "That's what you think, buster." She said she was keeping the Polaroid for evidence and had half a mind to have Lacey prosecuted for corrupting a minor. "You're still a child," lectured Mom, taking multiple deep drags on her cigarette. "You should be out playing sports. Not looking at disgusting pictures of naked harlots."

I replied that Millie Filbert had played softball for years, but that hadn't stopped her from getting knocked up.

Mom told me to get my mind out of the gutter. So much for trying to reason with a woman.

WEDNESDAY, August 15 — A sunny day, so I put on my sunglasses and my I'M

SINGLE LET'S MINGLE tee-shirt and walked all the way downtown to the library. We live about three miles up from the center of town—in the nervous zone between the affluent hills and the seething flats. Seeded baguettes in one direction, barbecue in the other—it's a short trip either way.

Because of the heat, the library smelled even worse than usual. I wish some wealthy philanthropist would endow a foundation to distribute Right Guard to the homeless. In the library bathroom a bookish-looking gentleman about 30 glanced at my sunglasses and asked me if I wanted to go out for coffee. I said no I was too young for dating. He seemed disappointed. I'm glad that in spite of my zits and incipient baldness at least one person in this world finds me attractive. If only he were a cute 16-year-old girl. But then what would she be doing loitering in the men's room?

I sat in the periodicals room for a few hours reading computer magazines. This always fills me with extreme hardware lust. Unrequited, of course, like all my other passions. My bankroll is down to $72 and falling fast. At the opposite end of the table a short fat girl about my age was reading Atari magazines. She kept looking over at me. Finally, she got her fat composed in a friendly expression and asked me if I had a computer. I didn't want to encourage her, but out of politeness I said yes I had an IBM AT clone. She said she had an Atari ST and loved its color graphics for games and drawing. I said I used my IBM mostly for word processing and "other serious tasks." That took the starch out of her sails. She was going to reply, but fortunately a librarian shushed for quiet. When Ms. Atari got up to get another magazine, I sneaked out.

After dinner tonight, we heard a semi-tractor hiss to a stop out front. It was the assless Don Juan back from his Iowa assignations. Jerry pretended nothing was amiss and feigned surprise when my mother lit into him. He disavowed any knowledge of the incident and said if a woman answered his phone (which he doubted) it must have been the maid bringing more toilet paper. What a feeble and transparent liar! To my shock, Mom bought it. She even kissed him!

As Mom fixed Jerry a much better dinner than she had served me, she asked him what he intended to do about the deceased camouflaged hulk in the driveway. Jerry viewed the matter with cool detachment. He said as much as he would like to move the car, he could not—because, of course, it was someone else's private property. He suggested Mom call the city and have it towed.

What about the angry sailor and his $900?

Jerry said if the sailor came back, Mom should simply remind him he had purchased the car with Jerry's standard guarantee: "Thirty days or thirty feet. Whichever comes first."

"I'm in the right," announced Jerry, carving his steak. "That $900 is already invested in my new car. I pick it up tomorrow."

"What did you get this time, honey?" asked Mom.

"A slab-sided Lincoln," said Jerry. "A cherry '62 convertible. Like the one Kennedy was shot in. Only this one's white instead of black."

With Jerry, that stands to reason.

THURSDAY, August 16 — When I got up, the big tractor truck was still parked outside. Thinking it would be fun to have extra guests for breakfast, I sneaked downstairs and called the midshipman in Alameda (I found the number in Mom's purse). He was very happy to hear Jerry was back.

At 8:12 we had three sailors at the front door and two at the back door. When the doorbell rang, Jerry was slumped in a kitchen chair trying to wake up enough to swallow coffee. He perked right up when Mom yelled the fleet was in. He turned white, hissed at Mom to get rid of them, and ran upstairs. The sailors cornered him in Joanie's closet. (They hadn't stopped to chat with Mom.) When they grabbed him, Jerry went limp like a house cat caught with the missing family hamster. Two big guys with bad haircuts held him off the ground while the erstwhile Chevy owner went through his pockets. They found $63 and change. Jerry said that was his entire life savings. The sailor poked him hard in the beer gut. Mom whimpered, "Don't hurt him!" I was shaking with excitement. The sailors were breathing hard. Jerry looked like he trying to climb out of his body.

"Honest guys," said Jerry, "that's all I got!" The sailor hit him again. Jerry lost his coffee down the front of his shirt. Mom screamed. I felt like screaming. Jerry started to cry. They carried him downstairs and dragged him outside to go through the cab of the truck. Mom yelled at me to call 911, but one of the sailors said, "Touch that phone, kid, and I'll slice your balls off." I didn't have to be warned twice. In the truck they found Jerry's jacket with his credit cards and bankbook. So all five sailors and the rumpled truck driver piled into a Navy van ("For Official Use Only") and drove off to wait for the bank to open.

Mom didn't go to work. She spent the morning crying in the kitchen. I feel terrible for ratting on Jerry. But what a stimulating way to start your day!

1:30 p.m. No sign of Jerry. Mom is frantic. The big question: if they murdered him, am I an accessory?

3:20 p.m. Jerry pulled up in his big white Lincoln. He had put the top down, changed into his nice (for him) clothes, and was smiling from ear to ear. He took us for a ride. What a beautiful car! The interior is as cherry as the outside—all chrome, plush carpet, and white leather seats.

Driving down to the bay, Jerry told us how he had outsmarted the U.S. Navy. In the bank, when they found out he didn't have any money in his account, the sailors made him get a cash advance of $836.72 on his Visa card. Jerry agreed, but asked the teller for a cashier's check instead of cash. The sailor was pissed, but took it anyway since it was a bank-guaranteed check. Then, when the sailors let him go, Jerry called up Visa and reported his credit card had been stolen. The night before! "Boy," chuckled Jerry, "is that dumb sailor going to get a surprise when he tries to cash that check!"

FRIDAY, August 17 — Mom and I are going to Clear Lake for a week with Jerry. We leave early tomorrow. The arrangements are being made sort of suddenly. Don't ask me why. I'm never consulted about these things. All I was told is we're going to be staying in a cabin on the lake owned by a friend of Jerry's.

I packed my grip. I'm taking my sunglasses, my harmonica, my zit salve, three books: *Bleak House, Atlas Shrugged,* and *The Function of the Orgasm* (by Wilhelm Reich), four F.S. albums, my favorite issue of *Penthouse* taped inside a portfolio of harmonica sonatas, and some clothes. I couldn't decide whether to take my baggy swimsuit or my skimpy, form-fitting trunks. The baggy suit looks dumpy, but the tight, form-fitting trunks don't have enough bulging forms to fit. So I packed both. Maybe the lake air will revive my dormant growth hormones.

I let Mom pack the cooking gear and sleeping bags. This always makes her a bit touchy. Right before she and Dad split up, he went on a four-day fishing trip to Lake Shasta with the guys. Later, when Mom was putting away his camping gear, she found a brassiere (size 42D) in the bottom of his sleeping bag. Ever since then, the sight of rip-stop nylon or a Coleman lantern always puts Mom in a bad mood.

Lefty came over to say goodbye. He was acting kind of jumpy. I suspect vitamin poisoning. Martha has stopped tormenting him with Joe Cocker and has switched to their parents' old Barry Coma records. We both agreed that is hitting below the belt. Lefty threatened to tell their parents about the diary revelations, but Martha has burned the evidence and says they'd never believe him. Until he gets some leverage over her, his life will remain a living hell. Of course, he searches her room every time she leaves the house, but nothing has turned up so far. She left an armed mouse trap in her panties drawer, but he saw it just in time. He moved it two drawers down, and right as he was leaving he heard a snap, followed by a piercing scream.

8:30 p.m. Lefty just called, sounding worried. I could barely hear him over Barry in the background warbling "Bali Hai" at concert volume. Martha has two bruised fingers and war has been declared.

SATURDAY, August 18 — I'm on vacation! Believe it or not, I'm actually writing all this down in longhand on a legal pad for transcription later into the computer. What a tedious process. I suppose, though, back when the pencil was a new invention people must have thought it was a marvelous labor-saving device. Then some genius thought of adding an eraser and everyone had to upgrade.

We hit the road right after breakfast. The phone rang steadily from 6 a.m., but Mom was under orders from Jerry not to answer it. I called Lefty before we left to check on battle casualties. His mom answered and said he was still asleep in the back yard. He had pitched a tent and was now camping out. "I hope the damp ground doesn't aggravate his condition," she said. I said probably not if he slept on his back. She wished me a good trip and I said I'd send them a postcard.

We took the Lincoln, of course. Jerry insisted on driving with the top down. He had on baggy bermudas, a TRUCKERS DO IT IN OVERDRIVE tee-shirt, and a hat made from Coors beer cans. Mom wore a halter top that looked like an advertisement for Droop City. I was a bottle baby so don't blame me. She also had on short shorts to show off her legs, which are nice if you like bulging blue veins.

I sat in the back-seat wind tunnel. The whole four hours up to Lakeport I was smashing bugs with my face at 70 miles per hour. After awhile I looked like Jeff Goldblum about an hour and ten minutes into the movie "The Fly." A couple of unidentified specimens dive-bombed my mouth and were swallowed reflexively, leaving behind the lingering taste of brackish bug. Yuck.

As we passed trucks and motorhomes, Mom waved to the drivers like she was Miss Corndog of 1954. Just as we were overtaking a Greyhound bus, Jerry went into a prolonged session of crotch rearrangement. Even through the glaze of bug slime, I could feel the passengers' curious stares.

Finally, the blue waters of Clear Lake came into view. Jerry wanted to stop for lunch, but Mom was all for driving straight through to the cabin. It took us 45 minutes to find the address—which turned out to be not a private residence, but the Restless Axles Trailer Park! Six busy, motel-clogged blocks from the lake.

Our trailer is a long, green, turd-shaped vehicle from some time in the Truman administration. It has a little patch of grass with a wagon wheel and some concrete dwarves, a dusty canvas awning over a small cement patio, and a decrepit picket fence with a sign that reads, "My Green Haven." Mom looked like she was going to cry, but Jerry said it was "real cute" on the inside.

He was right. Inside was kind of dim and cool and cluttered and musty smelling. Lots of old polished dark wood and 3-D religious art. Everything was in miniature. Up front was a miniature kitchen. Then came a compact living room, followed by a condensed bathroom, a long closet with bunkbeds opposite, and then a tiny master bedroom with a shrunken double bed flanked by little built-in tables with milk-glass lamps topped with rose-covered shades. It was real cute.

Mom perked right up after she got the windows open. She resumed her reign as Corndog Queen and waved to all the curious neighbors as we unloaded the big Lincoln. After washing my face in the toy-like sink, I unpacked my gear and put Frank on the tiny record player while Mom fixed lunch. After hotdogs, potato chips, and iced tea, Jerry scratched his balls, checked out Mom's low-slung halter, and suggested I go look at the lake. I got the message.

I took my sunglasses, zit salve, sun block, beach towel, and *Atlas Shrugged.* This book weighs about five pounds and should come with a fold-out handle and wheels. I lugged it along in hopes it might impress any literary chicks I met on the beach.

I circled through the trailer park on the way toward the water. Most of the trailers were old and looked like they had retired from the call of the open road.

A few trailerites were about—mostly old folks in their 30s and 40s. No kids my age, unless they were all at the beach.

I walked past the drive-ins and motels toward the lake. It was awesomely hot. Lots of high-school kids in souped up cars and cute girls in skimpy bathing suits. The beach was noisy and crowded, but I found a vacant spot in the shade under a tree. There was a bit of a breeze off the lake, which is several miles wide at this point. Mt. Konocti rose, brown and sun-baked, above the distant shore.

I read my book for a while, but kept getting distracted by the passing bikinis. What a fantastic invention! All those enticing curves wrapped in small bits of thin fabric. Here and there the teasing outline of a nipple or a faintly perceptible furrow in that softly swelling vee below the navel. I got a killer T.E. (Thunderous Erection) beneath my weighty book and could feel the sticky warmth of lubricant oozing optimistically from the tip. In the shallow water beyond the sand, tanned couples wrestled and splashed, pausing in their noisy games to touch with their bodies and lips. I need a girlfriend!

After my T.E. subsided, I toured the town in the late afternoon heat—the local idle youth eyeing me suspiciously. Not even a book store or movie theater. What am I going to do here for six days?

When I got back to "My Green Haven," Jerry was kneeling on the cement patio with his shirt off trying to light the propane water heater. His beer gut bobbled and hopped with each cuss word. No luck. We could hear the hiss of gas, but the pilot refused to light. Six days of cold water loom ahead.

The Corndog Queen has mastered the abbreviated kitchen and made a great dinner of fried chicken, potato salad, and corn on the cop. Rhubarb cobbler for dessert. Jerry guzzled Coors and rhapsodized at length on the nomadic life. He is hot to buy a trailer he can hitch to the Lincoln. "Just big enough for the two of us," he said to Mom. They exchanged a sloppy kiss, while I sat there feeling like an unexpected guest on a honeymoon cruise.

I *was* welcome to do the dishes. While I battled chicken grease with cold water, Mom tweezed hairs out of her legs and Jerry scanned the local paper for trailer ads. We were interrupted by a knock on the door. It was a thin, ancient lady in white gloves and a flowered dress. She introduced herself as Mrs. Herbert Clarkelson, our neighbor, and invited us to a prayer meeting. Surprise! This is a church-run trailer park with its own meeting hall. They have services every day. Mom declined the invitation, but said maybe we'd come tomorrow. I can't wait.

We went to bed to the sounds of hymn singing in the distance. Mom pretended that the issue of sleeping accommodations had just occurred to her and suggested I take the bunkbed while the "adults" took the back bedroom (as if they hadn't been flogging the mattress back there all afternoon). I agreed. Everyone flossed, brushed, peed, and climbed into their tiny beds. What trailers lack in space they make up for in lack of privacy. As soon as I switched off the lamp, my afternoon T.E. reasserted itself. I was all for putting it out of its misery, but any sort of vigorous arm movement shook the entire trailer. I went at it anyway, and just as I was about to blast a hole through the ceiling, Jerry kicked the wall and yelled, "Hey kid, you wanna beat your meat go outside!" I told him I was scratching my foot.

Just wait 'til that jerk wants some privacy. I'm going to stick to him like glue. Meanwhile, I hope I don't get terminal blue balls.

SUNDAY, August 19 — This may not be very coherent. I got about two hours sleep last night. Interruptions included returning church-goers chatting about Armageddon timetables, barking dogs, Jerry's snoring, Mom talking in her sleep, Mom and Jerry trooping past me to the bathroom, trucks roaring by on the highway, and Mrs. Clarkelson knocking on the door at 6 a.m. to announce that early church services began promptly at 7:15. Donuts would be served.

Since our trailer shower had no hot water and was only big enough anyway for bathing a penguin, I put on my robe and walked sleepily over to the park restroom. This turned out to be an austere cement shed with three dripping shower heads and no privacy walls. A fat bald man was toweling himself off when I arrived. I brushed my teeth (for about 10 minutes!) while he slowly dressed. Finally he left and I disrobed and turned on the shower. Ten seconds later, Jerry entered, stripped, and stepped under the shower next to mine. Guess what? The guy has more hose than a nervous fireman. No wonder ladies go for him. If Jerry had been my father, I'd be dumb, happy, and have a penis length in the 99th percentile. I'd also stand to inherit a nifty Lincoln convertible. Still, would I make the switch if I had the choice? I wonder!

Jerry is a very athletic showerer. He hopped around, splashed, gargled, spit, belched, and warbled truck-driving songs. I cut short my ablutions and left as soon as I could. As I walked out, red and damp, I passed a cute girl about my age going in the women's door. Garbed in a modest but nonetheless alluring flannel robe, she had chestnut shoulder-length hair, pretty blue eyes, and an aristocratically chiselled nose. She smiled at me! I panicked and returned a philosophical scowl. As we passed, she whispered softly, "Your robe's open." Flustered, I looked down. No winkie in sight. That was a bald-faced tease!

After breakfast, I walked through the trailer park hoping to run into her again. No luck. I figured she must be having donuts with God like the rest of the residents. Then, when I got back to our row, there she was—sitting on our patio drinking coffee with Mom. She now had on sandals, yellow shorts, and a white blouse just sheer enough to reveal the shape of her bra. She was thin, but interesting developments were in progress. As I walked through the gate, she looked me straight in the eyes and said, "Hi, stuck up." I stammered an incoherent reply. Mom said, "Nick honey, meet Sheeni."

Sheeni had to go to the grocery store, and invited me along as her bearer. I would have carried a Volkswagen. As we walked into town, my panic started to subside. I can actually talk to girls!

She is 14, is one of two intellectuals living in Ukiah, California, and is an atheist. This causes terrible fights with her Bible-thumping parents. She refuses to go to church and now the entire trailerite congregation is praying for her salvation. Her father is a big-time lawyer in Ukiah. I told her I never heard of a born-again lawyer. Sheeni said yes and he's prepared to sue for Christ.

She has been reading the existentialists this summer—Camus, Sartre, and other guys I never heard of. She said Ayn Rand is deplorable and will damage my "inchoate mind." She promised to draw up a study list of books for me to read. When she's 18 and free of "parental bondage" she wants to go to Paris and study philosophy. She is the only person in Ukiah studying French language tapes.

In the grocery store, Sheeni bought a large watermelon and permitted me to buy her a Popsicle. We walked back slowly in the heat, the watermelon progressively dislocating my shoulder. Sheeni said the arrival of the Lincoln excited considerable interest in the trailer park. Most residents are still reserving judgment, although Jerry's large beer cooler on the patio has been disquieting to some. Sheeni said she liked my Mom, but thought my father was "perhaps rather dim." I hastened to point out that Jerry was only my mother's consort and that I had absolutely no blood links of any kind to him. This seemed to put her mind at ease.

As we passed the cement-block meeting hall, we could hear the congregation inside shouting and stomping. Sheeni said that even though she was no longer a believer, she had to admit that the services were "wonderfully aerobic."

"You could say the same thing about sex," I surprised myself by saying.

Sheeni stopped and looked at me intently. "I hope, Nick," she said, "you're not going to turn out like all the other young men and have nothing on your mind except carnal pleasures."

I assured her that was not the case. "I hardly ever think about sex," I lied.

"I think about it all the time," Sheeni said. "It's the hormones at work, you know."

We walked on in silence. I felt confused. Sheeni ate the last of her Popsicle. I longed to taste the orange sweetness on her lips. She has lovely, full lips that cry out to be kissed. Sheeni turned in at a trailer I had noticed before. It was a 1959 Pacemaker (not to be confused with the medical device) and was the only two-story mobile home in the park. "Father bought it so he could look down upon the world," Sheeni explained. "For him Christian humility has always been a struggle."

I carried in the three-ton watermelon and Sheeni gave me a tour. Downstairs was a kitchen, living room, master bedroom, and bath. The usual dark paneling and (somewhat more tasteful) religious art. Up a short flight of stairs were two tiny bedrooms and a bathroom you couldn't stand up in. My heart was pounding furiously as Sheeni slid open the door to her miniature bedroom. It was cluttered with books, but otherwise was very neat. On the wall above the tiny, girlish bed was a poster of John Paul Belmondo holding a revolver in a sexually suggestive manner.

"Didn't you love 'Breathless'?" Sheeni asked eagerly, sitting on the bed.

"Yes," I lied, hunched over under the low ceiling like a nervous teenaged Quasimodo.

"It's my favorite film," she announced. "What's yours?"

I tried to think of a suitably high-brow movie. "'Tokyo Story'," I said. "I think Mizoguchi is a great director."

"'Tokyo Story'," said Sheeni. "A great film. But wasn't it by Ozu?"

I may be completely out of my league.

Sheeni jumped up, checked her face in the tiny dresser mirror (it was still beautiful), and led me downstairs. With extreme anxiety, I asked if she would like to go to the beach that afternoon. Sheeni smiled and said she would love to, but had to visit an "indigent ill person" her father was suing. We made a date for a swim after breakfast tomorrow. As I left, Sheeni waved from the doorway and said, "Goodbye, Mr. Twisp."

I forced myself to laugh. She may imagine that jest is original with her, but I have been hearing it since pre-school days. When people ask what writer I think is overrated, I always say James Hilton. I wish the twit had caught beri-beri in Shangri-la.

I walked home in a state of supremely exulted exhilaration. I wonder if this is what religious ecstasy feels like? Perhaps I should ask Mrs. Clarkelson.

The rest of the day passed in a fog. I think we had some sort of meat for dinner. Jerry drank too much beer and asked Mrs. Clarkelson, when she stopped by to invite us to the evening prayer service, to come in and sit on his face. She looked quite shocked and left in a huff. Mom got mad. She has managed to sunburn most of her chest and is irascible in the extreme. I played a lot of F.S. love ballads and thought about my future life in Paris with Sheeni. Where can you buy French language tapes?

MONDAY, August 20 — Another embarrassing shower episode. I may have to give up bathing on this trip. All night I slept in a state of lingering tumescence (I wonder why). Then, in the shower my hard-on returned—just as the fat, bald guy walked in. He smiled a lot at me and, while lathering his hairy white flab, kept stealing fond glances at my perky pecker. His got kind of perky too. (Not that I was looking!) I got out of there as fast as I could.

Back in the trailer I was trying to decide which bathing suit to wear, when Mom and Jerry waltzed through from the bedroom. Jerry said, "Look, Estelle, your kid's got a load in his peashooter." Mom looked. "Better put something on," she said. "If you're going out."

No, I was going to walk to the beach naked!

For my first semi-clothed date with Sheeni, I decided the baggy trunks would be better—especially in view of the present hair-trigger on my erectile response. For this beach excursion I packed along a towel, sunglasses, sun block, notebook, wallet, pen and pencil, book (*The Function of the Orgasm*), and condom (one must always be prepared, should the times demand it, to grow up fast).

Sheeni answered the door in a knockout yellow swimsuit that concealed yet paradoxically revealed her flowering nubility. She was so breathtakingly lovely, the pleasure I felt in gazing upon her jonquil-draped curves bordered upon physical anguish. Sheeni invited me in and introduced her father—an immense, out-sized, larger-than-life, gray-haired, florid-faced, verdant-eyebrowed, loud-voiced ogre in a rumpled blue suit.

"I understand you have invited my daughter to the beach," he boomed.

"Er, yes, Mr. Saunders," I stammered.

"Aha!" he bellowed, his great eyebrows rising. "Then I trust, sir, you are aware that in doing so, you have entered into an oral contract to perform *in loco parentis*, i.e, to provide for the safety and well-being of aforementioned minor female."

Sheeni told her father to shut up. He didn't seem to mind. She picked up a large straw beach bag and pushed me out the door. "Bye, Father," she said.

"Vaya con Dios!" he rumbled.

We walked along in the warm sunshine toward the beach. I wanted to take Sheeni's hand, but was paralyzed by adolescent indecision. My companion brazenly looked me over. "You're all skin and bones," she said. "Your haircut is impossible. Those sunglasses are an optical outrage. And I believe you could invite my father in to share those awful swim trunks with you."

The thought was repellent in the extreme. "I wasn't thinking of inviting your father," I said suggestively.

Sheeni smiled, wrinkling the faint but lovely freckles on her nose. "Well, I don't think my mother would be particularly interested."

"I wasn't thinking of your mother either," I said. We passed Mrs. Clarkelson, who cut us dead.

"How about, Mrs. Clarkelson?" asked Sheeni. "I hear she's hot for your bod."

"She's a bitchin' chick," I replied. "But wrinkles aren't my scene."

"You like them younger?" Sheeni inquired.

"About 14."

"That's statutory rape. A felony, I believe."

"Not if you're married."

"God!" exclaimed Sheeni. "Don't make me barf!"

Since it was a weekday, the beach was pleasantly uncrowded. We spread our towels in the sand and lay down in the hot sun. Sheeni's book was *The Red and the Black* by some well-dead Frog named Stendhal. She inspected my reading material approvingly and said Wilhelm Reich was one of the great thinkers of the 20th century. "His death in a U.S. federal prison was both a tragedy and a travesty," Sheeni declared. I was shocked. I didn't know you could be sent to prison for writing a sex manual.

Sheeni handed me her tanning lotion and asked if I wanted the arduous task of applying it to her "exposed areas." I gulped and assented. She rolled over on her stomach, exposing her exquisite back. My hands shook as I smoothed the sweet oils into her tanned, warm flesh. Instantly I got a killer T.E., which I hoped my billowing trunks would conceal.

"My you get turned on easily," Sheeni observed.

My hands froze on her back.

"Oh, don't stop, Nick." she said. "We all have our hormones to cope with. Girls are fortunate in that it doesn't show. For all the world knows, my vagina could be moist with desire as we speak."

"Is it?" I asked nonchalantly.

"That's none of your business, I'm sure."

"Well," I said, "then why are we discussing my penis?"

"Oh, I suppose because the subject came up. I find it very boring."

"The topic or the penis?" I asked.

"Both," she replied. "Shall you do my front too?"

I gulped. "OK. I'm up for it."

Sheeni rolled over on her back, her young breasts straining up against the yellow Spandex. "I hope you don't find it too stimulating, Nick."

"I'm coping," I said. I started with her flawless legs, gliding on the oil all the way up to within a finger's reach of her sweet apex. I could feel her muscles tense as the slippery hand approached, then swerved away in the final split-second before contact. With each daring pass, a roar of approval rose from my groin. Then finally, the reckless hand swerved too late, and a finger lightly grazed the softly yielding vee.

"Uh, Nick," said Sheeni, looking up over her sunglasses. "Maybe you better do the top now." I moved upstream, lubricating her tanned arms, shoulders, and neck. I saved the chest for last, smoothing oil on the softly undulating foothills in the public domain. So close, but off-limits (for now!) rose the tantalizing, Spandex-shrouded highlands. Desperately over-stimulated, my T.E. throbbed, my balls felt like they were going to explode.

"Thanks, Nick," said Sheeni with sickening finality. I handed her the tanning lotion, hoping she would volunteer to do me. She didn't. She opened her book and soon was engrossed in Great Literature. I did the same. Incredulous that relief was not at hand, my erection clung on defiantly, forcing me to lie on my stomach. Soon I could feel my back barbecuing. I read through 27 difficult pages of *The Function of the Orgasm* and did not encounter a single tantalizing sex tip. Meanwhile, Sheeni read avidly, pausing frequently to make long notations in the margins.

3 p.m. Sheeni and I are sitting in a cafe drinking coffee and writing in our journals. Except for the smell of burgers, the sound of the C&W jukebox, and the sight of two loutish truckdrivers eating apple pie, we might be in a Paris bistro. Sheeni has been keeping a journal since the age of eight and claims to have written more than one million words. She writes rapidly in a charming ovoid script, pausing now and then to look up in abstracted concentration. I saw

her writing my name! Then she asked if 'puerile' was spelled with one 'l' or two.

We have to go. The slatternly waitress just shuffled over and told us to leave. Apparently we are violating their "no loitering" policy. Sheeni became incensed, her fine nostrils flaring dramatically. She told the woman she found their coffee "unpalatable," their premises "unsavory," and their rudeness "unalloyed." Unchastened, the waitress hollered, "Get out!" We did so, but not before Sheeni proclaimed in a loud, clear voice her contempt for "rural America and all its denizens." I backed her up with a gesture of protest. I withheld the tip.

8:15 p.m. Dreadful news! Sheeni has a boyfriend! She dropped this bombshell on the walk home as I fumbled for her hand. He is 15 and is Ukiah's other intellectual. He is six-two, speaks French, plays the piano, is a champion swimmer, and writes "Futurist Percussive" poetry. The affected twit is named Trent Preston. Sheeni recited this recent work by him:

RamDam 12

Sizzle mop
Crunch down
Safety net
Hot! Hot! Hot!
Void.

If that's poetry, I'm a turkey scrotum. She says Trent has a brilliant mind, and daily writes her an "intellectually stimulating" letter. I just hope it's only her intellect he stimulates.

Temporarily deranged by this shocking revelation, I announced that I too receive daily missives of a culturally enlightened nature from my sweetheart. Sheeni probed for details. I said her name was Martha, she was 16 and had just returned from Nice where she had been conducting sociological research on the assimilation problems of Italian migrant workers. In addition, I said she was a trained musicologist, earned a large income as a professional model specializing in lingerie, and her IQ was registered in Washington with the FBI as a national resource.

Sheeni looked somewhat taken aback. She said Martha sounded like a "wonderful person" and hoped that someday soon she would have the pleasure of meeting "this remarkable teen."

I said that was unlikely as Martha rarely ventured out of the city "to small, out-of-the-way places like Ukiah."

"I certainly can't blame her for that," said Sheeni bitterly. "Trent feels even more stifled there than I do."

Poor Trent!

We walked on in angry silence to the Saunders' towering trailer. Sheeni looked pensive. I felt terrible. She stopped by their patio gate and asked me how my sunburn felt. I said it was no worse than medieval torture. She said thank you for the lovely time. I said don't mention it. We stood there awhile, not saying anything, and then I left. As I turned the corner, I saw her extract a letter from their mailbox (shaped like a miniature two-story trailer). No doubt Trent's latest literary masterpiece.

I am miserable. Plunged from exaltation to suicidal depression in one sunny afternoon. My only diversion from black despair is the bracing contemplation of more and more violently disfiguring deaths for the pining Poet of the Redwoods. As he is older, taller, better looking, and more accomplished than I, he must die. The gods demand it.

Things were generally tense at "My Green Haven." Mom went to the park laundromat this afternoon and was pointedly snubbed by all the ladies. Then, Jerry came back from a beer run to discover someone had scrawled "SHAME SINNERS!" in scarlet lipstick across the windshield of his Lincoln. Mom speculates that somehow word has gotten around that she and Jerry are co-habitating without benefit of wedlock. I fear the source of the leak may be a beautiful young temptress who has ripped out my heart and stomped on it.

TUESDAY, August 21 — Here's an hour-by-hour chronology of the worst night of my life:

1 a.m. I decide it was just a case of puppy love and look forward to all the interesting women I shall meet in the future.

2 a.m. I conclude the only way out is suicide. I turn on the light to write a poignant suicide note. Sheeni will see Trent for the shallow pedant he is and will always treasure my memory. Jerry yells at me to turn out the light.

3 a.m. Running through the options, I decide I am too chicken for any of the manly, violent means of suicide. I shall swallow sleeping pills. Where to get them though?

4 a.m. I decide I can't die an inviolate virgin. Either I find a way to get laid soon or suicide gets postponed until after high school.

5 a.m. I decide it will be too painful to see Sheeni again. I shall ask Mom and Jerry if we can cut short our vacation and return to Oakland. Someday, Sheeni will read about me in *The New York Review of Books* and will realize she has wasted her life.

6 a.m. Violent panic! I have to see Sheeni again! We have only three days left together! Maybe she'll like me better than Trent. Even if she doesn't, and I am completely humiliated, it will still be worth it. Why did I waste all of yesterday evening when I could have been with her? Even if she does marry Trent someday, I could still be their loyal best friend—like Sidney Carton. I could even save their child from a runaway horse. Then when Trent goes to a tragic early death (poets have a high mortality rate), Sheeni could turn to me for solace. Everything will work out!

6:05 a.m. I drag my weary body out of bed and stumble over to the men's shower room. At least I will avoid the amorous fat bald guy. Wrong! He enters quickly and sheds his robe with a leer. He approaches, grossly naked. I retreat under the steaming spray.

"Mind if I share your shower?" he asks coyly. "I hear there's a drought on."

As the corpulent blob looms ever closer, I grope for the knob. Finally, my hand touches metal and I give it a turn. The steaming spray turns to a chilling blast. The blob leaps back.

"Sorry," I say, my teeth chattering. "I like my showers cold."

Ten minutes later, dressed, teeth brushed, ready for a busy day, I knocked on the door of Sheeni's trailer. I prayed Mr. Saunders wouldn't answer. Improbably, God was listening. After several tense minutes, the door opened and Sheeni peered out sleepily. My heart leaped! Oh, to roll over some morning and meet those beautiful, sleep-fogged blue eyes. Sheeni clutched the undiaphanous terry cloth to her exquisite form.

"Nick? God, what time is it?"

"Sheeni, hi! Nice to see you. I was out for a walk and thought I'd drop by. I'm sorry I got upset about Trent. That was very immature. He sounds like a great guy. I'd like to hear more of his neat poetry. Would you like to go to the beach? How about breakfast?"

Sheeni told me to come back in two hours. She said she was going on a hike and I could come along "if I liked." Just the two of us together in the primeval wilderness. What rapture!

Suddenly, I was ravenous. I walked into town, found an open cafe, and ate six chocolate cream-filled donuts. As the life-giving sugar entered my bloodstream, I felt immediately restored. I also figured I'd be safely back in Oakland before the zits started erupting.

Sheeni was ready when I returned promptly at 8:15. She was wearing stout hiking boots, khaki shorts, brown work shirt, red bandanna neckerchief, and an Australian bush hat. A large canvas knapsack was slung over her shoulders. She looked like the world's most desirable Girl Scout.

"Nick, where are your hiking boots, water bottle, provisions, survey maps, and compass?" she inquired.

I said I wasn't hungry, wasn't thirsty, had an infallible sense of direction, and preferred to hike in running shoes. "Like John Muir," I said, "I enter the wilderness with nothing more than my journal and a childlike sense of wonder."

Sheeni said OK, but she didn't plan to baby "any slackers." She set a fast pace out of town. We walked through rolling brown hills that seemed, mostly, to roll uphill. She asked me if I had heard from Martha. I said yes, Martha reports she is busy modelling and has almost finished her monograph on B. Coma, an early blues singer. I asked if Trent was well. Sheeni said he was very well, thank you, and was hoping to visit Lakeport that weekend. The miserable jerk! I said how unfortunate I wouldn't get to meet him as we were leaving on Friday. Sheeni said yes that was unfortunate as she was certain the two of us "would become great pals." I said any friend of hers was a friend of mine.

"Likewise, I'm sure," she replied.

Despite the heat, Sheeni maintained a torrid pace. All those aerobic church services have left her awesomely fit. I followed as best I could, keeping up my spirits by concentrating on the rhythmic movement of her exquisite ass inside her hiking shorts. After a while the exertion, fatigue, lack of sleep, nervous excitation, and six greasy donuts began to be felt in my lower digestive tract. I excused myself and ran into a clump of trees. Some time later, I stumbled back down the trail to find Sheeni reading my journal!

I grabbed it away from her. The brazen sneak wasn't even embarrassed. She said I had egregious handwriting, a fairly decent vocabulary, and Trent was not an "affected twit." I replied that my private thoughts were "none of her damn business." How would you like it, I demanded, if I read your journal?

"Read it if you like," she said, pulling the blue notebook from her pack. I opened it to the last entry and squinted at the neat script. Except for names (a lot of them mine!), it was undecipherable gibberish.

"It's a shorthand of my own devising," said Sheeni smugly. "A necessity for an intelligent child in a household with two prying Christian parents."

"What does this say?" I demanded.

"Wouldn't you just like to know," she teased, taking back her notebook. "That last passage would be of particularly compelling interest to you too."

I grabbed her by her thin, delicate wrists and demanded she spill the beans. She refused. We wrestled. Sheeni protested. I held on tighter. Her perspiring, squirming body brushed against mine. Instant T.E. She saw it. "Hard-on!" she chanted, "Nickie's got a hard-on. Nickie's got a hard-on!" I turned baboon-ass red and let her go. She continued to chant. I told her to stop. She went on. "Nickie's got a hard-on!" I put my hand on my zipper. "Stop or I flash," I said.

"You wouldn't dare," exclaimed Sheeni.

"I will too," I said.

"You haven't the nerve," she taunted.

I unzipped and fished around in my shorts. My erect pecker blinked, surprised, in the bright sunshine. Sheeni studied it with interest.

"It's extremely ugly and not very big," she said.

I suddenly felt very shy and put away my wilting tool.

"I don't know why boys always want to expose those ugly things," Sheeni said, sitting on a tree stump. "Trent is obsessed with showing me his. He imagines it gives me a thrill."

"I suppose it's quite good-sized," I said.

"Oh enormous," she replied. "Mother Nature can certainly be quixotically extravagant at times." (I hate you Trent.)

I had to know. "Have you and Trent got it on?" I asked, sitting on the tree trunk beside her. Our bodies touched, but Sheeni didn't pull away.

"I haven't made love with Trent, if that's what you want to know," she said. (Thank God!) "But I'm not a virgin." (Rats!)

Sheeni said when she turned 13 she resolved to discard the crushing burden of her virginity. She promptly gave it up to a convenient high-school jock in her neighborhood named Bruno.

"Did you enjoy it?" I asked.

"Hardly," she said. "The clod was a clumsy dolt, but fortunately it was all over in five seconds. I found the act slightly less erotic than a gynecological exam. But according to the sex manuals I've read, it's supposed to get better with practice."

"Why not practice with Trent?" I asked. (Or me!)

She explained she was waiting for "grand passions in romantic European venues," not "furtive back-seat gropings in the California boondocks."

I said I could see her point.

"You're still a virgin, I can tell," said Sheeni, smiling. (It shows!) "Maybe that's why I like you."

Sheeni looked at me expectantly. I looked back and gulped.

"Kiss me, you weinie," she said.

I put my arms around her and tentatively approached her luscious mouth. Our noses dodged successfully and our lips met. Hers were soft and warm and wonderful. Her lips parted and I tasted her sweet tongue. The experience was awesome. We're talking life-threatening heart palpitations and instant, killer T.E. After a very long time, we broke off.

"My hard-on is back," I confessed.

"That's to be expected," said Sheeni, jumping up. "OK, lover. Break's over. Let's go!"

We hiked on. For twelve miles. In the heat. Straight up. My feet never touched the ground.

Later, walking hand-in-hand through town on the way home, we passed the fat, bald guy shuffling toward the beach in a grossly skimpy bathing suit. He pretended not to know me. Sheeni smiled at him and said, "Hello, Reverend Knuddlesdopper." He mumbled an incoherent reply and hurried on.

That fat pervert is the minister for the trailer congregation! Sheeni was shocked I'd gotten in the shower with him. "Knuddy has the hots for boy," she said, matter-of-factly. "Everyone knows it. He says extreme pedophilia like his is irrefutable proof of the existence of the devil. The congregation says special prayers for him—especially the younger boys."

"Well, they haven't helped," I said.

"Get up early tomorrow," said Sheeni. "And you can shower with me in the ladies' room." She looked me in the eye. "If you dare."

I said it was a date.

8:45 p.m. Hot and tired, the sun is beginning to set behind Mt. Konocti. Sheeni and I are sitting at the tiny green picnic table on my trailer patio writing in our journals. Mom, after another day of righteous ostracism, was happy to have Sheeni's cheerful company for dinner. During the meal, Sheeni was endearingly polite, mature, and even tried to make intelligent conversation about trailers with Jerry. He mostly leered and stared at her chest. I may murder him later in his sleep.

Can't write any more. I am completely brain dead. I am looking forward to a good-night kiss (and possible furtive grope) with you know who.

9:30 p.m. I returned from grappling in the warm darkness with Sheeni to find this note in my back pants pocket (and I thought she had been caressing my ass!):

Dear Nick,

Please excuse me for reading your journal. I have found that people who can successfully resist temptation invariably lead depressingly stunted lives. Fortunately, any willpower I ever had withered long ago.

Naturally, I was charmed by what you wrote about me. Your contemplation of suicide and your invention of Martha—both clearly prompted by your regard for me—cannot help but evoke a strong emotional response in my breast.

We are both young. At least one of us is innocent. The future is so precarious. Yet I look forward to our times together. Let's just live and what happens will happen.

Yours affectionately,
Sheeni

I'm lying in bed, reading her wonderful note over and over again. My first love letter! " . . .what happens will happen." I hope that means what I think it means.

WEDNESDAY, August 22 — Another perfect California summer dawn: a cool breeze smelling of brown grass and eucalyptus, crystal sunshine, a pale moon lingering in the blue morning sky, birds singing, dogs barking in the distance. A good morning to linger in bed, thinking about life and idly scratching your dick. But I bounded up at 5:45—a man with a mission. I slipped a robe over my nakedness, struggled for what seemed like hours to piss through an anticipatory erection, brushed my pearlies, then quietly slipped out the trailer door.

Except for birds twittering in the trees, the trailer park was absolutely still and silent. As I approached the shower building I could hear the sound of running water from the women's side—enticing music to my ears. I feinted a pass at the men's entrance, then darted quickly around the corner and entered through the forbidden door.

To my surprise, the women's shower room had real stalls and privacy doors. Sheeni, wisely, had selected the last stall in the row. I walked toward the cloud of steam billowing over the old green plywood, my robe bulging out in front like the prow of a Roman galley. In one smooth, effortless motion I shed my robe, hung it on a hook, kicked off my slippers, opened the shower door, and stepped into the steaming spray.

Sheeni looked up startled. Pendulous breasts! Sagging skin! Patch of white hair under the drooping belly! Wrinkles! It was Mrs. Clarkelson!

"Excuse me!" I stammered. She screamed and hit me in the eye with a bar of Lifebuoy. Blinded, I stepped back and slipped on the soap. I fell, knocking the naked old lady down on top of me. She struggled for a handhold, grabbed my boner, and screamed. "Rape! Rape!" Pinned to the wet cement, shower spraying directly in my face, I gulped for air but kept swallowing water. Mrs. Clarkelson pummeled my nuts with her fists. I groaned and pushed her away, fingers repelling from contact with the ancient flesh. Then the door swung open and a hand reached in and pulled me up. It was Sheeni. "Get out quick!" she hissed. I grabbed my robe and ran, while Sheeni—still wearing her bathrobe—dived into the hot spray to rescue the victim of my lust.

Back in the trailer, I threw on my clothes and woke up Mom. "I'm going into town for breakfast," I whispered. "If anyone comes around here, tell them it was all a mistake. A big mistake."

Startled, Mom wanted to know more, but I left before the inquisition could begin. As I ran through the park, a few of the residents out on their patios eyed me suspiciously. Jet-propelled by adrenalin, I raced into town—not stopping until I reached the donut shop. Too scared to eat much, I gulped down four buttermilk bars, then lingered longer over a maple bar. A sheriff's car roared down the street (toward the trailer park), its siren wailing. I wondered if I would be sent to the California Youth Authority for this first offense. There to be brutally gang-raped and to contract AIDS. I would be dead before I was 20—never to have had a sexual experience with a woman under age 79. With nothing to lose now, I ordered a cream-filled chocolate old-fashioned. Zits were the least of my worries.

Sheeni found me on the beach an hour later. I was down by the water, trying to wash human vomit (mine) from my tee-shirt. She walked toward me across the sand—a vision in lavender. Pale lavender blouse, unbuttoned, over an aubergine two-piece bathing suit. Someday, I thought, this beauty will look like Mrs. Clarkelson. How cruel is the hand of time. Better to die young than witness such ravages.

Sheeni smiled, leaned over (a view of exquisite breasts, nestled in purple), and kissed me. "Yuck," she said, "you taste awful. What have you been doing?"

"Puking donuts," I answered. "They taste better going down than coming up. Should I go to the sheriff's now?"

"Not this time," said Sheeni, plopping down on the sand. "I saved your ass."

"She's not going to press charges?"

"I don't think so. I managed to convince her it was an accident. I told her you were retarded and couldn't read the sign. Odd, though, she initially had some trouble believing that."

"Thanks a pantsfull!" I said.

"She wanted to know why—if it was all an innocent mistake—your privates were elevated."

"My what?" I asked.

"That was the expression she used. Rather charmingly quaint. She doesn't know your privates are always getting elevated. They look a bit elevated now, for example."

I looked down. She had a point there.

Sheeni went on. "Thinking fast, I said, of course, any man would get excited by the sight of her feminine charms—however innocent their intentions. She did agree with that. So, anyway, from now on when you see her you have to act retarded. Drool on your shirt and pick your nose—you know, sort of like you're always doing."

"Oh yeah!" I leaped at her and wrestled for a kiss. As she squirmed in my arms, my hand grasped the soft roundness of a breast. She laughed and pushed me away.

"Off, off, Sir Vomit! Away with thy gastric breath!"

I desisted and lay back on the warm sand. Sheeni leaned over and dribbled sand on my chest. "Say, where were you anyway?" I demanded. "We said five minutes to six."

"Women are always discretely late. It's expected of us."

"Swell. And the punctual guy fries in the chair for rape."

"Don't complain. At least you got to shower with a naked woman." Sheeni smiled slyly and leaned closer, pressing her warm breast into mine. Grains of white sand clung like sugar to her tanned shoulders.

"Yeah, that's true," I said. "Better Mrs. Clarkelson than Rev. Knuddlesdopper. But I wish it was you."

"Me too," Sheeni said.

This time, she let me kiss her.

We spent the rest of the morning on the beach. Sheeni went in the water for a swim, then came out—shivering, nipples tantalizingly erect under the purple Spandex—to towel off in the warm sun. She told me more about her life. She has one sibling—a much older brother named Paul, who, in between sampling advanced psychedelics, plays jazz trumpet. He called once about six years ago to request they send his high school lifeguard certificate to a post office box in Winnemucca, Nevada. "An arid region," remarked Sheeni, "not known for its water sports." That's the last they've heard from him.

Despite Sheeni's brilliant mind, she attends public school. Every kid in Ukiah does. She's known Trent since she was in kindergarten and he was a glamorous first-grader. They've always been smarter than everyone else in their school (especially the teachers), and therefore have had to deal with much resentment and jealousy. That's one of the bonds that unites them. (But not, I hope, for long!) Trent has it a bit easier since he can use sports to prove he's still one of the guys. But since developing beauty to match her brains, Sheeni has had to cope with outright overt hostility.

"Sometimes I wish I were plain and dull," lamented the ravishing intellectual.

"So do I," I said.

"But honey, you are," she teased.

To make her retract that slur, I had to resort to hand-to-hand (and hand-to-other-places) combat.

Later in the afternoon we drove around the lake with Jerry and the Corndog Queen in the slab-sided Lincoln. Exiting the trailer park, we passed Mrs. Clarkelson watering the petunia bed (shaped like a cross) in front of the cement-block church. She peered at me with fierce suspicion, so I crossed my eyes and probed for a booger. Beside me in the back seat, Sheeni bit her hand to stifle hysterics. Mom told me to "take my finger out of my nose and act my age."

Sheeni didn't seem to mind the wind tunnel. She tied a scarf around her chestnut locks and sat back in the breeze, casually resting a hand on the inside of my thigh. As we rounded a curve at 60, she reached over, yanked the sunglasses off my nose, and tossed them over her shoulder into the lake.

Our destination was toward Middleton where Jerry had sniffed out a trailer for sale. The place was deep in the boonies, but after a few wrong turns on back country roads, we came to a tiny, run-down shack perched on stilts over a steep hillside. The dusty yard was littered with dead cars, rusty school buses, old fruit processing machinery, and a decrepit ferris wheel from some long-extinct midway. Residing in the rusty junk were assorted ill-kept dogs, cats, chickens, goats, and a pig or two. The squire of this manor was a toothless old geezer with the world's largest beer gut. Jerry's third-trimester bulge wasn't even in the competition.

The geezer led us up a dusty track to a corrugated iron shed. The trailer was inside. It appeared to be an RV for midgets. Over twenty feet long, it was little more than four feet high. Mom looked concerned. "Jerry, what do we do?" she whispered, "crawl around inside on our hands and knees?"

The geezer laughed. "Watch this," he said. He opened a small compartment above the back bumper, turned a knob, and began pumping a metal handle. With each stroke, the trailer rose a notch, until it had miraculously doubled in height. "Saves on gas," said the geezer.

Sheeni elaborated, "The lowered profile yields reduced wind resistance on the highway."

Jerry, I could tell, was enthralled. We all trooped through the tiny home on wheels. It was newer than "My Green Haven" but not by much. In the front was a dinette for four, then came a miniaturized kitchen, followed chastely by two single beds separated by a modesty aisle. In the tail was a compact bathroom complete with sink, marine toilet (smelling of old piss), and a shiny, stainless steel bathtub big enough for an adult human. Mom and Sheeni exclaimed over the amenities, while Jerry—ever the shrewd bargainer—pointed out the flaws. For example, he was not happy about the twin beds.

The geezer sucked his gums. "Better though, if you snore," he said.

"I don't have that problem," countered Jerry. (What a liar!)

"Well, maybe you wet the bed."

"Nope," said Jerry. "Don't do that either."

"Well, you might someday," said the Geezer. "When you get old. I've been known to dribble a drop or two. I snore now too. Never did before."

I shuddered to contemplate what life as the geezer's bed partner must be like. I looked over at Sheeni, who was inspecting the wardrobe closet. Yes, I could imagine honeymooning in this trailer with her—twin beds or not. I bet if we tried we could both squeeze into that cozy bathtub. I happily contemplated that scene, and had to sit down on one of the beds to conceal a sudden T.E. The mattress sagged and smelled of mildew. Jerry and the geezer began their final dance.

"What's your cash price?" asked Jerry.

"I said in the ad," replied the old man. "$1,000 firm."

"Thousand, huh?" Jerry looked dubious. "That must be with a guarantee."

"As is, where she is," said the geezer.

"I don't know," replied Jerry. "You can smell the dry rot. The roof probably needs work and I really don't want twin beds. I couldn't go over $800."

The geezer pondered this bad news.

"There are mouse droppings in all the closets," said Sheeni. "And the electrical outlets aren't grounded."

Jerry looked impressed by my taste in women.

The geezer cleared his throat. "I might take $950."

"$900," said Jerry.

"$925," countered the geezer.

They agreed on $910, with the seller writing out a false bill of sale for $200 to save on sales tax at the DMV. Mom, as a salaried employee of the Department of Motor Vehicles, looked a bit uncomfortable about this, but did not object. While the men counted the greenbacks and did the paperwork, Sheeni and I wandered around the junk-strewn lot, scattering the clucking chickens before us.

Sheeni knelt beside an old cardboard box. "Oh look, Nickie!" she exclaimed. "Aren't they cute!"

In the box were a half-dozen squirming puppies. They were mostly black with a few spots of white divvied up, here and there, among them. They had short droopy ears, curled-up tails, and tiny bat-like faces. The mother, lying limp in the heat nearby, appeared to be part pug. She had bulging black eyes, a pushed-in nose, and a prominent underbite. She was the second ugliest dog I had every seen. The father, snarling at us from the end of a rope tied to smashed pinball machine, was the ugliest.

Sheeni picked up the puppy with the most white spots. Thrilled to be singled out, he peed on her blouse. She didn't seem to mind and let him lick her lovely mouth. "Isn't he cute?" she said.

"He's adorable," I lied. I made a mental note not to kiss her again until she had brushed and gargled.

"I wonder if they're for sale?" Sheeni said. "Do you suppose?"

"Wouldn't surprise me," I said. "But will your parents let you have a dog?"

"Of course," said Sheeni, "they love animals."

The geezer priced the dog at an exorbitant $10. This was more than Sheeni and I had between us. Broken-hearted, close to tears, she clutched the puppy to her breast. This was too much for the geezer. He studied her chest awhile, then said she could take the puppy for free. (Very close to the dog's actual value, I thought.)

Sheeni was overjoyed. For a moment I feared she was actually going to kiss the old geezer. More than mouthwash would be required to slay those cooties. Instead, Sheeni smooched her puppy, who she promptly named Albert (pronounced "Al-bare"), after the existentially deceased French writer Albert Camus.

Albert could tell he was moving up in the world and seemed pleased to be turning his back, at last, on his sordid origins. He looked over to make sure his brothers and sisters could see him seated in a Lincoln Continental convertible. Fortunately for his self-esteem, we were not hauling the trailer that afternoon. Jerry planned to return for his prize tomorrow after getting a hitch welded to the Lincoln. So, for the drive home, Albert sat proudly on Sheeni's lap, hopping down only once to take a dump on the white carpet. Jerry was incensed, but Sheeni put her charm in overdrive and appeased him with the promise that Nick would "clean up every last morsel."

Protesting vehemently, I forgot to dodge when she moved in and planted a wet one on my mouth. Yuck. The woman I love has dog breath.

Back at "My Green Haven," Sheeni hopped out of the car and was off with her dog like she'd been shot from a gun. Jerry examined the fecal matter on his carpet and gave me ten minutes either to remove it completely or "take a slug to the head from a .357." I went to work with paper towels, cold water, and detergent. As I was bent over my labors, the always-suspicious Mrs. Clarkelson walked by to snoop. I drooled, chuckled to myself, and playfully tossed a dog turd in her direction. She screamed and jumped back. This brought out Mom to investigate. Mrs. Clarkelson, red-faced, said to Mom, "Look into your soul, sinner. And you will see why God punished you with this child."

"Up yours, bitch," replied Mom with cogent succinctness.

Too shocked to reply, Mrs. Clarkelson stormed off.

"What did you say to that woman?" Mom demanded.

I felt a discreet lie was called for here. "She asked me if you and Jerry were married," I said. "I told her it was none of her business."

"Good for you, Nick," said Mom. "The nerve of these people!"

8:30 p.m. Sheeni and I are sitting at the little green table on the patio catching up on our journals. Albert is asleep at Sheeni's feet. After a tumultuous struggle, Sheeni persuaded her parents to let her keep him—even though her mother declared he has "the face of Beelzebub." (She's right.) But Sheeni had to agree to attend church "no fewer than two times per week." She was not happy about being forced into this concession, but felt, on balance, that Albert was worth it. "Besides," she said, "I can always use the exercise."

I am amazed at the affection Sheeni lavishes on that smelly, repugnant beast. If only she were so attentively loving with me. Now I have the egregious Trent to be jealous of, plus a dog. Falling in love has certainly not improved my peace of mind.

10:30 p.m. Sheeni gave me a long, deep goodnight kiss in the dark and let me put my hand under her bra. I cannot begin to describe the tactile pleasures of her nakedness: the soft round fullness, the smooth warm flesh, the firmness of the erect nipple under my busy thumb, the intoxicating girl aromas. Tomorrow I go for third base.

When I came into the trailer (after waiting for my throbbing T.E. to subside), I discovered a stain on my jeans. No, lower. The jealous Albert had peed on my leg.

THURSDAY, August 23 — I awoke to a dreadful thought. This was my last full day with Sheeni. Tomorrow we return to Oakland. How can I exist without her! Soon, she'll be back in Trent's tanned, muscular arms, feeling the press of his manly physique against her delicate body. This thought is pure, physical torture for me. I will have to kill Trent and accept the consequences. I can see no other alternative. I wonder if Jerry really has a .357. What if it's not loaded? Can 14-year-olds legally buy bullets? Probably they can. Thank God for the NRA!

My homicidal ruminations were interrupted by a knock on the door. I put on my robe and opened it. There in the early morning sunshine—panic-stricken, eyes red from crying—stood my beloved. Now the hour was at hand for young Sidney Carton to perform a noble deed for the woman he loves.

Sheeni told me the whole ugly story as we walked to the donut shop. She had retired to her tiny second-story bedroom with Albert curled up in her arms. (Oh lucky Albert!) During the night, while she slept, dreaming her sweet girlish dreams, he had slipped downstairs for some after-hours puppy mischief. When Sheeni's parents woke this morning, they came into the living room to find the treasured family Bible (actually the paperback vacation-home copy) shredded all over the floor. Even then, the godless canine was masticating through the last of Corinthians. For Mrs. Saunders, this singular act of desecration confirmed Albert's diabolical origins. He has been banished, and none of Sheeni's entreaties or cajoleries could overturn the parental edict. Albert has been temporarily imprisoned in their patio storage shed until his fate can be decided.

"What am I going to do?" implored Sheeni, biting into a powdered donut. I liked the way the sugar dust clung to her upper lip.

I chewed my maple bar and considered her options. "Let's get married," I said. "Albert can come live with us."

"Oh, Nickie, be serious!"

I was never more serious in my life. But I could see Sheeni wasn't quite ready to follow in Millie Filbert's matrimonial footsteps. A pity!

Then I recognized the signs: Sheeni was preparing to put her massive charm in overdrive. I braced for the onslaught.

"Nickie, honey," she purred, "why don't you take Albert? He could be our love child."

"No way," I said.

Tears welled up in Sheeni's beautiful blue eyes. "At least you could consider it, honey. For me. I never asked you for anything before."

I considered it. On the one hand was a dumb, smelly, ugly dog who had already proven he could be trouble. On the other hand, keeping him with me would provide a concrete (well, at least a canine) link with Sheeni. Then I had one of those sudden flashes of inspiration that come only once or twice in a lifetime. Albert was a bargaining chip sent from heaven. (Or perhaps from hell?)

"Maybe I could take him," I said, biting into a glazed old-fashioned.

Sheeni waited expectantly. I chewed my donut thoughtfully.

"But I have certain conditions."

"What sort of conditions?" she asked nervously.

"If Albert is going to be our love child, I'd want to feel like the only dad on the scene. Trent has to go."

Sheeni pondered this. "That's asking a lot," she said at last.

"Is it?" I asked.

"We're very close."

"I want to be even closer."

"Trent has a brilliant mind," Sheeni observed.

"I'm not exactly retarded."

"He's very good looking."

"Looks aren't everything."

"He has a great body."

"OK, I can take up body-building."

Sheeni bit her lip and thought some more. "Trent worships the ground I walk on."

Welcome to the club Trent! "It's your choice," I said. "Life with me and the dog you love. Or a pet-free existence with a shallow, egotistical poet."

Sheeni swallowed the last of her donut and licked her lovely fingers. "OK, Nick. I guess I don't have any choice. I'll break up with Trent. But if he kills himself, it's on your conscience."

"I accept full responsibility," I said. "For the dog. And the deserted lover."

Sheeni beamed. "Well good. That's settled."

"Not quite, darling," I said. "I want one thing more."

"What?"

I looked Sheeni straight in the eyes. "You know," I said.

"Oh no," protested Sheeni. "Not that. You're too young. I don't want that on my conscience."

"What do you mean!" I said. "You were 13!"

"That's different. Girls mature faster."

"But how else can I really feel bonded to my love child?" I demanded.

Sheeni looked like she regretted ever having introduced that phrase into the conversation. "Do you have a condom?"

Now we were getting somewhere! "Of course," I said.

"What brand?"

I checked my wallet. "Uh, it's a Sheik."

"That's bad," said Sheeni. "Those are made for big guys. It might slip off you. And motherhood is definitely not in my plans."

For a woman with just one sexual experience, Sheeni seemed to know a great deal about male contraceptives. "OK," I said, "I'll get another kind. Any brand you want."

Sheeni thought some more. "It has to be in a safe place. A nice comfortable bed. With no threat of interruptions. And for relaxation and mood setting, some good red wine—preferably French."

I was suddenly aware the woman I loved was definitely the daughter of a successful attorney.

"OK," I said. "Anything else?"

"I want a new condom. Not one that's been riding around in your wallet for years. *Consumers* rated them a while back, I suggest you get their top-rated brand. This may take some research in the library. I'd appreciate a photocopy of the article. Plus, for supplementary protection, I want a name-brand spermicide."

"How about I have a quick vasectomy just to be on the safe side?" I asked.

The sarcasm didn't register. "Well, Nick. That, of course, is your decision to make," Sheeni said.

"Don't you want to have my children someday?" I asked.

Sheeni was shocked. "Don't be silly. I don't plan to marry until I'm at least 30. And the father of my future children is probably now at the Sorbonne, studying philosophy."

How I hate that unknown pretentious Frog!

Pensively, I watched Sheeni sip her coffee. I had a tall mountain to climb, with many treacherous glaciers still to cross, but finally, at last, I had obtained a stamped and signed entry visa to the paradise that lay beyond. Now, I could begin to believe that tantalizing but abstract concept, commonly termed "sexual intercourse," might actually become a part of my everyday reality. In short, I had a real prospect for getting laid.

"Well," I said, chugging my coffee, "if I'm going to get all of this ready before tonight, we'd better get started. I wonder what time the library opens?"

"Don't be ridiculous, Nickie," said Sheeni. "You couldn't possibly get everything arranged today. Besides, I'm not in the mood."

"Well, what should we do then?" I asked dejectedly.

"Let's go rescue darling Albert!"

The smelly beast was overjoyed to be liberated from his patio sweat box. While Sheeni lavished kisses on him, he cast a smug glance in my direction— just like Dad with his bimbettes. Boy, will that ugly dog be surprised when he finds out who's going to be exercising suzerainty over his food bowl. I expect to see lots of humble doggy groveling then.

As we were leaving, I noticed a pale, ghostly face peering at us from behind a curtain in the trailer. The woman looked like Sheeni in the year 2174 A.D.

"Was that your grandmother?" I asked.

"No, my mother." Sheeni squeezed her puppy and said no more.

I sensed a terrible dark secret lay beyond those high aluminum walls. My heart overflowed with emotion, and I felt a powerful urge to shelter my inamorata from life's adversities. I can only hope this does not cause some future therapist to label me a "rescuer."

We went back to "My Green Haven" to discuss dog adoption with Mom, but she and Jerry were out. No doubt off shopping for trailer hitches. With just the two of us (plus Albert) alone in the trailer, the atmosphere quickly became charged with intense erotic energy.

Soon, we were in each other's arms on the tiny couch—our locked mouths mixing the lingering bitterness of coffee with the sweet taste of desire. Emboldened by passion, I pushed up Sheeni's bikini top. In the bright light of day I could finally view her fabulous breasts—made even more delectable by the contrast of virginal white skin rising from deep tan. Sheeni moaned as my eager mouth closed around her warm nipple. She moved her hand down my body and found the T.E. throbbing in my pants. I unzipped and Sheeni pulled out my granite-like tool as the Lincoln rumbled to a stop outside.

Damn!

Furious barking from Albert. Sheeni instantly unclinched and pulled down her top, expertly tucking away her incomparable charms. I lurched up and stepped on Albert, who began to howl. Sheeni reached down to comfort him, as I lumbered painfully toward the bathroom, my out-thrusting T.E. preceding me by several feet.

From within the tiny, dim bathroom I heard Sheeni greet Mom and Jerry.

"What's wrong with that damn dog?" asked Jerry.

"I fear it's separation anxiety," answered Sheeni.

Jerry did not reply.

"Where's Nick?" asked Mom.

Coolly Sheeni replied, "Oh, he's in the bathroom putting on his bathing suit. We're going to the beach."

I contemplated my record-setting T.E. Without relief this vast erection would take several months to subside. I couldn't wait. Nine quick strokes (one for each inch?) and a monumental gusher splattered the walls like milky buckshot. My entire nervous system felt like it was pulsing up through my urethra. If light petting was this intense, could I really live through intercourse? Only time will tell.

After wiping down the walls and ceiling, I quickly changed into my bathing suit, grabbed my beach gear, and calmly walked into the living room. Sheeni was cuddling our love child.

"Mrs. Twisp," said Sheeni, "Nick has something to ask you."

Mom assumed a wary parental posture. I flashed a cautionary glance at Sheeni.

"Uh," I said, thinking fast, "is it OK if Sheeni goes out to dinner with us tonight? It's our last night together."

Mom smiled. "Sure, that would be nice. Sheeni, our reservations are at seven."

"Wear something low cut," suggested Jerry with a leer. Mom gave him a dirty look.

"Just kidding, doll," he said, slapping Mom on the ass. His hand lingered on her shorts. "You people leaving now or what?" he asked.

We left quickly. Sheeni snapped a leash on Albert and the three of us strolled toward the lake in the hot sunshine.

"Sorry I jumped the gun on asking your mother about Albert," Sheeni said. "There won't be any problem keeping him will there?"

"Nothing insurmountable," I replied. "Of course, a big request like this requires careful strategic planning. You can't just waltz in and pop the question. That invites the Big No. And once you get parental ego invested in a 'no,' then you have to contrive some convoluted face-saving way for them to say 'yes'."

"Well at least, Nickie, you don't have to deal with constant interference from God. Be thankful for that."

"I am!"

We passed Mrs. Clarkelson, who was out on her tiny patio folding newspapers into tsetse fly swatters for the missionaries in Africa. I stuck a finger in my nose.

"Sheeni, why are you holding that boy's hand?" the old lady demanded.

"I'm taking him to the lake, Mrs. Clarkelson," replied Sheeni brightly. "It's for his hydrotherapy."

"Oh, I see. Well, I suppose that's all right then."

I held out my finger. "Want a booger?" I grunted. "I've got lots."

Mrs. Clarkelson shuddered. "No, thank you, young man. That's filthy and nasty."

"Be nice, Nickie," Sheeni scolded, "or I won't buy you a Popsicle."

I started to slobber and pule, continuing until we were out of sight of Mrs. Clarkelson.

"You do that marvelously well," said Sheeni.

"Thank you, my dear," I said. "I hope to study with Stanislavsky some day."

"That will take some doing," replied Sheeni. "He's been dead for 50 years."

Loving Sheeni, I decided, is at times like being romantically involved with the *Encyclopedia Britannica*.

We walked through town. The motel-lined streets were busier now that the weekend was approaching. A slow parade of over-heating motorhomes, campers, and big pickups towing speed boats inched toward the blue water. Three rednecks leaned out their windows to whistle at Sheeni, and two fat women called out rude comments about the ugliness of our dog. Sheeni and Albert pretended not to notice.

Large signs at the beach proclaimed "No Dogs Allowed," but Sheeni blithely ignored them. We spread our towels in the hot sand and worked on our tans. Albert quickly went to sleep in the shade under Sheeni's overturned straw basket—snoring noisily through his pushed-in snout. I oiled up my date and got a T.E. you could spot three miles off-shore.

"Maybe, honey, you should have your pituitary checked," Sheeni said. "I've never seen anyone with such overactive hormones."

I assured her the treatment I required was a simple in-home procedure that could be performed without medical supervision.

"Soon," said Sheeni. "Be patient, Nickie. I'll figure out some way to come down to see Albert and you."

"God, I hope so!"

The rest of the afternoon (the last with Sheeni until who knows when) passed in a warm haze. I remember the smells of suntan lotion and hotdogs, the heat of the sun on my back, the inch by inch shock of cold water, the taste of lake water on sweet lips, the touch of a hand slipping into my trunks under murky green water, the mystery of a soft cleft felt only for an instant through thin wet Spandex.

When, tired and sun-baked, we got back to Sheeni's trailer, she paused to remove the mail. One letter, I could see, was addressed to her in a bold masculine hand.

"Shall I tear that up for you, honey?" I asked.

"Why no, darling. That wouldn't be quite fair to the sender, would it?"

"I am not interested in fairness toward that person," I replied.

"Why not?" she demanded.

Because he has kissed you and fondled you and God knows what else with you! "Because I am not," I said. "I hope you will respect my feelings on this matter."

"I don't see what your feelings have to do with destroying U.S. Mail," said Sheeni obdurately. "Vandalism under any pretext is inexcusable. Besides, I have never asked you to tear up a letter from Martha."

"I don't get letters from Martha," I said. "And you know it!"

"Well, when you do, sweetheart," said Sheeni, turning in at her gate and handing me the leash, "bring them by and we'll make confetti of our love letters together." She leaned across the gate and kissed me. "See you at 6:30, lover. Bye-bye, Albert!" Clutching the offensive envelope, she disappeared into the multi-story trailer. Whimpering, Albert tugged at the leash to follow.

I turned away angrily and pulled him along. Albert skidded behind me like a small ugly dog trying to water ski on asphalt. Finally, I picked up the reluctant canine and carried him home.

Mom, still looking flushed from an afternoon of truckdriver wrestling, was standing in bra and slip in the tiny bathroom, putting on her face. From what I could observe, the small bottles of goop multiplied exponentially for each year past 35.

"Oh, there you are," she said. "Better get ready. And what are you doing with that dog?"

"Sheeni asked me to watch him while she dressed," I lied. "Where's Jerry?"

With great concentration, Mom painted on an artificial eyebrow. "He's taking a shower. Do you need one?"

I had a vision of the ever-lurking naked porcine minister. "No, I got clean in the lake," I said. I closed the meager privacy curtain that separated my room from the front of the trailer and pulled down my still-clammy trunks. My damp, sandy member had shriveled to the size of a small, unshelled peanut. Hard to believe this was the same robust organ a feminine hand had been fondling under water only hours before. Knowing my privacy was transient, I dressed quickly. Albert lay on the linoleum and watched me sullenly.

When I finished and pushed back the curtain, Mom was still applying layers to her face. She gave me a quick once-over.

"Oh, you look nice, Nick." She always says this. I could have 47 draining boils on my face (and probably will someday), and as long as my pants were pressed, Mom would say I "looked nice."

"Thanks, Mom. You do too," I lied. I decided to do some preliminary dog adoption spade work. "I found out what kind of dog Albert is," I said casually.

"Oh. What kind?" Mom was brushing on a top-coat sealer that looked like shellac.

"The man in the pet store in town says he's a pure-bred Spanish Tonzello." Albert looked up skeptically.

"Tonzello? Never heard of it."

"Sheeni hadn't either. So we went to the library and looked it up. Turns out that's Spain's famous sports dog."

This piqued Mom's interest. She put down her paintbrush. "What kind of sports?"

"Well, they have this competition. Called a Tonzello-athalon. Each team consists of one athlete and one dog. It's sort of a combination of running, acrobatics, and precision gymnastics. Quite a spectacle to watch, according to the encyclopedia."

"Do they play it here?" Mom asked.

"Not too much," I said. "But Spain is always petitioning to have it made an Olympic sport. If they ever did, it'd be real easy to make the U.S. team, because there are so few Tonzellos in the country."

"The Olympics. My goodness!" Thoughtfully, Mom buffed her varnish. I hoped she was contemplating life as the mother of an Olympic gold medalist.

I picked up the young Tonzello and gave him an affectionate squeeze. "I hear they're real easy to train too." Albert squirmed in my arms, nipped at my hand, and dribbled on my shirt. I hastily put him down.

At that moment, the door opened and Jerry entered. Pink and damp, he was dressed in an off-the-shoulder bathrobe that showed off his lush back hair.

"Hi, Nick," said Jerry, toweling his hair. "You get a piece off your cupcake yet?"

"Jerry, that's not funny," said Mom, walking toward the bedroom. Jerry hungrily eyed her bra and slip.

"I was just kiddin', Estelle," he said, following her. They shut the door. I heard Mom say, "Not now, Jerry. I just put on my make-up." Then came the sounds of a scuffle followed by a slap. I was wondering if this county had 911, when things suddenly became ominously quiet.

"You OK in there?" I called.

After a pause, Mom answered, "We're fine."

Disgusted by parental lust, I put on a record and turned it up loud. "Albert," I said, "this is Frank Sinatra. You are going to be hearing a lot of him."

A half-hour later, everyone except Albert was out on the patio waiting for my date. The Tonzello was locked in the trailer practicing his whimpering skills. Mom was wearing a flaming red, low-cut dress that looked like it had been mail-ordered from Hell, Carnal Sins Division. Jerry apparently had dressed to coordinate with his car: white linen suit, white shoes and belt, lime-green shirt, and yellow bow tie. I had on my usual dress-for-invisibility outfit: flannel trousers, beige shirt, conservative knit tie, and generic tweed jacket. I looked like a Young Americans for Freedom volunteer waiting for Dan Quayle's motorcade to pass by.

We looked up to see a beautiful woman approaching. Improbably, she spoke to us. "Hi, Nickie. Good evening, Mrs. Twisp. Jerry."

It was Sheeni. Make-up, pearl necklace, earrings, and chestnut hair artfully pinned up had added ten stunning years to her age. She looked like the world's most beautiful graduate student. Her exquisite tan glowed like 24 karat gold against the deep blue of her gossamer dress. My heart thumped wildly. I was speechless.

"Good evening, Sheeni," said Mom. "You look nice."

Nice! Nice! How we violate our language!

"You look beautiful," said Sheeni, compounding the language debasement. "And that suit is terrific, Jerry."

"Thanks, doll face," said Jerry.

My paralysis continued. Sheeni looked at me quizzically. "Something wrong, Nickie?" she asked, taking my hand.

"You. You . . . you're beyond rapturous," I stammered.

Sheeni frowned. "No, Nickie. Rapture is a mental state. I don't believe the adjective rapturous can be used to describe someone's physical appearance. That usage is incorrect."

Jerry rescued me from this grammatical conundrum. "OK, let's blow," he said.

We all piled into the big Lincoln—now equipped with a shiny chrome ball on the back bumper. Fastened under the steering wheel was a trailer brake mechanism. Every time Jerry stepped on the brake pedal, a lever on the mechanism pointed obscenely at his crotch.

Mom insisted Jerry put up the top to preserve "the ladies' hairdos." He complied reluctantly, so we had a relatively breeze-free drive to the restaurant. I held Sheeni's warm hand and tried to regain control over my tongue. I felt like Quasimodo on a double-date with Esmerelda. Any minute I expected Trent and the king's soldiers to stop the car and send me back to the bell tower for my presumption. Meanwhile, Esmerelda was giving off fabulous aromas.

"Is, is that perfume?" I inquired.

"Yes," said Sheeni. "Like it? It's Joy, my favorite. It was a gift from—" She stopped just in time.

"Oh," I said. "Well, I like it anyway."

Sheeni leaned over and kissed me. "I like you too."

I took advantage of the occasion to look down her dress—and caught Jerry leering at me in the rear-view mirror. At that moment I felt like the world's youngest dirty old man.

Jerry pulled in and parked at a large lakeside restaurant called Biff's Bosun's Barge. Mounted on a tall steel pole at one end of the crowded parking lot was a World War II landing craft. Anchoring the other end of the lot was an immense plywood cutout of the Flag Raising at Iwo Jima. In between was the restaurant: a rambling, one-story wooden structure with vast expanses of blue-tinted glass facing the lake. Above the windows swam a school of blue neon fish.

Biff himself greeted us in the fishing net-draped lobby. I knew it was Biff because all over the walls were framed photographs of him shaking hands with Famous Celebrities. I recognized Regis Philbin, Barbie Benton, Gary Hart, and—believe it or not—Frank Sinatra, Jr. After brazenly eyeing my date, Biff led us to our table—a choice one beside the windows. Biff held Sheeni's seat out for her and casually laid a liver-spotted paw on her bare shoulder as he was handing her a menu. In retaliation, as I was taking my seat I ground my heel into his toes. After that, I thought, Biff looked at me with new respect.

As usual, we were on the very fringe of the smoking section. Jerry always requested this location so he could blow smoke at anyone he suspected of harboring anti-smoking sentiments. He felt strongly that freedom to smoke was a constitutionally protected right. As he lit up his first unfiltered Camel, I could see him scanning the nearby non-smoking tables for potential fascists. But since this was the boonies, not Berkeley, no one seemed to mind the noxious fumes wafting their way.

"Isn't this nice?" said Mom. We all agreed it was. The sun was setting on the opposite shore, painting the sky and water with pinks, blues, and fluorescent oranges. Power boats zipped by, the people on board laughing and holding aloft cans of beer.

Jerry ordered three margaritas and a root beer from our waitress—a 50-year-old country housewife in Biff's regulation mini-skirt and push-up bra. (Marketing question: do grandmotherly boobs swelling above low-cut bodices sell fish dinners? From the size of the diamond glinting on Biff's pinkie I guess they do.) The waitress looked at Sheeni and didn't even ask for an I.D.! So I slurped my soft drink while the three "adults" sipped their cocktails. Sheeni did offer me a taste of hers. It was intoxicatingly delicious. So far, I have enjoyed every alcoholic beverage I've sampled. Perhaps this means I shall grow up to be an over-sexed alcoholic writer.

We studied the menu. Nouvelle cuisine it was not. Anything that was not deep-fried in molten grease was tossed—raw and bleeding—onto the grill. Mom decided on scallops, Sheeni requested sea bass, and the men ordered steaks. Jerry asked for his medium, so I asked for medium rare, so he asked for medium rare, so I switched to rare, so he decided on rare too. Since I didn't want to eat raw cow the competition stopped there. Surprisingly, both of our steaks arrived grilled a perfect medium rare. (Perhaps it was something Mom whispered to the waitress.) We also had French bread with butter, corn muffins with butter, buttered asparagus, and baked potatoes with butter and sour cream. Butter also appeared to be melting on the sizzling steaks when they arrived. Alas, there was no butter in the salad—only sour cream and blue cheese.

Everyone except the child had a second cocktail and soon the conversation grew loud and boisterous. Sheeni told amusing stories about life in Ukiah and Mom related painfully embarrassing anecdotes about my childhood. From early toilet training mishaps to my brief but mortifying kindergarten crush on Miss Romper Room, Mom trotted out them all with total recall—egged on by an inebriated truckdriver and The Woman I Love. Gamely I smiled and tried to think of it as a celebrity roast.

I was made even more uncomfortable when Sheeni took a Camel from Jerry. It pained me to think of those carcinogenic tars sullying her perfect pink lungs. It saddened me even more to contemplate her Parisian future amidst hordes of nicotine-stained, debauched Frogs. At least I will be there to defend her honor and insist we sit in the non-smoking sections at artsy left-bank cafes.

For dessert we all decided on the specialty of the house: chocolate cheese-cake. It was nice, but a bit on the heavy side. Only the men finished their huge, 3,000-calorie slabs. Jerry also cleaned up Sheeni's and Mom's. But, of course, he has a gut to keep in tone.

By then I was practically comatose, but the other three perked right up when the band started to play. This was a C&W quartet: Ginny and the Country Caballeros. Ginny was fat, 50, and flat (musically only). She sang and played the guitar. Backing her up were three skinny, middle-aged guys who looked like they could have constituted the day shift at the local Shell station. They commanded fiddle, drums, and accordion.

To my horror, couples at tables around us started getting up and drifting toward the dance floor. Like most 14-year-old white youths, I have a morbid fear of being compelled to dance in public. I prayed Sheeni shared my senti-ment. Alas, she did not. First Mom and Jerry got up. Then Sheeni took my hand and led me toward the dreaded Platform of Public Humiliation.

Except for the extremely pleasant sensation of Sheeni's firm breasts against my chest, the experience was a nightmare. When it comes to dancing, I have no talent, no training, and no rhythm. I was also cold sober (unlike my partner), and was acutely aware that my rival in love had doubtless already proven his Terpsichorean mastery. It did not improve my concentration to imagine them clinched cheek-to-cheek (and, even worse, chest to chest), gliding gracefully across some Ukiahan ballroom.

So we danced. Sheeni danced like gay pre-war Paris. I danced like the German Army retreating from Stalingrad. And then, finally, the struggle came to an end. We were out in the cool night air—walking arm-in-arm toward our waiting Lincoln. Jerry was singing, the Corndog Queen was whistling, Sheeni was humming, and I was immensely relieved.

In the dark back seat, Sheeni planted a long, ripe one on my lips. She tasted of tequila, cigarettes, and chocolate—a provocatively volatile mixture that ignited my nervous system. I longed to take her right there—even with my condom expired and my mother seated three feet away. I gasped as her exploring hand found the bulge in my trousers. "What about Albert?" she whispered.

"Just go along with anything I say," I whispered back. She gave my throbbing T.E. an assenting squeeze.

I reluctantly removed her hand and leaned forward. "Mom," I said, "Sheeni and I have been talking, and she's willing to give up Albert if it will help me get in the Olympics."

"You don't say!" exclaimed the tipsy Corndog Queen. "You'd do that for Nick, Sheeni dear?"

"Uh, yes, Mrs. Twisp. I guess I would," said Sheeni.

"Oh, that's marvelous, Nickie," replied Mom. "Sheeni, we'll take good care of your dog."

"Thank you, Mrs. Twisp," said Sheeni. She looked wonderingly at me.

I smiled and kissed her. Trent, I thought, you are history.

Jerry was in no condition to be driving anything larger than a golf ball, but soon we were lurching safely to a stop in front of "My Green Haven." Sheeni said good night, and gave Mom and Jerry a hug. The latter also swiped a kiss, which the surprised recipient later confided to me had been of the most intimate French variety. I added that to my long list of wrongs to be avenged.

I escorted Sheeni home. We have a donut date for tomorrow morning, but this was to be our last few moments of (comparative) privacy. As we walked arm-in-arm past the darkened trailers glinting silver in the warm moonlight, I explained Albert's metamorphosis from generic ugly mutt to glamorous, Olympic-caliber Tonzello sports dog.

"You are a genius," exclaimed Sheeni, laughing. "An absolute genius!"

I said it was nothing, but, in truth, these were the very words I had always longed to hear from the lips of a beautiful woman. And I was only 14! Some men wait a lifetime and die, never having heard those sweet syllables.

In the deep shadows under Sheeni's trailer awning, our eager bodies joined in unrestrained passion. Cautiously, I tasted her hot lips, happily detecting not a trace of the vile truckdriver. Soon, we were exploring the erotic limits of the human kiss. My tongue found her tongue, her teeth, her molars, her gums, her uvula, and even dislodged an unchewed morsel of sea bass. As I was attempting to introduce my right hand into her dress, a light came on in the trailer and the door opened. Looming in the doorway was Sheeni's 5,000-year-old mother.

"Sheeni," she croaked, "is that you?"

Sheeni smoothed her hair and strolled over into the pool of light.

"Yes, Mother," she said calmly. "I'm here with Nick."

"Let's see this young heathen."

Sheeni motioned me over. I gulped and edged into the light. "Hello, Mrs. Saunders. Nice to meet you."

"I doubt that very much," said the bathrobed crone. "I've been discussing your case with Mrs. Clarkelson. Her reports are most unsettling. I fear for your immortal soul, young man."

"Nick is a very sweet boy, Mother," said Sheeni. "He's agreed to adopt Albert."

"That is no step toward spiritual redemption. That dog should be stabbed through the heart with a silver dagger one hour before the cock's crow on a moonless night."

Even for Albert that seemed a bit extreme. I was at a loss for a reply.

Sheeni shook my hand. "Good night, Nick. Thank you for dinner. I'll see you tomorrow."

"Uh, good night, Sheeni," I said. "Good night, Mrs. Saunders."

"Look into your soul, young man. Before it's too late!"

"OK, I will," I said, edging toward the gate. I waved to Sheeni as she entered the towering trailer. Pale and expressionless, she didn't wave back.

When I got back to our trailer, I was surprised to see Albert outside tethered to the patio shed. He tugged glumly at his leash and barked. Inside was another surprise. Mom was still cleaning up the mess. Someone had gone systematically through the trailer ripping down and destroying the art. Scattered across the floor were shards of broken glass, chewed pieces of plastic frames, and torn bits of three-dimensional apostles. Oddly, the vandal had spared the one piece of secular art: a 3-D portrait of a pale, over-fed Elvis.

"Look what your horrible dog did!" exclaimed Mom, gingerly picking glass out of the rag rug.

I tried not to panic. "How could Albert have done that? They were way up on the walls! He'd have needed a stepladder."

"All the doors and windows were locked," declared Jerry, sounding like Perry Mason (except Perry usually didn't address the jury while lounging about in his tee-shirt, drinking beer out of a can and scratching his gut). "No one else was here. And there are dog teeth marks everywhere."

"That dog is going back to Sheeni in the morning!" announced Mom.

Rising alarm. "Aw, Mom. He's just a puppy. He'll learn. I'll watch him!"

"No!" said Mom.

Horrors, the dreaded parental 'no.' I floundered for a life rope. "I'll keep him outside. I'll make him a dog house in the back yard!"

"No," said Mom, with sickening finality. "That dog scares me. There's something funny about him."

"But what about my athletic career?"

Jerry snickered. Mom tweezed a sliver of glass from the rug and winced as it pricked her. "You'll just have to stick to baseball, Nick. You already have all the equipment."

I couldn't argue with that point. "Great!" I said. "Ruin my love life! But remember, if I turn gay, it was all your fault!" I stomped off to my room and yanked the curtain closed.

"If you ask me, Estelle," observed Jerry, "I'd say the kid's at least half queer already."

"Oh, hush, Jerry," said Mom. "You're not helping matters."

Jerry replied with a loud, deep, prolonged belch. I resolved to murder him that very night while he slept.

SATURDAY, August 25 — I lost my nerve. I had the butcher knife out of the drawer at 2 a.m., but couldn't go through with it. I considered using it on myself, but I didn't want Sheeni to pine away and die from a broken heart. So I went back to bed and tossed and turned until dawn.

I kept thinking about what Mom had said: "That dog scares me. There's something funny about him." He does seem a bit odd, come to think of it. Why this compulsive streak of profane desecration? And what was his strange hold over Sheeni? Why should she give up Mr. Wonderful (T—-t) for lowly me—just to keep a small, ugly, smelly dog? It didn't add up at 2 a.m. It didn't add up at 5 a.m.

And at 6 a.m., when I crawled out of bed, it still didn't add up. But I had decided one thing: Albert's adoption, though troubling, was still going through. Not without a struggle would I relinquish our love child.

I slipped on my bathrobe and stepped outside. Another beautiful summer morning. On the patio, Albert was asleep on the concrete beside a pile of vomited religious art. He woke with a start and growled. I ignored him and shuffled off for my last shower. I wanted to be well scrubbed for my farewell donut date.

To my surprise, I found my date lurking in the bushes outside the entrance to the men's shower room. She was wearing her fabulously modest bathrobe and (I hoped) nothing else. She waved and motioned me over. "Sheeni!" I said, "what are you . . ."

"Shh-h-h!" she whispered, "Crouch down!"

As I crawled into the bushes beside her, my robe came untied. Neither of us was surprised to discover I had already developed a massive T.E. Sheeni kissed me and squeezed my boner. One of the (many) things I like about Sheeni is her easy familiarity with my penis. "Good morning, sweetheart," I whispered, trying to reach into her flannel.

She pushed my hand away and tugged my robe closed. "Not now, darling," she replied. "You arrived just in time. Mrs. Clarkelson just went into the ladies' shower."

"No way!" I hissed, "I'm not . . ."

"Shh-h-h! Quick, put this sign on the men's door," she instructed, whispering the rest of her bold plan.

"But I can't walk anywhere in my present condition," I protested.

"Nonsense," said Sheeni, "it adds to your appeal."

I was pleased she thought so. I sighed. Blind love compelled my obedience.

I crawled back out of the bushes and hung the sign on the doorknob. Neatly lettered, it read: "Closed for Repairs. Men use ladies' showers 6-7 a.m. only." I then circled back through the trailer park—trying my best to conceal with my towel the monstrous protrusion in my robe. As I passed Rev. Knuddlesdopper's trailer, I bent over provocatively (I hoped) and scratched my bare leg. Walking back toward the shower building, I heard his trailer door open and close behind me. As I came around the corner of the building, I darted into the bushes and crouched beside Sheeni. Ten seconds later, the bathrobed minister appeared. He paused, read the sign, and continued on around the building toward the inviting sound of running water.

Sheeni looked at me and started to count softly. "One, two, three, four . . ." When she reached 14, we heard a blood-curdling scream, followed by a deeper yell, followed by a loud crash. Sheeni continued to count. Between 15 and 23 there were more screams, some muffled howls, and a sharp thud. At 27 we heard a door slam. At 28, Rev. Knuddlesdopper reappeared, rounding the corner in a flat-out sprint. He was beet red, dripping wet, and nude. At 32, the door slammed again. At 34, Mrs. Clarkelson appeared, moving at a fairly rapid clip for her age. She was a somewhat paler red, just as wet, and also naked. She was shouting more or less incoherently, but I thought I made out "pervert," "rape," and "911."

Sheeni stopped counting, stepped briskly out of the bushes, and slipped the sign into her robe. I followed. "Good work, Nick," she said. "Pick me up in ten minutes."

I nodded as she strolled away. I walked casually in the opposite direction, working my way upstream against waves of excited and disturbed trailer residents. I feigned disinterest amid the hubbub. Ten minutes gave me just enough time for a sponge bath in the tiny trailer bathroom. I had to look my best for the woman of my dreams.

In the condensed kitchen, Mom was staring moodily at the kettle warming on the miniature propane range. "What's all that shouting about out there?" she asked in sleepy irritation. "It's enough to wake the dead."

"I don't know," I lied. "People are running about all wet. Maybe it's some kind of religious rite."

"I'm glad we're leaving today," she said, pouring hot water into a mug.

"This place gives me the creeps." She dumped in a spoonful of instant coffee and gave it a slurp. I thought of Jerry having to wake to this apparition every morning and felt a fleeting twinge of pity.

After a vigorous sponge bath, followed by an extra-heavy spritz of deodorant, I dressed quickly and counted out my remaining cash: $43.12. I hoped it would be enough. As I was leaving, Mom looked up from her package of powdered donut gems. "We're leaving at nine," she announced.

Less than two hours remained with my beloved! "But Jerry isn't even up yet," I protested.

"He will be," said Mom. "Don't be late or you walk back."

"OK, OK," I said, slamming the door. I untied my dog and pulled him along.

Sheeni was waiting on her patio. She had changed into a bright yellow tube top (no bra!) and dramatically short cut-off jeans that were unravelling provocatively just millimeters below her reproductive organs. She and Albert were thrilled to be reunited. If only she displayed such unrestrained affection with me. I watched them jealously and fantasized about pulling down her tube top—with my teeth.

To avoid the boisterous crowds in front of Mrs. Clarkelson's trailer, we slipped out through an alley. As we walked into town, Sheeni carried Albert like a baby, lifting him to her face occasionally for a wet doggy kiss (yuck). I wondered if she'd object to gargling with a strong antiseptic before kissing me goodbye.

Fortunately, in the interests of health, the donut shop prohibited dogs. Tethered to a newspaper rack, Albert waited forlornly on the sidewalk while the humans went inside for breakfast. We ordered a combination dozen to start with and settled into "our booth" in the corner. Sheeni sipped her coffee and tackled a maple bar. I experimented with the house specialty: a blueberry-filled raised roll, topped with peanut butter and chocolate chips. It was good, but somewhat lacking in focus.

I was exhilarated by love and the extreme sugar rush, but also felt a fearful panic at the thought of our imminent separation. Sheeni assured me her father often went to San Francisco on legal business and she would wrangle a way to come along. "Dad is much more tractable than Mother," she observed. "It's the difference between pragmatism and zeal. I seem to have inherited their characters in equal measure, which explains the dichotomy in my nature."

"What dichotomy is that?" I asked, munching on a cinnamon twist.

Sheeni picked up an orange-frosted cake donut and licked the frosting. "Surely you've noticed, darling. I approach every aspect of my life with a zealot's intensity. Yet, I am also capable of dramatic compromise. My decision to forsake the love of Trent being an outstanding example of this capacity for self-sacrifice."

I didn't much like the sound of that. I decided to change the subject. "Then that woman I met last night is your natural mother?"

Sheeni frowned. "Of course. Why wouldn't she be?"

"Did she have you late in life?"

"You might say that. She was over 40."

We ate our donuts in silence. When she is emotionally distraught, Sheeni is even more heart-breakingly lovely than usual. Finally she looked up. "My mother, Nick, is a brilliant woman. A very brilliant woman. Her life has turned some strange corners. She has travelled in directions that perhaps we would not choose. But she has been places and seen things that we could not begin to appreciate. Or even understand. These journeys have been difficult and have exacted a fearsome physical toll. Now do you understand?"

It was all as clear as mud. "Sure," I said. "That's OK. She seemed very nice to me."

"She was abominable to you. And you know it. Let us speak the truth to each other always, Nick darling."

"OK, I promise." I even decided to try it. "Sheeni, I think I love you."

Sheeni smiled, a smear of orange frosting heightening the allure of her kissable lips. "Of course you do, Nick. Well, your hormones certainly do. And oddly enough, my hormones like you too."

I'm not sure, but I think that was a declaration of love.

After breakfast, we walked hand-in-hand to the bus station, where I spent my last nickel on this planet shipping a small black dog to Oakland. Not wanting to put my relationship in jeopardy (and knowing the loathsome Trent was expected that afternoon), I was forced to retreat from my vow of candidness. I told Sheeni that Jerry adamantly refused to transport Albert in the Lincoln. I did not mention, of course, that her blasphemous dog once again had been banished. Nor did I confide that I was now facing the daunting task of revoking an overt parental "no" while attempting to conceal my open defiance of it.

Sheeni, as ever supremely confident of her overpowering charms, volunteered to persuade Jerry to change his mind. But I finally convinced her Albert would have a happier and safer trip on the bus. As a family of Berkeley-bound '60s hippies looked on (what was it about that weird decade anyway?), mother and love-child had a touchingly tearful farewell. Then Albert was stuffed into a cage and carried off—howling pitifully. I hoped he had a long and miserable trip. And if, God forbid, the bus were to overturn, at least Albert would die happy in the knowledge that his life was insured—for $500 (payable to me).

A half-hour later Sheeni was distressingly dry-eyed as we said our farewells. Not even my last minute gift to her of my favorite F.S. album ("Songs for Lonely Lovers") activated her tear glands. She hugged the Corndog Queen, shook Jerry's hand, and gave me a sisterly peck on the cheek. Then she whispered in my ear, "Don't forget, darling. Red wine and *Consumer Reports*."

They were the sexiest words that ear had ever heard. I grabbed her and kissed her. She tasted of donuts and dog. Then Jerry fired up the big V-8, and suddenly Sheeni was a small figure retreating in the distance. Then we turned a corner and she was gone. I felt alone. Alone and numb.

The trip back was ineffably sad. We picked up the trailer without a hitch, or should I say, without a mishap. In the harsh light of day it looked much shabbier than it had in the dimness of the shed—especially shackled to the shiny white Lincoln. We looked like the new poor—forced by circumstance to flee California, perhaps to take up tenant farming in rural Oklahoma. As we drove off, the geezer waved and called out, "Happy trailering!" I couldn't help but wonder if that comment was made tongue in cheek. Perhaps it was just my state of mind.

Happy to be back on the road and towing something (a trucker's mission in life?), Jerry popped a Hank Williams tape into the dash and put the pedal to the metal. We roared down the highway, passing everything in sight (including a poignant turn-off sign for Ukiah). Needless to say, the top was down. I sat in the back-seat wind tunnel, dodging bugs and trying not to think of Sheeni getting ready to welcome Trent. (Though I certainly hoped she'd have the decency to change out of that yellow tube top.)

Mom, I noticed, was being coldly correct with Jerry. Women do this to drive men to the brink of insanity. She and Jerry had had words this morning over that always controversial topic, "Where do we park the trailer?" Since Jerry's apartment (the world's smallest in-law studio) doesn't come with parking (or anything else), he proposed to store their Love Mobile in our driveway. Mom pointed out that this valuable space was already occupied by his dead Chevy. Jerry replied he didn't own a Chevy, and the battle was on. I wasn't sure how it turned out, but no one had any obvious bruises.

To our surprise, when we got back to Oakland (even drearier now after a week in the country airing out our aesthetics), we discovered the issue was now moot. The camouflaged Chevy was gone. Apparently, the sailor had had a change of heart and had readopted his sick car. Here Mom made a tactical mistake. While she was thinking up some coldly correct comment to make on this new development, Jerry quickly and professionally backed the trailer up the driveway—threading it neatly between our house and Mr. Ferguson's ramshackle garage with just inches to spare. Faced with this *fait accompli*, Mom could only say, "Jerry, this is just temporary."

"Sure, babe," was his smug reply. He hopped out and began to unload as Mom bustled into the house.

Flecked with bug splatter, I climbed out stiffly and looked about. Here was the place where I had lived before I knew the sweet taste of a woman's lips. Or the tangy taste of a warm nipple. I had left a child and returned a man—a man with lash marks on his heart and feminine fingerprints on his privates. These profound thoughts were interrupted suddenly by a woman's scream. I dropped my bags and ran into the house. Mom was standing in the doorway to the living room, her face twisted into an ugly mask of shock and horror. I looked beyond her. There in the living room, surrounded by all the furniture pushed neatly against the walls, was Jerry's old camouflaged Chevy.

Jerry joined us and stared in stunned disbelief. "Holy shit! How in the name of God?" he muttered.

"How indeed!" exclaimed Mom. "And why!" She stared accusingly at her paramour. "You should've given that man his money back!"

"No way, babe," replied Jerry obstinately. "It wasn't in the code."

Mom looked confused. "The California Vehicular Code?"

"No, babe. The code of the streets." Jerry lifted up the hood and whistled. "Boy, everything's complete. There's even water in the windshield washer."

"How did they ever get it in here?" demanded Mom. "My front door couldn't be more than three feet wide."

"Looks like they brought it in piece by piece, babe. Then reassembled it. See, all the bolts show recent wrench marks."

Mom looked incredulous. "But it would take an army of mechanics to do all that!"

Jerry slammed down the hood—a startlingly loud noise in a living room. "Or a navy, babe," he said. "Or a navy."

"Quick, Nick!" shrieked Mom. "Get a pan from the kitchen. It's dripping oil all over my new shag!"

After we unpacked and ate lunch, Mom made Jerry call the sailor in Alameda. Bad news. His ship had sailed and he wasn't due back for ten months. Mom was livid.

"Jerry, what are you going to do about this?" she demanded.

Jerry sucked his beer and thought about it. "Well, Estelle. You'd been talking about wanting a new couch. Now you've got two of them. Plus a trunk."

"That's not funny. I want that car out of here!" Mom looked like she was ready to "fly off the handle" (as Dad used to say)—never a pleasant experience for her loved ones.

Jerry recognized the signs too. "OK, babe. Just kidding. I guess I'll have to come by in the evenings and take it out bit by bit. But I'm not putting it back together again."

"I don't care what you do with the pieces," said Mom. "Just don't leave them around here!"

"You're the boss," answered Jerry, sipping his beer. "I'm the peon." He looked at me. "Hey, kid. Want to learn how a car is put together?"

"No, thank you," I replied. "Auto mechanics don't interest me."

"See, Estelle," said Jerry. "I told you the kid was queer."

Once again, Jerry zoomed to the top of my shit list. Only the execrable Trent rates higher.

I went up to my room and sorted through my meager stack of mail. Thank God, Dad came through with an allowance check. Now I can buy dog food. Joanie sent a chatty letter and a newspaper clipping. Seems a guy in Florida slid into the handlebars when his motorcycle hit a wall at 50 mph. The reconstructive surgery failed and now he wears a dress, answers to the name of Susan, and is engaged to a former Boy Scout chum. They're planning to adopt.

He says probably none of these good things would have happened if he'd been wearing a helmet. "The brain damage improved my emotional flexibility," he told UPI.

I cringed and checked my equipment to make sure it was still intact. It looked OK. I checked the erect length. Up one-quarter inch—I'm now officially average! I checked the ejaculatory system. Still works like a charm. I just hope (for Sheeni's sake), my hydraulic pressure doesn't blast a hole through *Consumer's* check-rated condom.

I rode my bike over and found Lefty still camped out. His back yard now resembled Guatemala City after the big quake. The teen refugee was sitting on a camp stool amid piles of empty Coke cans and Pop Tart boxes. He greeted me with a dispirited "hi" and complained he hadn't received any postcards. I lied and said I had sent him three, including one with a naked woman lying spread-eagle on white sand.

"I bet the damn mailman stole that one!" he said bitterly. Lefty confided he was now dressing from the cast-off clothes box in People's Park. He looked like it too. A few days before, Martha had sneaked into his closet and dribbled motor oil on the crotches of his pants. The stains won't wash out and now all his trousers have permanent peter tracks. "My life is a living hell, Nick," said Lefty in despair. "A living hell."

This was the opportunity I had been waiting for. I told Lefty all about Sheeni and Albert. He was flabbergasted at my romantic progress and demanded a complete accounting. I filled him in on the torrid details. Understandably incredulous (I would be too), he demanded photographic evidence. What a shock! I had neglected to ask Sheeni for a photo. But I did have her note apologizing for reading my diary, which Lefty accepted grudgingly as temporary evidence.

I laid out my proposition: "OK, you take care of Sheeni's dog for a week or so, while I work on my mom. And I'll get Martha off your back."

Lefty looked doubtful. "How are you going to do that?"

"Don't worry, I've got a plan." (I didn't, but hell the strategy worked for Nixon in '68.)

"But I'm allergic to dogs. I swell up."

"I'm not asking you to keep the dog in the house. Just tie him up out here. Allergens are dispersed outdoors, so you won't have any problems. Trust me."

Lefty contemplated life without peter tracks and round-the-clock crooners. "OK," he said, "it's a deal." We shook on it.

I asked him if the vitamins were having any effect on his disease.

Lefty looked even glummer. "I don't know, Nick. I'm so traumatized by it all, I can't get it up any more. I think I'm impotent."

He pronounced this word with the accent on the second syllable.

"Don't be retarded," I said. "You can't be impotent. You're only 14. That doesn't happen to guys until they're 30, and then only if they beat off too much."

"Tell that to my dick," replied Lefty. "It's been Limp City down there for a week."

"You need to get out of this depressing yard," I said. "This place is a slum."

So for a change of pace, we got on our bikes and rode down to the bus station in Oakland's skid row. Unfortunately, the bus hadn't overturned and Albert was waiting for us in the baggage room. The trip hadn't improved his disposition. He looked up at me and growled.

"What an ugly dog," said Lefty. "What did you say his name was?"

I decided for his life in Oakland Albert needed a more macho name. "It's Al," I replied. "His last name is Bear. We named him that because he has a face like a bear."

"Looks more like a bat to me," observed Lefty, "or what do you call those monsters on churches?"

"Gargoyles?"

"Yeah, gargoyles. He looks like a gargoyle."

This was too much for Albert. He sniffed Lefty's aromatic Peoples' Park pant leg and applied a new layer of scent.

"Damn!" yelled Lefty.

"He likes you, Lefty," I said. "He's staking you out as a territorial claim."

"Fuck you," replied Lefty. "Fuck your dog. And fuck your girlfriend."

I knew he was only bluffing. "And what about Martha?"

"Her we don't fuck. Her we hunt down and kill."

We stuffed Al in my backpack and headed home. On the way we stopped at Safeway. I bought a bag of generic dog crunchies and Lefty shoplifted a hotrod magazine. As a matter of pride, he tries to steal at least one item from every store he enters. Back at Squalor City, we tied up Al behind Lefty's garage and fixed him up with food, water, and a bed (a pile of sibling war surplus trousers). Al gazed about dazed, slurped some water, flipped over his food dish, and peed on his bed.

"What a retarded dog," commented Lefty. "Your girlfriend actually likes him?"

"Women," I explained.

"Yeah," answered Lefty. "I know what you mean."

When I got home, Jerry was sitting in the front seat of the Chevy, drinking a beer. His tool box was open on the carpet. The dented back bumper (with a TRUCKERS DO IT WITH MORE GEARS sticker) now drooped slightly. Mom, I noticed, had arranged some books on the hood to cover the spray-painted greeting "Pay up or die!" She had also rearranged the furniture to sort of work the car into her decorating scheme. Now the Chevy looked like the world's largest coffee table.

"How's the demolition going?" I asked.

"Not so good," replied Jerry dejectedly. "Those wackos used some kind of locking compound on all the bolts. Plus they rounded over the heads. I've been working like a dog for hours. All I got off were two bolts. Had to saw 'em off with my hacksaw. This will take forever."

Serves you right, I thought.

Jerry belched. "And it's not even my car. Or my house."

"But Mom is your girlfriend," I pointed out.

"Maybe," sniffed Jerry. "She likes to think so."

If I've said it once, I've said it a million times: the man is God's perfect asshole.

9:30 p.m. I just spent two hours writing my first intellectual missive to Sheeni. I managed to mention Nietzsche, Clausewitz, and John Stuart Mill—all in the same sentence. What a struggle! I have to be impressed that the ever-pretentious Trent can do this daily. I'd give my left ball for a copy of one of his letters—just to see what I'm up against.

After practicing harmonica awhile (I wanted a clarinet like my god Artie Shaw, but Mom said she couldn't afford one), I went downstairs and caught Mom and Jerry necking in the back seat of the Chevy. They had turned down the lights and tuned the radio to a '50s rock 'n' roll station. I wish they'd grow up. It's unnerving for a kid to have his parental figures trying to relive their childhoods.

I desperately want to call Sheeni, but am constrained by economic want. I have to find out when long-distance rates are cheapest. Probably, we'll be doing all our phone chatting at 4 a.m.

SUNDAY, Aug. 26 — Twenty-four hours without the warm touch and doggy taste of Sheeni's sweet lips. I fear I may go starkers before I see her again. These long-distance romances are murder on the nervous system. Everything reminds me of her now—the smell of donuts, the sound of church bells, even the color yellow (that tube top is seared into my memory for eternity).

I counted 28 hairs in the shower drain. I realize now I'm in a race against time. I have to get engaged to Sheeni before my hairline goes north for good. Otherwise, I don't stand a chance against those hairy French intellectuals.

Dad and Lacey beamed over two hours late. We fought our way through Bay Bridge backup and spent the afternoon museum hopping in San Francisco. Dad does this periodically to stockpile ammunition for his competitive cocktail chatter. Lacey had on a curve-hugging green knit jump suit that drew more admiring glances than all the Neo-surrealists put together.

Dad just cashed in a CD (expensive turbo trouble in his Beamer), so he splurged and took us to dinner in Ghiradelli Square. We sat outdoors on a terrace and watched Sausalito turn 64 shades of mauve. Beautiful view but paltry conversation. I have nothing to say to that man. I knew if I told him about Sheeni I would only be ridiculed. So I laconically ate my scampi and tried not to stare at Lacey's fabulous bod. She is a kick to watch in a restaurant. All the waiters fawn over her, so she adopts an attitude somewhere between the Empress of China and the Queen of Sheeba. She demanded a better table, complained her menu was "soiled," sent back her bottled water ("it's not Evian, I can tell"), sent back her water again ("didn't I tell you? no ice"), sent back her salad ("too lemony"), sent back her salmon ("bring me one without bones"), and demanded a dessert that wasn't on the menu ("sliced fresh fruit with honey and yogurt").

The waiters only got snotty once—when Dad tried to send back the chardonnay. They tasted it, pronounced the wine "absolutely superb," and refused to bring a new bottle. So Dad had to drink the "vile vinegar" while seething inwardly. Then there was another ugly scene when the head waiter and the manager refused to take the wine off the tab. (Their brilliant argument: the wine couldn't have been too undrinkable, since Dad and Lacey polished off the entire bottle.) To get back at them, as we were leaving Dad casually dropped the wine bucket over the balcony. But they saw him do it, and made him pay for that too. What a delightfully relaxing meal!

Then Dad didn't feel like driving "all the way back to Oakland," so he dropped me off at a BART station. I didn't get home until after 10 p.m. Mom had already gone to bed.

11:30 p.m. Desperate for the sound of Sheeni's voice, I just called her trailer. My hand shook as I dialed the number. With each ring, the pounding of my heart doubled. Finally, I heard the line click and Mr. Saunders boomed a sleepy "Hello, dammit." I asked to speak with Sheeni. He said sorry she was still down at the lake—with Trent! Did I care to leave a message? I considered asking him what punishment, in his professional opinion, a 14-year-old youth could expect from the State of California for a premeditated, double homicide. But I didn't and hung up.

I feel like my emotional system has just been processed by an agricultural combine: I have been up-rooted, plucked, debarked, shredded, pressed, centrifuged, filtered, separated into composite compounds, and baked in a retort at 5,000 degrees.

MONDAY, August 27 — After a sleepless night I awoke to the sounds of bedsprings creaking rhythmically through the wall. I'm not saying one's parents should not have sex lives. That would be unfair. I'm merely proposing these people not have sex lives once their children reach the age of reason. Later, when their offspring leave home, they can pick up where they left off.

Jerry, if the auditory evidence is to be believed, appears to have remarkable "staying power." In fact, I'd be quite surprised if my mother got to work on time this morning. I lingered in bed, feeling like yesterday's smegma, until they finally left the house. Thank God, Jerry's leaving town with a load today.

Then, while I was morosely chewing my way through a bowl of Cheerios, Mr. Ferguson from next door came over to inform me there was "a slight problem" with the trailer. I hardly felt this concerned me, but I rose from my lonely breakfast and followed him up the driveway. The back yard smelled like a third world sewage treatment plant on a muggy day.

Holding a hankie over his nose, Mr. Ferguson pointed to the source of the stench. A valve on the trailer holding tank was leaking. Apparently, the old geezer hadn't bothered to empty the tank. God only knows how many years the stuff in there had been marinating. Each brown, oozing drip contained the distilled aroma of 112 truckstop restrooms. "Maybe you can tighten the valve," suggested Mr. Ferguson.

Holding my nose, I stooped down and gave the valve a turn. The noxious dripping intensified. "The other way! The other way!" he screamed.

I turned the valve in the other direction and a brown tidal wave washed over my bedroom slippers. "Oh my God!" yelled Mr. Ferguson. Too stunned to move, brown from the knees down, I stood in the fragrant pool, idly contemplating the flecks of paper clinging to my pajamas. Life, it seemed, had reached its nadir.

"Shit!" exclaimed my bewildered neighbor.

How true. How very, very true, I thought.

Yet life really is wonderful. Because 45 minutes later the phone rang and a wonderful, enchanting, extraordinarily desirable voice said "Hi, Nickie." It was my darling Sheeni. She's officially dumped Trent!

"Of course, he was disconsolate," she explained. "But we talked day and night all this weekend and he's come to see this as an opportunity for growth. We both wept when he left for Ukiah this morning. I was struck by how his appearance had altered. Had matured. He said he would try to turn his pain into poetry."

I hope he turns it into malignant cancer tumors!

"Oh, and Nick," added Sheeni, "Trent wanted me to tell you he bears you no ill will."

"Nor I him," I lied. "I wish him all the best."

Then Sheeni asked me to put Albert on the phone. Since I dared not divulge Albert was living as a fugitive in Lefty's back yard, I had to impersonate doggy whimpering noises while Sheeni cooed into the phone. I never realized falling in love involved so much deception.

We talked for a few more exquisite moments, promised to write, declared our undying love (at least I did), then hung up. Unaccountably, during that all too brief conversation the clock on the kitchen wall had sped forward one hour and fifteen minutes. I hoped Sheeni's parents wouldn't mind the expense. Then I remembered. She had called collect!

Since my neighborhood still smelled like Calcutta during a sanitation work stoppage, I spent the afternoon at Lefty's plotting Martha-abatement strategies. We lay on army cots in his dad's old eight-man canvas tent, swatting flies and discussing torture.

"I don't want her crippled or permanently disfigured," said Lefty. "Just brought as close as possible to the ultimate threshold of pain."

I counselled a more moderate course. "Pain is nice while it lasts, Lefty, but then it's over. What you want is something more permanent. Something that keeps on hurting."

"Like what?" asked Lefty, nuzzling Albert. The dog still growled at me, but he seems to have warmed up to Lefty. I was surprised to see the affection was being reciprocated. Albert's pee-stained bed had been moved into the tent—rather reckless proximity, I thought, for a youth who claimed to be allergic to dogs.

"Like peer embarrassment," I replied. "That's good for some prolonged and acute suffering. Or guilt. A nice heavy guilt trip can blight a life for years."

"That'd be great!" exclaimed Lefty. "Can you do it, Nick?"

"I'm working on it," I replied. And I think an idea, dare I say a plan, may be germinating.

When I got home, Mom was in the back yard emptying big industrial-size bottles of bleach on the grass. Mr. Ferguson had called her at the DMV office, and she had left work early (after arriving late). Fortunately Mom works for the state, which is always pleasantly surprised if its many employees manage to do any work at all. Unless she assassinates the governor (or they outlaw cars), Mom has a job for life.

She was livid. "Wait 'til that friggin' truckdriver gets back!" she exclaimed, sprinkling a toxic rain—like the Goddess of Death—on the once-verdant weeds. "I'm tired of his goddam messes! I got a cesspool in the garden. His damn Lincoln in my driveway. A friggin' Chevrolet in my living room. He can take his little motel playmates and they can all go straight to hell! I've had it!"

Finally Mom was talking sense. But why can't she come out and say "fuck?"

"What the hell is this?" Mom had a stick and was poking something dead and ugly in the muck.

It was my erstwhile bedroom slipper. I pretended to study it with interest. "Looks like a drowned rat to me."

Mom screamed and ran into the house.

TUESDAY, Aug. 28 — Still no letter from Sheeni. Not even a doting postcard for her love child. For a literary person who claims to have written one million words, she is remarkably parsimonious with her epistolary prose. At this rate the *Collected Letters of Sheeni Dillinger* (I expect she will want to take my name after we're married) will be a slim volume indeed.

I managed to excrete another intellectually scintillating missive to her last night. What a tremendously brain-bruising task! I fear I may have exhausted my known reserves of scholarly allusions. The next installment in our correspondence may have to be copied straight from the encyclopedia. It's hell to compete in this league when you're only 14.

The way I figure it, a quarter of my lifetime I was a drooling, pre-conscious vegetable. Another quarter I was functionally illiterate. OK, now I'm a bright seven-year-old and my idea of great literature is *Bucky Beaver Builds a Dam*. So say it takes three more years to work my way out of the children's section. Four years remain. Now subtract one-third for sleep. In the few remaining months I have to go to school, do my homework, eat, get haircuts, watch TV, play video games, mow the lawn, have interminable father-son bonding experiences, squeeze zits, and ponder the mysteries of sex. Is it any wonder I've yet to read Dostoevski? Thank God I'm not athletic, I'd still be a total moron.

Yet, consider the example of Trent: perspicacious scholar, star swimmer. Of course, he's had the advantage of growing up in the white hot heat of the ultimate intellectual goad. I speak here of My Beloved. If every youth had a Sheeni behind him, ours would be a nation of mental titans.

I've worked out a plan for dealing with Martha. It's rather extreme, but the situation is dire. At 4 a.m. last night Lefty's tent blew down in a light wind— trapping him and Albert in the limp, musty canvas. The ropes showed evidence of having been tampered with. Then at breakfast Martha complained to Lefty's parents about Albert. She said she got a flea bite on her nose and now it's infected. Lefty replied it was just a big, gross, ugly zit, and she kicked him hard under the table. So he emptied his cereal bowl down her brassiere. Now they're both grounded, and Lefty's been ordered to clean up the yard and get rid of the dog within 24 hours. He's heartbroken because he says if he can't keep Albert his life will be even more of a "living hell" than usual. Needless to say, I am also gravely concerned.

WEDNESDAY, August 29 — Mr. Ferguson just brought over a large manilla envelope. Finally a letter from Sheeni! I swapped it for the latest issue of *Field and Stream* that had been delivered here by mistake. Mr. Ferguson said he would read it, then take it to the proper addressee. If our mailperson is going to be so ruthlessly incompetent, he could at least misdeliver a copy of *Playboy* or *Hustler* once in a while.

The thick weighty envelope contained not a multi-page outpouring of deep-felt affection and passionate longing, but several brochures on dog care and a short, businesslike note. Sheeni reports it weighs greatly on her mind that she must be separated from our dog during his "formative puppy years." She wants me to keep a daily journal recording his "experiences, growth, and developing personality." I'd sooner bite the heads off live garden slugs. She also wants me to buy a camera and take lots of photos "of darling Albert at play." Instead, I think I'll send her photos of "darling Nick at play" (with himself).

Sheeni also reports the Rev. Knuddlesdopper case has split the trailer congregation into warring factions. One camp, led by Mrs. Clarkelson, regards the pastor as a sinner beyond redemption. They're agitating for immediate expulsion. The opposing camp agrees the reverend has sinned, but views him as "moving in the right direction." They favor retaining their spiritual leader— but only if he "takes a wife as soon as possible." Several of the older maiden ladies have volunteered for this perilous duty. No one can agree and the acrimony grows more bitter daily. Already, as the factions begin to assert territorial rights, some trailers have been uprooted and moved. Worse, Sheeni's parents are divided, with her mother siding with Mrs. Clarkelson and her father favoring the moderates. "Life is full of confusion," notes Sheeni, "it's all quite stimulating."

She concluded this torrid love letter with a tepid "Love to you and Albert. As ever, Sheeni." So much for grand passion. And not even one intellectually challenging scholarly allusion.

Wait a minute. I just shook the envelope and out fell a small photograph of an impossibly beautiful young woman. In an ovoid hand, it is inscribed, "To my dearest Twispy—all my love, Sheeni." Once again, my heart overfloweth!

6:00 p.m. Mom is depressed. Jerry was supposed to call from Dallas, but the phone refuses to ring. I think she's anxious to tell him off. Meanwhile, I'm trying to lay low, as I'm the only living, breathing frustration outlet within these nervous walls. I wonder how childless people let off steam?

8:30 p.m. Lefty has written the note and packed his grip. "Operation Sibling Retribution" commences at dawn tomorrow. By the way, he says Sheeni is one "stoking hot chick" with "great taste in dogs." I fear I can only meet him half-way on that assessment.

THURSDAY, August 30 — A day packed with intrigue. I rose at 5 a.m. and met Lefty and Albert at the donut shop at 5:30. Lefty was having second thoughts about the plan, but by plying him with Pepsi (his morning beverage of choice) and marshmallow-filled chocolate donuts, I was able to stiffen his resolve. Even though I had instructed him to bring the note with him, he said he left it on the camp table in the tent. "They'll be sure to find it there," he explained. I said that was fine, but in the future to leave all the brain work to me.

By 6:15 Lefty and Albert were holed up in Jerry's trailer in my back yard. Of course, since their presence there had to be concealed, we couldn't crank up the roof. This was no hardship for Albert, but Lefty had to crawl in on his hands and knees. I told him just to keep thinking about all the suffering he would be causing Martha. This seemed to cheer him up. "What's that awful smell?" he asked. The back yard now smelled like a septic tank explosion in a chlorine factory. I told him not to worry, that the "slight odor" would obscure his scent in case his parents brought in bloodhounds.

With Lefty and Albert secreted, I rode my bike over to Lefty's house and found the note in the tent. There was no mistaking Lefty's child-like scrawl: "Dear Dad and Mom, I'm sorry but I'm going away forever. I can't take it any more. Tell Martha I forgive her. I hope she can live with her conscience. —Your desperate son, Leroy." (It's a good thing for parents their children can't sue for emotional distress caused by abhorrent given names.)

I folded the note and put it in Lefty's grungy backpack (veteran of countless shoplifting capers and itself acquired through a past five-finger discount). I also stuffed in his WHO FARTED? tee-shirt and a couple more easily identifiable Lefty clothing items. Concealing the backpack under my sweater, I sneaked out of the yard and rode back home for breakfast.

Mom was still on the warpath. No word yet from the wayward trucker. She watched me sullenly while I ate my Cheerios. She was having the French Legionnaire's breakfast: black coffee and cigarettes. She told me to clean my room. I said OK fine. She told me to clean the house. I said OK fine. She told me to do the laundry. I said OK fine. She told me to watch my smart mouth. I said OK. Having no luck picking a fight, Mom drowned her cigarette in her coffee and left for work. If Jerry doesn't call by tonight, I may have to run away from home too.

After checking on Lefty (he and Albert were napping on the trailer floor), I rode my bike down to the Berkeley waterfront. Only a few fisherpersons were out on the pier. I parked my bike, and—trying my best to look inconspicuous—walked with the backpack far out to the end of the pier. The morning fog still hung chilly and grey over the churning green water. Across the bay rose the shiny towers of San Francisco.

But I didn't stop to sightsee. I opened the pack, put the farewell note in the top pocket, tossed the clothing into the bay, leaned the pack against a deck piling, and sauntered over to a payphone beside the pier restrooms. Inserting my quarter, I dialed 911. When the call was answered, I affected a Latin accent. "Hey, man. I jes' saw some kid go off da end of da Berkeley pier!" The concerned policewoman wanted to know more, but I hung up, grabbed my steed, and pedalled off in overdrive. After a few blocks, I could hear sirens in the distance.

Of course, I should concede here that when Lefty wrote down the note I dictated, he did not realize he would soon be taking the extreme step of suicide. For his own peace of mind, I let him believe he was merely running away. These days, though, kids run away all the time and parents hardly seem to notice. I think they've all come to expect it. But suicide, even in these jaded times, still packs a considerable emotional wallop. I expect not even Martha will be able to laugh this one off.

1:30 p.m. I fixed Lefty a nice tuna salad sandwich and carried it out to him on a tray. He crawled forward out of the gloom and blinked in the sunshine streaming in through the open door. "I'm bored, Nick," he said, taking the sandwich. "There's nothing to do in here. The air's kinda bad. I have to use the toilet. And I think Al does too." Albert looked up and growled at me.

"No problem," I said brightly. "Enjoy your lunch and I'll see what I can do." I found everything I needed in the garage. In five minutes I was back with an old black and white portable TV, three extension cords, and an empty mayonnaise jar. Lefty accepted the jar gratefully. "But what about Al?" he asked. "I don't think he can go in a bottle."

I replied that Albert would just have to hold it until I could take him for a walk after dark. I put the extension cords together, but came up five feet short of the outlet by the back door. So, I sneaked through the bushes and plugged into Mr. Ferguson's patio outlet. In the trailer, Lefty flipped through the channels on the TV. "I can't get anything except Channel 2," he complained. I looked in. Even Channel 2 was coming in poorly.

"Must be interference from the aluminum walls," I said. "I tell you what. You watch TV for a while. Then I'll bring you out a lamp and some of my *Penthouse* collection."

"OK," said Lefty, brightening. He and Albert settled down to watch "The Dating Game for Seniors."

3:00 p.m. I just cruised by Lefty's house. Three police cars were parked out front. And a Channel 2 news van!

5:30 p.m. Damn Kate Cruikshank! Damn Mitch Malloy! Damn the entire EyeSocket-2-You News Team! How was I to know this week's Eye Opener Issue was teen suicide? Talk about playing into the hands of the media. They're covering this story like Lefty was Elvis' baby brother.

Thank God I had the perspicacity to get Lefty distracted with *Penthouse* before the news came on. I tried to confiscate the TV, but he threatened to set Albert on me. Fortunately, Lefty has never manifested the slightest interest in news, current events, or public affairs. He probably wouldn't even sit through a news show.

At least "this unfolding tragedy" (Kate Cruikshank's words) has had a salutary effect on Mom. After coming home and haranguing me for not cleaning my room, vacuuming the house, or doing the laundry, she got very quiet when Channel 2 launched into their maudlin sensationalism. Especially when the Berkeley psychologist being interviewed live from Lefty's back yard said any teenager "was a potential suicide." Mom glanced over like she was trying to see if I had any razor blades hidden in my pockets.

"Did, did Lefty seem depressed?" Mom asked.

"Well, I don't know," I replied thoughtfully. "His parents were giving him a lot of grief. Always bugging him to clean his room."

Mom gulped. "I know you must be upset, honey," she said. "How about I fix you a nice steak for dinner?"

"OK, I guess," I said. "Lefty always liked steak."

"Did they find his body yet?" Mom asked.

"Not yet," I said. "According to Mitch Malloy, the Coast Guard is still sweeping the bay for him. They did find his tee-shirt, though. Mitch says his body may have been swept out to sea."

"Oh, how awful for his poor parents!" Mom exclaimed. "Have they made a statement yet?"

"Not yet. But every few minutes Kate Cruikshank pounds on their front door. They did show Lefty's sister Martha arriving home from a tennis match. She looked kind of glum, but she swung her racket at the camera and refused to comment."

"Poor Lefty," said Mom. "I wonder why he did it?"

"He was a troubled teen," I said sadly. "His parents wouldn't let him keep a nice dog he found."

Mom's face was a mask of guilt. "I'll get dinner started," she said, "you sit there and relax, Nickie."

8:45 p.m. After a nice steak dinner, I sneaked out to take Lefty another tuna salad sandwich. Someone whispered my name. It was Mr. Ferguson lurking in the bushes.

"Nick!" he called, *sotto voce*, "I think there's someone in your trailer. They plugged into my outlet."

I thought fast. "Uh, I know, Mr. Ferguson. It's, uh, refugees. From Central America."

"Fleeing political oppression, I expect," said Mr. Ferguson sympathetically. Although he doesn't look particularly subversive, Mr. Ferguson was once on J. Edgar Hoover's list of radical communist anarchists. Politically he was still somewhat to the left of Fidel Castro. "What can I do to help, Nick?"

"Well, Mr. Ferguson. I'm not much of a cook . . ."

"Say no more, Nick. I'll bring them some food. How many are there?"

"Just one," I replied, "and his dog."

"I'll make some spicy beans and rice," said Mr. Ferguson. "And some nice tortillas."

"Well, actually, I think he might prefer a hotdog and some potato chips. Maybe chocolate cake for dessert."

Mr. Ferguson looked puzzled.

"Uh, Mañuel," I said, "is trying to become acclimated to this culture."

"Of course," said Mr. Ferguson. "I'll bring it over in about a half-hour."

I told Mr. Ferguson that because Mañuel was so paranoid about the INS, he should put the food down on the ground, knock softly on the trailer door, then leave quickly.

"Of course," said Mr. Ferguson. "And what time does the brave lad want breakfast?"

"Early," I said. "How about six?"

"Fine," said Mr. Ferguson, retreating into the bushes.

What a swell neighbor!

Lefty, when I opened the door and crept in, was still deeply engrossed in *Penthouse.* "Good news, Nick," he said, "My hard-on's back!"

"Great," I replied. "How's the curvature?"

Lefty frowned and felt along the bulge in his trousers. "'Bout the same, I'd say. Damn! I forgot to bring my vitamins."

I gave Lefty the sandwich and told him to expect a nice meal in a few minutes. "But whatever you do," I warned, "don't let Mr. Ferguson see you. And if he tries to talk to you through the door, just reply in Spanish."

"But I don't know any Spanish," said Lefty.

"Do your best," I said. "Imitate Carlos." Carlos was Lefty's Mexican-American neighbor.

"That kid speaks dynamite Spanish for a three-year-old," he observed. Lefty bit into his sandwich and tore off a piece for Albert, who greedily devoured it. Lefty looked thoughtful. "I wonder, Nick, if they found the note yet?"

"Oh, I expect so," I said.

"I wonder if Martha is suffering?"

"I expect more than you even imagine."

This cheered Lefty immensely. "Life is finally looking up!" he exclaimed.

I gave Albert an accelerated tour of the back yard greenery, tossed him back in the trailer, and wished them both a good night. "Going to watch any more TV?" I asked nonchalantly.

"I might," said Lefty. "Why?"

"It's just that Mr. Ferguson asked that you go easy on his electricity. He's on a pension, you know."

"Oh all right," said Lefty. "What a cheapskate!"

9:45 p.m. I just got a phone call. It was Mitch Malloy in person! Somehow he found out I was a friend of Lefty's and wanted to send over a film crew to interview me. I said I was too grief-stricken to talk and didn't they have more important stories to cover. Then I asked him if it was true he was boffing Kate Cruikshank. He replied that was none of my business and hung up. Those news people are such hypocrites. Always exposing everyone's dirt except their own.

11:30 p.m. Eyesocket-2-You News just hit a new low. All I can figure, it must be ratings week. First they did Lefty's entire life story—full of shocking errors of fact like calling him an honor student. Then they had Kate Cruikshank live from the front porch reading a statement from Lefty's parents. They said Lefty was despondent because he had recently been diagnosed with Peyronie's disease. Don't those idiots know how to read a suicide note? Or are they trying to spare their guilt-wracked daughter? Then Mitch Malloy, back at the news desk, did an in-depth report on Peyronie's disease—complete with X-rated diagrams. I hope for Kate's sake, it wasn't Mitch who posed for the drawings. (I also pray Lefty wasn't tuned in. He'd kill himself for sure.)

Mom, needless to say, was pinned to the screen with ghoulish absorption. "Honey, if you ever have any problems like that," she said, "you won't be afraid to come to me about it, will you?"

"Oh, of course not, Mom," I lied.

FRIDAY, August 31 — 2:30 a.m.! A ringing telephone roused us from our beds at this ghastly hour. I feared it was Mitch Malloy, hot on the scent of a counterfeit suicide. But they wanted to speak to Mom. It was Jerry's dispatcher calling with shocking news. Jerry had a heart attack in a Dallas bar and took it rather badly. He died!

How unpredictable life can be. One minute, you're swilling beer and being obnoxious. The next minute, you're in front of St. Peter, answering for a lifetime of sexism, adultery, and odometer tampering. What a lesson!

Numbly, Mom asked when the body would be arriving. The dispatcher replied it had already been shipped. To Los Angeles. To Jerry's wife!

Mom hung up, too stunned to speak.

That's Jerry, I thought, a rat to the end.

6:00 a.m. I heard Mom crying in her room last night. I guess she must be upset that Jerry passed on before she could tell him off. I hope this doesn't make her late for work. I want to give Lefty an airing in the back yard this morning. We have to keep the brave lad's spirits up. I figure it will take at least a week to inoculate Martha fully with guilt. What luck that Mr. Ferguson has volunteered to serve as caterer. I just saw him bring over a very nice breakfast tray—complete with daisies in a vase.

The *Chronicle* had Lefty's story on page three, under the headline "Diseased Penis Sparks Apparent Youth Suicide." More diagrams and this time the guy was much better endowed. Again, no mention of sisterly tormentors. When are the media going to take off their gloves and give Martha the pummeling she deserves? Thank God, the Coast Guard called off its search for Lefty's body. I was beginning to get a little nervous about those federal tax dollars being consumed.

9:30 a.m. Triple disaster! Mom decided she was too distraught to go to work. Then she dropped the bombshell that Joanie has agreed to fly up from Los Angeles and stay with her for a few days. And now Lefty looks like the "before" photograph in a fat farm ad!

He said he could start to feel himself swelling up in the middle of the night. "It's like my whole body was getting an erection," mumbled Lefty through swollen lips. "Except it feels kind of bad instead of good. I feel awful 'cause Al is such a terrific dog."

Albert whimpered guiltily in a corner. Apparently the confined space of the trailer had concentrated the doggie dander until it reached critical mass. Worse, according to Lefty, the swelling won't go down until all traces of dog are removed.

Lefty stretched out a fat arm and switched on the TV. Kate Cruikshank was doing a live report. Hurriedly, I flipped it off.

"Gee," said Lefty, "that almost looked like my house."

"Don't be retarded," I said. "We don't have time to watch TV. We have to make plans."

"Why can't Al and I stay here?" asked Lefty. "The eats are great. And I don't mind too much being swelled up." His pneumatic features, I noticed, lent him a vaguely oriental appearance.

"Because my sister Joanie is coming home tonight," I replied.

"So what?" asked the rotund youth.

"So Joanie," I replied, "is Queen of the Snoops. One look at me and she could tell I was hiding something. Then she'd look at my left eyebrow and know it was something in the back yard. Then she could see from my right nostril it was a runaway hiding in a trailer. Then, from a twitch in my left earlobe, she'd deduce it was a fat 14-year-old with curvature of the dick and an allergy to canines. There's no hiding anything from Joanie."

"She should be a detective," observed Lefty.

"I don't think so," I replied. "From the string of losers she's gone out with, it appears I'm the one and only male she's ever figured out."

We lay on the cool trailer floor, inhaling dust mites and pondering our next move.

"Lefty," I said finally, "how would you like to go visit Sheeni in Lakeport?"

"Up at Clear Lake? Great!" he replied. "Can I take Al?"

"No. But you can take his bed."

3:30 p.m. I just put Lefty, his grip, and Albert's pee-stained bed on the bus to Lakeport. I borrowed the fare from the obliging Mr. Ferguson, who even chipped in 40 extra dollars "for the brave lad" (which I, needless to say, immediately pocketed).

Sheeni was nothing less than magnificent when I telephoned. She even claimed to be sorry to hear about Jerry. (Women can be such forgiving creatures!) She immediately grasped the Lefty dilemma and proposed a brilliant solution. Her parents are delighted they will soon be hosting a visit by a Bible exchange student from Burma named Leff Ti. He's from Burma because, as Sheeni pointed out, "No one has the slightest knowledge of or interest in that country." She promised to keep Lefty swelled up from dog dander and away from TV and newspapers. "He'll want to go to all the services, of course," Sheeni observed. "Fortunately, as the congregation is still divided, there are twice as many as before." For his part, Lefty promised to speak halting English, demonstrate at least some pretend piety, and keep his fat mitts off my girlfriend.

Meanwhile, once again I am left holding the proverbial dog leash.

4:30 p.m. Mom said I can keep Albert! She even helped me make a bed for him in the back seat of Jerry's dead Chevy. I fear she may still be so distraught she doesn't know quite what she's doing. She certainly looks like hell. In fact, she didn't even inquire how Albert happened to turn up. (I was going to suggest a miraculous homing instinct had guided him on an incredible journey.) Anyway, the loathsome mutt is in for now. As a prophylactic measure, I have removed from the house all items of an even vaguely religious nature.

6:30 p.m. The tragic story of Lefty is becoming stale news. All Mitch Malloy had to say was one brief sentence, noting the body still hadn't been found. Meanwhile, Kate Cruikshank did a tasteful live report from a local cemetery, solemnly concluding their week-long Eye Opener Report on teen suicide by panning across the headstones as a lone bugler played "Taps." This set off a gusher of tears from Mom. I never knew she cared that much for Lefty.

Uh-oh, the cab just pulled up with Joanie. I must try to make myself inscrutable.

10:05 p.m. Joanie and Mom are talking in her bedroom. Fortunately they've been closeted together since Joanie's arrival, sparing me a sisterly inquisition. Joanie has a new haircut, a new hair color, and a new figure (padding? cosmetic surgery?). I don't know, but she looks terrific. I only hope her new look is attracting a better class of men.

As I write this my best friend is going to sleep under the same roof as The Woman I Love. I would gladly sacrifice my left nut to be able to trade places with him. I know that is a common expression, but in this case, I actually mean it. My left nut!

SEPTEMBER

SATURDAY, September 1 — Where did the summer go? You're 14 only one summer of your life and now for me, it's almost over. Already, I am feeling nostalgic for my transient youth. Of course, another part of me would just as soon fast forward to age 21. I'd have money in my pockets, freedom to do as I please, and a beautiful young wife. Best of all, I'd have squeezed my last oozing zit. There's a furuncle erupting on my chin right now that looks positively life-threatening. Against my will, every five minutes I am drawn to the bathroom— there to be newly revolted by the horror in the mirror.

Still, life (and death) must go on. I just got back from a sad and deeply moving memorial service for Lefty. I kept wishing he could have been there. He would have enjoyed it immensely. (Fortunately though, it was all captured on video tape.)

Before the service, Mom, Joanie, and I went out to breakfast. Mom drove us in style in Jerry's Lincoln. Starting the powerful engine, she announced, "I'm not giving up this car to that woman." (Her term for Jerry's surprise widow.) Joanie told her she should keep the trailer too. "I intend to," said Mom. "Jerry bought it just for the two of us. That woman can buy her own damn recreational vehicle."

I asked Mom if I could drive the Lincoln when I turned 16.

She replied she had been thinking about it and had decided that when I get my license, if I've kept up my grades and haven't become a crack addict, she was going to give me Jerry's old Chevrolet.

Great! If I ever get it running, I can play bumper cars with the sofa. "Wow, gee," I said, "I'm truly underwhelmed."

Joanie turned around angrily and said if I really wanted to help Mother in her time of need, I could start dismantling "that eyesore."

"No thanks," I replied, "auto mechanics is not where my ambitions lie. I think you must have me confused with Phil Polsetta and your other high school boyfriends."

Joanie was going to reply, but decided, for Mom's sake, just to seethe inwardly. Then, in the restaurant, she started peering at me suspiciously over her waffles. "You've been up to something, Nickie," she said. "I can tell. What have you been doing?"

I decided the best defense was a good offense. "What have *you* been doing?" I demanded.

"What do you mean?" asked Joanie nervously.

I puffed out my chest.

Joanie blushed. "Not that it's any of your business," she replied, "but I've taken a class to improve my posture."

Not even Mom looked like she believed that lie. "I think Joanie looks very nice," said Mom. "She has a new boyfriend too."

"Oh, what make of cars does he work on?" I asked.

"He happens to work on atomic accelerators," replied Joanie. "He's a nuclear physicist."

"Did you meet him in posture class?"

Joanie looked very much like she wanted to bash me one. She had spent much of her early life pummeling me and probably missed this therapeutic outlet. "Still the smartest mouth in town," she observed.

"Just like his father," added Mom.

That, I thought, was hitting below the belt.

More than 150 people jammed into the funeral home chapel for Lefty's memorial service, including—much to my surprise—Millie Filbert herself. Conspicuously absent was her alleged fiancé Willis. Since the body of the deceased was also absent, the morticians in their dark suits stood around looking awkwardly unoccupied. With nothing to focus their attention on, the mourners sat on hard folding chairs and studied the profusion of floral wreaths. This was somewhat ironic, I thought, since the only interest Lefty had ever shown in flowers was in riding his mountain bike over his neighbors' landscaping.

How did Martha look? Her bloated face wore the unmistakable treadmarks of out-of-control remorse. So what if her parents refused to face reality, she knew who had murdered her unfortunate brother. The guilt was eating her alive.

Lefty's parents also appeared to be taking it rather badly. I regret, of course, making them suffer in this way. But I figure it's only temporary. And anyway, it's all for a good cause.

Besides his ubiquitous camcorder, Lefty's dad also brought along the family VCR. A big TV had been set up in the lobby and was showing home videos of the decedent in younger and happier days. Some I recognized from their recent vacation in Nice.

After a respectful silence, Lefty's minister stood up and read what sounded like a generic, death-of-a-teen funeral eulogy. He didn't even get all the blanks filled in right. Twice he referred to Lefty as "dear Nerine," prompting an old woman behind me to whisper, "Who's Nerine? Did she drown too?"

When the minister had concluded his somber banalities, family and friends stood up to recall what they remembered most about the dear departed Leroy. These reminiscences were so embarrassingly maudlin, everyone in the chapel (including me) was soon sniffling. A couple of times Joanie nudged me to get up to speak, but—not wishing to wallow in hypocrisy—I demurred.

Among the speakers was Millie Filbert, who confessed sadly that although she had not known Leroy well, she had always felt the presence of an unspoken bond between them. "I only wish I had had the courage to reach out to him," she said wistfully.

I only wish I could relay this fabulous news to Lefty. But since he is unaware of his death, revealing the context of her admission could prove troublesome. I just hope she doesn't go and marry Willis before Lefty is officially resurrected.

To my extreme embarrassment, Mom stood up and announced that she too had experienced a recent grievous loss, and therefore knew how much Leroy's family and friends were suffering. "We're all in this together," declared Mom. "Life is sometimes just the pits." On that profound note, she sat down.

Later, at the home of the grieving family a light buffet was served. I was shocked to see the refreshments included asparagus, a vegetable for which Lefty reserved his fiercest loathing, and which his sister invariably served when she made dinner. Even on this day of mourning, I noticed, Martha could not resist the vile green spears. She looked up and paused in mid-chew.

"Hello, Nick," she said glumly.

"Hi, Martha," I said. "How's the asparagus?"

"Mmmm, very good," she replied, resuming her dispirited mastication.

"So," I said, after a pause. "Heard any new Barry Coma records lately?"

Martha turned white. "What, what did you say?" she stammered.

"Oddest thing," I said. "I had a dream about Lefty last night. He appeared—dripping wet and ghostly pale—and asked me to ask you that."

Crash! Martha's plate shattered against the tile floor. She turned and bolted from the room.

No, diary. In sibling warfare we take no prisoners.

SUNDAY, September 2 — Things are tense, very tense around here. This is the day Jerry was due back, so Mom is in an even blacker mood than before. Plus, the 24-hour grace period has expired, so Mom and Joanie have resumed their lifelong habitual bickering. I have yet to see them spent two entire days together without shrieking at each other. Then Dad called to see if I was interested in any court-ordered bonding experiences. Joanie answered the phone and within 90 seconds was screaming profanities into the receiver. She has nothing but contempt for Dad (who doesn't?) and is commendably up front about expressing it. After Joanie warmed up the phone, I got on the line and told Dad I did not appreciate "vague proposals" of Sunday activities, as these invariably turned into my washing his car or mowing his grass.

"All right," said Dad. Even over the phone, you could tell he was seething inwardly. "Would you be at all interested in coming over and helping me clean out the garage?"

"No, I don't think so," I replied. "But thanks for the concrete proposal."

"You're entirely welcome," said Dad, hanging up.

Meanwhile, in between defending her lifestyle to Mom, Joanie continues to eye me suspiciously. I struggle to remain inscrutable.

Joanie made the mistake of divulging that her new boyfriend Philip, besides having a doctorate from Massachusetts Institute of Technology, has a wife and three children in Santa Monica. Joanie met him because he is a frequent flyer to assorted accelerator locations. "It was love at first sight," she said. "I asked him if he wanted a magazine. And he asked me if I had *Bulletin of the Atomic Scientists.*"

Shocked, Mom flew off the handle and called Joanie a "home wrecker."

Joanie got livid and said, "Oh really? I understand your last boyfriend didn't exactly qualify as bachelor of the month!"

So much for comforting Mom in her hour of need.

This emotional turmoil has played havoc with my erupting zit. My chin looks like an explosion at an earthworm ranch. I wonder if there's such a thing as malignant acne?

I have lost interest in my *Penthouse* collection. Now I am only interested in the real thing. I think about Sheeni constantly. She is the one bright, dazzling star in my gray world. Which reminds me, I have to go walk her stupid dog.

MONDAY, September 3 — Labor Day — Just think, if I had a job, I'd be paid all day for sitting around being bored. Instead, I get to do it for free. What a laborious holiday. And all those ominous back-to-school ads in the newspapers.

Mom and Joanie aren't speaking to each other. This is better than screaming, but still palpably tense. Mom got mad at Joanie for not helping with the breakfast dishes. "I don't understand it," said Mom, tossing a plate against the wall for emphasis. "After 18 years of not lifting a finger around here, you go out and get a job waiting hand and foot on total strangers. Why is that?"

"Because," replied Joanie, slamming down her book (*Particle Physics for Laypersons*), "occasionally one of those strangers displays a fucking particle of gratitude."

"Lazy, foul-mouthed home wrecker!" reasoned Mom.

"Over-bearing, never-satisfied shrew!" rebutted Joanie.

No wonder people have to escape family life through drugs. I just hope Sheeni and I have better rapport with our gifted children.

Lefty's mom just called and asked if I wanted Lefty's baseball card collection or computer. They're clearing out all his stuff! I suggested maybe they wait a few more days, since the body still hasn't been recovered. But she said no, she now has an absolute conviction that her son has "discarded his deformed body and departed this sphere." (So much for motherly intuition.) She wants to distribute his possessions to "needy youths" as soon as possible. (So much for being paralyzed with grief!) Already, she's given away his bike, stereo, and most of his clothes. So I said I would take the baseball cards *and* the computer. I just hope the other legatees will be as amenable to returning their bequests.

Mom and Joanie have made up and are organizing a "holiday picnic." I've been drafted to go to Seven-Eleven for some chips and charcoal. Can this day get any drearier?

7:30 p.m. Yes, improbably it could. When Albert and I returned with the groceries, we found Mom and Joanie in the back yard. They had moved the grill out of the garage and set up the lawn chairs. Unfortunately, Mom, seeking a more Sierra-like ambience, had also cranked up the trailer—thus discovering the TV, tuna salad remains, and a large portion of my *Penthouse* collection. When the interrogation began, I proposed as one possible explanation a visitation by the homeless. Mom, however, refused to buy it.

"You are disgusting," she bellowed, "a disgusting, sick pervert."

"Oh, Mother!" interjected Joanie, "all boys his age are interested in those kinds of magazines. You should be grateful, at least, the pictures are of women."

"Thank you, Miss Home Wrecker," replied Mom. "When I want your opinion on raising my child, I'll ask for it."

Joanie sighed, sat down in a lawn chair, and picked up her book. I sighed, sat down in a lawn chair, and picked up a magazine. Mom ripped the magazine from my hands and tossed it across the yard. Albert dashed after it and brought it back. Mom grabbed the magazine, smacked Albert on the nose with it, threw it at me, and stalked into the house. Joanie looked over from her book.

"When are you leaving?" I asked.

"I escape tomorrow morning at six."

"Wish I was going with you," I said.

"Your day will come," said Joanie. "I never thought mine would, but it did." Joanie studied me for a moment. "Can I ask you one question?"

"OK," I said.

"Is Lefty dead?"

"Not as dead as Jerry," I replied. "Did you really take a posture class?"

"Implants," said Joanie. "I wanted them all my life."

Mom walked out of the kitchen door carrying a tray of hamburger patties. "OK," she said brightly, "let's get that charcoal started!"

Later, as we were cleaning up from the gala picnic, the doorbell rang. It was Lefty's dad and Martha delivering his computer and famous baseball card collection. Helping them unload, I was appalled to see their station wagon was jammed to the roof with Lefty's worldly goods (much of them, of course, unlawfully obtained).

"Gee," I said, "I could take all of this if no one else wants it."

"Aren't you the greedy little friend," observed Martha.

Lefty's dad showed me his delivery list. "Sorry, Nick," he said, "everyone wants something to remember Leroy by."

The list must have had at least 20 names and addresses on it!

"Maybe you should keep a copy of that list," I suggested. "Just in case Leroy happens to turn up."

"That won't be necessary," said Lefty's dad. "If my son's alive, I'll buy him anything he wants. Brand new."

What commendable generosity. Now I've got two computers. And I can get big bucks for the card collection too.

10:30 p.m. Sheeni took advantage of the holiday rates to call collect. Thank God, I happened to answer the phone. Just the sound of her voice gives me the most amazing adrenalin rush—and immediate T.E. It seems almost incredible that someday soon she and I will be experiencing—as passionate beings—the ultimate expression of human union. (Which reminds me, I have to go to the library and drugstore.)

Sheeni reports Lefty is the sensation of the trailer park. Everyone wants to meet this pious youth from Burma. "He had a full social calendar today," Sheeni said, "starting with a 7 a.m. prayer breakfast with Mrs. Clarkelson's faction. Everyone is amazed by his mastery of English and his ignorance of theology."

"Is he staying swelled up?" I asked.

"Perfectly," replied Sheeni. "He sleeps with dear darling Albert's sweet little blanket and that keeps him swollen nicely. He's a remarkable sight in a bathing suit. Father loaned him a pair of his old trunks and we went swimming between church services and the afternoon prayer meeting. Then this evening Rev. Knuddlesdopper's faction had a barbecue in his honor on the lawn by the bath house. Lefty ate four hamburgers, five ears of corn, half a German chocolate cake, and, in between bites, talked about his native land."

"My God, what did he say?" I asked. "I doubt if Lefty even knows what planet Burma is on."

"He said quite a lot," Sheeni replied. "Let's see. He said the national sport was volleyball, although video games were big too. He said chili dogs were the national dish. He said that most of the people were poor and could only afford to drive Toyotas and Plymouths. Oh, and he said if sisters became obnoxious, boys in the family had the legal right to send them away to convents—for life."

"He hasn't made any passes at you has he?" I asked. "I mean while you were at the beach together in your bathing suits. I hope you weren't wearing that purple bikini."

"I was as a matter of fact," Sheeni answered. "For your information, Lefty was the perfect gentleman. He is very nice, if a bit dim. Of course, he got somewhat excited applying my tanning lotion. That's only to be expected. Odd, he looked a bit crooked, but perhaps it was only the weave of Father's bathing trunks."

I suggested to Sheeni that in the future she consider applying her own tanning lotion.

"I'll remember that, darling," said Sheeni, "the next time we're at the beach together."

"I didn't mean me," I said. "It's OK for me to do it. But not Lefty."

"Oh, I see," said Sheeni. "You are an advocate of discrimination. And against Asians. I should have thought the era of such reactionary prejudice was behind us."

I changed the subject. "Your dog is doing well."

"Oh, Albert!" exclaimed Sheeni. "I miss him terribly. Tell me all about the little sweetie!"

Since I wasn't going to run up Mom's phone bill talking about Albert, I made it brief, and soon I heard Sheeni's sweet voice saying, "Goodbye, darling. I love you." Then I put Albert down and she said goodbye to me.

Thus ends another laboriously labored Labor Day. Only one labor remains before I sleep. This involves some precision handwork on a T.E.

TUESDAY, September 4 — Joanie departed for the freedom of the open skies hours before I got up. She left me an envelope on the kitchen table. Inside was a short farewell note and $50 in tens and twenties. My wad is now back up to $90! And that's not even counting my ever-appreciating baseball card collection.

I celebrated by going out for donuts. Mom made me take Albert. It's always embarrassing being seen anywhere with that dog as he invites ridicule from strangers. People on the street stop to say, "My goodness, that's an ugly dog. What kind is it?" I've taken to replying he's a special pit bull bred for leg amputations. This usually terminates the conversation.

When I got back, Mom was in Joanie's room painting the walls. An ugly pale pink. I hope she cleared the color choice with Joanie. I learned the hard way when I was younger—never mess with Joanie's room. The bruises take too long to heal. Mom's asked for bereavement leave from her job for the entire week. Needless to say, her constant presence here will be cramping my already crimped style.

11:30 a.m. Total unmitigated disaster! I just got a call from Lefty's mom. She asked me—all excited—if I knew where Leroy was. I said well, ocean currents being what they were, he was probably halfway to Hawaii.

"That's interesting," she replied. "Because we just got a postcard from him. Dated Saturday. And postmarked Lakeport, California! Weren't you just up at Clear Lake?"

"No, I went to Tahoe," I lied. "What does the card say?"

Lefty's mom read the short inscription: "Dear Mom, Dad, and Creep. I am enjoying my new life as your former son and/or brother. Too bad I didn't bring my swimsuit, the lake looks great. I will write again when I get a job and get married. Regards, Leroy."

"Do you think he ran off with some woman?" asked Lefty's mom. She sounded quite distressed.

"That would surprise me," I said. "Lefty's always been pretty shy around girls."

"Well, if you hear from him, Nick, please tell him to call home immediately."

I said OK and hung up. Damn that bent retard!

I immediately called Sheeni. Her ancient mother answered and said Sheeni and Leff Ti had taken their Bibles to read down by the lake. I felt like asking if

Sheeni had also packed along her suntan lotion, but instead requested that Sheeni telephone me immediately when she returned. Without fail!

"What may I ask is this in regards to, young man?" asked the prying old crone.

"I can only say it involves international ramifications," I replied.

"Goodness!" she exclaimed. "I knew there was something fishy about that young man. I can always tell. I saw through you immediately."

I said, "Thank you, Mrs. Saunders" and hung up. I hope, after we're married, Sheeni won't expect me to do much socializing with her parents. I don't think I could stand it.

2:00 p.m. No call from Sheeni yet! I can feel the tension churning directly into zits. Mom was gabbing on the phone with some girlfriend for 42 minutes about her deceased lover. It was all I could do to keep from strangling her.

3:45 p.m. Finally, Sheeni called (collect, of course). I told her what happened and asked to speak to the Burmese idiot. Lefty, of course, was quite surprised to hear that the postcard was a tactical error. "I always send postcards when I go places," he observed. "I sent you two from France this summer. The stamps cost me over a buck."

"Yes, but you weren't running away from home then," I replied. "People who run away from home don't send postcards to their parents!"

"Oh, well I never heard that rule," said Lefty. "I just didn't want them to worry too much."

I started to explain that that was the point of the entire charade, but gave up in exasperation. "OK, Lefty. The vacation is over. You have to take the next bus home today."

"But what will I tell the Saunders?" protested Lefty. "And Sheeni and I were going to rent a video tonight. Some Frog movie called 'Breathless'."

Great! Just the two of them sharing an evening together on the sofa. "Sorry to interrupt your plans, Romeo," I said icily. "But you have to get home as soon as possible. Sheeni will think of an excuse to tell her parents. Here's what you have to do. Now pay attention."

"I'm listening," grumbled Lefty.

"OK. You fell off the Berkeley pier . . ."

"I did?" asked Lefty, surprised. "When?"

"The day you disappeared."

"Why'd I do that?" asked Lefty. "I can't swim."

"Just listen and don't interrupt! You fell off the pier. You swam—OK, no, you dog-paddled across the harbor. You got out of the water. You were too afraid to go home. So you hitchhiked up to Clear Lake."

"Can't we say I walked to Clear Lake?" asked Lefty, worried. "If my parents hear I was hitchhiking, they'll pound me for sure."

"Your parents won't care this time. I guarantee it. Just, whatever you do, don't mention me, Sheeni, or the Saunders. You did this all on your own."

"I did it all on my own," repeated Lefty doubtfully. "But it was your idea,

Nick."

"That's true," I conceded. "And it was working fine until you screwed it up. But everything will still turn out OK. Just get home—quick!"

"Oh, all right," said Lefty. "Anyways, I'm getting tired of being swelled up and going to church all the time."

"If you do as I say—keep my name out of it—I'll let you in on a nice secret."

"What kind of secret?" asked Lefty suspiciously.

"I'm not going to tell you now," I replied. "But you'll like it a lot. Just don't mention my name."

"I heard you," said Lefty.

"Nobody likes a squealer."

"I'm not a squealer," said Lefty.

I still needed more insurance. "Good," I said, "because I'm sure you wouldn't want your parents to find out how you got all your hotrod magazines and baseball cards and stuff."

"I'm not a squealer!" insisted Lefty. "My lips are sealed."

Eight more hours of hell. I figure everything should be over—one way or another—by midnight. I just hope the tension doesn't pockmark my face for life.

5:00 p.m. Tired from painting, Mom whipped up a fast meal of fried beef liver, boiled red beets, and steamed lima beans—the three food substances I find most despicable. I gazed in horror at my plate.

"You might as well eat it," said Mom, chowing down with alacrity. "If you don't, it's all coming back tomorrow in a casserole."

Are there no bounds to parental sadism? I picked up my fork. With each bite, my body shuddered in revulsion. The lima beans and beet slices I swallowed whole, like horse pills. The liver—tough, gritty, stringy with real cow veins—necessitated actual mastication. My palate recoiled in shock with each chew. Swallowing ensued as a horrible relief.

6:05 p.m. A worried call from Sheeni! Her father took Lefty to the bus station more than an hour ago and has not returned!

"Maybe he stopped at a bar for a quick one," I suggested hopefully.

"Would that he would do something so normal," replied Sheeni. "Both of my parents are zealous abstainers. Yet a prolonged alcoholic binge is precisely what each of them needs. I think it would do them such a world of good."

"Well, where can he be?" I asked.

"I fear the worst," said Sheeni. "Oops, here comes Mother."

Sheeni hung up. Panicked, my stomach contemplated its vile contents and decided to revolt. I ran to the bathroom and re-experienced my meal—in reverse. Up came the gritty liver, up came whole lime beans, up came pellets of boiled beets—red as clotted blood. Hot acidic wave followed hot acidic wave— each bilious spasm so horrific, I fear my aesthetic may never fully recover. From a corner under the sink, Albert watched with ghoulish delight.

Mom barged into the bathroom and demanded what was going on.

"Food poisoning!" I exclaimed, still prone upon the cold tiles.

"Don't be silly," replied Mom, handing me a towel. "Food poisoning indeed! That was a good, nourishing meal. Better than the homeless had tonight. You should be grateful."

"I'm grateful I'm still alive," I said, struggling to my feet. "Now I can go kill myself."

"Don't say things like that!" exclaimed Mom. "It's disrespectful of the dead. Think of poor Jerry and poor Lefty."

"They're better off," I said. "At least they never have to eat liver again."

"Jerry loved liver," snapped Mom. "I fixed it for him all the time."

"Yes," I replied, "and look what happened to him."

Mom swung back to clout me one, but decided—for once—to resist her deep-seated impulse toward child abuse. "You get to bed!" she exclaimed.

"Can I get a razor blade first?" I asked.

"Get to bed, smartypants!" yelled Mom, shoving me out of the bathroom. Thrilled by this display of violence, Albert barked excitedly. "And don't forget to walk that dog," added Mom.

"How can I walk him in bed?" I asked. That was a mistake. Mom officially lost it and flew off the handle. She delivered a stinging, flat-hand slap to my right cheek. Albert encouraged her with another lusty bark.

"OK, smart mouth!" bellowed Mom. "I'll walk the dog. You go to bed!"

"All right," I said appeasingly. "I was just asking."

"And I'm telling you!" screamed Mom. The veins on her forehead were beginning to stand out and turn purple—always a cautionary sign. I turned and hurried down the corridor to my room.

"Why do I put up with that kid?" Mom asked Albert. "Why?" The traitorous canine looked in my direction and sneered. I could tell he wanted to add some slander of his own, but words—as usual—escaped him.

9:30 p.m. I heard the phone ring downstairs and Mom answer it. I opened my bedroom door and slipped silently up the hallway to the head of the stairs. What I heard chilled my blood.

"I'm sorry, Sheeni." said Mom. "Nick can't come to the phone now, he's being punished. . . . I'm sorry, I don't care if it is an emergency. . . . All right, I suppose I could give him a short message. . . . You don't say! OK, I'll tell him. And please don't call here collect again. I can't afford the expense. I'm sorry to hear about your father . . . No, Nick won't be calling you tomorrow. He's not permitted to make long-distance calls. I suggest you write. Good night, Sheeni."

I hurried back to bed as Mom climbed the stairs. She looked in from the hall and scowled.

"Don't pretend to be asleep. That was that girl Sheeni. She told me to tell you her father has been arrested at the Greyhound bus station in Lakeport."

I was paralyzed with horror. "Why?" I croaked.

"For kidnapping some boy," replied Mom with distaste. "It all sounds quite sordid to me."

"Did, did she say anything more?" I stammered.

"That was all," replied Mom. "I don't see how it concerns us anyway. Now go to sleep. You're grounded."

"For how long?"

"Until I see a change in your attitude," said Mom, slamming the door.

Great! An indeterminate sentence, the worst kind. But I don't think it's going to matter to the FBI that I'm grounded when they come to haul me off to jail.

WEDNESDAY, September 5 — 12:30 a.m. I can barely type from the trembling in my fingers. Thank God, correcting mistakes is so easy on a computer. How I pity those troubled, literary teens of the past who had to type their journals on ordinary typewriters.

After Mom delivered her doomsday message, I lay in bed, listening to the muffled sounds of the TV from downstairs and contemplating my forthcoming years in the custody of the California Youth Authority. I wonder if anyone has ever gone on from reform school to literary renown? Probably not.

It was well past 11 before Mom switched off the TV and climbed the stairs to bed. I waited until I heard her begin to snore (everyone in my family snores, including—much to Sheeni's likely future distress—me), then I sneaked downstairs to the phone. A growl from the dead Chevy caused me to jump. It was my repellent dog, reclining in the dark on his Body-by-Fisher bed. I whispered for him to hush and dialed Sheeni's number. After two rings a strange man's voice answered.

"Deputy Riffman," it said. "Who is this?"

I hung up. Are they arresting Sheeni as an accomplice? Am I dragging the woman I love down a sorry, sordid path to perdition? What exactly does "perdition" mean? These questions torment me.

I've decided to sleep (as if I could!) beside the phone. I must know what is happening. This uncertainty is living torment.

4:20 a.m. The jangling telephone jarred me to consciousness. I had turned down the bell, so it didn't wake Mom. As usual, it was the operator asking if I wished to accept a collect call from ... "Yes, yes!" I interrupted, whispering eagerly.

"Nickie, darling. Is that you?"

It was The Voice of the Woman I Love. She sounded very far away.

"Yes, it's me Sheeni. What's going on? Are you all right?"

"I'm fine. A bit chilled. I sneaked out to call from a payphone. It's a little scary. I hope all the Lake County rapists have retired for the night. I'm just in shorts and a tube top."

"Not the yellow one I hope," I said, alarmed.

"Yes," replied Sheeni, "how did you know?

"Why must you dress so alluringly?" I demanded. "Especially when you're sneaking out in the middle of the night."

"It's just my nature I suppose," replied Sheeni philosophically. "Although, this evening's upheavals, I feel, may at least partially excuse this particular sartorial lapse."

"What is happening?" I asked.

"What is not happening might be a more appropriate question," said Sheeni. "It has been a night to remember. Father is back finally. I don't think they're going to charge him with anything. Although he should not have struck that sheriff's deputy."

"Why was he arrested?" I asked urgently.

"Lefty's parents notified the sheriff's office here. They were watching the bus station. Father, you'll recall, was somewhat in the dark at that point. At first he thought it was some kind of immigration matter. Then, when they said he was under arrest for kidnapping, he thought it was a joke. Some sort of a gag arranged by his law partners. Then, when the deputies persisted, he got angry. Father, as you may know, is apt to do anything when he gets angry."

"What about Lefty?"

"He went back home with his parents. They're probably getting into Oakland about now."

"Did he talk?"

"Like ZaSu Pitts on Ecstasy. First he clammed up. Then he got rattled by all the uniforms. His mother screaming hysterically didn't help his composure either. So, I'm afraid, Nickie darling, your pal spilled the beans."

"All of them?" I stammered weakly.

"Apparently so," sighed Sheeni. "Your name came up rather prominently. My parents have forbidden me ever to speak to you again."

"What!"

"Yes," said Sheeni. "Exactly so. You've been banned from my life. Of course, you realize this parental edict now makes you even more desirable in my eyes."

"It does?" I asked wonderingly.

"Well, yes," replied Sheeni. "Frankly, Nick, I was always somewhat appalled by my parents' approbation of Trent. In some ways it was the only chink in his armor of perfection."

"Then I'll get to see you again, Sheeni?"

"Of course, darling. But it's going to be difficult. We'll have to sneak around and lie to our parents. Can you do that?"

"I do it all the time," I replied.

"Good," said Sheeni, "I hoped you'd say that. I was worried you might be a bit of a Goody Two Shoes."

"Hardly," I said. "I'm in a state of permanent open revolt around here. That's why my mother wouldn't let me come to the phone."

"Then, darling, I shall take strength from your outlawhood. We shall revolt together. This will be the bond of our love. This and darling Albert. You must affect a girlish handwriting, Nickie, and communicate by letter daily. Write the name 'Debbie Grumfeld' as the return address on the envelope. She's a friend of mine who moved to Oakland last year. We're returning to Ukiah tomorrow, so send the letters to my home there."

"And will you write to me, darling?" I asked.

"As often as I dare," said Sheeni. "Unfortunately, this episode could not have come at a worse time. School starts Monday and I've yet to complete my fall wardrobe purchases. So, some parental appeasement will be required—at least temporarily."

"I'm sure you'll be lovely," I said wistfully, wishing with all my heart that I could walk the halls of Ukiah's Redwood High School, hand-in-hand with my love.

"Thank you, darling," said Sheeni. "Well, I'm shivering from the cold, and I don't like the way my erect nipples are outlined enticingly against this thin fabric. So, hugs and kisses. I'll talk to you soon. Say hi to Lefty for me. 'Bye, darling."

"Goodbye, sweetheart," I whispered.

At that moment, the overhead light snapped on, blinding me. I dropped the phone and turned around. It was Mom, standing in her robe by the light switch. If looks could kill, I'd be a cinch for the Channel 2 news.

"What the friggin' hell do you think you're doing?" she demanded. Albert growled at me from his ringside seat.

"I, I couldn't sleep. So I phoned for the time."

"You better be telling the truth," said Mom. "Because I'm calling the phone company tomorrow. And there better not be any more collect calls on this line."

Guess what, Lefty (wherever you are)? My life is a living hell.

10:15 a.m. I never got back to sleep. I lay in bed, feeling like moldy road kill, wishing I could fast forward through the coming week. The day dawned appropriately grey, gloomy, and cold. I thought of whacking off for some brief, transitory pleasure, but my libido is off somewhere hiding out.

The liver had its revenge on Mom too. I heard her go in the bathroom and toss her cookies. Not even the sounds of her violent bodily distress gave me pleasure.

Dreading another confrontation, I didn't go down for breakfast. Mom didn't call me. After a while, she walked into my room (without knocking) and said I owed her $83.12 in long-distance fees. To her surprise, I took out my wallet and paid her in cash. "Where'd you get all that money?" Mom demanded.

"Dealing dope," I muttered.

"What'd you say?"

"It's my savings," I replied. "My entire college education fund except for $7."

Mom, though, was impervious to guilt. "That phone is off-limits to you," she said, pocketing the greenbacks. "You want to talk to somebody, you write them a letter."

"I'm not going to talk to anyone," I replied. "I'm going to stay in my room and become a maladjusted, anti-social hermit."

"Good," said Mom, "that's sounds like an improvement to me. But first you're going to walk that dog."

Albert was in a bubbly mood and ready for exercise—even with me. We walked to the donut shop, where I blew four of my last seven dollars on the extreme depressive's breakfast: a large coffee, two maple bars, a cinnamon twist, a blueberry turnover, a chocolate old-fashioned, and a dozen donut holes. Even the clerk (an immense, middle-aged black woman), who doubtless deals daily with the profoundly sugar-compulsive, seemed impressed.

On the way back, I had to rescue Albert from a large doberman who trotted over menacingly to sniff his hienie. Albert's defense was to growl nervously, sit down, and look around to me for protection. I felt like maintaining strict neutrality, but for Sheeni's sake, I hoisted Albert out of danger range. He thanked me by dribbling on my shirt.

When I got home, Mom was in Joanie's room hanging frilly baby blue curtains on the windows. The effect is strikingly juvenile. Joanie, I am sure, will be pissed. Albert sauntered in and hopped up on the bed to watch Mom. She didn't object, and greeted him affectionately—while lobbing a scowl in my direction. Frankly, I think the two of them deserve each other.

I went to my room and sat at the computer. Any second now, I expect the phone to ring and the next stage of my life (as a juvenile offender) to commence.

12:45 p.m. The phone never rang. At 10:30 Lefty's parents showed up without an appointment. I heard the car stop out front and watched from my bedroom window. Lefty was in the back seat looking red-eyed, subdued, and just slightly swelled up. He spotted me in the window and quickly looked away. He didn't get out of the car.

When the doorbell rang, I felt a strange tingling at the base of my scrotum. This, I realized, is the physical sensation of extreme terror. It's probably what the noblemen in France felt right before the blade of the guillotine hurtled down.

I heard Mom open the front door and exclaim when she saw Lefty in the car. Five seconds later, I heard Lefty's parents exclaim when they saw the be-doilied Chevrolet in the living room. Then there were muffled conversational sounds interrupted periodically by loud expostulations from Mom. Then heavy footsteps stormed up the stairs and my bedroom door exploded open. Mom, several frightening emotional states past livid, stood in the doorway. "Get . . . get downstairs!" she raged.

I darted past the erupting volcano and hurried downstairs. Mom thundered down after me. From the couch next to the Chevy, Lefty's parents looked up in reproachful indignation. The next 15 minutes were an excruciating blur. I remember hysterical screaming (the two moms'), tears (mine), outraged bellowing (Lefty's dad's), expressions of heartfelt remorse (mine), threats and recriminations (Mom's), and abject cowering (mine). Finally—my emotions shredded, my self-esteem in tatters—I was sent upstairs to await punishment. (What do they call what they just put me through?)

Thank God it looks like Lefty's parents aren't planning to call in the cops—though Lefty's mom did say she was going to send us the bill for her daughter's "psychological counseling." I fear I may have applied too freely the red hot poker of guilt. I just hope Martha recovers her mental equilibrium in a hurry. God knows, psychological counseling is a luxury we can't afford.

Then I had to endure more abuse as I was carrying the computer and baseball cards out to Lefty's car. (His dad turned out to be a both a liar and an Indian-giver.) Lefty didn't even look at me as I was loading his computer into the back seat. Just see if I ever try to help out a pal in trouble again. He can walk around with permanent, day-glow peter tracks for all I care.

Mom has been phoning around trying to locate Dad. Whenever there's serious abuse, I mean discipline, to be handed out, she likes to rope in Dad to foster the illusion of parental consensus. Thus the tyrannical misuse of power is cloaked in a sheen of ersatz legitimacy. Naturally, I've been trying to anticipate what forms the parental decrees may take. Knowing Dad, I can expect some radical diminution in my allowance. I may also have to mow his yard gratis for the next 2,000 years. Mom, though, is harder to predict. She has a sadistic side that probes for deep emotional wounding through creative discipline. My worst nightmare is that she'll banish Albert. If she uses that sword against me, I don't know what I'll do.

2:15 p.m. Mom just burst into my room. "Your father is falling down drunk!" she exclaimed accusingly.

"Oh," I replied. I didn't see quite how I was at fault here.

"I'm going to Marin," continued Mom. "Don't you dare leave this house."

"OK."

"While I'm gone, I want you to take Joanie's bed apart and put it in the garage."

"OK," I said meekly. I didn't point out that to accomplish this task I would have to leave the house.

"It's none of your damn business why!" said Mom.

"OK," I said. "I didn't ask."

"Well, don't!" she added. "Just do it!"

5:30 p.m. Joanie's bed came apart with great reluctance. It's a vast oak monstrosity custom-built for athletic newlyweds. (Joanie inherited it at the age of seven when my parents moved on to twin beds.) I had to wham on it with a sledgehammer to free the bed rails—splintering some of the fine oak in the process. Then the mattress got away from me on the stairs, narrowly missing a small ugly dog.

Later, when I was closing the garage doors, Mr. Ferguson called my name from the bushes.

"Great news, Nick," he said, peering through the foliage. "I just heard on Channel 2 news that your friend Leroy is alive. He didn't drown after all!"

"That's nice," I said, walking quickly toward the house. I didn't feel much like talking to Mr. Ferguson.

Then, as I was watching Kate Cruikshank giving an exclusive live report from Lefty's front yard, the phone rang.

"I hate your slimy guts," declared a familiar voice.

"Lefty, I don't think you're being entirely fair," I replied.

"All my stuff is gone. My parents think I'm a sicko. And the whole world knows I've got a crooked dick. Thanks a pantsfull, Nick."

"What about Millie Filbert?" I said. "Did you hear what she said at your funeral?"

"Yeah, I watched the tape. So what? I'd be too embarrassed ever to speak to her again. Did you see that article about me in the *Chronicle*?"

"How did you get a copy of that?" I demanded.

"Martha saved all the newspapers. She also taped all the TV news reports. God, no way I can face school on Monday. I'm going to kill myself for sure now."

"Don't be retarded, Lefty," I said. "You know what you are now?"

"What?" he asked suspiciously.

"You're a big-time celebrity. A famous personality. And what do media superstars all have coming out of their ears?"

"What?"

"Girlfriends. Think about it, man. You can ask out any chick in the school."

"What about my wang condition?" asked Lefty doubtfully.

"It's only a negative if you make it a negative," I said. "Why not look on it as an asset? Flaunt it, guy! You have something that's out of the ordinary. Something unique. I bet there are lots of curious chicks out there now just dying to get their hands on your zipper."

"You think so, Nick?"

"I know so, man."

Lefty pondered that for a moment. "What'd your mom say?" he asked.

"She's still working on the terms of my punishment. She went over to Marin to talk to my dad."

"That sounds bad," said Lefty.

"I expect it will be pretty horrible," I said. "What did your parents do?"

"I'm grounded for two weeks."

"Is that all?"

"Yeah, and I can't play video games for a month."

"That's all you got for an attempted suicide?" I asked. "Boy, Lefty, your parents are pretty lenient."

"Yeah, well they also wanted me to go for counseling like Martha, but I talked them out of it."

"How did you do that?" I asked.

"I said it was all your idea. That I really never wanted to run away or commit suicide."

"Thanks!"

"Sorry," said Lefty. "I'm sorry I ratted on you, Nick. Thanks for not ratting on me."

"That's OK."

"Well, I better go," he said. "I'm not really allowed to talk to you."

"Why not?"

"My parents say you're a bad influence. And Martha hates you too. Funny, though."

"What's that?"

"Martha's attitude," replied Lefty. "What a change. She's been really nice to me ever since I got back."

9:30 p.m. Disaster to end all disasters! Dad's been on a three-day binge since Monday. He tried to run some old guy off the road for cutting in front of him on the freeway. Turns out it was Mr. Flagonphuel, the president of Agrocide Chemicals—the ad agency's biggest account. So on Monday, Mr. Flagonphuel demanded—and received—Dad's head on a silver platter. He's been canned!

Dad has no job prospects, no savings, and no funds for next month's child support. What does this mean exactly? It means—Mom informed me with malicious relish—that there are no tuition funds to send me to St. Vitus Academy. IT MEANS I HAVE TO GO TO THE OAKLAND PUBLIC SCHOOLS!

The horrors don't end there. My allowance is reduced to ninety cents a day for lunch money only. I am grounded for two months. And I am not allowed to phone or write Sheeni. Not for a week. Not for a month. Not for a year. Never again! (But I can keep her lousy, stinking dog.)

"Why?" I demanded, stunned and incredulous.

"Because," said Mom, "your father and I don't feel she has been a good influence on you."

"My father has never met her," I objected. "And besides, he's an unemployed drunk."

"That's just what I mean," replied Mom. "Backtalk like that. You've been willfully disobedient ever since you met her."

Willful disobedience? Willful disobedience? Lady, you have not yet begun to experience willful disobedience. But keep your eyes open. And stand back.

THURSDAY, September 6 — Another tormented, sleepless night. I bet if you totalled up my stress factors, they'd go right off the chart. I hope I don't have any unsuspected aneurysms in my brain—I'd be dropping dead from a stroke any minute now.

Being an iron disciplinarian must be getting to Mom. She chucked her chips again this morning. I rose to the bracing aroma of warm vomit wafting down the hall. Fortunately, we're not speaking to each other, so I didn't have to offer any phony filial commiseration. She left right after breakfast for God knows where.

Then, while I was eating my Cheerios, Mr. Ferguson knocked on the back door. He had been talking with Mom and wanted the bus fare and his $40 back. So, I invited him in and told him the whole ugly story. He was so sympathetic, he cancelled the debt. And gave me another crisp $20 bill to boot! It's a relief to know there are some decent adults in this world—even if they are left-wing commie pinkos.

After breakfast I gave Albert the executive dog walk (condensed to save me time), and—willfully disobedient—phoned Sheeni's number in Ukiah. Thank God, it was her incomparably desirable voice that answered. Quickly, I filled her in on all that had transpired. She was alarmed—and indignant—to hear that she had been banned from my life.

"I knew my parents were meddlesome and short-sighted," said Sheeni, "but yours, Nick, seem determined to pursue unenlightenment into hitherto unsuspected regions."

"What should we do?" I asked. "I'm desperate."

"Well," said Sheeni, maintaining her composure, "we might look upon your father's firing as a blessing in disguise."

"How so?"

"Because, Nickie, if we are both destined to have second-rate public school educations, at least now perhaps we can acquire them in the same school system."

"You mean you'd transfer to the Oakland schools?" I asked, amazed. Did Sheeni really love me that much?

"Don't be ridiculous," replied Sheeni. "I'm proposing that you move up here. We'll get your father a job in Ukiah and you can come live with him."

"I don't know if I could live with my father," I said doubtfully. "My father is a moron."

"Well, your mother doesn't sound so compellingly congenial at the moment either," Sheeni pointed out. "At least if you lived here we could be together. And I could see darling Albert too. Yes, I think we should find him a job. What does he do?"

"He's a writer—sort of. He writes advertising copy."

"That's bad," said Sheeni. "The employment opportunities for writers up here are necessarily slim. I don't suppose he'd like to change careers?"

"Maybe. What sort of jobs do they have up there?"

"How about a short-order cook?"

"No," I replied, "my father isn't interested in any job that involves actual work. I think it would have to entail some kind of bogus brain work. And preferably high paid."

"OK," said Sheeni, "I'll see what I can do. Do you think he'd be amenable to moving?"

"Maybe, if the rents are cheap enough. He's always complaining about the high rents in Marin County. And if I was with him in Ukiah, he wouldn't have to pay child support. Plus, he'd have his own live-in slave."

"That could be a powerful incentive right there," agreed Sheeni. "And housing up here is relatively inexpensive—especially if you're willing to live in a mobile home."

"I'd live in a drainage culvert to be with you," I confessed.

"Let's hope that won't be necessary, darling," said Sheeni. "Especially if you ever intend to invite me over. Yes, Dolores, I'll be taking the advanced math class too."

I could tell one of Sheeni's loathsome parents had entered the room. I promised to rush Dad's résumé to her, then reluctantly said goodbye.

"Goodbye, Dolores," said Sheeni, "I hope to see you in class very soon."

Oh, if only that miracle could happen! Yes, to be near The Woman I Love I would willingly live in the boonies with an insensitive, competitive, penny-pinching jerk.

4:30 p.m. I just mailed Dad's résumé to Ukiah by Express Mail. I hope Sheeni's parents don't question why their daughter's old school chum Debbie Grumfeld has suddenly begun marking her correspondence "extremely urgent."

I found one of Dad's old résumés in a desk drawer and doctored it slightly (he is now a graduate of Yale). Since Dad's version itself was not unremittingly truthful, the document is now almost entirely a work of fiction. Still, if Vice-presidential candidates can do it, why not lowly copywriters? I even managed to dredge up some snappy writing samples from back issues of *California Farmer*.

Mom came home with the Lincoln jammed with bags and boxes. Since we're not speaking, I saw no reason to volunteer to help her unload. She lugged the packages up to Joanie's room—which she is now keeping locked. Perhaps she's starting a small in-home business fencing stolen merchandise. I certainly hope she didn't buy all that stuff. She should be saving her money for school tuition.

Mom unwrapped one package in the living room—a large, framed color photograph of her deceased paramour, which she hung above the fireplace. From this hallowed vantage point, Jerry can gaze down for eternity upon his penultimate automobile and the rebellious youth who loathed him.

7:15 p.m. Liver, beets, and limas for dinner again. Mom must really hate my guts. We ate in silence—her chewing and me gagging. Then I did the dishes and it was back to my room. These four walls are certainly beginning to seem familiar. I figure this enforced captivity is good practice in case I am ever sentenced to a long prison term (for matricide?).

9:30 p.m. Lefty just called with some amazing news. (Mom let me take the call, but limited me to three minutes lest my life seem too normal.) My pal has a date with Millie Filbert!

"How did you ever work up the nerve to call her?" I asked.

"It wasn't too hard," replied Lefty. "She called me."

"What about Willis?"

"Oh, that's over and done with," said Lefty. "She's dropped that turkey."

"And the kid?"

"I don't know," said Lefty, "it sounds like that might have been dealt with."

"You mean she got an abortion?"

"No way. She wouldn't do anything like that. Probably she had a miscarriage."

"But she's definitely not pregnant?" I asked.

"No way," said Lefty, offended. "I don't think she ever was either. If you ask me, it was all a nasty rumor."

"Well, what does she say? Did you ask her?"

"No way," said Lefty. "I can't ask a girl that. I just know she's not knocked up."

"When are you going out?"

"In two weeks. As soon as I'm ungrounded."

"Wow, Lefty," I said, "you have a date with an experienced woman."

"I know, Nick. This could be the start of something big."

"Let's hope it doesn't suck its thumb and call you Da-Da."

"You're gross," said Lefty. "Anyway, I'm going to swipe some condoms. Just in case I need them."

"Good idea," I said. "You'll need them. Kid, the days of your cherry are numbered."

"You really think so?" asked Lefty.

Mom, wearing her best liver-fed scowl, came back into the room. "Yes, Lefty," I said, "I won't be seeing you Monday at St. V's. My parents are too poor to provide their son with a quality education."

One of Lefty's jailers must have entered his room. "OK, Jim," he said, "I'll swap you a Stan Musial for a Bob Feller."

FRIDAY, September 7 — The last day of summer vacation. I awoke a grounded, estranged, love-sick, virtually penniless, balding teen with zits. Soon I shall be another casualty of the tragic neglect of our public school systems.

Mom made it three mornings in a row. She catapulted her kibble just like clockwork at 7:06 a.m. I wonder if the liver was as delectable for her on its return flight? I hope she goes to the doctor soon—I'm beginning to experience parental regurgitation guilt. Of course, no one claimed it was easy raising a teenager.

At breakfast Mom broke her vow of silence long enough to tell me to go register at the local junior high school.

"But come straight home afterward," she added in her sternest warden-like voice. She shuffled over to the stove for a coffee refill. I noted with some trepidation that her ankles were grossly swollen. God, I hope Jerry didn't give her the clap! And all this time I'd been doing my usual indifferent job of washing the dishes. From now on everything Mom touches gets sterilized in bleach.

The junior high school was a tired-looking collection of stucco buildings lavishly autographed in spray paint by the local hoodlum associations. Crudely lettered signs on the entrance doors directed new students to the cafeteria—a large, low-ceiling room teeming with Future Dropouts of America. I signed my name on a sheet and took a seat. If only I had thought to bring a book. No such novelty as reading material was in evidence anywhere. So I sat and studied my fellow prospective students. The melting pot, it seemed, was aboil. Many diverse tongues were being spoken, but conspicuously absent was English.

After 94 minutes by the clock, a thin, harassed-looking man with glasses called my name. He said he was Mr. Orfteazle, my guidance counselor. He led the way to a tiny, windowless office knee-deep in computer printouts. I sat in a tiny chair (grade school surplus?) facing Mr. Orfteazle's cluttered, battle-scarred desk.

"So you want to transfer from St. Vitus?" he asked, studying me with evident interest over the top of his glasses. No wedding ring on his hairy fingers. Probably subscribes to *Mandate*, I concluded.

"Yes, sir."

"We don't get many transfers from there. Your father drop a bundle in the stock market?"

"He got fired from his job," I replied.

"It's usually something like that," he said. "Well, Nick, you look like a bright kid. Too bad you didn't drop by last month. I might have got you in some of the tracked classes. But those are all filled now."

"What does that mean?" I asked uneasily.

"It means we have to put you in the regular classes. At least for the first semester. The pace may be a little slower than you're used to."

"How slow?"

"Bring a good book," said Mr. Orfteazle with a conspiratorial wink. "Only kidding, of course. We have an excellent teaching staff here. You'll do fine." He hit a few keys on a battered computer terminal attached to the desk with what looked like ship's anchor chain. "Now, let's see what classes are still open."

A half-hour later I left with a school ID card (to get me past the armed guards) and a computer printout of my fall schedule. Assuming Dad doesn't move to Ukiah or I don't run away from home, I shall be taking gym, English, American history, biology, study hall, lunch, Spanish I, wood technology, and basic office skills. How's that for a curriculum guaranteed to wow the admissions officers of elite eastern colleges?

As I was walking down a long, grimy hallway toward the exit, someone said "Hi!" I turned around. It was fat Ms. Atari from the library. She had a construction paper badge labeled "voluntere" (sic) pinned to her already matronly bust.

"Are you going to be going to our school?" She posed this question so beamingly I wondered if she was high on drugs. Probably it was just her repellently upbeat fat personality.

"Maybe," I replied. "I mean, I hope not."

"If you do," she said, "I hope you'll join our computer club. I'm the president!"

"That's nice," I said, edging toward the door. "But I don't think I'll have time for extra-curricular activities."

"Why not?" she asked, following me.

I tried to think of a sufficiently irrefutable reason. "I'm on parole."

"Oh!" said Ms. Atari, beaming with even more interest. "You don't say!"

"Yes," I replied, finally reaching the door. "And I'm late for a gang meeting."

Ms. Atari had one last question. "What's your name?"

"Nick."

"Mine's Rhonda," she called, still beaming.

It figured. She looked like a Rhonda.

When I got home, Mom was banging away in Joanie's room with the door closed. Perhaps she's constructing a teen torture chamber. She might as well. When I opened the refrigerator to fix some lunch, I got the shock of my life. Mom had been shopping. We now have 23 frost-free cubic feet filled with jars of red beets, packages of frozen lima beans, and tubs of beef liver. Dietary war has been declared!

I extracted Mr. Ferguson's $20 bill from its hiding place (the thumb cavity of my official Rodney "Butch" Bolicweigski first baseman's glove), and sneaked out of the house to McDanold's. I ate slowly, savoring the burgers and fries. This could be my last decent, greasy meal for a long time.

When I got back, Mom was gone. She had left behind a note affixed by a magnet to the liver refrigeration chamber. It read in stark simplicity: "You're in trouble, buster!"

SATURDAY, September 8 — I am writing this in pencil. Mom has confiscated my computer keyboard for a week for violating my prison sentence. If my dick unscrewed, I'm sure she'd have that hidden somewhere too to prevent unauthorized access to bodily pleasures.

Mom went for the grand slam this morning. At 7:12 a.m. she pitched her pabulum. The slight delay I attributed to a more leisurely pace on the weekend.

Later, while Mom was hammering in Joanie's room, the phone rang. In breathless anticipation, I accepted another willfully disobedient collect call from Sheeni. Great news! She has actually dredged up a writing job in Ukiah.

"*Progressive Plywood* is looking for an assistant editor," reported The Woman of My Dreams. "It's perfect for your father."

"What's *Progressive Plywood* and how much does it pay?" I asked.

"It's a trade magazine," explained Sheeni. "All about the wonders of plywood, with occasional digressions on wafer board. The salary starts at 32."

"Wow, that's kind of low," I said doubtfully. "And Dad's not much of a woodworker. I'm not sure he knows what plywood is."

"That's OK," said Sheeni. "They're just looking for basic writing skills. The salary is quite generous for up here. And I had to pull some strings to get even that."

"Oh," I said suspiciously, "you have clout with trade magazine editors?"

"Indirectly," replied Sheeni. "The owner is the father of a friend of mine."

"Anyone I know?"

"OK, it's Trent's father. So what?"

"So, why should Trent want to help my dad move to Ukiah?"

"I told you, darling. Trent harbors you no ill will. In fact, he's looking forward to meeting you."

I didn't believe that for a second. "And I'm looking forward to meeting him," I lied.

"Can you call your father today?" asked Sheeni. "They're anxious to fill the position."

"I can't do that. My father would never take a job I found for him. It would violate his competitive Type-A standards."

"You're probably right," said Sheeni. "OK. I'll pretend to be a headhunter and I'll call him up."

"Flatter his ego," I advised. "He'll go for that."

"That's a good idea."

"Put your charm in overdrive," I added.

"Why, Nick," said Sheeni innocently, "I don't know what you mean."

After lunch, Lefty came over with a steak bone for Albert. Both dog and bone giver were happy to see each other. Lefty's body has returned to what passes for normal for him. He is still grounded (aren't we all?), but since both his parents work, he is free to be willfully disobedient during the day. By 4:45, though, Lefty is back in his room—pretending to be bored and cranky from a day of tedious confinement.

Mom was in the kitchen baking cakes when Lefty arrived. She greeted him with cold correctness. Perhaps she's jealous that Lefty rose from the dead but Jerry hasn't so far.

"Gee, that smells good," commented Lefty, after we went upstairs to my room. "What's your mom making?"

"Cakes, cookies, brownies, pies. You name it. She's going all out."

"What's the occasion?" asked Lefty.

"I don't know. She's not talking. My theory is she's planning a big surprise party for me to tell me all is forgiven and to make up for my having to go to public school."

"Well, I didn't get an invitation," complained Lefty.

"Of course not. You're grounded."

"So are you."

"True. But I don't have to leave the house to go to the party."

Lefty, I noticed, had something flat and rectangular concealed under his shirt. "Don't tell me you've been to the library," I said.

"No, a bookstore," he replied, pulling out a large hardbound volume. "I got this for my date with Millie." The book was titled *Lovemaking for Advanced Gourmets*. "I was reading it all last night. Boy, having sex is a lot more complicated than I thought. Did you know you were supposed to stick your pinkie up her bumhole?"

"You lie!"

"No way man," said Lefty indignantly. "Here, I got the page marked. Read that!"

I read the paragraph in question. Although phrased somewhat more delicately than Lefty's crude summary, there was no doubt this was precisely what the authors were advocating. "Well," I said, reading the passage again in disbelief, "I think this is for people who've been married so long they're kind of revolted by the sight of each other. Like your parents. I definitely wouldn't try this on a first date."

"I'm not planning to," stated Lefty with conviction. "If Millie wants that kind of action she can go back to Willis. See if I care."

I leafed through the book with interest. Every page was illustrated with tasteful drawings of yuppie couples participating in sophisticated lovemaking.

"Check out the chapter on cocksucking," suggested Lefty.

"Looks pretty spicy," I agreed. My T.E. was throbbing in my pants.

"Do you suppose our girlfriends will actually do that to us someday?" wondered Lefty, adjusting his crotch.

"Certainly," I replied, "it says right here most women enjoy performing fellatio. Once they overcome their feelings of revulsion and impulse to gag."

Lefty unzipped. "Want to try it?" he asked shyly.

"Maybe we should," I replied matter-of-factly. "Just so we'll know what it's like for our girlfriends."

I went first. In spite of the fetid crotch odors, Lefty's cock was surprisingly tasteless—except for some mild salinity at the tip. The experience was not unlike sucking a nailless, oversize, somewhat crooked thumb. I found I could take about three-quarters of the warm shaft before gagging. Lefty groaned with pleasure as I rolled my tongue around the sensitive glans. Thankfully, he pulled away just before he came and finished the job by hand.

Then, when Lefty was doing me, Mom walked into the room carrying two chocolate cupcakes. She screamed, Lefty bolted upright, I zipped. *Zingggg.* The first cupcake whizzed past my left ear and splattered against the wall. The second one slammed into the side of Lefty's head.

"Perverts!" screamed Mom. "Friggin' goddam perverts!"

Panicked, half-blinded, Lefty bolted toward the door and ran into Mom. She shoved him aside like a wild woman and lumbered toward the bed with murder in her eyes. I assumed the abused child's Basic Defensive Posture (knees against chest, arms shielding head) as Mom grabbed the nearest object (a heavy volume on advanced lovemaking) and began flailing me with it.

"In my house! How dare you!" she screamed. "Pervert! Friggin' pervert!"

After what seemed like ten minutes, she paused, examined her now tattered weapon, screamed, and flung it across the room. She looked around wildly. "Where's, where's that other degenerate?" she demanded, gasping for breath. But Lefty had long since beat it. "He won't get away!" she exclaimed, "I'm calling his parents!"

Futilely I whimpered for compassion. "Aw, we didn't mean anything by it, Mom. Don't tell his parents!"

Mom wasn't buying it. "I don't want to hear another word!" she bellowed. "Wait until your father hears about this!"

I decided to go on the offensive. "Well it's all your fault! You told me I couldn't see my girlfriend any more!"

"Shut up!" she screamed. (But I think the point had struck home.) "Don't you dare leave this room! I'm going to have you locked up!"

Mom walked out and slammed the door. I sat up, still somewhat dazed, and wiped chocolate frosting out of my hair. All this unpleasantness could be avoided, I thought, if only the woman would learn to knock before entering.

5:15 p.m. Mom is downstairs having an animated conversation on the telephone with someone. I fear it may be Lefty's mother. I also smell the unmistakable aroma of liver frying. Running away from home has never sounded more appealing than it does at this minute.

8:07 p.m. Mom is entertaining about 45 noisy truckdrivers downstairs. She's had the poor taste to host a wake for Jerry. I can barely think over the raucous country and western music. Periodically over the noise, an annoying peal of laughter rises from Mom. One would hardly suppose that just hours before, she was beating her only son for illicit homosexual congress. Why are adults so two-faced?

Me, I'm surprisingly nonplussed by the whole affair. It's occurred to me that a kid can get in just so much trouble and then you bump against a plateau. No matter what other heinous acts you commit, you're still in the same deep shit. So, that being the case, why not hold your nose, let 'er rip, and enjoy life? That's my philosophy.

I've been reading Lefty's book and taking notes. These are the practical, tab A in slot B pointers I was seeking (and not getting) from that late alleged genius Wilhelm Reich. I can't wait to try out some of the more improbable maneuvers on My Future Wife. Am I wrong to expect that our sex lives will be nothing less than sizzling? I think not.

SUNDAY, September 9 — Figuring Mom would be sleeping in from her late-night funereal debaucheries, I sneaked downstairs bright and early to call Sheeni. The living room was totally trashed—with the picked-over remains of a large buffet spread over the hood of Jerry's dead Chevy. I flicked cigarette ash off a brownie and gulped it down as I dialed the number. That Wonderful Teen herself answered on the second ring. As expected, Sheeni's pious parents were away at church, so she could talk without fear of interruption. She had bad news to report.

"Alas, darling," she said, "your father listened to my employment proposal most graciously. But he's declined to come for an interview."

"He declined!" I exclaimed. "Why?"

"He says he thinks this is a wonderful opportunity for him to resume work on his novel."

"His novel! He's been working on that piece of trash since before Joanie was born. I don't think he's past page five!"

"He says he's up to page 12 now."

"And what's he planning to live on?" I demanded.

"I asked him that, of course," replied Sheeni. "He said he's going to move to a cheap apartment and live on unemployment compensation. He said his check will just cover rent, food, and BMW payments. Oh, and he thought his girl-friend might move in and help with expenses. He also suggested that if she did not perhaps I could come down and have dinner with him some time."

"That lecher!" I exclaimed. "That lazy, parasitic lecher!"

"He seemed rather sweet to me," observed Sheeni.

"And did he mention how he proposed to meet his legal obligation to pay child support?"

"No," admitted Sheeni, "I don't think that issue is weighing particularly on his mind."

"Well, it will be shortly," I said. "I'm not going to stand for this lawless neglect."

"Good for you, Nickie," said Sheeni. "Parents should be reminded pe-riodically of their responsibilities. In fact, my father received quite a sobering reminder yesterday. Mother and I drove down to Santa Rosa and spent $2,683 on my fall wardrobe. It was quite an exhilarating day."

"Santa Rosa!" I said. "That's half way to the Bay Area."

"Yes," she replied, "I thought of you, Nickie, in the lingerie department. So close, and yet still hauntingly out of reach."

"Did you get some nice lingerie?" I asked, nearly swooning.

"Oh yes! Something sheer and lacy and ever so alluring. I'm not going to tell you precisely what it is. I'd rather it be a surprise. Frankly, though, I was amazed my mother consented to purchase it."

I heard a noise that sounded like feminine vomiting upstairs. "Oops, I better hang up now," I said. "The forces of darkness are astir. I can't wait to explore your surprise."

"Soon, darling, soon," promised Sheeni. "Bye-bye, and kiss darling Albert for me."

Two seconds after I hung up, Mom dragged herself downstairs. "What are you doing?" she demanded.

"Waiting for the newspaper," I said. "It's late again."

"I've got something to tell you, Nick," she said, giving off a familiar aroma of gastric evacuate.

"Uh-huh," I said.

"I've decided to accept it," Mom said, "I don't mind that you're gay."

"What!"

"But please, be careful. Don't get any, you know . . . diseases."

You should talk, I thought. "Thanks," I said, "I'll remember that." I thought of making an effort to convince her I was a card-carrying heterosexual, but what's the point? She'll believe what she wants to anyway. Reasoning with parents is like spelunking in a sewer: it's dark, scary, and almost always results in a lot of shit coming down on your head.

I actually had a pretty good morning. I read the Sunday paper and ate leftover wake pastries until my eyes could no longer focus from the sugar rush (though I pointedly boycotted the chocolate cupcakes). Mom fixed herself a nice plate of scrambled eggs and fried liver. As she was digging in she looked up and apologized for tilting the menu so heavily toward the organ meats. "I have this incredible craving for beef liver," she remarked. "I can't get enough of it."

"Oh," I said, "too bad it's not steak and French fries."

"No, I never craved steak when I was . . ." Mom stopped. "When I was having cravings before."

The woman is sure acting strange. Maybe it's dreaded menopause. I hear that can be hell on innocent family members.

Just as Mom was finishing her second helping of liver, the doorbell rang. She was off like a jackrabbit to answer it. "Good morning," I heard her say to someone. "So you came by after all. Nice to see you."

A moment later, Mom walked back into the kitchen followed by an immense, seven-foot-tall giant in a plaid shirt and bib overalls. The giant had to duck to come through the doorway.

"Oh, Wally," said Mom, "this is my son. Nick, this Mr. Rumpkin, a friend of Jerry's."

The giant leaned over and stretched out a frighteningly huge hand. Timidly, I offered mine and the Brobdingnagian fingers enveloped it in a shockingly mild grip. The giant blushed, looked at his shoes, and mumbled, "How do?"

"Fine, thanks," I replied. I noticed that instead of being completely hairless, as I had first supposed, Mr. Wally Rumpkin's immense pink head was covered with wispy blond hair of such fineness as to make even the most delicate infant green with envy. His features were also babylike, with a tiny pug nose and watery blue eyes forming a lonely oasis in a vast desert of puffy pink skin.

"Wally volunteered to help with the clean-up this morning," said Mom, beaming. "Wasn't that nice of him?"

Wally blushed and looked at the ceiling. From his vantage point no flaw in the plaster escaped his scrutiny.

Mom and Wally set to work on the clean-up while I helped by staying out of the way. As the laconic pink giant carried tray after tray of soiled dishes into the kitchen, he would sometimes glance in my direction and blush fiercely. Twice I looked down to make sure my robe was closed. No winkie in sight. The source of Mr. Rumpkin's acute embarrassment remained a mystery.

Most intimidated by Mom's new helpmate was Albert, who scurried into the Chevy and burrowed under the front seat until only his black nose and two frightened black eyes were visible. Perhaps Albert feared being crushed under Wally's size 26, triple-E boots.

Even with Wally's gigantic assistance, the clean-up took nearly two hours. Mom talked gaily all the while and Wally mumbled semi-incoherent replies in his deep, giant's voice. David Susskind he is not.

Later, while Wally was showing Mom his new semi-tractor out front, the phone rang. It was Dad making his court-ordered Sunday check-in call. He said he wanted to take me to Pier 39 for a fun afternoon of video-game playing, but couldn't because I was grounded.

"And what's this I hear about your being gay?" he asked.

"What's this I hear about your being unemployed?" I answered.

"Yes," said Dad competitively, "but my condition is only temporary. I can change it."

"I hope you do," I said. "We need the money."

"Nick, there are more important things in life than money."

"I know, Dad. Like getting a good education. And being able to respect your parents."

"Take it from me, kid, there's no greater experience a man can have than the love of a good woman."

I was feeling reckless. "How about the love of a dozen good women—all under the age of 20?"

"I can see you don't wish to discuss this," said Dad, seething inwardly.

"What's there to say?"

"I've got two words of advice for you then," he went on.

"OK."

"Safe sex."

"Thanks, Dad."

Now I know why I dislike Sundays so much.

1:30 p.m. I'm writing this on my computer! Mom gave me back my keyboard. Perhaps she feels sorry for me for being gay. She and Wally went to Berkeley in Jerry's Lincoln. They're going to an antique book fair. Wally, believe it or not, collects books. Admittedly the books he collects are about trucks. But still, they're books.

6:15 p.m. Mr. Rumpkin stayed for dinner. As you might expect, he has a fairly colossal appetite. Fortunately Wally dislikes liver, so we had barbecued chicken, fried potatoes, and corn on the cob instead. I discovered eye contact makes him blush, so you have to keep your eyes pinned elsewhere when you talk to him.

"Mr. Rumpkin is very smart," said Mom, offering him another piece of chicken. He blushed and held the chicken breast up to his face, as if trying to hide behind it. "Ask him a question, Nick."

"OK," I said. I looked at the ceiling. "Mr. Rumpkin, what famous actress was married to Frank Sinatra, Artie Shaw, and Mickey Rooney?"

"Ava Gardner," mumbled the giant.

"Correct," I said, impressed.

"No, ask him a proper question," insisted Mom.

"OK." I tried to think. "Mr. Rumpkin," I said, studying my water glass, "can you name all of the United States' female winners of the Nobel Prize for Literature?"

"That's easy," mumbled Wally, "There's only one: Pearl S. Buck."

"And what does the 'S' stand for?" I demanded.

Wally gulped. "Uh . . . oh, I know, Sydenstricker."

The man is an absolute genius. He may turn out to be a great scholarly allusion resource for my intellectual correspondence with Sheeni.

8:30 p.m. Wally and Mom are still doing the dishes. At least, they're down in the kitchen being awfully quiet. Lefty just called with some good news and some bad news. The bad news is his parents are sending him to a shrink to get his sexual orientation reprogrammed. The good news is there's been an emergency cancellation of his grounding so his date with Millie Filbert could be moved up to this coming Friday. The further bad news is they screamed at him for two solid hours for violating their ban on associating with me.

"It's depressing," said Lefty, "all my dad did today was pester me to shoot some baskets with him or go fishing. You can tell he thinks I'm a pansy. I wish your mother had kept her trap shut just this once."

"So do I," I replied. "Odd thing is, ever since she told me it was OK to be gay, she's been really nice to me."

"Parents really suck," said Lefty.

"The hairiest fur ball they can find," I agreed. "Are you going to see Millie tomorrow at school?"

"Yes, and I'm really nervous."

"Just be natural," I said. "You'll do fine. She likes you a lot."

"OK, Jim," replied Lefty. "I'll trade you a Juan Marichal for a Peewee Reese."

"Say hi to the guys at St. V's for me, Lefty."

"OK, Jim," he replied. "I'm sure sorry you won't be there."

10:30 p.m. I just heard Wally's truck pull away. I hope to see him again. Maybe he can keep Mom distracted and off my back.

I laid out the best of my 1973 wardrobe to wear to school tomorrow. The question that haunts me: Are bellbottoms totally, totally out of it?

MONDAY, September 10 — Today I entered the gulag of the Oakland Public Schools.

I was neither stabbed nor shot, though as I approached the school grounds this morning, I was compelled to hand over my 90 cents in lunch money to two 12-year-old thugs with beepers on their belts. You'd think they'd stick to robbing kids their own age.

Once past the sullen guards at the doors, I felt a little safer, though still exposed. When you're one of two dozen white kids (and the only one wearing bellbottoms) in a big inner-city school, some degree of self-consciousness may be excused.

The ever chipper, always rotund Rhonda Atari was in my homeroom class. She greeted me effusively.

"Like your bellbottoms, Nick," she cooed.

"Thanks. I like your mou-mou."

"It's not a mou-mou," she said, offended. "It's a dress. My mother made it."

"She's very talented," I lied.

Rhonda beamed. "How was your gang meeting, Nick?"

I said I couldn't discuss it because of my vow of secrecy.

"What are the principles of your gang?" she asked.

"The usual," I replied, "theft and mayhem."

"Wow!" she exclaimed, "that's heavy."

Not as heavy as you, I thought.

The first period was gym, taught by a grizzled old white guy who may have been a plantation overseer in a previous life. "OK, you slackers," he bellowed, "get out on that track!"

And so, without any conditioning, without any preliminary stretching, 30 African-American youths and I did eight laps of the track. Then six more. I thought I was going to faint. Back in the locker room, I was among the last to hold onto my breakfast. But as the world heaved around me, my three chocolate cream donuts lost their grip and joined the fragrant buffet on the floor. Still, sick as we were, the whip-cracking overseer made us all take showers. Was my pale winkie the most abbreviated in the room? Does the Pope serve refreshments on Sundays?

The rest of the morning was a blur. I received my English, history, and biology textbooks—all nicely broken in by untold generations before me. In every class, the teacher called the roll. Yet each time, when they came to the "t"s, my name was not mentioned. Am I enrolled or not?

Since I had study hall right before lunch, I skipped out and went home to make a sandwich and perform some leakage. (I had ventured into a restroom at school, but not wanting to smoke dope, buy drugs, or converse with 20 robust fellows in Raiders jackets hosting a switchblade show-and-tell, I quickly turned around and left.)

Mom wasn't at home. Her bereavement period has expired and she's gone back to work—leaving behind the lonely Albert. He lay in the dead Chevy, pining for a prayer book.

While I was home, I called the State Office of Human Resources in Marin and asked to speak to the caseworker for Dad. After a lot of festive music on hold, I was finally connected to the proper bureaucrat. Oddly, I couldn't think of any better strategy than the truth. The woman seemed quite interested and sympathetic. I said Dad was in arrears on his child-support payments, was not seriously looking for work, and had turned down the offer of a very good job. As a consequence, I had no new clothes for school (technically true) and had to go to public school in Oakland.

"Not the Oakland schools!" exclaimed the woman, appalled.

"Yes," I said. "And I was robbed of my lunch money this morning."

"Don't you worry, young man," she said, "I'll get right on this."

"You won't tell him I was the one who snitched on him, will you?" I asked. "He has a violent temper."

"Of course not," she replied. "And don't worry. We'll light a fire under that deadbeat."

My first class after lunch was beginning Spanish. I had requested French (in preparation for my life in Paris with Sheeni), but those classes were full. To my surprise, about three-quarters of my fellow Spanish scholars were hispanic. For 45 minutes they conversed among themselves in their mother tongue, telling jokes and making fun of the teacher's accent. Miss Talmadge, an aging '60s peace warrior, had learned her Spanish dodging bullets in the Peace Corps in El Salvador. Perhaps this is why she now chose to teach in Oakland.

Wood technology class was next. This, it turns out, is just wood shop with an upscale name. Our first project is to transform a large block of pine into a small doorstop. This could be done quite accurately on a table saw in about 10 seconds. We've been given a not-very-sharp hand plane and two weeks. I think they should re-name it wood technology for serfs.

Basic office skills was the final class of the day. What a relief to gorge the brain at last on true intellectual meat. In 45 minutes we learned all the size classifications, types, styles, and uses of the paper clip. Tomorrow we move on to thumbtacks and pushpins. I can't wait.

Mom was feeling pleased with herself when she got home from work. She has accessed the DMV computer and changed the registration on Jerry's Lincoln and trailer into her name. "That woman may have Jerry's body," boasted Mom, "but I've got his entire rolling stock." (Definitely the better of the bargain it seems to me.) To obscure the paper trail even more, Mom registered them in her maiden name (Biddulph, rhymes with "bit off") at Mr. Ferguson's address. Not even the KGB could track down those hot vehicles.

Dinner was delayed for one hour while Mom chatted on the phone with Wally. He must be somewhat more articulate in that medium—Mom was only doing about 85% of the talking. He's on the road, hauling malted milk balls to Salt Lake City. Dinner was potroast and sweet potatoes. The liver crisis may be over.

7:30 p.m. Lefty just checked in by phone. He said the ravishing Miss Satron expressed her regret that I was no longer enrolled at St. V's and would not be taking her English lit class. "You should have seen the sweater she had on today," exclaimed Lefty. "It was like dual nose-cones on an F-16 fighter jet."

"Did the kids razz you about your suicide attempt?" I asked.

"Not too bad," he replied. "Dinky Stevens asked me if I was going out for the swim team. Then dumb Tatar Collins asked me if it was true I was allowed to park in handicapped zones. I told her anyone who parked in her zone would have to be handicapped."

"Good for you," I said. "Did you talk to Millie?"

"Sure," he replied, "we ate lunch together. Boy, does Millie look sexy biting into a ham sandwich. I had to hold my lunch bag over my lap."

"What did you talk about?"

"Mostly my baseball card collection. I'm not sure she was too interested either. But, I mean, what do you talk to girls about, Nick?"

"Well, you could talk about movies and books and current affairs. You know—the issues of the day."

"You mean those guys I see driving around in jacked up pickup trucks with hot babes all snuggled up against them are talking about movies and books?"

"I expect so," I replied. "That's what Sheeni and I talk about."

"Yeah, well, you guys are a couple of eggheads. Half the time I was up at Clear Lake, I didn't have a clue what your girlfriend was talking about. But I wasn't too surprised considering the wacko parents she's got."

I felt this criticism of his recent hosts was most ungracious. Mr. and Mrs. Saunders may be somewhat eccentric, but let us not forget they will be contributing half the chromosomes of my future children.

"Speaking of mental illness," I said, "when's your appointment to see that psychologist?"

"Tomorrow after school," replied Lefty gloomily. "I wonder if he'll give me a test."

"What kind of test?"

"You know, show me a *Playboy*. Then *Playgirl*. See which one gives me a hard-on. I hear they do that. Then, if you go for the wrong pictures, they zap you with electric shocks."

"That's sounds like it might be effective."

"Yeah," said Lefty, "I hear it's painful as hell. That's why I'm laying off my meat tonight. One peek at that first tit tomorrow and prong, I'm going to prove to that shrink I'm straight."

"Straight in a crooked sort of way," I observed.

"Damn those fucking vitamins," replied Lefty. "They haven't done jack shit."

TUESDAY, September 11 — I had a pleasant day at school today. I didn't go. I got within a half block of its grim walls, but couldn't proceed any further—almost as if an invisible force had glued my Reeboks to the pavement. It didn't help that those grammar-school stick-up artists were lurking by the main gate. So, I crossed the street and kept on walking. I spent the day downtown at the library. At first I was worried someone was going to ask why I wasn't in school. But nobody paid the slightest attention to me.

I spent most of the morning getting caught up on all the computer magazines. Then I started to feel somewhat guilty, so I took down a book on biology and read it awhile. Very boring stuff. Next I had a nice lunch at McDanold's. Then I went back and mined the fiction section for dirty passages. All and all, I think I improved my mind considerably more than I would have at school. And it was ever so much more pleasant. Perhaps I am destined to be one of those great self-educated renaissance men.

Mom remains cheerful despite her bereavement and daily morning chow chucking. She had another long phone conversation with Wally; the next phone bill should be quite a whopper. (Our family only falls in love with people who telephone collect. I wonder if Joanie's physicist reverses the charges when he makes his surreptitious love calls.) Wally, reports Mom, is now on his way back—hauling a load of religious tracts from Salt Lake. Perhaps he'll put one aside for Albert.

8:15 p.m. Further telephonic communication with Lefty. He reports that while walking from English to math class, he successfully reached for and grasped Millie's hand.

"She has a nice sexy hand," said Lefty. "Warm and soft. Not too clammy."

Lefty said he mentioned this to Dr. Browery, his shrink, right away, but the guy wasn't particularly impressed.

"Why not?" I asked.

"He said I didn't have to prove anything. That he wanted to help me become more accepting of my latent tendencies."

"That sounds bad," I said. "Did he show you any pictures?"

"No, we just talked. He asked me if I thought a lot about suicide and touching guys on their private parts."

"What did you say?"

"I told him all I thought about was baseball cards, computers, going out with Millie Filbert, hating my sister, and getting my dick straightened. Of course, I said 'penis' to him."

"What did he say?" I asked.

"He asked me what I thought about my mother. So I said I thought she should lose some weight and stop dying her hair orange."

"Did he ask you what you thought about your dad?"

"No. He was a lot more interested in my mother. Maybe he's got the hots for her."

"Did he ask you about Martha?"

"Yeah. That was bad. He asked me if I ever had lustful thoughts toward my sister. So I told him about beating off once with her brassiere."

"What did you tell him that for?" I demanded.

"You don't know what it's like," replied Lefty. "These guys release chemicals in their office to make you tell the truth. You can't hide anything."

"What did he say?"

"Not much. He wrote it all down though. Maybe he's going to blackmail me with it when I grow up and get a good paying job. The guy drives a gold Porsche. I just hope he doesn't tell Martha."

"Why would he do that?"

"I don't know. He's her shrink too."

"You're going to the same psychologist?"

"Sure," answered Lefty. "Mom got us a package deal. Fifty bucks a session and the bill goes to your house."

"You mean my mom has to pay for you too?"

"I guess so. It was your cock I was sucking."

"Yes. But it was your idea!" I replied.

"That's true," he admitted. "Gee, maybe I am gay."

"Don't be retarded," I said. "We were doing research for our girlfriends."

"Oh right. I forgot. That's a relief."

"Do you have to see Dr. Browerly again?"

"Next week," replied Lefty. "Yes, Jim, next week I can trade you a Joe Jackson for a Bob Feller."

"Maybe you'll have laid Millie Filbert by then."

"Yes, Jim," said Lefty. "That would certainly be a great day in major league baseball."

10:30 p.m. Mom was watching TV in her bedroom when the phone rang downstairs. Thank God I had had the foresight to sabotage the extension next to her bed. It was Sheeni, calling collect with marvelous news. Dad is going to Ukiah tomorrow for an interview!

"He sounds quite eager to accept the position now," said Sheeni. "I don't know how to account for such a complete reversal of mind."

"I do," I replied. "It was extreme fear."

"Extreme fear of what, darling?"

"BMW withdrawal," I replied. "Dad couldn't survive if his Beamer were repossessed. The yuppie shock would kill him. Let's just pray he gets the job."

"He shouldn't have any trouble. The only other candidate is my brother Paul."

"Your brother's back?" I asked, surprised.

"Yes," replied Sheeni. "Didn't I tell you? He turned up last weekend. Six years without a word, and then he walks in while we're having breakfast and asks for his toast medium brown. He's living out in the studio over the garage."

"Where was he all that time?"

"Maybe Tibet. Or Nepal. He's not very coherent at the moment. He mostly talks in a language that sounds like Mandarin Chinese, but is not. Too bad Leff Ti isn't here. Perhaps it's Burmese."

"You don't think he could get the job?"

"Not likely," said Sheeni. "Father, of course, is twisting arms—including Paul's. Paul had an interview with Trent's father and said he was more interested in plywood than anything else in the world except spiritual nirvana. His résumé also displays some troublesome gaps in employment. Therefore, I should have to rate him the weaker candidate—even if he has been supplying me with some wonderful psychedelics."

"You've been taking drugs?" I exclaimed in alarm.

"Just a few mushrooms, darling," replied Sheeni. "Nothing heavy. They're wonderfully mind expanding. I've put some aside for us to take together. In the interim, I suggest you read *The Doors of Perception* by Aldous Huxley."

"OK," I said doubtfully. "Just promise me you won't get addicted to crack before I get a chance to move to Ukiah."

"I promise," said Sheeni, laughing. "You know why I like you, Nick?"

"Why?"

"You're such an adorable throwback. A relic of a bygone epoch."

"I'm as hip as the next cat," I protested.

Sheeni laughed. Her wonderful, lyrical laugh. (The most addicting drug I know.)

WEDNESDAY, September 12 — Another stimulating day at the library. With the nice weather we've been having, most of the homeless were outdoors working on their tans. So the library was pleasantly uncrowded with only occasional pockets of bad b.o. And some of the most malodorous offenders were library personnel themselves. What a collection of dispirited, ill-garbed misfits. They really have no excuse either, since the library subscribes to both *Vogue* and *GQ*. I think a monthly perusal of those magazines should be compulsory for all employees (and perhaps the homeless as well).

I found the Huxley book and read it most of the morning. Its pages were heavily annotated by generations of drug groupies. Al may have achieved brilliant insights through chemistry, but the evidence left by his acolytes suggests this is not always true. Still, he makes a persuasive case so I am keeping an open (though as yet unexpanded) mind.

Seeking more variety in my diet, I went to Burger Prince for lunch. I must confess I felt a little nervous gazing at the minimum-wage burger jockeys as I munched my fries. How many of them were once-budding intellectuals who dropped out of stultifying public schools? I may consider myself a self-educated renaissance man, but what if the world views me only as an ninth-grade dropout? Will Sheeni be embarrassed to introduce me to her high-brow Parisian friends? Will Knopf return my manuscripts unread? Will I be flipping spatulas instead of signing autographs? The conclusion is inescapable: at some point soon I shall have to rejoin the educational establishment.

In the afternoon I photocopied the *Consumers* article on condoms and wrote a long, penetrating missive to Sheeni. Having the resources of the library's reference department at hand makes this task somewhat easier. At one point, all five staff members were at work tracking down allusions for me. I enclosed the prophylactic rating sheet with the letter, remembering to address the envelope in the flamboyantly cursive hand of Debbie Grumfeld. Then it was home for another evening of oppressive grounding with Mom and Albert.

After dinner, while I was watching TV, Mom came in and demanded to know why I wasn't upstairs doing my homework. I replied that I didn't have any to do.

"Why not?" asked Mom.

"Public schools don't give out homework," I replied.

"They don't?" she asked, surprised.

"No. Too many teachers were getting beat up. So they stopped assigning it."

"Then how are you supposed to learn anything?" demanded Mom.

"What's to learn?" I replied. "You don't have to know algebra to sell crack."

"Watch your smart mouth," retorted Mom. But was that guilt I saw flickering across her countenance?

THURSDAY, September 13 — Dad got the job in Ukiah! Sheeni called collect in the morning while Mom was upstairs in mid-puke.

"Everything's working out beautifully," said Sheeni. "Of course, Father is livid. But Paul is accepting his rejection philosophically."

"When does my dad start?"

"Next Monday, believe it or not. Trent's father is going to help him look for housing today. And they've given him some plywood samples to study over the weekend."

"Wow, that's great! Now all I have to do is get him to agree to let me live with him."

"And darling Albert too," reminded Sheeni.

"Oh sure."

"How does your father feel about dogs?" she asked.

I tried to think. It seemed to me that Dad disliked all life forms except under-20, bra-less, sexually uninhibited human females. "I'm not sure he likes them very much," I admitted.

"Damn," said Sheeni. "If I'd known that, I would have had Trent's father specify dog ownership as an employment condition. I suppose now it's too late."

"Well, I can probably persuade him. I'll tell him you need a dog for protection in the country."

"That's a good idea," she said. "Yes, Dolores. The French test promises to be most exacting. Perhaps we shall be able to get together next week to study."

"That is my greatest hope," I whispered.

"Goodbye, Dolores," said Sheeni. "Say hello to your dear black friend for me."

Right as I hung up, the phone rang. It was Lefty. He was preparing for his hot date tomorrow and wanted some advice on what brand of condom to swipe after school. I told him the name of the brand recommended by *Consumers* and asked him to pick up a dozen or two for me as well. He said in the course of boning up for his date, he asked his sister to describe the seduction techniques employed on her by Carlo, her Italian waiter, but she refused, calling Lefty a "truly degenerate dweeb."

"I found her diary again," noted Lefty. "It was taped inside the furnace duct."

"Anything spicy?"

"Jalapeño City, as usual. Guess who she's got the hots for now?" he asked.

"Me?"

"Dream on. You're off about 30 years. It's Dr. Browery."

"Your shrink?" I exclaimed.

"Yep. And boy does she want him bad—wrinkles, bald head, and all."

"How do you know that?" I asked.

"She says when she leaves his office her panties are drenched with desire. That was the word she used, 'drenched.' In fact, she's thinking of mailing him a pair."

"Jesus, Lefty, your sister's crazy."

"You can say that again," agreed Lefty. "It's a good thing she's going to a psychologist."

I had another pleasant, uneventful day at the library until 3:30 p.m. when fat Rhonda Atari lumbered in. She spotted me, smiled inanely, and steered her flab in my direction.

"Hi, Nick!" she beamed, docking against a table. "Have you been sick?"

I replied I was in the best of health, thank you.

"I got worried when I didn't see you in school," said Rhonda. "Especially when Mrs. Tiffin didn't call your name in homeroom. I was afraid you transferred. Turns out it was all just a computer error."

"What?" I asked, startled.

"Yes," smiled Rhonda. "I asked Mrs. Tiffin to check and she discovered that Mr. Orfteazle had hit F5 instead of F7 on his computer. You almost got left off the enrollment! It's all fixed now, though."

"Thanks a pantsfull," I muttered, noticing with alarm that someone had written "Nick" inside big red hearts all over the notebook Rhonda was clutching to her massive bosom. I prayed I was not the only Nick of her acquaintance.

"Will I see you in class tomorrow, Nick?" Rhonda inquired coquettishly.

"If my brain tumor permits," I sighed.

"Your brain tumor!" she exclaimed. "I thought you said you were fine."

"I am," I replied. "Except for my malignant brain tumor. It's the size of a grapefruit."

Rhonda screamed. Fat girls can scream quite loudly. It must be that extra-big resonation chamber.

5:30 p.m. Wally Rumpkin is back. I came home to find him stretched out on the floor under Jerry's dead Chevy with a wrench in his hand. The big sap has volunteered for automotive disassembly duty. I can't believe he would go to all that work just for the privilege of hanging around my mother. He is making some progress though (romantically speaking). Mom has removed Jerry's memorial portrait from its place of honor over the fireplace and hung it in the back hallway next to the laundry room. How quickly are the deceased prised from the hearts of the living. I am resolved to avoid this through a clever strategy—

I shall simply outlive all my loved ones.

"Hi, Wally. How's it going?" I said, peering under the rusty Nova.

Wally peeked out, blushed, then examined the muffler as if he had never seen one before. "OK, Nick," he mumbled, "It's a hard . . ."

He was interrupted by Albert, who lunged at him in the semi-darkness and planted a wet, juicy one full upon the lips. Evidently Albert has worked through his shyness toward Wally.

Wally put down his wrench and gently pushed Albert away. "Now doggie, I've told you not to do that."

"Here Albert!" I called.

As usual, the repellent canine ignored me and—dodging right, then left— landed another deep, probing kiss on the prone truckdriver. Again, Wally pushed him gently away. "Doggie, you're going to have to stop that." Albert kissed him again.

"Looks like he likes you," I observed.

Wally slid out from under the car, sat up, and studied a door handle. "Maybe I'll work from the top down," he said. "I wasn't having much luck under there anyway."

"The bolts aren't loosening?" I asked.

"Not a single one," he sighed.

Just then, a canine torpedo catapulted out from the passenger window and slammed tongue first right on target. Wally recoiled from the salivatory assault.

If I didn't dislike that mutt so intensely, I'd wonder why he seems to like everyone except me.

9:45 p.m. Mom and Wally are downstairs listening to a '50s radio station and petting in Jerry's Chevy. Talk about recycling your déjà vu. I went down to get a book a while ago and all the car windows were steamed up. Even through the mist I could tell some buttons were awry. Why don't they just come upstairs, go into the bedroom, and screw? I certainly would.

Speaking of sexual union, for the first time I am allowing myself to believe that I may soon be living in Ukiah. My brief week with Sheeni seems now almost to have been a dream. Slowly, the "realness" of our days together is draining away. If only she would write to me. One of the great teen stylists of the age and all she can do is pen one measly (though masterful) letter.

So, while millions in this great metropolis happily copulate, I am left to experiment with different handgrips, manual lubricants, and stroke speeds. Thus, the solitary teen chips away at the Mountain Range Called Desire.

FRIDAY, September 14 — I went into the bathroom this morning and there was Wally Rumpkin in the buff, combing his fine baby scalp flocking. No, curiosity seekers, all of his bodily parts are not in proportion. Flaccidly speaking, I'd say I've got at least three-quarters of an inch on that giant. No wonder the guy can't look you straight in the eye.

Wally turned red, let out a squeal, and dived behind the shower curtain. I apologized and hastily shut the door. Why such girlish modesty? Maybe Mom told him I was gay.

Returning to my room, I passed Mom in the hall. "Oh, Nick," she said, "Mr. Rumpkin may be dropping by for breakfast this morning."

"OK by me," I replied. "As long as he puts some clothes on first." I smiled innocently. After all, it's none of my business she's an easy lay.

Then at breakfast Wally proved he could eat an entire bowl of Cheerios without once removing his eyes from the ceiling. At least he doesn't slurp hideously like Jerry. In her post-coital glow, Mom was actually nice to me. She even dragged out the waffle iron (unheard of on a weekday) and made pecan waffles. Of course, the ever-laconic Wally had some too. While we dined, Albert nuzzled Wally's ankles under the table—tugging down his socks so he could lick the bare pink flesh. The dog is either completely love-sick or is about to evolve into a man-eater.

The chilly weather has brought throngs of literature-mad homeless back into the library. I wonder if anyone would object if I pursued my self-education there with a clothespin on my nose? After lunch, to escape the stench, I went on a one-man field trip to the thrift shops in Oakland's Chinatown. I found a nice pair of real pearl earrings for Sheeni for 35 cents, a switchblade comb for ten cents, a slightly scratched F.S. album for a buck, and a pair of genuine surgical steel gynecological forceps (at least I think that's what it is) for five dollars. Since I didn't have five dollars, I was obliged to make this last purchase via Lefty's discount strategy.

Boy, is larceny nerve wracking. No wonder people go into white-collar crime instead. The forceps, though, were definitely worth the risk. They are wonderfully erotic to fondle and a great confidence booster. There's nothing like having the proper professional instruments on hand in case someone cute invites you to play doctor.

6:30 p.m. The shit has hit the wind tunnel. Mom got the latest phone bill today. $107.36 in willfully disobedient collect calls from that suspicious number in Ukiah. Plus, Dr. Browery mailed in his first payment demand—for $350. (Maybe it's his big bank account that gets Martha excited.) Then, in mid-harangue, the phone rang. It was Mrs. Tiffin, my homeroom teacher, inquiring of Mom how my brain tumor was and did she want my homework sent to the hospital or the house since I had missed four days of school. (Thank you, Rhonda the Rotund!)

With this fresh outrage, Mom totally lost it. She FLEW OFF THE HANDLE as never before. I thought for sure she was going to rupture an internal organ. She would have ruptured some of mine, but I fled the house when she picked up a floor lamp and started swinging.

When the screaming died down, I slunk up to my room. Here I sit awaiting final sentencing and execution. In my present grounded, privilege-deprived, penniless state what further exactions can be made? This is the great dilemma facing the modern parent. Once you've made your child's life a living hell, what do you do for an encore? What's next—ritual disfigurement?

8:15 p.m. Mom just came up to impose sentence. In addition to the prior two-month grounding, I am now facing one-month of confinement to my room. (It's still unclear whether these sentences are to run concurrently; I was too afraid to ask.) For a full 30 days starting now I am not allowed out of my room except to go to the bathroom or to school. All spending money is frozen. I will be given a bag lunch to take to school and 25 cents for milk. In addition I am denied all mail or phone calls. My isolation is to be total. Yes world, Hitler lives.

10:30 p.m. The phone rang downstairs and I heard Mom answer it. A few minutes later she walked into my room. To my mother, knocking is something you do on your kid's head, not on his bedroom door. Under the bedclothes, gynecological forceps were clamped to my erect member.

"I have a message for you from Lefty," she growled.

"What is it?" I asked, nonchalantly leaning forward and raising my knees. The cold steel bit into my groin.

"He said to tell you Honus Wagner is safe on second base."

Wow! Lefty got to second base with Millie Filbert on the first date.

SATURDAY, September 15 — The day dawned warm, sunny, and beautiful. A great day for tossing a baseball around in the park. Thank God I'm devoutly unathletic. Otherwise, I'm sure I'd feel the pain of 30 dreary days in the hole even more acutely.

Wally spent the night again. No screaming yet from Mom. I hope this doesn't reflect poorly on his sexual performance. I could tell Wally slept over because Albert spent the night whimpering for his buddy outside Mom's bedroom door. Perhaps, though, it's only a case of puppy love.

By imposing such a tyrannical sentence, Mom has ironically turned herself into my servant. At 8:15 she was obliged to bring me my Cheerios, crumb donut, and orange juice on a tray. She glared at me, slammed down the swill, and marched silently out of the room. What a termagant. Even in San Quentin the guards at least give you a grudging "hello."

Mom has also forced on herself the burden of walking loathsome Albert, washing the dishes, cleaning the toilet, and mowing the yard—irksome tasks formerly palmed off on me. Serves her right!

11:15 a.m. Ear pressed tightly against the floor, I heard Wally downstairs suggest to Mom they go to a show of customized pickup trucks at the Cow Palace. Sure enough, five minutes later Mom barged in and said she was "going out for a few minutes." (A lie! The Cow Palace is way on the other side of the bay.)

"Don't you dare leave this room," threatened Mom.

"What about lunch?" I demanded.

"You can fix it yourself," she replied. "While you're at it, you can do the dishes, mop the kitchen floor, and clean the bathroom."

"I thought you said I wasn't allowed out of my room."

"Don't ask questions," she yelled. "Just do as I say!"

The woman is a total Nazi.

As soon as I heard Wally and Mom drive off in Jerry's Lincoln, I went downstairs. In the wastebasket under the kitchen sink I found a letter from Sheeni. Torn to bits! For this atrocity, Mom is going to suffer.

After retrieving the tiny shreds for later reassembly, I called Dad in Marin. His bimbette answered. She said Dad was still up in Ukiah looking for a place to rent.

"Isn't it exciting?" asked Lacey. "I'm going to move up too. We're going to live in a cute little cabin out in the redwoods and I'm going to get a job in a beauty salon in town."

"Gee, Lacey, you don't suppose you'd have room for me and my dog?"

"Things aren't going so well at home, Nickie?" asked Lacey solicitously.

"The pits," I replied. "And I really miss not spending more time with Dad," I added untruthfully.

"A boy should be close with his father," averred Lacey. "Well, I'll certainly suggest it to Thunder Rod when he gets back. I expect him tonight. We have to pack up tomorrow. Oh, it's so exciting!"

I imagined Lacey excited and found the thought quite thrilling. Having the alluring bimbette under the same roof definitely made the prospect of living with Dad more palatable. Perhaps Dad will find a cabin with a hot tub and be forced to work late at the office on warm summer evenings when the air is sticky with desire. As the dying sun flickers through the sequoias, Lacey will wiggle innocently out of her clothes and suggest a dip in the soothing waters. I will follow, of course—not forgetting that my heart is Sheeni's alone, but not fearing to taste deeply of all the experiences life places before me. After all, I owe it to my art.

After Lacey rang off, I called Lefty's house. His fat mother answered. I affected a sultry woman's voice.

"May I speak to LeRoy, please?" I purred.

"Who is this?" demanded the prying parent.

"Miss Satron, his English literature teacher. I wish to discuss a matter pertaining to William Blake the poet."

"Oh yes, Miss Satron," she said, suddenly respectful. "I'll run and get him. He's out playing basketball with his father."

After a minute Lefty answered. "Hello, Miss Satron," he said.

"Young man I understand you had a date last night with Millie Filbert."

"Yes, Miss Satron, I did," he said wonderingly. "How did you know?"

"Never mind. What I want to know is did you remove her panties and suck her throbbing pubes?"

"Of course n—Hey, who is this?"

"Who do you think it is?" I said, reverting to my normal voice. "Meet me in the park in five minutes. Or do you want to shoot some more baskets with your dad?"

"Miss Satron," said Lefty, "you called just in the nick of time."

I took Albert to the park with me. That way, if somehow Mom got home before I did, I could always claim Albert had demanded a walk. Lefty was overjoyed to see his old companion, but the dog was rather cool. Clearly his heart now belongs to another. Fortunately, Lefty didn't seem to notice.

"So tell me about your date," I said. "You got to second base?"

"Both of them," he replied, scratching Albert's ears.

"Over or under?"

"Under, of course," said Lefty, offended. "Second base doesn't count unless you're actually under the bra. At least not in my league."

"So let's get the story!"

"It was great," he replied. "We went out to Berkeley. Dad offered to drive us, but I nixed that. We took BART."

"Did you go to a movie?"

"Naw, we went up to Telegraph Avenue and checked out the record stores. Millie had a whole list of tapes she needed. It was tough too, 'cause they have hidden cameras and those magnetic detectors. But I managed to get her most of what she wanted. She was quite impressed."

"You're the pro," I agreed. "Where did you have dinner?"

"We bought pizza slices and ate them on the street. Boy, does Millie look sexy scarfing down the pepperoni."

"Then what did you do?"

"Well, you know she wants to be an anesthesiologist when she grows up. So we walked down to Herrick Hospital and hung out in the emergency room for a while."

"How was that?"

"Not bad. There was a neat stabbing victim they brought in with the sirens going. Blood all over the place. He lived though."

"Then what?"

"Then we went back to Millie's house and sat on this swing thing they have in her back yard. It was nice and dark and private."

"You made out?" I asked.

"Eventually," said Lefty. "It took me a while to work up my courage. It was great though. She has incredible lips."

"Instant hard-on?"

"Are you kidding? I had a hard-on when we sat down."

"Did she mind when you touched her chest?"

"Mind? She put my hand on them! God, it was great. It was almost like I was in a dream."

"Are her tits nice?" I asked.

"Fabulous," said Lefty, "totally fabulous. Better than Sheeni's, I'd say."

"No way," I replied.

"Well," said Lefty, "in my opinion, they're bigger."

"Yeah, if you like them drooping."

"They don't droop. They're hard as baseballs."

"Well, they'll droop someday," I reasoned. "Big ones always do. Look at your mother."

"Let's leave my mother out of this," said Lefty. "I don't look at your mother's chest, you don't look at mine."

"It's a deal," I said. "So when are you seeing Millie again?"

"Tomorrow afternoon. She's coming over and we're going to study together."

"Are you going to try for a triple?" I asked.

"Triple nothing," he replied, "I'm swinging for the fences. Bye the way, I got you your rubbers."

From his backpack Lefty extracted a box of a dozen purloined prophylactics. Nervously, I slipped the hot goods down the front of my shirt.

"Thanks, pal," I said. "I'm not leaving you short am I?"

"Naw," replied Lefty, "I got enough for a few weeks. Just to be on the safe side, I picked up a whole case."

2:15 p.m. I came home to find the front door ajar. It had been kicked in. The house was ransacked. We've been burglarized!

4:30 p.m. I just came upstairs after being interrogated by Mom, Wally, and Officer Lance Wescott of the Oakland PD. The cop was a big, beefy authority figure around 45 with a flattop, watery red eyes, and assorted protruding guns, flashlights, billy clubs, stun guns, tear gas canisters, walkie-talkies, and hand grenades. In my opinion, he was also wearing a bulletproof vest.

Mom was near hysteria because the thief (or thieves), besides swiping the TV, VCR, $46 in cash, and Mom's jewelry box, also jimmied out the radio from Jerry's dead Chevy. No more musical excursions down lovers' lane with Wally. As for Wally, he was doing his ineffectual best to comfort Mom, while arousing the suspicions of the cop for gazing so earnestly at the ceiling.

"What kind of radio was in the car, ma'am?" asked Officer Wescott, writing in a small blue notebook.

"It was a Chevrolet radio, of course," replied Mom.

"Did it have a tape player?" he asked.

"No. It was just an AM radio. But it had excellent tone," she added.

"Why exactly is this car parked here, ma'am?"

Mom looked like she thought that was an incredibly impertinent question. "It belonged to a friend of mine who is now deceased. He left it here."

"Uh-huh. And you listen to the radio in it?"

"Sometimes," retorted Mom. "Is there any law against that?"

"Off hand, I can't think of any," replied the cop. His watery gaze shifted to Wally. "Who are you?"

Wally blushed. "I, I'm a friend," he mumbled, shifting his feet. Albert was licking his ankles.

The cop glanced suspiciously at the dog, at Wally, and up at the ceiling.

Then he looked at me.

"Where were you when the crime took place?" he demanded.

"I, I was upstairs in my room," I lied.

"Then you must have heard the break-in."

"Uh, yes. Of course," I stammered.

"What did you do?"

"I, I stayed in my room."

The cop was perplexed. "Why didn't you call the police? Or leave the house?"

"I'm not allowed out of my room," I explained.

"He's being punished," volunteered Mom. "But he should have known to run away. Nickie, you could have been killed!"

Fat lot you'd care!

"Well," I said, "I figured I had Albert with me for protection."

"Who's Albert?" demanded the cop.

"My dog," I said, pointing to the ankle nuzzler.

An ill-concealed sneer darted over Officer Wescott's bloated face. "Did you get a look at the suspects?" he asked.

"No," I replied. "I had my door shut."

"They didn't come into your room?" he inquired, smelling a rat.

"No," I lied. I dared not confess the thieves had made off with my entire sports equipment collection, including an official Rodney "Butch" Bolicweigski first baseman's glove in mint condition. Thank God the perpetrators preferred baseball gear to computers.

Officer Wescott peered at me. I could tell he was thinking that all it would take to get the truth out of me was an expert application of a rubber hose. Unaccountably, he must have left his in the patrol car. He turned to Mom. "OK, ma'am. If you discover anything else is missing give me a call."

"Will you catch the criminals?" asked Mom.

"More than likely we won't," confessed the cop, "but we'll let you know if there are any developments."

7:05 p.m. In honor of my narrow escape from homicidal maniacs, Mom let me come downstairs for dinner "just this one time." Over tuna noodle casserole, she announced to Wally and me that she has decided the burglary was "a sign from Jerry."

"I can see now that Jerry does not want that automobile tampered with," said Mom. "Wally, you'll have to put back all the parts you took off."

Wally blushed. "But Estelle," he said, "I didn't actually remove any. The bolts were too tight."

"Good," she replied. "Tomorrow we can go out and get a new radio—if, Wally darling, you'll be a doll and put it in for me?"

"You know I will, baby," said Wally.

The guy is such a sap.

10:30 p.m. After two frustrating, tedious hours I was able to reassemble

Sheeni's letter—minus a few strategic pieces here and there. Perhaps Mom swallowed those. Thank God she doesn't have a shredder yet.

Sheeni reports she is in all the accelerated classes and already has her teachers "thoroughly intimidated." In fact, she says after correcting over a dozen errors of fact made by Mr. Perkins, her English teacher, he is now virtually "tongue tied" in class. She also reports her fabulous new wardrobe has inspired such "egregious envy" among her female classmates she fears "a sinister cabal" may be forming against her. "Why, darling Nickie," wrote Sheeni, "in the presence of fashion, style, and beauty, do people respond, not with admiration, but with an impulse toward destruction? Why are human beings so determined to enforce a dreary ordinariness in appearance, thought, and conduct? More than ever, my darling, I am resolved we must flee to Paris with Albert as soon as possible."

Sheeni is ready to emigrate and I've yet to learn a word of French. I must begin foreign language study at once—whatever the consequences!

SUNDAY, September 16 — No screaming last night either. Not even the telltale creakings of the bedsprings. Has the bright flower of passion faded so quickly?

At 7:06 a.m. Mom slunk into the bathroom and hurled her halibut. She really should go in for a blood test. Maybe that's what Jerry was trying to communicate by the burglary.

This time, Wally brought up my breakfast tray. I knew it was Wally because he actually knocked on the door.

"Good morning, Wally," I said. "Sleep well?"

Wally put down the tray and blushed one of his darkest crimson hues. Perhaps he imagined I was making some sort of thinly veiled allusion to his celibate night. Was I, in fact?

"Very well," mumbled the giant. He turned to go, then paused. "I, I put in a good word for you with your mom," he said, addressing the ceiling light.

"Thanks, Wally," I said, actually meaning it.

Wally Rumpkin may be a total sap, but he's a much nicer guy than my mother deserves.

11:30 a.m. After Mom and Wally left to go radio shopping, I sneaked downstairs to make some calls. Willfully disobedient as ever, I dialed Sheeni's number in Ukiah.

"It's your nickel," answered a strange male voice.

"Uh, may I speak to Sheeni," I said.

"You want to speak to Sheeni? The world wants to speak to Sheeni. Why are you so special?"

"Uh, is this Paul?" I asked.

"If the name palls, try another," he said. "Call me Nick."

"Uh, that's my name," I said.

"Then call me Rick. What's up Nick?"

"May I speak to Sheeni, please?"

"Sheeni is out, Rick. She left a message for Nick. I'll get it quick."

I heard the sounds of paper rustling and then the voice returned. "Through the hand of Sheeni moves the message genie: 'Nick, everything is set. Your father found a place to live that takes dogs. Love to Albert.' What do you think, Rick? Sounds like code to me."

"Uh, Paul," I said, "could you give her a message for me?"

"Not if it involves writing," he replied. "Today is the sabbath."

"OK. Just tell her I'm in total lockdown for a month and I'll call her again when I can."

"Thirty days of total lockjaw," repeated Paul. "And you'll can the calls when you gain the upper hand."

"Uh, just tell her Nick called."

"OK, Trent," said Paul. "Thanks for calling."

Or did he say "bawling?" Or was it "balling?" And why did he call me Trent?

Still confused, I dialed Dad's number in Marin. After six rings, Dad answered, sounding harassed.

"Hi, Dad. This is Nick," I said, trying to chisel some ersatz affection into my voice.

"Nick, I got a truck here costing me $39.50 an hour. What do you want?"

"Uh, I hear you and Lacey are moving to Ukiah," I said brightly.

"We're certainly trying to," he answered peevishly.

This conversation was proving even more painful than I had imagined in my worst moments of anticipatory dread. "Well, did Lacey talk to you about my staying with you awhile?"

"Gee, I don't know," said Dad. "That's a big responsibility."

"I know, Dad. But you wouldn't have to pay child support. Mom might even pay you some. And I'd be happy to go to public school and get a job and do lots of chores around the house—for free."

"Well, I don't know," repeated Dad. "I don't want any swishy characters hanging around."

"I'm not gay, Dad."

"Since when?" he asked, surprised.

"Since always." I considered mentioned Sheeni, but feared the mention of another female might trigger his competitive instincts.

"Well," sighed Dad, "I guess we could do it on a trial basis. But don't bring too much of your stuff—in case it doesn't work out. And I need your mother's OK too."

"Great! Dad, you won't regret this."

"I doubt that," he said, "I regret it already."

What a prize-winning asshole. Still, he did say yes. But his consent was so tentative, I dared not mention Albert. I'll just have to cross that canine when I come to him. At least, it shouldn't be hard getting Mom's consent. At this point she should be thrilled to be rid of such an incorrigible truant.

2:30 p.m. WRONG! WRONG! WRONG! I have been stabbed in the back by a mother's wanton lust! Here is the shocking conversation:

"Great news, Mom! Dad is moving to Ukiah and he says I can come and live with him."

Mom slams down box with new car radio. "Oh yeah? Well you can just forget that idea, buster!"

"But, Mom! Why?"

"I'm not going to go through this alone. You're going to help me!"

Nick scratches head in confusion. "Help you do what, Mom?"

Mom fumbles in purse; Wally ponders ceiling. "Go upstairs and look in Joanie's room!" shouts Mom. "Here's the key."

Distressed, alarmed, puzzled, Nick races upstairs, unlocks door, stares into room in horror. Pink walls, frilly curtains, framed scenes of bunnies and lambs, toys scattered about, big crib in center. Only one conclusion is possible: Joanie IS PREGNANT BY A MARRIED MAN! Oh the shame! The inconvenience!

Nick races downstairs. "Mom, when's Joanie having her baby?"

"Don't be stupid," declares Mom, "Joanie's not pregnant. She's been on the pill since she was 12."

"Then who . . ." Nick stops as dreadful realization dawns. "Mom! It's not . . . you!"

"Who else, buster?"

"But, but . . . you're . . .old!"

"Oh yeah? Well, some men don't think so. Right, Wally?"

"Er, that's correct," states giant.

Nick collapses on stairs in shock.

Second jolting realization: PROBABLE FATHER IS JERRY, LATE KING OF THE MORONS!

Third alarming realization: NAME OF THE PUTATIVE HOUSEKEEPER, AU PAIR, AND GENERAL BABY-CARE SLAVE: NICK TWISP!

Fourth horrifying realization: FUTURE PROSPECTS FOR NICK/SHEENI RELATIONSHIP: VIRTUALLY NIL!

Fifth paralyzing realization: NICK'S LIFE IS NOW AND LIKELY TO REMAIN A LIVING HELL!

10:30 p.m. All is black. Too depressed to write. Hateful enceinte mother just barged into bedroom with telephonic message from Lefty: "Mrs. Honus Wagner had a snack on third base." Happy, at least, that friend is progressing in love.

MONDAY, September 17 — Stayed home all day. Have not killed self yet.

TUESDAY, September 18 — Stayed home all day. Refuse to speak to despicable mother. No progress on suicide front.

WEDNESDAY, September 19 — Stayed home all day, except for trip to doctor instigated by hateful mother. Doctor says youth is depressed, recommends counseling. Hateful mother says, "He'll snap out of it."

THURSDAY, September 20 — Stayed home all day. Hateful mother suspends 30-day lockdown; 60-day grounding remains in effect. Still stay in room except when harangued by hateful mother to come to meals. Do not eat. Look gaunt, but lack of food improves skin condition. Hear voices downstairs. Go down to investigate. Hateful mother is having tea and cookies with Officer Lance Wescott of Oakland PD! Wally Rumpkin not in sight.

FRIDAY, September 21 — Stayed home all day, despite continued haranguing by loathsome mother. Try to write farewell letter to Sheeni, but can't find words. Hateful mother comes home from work in cheerful mood, gets dressed up, goes out for evening with surprise date: Officer Lance Wescott of Oakland PD. Hapless Wally on road to Iowa.

SATURDAY, September 22 — Early a.m.: wake to sounds of hateful mother screaming. Attribute vociferation to sexual ecstasy. Wonder if energetic intercourse safe for fetus. Hope not.

Hours later: surprise large naked cop gargling in bathroom. Looks like partially shaved bull. Could feed family of six for long winter. Pendulous testicles hang down halfway to knees. Cop not bashful, says: "Hi, Nick. You know what you need, kid? A swift kick in the kiester. And I'm just the fella to do it." Contemplate pilfering naked cop's service revolver and shooting everyone in sight (commencing with him). Pass loathsome mother in hall. She says, "Oh, Nick. Officer Wescott may be dropping by early to ask us some more questions about the crime." Which crime is that: Fornication? Betrayal of Wally? Corrupting the morals of a minor?

Half-hour later: small, ugly, black dog bites Officer Lance Wescott in left ankle. Possible motive: avenging wrong against Wally. Only light bleeding. Hateful mother swats dog with newspaper, invites bellowing policeman out for brunch. Invitation not extended to son.

10:15 a.m. The phone rang, I answered it, and God switched the sun back on. It was Sheeni. She's in San Francisco with her parents!

"Darling, I was worried sick!" exclaimed Sheeni. "Nothing's happened to Albert has it?"

"No," I replied, "I've been stabbed in the back. By my mother. She says I can't move to Ukiah."

"But why, darling!"

"She's pregnant."

"Who's pregnant?"

"My mother."

"Your mother! But your mother's old!"

"She's ancient," I agreed. "But she's still knocked up."

"Let that be a lesson to us all," said Sheeni. "Who's the poppa?"

"Old moldering Jerry, one presumes. Meanwhile, her new boyfriend's out of town, so she's shanghaied yet another guy into her bed—a fascistic cop. Even for this family, it's all amazingly sordid."

"You don't say, Debbie," said Sheeni. "Yes, I would love to get together this afternoon. Why don't I take BART over and meet you in downtown Oakland around one? We could do lunch."

"That would be wonderful," I said. "I'll meet you in front of city hall."

"Great, Debbie," said Sheeni, "and do bring that dear black friend of yours."

Lunch with Sheeni! Suddenly, I was ravenous. Five days without food. What was I thinking of? But what smooth, virtually zit-free skin to bring to those intimate embraces. Oops, instant T.E. Life is looking up!

7:30 p.m. A whole afternoon and part of an evening with The Woman I Love. What an exquisite day—even if there was hell to pay when I got home. Mom didn't buy it that I'd been taking Albert for a six-hour walk. She came dangerously close to flying off the handle again. Doesn't she realize how damaging these tantrums are to young Jerry Junior? Of course, the kid is facing many, many years of life with Mom. So perhaps it's best that he come into the world with that first layer of emotional scar tissue already formed.

I was a half-hour early and Sheeni was 15 minutes late—ample time to work myself into a state of near nervous collapse. When she finally appeared, the adrenalin rush almost killed me. I'd forgotten how excruciatingly lovely she is. She strode toward me in the bright sunshine in a pale blue sleeveless dress the color of her eyes. She had a white cashmere sweater slung over her tanned shoulders and a big canvas bag under her arm. She was also wearing her patented Sheeni smile: quizzical, ironic, faintly bemused.

Fortunately, Albert went ape-shit when he saw her, so I had several seconds to compose myself before she transferred his doggie germs to my famished lips.

"Hi, Nickie," said Sheeni, "miss me?"

"It's been years," I stammered.

"Decades," she replied.

"Centuries."

Sheeni frowned. "Centuries, I fear, may be transporting us to the realm of hyperbole."

We had lunch in a small Thai cafe selected for its authentic Third World atmosphere, cleanliness, and prices. Sheeni chose a booth by the front window so she could coo and wave to lonely Albert, tied up outside. "Do sit beside me, Nickie," said My Love, sliding over in the tiny booth. I squeezed in beside her. Slowly, the unexpected shyness I felt in her presence was beginning to thaw.

Sitting beside her, I could admire her new pearl earrings. When I presented them to her, Sheeni exclaimed, "Oh, Nick, genuine clip-on faux pearl earrings. How exquisitely retro!" I knew she'd like them.

Over spiced coffee and lemon-grass chicken we caught up on all the news. "How long are you in San Francisco?" I asked.

"Only today, I regret," said Sheeni. "Father and Mother are here to interview a new minister for the congregation."

"What happened to Rev. Knuddlesdopper?"

"Canned, I'm afraid," she replied. "There was another incident in the men's shower room. Mrs. Clarkelson's faction waged an intensive letter-writing campaign among the church hierarchy that finally bore fruit. Knuddy has been defrocked."

"Happens to us all sooner or later," I leered.

"Alas, much later than some people anticipate," replied Sheeni.

I sighed. "Damn that Jerry. There should be compulsive sterilization laws for morons like him."

"I'm amazed your mother wants to go through with a pregnancy at her age," said Sheeni. "It seems to me a timely miscarriage at this point would be greatly beneficial to everyone concerned."

"Well, I have thought of loosening some treads at the top of the stairs."

"Too Hitchcockian," said Sheeni. "Strategies like that never work in real life. Chances are someone else would fall and then you'd be tormented by remorse. Or you'd forget and trip yourself, and then be paralyzed for life—probably from the waist down."

"That would certainly be inconvenient," I agreed. "Well, what can we do?"

"How about a reconciliation between your father and mother?" suggested Sheeni. "The entire family happily reunited in Ukiah."

"Out of the question," I sighed. "They hate each other—as well they should. Besides, Dad only goes for younger women."

"Yes," said Sheeni, "I'm told all work came to a complete halt at *Progressive Plywood* yesterday when his friend Lacey dropped by. She certainly made quite an impression on Trent."

I didn't like the wistful way Sheeni lingered over that despised name. "You sound like you're jealous," I observed pointedly.

"No one enjoys being replaced in the affections of former sweethearts, Nickie. Think of how you'll feel when I marry Francois."

"Who's Francois?" I demanded.

"My future French husband," she replied. "I've had a presentiment that he will be named Francois. It came to me while on mushrooms."

How I hate that ethereal, drug-induced Frog!

After lunch, Sheeni, Albert, and I took a long stroll around Lake Merritt. I held her slender hand and wondered if I could live with the name Francois Dillinger. It was better than Nick Twisp, but not by much.

We came to a pleasant hillside overlooking the lake and lay down in the warm grass. Sweating joggers trotted by on the path above us; below us, a few paddleboats churned across the polluted green water. In a minute, Albert was noisily asleep. I leaned over and kissed the future wife of Francois. My sense memory confirmed they were the same sweet lips I had tasted in Lakeport.

"Oh, Nickie," sighed Sheeni, "what are we going to do?"

As we lay on our sides facing each other, I could peer past the neckline of her dress and see a pink nipple nestled in white lace. I have tasted that part of her too, I thought, and felt a deep thankfulness that the world permits such miracles. "I don't know," I said. "But I'm getting pretty desperate. Last week, my mother tore up one of your letters."

"That's awful," said Sheeni. "And my parents are questioning the sudden boom in Debbie Grumfeld correspondence. They're extremely suspicious. I had to take a holy oath it was she I was visiting today, not you." Sheeni lay back and looked wistfully up at the sky. "If only, Nickie, you were a tad more rebellious."

I sat up. "What do you mean!" I demanded. "I'm extremely rebellious! I've cut every single day of school so far except one. I'm in deep shit with my mother at all times. I've had my allowance and privileges suspended. I always accept the charges when you call collect. What do you want? Grand theft? Drug smuggling? Political assassinations?"

"Nickie, you're ranting like my father."

"Well, I thought we were going to be revolting together. I don't see you racking up any forbidden calls on your parents' phone bill!"

"You're entirely correct, Nickie," said Sheeni, placing a gentle hand on my arm. "I've shown an unconscionable lack of contumacy. Perhaps it is my middle-class upbringing. I'll endeavor to do better. It just seems to me that if your behavior were unrestrainedly insubordinate—and I know that is asking a lot from one so virtuous as you—your mother might eventually be persuaded that life without you is preferable to life with you."

I had to admit she had a point there. "What exactly should I do?" I asked.

"Nickie, darling," said Sheeni, "you must become a rebel. Yes, even an outlaw. I propose you rent the film 'Breathless' as soon as possible. You must emulate Jean Paul Belmondo."

"But our VCR was stolen," I pointed out.

"Then steal one yourself!" replied Sheeni.

Of course. What a liberating concept!

As the setting sun dyed the sky a vivid magenta, we resumed our walk around the lake. Sheeni was under strict parental orders to return no later than five, but—in a willful act of filial rebellion—she delayed her departure until after six. As we said our farewells outside the BART station, Sheeni kissed me nearly as fervently as she did Albert. "Be good, Albert," called Sheeni. "And Nickie, be bad. Be very, very bad."

"I will, darling," I replied, choking back the tears as The Woman I Love descended the escalator and disappeared again from my life. "I will!"

SUNDAY, September 23 — Another night interrupted by through-the-wall bedspring gymnastics. Officer Lance may be even more frenetically rabbitlike in his mating than the over-sexed Jerry. I can only pray he is similarly predisposed to life-shortening heart disease.

As I lay awake in the dark, I decided one of Francois' first tasks will be to rid the house of all uniformed policemen. To overcome the inhibitions that compel me to be law-abiding, polite to elders, and excessively "nice," I have decided to create a supplementary persona named Francois. Bold, reckless, contemptuous of authority, and irresistible to women, Francois is just the sort of atavistic sociopath who can wage and win a war of nerves. In my new split personality, Francois is the side with the calculating intelligence, itchy trigger finger, and *cojones grande*.

This morning, Francois got out of bed feeling more than usually dangerous. As he passed the bathroom, he heard male and female voices inside. "Shit!" he muttered, "those fuckers are taking a shower together. How repulsive." So Francois sauntered downstairs and closed the valve on the hot water heater. This produced loud shrieks from above. Then Francois untied Albert, who sniffed the air, growled, and darted up the stairs salivating for cop blood. More screams and bellowing ensued.

At breakfast, Francois made no effort to conceal his contempt for the Cheerios-slurping cop. "What was all that racket last night?" he demanded coldly.

Mom put down her cereal spoon and blushed. "I'm, I'm sorry, Nickie, if we disturbed you."

Francois was unappeased. "You know this is my home too. All of a sudden some stranger starts sleeping over. I'm not even consulted." Francois was amazing Nick with his outspokenness. He also was clearly amazing their mother.

"What's it to you, kid?" demanded the cop. "Mind your own damn business."

"You mind your business, Lance!" said Mom. "He's my son. I'll talk to him. Nickie, you're right. I should have informed you that Officer Wescott would be spending the night. I'm sorry."

My mother actually apologized to me! But Francois was determined to draw blood. "I thought there were laws in this city against illicit cohabitation. Or are they just another big policemen's joke—like the laws against burglary?"

The red-faced cop was really steaming now. "Kid, you are asking for trouble . . ."

"What are you going to do, shoot me with your gun?" taunted Francois.

"Why you little worm, I'll . . ." The cop lunged toward Francois, but Mom flung herself against his great hairy arm.

"No, Lance," she shouted. "Nickie, go to your room!"

Francois rose coolly, flung down his napkin, and walked toward the back door.

"Where are you going?" demanded Mom.

"Out," replied Francois.

"You're grounded, buster!" she screamed.

"Not any more," said Francois, banging the screen door as he departed. He strolled across the lawn, expecting two angry adults to fly out after him. But curiously, they did not. "Showed those fuckers," muttered Francois.

"You certainly did," I agreed.

I walked down to the corner and called Lefty from a payphone. His sister Martha answered. "Hi, Martha," I said. "How's the psychotherapy going?"

"None of your damn business," she replied. "And why hasn't your mother paid Dr. Browerly's bill?"

"I don't know. Maybe she has an emotional block against it. Can I speak to Lefty?"

"You tell her that Dr. Browerly says if he is not paid this week, he will have to suspend our consultations."

"That would be tragic," I agreed. "Maybe you could send him something else in the mail in case Mom's check doesn't come through."

"What do you mean?" demanded Martha.

"Nothing," I said. "Can I speak to Lefty?"

"The dweeb went up to Tilden Park," she replied. "And what did you mean by that?"

"Forget it, Martha. See you around."

The receiver was still squawking when I hung it up. Uh-oh, I thought, loose lips sink ships.

Lefty was not alone in the park. When he spotted me approaching on the trail, he dropped Millie Filbert's hand like it was a red-hot report card. "Hi, Nick," he said nonchalantly, "long time no see."

"Hi, Lefty. Hi, Millie," I said.

"Hi, Nick," answered Millie. She was looking tremendously alluring in pale-peach shorts and thin cotton tee-shirt. Perhaps for the convenience of her date, she had left her bra at home. Lefty was right. Improbably, they did not droop.

"What are you guys up to?" I asked.

Poor choice of words. They both turned red. "Just hanging out," said Lefty. "Want to go on a hike with us, Nick?"

Francois knew what he wanted to do. He wanted to brain Lefty and drag Millie Filbert into the bushes. But ever-tactful Nick was in charge. "Sorry, I can't stay," I said. "I'm running some errands. Call me tonight, Lefty. OK?"

"OK," said Lefty.

"Bye, Nick," said Millie sexily.

Lefty and Millie headed off up the trail. In that direction, I knew, lay the remote glen Lefty and I had discovered just a few weeks before. After wrestling my conscience into submission (Francois helped), I decided to follow them surreptitiously. Lefty wouldn't mind, I decided. As best pals, our sex lives are open books to each other.

As expected, Lefty and Millie soon departed from the main trail and headed down into the ravine. I hiked on another 200 yards, then circled down toward the glen from the south end of the canyon. Threading my way silently through the thick brush, I reached a clump of bushes on a small rise. About 30 feet below, the two lovers were making themselves at home in the tiny cloistered clearing. I ducked down and peered out through the foliage. At this close range, I could easily overhear their conversation.

"Are you sure this is private, sweetie?" asked Millie, looking around.

"Sure, baby," said Lefty, unzipping his backpack. "Nobody comes down here. And if anybody did, we'd hear them in plenty of time." From the ancient pack, he extracted a blanket (brand-new and still in its plastic wrapper), a split of screw-top champagne, two plastic cups, and a box of condoms. Whatever his conversational shortcomings, Lefty certainly had the makings of a good provider.

Millie helped Lefty spread out the blanket, then nestled down beside him, poised expectantly for a torrid kiss. Instead, Lefty handed her a cup and poured her some bubbly. His hand, I noticed, was shaking. (So were mine!) Lefty emptied the champagne into his cup, clinked it against Millie's, said "Many happy returns," and took an exploratory sip. Millie gulped hers.

"I love good champagne," said Millie, setting aside the empty cup. She reached down, lifted her tee-shirt over her head, folded it neatly, and lay back on the blanket—her fabulous breasts bobbling pale white in the dappled sunshine. There was no question she had undergone major developments this summer.

Lefty continued to sip his champagne. "I feel this wine lacks body," he commented, his voice quavering.

"How about mine, honey?" cooed Millie, slipping off her shorts. A vivid patch of black between creamy thighs confirmed her undergarment boycott was total. I felt the blood drain from my head. Most of it was going, I noticed, straight to my pecker. As Millie casually picked lint from her navel, her smoldering sexuality finally overwhelmed Lefty's fear. He jumped her. After a brief tussle (what exactly was he trying to do?), she helped him pull off his clothes, then reached for his ramrod stiff (if not ramrod straight) tool.

Lefty groaned as Millie's luscious lips closed over his scimitar-shaped sword. Then it was his turn to triple up the middle, as Millie opened her legs and he lapped eagerly at her soft pink center. I watched in stunned amazement as my boyhood chum hurtled past me in sexual experience. While I was stalled on a siding, Lefty was riding the express straight out of virgin territory.

"Shall we do it, honey?" inquired Millie.

"Oh yes!" whispered Lefty.

As Millie expertly slid a condom over Lefty's gnarled spruce, my left foot slipped, I grabbed for a branch, missed, and tumbled forward over the bushes. As the sky, earth, and forest swirled around me, I felt an explosion of pain in my back and heard a woman scream. The rest was a blur. I remember striking my head on a rock just before coming to a halt, followed by more yelling, then I think someone kicked me. Then it was quiet for a long time. Then I had a dream

(I think it was a dream) that a naked Millie Filbert was walking over my body. I remember realizing with surprise as her bare toes gouged into my privates that agony could be fun. Then I woke up and somehow struggled out of the canyon and got back to my bike. But my shoulder hurt too much to ride. So I walked the bike back home, feeling all the while like I was going to faint or barf or drop down dead. Then I remember Mom yelling at me as we drove to the hospital in Jerry's Lincoln. Then an old bald doctor said "This may tingle" right before he pushed my dislocated shoulder back into place. It hurt like hell. Then, a pretty nurse washed out all my cuts and applied about 12 miles of duct tape to my upper torso. Then I came home (somewhat less yelling this time) and took a long nap. Could it have been the pill that nice nurse gave me?

9:30 p.m. If my pain-racked body were any stiffer, typing would be a physical impossibility. I just had a disquieting phone call from Lefty. I could barely hear him over Barry in the background crooning "Til the End of Time." Martha is back on the warpath. And Millie Filbert has terminated their relationship. Unfairly, my friend blames me for both of these developments.

"Some pal you are," complained Lefty. "Millie thinks I arranged in advance for you to spy on us. She thinks we're both sickos!"

"How come you guys left me there?" I demanded, strategically changing the subject. "I could have died!"

"Serve you right," replied Lefty. "Do you realize how close I was?"

"Only too well," I said. "Gee, I'm sorry. Don't worry, I'll write Millie a letter and tell her you didn't know anything about it."

"Sign it in blood!" he demanded.

"OK," I said. "And how about I staple on my right testicle too?"

"Sounds good to me," said Lefty. "Write it tonight and I'll pick it up on the way to school tomorrow. I want to give it to Millie before some other guy puts the moves on her."

"I don't blame you," I said. "With a body like that, she's bound to be popular."

"Don't you talk about my girlfriend's body! And what are you going to do about Martha?"

"That's easy," I replied. "Tell Martha if she doesn't can the music you'll be compelled to reveal the contents of her diary to Dr. Browerly. That should get her off your back. And stop snooping in your sister's damn diary. You should respect other people's privacy."

"Look who's talking!" exclaimed Lefty.

He had a point there. Even Francois grudgingly conceded that.

11:15 p.m. Time for bed. I just composed this letter of contrition for Lefty:

Dear Millie,

I am sorry to have violated your privacy so intrusively. Please accept my heartfelt apologies. I can assure you my presence in the canyon was as much a horrifying surprise to Leroy as it was to you. I was certainly not there at his invitation nor through any premeditated conspiracy. I have been thoroughly

excoriated by my friend for my heinous and depraved voyeurism. My remorse is all-consuming. I am abject. Forgive me!
Your friend,
Nick Twisp

I hope that is servile enough for Lefty. What a day! Francois certainly has a lot to answer for. I'm a mass of cuts and bruises, my body looks like something from the Egyptian Room of the British Museum, and the tenderness of my shoulder precludes any sort of relief-giving rhythmic arm movement. I must not think about s–x. I must not let my mind dwell on M.F.'s alabaster b—y.

Oh no! Creaking bedsprings through the wall. I'd like to boil that Lance!

MONDAY, September 24 — My body is driving me insane! I awoke at 3 a.m. gripped by a frenzy of uncontrollable itching. Under the surgical tape and bandages, every skin pore shrieked in prickly rage. Poison oak! Leaping out of bed, I tugged at a piece of tape. Agony! Each pull felt like I was skinning myself alive with a rusty fish scaler. Not daring to remove the tape, I scratched furiously, then ran to the bathroom, filled the tub with cool water, and hopped in. The firestorm of itching slackened slightly.

I spent the rest of the night in the tub. Only when I heard Mom and Lance stirring, did I sneak back to my room. Almost at once my skin flamed out of control anew—the wet tape still clinging resolutely to my tortured epidermis. "Mom!" I called, feebly. "Mom, help me!"

Looking none too cheerful, Mom eventually answered my pleas. "What is it now?" she demanded.

"Poison oak!" I croaked.

So Mom and Lance ripped the tape from my screaming flesh. It was difficult to tell which of them enjoyed it more. As for me, I was incredulous that a human being could retain his reason through such agony. When at last the final piece of tape was plucked from my raw, inflamed, now virtually hairless torso, Mom rubbed on a soothing salve. Slowly, the torment began to subside.

"Thanks, Mom," I said.

"The way you've been behaving, I should have let you suffer," replied Mom. "That'll teach you to disobey me."

"I already know how to do that," mumbled Francois.

"What did you say, buster?"

"I said I know better than to do that."

5:30 p.m. I stayed home from school, of course. As the itching subsided, my nervous system regained the circuit capacity to register the merciless throbbing in my shoulder. So after Lefty stopped by for the letter, I crawled into bed and spent many miserable hours in deepest ennui-land. Around 3:30 I was startled out of my delirium by a light tapping on my door.

"Yes?" I croaked.

The door opened slightly. "Can I come in?" asked a hesitant female voice.

"Why not?" I replied, "everyone else does."

The door swung open and Millie Filbert walked in. Fresh from the rigors of private school, she was wearing a neat forest green skirt and simple white blouse. A stack of books was cradled in her arms against her left breast. Oh, to be a ninth-grade math textbook, I thought.

"Hi, Millie," I exclaimed, startled.

"Hi, Nick," she said. "The door was open downstairs so I let myself in. I hope I'm not disturbing you."

"Not at all. Come in."

Millie smiled shyly and walked over. "I hope you're feeling better."

"A little," I replied weakly. "Nice to see you. Have a seat."

Millie put down her books and sat on the edge of the bed. (Brazenly ignoring the nearby chair!) "That was a very nice note you wrote me, Nick," she said. "You have an excellent vocabulary."

"Thank you, Millie," I replied. "I've always admired your . . . vocabulary as well." I liked the way her lacy bra showed through the sheer fabric of the blouse.

"I'm sorry I kicked you yesterday, Nick."

"Quite all right. I deserved it. I had no business spying on you and Lefty."

"Did you see very much?"

"No," I lied, "my view was blocked by some foliage."

"Oh," said Millie, sounding disappointed. She reached out a pale white hand and touched the bandage on my forehead. "Does it hurt much, Nick?"

"Nothing I can't stand," I replied bravely.

Millie smiled. "I like a man in bandages."

"Yes. Lefty has remarked you want to be an anesthesiologist someday."

"I ask you," said Millie earnestly, "what profession relieves more pain?"

"I can't think of any," I admitted.

Millie gazed around the room, no doubt admiring my mottled green and khaki wall treatment. "Is this your girlfriend?" she asked, pointing to the photo of Sheeni pinned to the wall above my bed.

"Uh, well, she's not really my girlfriend," I was amazed to hear Francois reply. "I hardly know her really."

"Then why do you have her picture on your wall?"

"Oh, I like the stylistic composition of the visual elements in that photograph."

"So you don't have a girlfriend, Nick?" asked Millie.

Francois put a warm hand on Millie's exquisite knee. "No, but I'd like one," he said.

Millie leaned toward me and whispered, "You, uh. You don't have a baseball card collection do you, Nick?"

"Not at all," I replied. "Sports bore me."

"Well, outdoor sports," added Francois.

Millie smiled and leaned even closer, applying a soothing breast to my injured shoulder. "Is there anything I can do for you, Nick?"

"How about unbuttoning your blouse," replied Francois.

"Certainly," said Millie. She unbuttoned her blouse, removed it, and folded it neatly on a corner of the bed. Her milky white breasts swelled above the constricting lace.

"Does that bra unsnap from the front?" asked Francois.

"Yes," replied Millie, demonstrating how it worked. "I find this design much more convenient." She folded the brassiere and placed it on top of the blouse. I marveled at her neatness.

"If you take off your skirt, we could play doctor," suggested Francois.

"That's a great idea," agreed Millie. "But you have to remove your pajamas too."

"It's a deal!" Hindered by my stiff shoulder, I was much slower than Millie in my shedding my clothes. She stepped out of her skirt and panties, then helped me remove my pajama bottoms. Moving her hand slowly up my thigh, she gently grasped my swollen rod and examined it with professional interest.

"This growth looks serious," said Millie. "Does it hurt?"

"It aches for you," replied Francois, thrilled by her touch. "Now let me examine you."

"Certainly, doctor." Releasing her grip, Millie lay back on the rumpled bed and shyly opened her legs. Under the triangle of dense black hair, a sheen of moisture glistened on her delicate . . .

The door flew open and Mom walked in. "What do you think you're doing?" she exclaimed.

"Typing on my computer," I replied.

"Get back in bed! You're supposed to be resting."

So I got back into bed. And I never even got to the part where I took out the gleaming forceps. Yes diary, I confess. This account of Millie's visit was complete fiction. Well, I told you it was a boring day.

7:45 p.m. The loathsome Lance was here again for dinner (I had mine in my room on a tray). His patrol car is still parked outside. Meanwhile, parked across the street and staring moodily toward the house is Mom's erstwhile lover, Wally Rumpkin. I fear she must have given him the word that his services would no longer be required. I only hope if Wally is packing a gun, he is an accurate shot. I would hate to catch a misdirected bullet intended for a fat policeman.

I just had another unpleasant shock. Someone knocked on my door, I said "enter," and beaming Rhonda Atari waddled in. Talk about kicking a guy when he's down. It's bad enough coping with her cloying ministrations in public, let alone having to confront her in one's very own private chambers. I'm afraid Francois was not very polite.

"Hi, Nick!" she bubbled. "How are you feeling?"

"The doctors give me one more week at the most," replied Francois weakly. "What do you want?"

Rhonda beamed. "Oh, Nick, you're so funny. Your mother told me you don't have a brain tumor at all. And I was so worried. You have a strained shoulder and poison oak. No one dies from that."

"What do you want, Rhonda?" repeated Francois.

"Oh, I brought you all your homework," she said, dumping a frighteningly large stack of books and papers on my desk. "I'm afraid you're getting a little behind."

"You'll never have that problem," commented Francois. "Yours is immense."

"Gee, what's wrong with your walls?" asked Rhonda, ignoring the jibe and scrutinizing my private sanctuary uninvitedly.

"I painted them during one of my psychotic states," explained Francois. "I prefer a hallucinogenic environment."

"Oh, Nick, you're so weird," said Rhonda, clearly implying she found weirdness extremely endearing. "Who's this person in the photo?"

"That is the one great and magnificent love of my life," replied Francois. "Isn't she beautiful?"

Rhonda's crest had clearly fallen. "She's OK. She looks kind of dumb though."

"Oh, quite the contrary. She is by far the most intelligent person I have ever met."

"Well, she doesn't look very truthful," said Rhonda, obviously clutching at straws. "Her eyes are kind of shifty like."

"Her eyes are shimmering azure pools of deep sincerity," I countered. "She is altogether wonderful. In fact, we're engaged to be married."

"You are no such thing," insisted Rhonda. "You're too young to be engaged."

"That is your opinion, of course," said Francois. "Not that the matter is of any concern to you."

"I don't care who you go and marry," she announced. "I'm going to study hard, go to college, and get a good paying job before I get married. By then, you'll probably be divorced and paying alimony!"

"I think not," said Francois. "Sheeni and I are destined to cleave for all time."

"Well, Nick, I hope your cleaving doesn't interfere with doing your homework. You've got lots. And personally, I think IBM computers are boring!"

With that, Rhonda activated her immense bodily mass and flounced out.

I must insist to Mom that she screen my visitors. I'm not a well person.

TUESDAY, September 25 — Another day alone in my room. A couple more weeks of this and I'll have tied Nelson Mandela's record. What with the bruises, bandages, and patches of distressed skin, one might almost suppose I was in the custody of the South African police.

Speaking of police, there was a mild altercation on our street at 2 a.m. last night. When Lance discovered that Wally was still parked out front, he phoned in a request to his colleagues for some middle-of-the-night police brutality.

Three squad cars answered the call and within 20 seconds a half-dozen cops had Wally out of his car and spread-eagled face-down on the asphalt. Then one cop "found" an open container of beer on Wally's front seat, so they cuffed him and carted him off for driving under the influence. I hope the charge doesn't jeopardize Wally's trucker's license. I've decided Mom's boyfriends are a lot like U.S. Presidents. You keep thinking they can't get any worse. And then she comes up with a Lance Wescott.

11:00 a.m. Sheeni just called. After the phone rang 35 times I knew it couldn't be one of Mom's friends, so I answered it. It was My One and Only Love, dialing direct.

"Hello, darling," said Sheeni. "I guessed you'd be cutting school. How wonderfully bad of you!"

I decided not to divulge to Sheeni that I had a valid medical excuse. "Yes, I'm being flagrantly rebellious as usual," I said. "Where are you calling from, sweetheart?"

"From the hallway of dear old Redwood High," she replied. "Some boys in the electronics shop altered the payphone so you can call anywhere in the U.S., Canada, or Europe for free. It's proving a great boon to the study of geography."

"Were your parents angry when you got back late?" I asked.

"Furious. I had to invent an elaborate story about Debbie Grumfeld having Parkinson's disease. So when you write, Nickie, you must now affect a girlish handwriting with a tremor."

"Will do," I said. "How are you, darling?"

"Missing you and Albert terribly, darling. Any sign of your mother's resolve weakening?"

"Some," I lied, "I'm being unrelentingly obnoxious. I'm also insulting her new boyfriend every chance I get."

"Very good," said Sheeni. "Women hate that. What other misdeeds do you have to report?"

"Uh, well, let me see . . ." I hadn't realize I was going to be put on the spot.

Sheeni didn't wait for a reply. "I've been thinking," she said, "you know your mother's nice Lincoln?"

"Yes."

"Wreck it."

"Wreck it? But I don't know how to drive!"

"Exactly my point," said Sheeni. "That makes taking such a rare and valuable car out on the highway even more of a wantonly rebellious act. Just wear your seatbelt, darling, and don't get hurt."

"I, I don't know, darling. It's a really nice car."

"Maybe you should hook up the trailer too. I'm told they splinter into pieces spectacularly."

"Not the trailer!" I objected. "I was thinking someday, maybe if you came down, it might be a good place to, you know, well . . ."

"I don't think so, Nickie," said Sheeni. "As I recall that trailer smelled rather badly. No, it is not the sort of venue a young woman dreams of for a romantic assignation. You'll have to do better, much better than that. I suggest you wreck it also."

"Well, I'll, I'll give it some thought." I looked around for Francois. He seemed to be off on a coffee break somewhere.

Through the phone I heard a male voice say, "Come on, Sheeni. Let's go."

"Who was that, Sheeni?" I asked.

"Oh, just a friend, Nickie," she replied, "I have to go. My next class is about to start. Kiss Albert for me, darling. Be bad. Be more than bad, darling, be awful!"

"I will!" I replied.

Francois clearly did not like the possessive tone of that cultured voice he had just overheard. "You know who that was don't you?" asked Francois. "It was that asshole Trent!"

"I know," I said. "And what are you going to do about it, tough guy?"

"Just watch me," replied Francois, his steely eyes glinting with dark intentions.

4:30 p.m. Lefty dropped by with a get-well card and a two-pound box of chocolates—both purloined, of course. Still, his thoughtfulness is appreciated. Lefty has decided he violated the code of the streets by abandoning me injured and dying in the woods—even if I had contributed to the needless prolongation of his virginity. Hence, these small gestures of contrition.

Having just come from a check-up with his lady penis doctor, my pal was even more down in the dumps than usual.

"Did you have the same cute young doctor?" I asked, helping myself to another chocolate. I could see I would have to eat fast if I hoped to keep up with Lefty. He struggled to swallow the three in his mouth before replying.

"Yeah, same one. This time I kind of enjoyed it when she examined my hard-on. Maybe because I'm more experienced now with chicks." Lefty adjusted his crotch and took another handful of chocolates.

"Well, what did she say? Are you any straighter?"

"I think I am a little, but she says no. So she wants to operate!"

"Jesus, why? So what if you're a little crooked."

"That's what I say!" exclaimed Lefty. "I mean, I can piss straight enough. If I'd been able to get it on with Millie, then I'd of known for sure it would work OK for sex. I've decided I'm not going to let them cut on it 'til I've had a chance to try it out first."

"Good for you," I said.

"I mean, if it works OK, I'm just going to live with it crooked. I don't care how much my mother bugs me. It's my dick, isn't it?"

"It sure is," I agreed. The chocolates were disappearing fast. I took two more. Lefty gulped another handful. "Lefty, I'm really sorry about Millie. Did you give her my letter?"

"I did," said Lefty. "She's still acting pretty frosty though. She said your note was pretentious and insincere."

I was surprised by the acuity of Millie's perception. She rose yet another notch in my growing esteem. "But she believes you now, doesn't she?" I asked.

"I guess so," said Lefty. "She said she'd go out with me on Friday."

"That's great!"

"Yeah, but where are we going to go? I'll never get her back into the woods. What am I supposed to do? Bring her home and say: Mom, Millie and I are going upstairs to test out my equipment, we don't want to be disturbed?"

"What about her house?"

"Are you kidding? After what happened with Willis, her parents are watching her like a hawk."

Here at last was a chance to make up for the wrong I had done my friend. "Then bring her over to my house, Lefty. You can do it right here in my bed. I'll get Mom to take me to a double-feature, and I'll leave a key under the door mat. I'll even make sure the sheets are clean."

"I don't know," said Lefty, laboriously masticating four cherry-filled bonbons. "You sure you won't be hiding in the closet?"

"I promise. You'll have total privacy. How about it?"

"Sounds good to me," said Lefty, swallowing at last. "Gee, Nick, you're a real pal."

"Glad to be of service. That reminds me. Did Martha cool off?"

"Yeah," said Lefty. "She's back on the reservation. I told her if I heard another peep from Barry I was going to be on the phone with Dr. Browerly talking diaries. Her eyes got very big and I thought she was going to bust me one, but she didn't. She's really a mess because the doc cancelled our sessions."

"My mom didn't pay him, huh?"

"Not yet," replied Lefty. "And Martha can't understand why after she poured out her soul to him, he won't go on for free. I told her the guy was only in it for the bucks. That's when she punched me. I just hope your mom doesn't pay."

"You don't wish to continue therapy?" I asked, incredulous. Personally, I can't wait to commence intensive, interminable analysis.

"No way!" said Lefty. "Those guys are so nosy. I know if I'd seen Dr. Browerly this week, I'd have wound up telling him that I'd eaten out Millie Filbert. And I'm sure he's required by the state to blab stuff like that to your parents. If he did, man, I'd be a virgin for life."

"How was that anyway?" I asked.

"Great! It tastes a little like chicken. Only thing is your tongue gets kind of tired. So I'm doing tongue pull-ups every night when I tape my dick down."

"That's a good idea," I said, making a mental note to do some myself. At last, exercise I could relate to.

Lefty picked up the last morsel of chocolate and flipped it into his mouth.

"Aren't you feeling a little sick?" I asked. "I am."

"Nah," said Lefty. "And I ate another box on the way over. I like chocolate a lot."

"You're lucky you don't get zits."

"I'd rather have a crooked dick any day than zits," he declared.

Lefty has a point there. Or does he?

8:15 p.m. Mom made me come downstairs and eat dinner with her and that repulsive cop. She must not realize the awesome depths of our mutual contempt. From that first post-burglary interrogation, Lance Wescott and I have loathed each other with a compellingly visceral potency. I chafe in his presence. I despise the air he sucks into his vile, nicotine-stained lungs. I covet the very gravity that holds his putrefying flesh to this planet. Yes, I could happily turn Officer Wescott over to Thai pirates, Guatemalan death squads, Medellin drug lords, or Pol Pot's Khmer Rouge. Better yet, let them all have a go at him. No doubt he feels the same way about me.

Lance glared at me with his red watery eyes as he shoveled mashed potatoes into his churning maul. Francois glared back.

"I don't think that was fair what happened to Wally last night," commented Francois. "I think the ACLU should be alerted."

"You would squeal to those commie flag burners," replied the cop. "That asshole got what he deserved. He won't show his big ugly mug around here again."

Talk about the pot slandering the kettle!

"I hope Wally's OK," said Mom guiltily.

"The bigger they are, the harder they fall," noted Lance smugly and unoriginally.

"And the fatter they are, the bigger the grease spot," added Francois.

Lance glared at me even more fiercely. "Estelle," he said, "you want me bash him one? He's really asking for it now."

"Nick," yelled Mom, "you watch your smart mouth! You should act respectful toward Officer Wescott."

"I'm trying as hard as I can," replied Francois. "But he's not making it very easy for me. And how come he took three pork chops and I only got one?"

"Officer Wescott is our guest," said Mom.

"So I have to go hungry?" demanded Francois.

Lance turned even redder, tossed down his napkin, and stood up. "Estelle," he bellowed, "if you don't smack that kid right now I'm walking out of here!"

Not wishing to break up her pleasant dinner party, Mom complied. She walloped me one across my head.

Lance sat back down and I stood up. "You'll be sorry you did that!" exclaimed Francois, storming out of the room.

"I'm sorry about my son," I heard Mom say to Lance.

"Nothing wrong with him a few bruised ribs couldn't cure," replied the compassionate cop.

10:30 p.m. Wally is back! I was alerted to his arrival by Albert whimpering for his buddy from his new doggie prison down in the basement. Not taking any chances, this time Wally got out of his car, locked all the doors, extracted a lawn chair from the trunk, unfolded it beside the curb, and sat down—facing our house. You have to admire his courage, if not his intelligence.

Ten minutes later: I just heard some bellowing downstairs from Lance. Trouble is brewing. Hard to believe all these gallons of male testosterone are being shed over my mother.

11:10 p.m. Well, Wally's gone. The cops just carted him off on his second trip to jail in two days. This time I think the charge is likely to be assault on a police officer (Lance) with a deadly weapon (an aluminum lawn chair). But I am willing to testify the defendant acted in self-defense. Lance had no business pushing Wally over backwards in his chair. He could have cracked open his head on the sidewalk. Luckily, a rose bush was there to break his fall. Probably it was the thorns that made Wally respond with such uncharacteristic belligerence. You could hear the clang of aluminum impacting policeman's skull for blocks around. Needless to say, it was sweet music to my ears.

Good news. My shoulder has improved enough to permit some degree of normal arm movement. I am now able to reflect freely upon Millie Filbert's voluptuous charms. After wiping up, I slathered a new coat of salve on my poison oak. Mostly the itching has subsided, except for the occasional spasmodic twitch. I did ten minutes of tongue pull-ups and already can feel that vital muscle toning up.

Oops, loud shouting downstairs. Mom and Lance are going at each other. Dare I hope this is the beginning of the end?

WEDNESDAY, September 26 — My dream came true! I went down for breakfast, and there was Mom in her EAT IT AND LIKE IT apron, making pecan waffles for the felonious truckdriver. Under the table lay Albert, contentedly nuzzling a giant pink ankle. Unaccountably, truth and goodness have triumphed over evil. The long nightmare is over. Lance is gone!

"Hi, Wally," I said. "Did you break out of jail?"

"No," he replied, inspecting the ceiling. "Your mom bailed me out."

"You really walloped that turkey!" I said.

"It, it was an accident. I didn't mean to."

"Well, Lance—I mean, Officer Wescott had it coming," said Mom, plopping another steaming waffle onto Wally's plate. "I told him you weren't doing any harm sitting there on the curb. Some men are just too macho for their own good."

"I didn't trust him," said Wally. "I wanted to be there, Estelle, in case you needed me." This was a long speech for Wally; he blushed at his loquacity.

"That's very sweet of you, Wally," said Mom. "Isn't that sweet, Nick?"

"Very sweet," I agreed. "Gee Wally, did they rough you up down at the jail?"

"Not really," he replied. "They were mostly nice once they got the handcuffs on. Officer Wescott was the only one being disagreeable."

"That neanderthal!" exclaimed Francois, "I don't see how Mom ever went out with him."

"Officer Wescott has his good points," retorted Mom. "And it's none of your business who I go out with."

"It is if they're continually threatening me with bodily injury," I said.

"Officer Wescott is a strict disciplinarian," said Mom. "That's exactly what you require. I need a man around here who can keep you under control."

"What about Wally?" I asked. "If ever there was a man I could look up to, it's Wally."

Mom glanced at Wally; he blushed. "You eat your breakfast, Nick," she said. "And don't bother Mr. Rumpkin."

"It's no bother," said Wally. He leaned over and looked down. "Doggie, I asked you not to do that." Albert paused, flashed a gargoyle grin, and—leaping up—planted a juicy kiss.

"See, Mom," I said. "Everyone likes Wally. I'll bet he's nice with babies too. Aren't you, Wally?"

Wally blushed.

"Eat your breakfast, Nick," replied Mom. "And shut your mouth."

No wonder I'm a disciplinarian problem. My parents are always giving me mixed messages.

5:00 p.m. I just made $20! Still too ill to go to school, I stayed home and helped Wally remodel the living room. He paid me in cash.

After Mom left for work, Wally brought in his tool box, a big carton of miscellaneous supplies, and a hydraulic car jack on little steel wheels. We started by piling all of the furniture along the front wall. As his assistant was still nursing a tender shoulder, Wally did most of the heavy lifting. Boy, is he strong. He hoisted the couch all by himself—with Albert on it.

Next, Wally got the jack under Jerry's Chevy and swiveled the dead hulk against the wall that adjoins the dining room. Then, borrowing Joanie's old slide projector, he shone a beam at the car—thus projecting its silhouette on the wall. This we traced in pencil, following the shadow precisely.

After a short break for coffee and donuts, Wally jacked up the car again and pulled it away from the wall. Then he fired up his reciprocating saw, and—having ascertained that the wall was not load-bearing—cut through the plaster and studs along the Nova-shaped line. The only mishap came when the buzzing blade sliced through the electrical cables to the second floor. Fortunately for the saw operator, the circuit breakers tripped in time to prevent complete electrocution. "Damn," said Wally, shaking off the jolt, "I should have checked the wiring routes in the basement."

Rerouting and patching the cables took about an hour. While he was at it, Wally put in a new triple wall switch and wired in an AC to DC rectifier and a 12-volt transformer. He is certainly handy with tools.

That done, Wally resumed cutting. When at last the restless blade bit through the final inch of pencil line, Wally put down the saw and gave the wall a gentle push. It swayed indecisively, then fell slowly back and crashed to the floor. As the clouds of plaster dust settled, a neat Chevrolet-shaped portal to the dining room was revealed.

After lunch, Wally jacked up the car and, with much grunting and heaving, we pushed it into the cutout—stopping when the wiper blades were neatly centered between the wall. Already, it seemed to me, the living room looked so much less cluttered.

Next, Wally patched the seams between Detroit sheet metal and Oakland plaster. In both rooms he applied drywall compound and paper tape to the joints, smoothing everything neatly until the wall and car blended together seamlessly. While that dried, I masked the car windows, handles, trim, bumpers, and tires.

"Nick, would you by any chance have some left-over wall paint?" asked Wally.

"Sure," I replied. "Out in the garage. There's at least a gallon or two."

"Uh, get it," said Wally, almost assertively. He was much less shy when he was doing something masterful.

I rollered on the paint while Wally completed the final wiring connections. Rust, dings, camouflage coloring, unsightly road tar—all disappeared under gleaming off-white latex. Only the hood required an extra coat to obliterate fully that prophetic message "Pay up or die!"

We were just moving the last of the furniture back into place when Mom arrived home from work. Tired, dirty, sweaty, we stood beaming as she gazed dumfounded at our handiwork.

"Goodness!" exclaimed Mom.

Wally flipped a wall switch. The Chevy's taillights began to blink.

"Oh my!" exclaimed Mom.

Wally flipped another switch. The headlights beamed on, shining bright circles on the opposite wall.

"Far out!" exclaimed Mom.

Wally flipped the final switch. The car radio flickered on; Elvis was singing "Love Me Tender."

"Oh, Wally!" exclaimed Mom. "You're wonderful!"

For once, I had to agree with her.

THURSDAY, September 27 — I just got my official Rodney "Butch" Bolicweigski first baseman's glove back. Plus the rest of my impressive sports equipment collection. Officer Lanced Wreckedcock showed up with it and all the other burgled items while we were having breakfast. Thank God in the excitement no one thought to inquire why my jock-related losses had gone unreported.

Poor Wally had to sit there meekly drinking his coffee and staring at his shoes while the big-mouthed cop boasted of how he cracked the case. The confessed criminal is none other than 18-year-old unemployed dropout Leon Polsetta from down the block. Even though I always sensed Leon was destined for a life of crime, I received the news of his arrest with regret. When I was nine,

Leon took me into the garage and introduced me to an entertaining activity called beating off. He also patiently answered all my eager inquiries about sex, illustrating his lectures by pulling down his kid sister's pants to point out areas of interest. Leon also told me a dark secret: he had sneaked into the garage once and watched his big brother Phil get it on with Joanie. I knew my sister once "went steady" with Phil Polsetta (today a successful radiator brazer), but I've never managed to work up the courage to ask her if it was true she had her first sexual experience leaning up against Dad's old Subaru.

Unsettlingly, Mom was clearly impressed by Lance's detective genius. She didn't even object too much when Lance called Wally's masterful remodeling job "a gross eyesore." All Wally could do was seethe inwardly and restrain Albert, squirming with eagerness to clamp onto a juicy cop ankle. "Let go, Wally!" I mentally telepathized, but my silent entreaties fell on deaf ears.

As Mom and Lance flirted outrageously, I found little consolation in the fact that Wally had spent the night. The bedspring creakings had been alarmingly short-lived and constituted the only auditory evidence of sexual activity. I must find a way to loan Wally my copy of *Lovemaking for Advanced Gourmets*. Clearly, the guy needs help in this department. I only pray his shortcomings are in technique, not in equipment.

After the loathsome cop finally left, I moved quickly to repair the damage. "Gee, Mom," I said, "I see where two of your favorite films are playing at the UC Theater tomorrow night."

"Which ones?" she asked suspiciously.

"'Hair' and 'Woodstock'," I replied. "Why don't you and Wally make a night of it?" Hard to believe my rigid, uptight, cop-loving mother had once frolicked through the sixties a quasi flower child. As far as I can tell, the only vestige of that liberated decade that had persisted into middle age was her tendency toward multiple sex partners.

"I'd like to go, Estelle," declared Wally wimpily.

"Well, I don't know," said Mom. "Officer Wescott might want me to testify against Leon."

"The trial won't be for weeks," I said. "And you don't want to miss Dylan."

"OK, I guess so," said Mom unenthusiastically.

"Swell," said Wally, hugging Albert in his immense pink arms. "It's a date. You want to come too, Nick?"

"No thanks, Wally. I know three's company. You two have a nice romantic evening. I'll find something else to do."

Anyway, Francois has something planned for tomorrow night. Something ruthlessly Belmondoesque.

Although my shoulder was feeling much better, I didn't want to risk a relapse by subjecting it to the pressures of contemporary public education. So I skipped school and rode my bike down to the library. I didn't stay long. Some sadistic kindergarten teachers had organized a field trip; the building was overrun with screaming five-year-olds. Even the homeless were fleeing in droves. I checked out one book, *Safe Driving for the Modern Teen,* and came straight home. I'm not sure I really qualify as a "modern teen," but the librarian didn't object.

As I was biking home, I stopped to chat with fellow truant, Patsy Polsetta, whose prepubescent privates I formerly studied. Little Patsy is maturing rapidly. She now wears a grimy bra and smokes Lucky Strikes. As we talked I found myself wondering if she'd care to visit the garage again with me (just for old time's sake). But not even Francois had the nerve to ask her.

Patsy disclosed how her brother Leon was brought to justice. Her mom found his burgled stash and called the cops! The only detective work Lance Wescott had to do was track down the Polsettas' doorbell when he came to arrest Leon. And even then, he probably knocked. Mom will certainly hear of this.

I read my driver education book in the front seat of our new modular wall unit: Jerry's dead Chevy. This gave me a chance to simulate all the high-speed maneuvers (labeled "Bad Habits of the Immature Driver") condemned by the book's prim authors. I now know how to peel out and lay rubber. I also know how to be discourteous, drive offensively, fail to yield the right-of-way, ignore warning signs, and travel in excess of posted speed limits. Perhaps this is the book Dad studied when he was learning to drive.

7:30 p.m. Mom looks distracted. She made Swiss steak and fried potatoes tonight for dinner—even though it is a truth universally acknowledged that Swiss steak is to be served with *mashed* potatoes. Of course, I prefer fried potatoes, which makes her choice even odder. No boyfriends were invited. Mom laments her food bills have gone "out of sight." When I filled her in on the latest developments in the "Lance Wescott, Ace Detective" saga, her only comment was, "Gee, it's a good thing Joanie didn't marry Phil Polsetta, even though married life can be wonderful."

Mom must have an elastically forgetful memory to say that with a straight face. Is it possible she is contemplating cinching the love bridle on Husband Number Two? If so, who will be the lucky guy? And will he treat his new stepson with deference, respect, and courtesy? These questions haunt me.

After dinner, Lefty checked in by phone. Everything is set for his date tomorrow with Millie. Mom and Wally's movie starts at 7:05. At 7:30, the ardent teen couple arrives at Nick's We-Pay-No-Rent Love Emporium. They find the lights romantically dimmed, Frank softly crooning "Songs for Clandestine Lovers" on the stereo, bed covers thoughtfully turned down, Albert demurely tied up in the basement. Second movie lets out at 10:25. Satiated teen couple to depart Nick's Passion Pit no later than 9:50. Nice evening is had by all.

"What are you going to be doing?" asked Lefty.

"Oh, I think I'll ride up to Skyline and watch the sunset," I replied.

"Well, we're still going to check the closet for Peeping Toms," he said. "Millie told me she doesn't trust you."

"Don't forget to look for hidden cameras," I added sarcastically.

"She'll probably do that too," Lefty replied. "It doesn't matter that much to me, Nick. But with a body like hers, Millie really can't be too careful."

How true, I thought. How excruciatingly true.

FRIDAY, September 28 — So far so good. No boyfriends slept over last night, though Lance Wescott called this morning while Mom was in the shower. I told him Mom had instructed me to inform him that she never wished to speak to him again. Furthermore, I said that she was now engaged to Wally Rumpkin, who has agreed to adopt me. "From now on you may address me as Nick Rumpkin," I said. Lance replied by stating precisely how he would choose to address me. I don't think it's proper for a police officer to employ such language—especially with impressionable minors.

Mom is still distracted. She spent a frantic half-hour after breakfast turning the house upside down searching for the keys to the Lincoln. She never did find them. So she had to drive her old Buick to work. To her credit, Mom was unaware that Francois had sneaked the keys out of her purse last night and concealed them in the thumb cavity of his official Rodney "Butch" Bolicweigski first baseman's glove. Nonetheless, an organized person would have had the foresight to keep a spare set in reserve.

Later, as I passed the Polsettas' house on my way to the Chevron station with Dad's old gas can, little Patsy was out front decarbonizing the cylinder block of Leon's Harley. She seems to attend school as infrequently as I do. She looked up, pushed back a wisp of black hair with one greasy hand, and flicked the ash off her cigarette with the other. I prayed the solvent she was using was not explosive.

"Hi, Nick," she said, "better get out of here fast."

"What's up?" I asked.

"Ma bailed out Leon and he's looking to pound your ass."

"Why?" I exclaimed. "I haven't done anything!"

"He says you made him turn to stealing. Having all those neat gloves and bats and shit, and never using any of them."

"That's ridiculous," I replied.

"Maybe, maybe not. But you're in deep trouble, Nick. Leon said this morning he's going to castrate your cop-kissing balls. He's got a knife too."

"Thanks for the warning, Patsy," I called, hurrying down the street. I could feel the targets of Leon's ire quivering in my pants.

I took another, tortuously circuitous route back from the gas station. After stashing the full gas can in the trunk of the Lincoln, I closed all the drapes in the house and locked the doors. I also untied Albert and instructed him to attack anything that broke through a door. He yawned and trotted off to nap in the back seat of the Chevy. I just hope Leon doesn't cut the phone line before he breaks in.

2:30 p.m. No sign of Leon yet. Francois was getting cold feet, so I had to remind him of the young woman whose love he was fighting for. Think of

Sheeni up in Ukiah with odious Trent, I said.

"That asshole had better not cross me," muttered Francois. "And that goes double for Leon."

It's a comfort having Francois around. Though I wish he were better trained in the martial arts.

4:15 p.m. Leon Polsetta, his jailhouse pallor fixed in a menacing stare, just walked past the house. I wonder if I could appease him by making him a gift of my entire sporting goods collection?

6:05 p.m. Mom gave me two dollars to buy dinner out. Where does she expect me to go, the Salvation Army soup kitchen? She and Wally just left for Berkeley to have an upscale, pre-theater dining experience at some sumptuous yuppie cafe.

Francois is impatient to get started, so I have to go now. The next passage I write will be the words of a bold youth in open revolt.

9:30 p.m. Things are grim. Very grim. Francois is making a run for the Mexican border. I wish I could join him. I'm typing this as a conscious effort to keep my panic under control. And to leave a written record in case I should be killed or commit suicide tonight. Anyway, this is my side of the story:

After Mom and Wally left, I got the keys to the Lincoln and went out to hitch up the trailer. Problem number one. Mom had gone in Wally's car and left her Buick in the driveway blocking the Lincoln. Naturally, she took with her the only set of keys. Cursory inspection revealed every door of the Buick was locked, the brake was set, the transmission was in Park, and the steering wheel was locked. Two tons of immoveable steel were blocking my way, Lefty and Millie were due to arrive soon, and at any moment I could expect an assault from a crazed, knife-wielding felon. I decided to turn the problem over to Francois.

He fired up the Lincoln, backed it up against the Buick's front bumper, and goosed the throttle. Tires spun against asphalt, metal ground into metal, the Buick's insides clanged and clunked, but backward progress was achieved. Francois stopped when the Buick—its grill now extensively rearranged—was astride the sidewalk. This afforded the Lincoln a kind of Polish Corridor to the street across the front yard. By backing into the yard and maneuvering laboriously over the landscaping, Francois was able to swivel the Lincoln 180° and back it up the driveway toward the trailer. Not bad for a first-time driver.

By now, Mr. Ferguson had come out to see what all the commotion was about. "What are you doing, Nick?" he inquired mildly.

I tried to think of a logical explanation. "Uh, we're going camping tomorrow and Mom asked me to hitch up the trailer. Can you help?"

"Sure," he replied.

While Mr. Ferguson made cryptic hand signals, Francois struggled repeatedly to back the Lincoln's hitch ball under the trailer's socket. Finally, as tempers and bumper chrome wore thin, union was achieved. Mr. Ferguson cranked up the trailer jack and I plugged in the wiring cable. The rear of the

Lincoln sagged contentedly under its familiar burden.

"Aren't you supposed to connect those chains too?" asked Mr. Ferguson, pointing to two short lengths of chain dangling from the trailer A-frame.

"Yes, of course," I replied, unfastening the shackle and linking the chains firmly together. "There, that's that. Thanks, Mr. Ferguson."

"Don't mention it," he replied. "Have a nice time camping."

"We will," I said. I waved as Mr. Ferguson walked back into his house.

"OK," said Francois, sliding into the white leather seat, "let's blow this joint."

Francois paused to paste on the false moustache he had made from surplus Albert fur. That done, he examined his visage in the rear view mirror. Unquestionably, he now appeared old enough to have a valid driver's license.

Francois fired up the big V-8, shifted into Drive, and pulled forward. As he cut across the lawn to dodge the Buick, the side of the trailer clipped the corner of the house—making an alarming tearing sound. Francois didn't stop. Chunks of stucco fell like giant hailstones and a galvanized downspout shuddered and writhed, collapsing the long rain gutter across the front of the house. As the house clung obstinately to the trailer, the Lincoln's big whitewalls began to spin deep ruts in the thick sod. Francois gunned it. With a lurch, the trailer splintered free and the Lincoln shot forward. Masterfully, Francois dodged the birch tree, sacrificing instead the smaller Asian pear. Next, he successfully swerved around the newly emerged Mr. Ferguson, wide-eyed with wonder and fright. Then, the still accelerating Lincoln bounced over the curb and catapulted into the street, narrowly missing several parked cars. Fighting panic, Francois at last found the brake pedal and screeched to a stop—nearly jackknifing the trailer.

"Are you sure you know what you're doing?" demanded Nick.

"Relax, kid," said Francois, straightening his moustache. "I read the book. It's all coming back to me now."

Francois buckled his seatbelt, gripped the steering wheel at ten o'clock and two o'clock, checked his rear-view mirror, and proceeded sedately down the street. At the corner he came to a full stop, activated his turn-signal, waited patiently for on-coming traffic to pass, then negotiated a successful right-hand turn. Driving was just as easy and fun as he had always imagined. No wonder adults didn't let kids do it.

Francois followed his pre-planned route through the heavy Friday evening traffic, keeping well under the speed limit. Impatient Type-A drivers honked and pulled around him, gazing with curious stares as they sped past. At the Oakland border, Francois turned north into easy-going, tolerant Berkeley. His plan was simple yet bold: drive up into the hills to Tilden Park, stop in a deserted lot, unhitch the trailer, torch it, and drive home. His mother would be furious, his wish to emigrate would be granted, and the still intact, though now cosmetically marred Lincoln would be his to inherit someday.

The plan might have worked except for that bump in the road right before the stop sign on that long, steep hill. The car bottomed out, the trailer bounced up, and suddenly Francois noticed the Lincoln manifested new power—almost as if it had spontaneously acquired a turbocharger or been released from a great weight. The latter was the case. Frozen in terror, Francois stared at the horror scene unfolding in his rear-view mirror: trailer retreating rapidly, A-frame sparking against the asphalt, other cars careening out of the way. Then crash! The Lincoln's forward progress was arrested abruptly by the crumpling bumper and trunk of a Fiat stopped at the intersection. Dazed, Francois stumbled out of the car and, open-mouthed, watched the vehicular ballet unfold.

Down the hill, the speeding trailer side-swiped a delivery van, spun around, paused a split-second to ponder its options, then resumed its downward plunge toward the busy cross-street below. *Kwomp!* With that ominous sound, the still restive Lincoln parted from the broken Fiat and began to roll down the hill after its partner. "Oh no!" exclaimed Francois to the stunned Fiat driver, "I forgot to set the brake!" The driver bolted after the accelerating Lincoln and almost reached it in time. Too bad he didn't. Too bad he hadn't thought to set his own brake.

As startled motorists slammed on their brakes, the speeding trailer rolled unscathed across four lanes of traffic, jumped the curb, and disappeared silently through the plate glass window of Too Frank, a gourmet sausage shop. (Fortunately closed for the evening.) A split-second later, the deafening crash reverberated up the hill.

On its slalom run, the Lincoln generated even more momentum, thundering past the stopped cars and into the wrecked building like a runaway express train. *Whoosh!* A flash of fire rose up as the gas can in the trunk ignited. *Boom! Boom!* The trailer propane tanks went off like bombs, hurtling chicken-apple sausages through the air like savory shrapnel.

By then the Fiat's suicidal dash into the flaming building would have come as an anti-climax, except for the trail of gasoline left by its broken fuel tank. As a stream of liquid fire raced up the hill like God's divine vengeance, I screamed and fled. Propelled by tidal waves of adrenalin, I flew above the pavement, achieving speeds undreamed of by Olympic hopefuls. I passed curious spectators, I passed thrill-seekers and rubber-neckers, I passed clanging firetrucks and wailing police cars, I was unstoppable.

In downtown Berkeley I overtook an Oakland-bound bus, jumped aboard, tossed a buck at the driver, and fell—sweating and gasping—into a seat in the rear. Most of the passengers were looking out the windows at the plume of black smoke rising into the pale twilight sky. The rest were staring at me. Nonchalantly I reached a hand up to my moustache, discovered it missing, then located it on my left cheek. Hastily, I yanked it off.

"What's on fire?" one woman asked.

"I don't know," replied her seatmate. "But smell that garlic!"

On the ride home I tried to calm my racing heart, but each new siren prodded anew my quaking nervous system. It seemed like every firetruck in Oakland was racing toward Berkeley. Finally, the bus stopped at my street and I hurried homeward in the darkness.

Uh-oh! Flashing red and blue lights at the end of the block. I approached cautiously, then stopped. Parked in front of my house were two Oakland patrol cars, their radios blaring police chatter into the night.

I ducked behind bushes, reapplied my moustache, and peered out. Somewhere Albert was barking furiously. In the stark white glare of the police spotlights, the ravaged yard and ruined stucco looked like a post-apocalyptic disaster scene. Just then the front door opened and out stepped Officer Lance Wescott, leading a bruised and hand-cuffed Leon Polsetta. They were followed by two more beefy cops escorting a pair of scantily clad teens. Only Lefty was handcuffed. Millie looked like she might have been too hysterical to get the cuffs on her. One cop, I noticed, was carrying Lefty's backpack. With a great slamming of doors, all the prisoners were stowed away, and the cars screeched off into the night.

After a while, I crept out and nearly knocked over Mr. Ferguson, who had been lurking nearby in his bushes.

"The cops arrested some intruders in your house, Nick," he said, eyeing my moustache nervously.

I yanked it off. "Yes, I saw," I said.

"Is there anything I can do, Nick?" he asked.

"Just don't tell the cops anything."

"Oh, I won't," he replied, "I never do."

In the house, the living room was a shambles. Leon must have resisted arrest or perhaps Lance had just played handball with him awhile. The Chevy, I noticed, had a fresh head-shaped dent in the door. I opened it, and Albert rushed out, still barking excitedly. I looked at him accusingly. "All those cops and not a single dog bite among them. Some help you are." Albert growled a grovelling apology and grinned. At least he was having fun.

Upstairs, my bed was torn apart, a brassiere was draped over the lampshade, and on a corner of the nightstand was a torn condom wrapper. The actual prophylactic I found in the sheets. It was unrolled but otherwise in mint condition. All signs pointed to a clear case of coitus interruptus. Further investigation turned up Lefty's undershorts, but not Millie's panties. Either she arrived without them or Lance let her put them back on. He probably watched too, the sicko. The bra I put away in a drawer for later examination.

Too scared for rational thought, I switched on an all-news radio station. The big story was the five-alarm fire still raging out of control in Berkeley. Fed by large stocks of extra-virgin olive oil, flames had spread to a bakery, specialty grocery store, cheese shop, and Santa Fe-style restaurant. Now fire fighters were being hampered by the irritating smoke from burning jalapeños.

Uh-oh, sounds from downstairs. I recognize that scream. Mom's home!

11:15 p.m. I just turned on the radio to test my hearing. The fire's nearly out in Berkeley. For a time they were worried it might spread to a building housing 40,000 pounds of mesquite charcoal, but then the wind died down. My ears are ringing, but I guess I can still hear OK. For a while there, I was afraid I was going to be the first person in history deafened by his mother's voice. Thank God Wally was there to keep her physically restrained. Otherwise, I'd be a curiosity down at the morgue right now.

Since things had gotten so out of control, I figured the best course was just to deny everything. I've had pretty good success with this tactic in the past and can simulate veracity instinctively—even while under extreme emotional and psychological duress. Besides, what's a few lies when you've just destroyed over $5 million worth of epicurean delicacies? My opening moves were brilliant:

"Mom!" I yelled, running down the stairs, "Officer Wescott just arrested Leon! He broke in again!"

"Leon did all this?" she exclaimed, slumping stunned into a chair. "What happened outside? Who wrecked my car? Where's Jerry's Lincoln?"

"The trailer's missing too," mumbled Wally, fighting off an affectionate Albert.

"Where's my trailer!" demanded Mom.

"I don't know," I replied, "maybe Leon took them."

Mom eyed me suspiciously. "What do you mean you don't know? Where were you, buster? You're supposed to be grounded."

"I, I went to look for a birthday present for you, Mom," I said. "It was the only chance I had."

"My birthday's not until November!"

"I know, but I saw something neat on sale."

"What?" she demanded.

"It's a surprise!"

"Wally!" screamed Mom. "Call 911. Tell them to send Officer Wescott over right away. Tell them we need help. We've been attacked! We've been robbed!"

Lance didn't show up until a half-hour later. In the interim, Wally and I cleared up the mess in the living room while Mom lapsed into a mild catatonic state.

"Wally, how come you guys got home so late?" I asked.

"We stopped to watch that big fire in Berkeley," he replied.

"Oh," I said. "How was it?"

"Great. The flames were shooting hundreds of feet in the air. The aromas were wonderful."

"Was anyone hurt?"

"I heard some waiters got singed trying to rescue the chardonnays. They lost some very excellent wines. Doggie, please don't do that."

Albert had burrowed under Wally's cuff and was trying to climb up inside his pant leg. Wally reached in and gently extracted the obdurately affectionate canine.

"Did, did they know who started it?" I asked.

"Some arsonist. Boy, I'd hate to be in his shoes when they catch him. Damn, I wonder if I can get that dent out of the door."

While Wally and Albert contemplated the damaged Chevy, I brought Mom a glass of water. She was too distraught to notice my hand was shaking uncontrollably. But she revived when the loathsome Lance swaggered in without knocking. He looked even more pleased with himself than usual.

"Hi, Estelle," he said, ignoring me and Wally. "Busy night."

"Oh, Lance darling!" exclaimed Mom, "what happened?"

"Caught your friend Leon going in the front door again. Then I hear a noise upstairs and find two under-age minors fornicating in the bedroom."

"Nick!" screamed Mom.

"It wasn't me, Mom! It was Lefty and Millie. They love each other."

"Yeah, right," sneered Lance. "Well if her parents file a complaint, and I've advised them strongly to do just that, he's going down on a statutory rape charge. I just wish I could nail you as an accessory." Lance shot a bloated scowl in my direction. "But I've got other fish to fry with you, hot shot."

I gulped.

"Lance darling!" said Mom. "Where's my car and trailer? What did Leon do with them?"

"Leon's clean on the car-theft rap," replied Lance, dazzling her with his police lingo. "You might have better luck asking your kid those questions."

Mom gave me a look the temperature of liquid helium.

"I, I don't know anything about it," I stammered. "I don't know how to drive. I'm too young."

"You know that big fire in Berkeley?" asked the cop.

"We were there!" declared Mom.

"Well, it was started by a trailer. And an old Lincoln convertible. A white one."

Improbably, Mom looked even more shocked. "Nick!" she screamed.

"I didn't do it!" I screamed back.

"I'm sure Nick had nothing to do with it," interjected the always-credulous Wally. "Did they get a description of the suspect?"

Lance flipped through his police notebook. "A white teenage male, about five-seven, 125 pounds, dark hair, spotted complexion, and a moustache—a bushy one."

I flashed my most innocent, clean-shaven smile.

"Oh, one other thing," continued Lance, "he was wearing a tee-shirt. A yellow tee-shirt that read, I'M SINGLE, LET'S MINGLE."

I looked down. Oops, I had meant to change my shirt.

A prolonged period of violent recriminations ensued. While I was being roasted orally for my flagrant irresponsibility, the irony of the situation occurred to me. I was in deepest, darkest shit precisely because responsible Nick had overruled impulsive Francois. He wanted to torch the trailer where it sat. I nixed that idea, fearing the blaze would spread to Mr. Ferguson's old garage, a structure worth considerably less than $100. Had I only acted rashly this entire nightmare could have been avoided. Eventually, the abuse was silenced by the wail of a siren. The Berkeley police had arrived to interview Mr. Ferguson.

SATURDAY, September 29 — 2:15 a.m. The dam is holding so far. Mr. Ferguson didn't squeal. Lance didn't arrest me. He is overlooking his official responsibilities out of some inexplicable regard for my mother. Perhaps he doesn't want to be involved with a woman who is in hock to insurance companies for $5 million.

Mr. Ferguson came over after the cops left. He didn't want to say anything in front of Lance, but Mom told him it was OK. He said the Berkeley cops had sent a guy in an asbestos suit into the still-smoldering building to get the ID off the Lincoln. They didn't believe him when he said he didn't know an Estelle Biddulph and didn't drive a white Continental convertible.

"I told them I all my life I despised Henry Ford and his politics," said Mr. Ferguson. "Didn't make a hoot of difference. They were sure I was hiding something. They said they're coming back with a search warrant. I said fine, I hope you find the hacksaw I've been looking for since Tuesday."

"Thank you so much," said Mom weakly.

"I'll never shoot my mouth off to the cops," averred Mr. Ferguson, eyeing Lance distrustfully. "But I don't know about the other neighbors. Nick put on quite a show getting that trailer out of the drive. Somebody else might have seen him."

"Well, there's one way to find out," said Lance wearily. "I'll go question them."

"Right now?" asked Wally. "It's the middle of the night."

"Good. Then everyone should be home."

3:30 a.m. Lance returned from his interrogations looking grim. Our busybody neighbors had witnessed everything. People think just because the street has a Neighborhood Watch program it gives them a 24-hour-a-day license to snoop.

Lance looked over his notebook. "I got eight witnesses who say they saw a man with a moustache drive a white Lincoln and a trailer out of your driveway. Only one though made a positive I.D. on the driver as Nick. That's Leon's sister."

"Patsy Polsetta is a lying little whore," said Mom uncharitably.

"Will she make trouble?" asked Wally.

Lance addressed his reply to Mom. "She'll deal. She's willing to have a memory lapse if you drop all charges against her brother."

"I guess we don't have any choice," said Mom. "But you tell Leon I'm buying a gun. If he tries to break in again I'll shoot his nuts off!"

"Good for you, Estelle," said Lance. "I told you you needed more guns around here. I'll teach you how to fire it."

Now I definitely have to leave. I don't want to be around the next time my gun-toting mother flies off the handle.

Lance took out a clipboard. "OK, I'll make out a report for the stolen car and trailer. I'll put the time of the report as before the fire. It'll be less suspicious that way. But I'm going to take some heat for not putting it into the computer right away."

"Oh, Lance. You're wonderful," swooned Mom. "What would I do without you?"

Lance shot a smug glance at Wally. "Just trying to help out, Estelle," he said. "Now, this kid better not be here when the detectives start coming around. I'd send him away for a while. A long while."

"He can go make his father's life miserable!" declared Mom.

Did I hear what I thought I heard? I seized control of my facial muscles to prevent any possible appearance of a smile.

"But I like it here," I said solemnly.

"You're going, buster!" shouted Mom. "Wally, hand me the phone."

For the first time tonight Mom was enjoying herself. She didn't even give Dad a preliminary 'hello' when he finally answered. "Your kid just burned down half of Berkeley!" she screamed. "Come and get him!"

Dad thought it was a cruel practical joke, so Mom put Lance on the line. He explained Dad's potential legal and financial liabilities in his most draconian policeman's jargon. Even I felt a fresh quiver of anxiety. Lance pulled the squawking receiver away from his ear. "Boy, he's hot!" exclaimed the cop.

Mom got back on the phone and told Dad he had two hours "to get his ass down here." She hung up looking tired but satisfied. At least I'm giving her ammunition in her post-divorce marital wars. She looked over at me. "You get upstairs and start packing!"

"Wait a minute," said the cop. "Estelle, aren't you going to punish this kid? I'd say he deserves a hiding."

"He's too much for me any more," sighed Mom. "Can you do it, Lance darling?"

"Be glad to," he replied, eyeing me with sadistic anticipation.

"Wait! Estelle, he's suffered enough," interjected Wally.

"You mind your own business," hissed Mom. "You can go home now, Wally. Thank you for the lovely evening. I'm sorry this horrible child had to spoil it for everyone!"

Oh, surely not quite everyone, Mother dearest.

Wally got up reluctantly. "Everything will be OK, Nick," he said. "Have a nice time up in Ukiah."

"Thanks, Wally," I said. "I'll try to."

"Don't think you'll be seeing what's-her-name up there," exclaimed Mom. "I'm making sure your father keeps you away from that girl!"

"Twyt," I mumbled.

"What did you say, buster?"

"I said twyt."

"What's that mean?"

"Whatever you say. You're the boss."

My translation was inaccurate. Everyone knows twyt stands for That's What You Think!

After Wally left, I was sent upstairs to await my counseling session with Lance. Five minutes later he swaggered into my room carrying a stout tree limb.

"OK, hot shot. Drop your drawers," he said.

"You hit me with that and I'm going to scream bloody murder," I warned.

Lance grinned sadistically. "Scream away, hot shot. Now, drop 'em!"

I didn't scream—well, not much. As the red-faced cop thrashed my naked buttocks and legs, I thought of the noble Sidney Carton. Like him, I was making a painful sacrifice for the woman I love. My suffering possessed a beauty which elevated it above this sordid scene. Still, it hurt like hell.

Eventually, Lance delivered his last blow, a full body swing that broke his staff and knocked me into the maple bed post, cutting my lip. I hardly felt this last injury over the searing pain from my bloodied backside.

"Are you through?" I asked weakly.

Lance tossed aside the broken branch. "For now. Get packed, hot shot."

He's going to pay for this, of course. He doesn't know it. But he will. And so will Mom.

5:05 a.m. Dad just roared into the driveway. He must have flown down from Ukiah. I'm packed. Albert is on his leash. I can barely move (let alone sit) from my stiff, throbbing legs. Time to go. I shall write my next words in a cabin surrounded by beautiful redwood trees.

9:30 a.m. Well, not quite. You could call the house a cabin, but the county assessor knows it as a double-wide manufactured home. Redwoods are in evidence—on the distant hills across the valley. Dad's rural paradise is a flat and treeless quarter-acre, down a dusty road past a gravel pit and concrete plant. The house is an austere plywood rectangle perched on cement blocks. It has aluminum windows, a swamp cooler on the shallow-pitched roof, attached carport shading the south side, pre-cast concrete steps leading to the plain front door, and modesty strips crudely stapled over the seams joining the two halves. The landscaping consists of high brown weeds, which I am under orders to mow promptly. We are four miles from town. There is no bus service. I shall be walking it. Dad didn't have a bike rack, so my ten-speed had to be left behind. He didn't want to take the dog either, but Mom insisted. Albert has set up housekeeping in the dim crawl-space grotto under the floor.

To his credit, Dad has rented by far the nicest house in the neighborhood. At least our "cabin" has running (well) water, intact windows, and a sound roof. The swamp cooler even takes some of the bite off the baking heat—if you don't mind the extra humidity. The house is also quite expansive—the rooms are huge and I have my own bedroom. Soundproofing, though, appears to be nil. I shall have to master the art of living silently; Dad is very sensitive to noise. I have set up my computer by a window. The view is almost pleasant: weeds and falling down fence in the foreground, dusty tower of the concrete plant in the middle ground, forested green hills in the distance, and an occasional red-tailed hawk lending ornithological interest to the cloudless blue sky.

I should be sleepy, but I'm not. I suppose taking a shower has reset my internal clock. My brain thinks it's morning even if my body feels like it's still midnight in the concentration camp. While Dad and Lacey went in to town for breakfast, I made some calls. Sheeni wasn't in, but I expect she'll call me back soon (if her idiot brother delivers my message).

Dad, of course, did some energetic vociferating while we loaded up the car in Oakland. Mom helped (in the screaming, that is). She only stopped yelling long enough to cut Lacey dead. Even dragged out of bed in the middle of the night, Lacey was gorgeous. She was the only person who displayed any humanity, exclaiming in sympathy when I displayed a lacerated leg. Dad, I think, was disappointed he'd been cheated out of his chance to hit me. Perhaps he'll take his turn later.

I got in the car without saying goodbye to you know who. I hope her baby has three eyes, six legs, and a coat of thick brown fur. He probably will too with Jerry as his dad and Lance as his evil stepfather. I also snubbed the repellant policeman, who had draped a territorial arm over Mom's shoulder the entire time Dad was there. As if Dad wants her back! I did say goodbye to Mr. Ferguson, who came out to see me off and managed to slip me $20 when no one was looking. Him I'll miss.

Dad insisted on making a detour through Berkeley to inspect the devastation. Firemen were still spraying water on the smoking ruins. "Oh my God! Look what you did!" exclaimed Dad, as he drove slowly past the wrecked buildings. For once, I wished he'd step on it. Yes, I felt terrible. But geez, it was an accident.

Dad's mood wasn't improved when he got a ticket in Cotati for doing 92 in a 55 mile-an-hour zone. After the motorcycle cop roared off, Dad passed the ticket back to me. "Here, you pay this," he said. "If it weren't for you, I'd still be home in bed." Then he peeled out and resumed his lecture on how I should start taking responsibility for my actions. My first action after unpacking was to file his traffic citation in the trash.

One good thing you can say about being brutally caned by an irate policeman, it's a marvelously fast-acting guilt palliative. The pain assuages the conscience, relieving the mind from the hot pricks of remorse. Already I feel well on my way toward being absolved of responsibility for the damages and distress caused in the fire. Why should I torment myself when Lance did it so much more professionally?

After I called Sheeni's house, I put a long-distance call through to Lefty's. His mentally disturbed sister Martha answered. "My dad's going to get a restraining order against you, Nick Twisp," she announced.

"Tell him not to bother," I replied. "I just moved to Ukiah."

"I wish you'd move to the moon."

"Can I speak to Lefty, please?"

"You're not allowed to talk to him."

"Please, Martha. Just this one last time. I want to apologize."

"I'll see if he's receiving any calls from morons."

After a while, Lefty came on the line. "I hate your guts."

"I'm sorry, Lefty. It wasn't my fault!"

"I hate your slimy guts."

"How was I to know Leon was going to break in?"

"I hate your putrid guts."

"How's Millie?"

"She hates me. She thinks you planned it all."

"Are her parents going to press charges?" I asked.

"Dad talked them out of it. But I'm banned from her life. I can't see her ever again!"

"I'm sorry, Lefty. I really am. Did you at least get to home base?"

"Who knows. I couldn't tell with that lousy condom. No wonder the magazine rated it number one. Nothing could get through that rubber. It felt like I was wearing a truck inner tube. Millie might know if I made it, but I sure don't. Looks like I'm going to be a virgin for life. Thanks to you."

"Don't worry. It'll all blow over. Sheeni and I aren't allowed to see each other, but we manage."

"Yeah, well she wants to. Millie hates my guts."

"No, she doesn't. She's just upset. You wait. Monday at school she'll be making eyes at you again."

"You think so, Nick?"

"I know it. Just be persistent. You two are destined to cleave. It's in the stars."

"I hope so," said Lefty, sounding more optimistic.

"Were your parents pissed?" I asked.

"They yelled at me for about two seconds. That was all. And Dad's taking me out this afternoon to buy me a color monitor for my computer—a super high-resolution VGA display."

"Wow, that's great," I said enviously. I have to stare at my electronic words in 1950s black and white. No wonder my prose seems so monotonously behind the times.

"Yeah, and it looks like I won't have to play any more basketball with my dad either," added Lefty, now definitely brightening.

"So things may turn out OK after all," I said, relieved.

"Maybe so, Nick. Well, have a nice time up in Ukiah. Maybe I'll see you up there sometime."

"Sure, come for a visit," I replied. "We have a great ranch out in the country. With horses and everything."

"That sounds really cool," said Lefty. "See you, Nick."

"See you, Lefty."

OK, so we don't actually have horses. But you can certainly smell them from here.

All that talk about Millie Filbert reminded me of something. I took out my official Rodney "Butch" Bolicweigski first baseman's glove and extracted her brassiere from the thumb cavity. I lay on the bed and examined it closely. It still exuded wonderful girlish aromas. "Look on the bright side," said Francois, suddenly back from the Mexican border. "You're now living under the same roof as a gorgeous bombshell. And Monday you're going to be walking down the halls of Redwood High holding hands with the best-looking chick in the school."

"I love her," I replied.

"Yeah, well, don't let that distract you from the business at hand," said Francois. "You better check your equipment, guy. You're going to need it."

So I did. Still works like a charm.

4:30 p.m. Sheeni finally called back. She had to walk all the way downtown to a payphone. I was dripping with sweat from four hours in the blazing sun pushing an under-powered mower through over-developed grass. Except for the occasional explosive dismemberment of a lizard, it was entirely tedious work.

"Darling, you're in Ukiah!" exclaimed Sheeni. "It's so sudden."

"I wrecked the Lincoln and trailer, darling."

"That's wonderful, darling! I'm proud of you."

"Yes, darling. And I also destroyed half of Berkeley's gourmet ghetto."

"Darling, you set that big fire? We read about it in the paper. That's incredible!"

"My mother didn't want to get stuck with a bill for $5 million, so she had to send me away," I explained. "That was my strategy, darling, and it worked."

"Darling, you're a genius!" exclaimed Sheeni. "But wasn't a $5 million fire a bit excessive?"

"I felt a grand gesture was required, darling. When can I see you?"

"Oh, uh, did you get my letter?" stammered Sheeni uncharacteristically.

"No, I didn't, darling. Why?"

"Something wonderful has happened, darling," she replied. "You know how unhappy I was at school because of the envious behavior of my classmates?"

"Uh-huh."

"Well, Father and Mother have finally agreed to let me transfer."

A cold sweat broke out over my hot sweat. "Transfer where, darling?" I asked.

"To the École des Arts et Littératures, a wonderful school with a great reputation. All the classes are conducted in French. Isn't that marvelous, darling?"

"And where is this wonderful school?" I asked.

"It's, uh, in . . . or, that is to say, it is just outside of . . . Santa Cruz."

"What!" I exclaimed. "That's 500 miles away!"

"Not that far, darling! It's only a little over 200 miles."

"Sheeni, what are you trying to do to me? Couldn't you change your mind now that I'm here? Albert's here too."

"Oh darling, I'll miss you both. But Father's already paid a full year's tuition. And all my things have been shipped there. Don't worry, darling. We'll have wonderful times together over the holidays and all next summer."

For some reason, this thought did not lighten my despair. "When are you leaving?"

"That's the thing, darling. We were supposed to have left an hour ago. I had to sneak out of the house to call you. Father will be furious over the delay."

I was incredulous. "You mean I won't be able to see you before you go?"

"Sorry, darling. But I'll write. I promise. I'll write every day. Goodbye, Nickie. I have to go."

"Goodbye, Sheeni," I said, stunned. "I'll miss you!"

"I'll miss you too, darling. Squeeze darling Albert for me!"

The phone clicked. The line went silent. The red welts on my legs throbbed anew. I had endured a $5 million beating for nothing.

6:30 p.m. While I was masticating my way through an abysmal meal prepared by Dad's alluring but culinarily untalented girlfriend, the following conversation took place:

"Since you won't be getting an allowance, Nick," said Dad, "I think you should start looking for a part-time job."

"OK."

"There may be an opening down at my office doing filing and typing after school," he added.

"Isn't that what Trent does?" asked Lacey.

"Yes," replied Dad. "But I understand he's leaving."

"Does he have another job?" asked Lacey.

"No. He's leaving town. He's going away to school."

My heart began to palpitate uncontrollably. "Do you know what school, Dad?" I asked.

"I don't know. His father didn't say. It's some French-speaking prep school down south. Santa Cruz, I think."

I dropped my fork.

"That Trent is a great kid," said Dad. "Too bad, Nick, you're not more like him."

"And he's so cute!" exclaimed Lacey.

I've been stabbed. Stabbed in the back!

Book II

YOUTH IN BONDAGE

SEPTEMBER

SUNDAY, September 30 — Am I grounded, that is the question?

On the one hand, it is incontrovertibly true that two days ago I started a fire in Berkeley that caused $5 million in damages. At least my alter ego Francois started it. (I have been forced by circumstances to split my personality in half: 14-year-old Nick Twisp is in charge of flossing daily, improving our minds, dressing conservatively, and acting respectfully toadyish around adults. Reckless, darkly handsome Francois Dillinger takes care of swearing, holding authority in contempt, flaunting conventional sexual mores, and projecting a sense of menacing danger.)

On the other hand, my loathsome father, under whose despotic rule I have come to live while hiding out from the arson investigators, has not stated explicitly that I *am* grounded. Of course, I dare not ask him. As a test, after lunch I announced I was taking my dog Albert (named by my intellectual girlfriend, Sheeni Saunders, after the late existentialist Albert Camus) for a walk into town. Dad did not object. He did not comment at all, but continued to gaze fixedly at the sheerly draped bosom of Lacey, his alluring 19-year-old live-in bimbette. (I spend a lot of time gazing at her too; she's an incredible knockout.)

So, until told otherwise, I am proceeding under the assumption that I am free to do as I please. What a change from the endless weeks of solitary confinement suffered under my tyrannical mother in Oakland and her vile cop boyfriend Lance Wescott. Freedom is wonderful—even if all you're free to do is walk four hot, dusty miles into Ukiah, California: gateway to Mendocino County's clear-cut redwood groves.

This was my first look at my new home town, hallowed birthplace of The Woman I Love. Yes, I still love Sheeni. Even though she lured me here with promises of sweet sexual delights, and then promptly transferred (along with her allegedly former boyfriend Trent) to a Frog-speaking boarding school hundreds of miles away in Santa Cruz.

After exploring Ukiah's phlegmatic downtown, I walked west along the gracious old residential streets. 2016 Sonoretto Street was a rambling three-story Victorian with tall, narrow windows, wrap-around front porch, and a circular tower topped by a conical roof. Albert yipped excitedly, tugging on the leash and jumping up against the old wrought iron fence. Canine intuition told him this was the home of his (and perhaps someday my) mistress.

On the porch, a handsome but somewhat unkempt-looking man in his mid-twenties was blowing cool jazz on a beat-up old trumpet. This, I concluded, must be Paul, Sheeni's prodigal, psychedelic-ingesting brother. He put down his horn and took a long drag on a home-rolled cigarette.

"Hi, Nick," he called. "Want a hit?"

"How did you know my name?" I asked.

"Come on in," he replied, ignoring the question.

I opened the gate and walked up to the porch. Albert, wiggling uncontrollably, sniffed the landscaping as Paul handed me the aromatic cigarette. Francois sucked in a big gulp of smoke and our brain cells began to pop like popcorn. This was the real stuff.

"G-g-good," stammered Francois, handing back the joint. "How'd you know it was me, Paul?"

"We've met," he said, taking another drag.

"No we haven't."

"In a previous life," he elaborated, offering the cigarette again.

"Oh," said Francois, greedily puffing on the fast-disappearing butt. Even Nick had to concede watching his brain levitate 12 feet off the sidewalk was pleasurable in the extreme. Besides, he told himself, writers should experience hallucenogenics to get in touch with their previous lives. Somebody might still owe them some money.

"Sheeni cut out on you, Nick," observed Paul.

I shrugged. "What can you do? I'll see her at Christmas."

Paul blew a long mournful blast on his horn. "Nice fire," he said.

"Did Sheeni tell you it was me?" I asked, shocked.

"No. She didn't have to."

"Why? Was I an arsonist in a previous life?"

"No," replied Paul, making his horn wail. "But Sheeni was."

"Wow," said Francois.

"And is," Paul added.

Those words seared into my brain. "My God," I said, suddenly profoundly in tune with the cosmos. "What does she burn?"

"Men," replied Paul. "Men and boys."

Francois was thrilled. "Come on baby light my fire," he exclaimed.

Paul launched into a lyrical solo. I recognized the tune at once. It was Cole Porter's "Get Out of Town."

When I got back to the ranch (Dad's rented quarter-acre with a double-wide modular home set on cinder blocks), Dad and Lacey were out. Still feeling chemically levitated, I wandered into their bedroom. The immense king-size bed was in disarray, suggesting recent mixed-sex wrestling. I pulled back the blankets. Yes, there was the tell-tale wet spot, a geological curiosity that has, alas, never been detected in my bed. How unfair, I thought. Only five years separate Lacey and me, yet she sleeps with a balding creep 25 years her senior (practically a lifetime!).

I opened a dresser drawer: pantyhose, brassieres, and a jumbled rainbow of tiny bikini panties. What curious underwear Dad has, I thought. "Put some on," suggested Francois. "Why not?" replied Nick. I shed my clothes and slipped easily into lacy black panties. The matching bra required somewhat more effort to don. I switched on the radio and, swaying to the music, studied my reflection in the mirrored closet doors. I liked the way my T.E. (Thunderous Erection) bulged through the sheer panties, but I could never hope to compete with Lacey in filling out the dual C-cups. "This has to go," declared Francois. He unsnapped the bra, draped it over our head, and tied the straps under our chin.

"Ceremonial headdress of the black arts," commented Nick, bogeying to the beat. "Much more appropriate, don't you think, Francois?"

"What the . . .what the fuck?"

I froze. In the doorway stood Dad, open-mouthed, crimson-faced, clutching a Safeway bag.

Lacey, carrying another grocery bag, peered over his shoulder. "Is that my bra?" she inquired. She looked lower. "Oh my God!"

I yanked a blanket off the bed. "Hal-halloween's coming up, Dad," I sputtered, struggling to wrap the blanket around my torso while simultaneously tugging furiously at the recalcitrant brassiere. "I, I was looking for a costume."

"Get the fuck out of here, you sicko!" raged Dad.

7:30 p.m. Dad isn't speaking to me. Even Lacey still looks miffed. I have a tremendous headache. What was Paul smoking anyway?

I have laid out my circa-1973 school wardrobe. (Dad conserves vital cash by buying my clothes secondhand at flea markets.) Tomorrow I enter Redwood High, scene of brilliant scholastic triumphs by My One and Only Love. If only she were there to introduce me to her elite friends. Instead, I must enter alone. I do not have a single friend (male or female) within 100 miles. This is a daunting thought if you think about it. I'm trying not to.

9:45 p.m. Dad just walked into my room without knocking (he subscribes to the same parental charter as his ex-wife).

"We're calling that fruitcake display of yours strike one," he announced.

"OK," I muttered, somewhat confused.

"Two more strikes, pal, and it's back to Oakland for you. Is that clear?"

"Perfectly," I replied.

"Now, what do you have to say for yourself?" he demanded.

I gave the question some thought. "Dad," I said at last, "would you mind knocking before you enter?"

"I'll knock, pal," fumed Dad, "when you start paying rent on this room. Two-hundred bucks a month sounds about right to me. What do you say to that, smart guy?"

I say, Dad, when you die I'm going to turn your body over to science. Maybe they can identify a new gene—the one responsible for producing jerks.

OCTOBER

MONDAY, October 1 — Today I experienced my second day of second-rate public school education.

My first took place three weeks ago at an inner-city school in Oakland. Were the experiences as different as black and white? Surprisingly not. Again, I encountered the same odorous corridors teeming with bored, disinterested scholars; the same bedraggled ranks of discouraged, harassed teachers; the same officious administrators; the same scrupulously inoffensive textbooks; the same pervasive sense of a relentless institutional retreat from reality.

By lunchtime Redwood High School had made it perfectly clear it proposes to waste the next four years of my life. Furthermore, through a perfidious combination of ennui, rote repetition, peer pressure, reactionary doctrine, intellectual dishonesty, and school spirit, it intends to extinguish the curiosity of my mind and the independence of my thought. But at least it will be accomplishing these tasks on a pleasant, tree-studded campus surrounded by acres of manicured lawn. And here, at least, there are no uniformed guards insisting that Uzis be checked at the door.

Since I arrived sans transcripts, Miss Pomdreck, my aged guidance counselor, was unsure at first where to place me. But by strategic use of such words as elucidate, *rapprochement*, and quotidian, I managed to convince her I would not sink like a stone if assigned to the tracked classes.

"Normally these classes are all full by now," she observed, "but two of our best pupils just transferred. It was quite a shock to us all."

You're telling me, lady.

"One of the transferred students was a freshman like you, Nick," she went on. "Why don't we just give you Sheeni Saunder's schedule? Too bad you won't get to meet her. She was one of our brightest students."

Yeah, rub it in. I'm used to it.

"That sounds fine to me, Miss Pomdreck," I replied.

"Good," she said. "One thing. We'll have to switch you over to boys' gym. I'm sure you wouldn't want to shower with all those girls."

Oh yeah? Try me.

I was even assigned Sheeni's very own locker, still redolent with her exquisite scent. Reverently, I placed my lunch bag on the same shelf where, just a few days before, Sheeni had cached her own delicate refreshments. I felt like crawling in and closing the door, but instead I trooped disconsolately from class to class, following the ghost of My Departed Love.

In Physics I, my first class, Mr. Tratinni made me stand up and introduce myself. What a mortification. I turned red and mumbled incoherently to my shoes—almost as if I'd been studying elocution with Mom's giant jilted boyfriend Wally Rumpkin.

Then, 45 minutes later, I had to repeat the performance in Mr. Perkins' English class. Of course, since the audience had hardly changed (the ranks of Redwood High's intellectual elite do not run deep), I felt compelled to reveal something new about myself.

To my horror, each subsequent class began with mumbled redundancies by New Student Nick Twisp. Period after period, I addressed halting autobiographical revelations to the same sea of disinterested, increasingly hostile faces. I'm sure by the end of the day everyone had pegged me for a conceited buffoon, ever boasting of his exotic life in glamorous Oakland.

At midday, I ate my meager lunch alone in the boisterous cafeteria. No one spoke to me, not even the plain fat girls (who in Oakland had a history of finding me irresistible). I chewed my peanut-butter and jelly sandwich, while all around me teen gossips loudly imputed scandalous motives for Sheeni and Trent's recent departure.

"I hear she's knocked up and her dad's making Trent marry her," said one tittering slander monger.

"And he isn't even the father!" interjected her acne-blotched companion. "I hear it's some college guy down in the Bay Area she's had the hots for."

"Serves her right," said another shrewish teen. "She thought she was such hot stuff. So much smarter than everyone else."

"I just hope Trent gets away," said a fourth back-stabber. "He's much too good for her."

"Oh, he's a doll," assented the acne case. Her companions eagerly agreed. "God, and I was going to go to all the swim meets this year too, just to watch Trent."

"Did you see him last year in those tight trunks!" squealed her repellent friend.

The table erupted in giggles. Fighting a sudden impulse to gag, I departed hastily.

"Who's that?" I heard someone ask.

"Some new kid," a voice replied. "I hear he's stuck up."

"I don't know what for," answered the Zit Queen. "He looks like a monkey."

Peals of laughter followed me out of the room. Now I understand why kids bring guns to school.

7:30 p.m. I just forked my way through another one of Lacey's patented palate-punishing dinners. Like many young women of her generation, she harbors the illusion that human comestibles can be prepared in a microwave oven. The frozen peas were passable, but the porkchops arrived at the table looking (and tasting) like some sort of extraterrestrial life form. My hypercritical, competitive, Type-A dad refused to eat them, so I was obliged to proclaim the chops "delicious" and ask for seconds. He sat there seething inwardly, smoking Marlboros and sucking up the zinfandel. I wish this modular home had a non-smoking section. Already I can feel my lungs congealing from secondhand parental tars.

10:10 p.m. Lacey, dressed provocatively for bed (I don't see how Dad gets any sleep at all), just knocked on my door to tell me I had a call. I prayed it was Sheeni.

"I hate your slimy guts," said a voice. It was my old Oakland pal Lefty, whose trek beyond virginity I have been assisting. Despite his notoriety as the Bay Area's best-known teen Peyronie's disease victim, Lefty has on two recent occasions nearly united his eccentrically curvilinear member with the more conventionally curvaceous Millie Filbert. Success, he believes, would render unnecessary the penile corrective surgery his parents are clamoring for.

"What's the problem now?" I asked.

"Millie dumped me for Clive Bosendorf!" he exclaimed.

"Clive Bosendorf!" I replied, incredulous. "That midget's only three feet tall."

"You're telling me," complained Lefty. "He comes right up to her chest."

That may be far enough, I thought. I said, "She's only playing with you, Lefty. She's still a little angry about your being arrested in bed together. She'll get over it. She can't be serious about a shrimp like Clive."

"Well, they were holding hands at lunch today! I nearly threw up."

"Did you threaten Clive?" I asked.

"Of course," said Lefty in despair. "But he said if I pounded him, he'd blab to Millie."

"He would too, the little worm. Well, Lefty, what can I do about it? I'm 150 miles away."

"You could write to Millie. Tell her it was your fault the cops interrupted us."

"OK, I guess I could do that," I replied, not pointing out that the fault undoubtedly lay elsewhere. How was I to know Mom's perfidious cop boyfriend was going to raid the house for burglars just as Lefty was swinging for home plate up in my room?

"But, Lefty," I cautioned, "don't expect much from the letter. The way to get Millie back is to act indifferent. Women hate that."

"But I'm not indifferent," he complained, "I'm deeply in love."

"Yes, and Millie can sense it. That's why she's torturing you. What you've got to do is give her back some of her own medicine. I suggest you put the moves on some other chick."

"Like who?" he demanded.

"Anyone will do. Just make sure she's smart, popular, good-looking, and stacked. Otherwise, Millie might not get sufficiently jealous."

"Yeah," said Lefty, brightening, "and if she's that good, I might not want Millie back at all!"

"Oh, uh, sure," I said, somewhat shocked.

It's guys like Lefty who give teen romance its unfortunate reputation for shoddy insincerity.

TUESDAY, October 2 — No letter from Sheeni yet. I wonder if the postal employees in Ukiah are as ruthlessly incompetent as their colleagues in Oakland. Until she writes with her address and phone number we are totally cut off. It's all I can do to keep the panic under control.

Kind-hearted Lacey gave me a lift to school this morning. Dad could, but he thinks the one-hour walk each way is just what I need. Wait, though, until he has to buy me a new pair of shoes. We're so far out in the boonies, I may go through a pair a week at this rate.

Lacey drives (recklessly) the ubiquitous single career woman's budget Toyota. Not since Studebaker went belly up have cars been this boring. At least the driver is the deluxe, grand tourisimo sports model.

On the way, I asked Lacey if she minded Dad's non-stop criticisms, sarcastic comments, and put-downs.

"It gets on my nerves a lot," she admitted. "I wish George could relax for two seconds just once. You'd think all that booze would calm him down a little. Nope. He's like one big raw, exposed nerve ending 24 hours a day."

I had to ask. "Why do you put up with it?" It seemed to me Lacey could have her choice of any man on the planet.

"Oh, I don't know," she replied. "He's kinda cute. And he's real smart."

I guess when so many of your genes are devoted to alluring sexuality there aren't many left over to handle critical discernment.

Another depressing day at Redwood High. Being the new kid in school must be life's dreariest role—just slightly worse than terrorist hostage. I walk through the halls smiling amiably and am met with indifference, suspicion, or overt hostility. At least the classes are easy, if uninteresting. Except for Mrs. Blandage's French class. I'm three weeks behind and everything sounds like affected gibberish. I sit in the back of the class in a state of confused panic, my churning mind desperately seeking a familiar linguistic handhold. I feel like I was dropped into the middle of a bad Godard film—lots of murky dialogue and no plot.

Meanwhile, with every passing minute Sheeni doubtless grows ever more fluent in this accursed tongue. Why couldn't she aspire to emigrate to England instead of France? Or Ireland? Lots of great thinkers hang out in Dublin I'm told. What about Australia? We could read philosophy on the beach.

8:45 p.m. Lacey had a headache, so I was elected to make dinner. I made grilled sausage, scalloped potatoes, steamed yellow squash, and salad. Dad liked everything so much, he appointed me head chef. I get to slave over dinner every night.

"What does this position pay?" I asked uneasily.

"Room and board," replied Dad, taking thirds of potatoes. "And free hot showers every morning."

"Who does the dishes?" I demanded.

"Who do you think?" he replied.

I think the slave-driving creep better get ready for a run of one-dish meals. After cleaning up the kitchen (Lacey helped), I penned this missive to Millie Filbert:

Dear Millie,

Greetings from the Redwood Empire! Life up here on Dad's ranch is certainly a big change from the city. I just finished grooming Fire Walker, my Arabian stallion, and thought I'd catch up on some of my correspondence. I was shocked and appalled to hear of your unfortunate encounter with the Oakland police. Lefty tells me you acted with magnificent poise. He continues to express admiration for your unwavering courage through the grim trials of that traumatic evening. We are all taking strength from your sterling example.

Just for the record I'd like to confirm what I'm sure you must have concluded, that is, that both Lefty and I were entirely ignorant of the police surveillance of my home and thus cannot be held accountable in any way for the ensuing misunderstanding. I know I may rely on your sense of fair play to preclude any other possible interpretation of those events.

Lefty informs me happily that you have befriended little Clive Bosendorf. He is charmed by your goodwill toward the height-challenged and sees this as yet another confirmation of your innate beneficence. His admiration for you continues to bloom, even as circumstances have kept you apart. He prays earnestly this separation may be short-lived.

I have added French to my studies this year and find it a marvelously expressive language. Of course, I do greatly miss not sharing Miss Satron's English Literature class with you and Lefty. My regards to you all. I remain as ever . . .

your pal,

Nick Twisp

That's it for this night. Except for some grooming attention to a T.E. that's begun to kick angrily in its stalls. Time to take Fire Walker out for a canter. This magnificent stallion I ride bareback—hanging on with one hand.

WEDNESDAY, October 3 — No letter from Sheeni! Even Albert is depressed. He lies in the gloomy crawl-space grotto under the house and chews listlessly on a bone. The heat has everyone on edge. As I walked through town after school the sign on the bank read 107°. Perhaps it was registering my IQ. Hot weather certainly chips the edge off one's intelligence. Redwood High's football team (the sexually suggestive Marauding Beavers) was out practicing in full uniform. God only knows to what depths their mental abilities had plummeted. Even on a chilly day, most of those jocks barely register on the scale. The ham-handed quarterback, I've noticed (from reading the typo-ridden school newspaper) is named Bruno Modjaleski. I must try to find out if he is the "clumsy jock Bruno" to whom Sheeni impatiently yielded up her virginity last year.

Despite the heat, I did retain sufficient mental agility to achieve a near perfect 98 on a physics test—the top score in the class. I could feel the dagger-like glances of my fellow students as Mr. Tratinni (a genuinely nice man) singled me out for praise. No doubt about it, I have established myself as an academic force to be reckoned with. Even the Zit Queen looked at me with new respect.

French class, however, remains a nightmare. The simplest Frog phrases enter my mind with great difficulty and then slip quietly out the back door while the next one is bumbling about in the foyer. Patient Mrs. Blandage is beginning to look somewhat peeved. I fear she may have me pegged for a retard. I try to concentrate, but am constantly distracted by her immense eyebrows. As big as Brillo pads, they dance up and down with each syllable. So far the only word that has stuck for good is *sourcil*.

We're doing wrestling in gym class. Yuck. Who wants to thrash around on a smelly mat with some sweaty stranger while everyone else yells at you? Most of the guys cheat and try to knee you in the nuts when Mr. Hodgland isn't looking. I got stuck with a kid named Dwayne who outweighed me by at least 40 pounds and had the nicest pair of tits I've seen since Millie Filbert got naked in the woods. He really should wear a bra. With those perky, pink nipples in my face, I had such a morbid fear of getting an erection, I let him pin me after about four seconds. Dwayne must have enjoyed it, because it took him forever to haul his steamy blubber off my flattened torso. Perhaps he was only savoring his victory.

When I got home, Lacey was doing her aerobics in the world's smallest bikini. That's what I call an energy efficient alternative to wasteful air conditioning. The kitchen was so oppressive I couldn't face the stove. So I made a big plate of festive sandwiches (crunchy-style peanut butter and mixed fruit jelly). Dad took one look and left (with Lacey) for McDanold's. I watched TV and ate my fill, then gave the rest to Albert, who almost looked grateful as he bolted them down. I think he may have been a compost pile in a previous life.

Can't put it off any longer. I must study Frog-speak. Why couldn't the French language have gone to a tidy grave like Latin?

THURSDAY, October 4 — No letter from Sheeni! This is getting ridiculous. I am an emotional wreck. It didn't help that as I was sneaking a peek at the new *Hustler* this afternoon in Flampert's variety store, I looked up to meet the withering gaze of Sheeni's 5,000-year-old mother. The wrinkled crone was clearly shocked to see me.

"What are you doing in Ukiah, young man?" she demanded.

"I, I live here now, Mrs. Saunders."

"Oh you do, do you?" she said menacingly. "Well, we shall just see about that!"

What is she going to do? Have me deported to Oakland?

Sheeni's mother glanced at what I was reading. On that page, two gentlemen were pointing very large T.E.s at a lady's shaved pudenda.

"Filth!" she exclaimed. "I might have known!"

"I, I picked it up by mistake," I stammered, hastily returning the magazine to the shelf. "I was looking for *Boy's Life.*"

But she had already stomped off.

I only hope her behavior is a little more courteous at the wedding.

Two kids actually talked to me at school today. The first was Dwayne, who apologized again for "whomping" me "so bad" in gym class. He asked me if I wanted to eat lunch with him, but I said I was fasting for disarmament. The second was a short Chicano kid with a peculiar David Niven accent, who congratulated me for scoring highest on the physics test. I believe he was sincere, but in this competitive age one never knows for certain. I thanked him in my best guardedly friendly manner.

Another trying day for Mrs. Blandage and her *sourcils anime*. The topic today in conversational French was the weather. We were all learning to say "Yes, how pretty is the snow on the trees in the park" (it was 103° outside). But when my turn came I got no further than "Oui . . ." before my entire consciousness froze in contemplation of those bobbing eyebrows.

Mrs. Blandage muttered what I took to be some spicy French expletives and sent me to Miss Pomdreck with a note. The latter handed me a long dull test called "Ancillary Language Cognition Aptitude Evaluation Assessment" that I had to take in study hall. Perhaps it will reveal that I am such a naturally gifted linguist I can only thrive in the most accelerated classes.

The heat wave goes on. Why does summer in Northern California always arrive in the middle of fall? The swamp cooler broke down on our modular home, so Lacey was forced by circumstances beyond her control to slip into an even skimpier bikini. How ironic that her efforts to cool off cause everyone else to heat up. I had to go immediately into my room to attend to a private matter. And all through dinner, the sweat poured off Dad in buckets. The cuisine also may have contributed to his discomfort. Francois made dinner and, like many sociopaths, he has a heavy hand with the cayenne pepper. Even the molded salad packed a startling wallop. Dad put out the fire with his flame retardant of choice—cheap zinfandel.

If the world can be divided into sweet drunks and mean drunks, Dad definitely belongs in the latter category. Booze steeps his innate competitiveness in a strong broth of belligerence. Or, to roll the metaphor over and examine its backside, alcohol anesthetizes Dad's natural cowardice. All this can be reduced to a simple formula: Wine in, whine out.

"This tastes like shit!" slurred Dad.

"It's Thai food, Dad," I explained. "It's supposed to be spicy."

"Thai food!" he bellowed. "Who ever heard of Thai meatloaf!"

"It's a synthesis of Thai and American cuisines," I elaborated.

"You're doing this deliberately! You're taking expensive groceries and deliberately sabotaging them. To get out of doing your work!"

Obviously the alcohol had not entirely impaired Dad's analytical faculties.

Francois decided to join in the debate. "This isn't the middle ages. You can't make me your kitchen slave!"

"That's strike two!" rebutted Dad.

"Honey," interjected Lacey, "Nickie's right. He's no cook and neither am I. You're making a good salary. Why don't we hire a housekeeper?"

"Hire a housekeeper!" exclaimed Dad. "Who do you think I am, the Crown Prince of Siam?"

Well, you are losing your hair, I thought.

"Oh, poo!" scoffed Lacey. "Housekeepers aren't expensive. Up here you can get a very competent Spanish lady for practically nothing."

"That's just what I intend to pay," declared Dad.

Lacey and I exchanged wondering glances. Had the cheapskate actually gone for the idea?

"But that kid's not going to sit around here and get waited on," added Dad, swilling the zin. "Guy, you got two days to get yourself a job or a bus ticket back to Oakland. The choice is yours."

Wow, a choice. Can this be the thin edge of the wedge of enlightened parenting?

I doubt it.

9:30 p.m. Dad just barged into my room without knocking and yelled at me to turn off "that repulsive music."

"But, Dad, it's Frank Sinatra," I said. Frank was at that moment crooning through the great Jerome Kern classic "The Song Is You."

"It sucks," said Dad. "If you want to play that garbage, listen through your headphones."

Reluctantly, I turned down the volume. Why are parents such fascistic stuck-in-the-muds when it comes to their children's taste in music?

FRIDAY, October 5 — No letter from Sheeni! One entire, excruciatingly unendurable week has now gone by since I've heard from My Beloved. Does she know how much she tortures me by not writing? (Yes, probably she does.)

I got a frightening shock in school today. Miss Pomdreck made me drop French class. According to the test, I have no aptitude for foreign languages.

"But I'll study even harder!" I protested.

"Studying won't help, Nick," replied Miss Pomdreck. "Some people simply cannot learn other languages once they've acquired their birth language. It's not a matter of intelligence or application, it's simply the way their minds are structured. I'm afraid this test proves conclusively you exhibit all the characteristics of that syndrome."

"But I've learned some words!" I exclaimed. "*Sourcil*, for example. That means eyebrow."

"I'm sorry, Nick. Mrs. Blandage has seen your test results and insists you be transferred out of her class. I'm sure you wouldn't wish to impede the others.

Let's see what other classes are open that period. Oh, here's a nice one. How about wood technology?"

Swell. While Sheeni carries on intellectual discussions with affected Frogs in artsy, Left Bank cafes, I can sit there mute as a fromage, whittling a stick. Perhaps I am destined to become France's most celebrated silent woodworker.

Right before I was assigned my hand plane and doorstop-to-be lump of pine, I ate lunch with the anomalously accented Chicano kid, one of the star pupils in my erstwhile French class. He said he was sorry to hear I got booted out. His name is Vijay and it turns out he's not Chicano at all; he's from Maharastra state in India. His dad is a systems analyst (computer jock) with one of the big lumber mills in town. Vijay speaks English, Hindi, Marati, some Urdu, and now he's quickly mastering French. Needless to say, I'm extremely jealous. Worse, his exotic accent buffs his every utterance with a fine intellectual polish. He's been in Ukiah for nearly a year and finds it boring in the extreme.

"Pune is a great city with a lively cultural scene," he lamented. "This place, by contrast, is a desert. I trust my candidness does not offend you, Nick."

"Not at all," I assured him. "I can hardly stay awake here most of the time myself."

"The brain cries out for sustenance, but the famine is unabating. Of course, some of the girls are rather attractive."

"Do you have a girlfriend?" I inquired.

"Not at the moment," he admitted. "But I remain optimistic. How about you?"

"Yes, but she just transferred."

Vijay looked shocked. "You don't mean Sheeni Saunders? I heard she was interested in some brilliant and accomplished fellow down in the Bay Area."

"That's me," I replied. "I just moved up here and then she split to Santa Cruz."

"That sounds very much like Sheeni. So you are her new fellow. Well, I am surprised. You are not at all as I imagined."

"Uh, why's that?" I asked.

"To supplant the magnificent Trent one expects at least a minor deity. It is good to know that we short fellows have some appeal with the girls as well."

"I believe I am of average height for my age," I declared. I didn't point out that I towered at least three inches over my diminutive lunchmate.

"That is possibly true," he admitted. "But I believe your Sheeni dwells within a realm of superlatives, does she not?"

I had to admit she did.

"Yes, she is a remarkable girl," he said, "a most remarkable girl."

"I like her a lot."

"So you should, Nick. So you should indeed!"

As we were leaving the cafeteria, Vijay handed me several pamphlets. Despite his apparent intelligence, he is an active member of the Redwood

Empire Young Republican League. I wonder if I could actually be friends with someone who holds Ronald Reagan in high regard?

After school, I dropped by the dusty offices of *Progressive Plywood* (Dad's employer) to talk to Mr. Preston (father of despised affected twit Trent) about a position as a part-time filing and typing slave. Dad was in his tiny cubicle of an office pretending to be investigating some new lamination theories. A prim secretary showed me to the waiting room, where I leafed desultorily through back issues of you know what. After ten dreary minutes, the secretary ushered me in to meet Mr. Preston himself.

What an enchanting man! Tall and distinguished, he combines the elegant looks of a mature Cary Grant with the friendliness of Dale Carnegie, the manners of a renaissance courtier, the compassion of Albert Schweitzer, and the authoritative competence of Walter Cronkite. If only he'd had a courtly and compassionate vasectomy in his youth. Or, failing that, had met my mother before Dad stumbled on the scene. Am I saying I wish Mr. Preston had been my father? Does the Pope kiss airport asphalt?

After a long chat about my childhood, school interests, hobbies, vocational aspirations, and impressions of Ukiah, we agreed that I would work about 15 hours a week for the not-too-exploitative sum of $4.65 an hour (higher, at least, than the minimum wage). I was also free to miss work occasionally when I had exams or school activities. "You might even find the work interesting," said Mr. Preston. "Though I don't think it held much appeal for my son Trent. I was always finding him holed up in the coffee room working on a poem. You don't write poetry do you, Nick?"

"No," I said. And neither does your son, I thought.

"You'll get to meet him at Christmas," added Mr. Preston. "I'm sure you'll get on great. You boys seem to have a lot in common."

"I'm sure we do," I assented. Specifically, Trent is interested in seeing me dead. I am interested in assuring that his violent death is preceded by ruthlessly merciless torture.

8:30 p.m. After supper (microwaved TV dinners), I took Albert for a walk around the neighborhood in the warm blue twilight. The residents of our street tend to favor large dead cars as lawn ornaments. As I passed the shabbiest, most automotively littered bungalow, someone called "Hi Nick!" from behind the broken screen door. The door swung open and out bounded Dwayne, my provocatively breasted wrestling partner. His ripped tee-shirt displayed one jiggling tit and that evening's dinner menu: spaghetti, orange soda, and chocolate ice cream.

"Er, hi, Dwayne."

"Whatcha doin'?"

"Walking my dog Albert," I replied, briskly walking on. Dwayne matched me stride for stride.

"Neat dog!" he exclaimed. "Looks like a pit. Does he bite?"

"When provoked," I answered laconically.

"I seen you eatin' lunch with that spic today, Nick. I thought you was fastin' for dis'marment?"

"Just on Thursdays," I said. "And Vijay, for your information, is from India."

"I think he should go back where he come from. Like all the rest of them for'ners. They take all our jobs and steal all our wimmen!"

I could understand the source of Dwayne's prejudice. Clearly he faced a lifetime of scrabbling for dates and employment at the bottom of the pile. Still, I felt I should defend the principles of enlightened secular humanism.

"By and large, Dwayne, I think this country is enriched by its immigrants. I like Vijay and look forward to getting to know him."

Dwayne looked at me wonderingly. "You hang out with that spic, Nick, and the other kids are going to despise you!"

"I'm not sure of that," I replied. "And it wouldn't bother me anyway."

"Dontcha want to be pop'lar? I do!"

"I don't care much one way or the other," I lied.

"Gee, Nick, you're kinda fresh. I think it's zinky we live so close, dontchu?"

"Uh-huh," I lied.

"Want to sleep over tonight? I got a tent in my back yard. Or Mom'ld let us crash in the camper."

"No thanks, Dwayne," I replied, shuddering. "I'm allergic."

"To what, Nick?" he asked.

"Uh, to sleep. I have to stay awake 24 hours a day or I get hives."

"Wow! Dontcha ever get tired?"

"No. I've adjusted."

"Wow. I'm going to try that too. If I didn't have to sleep, I could play Nintendo all night long!"

SATURDAY, October 6 — At last our lethargic postal person brought a letter from Sheeni. That's the good news. The bad news is it was written in French. Every endearingly unintelligible word! After struggling without success to decipher it, I put the scented missive aside to open my second letter. This too was written in a charming feminine hand. It read:

Dear Nick,

Not that it's any of your business, but Clive Bosendorf happens to be a great guy. He's also grown two full inches since he started getting hormone injections this summer. By Christmas he expects to be taller than all you turkeys. So watch out!

I suppose I should thank you for showing me what a total zero Lefty is. When the Vice Squad broke in on us he acted like a spineless wimp. I was never so humiliated in all my life. I wouldn't go out with that jerk again if he was the last boy on Earth. I hear he's putting the moves on Wanda Fletcher. I could tell you some things about that b——h, but I'm not going to waste our country's finite paper resources.

I'm going to soccer camp in Hopland this weekend, so I'll call you Saturday night to come see your ranch. I love horses and would like to get a ride on Fire Walker. Don't worry, I got your phone number from a certain deformed wimp.
Regards,
Millie

Incredulous, I read that last paragraph three times. Each time the message remained the same. Millie Filbert is coming to visit me today. Why does this thought make my hands tremble? Why do I suddenly have The T.E. That Devoured Fresno?

12:15 p.m. Our kitchen looks like Guatemala City on market day. Lacey is interviewing prospective housekeepers. I didn't realize she *habla Español* so ineptly. She looks even more poignantly alluring than usual struggling to communicate by hand signals and pigeon Spanish. Dad's bilingualism is slightly more advanced. He keeps chanting "No tengo mucho dinero." For all I know he may be linguistically equipped to be a cheapskate in all the world's major languages.

I just called Vijay for some emergency Frog deciphering. Fortunately, there was just one listing for Joshi in the phone book. A female answered with the most exquisitely lyrical voice I have ever heard. She purred, "Vijay? Yes, I believe he is here. Please wait a moment, won't you?" Then Vijay came on the line and said he would be happy to translate a letter from "your remarkable Sheeni."

2:30 p.m. Vijay motored over on a flashy red mountain bike I would give Dad's left testicle to own. I wonder how many *Progressive Plywood* letters I'd have to type and file to buy a bike like that?

Vijay evinced polite interest in our residence. "A portable manufactured house. How intriguing. I've seen them, but have never been in one before. The rooms are surprisingly spacious. But why are the walls so obviously simulated wood? Does it really fool people?"

I replied that we Americans feel more comfortable in surroundings that are safely distanced from nature. "It has to do with issues of control," I explained. "We like to feel that nature is subjugated to our will at all times."

Vijay was more enthusiastic about Lacey. "What a fantastic stepmother you have," he exclaimed as we went in my room and closed the door. "Why is she wearing such a revealing swimsuit? Do you have a pool?"

I replied that Lacey dressed that way to stay cool and she was my dad's girlfriend, not his wife.

"Then they are living together," he whispered. "How racy! You are lucky to have parents who are open-minded. Mine are so strait-laced."

"Yes, Dad's a real Bohemian," I lied. "Say, Vijay, who was that who answered your phone?"

"My sister Apurva. She's 16."

Apurva! A name as beautiful as the voice. "Is she pretty?" I asked.

"She certainly thinks so. She's always pouting because Father won't let her go out with American boys."

"Why not?" I asked.

"He doesn't trust them—or her. He says she has to stay pure and marry some nice Indian boy. I don't think she wants to though."

"Stay pure or marry some nice Indian boy?"

"Neither," declared Vijay. "But I expect she'll do as she's told. My father is a tyrant on that subject you see."

"Can you go out with American girls?"

"Of course," he answered, "I just better damn well not want to marry one. Now, where is that letter?"

I waited impatiently as Vijay, smiling and chuckling, silently scanned Sheeni's letter. "Marvelous!" he exclaimed. "Sheeni is so clever. And her French is superb. It really is unfortunate you can't read it. My translation will never do it justice."

"Do your best," I urged.

So laboriously, with much stopping and backtracking, Vijay plodded through the letter, turning Sheeni's "superb French" into a confusing muddle of English. It appears that she is excited by her new school and finds her classmates and teachers much more stimulating than at Redwood High. She is also enjoying the total immersion in French. English cannot be spoken on campus "even if you are hemorrhaging from an accidental limb amputation." At first she wasn't certain she was prepared for the challenge, but now believes it is the only sensible way to acquire real language fluency. Her partial escape from parental bondage is also extremely liberating (not excessively, I hope). She has an interesting roommate from New York named Taggarty, who—though she is only 16—has already lived in London, Florence, Barcelona, and Paris. As further proof of her precocity, she already has slept with 17 guys and hopes to rack up 50 before college.

"I must meet this girl," leered Vijay.

Sheeni and Taggarty have been exploring Santa Cruz and find it not without its cultural attractions for a "small, provincial American city." They also like the beach and boardwalk, where Taggarty is conducting an on-going quest for the "cutest and dumbest" surfer. Trent has taken up windsurfing and has been designated "target number one" by all the girls in her class. Sheeni says she is trying not be jealous, but sometimes experiences "twinges of distress." She says Trent's appearance on campus came as a "complete shock" to her. He maintains it was merely a "fortuitous coincidence" that they both happened to transfer to the same school. (What a liar!) Of course, notes Sheeni, with his test scores and academic record, Trent has his choice of any school in the country. She says dorm food is not as bad as one might fear, and they have a view of the ocean from their bathroom window if they stand on the toilet. All in all, she is happy and looks forward to "further growth in this rich, intellectual environment."

Vijay sighed and folded the letter.

"Was that it?" I asked, startled. "Wasn't there anything about me?"

"Oh, yes. She said 'love to you and Albert.' Who's Albert?"

"Albert is our dog," I replied testily. "That's all?"

"I'm afraid so, my friend. That's the complete translation as best I can do it. Oh, and she's noted her address and the number for the telephone on their hall."

"I don't like the sound of this one bit," I said.

"No," agreed Vijay.

"Her roommate sounds like a decidedly bad influence."

"Yes, Nick, she certainly seems remarkably uninhibited. She must be good looking to be so attractive to boys. I wonder if she's made it with a Hindu yet?"

"This won't do at all. I've got to get Sheeni to transfer back to Redwood High," I said, thinking out loud, "as quickly as possible. She and Taggarty could be dating surfers as we speak."

"I wonder if Taggarty likes intelligent boys too?" speculated Vijay. "Of course, I could always pretend to be stupid."

"Vijay, help me!" I insisted. "We've got to get Sheeni back to Ukiah."

"You're right, my friend. Sheeni may be happy down there, but this town is a desert without her. She must return for the general welfare."

"We all have to make sacrifices," I pointed out.

"That is the road to enlightenment, so the philosophers tell us," he added.

"Sheeni," I announced, "I have to do this. For your own good."

"But what are you going to do?" asked Vijay.

"I don't know exactly. I haven't figured it out yet. But I'm desperate."

"Whatever it is," said Vijay, "let's make sure it involves meeting this remarkable Taggarty. At least once."

"I take it then, Vijay, you are still a virgin?"

"Yes, and I find it extremely galling. When Ghandi was my age, he had already been married three years."

No wonder Ghandi turned out to be a great man. When you get your lovelife nailed down that early, think of all the time it frees up to devote to Great Ideas.

6:10 p.m. Millie just called. Right as I was finishing the dinner dishes. She has a "horrible bruise" (from getting kicked in the leg at soccer camp), but is still sufficiently ambulatory for her ranch tour if not her stallion ride. I broke the news that an unfortunate outbreak of hoof and mouth disease had put the ranch under quarantine, but offered to sneak out to meet her downtown. She was disappointed, but agreed to the plan. Lacey has volunteered to give me a lift. I changed my clothes and Francois pocketed a condom just in case. He also slipped in Millie's brassiere (left behind in the police raid) as a conversational icebreaker.

11:40 p.m. I'm back. What a night! I'm too overwrought to sleep so I might as well get the story down on microchip. Millie, looking tantalizingly sunburned (does flawless alabaster skin not tan?), was lounging as specified in front of Flampert's variety store. She had dressed for the occasion in jeans, a brand new I GET A KICK OUT OF HOPLAND soccer camp tee-shirt, sandals, and scarlet toenail polish. All too evidently, I was the only person packing a bra.

"Well, Nick," said Millie brightly, "what's there to do in this town?"

"Uh, not much, Millie. We could go for a walk. I could buy you an ice cream."

"That sounds nice."

So we walked slowly up and down the empty streets in the warm twilight. We looked in the thrift store and dress shop windows, studied the array of washing machines and chain saws behind the plate glass in the Sears catalog store, peered into the noisy bars, examined the property-for-sale listings in the windows of real estate offices, commiserated with a nervous-looking rabbit sharing the front window of a reptile store with an immense boa constrictor, and—as darkness fell—refreshed ourselves with two triple-dip ice cream cones served up by a hostile youth in a ridiculous paper hat. From his manner I could tell he thought in a perfect world I would be scooping up the confections and he would be squiring the knockout brunette.

As we walked, licked, and wiped (our cones and lips respectively), Millie continued to ask me probingly knowledgeable equestrian-related questions. I continued to answer haltingly (why hadn't I been at the library all this afternoon boning up on Arabian horseflesh?), while endeavoring to steer the conversation back to her misjudged boyfriend Lefty.

"I don't think Lefty is a wimp at all," I declared.

"Oh, Nickie," replied Millie, "how can you say that?"

The appellation "Nickie" had been a recent, stimulating addition to our conversation. To match the pace, I had accelerated to "Mil."

"Well, for one thing, Mil, he may just be the best damn shoplifter in the state."

"OK, so the creep's a thief too. There are lots of wimps in San Quentin."

Clearly an unsubstantiated assertion, but I let the point drop for now. Millie's sugar cone had begun to drip from the tip onto her nice new tee-shirt. As the drips were falling in a provocative area, modesty prevented me from bringing it to her attention. Francois had no such scruples.

"Be careful, Mil," he said. "Your cone is dripping on your left breast area."

"Fuck!" she exclaimed, handing me her soggy cone and daubing the stains with her napkin. "I just got this shirt today!"

"Don't worry," I said. "The stains should wash out. It looks like a polyester blend."

"Not that I know anything about laundering fabrics," added Francois, mentally kicking me.

"No, you're probably right," she said. "Oh, throw that away!"

So Francois dropped the remains of Millie's cone on the sidewalk. The ever-frugal Nick went on eating his as they turned down a dark residential street. Crunching into the cone, he resumed his advocacy of his friend.

"What about the time in fifth grade when Lefty saved my life?"

"Lefty saved your life?" asked Millie, surprised.

"Yes," I lied. "Why do you suppose we're such great pals?"

Our stroll had brought us to an elementary school, looming anxiously in the black night like long division.

"Oh, Nickie, let's go swing on the swings!"

Millie grabbed my hand and led me toward the deserted playground. Lefty was right—her hand was warm and not at all clammy. While I sat on a swing and discussed Lefty's heroism, Millie soared back and forth in the dark.

"And so you see," I said, "if Lefty hadn't stopped the runaway bulldozer, the tent I was sleeping in would have been crushed."

Millie slowed slightly. "How did the bulldozer get started in the first place?"

"I told you. Some of the other Cub Scouts in camp started it."

"How can a kid start a giant bulldozer?"

"I suppose the loggers must have left the key in it by mistake."

"So Lefty jumped up on a moving bulldozer? That doesn't sound much like him. Why didn't he just get you out of the tent instead?"

"Well, there were more tents in its path farther on. The dozer had to be stopped at any cost."

"Oh, I see," said Millie. "So Lefty saved other people's lives that day too?"

"Oh sure. He was a real hero. They were thinking of renaming the camp after him, but it would have jeopardized their federal funding."

"Did you have horses at the camp?"

This woman has a one track mind, I thought. "No, just pack llamas," I lied. "Boy, you can sure swing."

"I was my grammar school champion," Millie announced. "Try it."

I tried, but concluded strenuous swinging was not an activity to do with a stomach full of melted ice cream. As I slowed, Millie spotted something dangling from my back pocket.

"What's that?" she asked, stopping.

This was Francois' cue. "Oh, Mil, it's your brassiere," he said. "I found it in my bedroom down in Oakland after the cops left."

Millie accepted her intimate apparel without evident embarrassment. "Thanks, Nick. Glad to have it. These are kind of expensive, you know."

"Like how much?" asked Francois.

"Oh, I don't know. I think this one was $18."

"That's only $9 apiece," he pointed out.

"N-N-Nick!" exclaimed Millie. "I didn't think you were that kind of boy."

"What kind is that?" I asked. We had twisted toward each other on the swings so our knees were almost touching.

"You know. Interested in girls' bodies. I thought all you cared about was English literature and computers. And telling me how great Lefty is."

"I'm interested in you," whispered Francois, leaning forward. "A lot."

Thank God it was dark. I had a T.E. the size of an old-growth redwood.

"Gee, Nick," whispered Millie, also leaning forward. "That's a surprise."

"Is it?" Francois asked.

Millie didn't answer. Her lips were blocked by Francois' feverish tongue. While he busied himself, I ruminated on a surprising discovery. Girls' lips were not all the same. Millie's tasted and felt entirely different from Sheeni's. The bold Francois soon discovered her breasts felt different as well.

"Gee, Nick," said Millie, coming up for air and looking around. "This is kind of exposed. Let's go over there where those trees are."

We crept furtively toward the even blacker shadows under tall fir trees, and lay down on the still warm grass. Within ten seconds, I felt an evening breeze and Millie's warm hand on my cock. I groped for her zipper as Francois nipped teasingly at her lips. "Be careful of my bruise," she cautioned, as Francois slipped down her jeans and tugged at her panties. He moved down and probed experimentally with his tongue for her fragrant moistness. Lefty was wrong, realized Nick. It doesn't taste at all like chicken.

Millie groaned, but not from pleasure. "Nick! Watch out for my bruise!"

"Sorry," I replied. It was so dark you couldn't see a vagina in front of your face.

"Here," she said, searching in her purse and taking out a small flashlight, "I'll show you." She shined the beam on a milky white thigh, discolored by a huge purplish-yellow bruise.

Mildly revolted, Francois moved up to what was probably a pink nipple, as Millie softly stroked the tip of my throbbing T.E.

"Do you have a condom, Nickie?" she asked. (The six most inflammatory words in the English language.)

"Right here," replied Francois, reaching into his pocket.

Emptiness. Zero. Total void.

Panicky, I felt around in my other pockets.

Desolation. The utter vacuum of space.

"Shit!" whispered Francois. "It must have fallen out somewhere. I know, I'll just pull out before I come."

"No way, tiger," she replied. "I learned my lesson. Here."

A dozen expert strokes later, Millie had a wet hand. When, some seconds later, I resumed command of my conscious mind, I asked, "What about you?"

"Do me with your tongue," she replied. "But watch out for my bruise."

So Francois set to work. Millie guided him on target. "Up. Down a little. To the right. There. Oh, yes!" While Francois labored linguistically, I pondered the flavor question. More like a mushroom and Guyere omelet with a small Greek salad on the side. Nice, but Lefty was right. Your tongue does get tired. Just as I felt the onset of crippling lingual paralysis, Millie shuddered and quaked in great convulsive waves. Wow, girls have orgasms too.

"You do that so well, Nick," said Millie later, as we lay in each other's arms. "And you don't stop to rest. That's nice."

"It comes with experience," replied Francois, shifting uncomfortably. He didn't like the way Millie was shining her flashlight on his shrunken member.

"There was just one thing I was wondering," she said.

"What's that?" I asked, with some trepidation.

"What were they doing logging in a Boy Scout camp?"

"They were thinning out the trees," I replied. "Too much masturbation in the woods."

When I got home an hour later, Dad was prone on the couch in his usual alcoholic haze.

"Some girl called for you," he slurred.

"Who?" I demanded.

"I don't know. Some funny name. It was long distance. From Santa Cruz."

My One and Only Love! "What did you tell her, Dad?"

"What do you think? I said the stud was out with some babe. Funny, I think I heard her voice somewhere before."

Total scrotum-tingling panic!

SUNDAY, October 7 — 1:15 a.m. After Dad and Lacey finally went to bed, I called Sheeni's number in Santa Cruz. Some girl answered. Speaking French.

"May I speak to Sheeni, please?"

Short Frog speak.

"Sheeni Saunders. She's a student there."

Longer Frog speak. Female tittering in the background.

"I can't understand you. Please speak English. This is important."

More Frog speak.

"I tell you, this is a life or death emergency!"

More Frog speak. More laughing.

"OK. Could you tell her Nick called? Please tell Sheeni to call Nick Twisp first thing in the morning. OK?"

Long, labored Frog speak.

"Oh, go stuff it in your sourcil!" I hissed, slamming down the phone.

10:30 a.m. A long, sleepless night followed by a glum breakfast. I am wracked by guilt. How could I have betrayed Sheeni so wantonly? And why did she have to find out? Even the milk on my Cheerios poured out sour. I ate the repulsive gruel anyway to atone for my treachery. Then the phone rang. Lacey said it was for me.

"Good morning, darling," I said brightly.

"I hate your stinking guts!"

"Lefty, what did I do now, guy?"

"You know what you did, traitor. Millie called me this morning. From soccer camp."

"Oh. She did," I mumbled, shocked. "What, what did she say?"

"She said she made it with you last night!"

"And I suppose you believed her? Lefty, the woman is desperate. She's trying to make you jealous because you've put the moves on Wanda Fletcher. By the way, that was a brilliant ploy on your part. Wanda is really hot."

"Millie said you would deny it. She gave me evidence."

"What evidence?" I asked nervously.

"The mole on your right nut. How did she know about that, traitor?"

"Oh, well . . . Uh, we were talking about birth marks. I happened to mention I had a mole down there."

"You were talking about *your* balls with *my* girlfriend?"

"Not my balls, Lefty, my scrotum. It was all very medical. She's going to be a doctor, you know. Face it, Lefty, in a few years she's going to be handling testicles all day long."

"Then you didn't eat her out? She said you did it very well."

"Total fabrication, Lefty. You know I'm only interested in Sheeni. I *did* see Millie last night. To tell her what a great guy you were!"

"Yeah, that's another thing. If you were going to make up some story about me saving your life, you could've at least warned me in advance. Now she knows it was all a big lie!"

"Sorry, Lefty. I was going to tell you. I had no idea Millie would talk to you so soon. She only called because your strategy was working so well."

"You really think so, Nick?"

"I know it. I could tell she was boiling with jealousy. How's Wanda by the way?"

"Oh, she's OK. She gets on my nerves."

"How so?"

"She's always bugging me to talk about my feelings. Like when I'm trying to get my hand in her blouse. I don't know if I have any feelings. I think I'm too young for that stuff."

"She wants to know if you like her."

"But I don't like her much. She bugs me. I like Millie. I've liked her since I was 10."

"Well, Wanda can probably figure that out. You'll have to do more sincere lying. That's my advice."

"I guess you're right. Did Millie say anything about Clive Bosendorf?"

"Hardly mentioned him. I could tell she doesn't really like the shrimp. I bet if you pounded him she wouldn't even care. In fact, it might go a long way toward correcting your wimp image."

"That's a great idea! Thanks, Nick. We've been best pals for a long time. I knew you wouldn't do anything that rotten to me."

"That's right, Lefty," I lied. "We guys have to stick together."

I belched. It tasted like sour milk and guilt. At least now I don't feel like I've betrayed Sheeni. Unfaithfulness doesn't count when you're only being used by the other person. Just see if I ever give Millie a ride on my Arabian stallion. Still, I am in her debt for broadening my sexual horizons. I might be a certified non-virgin this morning if the fates had not conspired against me.

12:20 p.m. Sheeni just called. Lacey and Dad were out taking Albert into the hills to pee on redwoods, so I was able to accept her collect call.

"Bon jour, Nickie," whispered The Woman of My Dreams.

"Hello, Sheeni darling," I replied. "I can hardly hear you. Is something the matter?"

"I'm calling from the dorm so I have to talk softly. We're not supposed to speak English on campus, even on the phone."

"I know. I had a hell of a time trying to reach you last night."

"Yes, I heard about that this morning. You told Darlene to do something obscene with her eyebrow."

"My French is rather rudimentary," I admitted. "Were you out when I called?"

"Yes. Taggarty and I went to a party."

"Oh, I see. How was it?" I imagined dim rooms full of debauched surfers.

"It was fun. The people here are so interesting. Your father said you were out when I called."

"Yes, I was counseling Lefty's girlfriend Mildred. She happened to be up in this area for a sports camp. They're having a difficult time of it and I think I may have helped."

"That was nice of you. Is she pretty?"

"No, she has a face like a potato," I lied. "But Lefty likes her."

"Well, Nickie, I want you to feel you are free to go out with other people. As Taggarty points out, we really are rather young to tie ourselves down. Especially with all the miles separating us."

"I love you, Sheeni," I replied. "I don't want to go out with anyone else."

"I feel the same way, Nickie. I just want you to know you are free to do as you wish."

A generous sentiment, Sheeni, but one with an alarming corollary. "Well, darling, it may be unAmerican to say this, but I don't want to be free. I'm perfectly happy being enslaved—to you."

"How sweet," whispered Sheeni. "Oh, did you get my letter?"

"Yes, darling. Your French was marvelous. Very clever."

"You didn't have any difficulty reading it then?"

"Not at all. Mrs. Blandage says I am a born linguist."

Sheeni then spoke animatedly for several minutes in French. When she finished, I said, "Uh, darling, I guess my oral comprehension still lags somewhat behind my reading level. Could you repeat that in English?"

"I was just describing my classes, Nickie. How do you like Redwood High? Have you made any friends yet?"

"Just a few. You know Vijay Joshi?"

"Oh, yes. He's a nice boy. Very cultured for Ukiah. Odd politics though. He once invited me to a rally welcoming an aide to Dan Quayle. Vijay's sister is quite beautiful. She's been writing letters to Trent."

"Does Trent write back?" I asked, shocked.

"Of course. I think he may be in love with her. The rat. Just kidding, Nickie. It's all hopeless, though, since her father is so strict."

I must meet this sister, thought Francois. We then talked for an additional one hour and fifteen minutes. Finally, my heart filled with love, my ear inflamed, I said goodbye and rang off. I can see I won't be buying any mountain bikes soon. All my hard-earned wages will be going straight to AT&T.

4:20 p.m. The familiar hiss of airbrakes brought me to my window. A big semi had stopped outside and there was no mistaking the driver. It was Wally Rumpkin, Mom's giant jilted lover. The immense pink seven-footer was just climbing down from the cab as I walked out to greet him.

"Hi, Wally! What a surprise!"

"Oh hi, Nick," said Wally, shyly addressing a scraggly juniper by the edge of the drive. "I was hoping this was your street. I had an awful time finding it."

A black blur darted between my legs and leaped—all wiggles and lapping tongue—into Wally's surprised arms.

"Doggie, please don't do that," said Wally, gently returning the squirming Albert to the ground. "I'm making a run to Tacoma, Nick. So I brought you your bicycle."

"That's great, Wally. Thanks!"

Wally opened the great swinging doors of his rig and carefully lifted down my old Warthog ten-speed (a $5 garage sale purchase presented to me on my eighth birthday by my loving dad.)

"You're a life-saver, Wally. Boy, can I use this. I've been walking 12 miles a day."

"No trouble, Nick," replied Wally to the concrete plant in the distance. "It was on my way. And it gave me a chance to see your mother."

"Oh, her. How is she?"

"Very bad, I'm afraid. She's engaged to be married."

"Engaged! Not to that fascist cop, I hope."

"I'm afraid so. They're going to Reno next Saturday."

In less than one week I will have an evil stepfather. And I wasn't even consulted.

"That's terrible, Wally. Couldn't you talk her out of it?"

"I tried, Nick, but she wouldn't listen. I think she may be doing it out of a misplaced sense of gratitude."

"Gratitude! For what?" I demanded.

"Oh, you know," said Wally, blushing. "Helping cover up after the fire."

"Oh, that." More guilt for Nick. "How's that going?"

"Fine, don't worry. The arson investigators have been out once or twice to talk to your mother. They searched your neighbor's house and got real suspicious when they found all the radical pamphlets. But they didn't have any evidence to arrest him on, so they let him go. Now the city's offering a $10,000 reward."

I swallowed nervously. $10,000 was a lot of money. Anyone might turn me in for a sum that large. Even I was tempted.

No time to write any more. I just told Dad about Mom getting married, so he's taking Lacey and me out for steaks to celebrate. His long nightmare of debilitating alimony payments may soon be over.

MONDAY, October 8 — The damning evidence against Bruno continues to mount. Vijay's friend Fuzzy DeFalco confirmed at lunch today that Redwood High's star quarterback (star so far of one tie and five defeats) lives on the same street as Sheeni's parents. Yet could Sheeni really have yielded up her delicate virginity to such an oafish clod? I recoil in contemplating such desecration. So instead I ruminate on tortures involving steam-heated jock straps and sharpened steel cleats grinding into low, hairy brows.

Speaking of hairy, I'm told Fuzzy acquired his nickname at the age of nine when he first came to the attention of scouts for the U.S. Olympic Body Hair Team. He could shave non-stop from his eyes to his toes, but instead maintains only a small facial clearing that ends arbitrarily about two inches above his collar. All his clothes float away from his body on a dense layer of red fur. Vijay has suggested he seek government recognition as a National Hair Transplant Reserve.

Fuzzy takes this ribbing good-naturedly, but gets mad when girls tape flea collars to his locker. They also pretend to scratch when he enters a room, which makes him even madder. Still, his perpetual five o'clock shadow remains zit-free, so he has no real reason for complaint. His parents have money, which in my book compensates for virtually all genetic disfigurements (excepting only the horror of penile abbreviation).

Vijay claims that despite all the evidence to the contrary, Fuzzy is extremely intelligent. "He's just misguided," says Vijay, "a victim of your media-promulgated American mass culture." Perhaps from watching too many beer commercials, Fuzzy aspires to be a jock, but is hampered by chronic klutzitis. He has tried out for all the sports teams (including the namby-pamby ones like golf), but has been rejected for incompetence by them all. Nonetheless, he continues to yearn for athletic stardom.

After school, I shuffled up the dusty stairs of doom and entered the World of Work. Only 10 minutes later I could feel brain cells starting to wither and die. Why are all the jobs offered to youths so cripplingly boring? You'd think the gods of capitalism would give us the interesting jobs. Then, when we're safely shackled into the system with marriages and mortgages, they could turn the tedium up full blast. Nope, we're immediately abandoned, naked and defenseless, on the icy tundra of ennui—and paid peanuts for our suffering to boot.

My job of the day was to file an immense stack of papers in a vast bank of musty green cabinets. This proved to be harder than it looked (but no more interesting). There was one cabinet for A-D, one for E-L, one for M-O, 28 cabinets for P, and one for R-Z. I doubt if anyone in the lumber industry consulted the file clerks when they decided to name particle board with the same first letter as plywood. And did no one think to remind them of that popular wood called pine? Not to mention panelling, pecan, poplar, and pecky cedar.

I got so perplexed and peeved among the P's, I fear my filing soon grew somewhat prankishly perverse. Plus, the obvious indifference of my predecessors to alphabetical rigor only encouraged continued capriciousness. I filed a report on Swedish furniture-grade plywood under G (for Greta Garbo) and a survey of decorative particle board panelling under O (for "only for the aesthetically impaired").

Dad, true to character, pretended we weren't related and ordered me about like the Despot of Constantinople. He even insisted I address him as Mr. Twisp to, in his words, "maintain proper business decorum." I complied, but let my pronunciation slide. "Yes, suh, Mr. Twit," I salaamed. It felt right somehow. This brought a smirk to the primly powdered face of Mr. Preston's secretary, Miss Pliny (first name Penelope—no, she does *not* wish to be called Penny).

Miss Pliny is either a prematurely faded 30 or a well-preserved 50. She wears soft-focus coordinated pastels, pins her sweater around her shoulders with a gold chain, sips gunpowder tea out of a china cup (with saucer), keeps a rose cachet in every desk drawer, speaks like an elocution teacher, and—anomalously—daubs her smoldering lips with flamboyant lipstick (color: autopsy red). As *Progressive Plywood's* official proofreader, she ruthlessly blue-pencils every contraction, giving the already wooden prose an oddly stilted quality—as if it were composed by 19th century scribes. Improbably, Francois finds her fascinating. I'm surprised—she doesn't seem at all like his type.

When I got home, I received the shock of my life. There at the dining room table, napkin tucked under his double chin, fat face composed in an expectant grin, slouched my girlishly breasted classmate Dwayne.

"Hi, Nick," he exclaimed, "Mom's makin' pork roast for supper!"

It was true. Despairing of bridging the yawning language chasm, Lacey has hired as housekeeper (for a one-week trial) the only Anglo applicant: Mrs. Flora Crampton, mother of you know who. Dad has agree to let Dwayne eat with us in exchange for a slight reduction in the already penurious wage.

"You must be . . . Nick," said a phonebooth-sized woman in a frilly orange apron as she carried a big pan of cornbread out from the kitchen. "I'm Flora . . . Go wash your hands, boy . . . I don't . . . serve two shifts." She spoke amazingly slowly, as if she were inventing the language as she went along. If you speeded up the tape, you might discover she speaks some obscure dialect of the rural Middle West.

I frowned and counted the place settings on the table. Five!

"Uh, Lacey," I whispered, "shouldn't the help and their children eat in the kitchen?"

Flora overheard. "Well aren't you . . . the stuck up . . . little snot!" she said, slamming down the pan and huffing back into the kitchen. I noticed she had to crab-walk sideways through the too-narrow (for her) doorway.

"That's all right, Mrs. Crampton," called Lacey. "Don't be silly, Nick. We're all going to have a nice meal together. Mrs. Crampton is a wonderful cook."

Well, she's an OK cook—if you're partial to white trash cuisine. God knows, we all seem to be. For dinner we shoveled down pork roast and gravy, bread stuffing, candied sweet potatoes (with multi-hued mini-marshmallows melted on top), mustard greens, and buttered cornbread with cherry jam. Dessert was homemade coconut cream pie. Dad had thirds of everything, his gustatory enjoyment dimmed only by the unnerving sight of the two Cramptons matching him calorie for calorie. Mrs. Crampton also helped herself freely to the zin jug. I suspect he may demand a further adjustment in the compensation package.

Dwayne did miss out on his third piece of pie. He fell asleep in his chair. "I don't know ... what's got ... into Dwayno," said his mother. "I been catchin' him ... up at all hours ... playin' with that damn Nintendo ... He thinks he ... don't need no ... sleep!"

Dad volunteered me to do the dishes, but Mrs. Crampton said no. "I hear he's a ... scholar, let him ... go do his school ... work." So she poked Dwayne awake and made him do them.

I fear I may have misjudged her. Sometimes you just can't trust your first impression.

I sauntered into the kitchen as Dwayne was scrubbing up the last of the pots and pans.

"Your mother calls you Dwayno," I observed.

"So what!"

"So how much is it worth to you not to have that fact repeated at school?"

Dwayne emptied his pockets. "All I got's 78 cents."

I took the proffered change. "It's a start. Dwayno."

TUESDAY, Oct. 9 — School, job, homework, dog walk, TV. Another boring day. Not even a letter from Sheeni. Do you suppose the human race invented boredom to make the prospect of death more palatable?

I just mailed my sister Joanie a belated birthday card. It's three weeks late, but that's what belated means. (You could look it up.) She's probably not home to receive her mail anyway. She's a flight attendant and is always on the road. She only returns to her condo in L.A. to sleep and entertain men without college degrees.

Another monstrously caloric meal by Mrs. Crampton. Dad, I fear, may have to moonlight on the weekends to pay his grocery bill—assuming he can heave his burgeoning blubber off the couch. Only Lacey eats lightly to preserve her traffic-stopping figure. It's hard to believe, seeing them side-by-side at the table, that Mrs. Crampton and Lacey are members of the same sex of the same species. One might almost suppose them to be from different solar systems.

In between bites, Dwayne has taken to playing footsie with me under the table. In retaliation, I try to dirty as many dishes as possible.

Mrs. Crampton is mad because Dad dared to suggest she put her obese offspring on a diet. "Dwayno needs . . . to eat good," she retorted. "They want 'em . . . big . . . in the NFL."

Apparently she's expecting Dwayne to buy her a nice house after he signs his multi-million dollar professional football contract. Perhaps someone should mail her an anonymous note informing her that her son is, next to Fuzzy, the most athletically impaired member of his gym period. I wonder how much Dad would pay for that information?

I committed a slight faux pas over dessert (egg custard with whipped cream). "Where does Mr. Crampton have his dinner?" I asked innocently.

Dwayne blushed. Mrs. Crampton lowered her spoon. "My man . . . takes his meals . . . down at San Q," she replied. "And will be . . . for the next . . . 10 to 20 years."

Later, as I was in the kitchen using three glasses to swallow three vitamin pills, Dwayne glanced over sheepishly from the sink. "You won't tell anyone my pop's in jail, will you, Nick?"

"I don't know," I replied thoughtfully. "What's he in for?"

"He cashed some bad checks."

"I didn't know you could go to prison for that," I replied, surprised. "My father does it all the time."

"Well, the checks were stolen," Dwayne elaborated, "off a guy he shot."

"Did the man die?" I asked, shocked.

"No, he's just, whatchamercallit, brain dead. But the jury said it weren't murder so my pop didn't have to fry."

"They gas people in this state," I corrected him. "Your father would have been executed in the gas chamber."

"Wow!" exclaimed Dwayne. "Do you s'pose they'd have let us watch?"

"Of course," I said. "The family's always invited. Otherwise, it would be cruel and unusual punishment."

Dwayne yawned. "I don't see how you stay awake, Nick. I try as hard as I can, but I'm always tired."

"Just keep at it. You only feel sleepy if you let your eyes close."

"But sometimes they just go and fall down on their own," he complained.

"Don't let them. When you feel your eyes shut, go splash water on your face and hop around on one foot. That's what I do."

"Wow, Nick. How did you get to be so smart?"

"Staying awake," I replied. "Sleep deprivation hones the mental processes." I opened the oven door. "Damn, some fool put the meat platter back in with the oven turned on high. Boy, that sure looks charred on bad. I suggest you use a Brillo pad and trisodium phosphate."

"Thanks, Nick," said Dwayne gratefully. "When I'm through, can I take Albert for a walk? Can I, huh?"

"I suppose I could do you that favor," I replied.

"Gee, Nick. You're great."

"Don't mention it," I said.

WEDNESDAY, Oct. 10 — I got a C- in wood technology on my doorstop. Mr. Vilprang said my edges were not planed to true right angles and my shellacking was blotched. This is the lowest grade I have ever received. I wonder if Stanford is this academically demanding?

While I was disconsolately starting in on my next project (a napkin holder), the no-neck jock Bruno came in to spend a free period sanding his Early American maple dry sink (at least that's what I think it's supposed to be). Bruno's in the advanced class and gets to work on all the power machines Mr. Vilprang says "would rip the thumbs right off you bozos." Ham-handed as he is, Bruno still retains all his digits. To my chagrin he survived that period intact as well. I must find a way to bump him while he's looking into the planer or doing close work on the shaper. He likes to stick his tongue out as he works—perhaps he could snag that appendage in the belt sander.

Now that the novelty has worn off, my after-school job has become even more excruciatingly mind-numbing. Today my assigned task was to enter into the computer a stack of incoherent and poorly spelled letters to the editor. To relieve the tedium, I selectively altered the occasional "now" to "not" and vice versa. This insidious typo often escapes detection by proofreaders and can greatly enliven even the dullest writing. I am hoping for the best.

Dad was in his cubicle the whole time keeping a low profile. Mr. Preston overheard him ask Miss Pliny how long she'd been "parking her pretty can at Regressive Plywood." She replied coldly, "I do not know to what you refer," while Mr. Preston gave Dad a look that could splinter mahogany.

Lacey made leftovers for dinner. Mrs. Crampton had a family emergency and couldn't come.

"What kind of emergency?" I asked.

"She had to take Dwayne to the doctor," replied Lacey. "She found him in her kitchen at 4 a.m. He was dripping wet and jumping around on one leg."

7:30 p.m. The phone rang after dinner and Dad handed it to me.

"Hello, Nickie darling."

It was my repulsive mother.

"Oh, hi, Mom," I replied coldly.

"How are you doing, Nickie? Are you getting along with your father?"

"Yes, he's great," I lied. "I really like it here a lot."

"That's nice, Nickie. I've been worried about you."

"Yes, my legs have almost healed from the beating. I still limp a little, but it looks like my injuries are not permanent."

"I'm sorry if Lance was a little too severe. We were all upset that night."

"Uh-huh," I replied.

"Did you hear that Lance and I are getting married this Saturday?" she continued brightly. "We were hoping you could meet us in Reno for the ceremony. I can send you a bus ticket."

"Uh, gee, I'd like to. But I have an appointment to get my teeth cleaned.

Maybe next time."

Long silence.

"Well, OK, Nickie. It sounds like you don't want to come. I think, though, if you gave Lance a chance you'd start to like him."

"Uh-huh." Sure, and I hear Joseph Goebbels was a riot on weekends too.

"We're driving to Winnemucca for our honeymoon. Lance's mom lives out there in the desert in a trailer."

"That sounds nice. Well, I have to go do my homework now."

"Nickie, will you write or call me? I'll be back here in a few days."

"I'll try. 'Bye, Mom."

"Goodbye, Nickie. I'll be thinking of you."

"Uh-huh." *Click.*

I think I'll write a letter to the *New England Journal of Medicine*. I just discovered the cause of clinical depression: parents!

THURSDAY, October 11 — Boy, am I tired. Dad and Lacey had a high-pitched screaming contest last night starting at 2 a.m. I couldn't tell what the spat was about, but at one point I heard her call him a "tight-assed, critical, stingy, non-feeling, sexist drunk." She also declared he was a "selfish, uptight, boring lover." I'd say that sounds like a fairly cogent assessment. She left out "lousy driver," but perhaps she was restrained by her own besmirched DMV record.

Several times the battle grew so heated Albert joined in from his dusty bed down in the crawl space. Finally, Francois had to yell out, "Hey, there are people here who have to answer difficult questions in physics class tomorrow. Could you people hold it down?"

"Fuck you, jerkoff!" replied my compassionate parent. But the verbal fireworks tapered off soon after that. This morning I discovered Lacey asleep, in a state of semi-nudity, on the living room couch. Perhaps they will have fights more often.

Fuzzy DeFalco, I learned at lunch, has just been named assistant manager of the Marauding Beavers football team. He hopes eventually to move up from this position to starting varsity offensive pass receiver. I wonder if that's how Red Grange started? In the meantime Fuzzy gets to hang out with jocks— taping assorted ankles, keeping the Gatorade chilled, and sweeping the field during timeouts for gouged out eyeballs. It should also leave him well placed to get the inside dirt on Ukiah's most illustrious no-neck jock.

The scent of burnt flesh hung in the air at work today. It was Dad sizzling on the hot seat. Mr. Preston called him into his office and informed him that their official fact-checker (Miss Pliny) discovered "31 major errors of fact" in Dad's article, "New Developments in Tongue-in-groove Flakeboard Subflooring."

Concluding Dad needs a stronger background in wood, Mr. Preston invited him to spend the weekend assisting him in his basement workshop. Working together, they are going to construct a four-drawer plywood filing cabinet (the "P" files are overflowing again). Dad agreed, but his ersatz enthusiasm fooled no one.

After Dad's dressing down, Miss Pliny sipped her tea and hummed selections from "Kismet." She also complimented me on the accuracy of my typing.

"I hope you don't mind, Miss Pliny," I said. "I took the liberty of correcting the misspellings and eliminating the contractions."

"You were quite correct to do so, Nicholas," she replied. "We must be forever vigilant in resisting the onslaught of linguistic impurity."

"Standards must be upheld," I concurred. "The Philistines are at the gates."

She glanced toward Dad's cubicle. "The walls have been broached, Nicholas. We are grappling with the Visigoths in the streets."

Lacey did not come home for dinner. Just as well, Mrs. Crampton had the galling effrontery to make fried cow's liver. Dwayne hates it as much as I do. We sat there in silent communion, staring in revulsion at our plates, while Dad and Mrs. Crampton packed it away. Later, as Dwayne was washing the dishes, he told me his doctor has prescribed a strong sedative to be administered nightly before bedtime.

"Mom gave me one last night, but I spit it out later," he confided.

"Good for you. You could get addicted to those drugs. What did you do with the capsule?"

"I hid it under my pillow," he replied.

"Good. Here's what you do. Right before bed, you ask your mother if she wants a hot drink, then slip the pill into it. That way she won't hear you if you have to get up and hop around for a while."

"That's a great idea!" whispered Dwayne. "Boy, Nick, I wish I had your brain."

"Sorry, Dwayne," I replied, offended. "I'm still using it."

"Can I walk Albert again tonight? Huh, can I, Nick?"

"Gee, Dwayne. I don't know. Dogs don't grow on trees, you know."

"I'll pay you 50 cents."

"It's a deal," I replied, pocketing the quarters. "Walk him as long as you like."

9:45 p.m. Vijay just called. I'm invited to his house for dinner tomorrow night. Finally, I get to meet the beautiful Apurva. He also said he'd had "a sudden brainstorm" he wishes to discuss privately with me.

10:15 p.m. Lacey, looking a bit tipsy, finally came home. She and Dad are now closeted in their bedroom, whispering. Oops, bedsprings rocking. Another domestic crisis successfully resolved. Too bad. Francois was going to suggest to Lacey she bunk with him tonight.

FRIDAY, October 12 — I'm going to Santa Cruz to visit Sheeni tomorrow! It was Vijay's idea and he has it all planned out. Fuzzy, Vijay, and I are driving down. We're going to "borrow" Fuzzy's grandmother's car. She's in the hospital hooked up to life-support equipment, so she won't be needing it. Fuzzy skipped shaving this morning. We figure by tomorrow he'll look at least 35, so he's going to drive. He says he's been borrowing his granny's car since he was 12, and once got it "up to 104" on the Redwood Highway. He should have no trouble getting a driver's license in two years. Since I have some experience piloting Mom's erstwhile Lincoln and trailer (alas, consumed in the Berkeley fire), I've been designated backup driver. This time I'll be sure to set the parking brake. As a cover, each of us is telling our parents we'll be sleeping over at another's house. I'm paying for the gas since Sheeni is my girlfriend. It's only fair.

Mr. Preston agreed to let me skip work tomorrow, after I told him I had to memorize "The Rime of the Ancient Mariner" in its entirety for English class. He said, "Fine. We'll expect a recitation here on Monday too."

Damn!

Dinner at Vijay's was fabulous: lots of mystery grains, alien vegetables cooked in bizarre sauces, weird flat bread blown up like balloons, and daubs of unidentifiable spicy matter in tiny stainless steel bowls. Piquant, but not too hot for my pallid American palate. Someone forgot the forks, so we ate with our hands. To drink, we had a watery, salty yogurt beverage called lassi, after the famous canine TV star. (Though not, I hope, brewed from dog's milk.)

Apurva was a total knock-out in a red sari and golden slippers. She has long black hair, burnished bronze skin, huge dark eyes, and a lilting voice that caresses the ears like distilled birds' song. Her dad (a big, gruff, scary-looking guy with a piercing gaze) makes her go to a chicks-only Catholic school, so she seemed especially eager for some male conversation. Francois obliged, and flirted outrageously even for him.

"Apurva is a beautiful name," he said. "Does it have any special meaning?"

"Yes," she replied, blushing slightly. "It means unique or wonderful."

"Of course," said Francois, "how silly of me not to have guessed."

Mr. Jhosi looked at me sternly.

"What does your name mean, Nick?" asked Apurva.

"It means shaving injury," I replied.

Apurva laughed. "Oh, Nick, I'm certain it must mean something nicer than that. You are too modest."

"Is that name the diminutive form of Nicholas?" inquired Mr. Joshi.

"Yes, sir."

"Then that makes you a practicing Catholic, I suppose?" From his tone, one might have supposed he had just inquired whether I was a practicing pederast. But if he hates Catholics, I thought, why does he send his only daughter to a school run by nuns?

"No, sir. I am a non-practicing Protestant. We tell the census-takers we're Methodists."

"Have you no spiritual life at all?" he demanded, shocked.

"I'm afraid not," I apologized. "Though we do have a Christmas tree every December."

"Your parents should be taken to task," he avowed. "They are neglecting their duties. A child should . . ."

"A child should eat his dinner before it gets cold," interrupted Mrs. Joshi, smiling. "Have another chapati, Nick."

Apurva's mother, to my surprise, was just as animated as her daughter and nearly as beautiful. She insisted I have seconds of everything, and looked genuinely stricken when I obdurately refused a fourth helping of curried moong beans.

Sitting in that tasteful dining room, listening to their lively, intellectual conversation, I couldn't help but feel, well, pissed. At that moment, I reflected, Dad was probably grunting "pass the fish sticks" to Mrs. Crampton as Lacey chattered away about the latest breakthroughs in hair dye and Dwayne probed listlessly for a booger. Why me, God? How come Vijay gets selected for "Masterpiece Family" and I get stuck in the reruns of "My Favorite Moron?"

10:30 p.m. Back among my own kind. Lacey and Dad aren't speaking again. Before he left with his mom, Dwayne paid today's dog walking fee and told me that Dad had threatened Lacey with a butter knife at the dinner table after he found out she had emptied his zin jug down the toilet. "It was just like when my pop was home," Dwayne whispered. "Only they didn't swear as much." Lacey is now making up her bed on the couch and Dad is sulking in his bedroom.

I tried to call Sheeni to alert her to my visit, but I couldn't get past the twittering Frog-speak barrier. Looks like I'll just have to surprise her. I am optimistic she will listen to reason and agree to transfer back to Ukiah. It's a small sacrifice to make for love.

I have counted my wad: $46.12 ($45.12 in savings and $1.00 in dog-rental profits). Grandmother DeFalco's car better get good gas mileage. Otherwise, I may not eat this trip.

SATURDAY, October 13 — (transcribed from pencil). 9:30 a.m. We're on the road to Santa Cruz! Motoring south on Highway 101, we just passed through greater Cloverdale. So far, Fuzzy appears to be a very competent driver. Of course, after riding with Dad, almost anybody seems like a good driver by comparison. Fuzzy showed up this morning proudly wearing a Marauding Beavers letter jacket, which we immediately made him take off. We want him to look at least post-college, not high school.

Granny DeFalco's car is a mint condition 1965 Ford Falcon (color: Denture Cream) with 38,000 miles on the odometer. A sharp car, but the interior smells like little old lady. I feel as if we should all be wearing white gloves and discussing Social Security reform. Under the hood is a small, gas-thirsty 260 cubic inch V-8, so we have plenty of reserve power to speed toward my complete impoverishment.

I have memorized the first two lines of "The Rime of the Ancient Mariner." Only 728 to go. Vijay is assisting me by making obscene alterations in each line.

He claims once you learn the dirty version, it's a snap to remember the original. Seems logical to me. Next time, though, I'm telling Mr. Preston I need time off for something vague like spiritual growth.

10:15 a.m. Our first crisis. The sun came out in Novato and Fuzzy's eyes locked into reflexive squint. We barely made it off the freeway alive. He forgot his sunglasses, so we had to stop at K-Mart to buy him a pair. While we were there, we picked up two dozen donuts (only eight apiece, but we're husbanding our funds). Fuzzy can see OK now, but he says the cheap lenses make it seem like he's piloting a low-flying airplane. His entire body is extra-sensitive to light. Maybe that's why he has all that fur.

1:30 p.m. Fuzzy made a wrong turn in San Francisco, and before we knew it we were heading east on the Bay Bridge. So I said hell, let's go to Oakland and see my old house. To my surprise, my front door key still fit. I figured Mom would have had all the locks changed by now. The place was deserted, of course, since Mom was up in Reno with Lance ruining her life.

Fuzzy and Vijay both agreed the in-the-wall-Chevy-Nova (installed by Mom's giant jilted boyfriend Wally) was radical in the extreme. Upstairs, we found much alarming evidence of Lance's loathsome presence, including six neatly pressed, size 48-long Oakland police uniforms hanging in *my* closet. Borrowing Mom's eyebrow trimmers, I snipped every third stitch along the rear seam in all his trousers. Next time he bends over to club a defenseless crack pusher, *r-r-rippppp!* I also borrowed some nail polish and painted a bull's-eye directly over the heart on his bulletproof vest.

Fuzzy and Vijay were inspecting my sister Joanie's old room, now transformed into a frilly pink nursery-in-waiting. "What's with all the baby stuff?" asked Fuzzy.

"My mom's expecting," I confessed.

"God, that's gross," replied Fuzzy. "Isn't she a little old to be cranking them out?"

"Freak of nature, I guess," I said. "I just hope the kid isn't born with two heads. The father was a real moron."

"Is it the fellow she's marrying?" asked Vijay.

"Nah. Another moron. This one croaked from a heart attack."

"Boy," exclaimed Fuzzy, "the kid's not even born yet and he's already half an orphan."

"In my family that can be a decided advantage," I replied.

Before we left, I went into Mom's bedroom and scrawled in scarlet lipstick on her dresser mirror: "YOU'LL BE SORRY!!!"

"Will your mother know who wrote it?" asked Vijay.

"Nah," I replied, "I disguised my handwriting. With any luck she'll think it's a message from some divine Dear Abby."

3:30 pm. As we reached the Santa Cruz city limits, a cold grey rain started falling. I hope this is not an omen. I have memorized the first six salacious lines of you know what.

We just filled up the gas tank: $24.53. I didn't know you could put that much gasoline into a Falcon. I wonder if I'm too young for those "sell your blood for subsistence money" places.

6:15 p.m. I just had an emotional reunion with My One and Only Love. My hands are still shaking. I feel immensely, exultantly alive. Sheeni was delighted, perhaps even thrilled to see me. We luxuriated in a passionate embrace—indifferent to the stares of Vijay, Fuzzy, a half-dozen leering students, and an indignant dorm matron. In her excitement, Sheeni even let out a few words of English. This provoked even more expostulations of outrage from the matron. We were forced to unclinch, but I anticipate an imminent resumption of intimacies.

I am writing this in the back seat of Fuzzy's car, parked just off the posh campus of École des Arts et Littératures. We are waiting for Sheeni and Taggarty to finish dressing and come down to join us. The plan is for all of us to go out to dinner and then walk along the boardwalk (if the rain lets up). They have promised to bring along a date for Fuzzy. (Vijay has laid dibs on Sheeni's sultry roommate.) I only pray they are also bringing along some money.

10:30 p.m. We are back in our parking spot, waiting for Sheeni to come out to tell us the coast is clear. Can only four hours have transpired? It seems like days. Sheeni has courageously agreed to sneak us into her and Taggarty's room to spend the night. This is a major violation of the school's police-state dorm rules. It will be Sheeni's and my first night together. I am hoping the presence of three other people does not limit excessively our opportunities for passionate lovemaking.

Fuzzy was thankful he had retrieved his letter jacket. His date turned out to be a strapping giantess named Heather, star forward of the girls' basketball team. She was dressed for combat in a short skirt that showed off her sinewy leg muscles. Upcourt was a tight red sweater encasing two near-regulation-size NBA game balls. To say Fuzzy was soon lost in the tall Heather would be an understatement. She, in turn, took an immediate shine to her escort after he announced he was presently leading the Redwood Empire Athletic League in pass reception yardage.

Vijay had a more difficult time. The alluring Taggarty (short dark hair, intense green eyes, Manhattan sophistication cloaked in fragile ripeness) seemed more intent on demonstrating that she possessed the largest forebrain in the group than succumbing to his exotic, sub-continental, right-wing charm. In her gratingly shrill, over-cultivated voice, she trotted out more scholarly allusions than an entire month of my letters to Sheeni. It's a wonder she finds any time for sexual conquests with all the fact-cramming she must do.

To his credit, Vijay more than held his own, especially after he commenced a long, florid recitation of Urdu poetry. Taggarty tried to steer the conversation toward a historical analysis of the *Ramayadan* (she must have read the trot on that one), but desisted abruptly when Vijay tripped her up in a glaring factual error. Still, Taggarty is such an intellectual heavyweight she makes everyone except the supremely formidable Sheeni nervous about expressing an opinion. I pity her future fact-riddled husband.

Sheeni is more alarmingly mature and beautiful than ever. She wore a soft, wine-red velvet dress that made her long hair glow like aged bronze. For me, our moments together pass in a fog of exquisite anguish. I want to clutch her to me, lest she pass beyond my humble orbit like some brilliant comet, streaking across the heavens. These sentiments, as you might expect, often render normal speech difficult. Plus, Francois is forever reminding me not to look so love-sick. He says it's bad for our image.

Everyone exclaimed over Fuzzy's rad '60s wheels, so he had to drive like a maniac to the restaurant. (A fancy one, specializing in expensive Mediterranean peasant food. At these prices, no wonder the peasants are impoverished.) Naturally it was Taggarty's choice.

Since the ladies were forgoing their dorm dinner, they all decided to eat heartily: the greedy Taggarty ordering (in Italian, of course) both the soup and an appetizer, plus the most expensive entrée and dessert. Heather made do with a salad, two entrées, and dessert. She's in training and has to keep up her vitality. Sheeni skipped dessert, limiting herself to an appetizer, salad, and entrée (an unappetizing grey blob of mystery animal parts passing under the name sweetbreads). Vijay the Vegetarian had the linguini in cream sauce, Fuzzy experimented with the pizza, and I ordered something called grilled polenta, which arrived looking and tasting suspiciously like fried mush. I almost asked the waiter for some maple syrup, but Francois put his foot down.

From 8:35 to 10:05 the check lay untouched on the table like an unexploded bomb, its menacing presence delaying our departure until it was too late to continue on to the boardwalk. Finally Francois coughed nonchalantly and turned it over. The numbers blew up in his face: $167.23.

Fearing the worst, the waiter had added in a generous 15 percent gratuity. The three men huddled and, after rifling all of our pockets (Fuzzy, to his surprise, found three crumpled twenties and a used condom in his varsity jacket), came up with $135.74. I was forced to write a personal IOU to our companions for the balance. They grumbled but coughed up the cash. Two hundred miles from home and we're now totally broke. Thank God we had the foresight to fill up the gas tank.

Fuzzy drove back to the dorm at 20 mph to conserve fuel. Perhaps he also wanted to prolong his enforced proximity to his nubile jockette. This time I made Vijay sit in the front with them so I could sit next to Sheeni in the back. I held her warm hand and tried, in between interruptions (in French) from the jealous Taggarty, to converse privately with My Love.

"So, Sheeni, how do you like Santa Cruz? Isn't it excessively damp being this close to the ocean?"

"Not at all, Nickie. I'm liking it more and more. The experience has been so broadening. My years in provincial Ukiah now seem like a fast-retreating nightmare. Of course, I do miss you and Albert. How is my darling dog?"

"A bit sluggish these days, I fear," I replied. "He pines for you dreadfully, you know."

"I'm so selfish," she sighed. "Always thinking of my own happiness first. I promise to make it up to you both when we're all reunited in Paris. Did I tell you Taggarty and I have an opportunity to study there next summer? Wouldn't that be wonderful?"

"Next summer!" I exclaimed. "But that was our time to be together in Ukiah."

"I know, Nickie, but this is too extraordinary an opportunity to pass up. I've never been abroad you know. Why don't you come and visit us there? We could go to all the museums and you could work on your French conversational skills."

"And how am I supposed to finance this excursion?" I demanded.

"With the savings from your job, silly," she answered. "You must begin to economize, Nickie."

With some effort of will I let that point drop. "Is Trent going to be studying in Paris also?"

"I believe he's submitted his application," she replied. "But he's trying to find out if they have facilities on the Seine for windsurfing. He's become quite tiresomely fixated on that sport. His poetry is suffering."

"Isn't the Seine polluted?" I asked, entertaining a rapturous vision of a lapsed poet felled by hepatitis.

"Oh, I don't think so," Sheeni answered wistfully. "It looks so poignantly blue in the photographs."

11:30 p.m. (written by flashlight). We are all chastely bedded down for the night (at least some of us are). Taggarty, feigning severe menstrual cramps, distracted the matron while Vijay, Fuzzy, and I—carrying our grips and sleeping bags—sneaked in through the side door. Sheeni and Heather led us on tiptoes up to the third floor. Despite extreme stealth, our presence became known instantly among the occupants of the floor, exciting much giggling in French and running about in near undress. Why do you suppose confining large numbers of teenage girls in one place produces such aberrant behavior? And why is it always the plain ones who take off most of their clothes?

The school buildings are grand mock Georgian on the outside, but the grim interiors (dorm rooms the size of hamster cages) would make Dwayne's incarcerated father restive. Sheeni and Taggarty share a cement block cubicle just big enough for a bunkbed, two small desks, one army surplus dresser, and a diminutive overstuffed armchair.

As the more intelligent and beautiful, Sheeni claimed the bottom bunk. On the wall above her desk she has taped her Jean Paul Belmondo 'Breathless' poster and a photo of Albert and me. Taggarty's wall displays several dozen bus-station photo-machine mugshots of sullen-looking youths, all of whom, presumably, have known her intimately. Written on each photo was a letter from A to F. Taggarty is a hard grader. Most of the guys, I noticed, earned a C-

or below.

"There's your competition," I whispered to Vijay.

"A distinguished group I would be happy to join," he whispered back.

To relieve the overcrowding, Heather suggested Fuzzy come sleep in her room.

"Your roommate won't mind?" he asked, surprised.

"Oh, Darlene went home for the weekend," Heather replied nonchalantly.

Fuzzy gulped. Vijay and I exchanged glances. "That sounds fine," Fuzzy said, picking up his grip. "Well, see you guys in the morning."

Ten minutes later, as we were unrolling our sleeping bags on the floor, we heard a woman's scream through the wall.

"Sounds like your pal plays rough," observed Taggarty.

"We are all of us quite hot-blooded," confirmed Vijay.

We got even more hot-blooded a few minutes later when Taggarty, ostensibly searching for her misplaced nightie, revealed her contempt for bourgeois modesty by walking about with her bra off. She gets a B+ for size, but I would have to subtract points for the droop and nipple hairs. Vijay, though, clearly was awarding her an A. Thankfully, at that moment my discreet girlfriend was in the closet changing into her nightgown (undiaphanous as usual). So Vijay and Francois felt free to stare brazenly. Taggarty didn't seem to mind.

Since the bathroom was down the hall, Taggarty (now clothed provocatively in pale green baby-dolls) stood guard outside the door as Vijay and I leaned over the grungy sinks and brushed our pearlies.

"I am in a state of sexual frenzy," he confessed.

"Welcome to the club," I said.

"What is your plan?" he asked.

"We drape a blanket over the lower bunk for Sheeni and me. You tackle Taggarty on the top bunk."

"Do you have any condoms?"

"Let's see. I slipped two to Fuzzy. So I've still got eight in my pack."

"That should do," said Vijay, gargling. He looked stricken. "What if they don't go for it?"

"They'll go for it," I said. "You can cut the sexual tension in that room with a knife."

Sheeni didn't go for it. She whispered, "Don't be silly, darling. Not with others in the room," gave me a peck on the cheek, and slipped—alone—into her narrow bed.

Taggarty climbed laboriously up to her bunk in the sky, flashing her guests a stimulating eye-full in the process. "Goodnight, boys," she cooed. "Do you need the light on to take off your clothes?"

"No," I said, flipping off the overhead light. "We can find our zippers in the dark."

Gloomily, we stripped down to our underwear and crawled into the sleeping bags. The concrete floor was cold and hard.

"This is most disconcerting," whispered Vijay. "I shall not sleep a wink. Do you think I dare sneak up to Taggarty's after everyone's asleep?"

"It's worth a try," I whispered. "I don't imagine she'd object."

Too tired to write any more, and Vijay keeps looking over and scowling impatiently at me. I wish I hadn't nervously sipped all that water at the restaurant. I have to pee again already.

SUNDAY, October 14 — 6:45 a.m. A disastrous night! We are on the road back to Ukiah. Vijay and Fuzzy are blaming me, but I don't see what they have to complain about. Fuzzy, thanks to some skillful ball-handling by Heather, is now a certified non-virgin. Vijay is about 65% certain he qualifies as one too. I should be so lucky.

The difficulties started when I got up to go to the bathroom. Yes, I was careful and made sure no one was in the hallway or restroom before I ventured forth. After pissing about three gallons, I suddenly developed a killer T.E. Maybe it was from being alone in a girls' bathroom with the exotic ambience and gleaming sanitary napkin dispenser. Anyway, I decided to take a nice hot shower and deal with the T.E. while I was at it. This I did, and as I was toweling off (with a towel I found labelled "Darlene's, Touch It and Die!"), I heard the outside door open. Feeling somewhat exposed, I slipped on my underpants, wrapped the towel around me, and tried to sneak out.

"Who are you?" asked a thin girl with short platinum hair and six earrings per lobe, glancing up from the sink into which she was vomiting.

I paused. "I'm Nick, a friend of Sheeni's. Sorry to disturb you."

"Wait! Don't go!" she gasped, in between heaves.

"Are you OK? Should I go get some help?" I asked, alarmed.

"I'm OK," she said, rinsing out her mouth from the tap. "It was just something I ate. Uh, could I borrow your towel for a second?"

Reluctantly, I handed over the damp towel. She wiped her mouth and looked me up and down with some curiosity. "So, what—are you Sheeni's boyfriend or something?"

"Uh, yeah."

"You're staying the night? Where's Taggarty?"

"Uh, she's . . . she's sleeping. A friend and I are just, just camping on the floor."

"I get it. A slumber party. Any more boys on the floor I should know about?"

"Well, there's my friend Fuzzy in Heather's room."

"Fuzzy. That's a cute name. My name's Bernice, by the way, not that you asked. Not that anyone does."

"Nice to meet you, Bernice," I added hastily. "I just feel a little, uh, uncomfortable standing here in my underwear."

"What for? You have an OK body."

"Thanks," I said. Francois added, "You do too."

"I'm totally gross," she replied with a sneer. "So, you really like Sheeni, huh?"

"Yes, don't you?"

"Personally, I hate her guts."

"Why?" I asked, shocked.

"I have my reasons." She read my mind. "Don't worry, I won't snitch on you. Well, pardon me, Nick. I feel like throwing up some more now."

"You're sure you're OK?"

Bending over the sink, she frowned and waved me away.

When I got back to the room, Vijay's sleeping bag was empty. The room was quiet except for some heavy breathing up near the ceiling. Exhausted, I crawled into my sleeping bag and dropped immediately into an uneasy sleep.

I awoke 20 minutes later—the beam of a powerful flashlight in my eyes and high-decibel French expletives in my ears. The matron! Behind her, peering into the room and smiling diabolically, stood Bernice. And to think just a short time before I had kindly lent her my towel. What ingratitude!

Two confused, frenetic, nightmarish minutes later, we were standing by the car in a cold rain waiting for Fuzzy, dressed only in a Marauding Beavers varsity letter jacket, to put on his pants so he could look for his car keys. Vijay, barefoot and naked from the waist up, was shivering uncontrollably from fright, the cold, and undischarged sexual tension. I had managed to toss on most of my clothes, but had misplaced my jacket. Fortunately, I remembered to grab my sleeping bag, which I was now wearing poncho-style. Vijay, distracted by his naked climb down from Taggarty's romantic mountaintop, had not been so quick-minded. He was without shirt, socks, shoes, jacket, or poncho. Worse, at that moment, we knew, our dates were somewhere locked in an office, being harangued in high-volume French.

Sheeni, through the tumult, displayed her usual magnificent poise. She rose placidly from her bed, replied to the matron's diatribes in demure, sedate French, and even had the presence of mind to hold a blanket up while Vijay stumbled into his shorts and trousers.

As we were bolting the premises, she spoke to me rapidly in French. Vijay translated after we got into the car and he had wrapped his shivering nakedness in my damp sleeping bag. "Sheeni said-d-d it would b-b-be wise for us to d-d-depart im-m-mediately," he chattered. "Sh-sh-she expressed a f-f-fear the ma-matron m-m-might call the c-c-co-co-cops."

But Fuzzy was already laying rubber, as he floored the aged V-8 and pointed our fleet Falcon homeward.

As we sped up the mountain road leading out of town, we reflected on that evening's developments.

"I did it three times," announced our driver. "Two quick ones, and then the last one lasted a long time."

"But I only gave you two condoms," I pointed out.

"I had to borrow the last one from Heather," Fuzzy replied. "She swiped it from her roommate's private stash."

"So how was it?" I asked, trying not to sound too envious.

"Great," he replied. "I thought it might be like riding a bicycle—you know, something you have to fall down a few times learning how to do. But it really does come naturally. I mean, you're lying there on top of her. She's squirming around, naked as a clam. And you say to yourself, 'this really does feel right. I know what to do next.' Didn't you find that was true with you and Sheeni?"

"Oh, of course," I lied. "It's all instinctual behavior. We're animals after all."

"I fear it could be terribly addicting," added Vijay. "This night has ignited in me a lust of disturbing insatiability."

"Me too," confessed Fuzzy. "So Taggarty put out?"

"Most enthusiastically. We were approaching the consummation of the act when the authorities broke in. I may in fact have passed beyond the portals. It was very difficult to tell with that damn condom. Nick, why do you buy such thick ones?"

"Sheeni insists on it," I replied. "That brand was top-rated by *Consumer Reports*."

"Well, she's safe," he exclaimed. "No organisms could penetrate those stout walls."

"What do you think they'll do with the girls?" asked Fuzzy.

"Notify their parents, I should think," said Vijay. "Perhaps even expel them."

EXPEL THEM! OF COURSE! IT'S ALL GOING TO TURN OUT FOR THE GOOD! SHEENI'S REACTIONARY PARENTS ARE CERTAIN TO BE OUT-RAGED AND DEMAND HER RETURN. THANK YOU, BERNICE, YOU SWEET ANGEL OF THE LAVATORY!

Only now I wish I'd had the guts to climb into Sheeni's bed. Surely being discovered in *flagrante delicto* is inextenuatory grounds for expulsion.

I just remembered. I forgot my copy of "The Rime of the Ancient Mariner." More disappointments for Mr. Preston from the Twisp family.

10:30 a.m. (Hitchhiking somewhere in San Jose). We ran out of gas on the freeway! After barely travelling 50 miles.

"This is impossible!" screamed Fuzzy, staring in disbelief at the gauge as we coasted to the shoulder. "We had a full tank!"

"Well," said Vijay, "either there's a leak somewhere or some wretched dacoit siphoned out our petrol last night. Does this car have a locking cap?"

"Are you kidding?" replied Fuzzy. "They didn't have crime back in 1965. Fuck! Now, what'll we do, guys?"

We sat in silence, looking out at the cars whizzing by in the cold grey rain.

"Well," I said, "we can't stay in the car. Sooner or later the Highway Patrol will stop and want to see Fuzzy's driver's licence."

"But what'll we do?" protested Fuzzy. "We don't have any money!"

"I don't have any shoes!" objected Vijay.

"We haven't had breakfast!" lamented Fuzzy.

"I don't have a jacket!" complained Vijay.

"I can't leave my grandmother's car!" whined Fuzzy.

"I'll catch pneumonia!" puled Vijay. "And die an indeterminate proto-quasi-virgin!"

"We'll all go to prison for car theft!" simpered Fuzzy.

"Exactly," I said, trying to remain calm. "That's why we have to ditch this car right now. We'll hitch as far as Oakland and I'll get some money in my mom's house. Then we'll take the bus to Ukiah. With any luck we'll get there tonight and nobody'll be any the wiser."

"But what about the car!" wailed Fuzzy.

"The cops'll find it and trace it on the computer. They'll get it back to your grandmother. Don't worry."

"But they'll know it was us!" whimpered Fuzzy, starting to cry.

"Not necessarily," said Vijay, thinking out loud. "We'll wipe down our fingerprints and leave them a red herring."

"What's that?" asked Fuzzy.

"Your jacket," replied Vijay.

"My jacket?" he gulped.

"OK, Fuzzy," I said, "'Fess up. Whose is it?"

Fuzzy clutched the jacket to his bare but furry chest. "Mine!"

"Well, my friend," said Vijay, "I have not been in your country very long. But one thing I am certain of: they do not award varsity letter jackets to the assistant manager of football teams."

"At least not on his first day," I agreed. "OK, Fuzzy. Spill it."

Slowly, Fuzzy opened his right lapel. Vijay read the name inscribed above the breast pocket. "Bruno Modjaleski. I might have known."

Bruno arrested for car theft! More than I ever dared hope for!

"Where did you get that jacket?" demanded Vijay.

"Bruno left it on the bus after Friday's game," sniffed Fuzzy indignantly. "I guess he was bummed we got creamed again. So I picked it up to bring to him on Monday. That's part of my job as assistant manager."

"I see," replied Vijay. "And I suppose it is also your job to wear it all weekend for purposes of wooing impressionable young women."

"Well, that's what letter jackets are for!" retorted Fuzzy.

He had a point there. Vijay was unpersuaded. "I'm sorry, Fuzzy, but you'll have to leave behind your emblem of athletic glory. We must employ it to divert the suspicions of the police."

"Vijay, you just want me to take off my jacket so I can freeze in the rain like you," protested Fuzzy.

"Don't complain," Vijay replied. "At least you've got shoes!"

Five minutes later, rubberneckers slowed, but no good samaritans stopped, as three half-naked youths, wrapped in one wet sleeping bag, trooped up the freeway offramp into soggy, grey San Jose.

11:45 a.m. Too cold, wet, and hungry to write much. No luck hitchhiking. Vijay is afraid we look too much like the homeless.

"In Pune I used to pass hundreds of barefoot and shirtless indigents and never give them a second glance," he confessed. "I never imagined that I myself someday would be experiencing hardships at a similar perceived social stratum. It is quite embarrassing."

Fuzzy and I are all for swiping another car, but Vijay is adamantly opposed.

"Too dangerous," he objected. "That's a felony, you know. With an automobile theft conviction on my record, I'd never win admission to Stanford University. Besides, you boys are citizens. The authorities might deport me. I dare not risk that disgrace to my family. And think what such an ignominy would do to my marriage prospects."

"But we already stole one car," I pointed out. "What is your future bride going to say about that?"

"She is going to remain entirely ignorant of all my misdeeds, both criminal and carnal," he replied. "That is the duty of a good Indian husband."

"Couldn't we call some of your bigshot Republicans buddies or the Indian Consulate?" suggested Fuzzy.

"I don't think so," replied Vijay. "But you just gave me an idea."

1:15 p.m. (on the road to Oakland). We're taking a taxi. We dredged up 35 cents and Vijay called the Khalja Cab Company. Our driver is a big Sikh fellow wearing a real turban. Vijay told him in Hindi that we were waylaid by bandits and promised, if he drove us to Oakland, that my wealthy parents would give him a big reward. The driver was suspicious, but Vijay's affluent accent and condescending manner finally persuaded him there could be some tall rupees waiting in Oakland. I just hope Mom left some money in the house. The meter has already clicked past $80 and I seem to remember from somewhere that these guys all carry knives.

2:30 p.m. Home in Oakland. I never imagined its dreary walls could ever look so welcome. An exhaustive search failed to turn up any money, so I had to offer the driver Mom's TV. He said it was old and insisted on taking the VCR too. Looks like Lance will have another burglary to investigate when he returns from his honeymoon. Fortunately, Mom lives in one of the crime capitals of America, so her dim new hubby-cop is unlikely to suspect an inside job. I have also taken the precaution of breaking a window on the back porch.

After everyone took prolonged hot showers to warm up, we scrounged up some clothes, then raided the kitchen. The pickings were meager all around. My companions were reduced to borrowing assorted parts of Lance's police uniforms. Since Lance's shoes were too big, Vijay borrowed a pair of my mother's. To his consternation, the only pair that fit were her most elevated red spike heels. His walk is precarious, but he appreciates the extra stature. "Look, fellows!" he called, tottering out of her bedroom. "I'm six feet tall!"

After helping Vijay down the stairs, we dined on Saltines with dill pickle slices and kidney beans out of the can. Not even a warm rootbeer to wash it down with. As we snacked, I called around to see if I could raise bus fare to Ukiah. I dialed the affluent and freely giving Millie Filbert, but her mother said she was out visiting Clive Bosendorf in the hospital.

"Uh, what's the matter with Clive?" I asked, fearing the worst.

"The unfortunate boy has a fractured arm and pelvis," she replied. "One of his school mates went berserk and assaulted him."

Uh-oh. Quickly I dialed Lefty's number. His obnoxious older sister Martha answered.

"My parents are going to get a restraining order against you, Nick Twisp," she announced.

"What did I do now?" I demanded.

"You know what you did. You goaded Lefty into beating up Clive Bosendorf. Now Lefty's in detention and Clive's parents are threatening to sue us for everything we own."

"The cops have got Lefty?" I asked, shocked.

"My mom and dad are bringing him home today. He has to go to juvenile court when Clive gets out of the hospital. Thanks to you!"

"I don't know what untruths Lefty may be spreading," I replied, with innocent calmness. "But I had nothing to do with his coming to blows with Clive. I suggest he call me tomorrow."

"I suggest you resign from the human race, Nick Twisp," she answered. "You are a menace to society." *Click.*

"Are they giving us the bus fare?" asked Fuzzy.

"Er, no," I said. "Looks like we'll have to go to Plan 2."

5:15 p.m. (on the road to Ukiah). Mom's left-wing, pinko, Fidel-loving neighbor, Mr. Ferguson, couldn't loan us the bus fare (his Social Security check was delayed by Republican red tape), but he offered to drive us in his old Toyota (hand-painted May Day red).

I explained that Fuzzy and I were smuggling a young illegal immigrant, fleeing political oppression on the sub-continent, to a sanctuary in Mendocino County. Ever compassionate toward the downtrodden, Mr. Ferguson agreed to help, and also promised not to divulge to anyone our presence in the neighborhood today—not even to Mom or persons purporting to be her husband.

The elderly radical positioned himself in the driveway to keep a sharp lookout for INS agents while we sneaked our charge through the bushes to the car. He struggled to hide his surprise when Vijay hobbled into view.

"By persecuting homosexuals," observed Mr. Ferguson, "our capitalist rulers divide the working class and pit workers against the intelligentsia. Sexual oppression is one of the oligarchy's most powerful tools in perpetuating its hegemony."

"Sodomy is an abomination that must be punished," replied the refugee with conviction.

Mr. Ferguson looked confused.

"Brainwashed," I explained, pushing Vijay into the back seat. "He's still undergoing doctrinal deprogramming."

However fiery his politics, Mr. Ferguson is all meekness on the highway. At our present rate of speed, we have an ETA of a week from next Thursday.

"Would you like me to drive, Mr. Ferguson?" suggested Fuzzy, tired of watching the telephone poles crawl by.

"How old are you, young man?" he asked.

"Twenty-six."

"Oh. Well, OK. My eyes aren't as sharp as they used to be. Try to keep it under 40."

Fuzzy soon had the ancient four-banger cranked up to top speed—62 miles per hour. It might have reached 65, were it not for the wind drag created by dozens of seditious bumperstickers plastered over the fenders.

Mr. Ferguson turned in his seat and looked back toward Vijay. "And how old are you, lad?" he asked kindly.

"I'm 37," Vijay replied.

"Goodness, I would have placed you still in school," he exclaimed.

"It is my non-Western diet," explained Vijay earnestly. "I eat only whole grains and the pit of the green mango. I also make it a practice to drink a generous cup of my own urine every morning."

"I see," said Mr. Ferguson. "That's a good tip. And may I ask why you wear those shoes?"

"It is to achieve elevation above the soil. Prolonged contact with the earth results in the draining off of vital electrons, leading to the imperfect cell division we know as aging."

"How fascinating," exclaimed our benefactor. "We Westerners have much to learn from the wisdom of the East."

"Perception is the first step toward knowledge," replied the youthful sage. "The mind follows where the chicken pecks, we like to say."

"Exactly so," agreed the radical pensioner, "exactly so."

I nodded off as Vijay and Mr. Ferguson continued their discussion. When I awoke, some time later, night had fallen, and Fuzzy was stopped at a light in downtown Ukiah. Home at last!

"Then why do the elites permit the establishment of universal suffrage?" Vijay was insisting. "Does this not give the masses the power to redistribute wealth through taxation?"

Mr. Ferguson snorted. "Not as long as the rich control the media and the nomination process, and finance the campaigns. Wake up, son. You're a pawn!"

"Perhaps," replied Vijay. "But at least I do not have some ignorant, unwashed, upstart ruffian telling me what I may and may not do, read, and think. That is the world you would create. People do not act according to your enlightened ideals. They are more inclined to destroy than build. A stable society must be structured to suppress man's innate evil. Humans are greedy, envious, covetous, and murderous."

"Well, at least the Republicans are," I observed.

Vijay poked me in the ribs. "You have deafened us with your snoring, Nick! Do not assault us further with your inane opinions!"

"Sheeni is a card-carrying liberal," I taunted.

"She is beautifully misguided," replied Vijay. "I hope someday I shall have an opportunity to change that."

What did he mean by that?

8:10 p.m. We dropped Vijay off first.

"What explanation shall I offer my parents concerning my clothes?" he whispered.

"Say you've been invited to join a fraternity at school," I replied. "Tell them the clothes are part of an initiation ritual. They won't mind. Parents love to think their kids are at the center of the social vortex."

"Good idea. I'll try it."

"Keep a sharp eye out for INS agents, young man," called Mr. Ferguson.

"I will," Vijay answered. "Thank you for your help. I hope my candid expression of contrary beliefs has not offended you."

"Nothing offends me any more, son. Except apathy."

Fuzzy drove on to his palatial home, parked, and handed the keys back to the owner. "Thanks, Mr. Ferguson. Nice car you got. See you tomorrow, Nick."

"Oh, Fuzzy," I said. "I meant to ask you. What was that scream we heard last night from your room?"

"That was Heather. She was helping me off with my shirt and I guess something scared her."

"Maybe it was your muscles."

"Probably so," he replied. "I've been working out a lot lately."

10:45 p.m. Since Mr. Ferguson looked tired from the long drive, I invited him to spend the night. It was the least I could do. And I figured it would give Dad a chance to reciprocate for all the nights he spent on Mr. Ferguson's couch before he and Mom finally tossed in the towel.

"Hi, Dad," I said. "Guess what? I ran into Mr. Ferguson downtown. Is it OK if he spends the night?"

"Hello, George," beamed Mr. Ferguson, holding out his hand. "Long time no see."

Dad, looking dazed, did not shake hands. His right hand, I noticed, was bandaged in gauze. "Oh, hello Judd. This is a surprise. Well, uh, let's see . . . I suppose we might be able to put you up."

"What happened to your paw, George?" asked Mr. Ferguson.

"Ran my thumb through a bandsaw, Judd." Dad declared proudly. "Almost sliced it clear off. The wound required 38 stitches to close."

"That so," Mr. Ferguson exclaimed. "I didn't know you were interested in carpentry, George."

"I'm not," Dad replied. "And if I didn't work for the son-of-a-bitch responsible, I'd sue the bastard for my injuries."

Uh-oh, sounds like *Progressive Plywood's* new filing cabinet may be slightly delayed.

Famished, I raided the refrigerator while they worked out the accommodations. By shifting the reluctant Lacey back into Dad's bed, they were able to free up the living room sofa for our guest.

11:30 p.m. With everyone snoring peacefully, I sneaked into the kitchen and dialed Sheeni long-distance. It was answered in French, but I recognized the shrill, over-cultured voice.

"Taggarty, this is Nick. Is Sheeni there?"

"Nickie, darling. How nice to hear from you. Sorry about that unpleasant scene last night. Bernice can be so tiresome. No one likes her, you know. Did you get home OK? How's Vijay? When you see him, can you ask him to send me a wallet-size photo? Now it must be wallet-size, I'm firm on that. Could you do that, Nickie, please?"

"Yes, Taggarty. I will. Now, can I speak to Sheeni?"

"Certainly, Nickie. She's right here."

"Hello, darling," Sheeni whispered. "Are you all right?"

"Yes, darling. We had a bit of car trouble on the way. But we made it back finally. Have you all been expelled?" I asked hopefully.

"Of course not, darling. The matron likes to bluster, but that's just her character. She's so delightfully French. We told her it was all very innocent, so she's agreed not to inform the dean."

"But Vijay was naked. And so was Fuzzy."

"Were they, darling? Oh, it was dark. I don't think anyone noticed."

"Are you kidding? The matron had her flashlight trained on Vijay's condom-equipped boner. I saw it with my own eyes!"

"Well, perhaps she doesn't see quite as well as you do, Nickie. Anyway, I think she's rather given up defending Taggarty's virtue. The last time she called Taggarty's parents about a similar incident, they laughed at her."

"You mean she didn't call your parents?" I asked, incredulous.

"No, thank God. I'm sure they'd be hysterical. It's a good thing we weren't doing anything but sleeping when the matron broke in."

"I've been meaning to complain about that, Sheeni. I go to all the trouble of stealing a car and driving 200 miles, just to have a totally celibate night while everyone else is going at it like crazed rabbits. Is that fair?"

"Well, you should have given me some notice, Nickie. We could have found another room for Taggarty and been alone together. Remember, darling, I'm just as frustrated as you are."

I doubt that.

Sheeni continued, "And you shouldn't have stolen that car. Or blabbed so much to Bernice."

"How was I to know she was the Mata Hari of the third floor? Why does she hate you so much?"

"I really have no idea, Nickie. I've made an effort to be nice to her. She thinks there's a conspiracy to exclude her from our activities. But it's just her rude unpleasantness that puts everyone off."

"What's her last name?" I asked.

"A rather grim one: Lynch. Why do you ask?"

"Oh, just curious. Well, darling, it was great seeing you."

"Oh, Nickie, I'm so happy you came down. I'm sorry things didn't work out."

Bernice Lynch, hmm. Yes, I think she will do nicely.

MONDAY, October 15 — I decided to stay home from school and my job today to rest up from the rigors of the weekend, duck my recital-anticipating employer, and attend to the needs of Mr. Ferguson. He's presently lying on the living room couch moaning with stomach cramps. He says it may be an allergic reaction to something he consumed this morning. Lacey offered to drive him to a doctor, but he refused politely and went on moaning. I hope he doesn't die, though at his age the prospect of death must loom larger with every miraculous breath—rather like the prospect of getting laid looms in the lives of people my age.

At 8:15 this morning a call came in for me. I knew who it must be.

"Hello," I said, "I suppose you detest my putrid guts."

"That's right," confirmed Lefty. "And I really mean it this time. I'm in the biggest pile of shit of my life, thanks to you."

"Lefty, I told you to rough up Clive a little, not murder him. What did you do, beat him with a two-by-four?"

"I just pushed him down! How was I to know the shrimp's glandular condition gave him brittle bones? His parents oughta make him wear a sign or something. Hey man, I got a glandular condition too."

"And a very important gland it is," I agreed. "Clearly, Lefty, you are not culpable here. Just tell the judge you were playing tackle football and mistakenly thought Clive was in possession of the ball. I'm sure he'll let you off."

"What about the leather jacket and the boombox?"

"Uh, what jacket and boombox?"

Lefty sighed. "The ones I had with me when the cops took me down to juvenile hall. The ones with the price tags still on them that I didn't have no receipts for."

"Oh those," I said. "Damn, they got you for shoplifting too, huh?"

"Grand larceny!" he exclaimed. "Even though the jacket's really cheap leather and the boombox doesn't even have a CD player."

"Did you admit you stole them?"

"No way. You think I'm stupid? I said I found 'em. The cops didn't believe me though."

"OK, Lefty. Here's what you do. You say you felt so guilty about hurting Clive, you didn't want to tell the truth. But now you realize you have to. It was Clive who stole the goods, and you were trying to persuade him to take them back when he accidentally got pushed down."

"Wow, Nick!" exclaimed Lefty. "That is pure genius!"

"You'll have to look sincere. Maybe cry a little. Can you do it?"

"Oh man, I'll put on such an acting job, even Clive'll think he's guilty."

"I know you can do it, Lefty. You're a really talented liar."

"Thanks, Nick. But what if they call Millie as a witness? She knows all about the stuff I've swiped. She could put me away for 20 years."

"You've got to win Millie back over to your side. Fast."

"How do I do that? She spends all her free time at the hospital visiting that faker Bosendorf."

"Millie has a natural affinity for the sick," I observed. "That's why she wants to be an anesthesiologist. To get her back, you simply have to be sicker than Clive. You have to get in the hospital too. Plus, it will give you some valuable sympathy points with the judge."

"But I'm not sick," protested Lefty. "I feel fine."

"Well, haven't your parents been bugging you to get that operation?"

"No way are those doctors going to cut on me down there!" he declared.

"Now's the time for it, Lefty," I insisted. "It's perfect. You'll get everything straightened out—your police record, Clive Bosendorf, Millie Filbert, and your dick. You'll have a completely clean slate."

"You think so, Nick?" said Lefty, starting to waver. "Would you do it? Really?"

"In a flash. As soon as we hang up, grab your crotch and start bellowing. By tonight, I guarantee it, Millie Filbert will be at your bedside feeding you restorative soup."

"Soup makes me pee," he complained. "What if it hurts? What if I get a hard-on from seeing Millie and I start ripping my stitches?"

"The doctors think of all that," I said. "Don't worry!"

"OK, Nick. But if this doesn't work, I am really going to despise you. Our friendship will be over for all time."

"Trust me, Lefty. This plan cannot fail. Plus, think of all the school you'll get to miss."

"Hey, that's true. I got a big chemistry test on Wednesday too. OK, I'll do it!"

2:15 p.m. I just finished transcribing my journal into the computer. What a lot of tedious typing. I'll be glad when I'm a prominent author and can hire Miss Pliny to do all my irksome secretarial tasks.

I also wrote this letter to my new friend in Santa Cruz:

Dear Bernice,

It was nice meeting you this weekend in the bathroom. I hope you're feeling better. I just want you to know I think you did the right thing by informing the matron of our presence. We had no business being there infringing on your privacy. Taggarty and Sheeni should be punished for violating the rules.

Unfortunately, Sheeni is conspiring with the matron to prevent news of her flagrant misconduct from reaching her parents. A sense of fair play compels me to ask if you would be so kind as to write a letter (preferably on official school stationery) to Sheeni's mother and father outlining the events of last Saturday night. I have enclosed their address.

In case it was not apparent, I should like to confirm that some of my companions were indeed completely unclothed when discovered. You also might mention that one of the youths in Sheeni's own bedroom was discovered to be wearing a sexual apparatus.

Did you know that when Sheeni went to school here in Ukiah she was universally disliked by her fellow female students? You were most perceptive to see so quickly through her pretense of genial affability. I think it would serve both our interests if you could keep me informed of any and all matters relating to Sheeni's relationships with the opposite sex, especially a recent transferee named Trent Preston. I appreciate your assistance and look forward to hearing from you soon.

Your friend,

Nick Twisp

P.S. Loved your earrings!

3:30 p.m. As Mr. Ferguson had stopped moaning in pain and was feeling better, he accompanied me and Albert on a walk down to the highway to mail my important letter.

"It's nice being out in the country," observed my companion, drawing fresh, dusty air into his aged lungs. "It's so peaceful here."

It was not quite so peaceful in front of the cement plant, where a line of militant-looking men with beer guts were marching back and forth carrying signs. The placards read "Unfair!"—a complaint, it seems to me, you could make about virtually any employment. Why, I wondered, did these whiners think they were so special?

Mr. Ferguson soon got the whole story. The men are cement truck drivers on strike for higher wages. As if $11.63 an hour weren't adequate! I'd take it in a minute.

Naturally, Mr. Ferguson was completely sympathetic and felt compelled to give an embarrassing speech about worker solidarity to boost morale. The men looked confused, but listened politely and gave a dispirited cheer when he finally stopped. I watched with alarm as a sheriff's deputy, posted at the gate to keep labor and management from armed conflict, retrieved a camera from his squad car and took Mr. Ferguson's picture. The elderly agitator didn't seem to mind.

Mr. Ferguson was still fired up as we walked back. "Nick, do you realize what it would mean if those courageous boys win their strike?"

"Sure, it means hundreds of big, noisy, fume-spewing trucks will start rumbling past the house again. Waking me up at 6:30 every morning, including Saturdays."

"No. It means higher wages, shorter hours, and better working conditions.

It means new hope for dozens of families!"

Why does that fail to suck the living socks from my feet?

6:30 p.m. Mrs. Crampton has passed her probation period. She is now a permanent employee, entitled to all the rights and privileges that that position does entail. She received the good news from Lacey with a yawn, then proceeded to shuffle through her duties like an apprentice somnambulist. She nodded off leaning against the stove and boiled the spaghetti for 45 minutes. This, it turns out, is just how Mr. Ferguson prefers it. He needs new dentures, but the appropriation was scuttled in Congress by reactionary Republicans.

Dad was surprised to find Mr. Ferguson still here and was even more surprised when Lacey invited him to dinner. Mr. Ferguson ate almost as much as Dwayne and helped himself to the wine too. He tried to get Mrs. Crampton to discuss her life as an exploited service worker, but extreme fatigue had brought her languid speech to a virtual standstill. I grew so impatient waiting for her next word to dribble out, it was all I could do to keep from screaming. You can imagine the reaction of my time-conscious, Type-A dad. I thought he was going to have a stroke and collapse face-first into his meatballs.

After dinner I had a private conversation in the kitchen with the dishwasher.

"Dwayne, there seems to be something amiss here," I said.

"You noticed, huh?" he replied. "Mom don't take hot drinks in the evening. So I been puttin' the pills in her morning coffee. I kinda like it, 'cause she don't pay much attention to what I do now. I didn't wear no underpants to school today, and she didn't even notice. I'm not wearin' none now, Nick."

I pretended I hadn't heard that last remark. "Dwayne, we need your mother awake to cook dinner. In her present inalert state she could accidentally thicken the gravy with rat bait. Then where would we be?"

"Dead?" suggested Dwayne.

"Some of us," I replied. "The heavy eaters at least."

Dwayne gulped. "All right, Nick. What should I do with the pills then?"

"Save them and give them to me," I replied.

"OK, Nick," he assented. "What you goin' to do with 'em?"

"That's confidential."

Strong sedatives: something every enterprising teen should have on hand for emergencies.

"Are you wearin' underpants?" inquired Dwayne conspiratorily.

"That is none of your business I'm sure. Gee, it's too bad Dad doesn't believe in Teflon. That meatball pan looks like something out of the Middle Ages."

10:15 p.m. Mr. Ferguson is bedding down on the sofa again. Lacey said he had too much to drink to drive home tonight. She is making up a bed for herself on the floor in the third bedroom, a chamber Dad pretentiously refers to as "his study." It contains his meager library, long-silent typewriter, and the scribbled notes to his magnum opus—a work of fiction presently stalled on page 12.

TUESDAY, October 16 — Fuzzy wasn't in school today. His grandmother died! In fact she and her wayward Falcon expired almost simultaneously. Vijay got the scoop from Fuzzy last night by phone. Things are very tense with the DeFalcos. Right when the doctors pulled the plug, Fuzzy's uncle Polly (short for Polonious) raced to Granny's house to claim her car. When he discovered it missing, he put two and two together and concluded that Fuzzy's dad had prematurely and unfairly jumped the gun. Meanwhile, Fuzzy's dad is convinced his lying brother has surreptitiously moved the car to an undisclosed location for purposes of cheating him out of his rightful inheritance as elder son. The families are now well past the name-calling stage. Since no one is willing to discuss funeral arrangements until the car is returned, Granny has been put temporarily on ice. Wisely, Fuzzy has kept his furry lips zipped tight through it all.

Vijay was thrilled by the news that Taggarty requested his photo for her love wall. He views this as confirmation that the act was indeed consummated. Unfortunately, the only photo he could produce was a school picture taken last term in which he resembles a more than usually nerdlike nine-year-old. Since Taggarty sounded pretty impatient, I told him it would have to do. He made me promise to find out from Sheeni as soon as possible his assigned love grade.

"I'm certain I did well," said Vijay confidently. "I know the *Kama Sutra* backwards and forwards."

"Speaking of enlightened sexuality," I said, "what did your parents say when you walked in wearing high heels?"

"They thought it was puzzling, but tremendously quaint. At times it is such an asset having parents from another culture. They believe the most improbable stories. My sister was more suspicious, but I bought her off by making her a gift of the shoes. I hope you don't mind. They were just her size—though I can't imagine Father permitting her to wear them out of the house."

I only got to line four of "The Rime of Ancient Mariner" at work today. I told Mr. Preston I was still so traumatized by Dad's injuries I couldn't concentrate. He swallowed guiltily, and excused me from the balance of the recitation. Dad, I noticed, has also been mining this rich vein. Every time Mr. Preston walked past, Dad let out a pitiful groan. Since Dad can't type (at least not with both hands), he's been excused from most of his work. He takes long coffee breaks, ventilates his bandage out on the fire escape with a cigarette or two, returns for a little light paper shuffling, then chats up Miss Pliny or the art director, Mr. Rogavere, until quitting time. What a role model. It's no wonder I have a bad attitude toward work.

7:15 p.m. Mr. Ferguson is still here. He spent the day on the cement plant picket line and was too tired to drive home. Diplomatically, he returned with an expensive bottle of zin to appease Dad and bouquets of carnations for Lacey and Mrs. Crampton. Dad grumbled, but said he could stay one more night. Lacey, of course, welcomes his company, since having such a chatty person around makes it easier for her to snub Dad. They talked at length about the brave strikers and evil bosses. Lacey was quite sympathetic and promised to visit the picket line on Saturday for some of her patented feminine morale boosting. Mrs. Crampton, looking alert and well-rested, promised to bake some brownies for Lacey to distribute to the "nice Teamsters."

"Can I have some to?" asked Dwayne.

"No! You're ... being ... punished," drawled his mother. "I don't ... know what's ... got ... into that boy," she continued. "I caught ... him ... this morning ... trying to sneak ... off to school ... without ... his underwear!"

WEDNESDAY, October 17 — Bruno Modjaleski's been arrested! Two Ukiah cops dragged him out of Mr. Freerpit's health class at 10:05 a.m. By 10:09 the news was all over the school. The charge is first-degree auto theft. Later at lunch Fuzzy confided that his uncle Polly wants Bruno prosecuted for manslaughter as well. "He thinks Grandmamma could tell her car had been tampered with," whispered Fuzzy. "He claims that's what killed her."

"Nonsense," hissed Vijay. "Your grandmother was a 92-year-old vegetable. Only the machines were keeping her alive."

"Did they get the car back?" I asked uneasily.

"Dad and my uncle left for San Jose this morning," replied Fuzzy. "It took them a while to work out the details. Dad's going to drive the Falcon back and Uncle Polly's driving Dad's car as a security deposit."

"A security deposit?" asked Vijay.

"To make sure Dad doesn't steal the Falcon," explained Fuzzy. "I can't believe they're making all this fuss over an old lady's boring car. You'd think it was something hot like a Camaro."

"When are they going to inter the deceased?" inquired Vijay.

"On Saturday. You guys are invited. Come on over. They'll be lots of good Italian food."

"There won't be any corpses lying about will there?" asked Vijay.

"Nah. Grandmamma's making her last ride in the morning. You guys come over in the afternoon. Maybe they'll rent a U-Haul and have her towed out to the cemetery by the Falcon. She might have wanted it that way."

7:30 p.m. Since it was raining, my generous dad offered me a ride home from the office. He's worked out a way to shift his fine German gearstick by gripping the metal shaft with his unbandaged pinkie. Despite occasionally grinding the gears and being forced by a Mexican in an old pickup truck to back down or lose a fender in a lane merge, Dad remained suspiciously cheerful the entire drive.

Dad's houseguest has finally departed, perhaps that's lightened his spirits. On his way back to Oakland, Mr. Ferguson stopped downtown for a long, friendly chat with Dad on the fire escape (now facetiously designated "Mr. Twisp's office" by Miss Pliny). Dad's been whistling like a cretin ever since. Maybe Mr. Ferguson filled him in on what a rat Mom just got shackled to.

When we got home, a large cardboard box from Sheeni was waiting for me in the middle of the living room. I tried to sneak it into my room, but Dad made me open it right there. Inside was a short mash note and assorted sleeping bags, packs, clothing, and a dog-eared copy of "The Rime of the Ancient Mariner."

"What's all this stuff?" demanded Dad.

"Earthquake relief supplies," I replied. "We're collecting them at school."

"That looks like the jacket I bought you last summer at the flea market," he pointed out.

"No, Dad," I replied. "The jacket you bought was much nicer."

"Well, yeah. I guess it was."

Lacey came home five minutes later with a used, soggy mattress (twin size) strapped to the roof of her Toyota. Dad cheerfully refused to help her unload, so Dwayne and I had to lug the damp, floppy bundle into Dad's erstwhile study. It appears Lacey won't be sleeping on the floor another night—nor, alas, exposing to passersby her incomparable charms on the couch.

During dinner (Mrs. Crampton's famous red-meat-down-the-sluice-gates potroast), Lacey steadfastly ignored her alleged boyfriend and conversed with me instead.

"I had a client in today who says she knows you," she announced.

"Who was that?" I asked.

"I didn't get her name. She was an Indian girl. Very attractive . . ."

Apurva!

" . . . Beautiful thick hair—she wanted it all chopped off, but I just evened up the edges and got rid of the bangs. I managed to convince her that short hair would be a mistake with her bone structure."

"Did she have feathers stuck in her hair?" asked Dwayne.

"No, she wasn't that kind of Indian," said Lacey. "She was from India. Where they don't eat cows."

"No potroast!" exclaimed Dwayne in wonder, displaying a large quantity of the comestibles in question undergoing mastication. I kicked him hard under the table.

"What did she say about me?" I demanded.

"She said she thought you were a very nice boy. Very charming and cute."

"Must be two Nick Twisps in this town," commented Dad, swilling the zin. We both ignored him. "What else did she say?" I asked breathlessly.

"Well let's see. She said she was mad at her father. That's why she wanted to cut off all her hair. She's fond of a boy who lives out of town, but her father doesn't approve of him. He keeps intercepting her mail and tearing up letters from her friend. Can you imagine that? In America? In this age?"

"My mother tore up my love letters," I pointed out.

"Your mother has had a difficult time," observed Lacey, glancing at the zin-swiller. "She's had a great deal to put up with. I am just beginning to appreciate that now."

"Are you by any chance referring to me?" slurred Dad.

"If the shoe fits," replied Lacey, mixing her metaphors, "suck on it."

"We'll see who's sucking on what soon," Dad replied ominously.

The guy has something nasty up his sleeve. I can tell.

8:45 p.m. Fuzzy just called with amazing news. He found out at football practice that reliable sources on the jock grapevine are reporting that Bruno Modjaleski doesn't have an alibi for last weekend.

"He doesn't?" I exclaimed.

"No!" said Fuzzy. "Coach told him after the game last Friday that next week Stinky Limbert would be starting at quarterback. Bruno got so bummed, he hopped on his chopper and roared off into the woods. He didn't come home until late Sunday night."

"Wow! And no one saw him?"

"Nobody! He didn't even call Candy, who he'd promised to take roller-skating Saturday night. Boy, was she pissed. Man, I would never keep that chick waiting."

Head cheerleader Candy Pringle was the senior class boys' unanimous choice for "Most Likely To Be a Future Playmate of the Month."

"What was Bruno doing all that time?" I asked.

"Camping, I guess," said Fuzzy. "Talking to the bunnies and squirrels maybe. Though if you ask me, I bet he was giving his passing arm a workout. Not that it would do any good. The guy throws like a girl."

"Wow! Do you think they'll convict him?"

"Looks bad for Bruno," admitted Fuzzy. "Coach says it's a good thing he's so untalented. Otherwise, he'd be jeopardizing a big-time athletic scholarship."

"Is the car back?" I asked.

"Yeah, it's back. Not a scratch on it, thank God. They parked it in Grandmamma's garage, and Dad and Uncle Polly each put their own padlock on the door. Looks like we won't be driving down to Santa Cruz again soon."

"Too bad, Fuzzy."

"You're telling me. I want to see Heather so bad I can hardly even think about football."

Bruno in disgrace and facing a long jail term. That will teach the brute to keep his repulsive mitts off my girlfriend.

THURSDAY, October 18 — Mr. Ferguson is back. My devious, unscrupulous, grasping father has rented him the third bedroom for $250 a month plus board fees. The aged radical pulled in just after supper with a small cargo trailer attached to his wheezing Toyota. Dwayne was out renting my dog, so I had to help Mr. Ferguson unload his stuff all by myself. He intends to stay until the strikers achieve victory or he is convicted of fomenting labor unrest. "It's a grand cause, lad," he said, carrying in his army cot, bullhorn, and riot shield. "I feel 30 years younger."

Lacey has been bounced back to the living room—having turned down roommate offers from Dad, Mr. Ferguson, and Francois. I think Mr. Ferguson's may have been made facetiously. Lacey thumbtacked a kingsize flowered sheet to the ceiling, walling off a privacy nook in a corner. Then she and I jammed in a dresser, lamp, and her still-damp mattress. Dad grumbled about this "outrage" to his decorating scheme, but Lacey silenced him with a menacing stare.

Redwood High's most notorious car thief was back in school today. Improbably, the authorities have released Bruno into his parents' custody. At lunch I overheard him telling his buddies he thought he had been set up by "that back-stabbing, ass-kissing Stinky Limbert." Just then, Stinky walked into the cafeteria holding hands with Candy Pringle. Bruno let out a strangled cry and hurtled over the tables toward his rival in a spray of flying potato chips and milk cartons. In the ensuing scuffle Bruno had his nose broken and Stinky was stabbed in his passing arm with a fork—earning Bruno another trip downtown with the cops and throwing the Marauding Beavers into turmoil. They are now a team without a leader—right before the big game with that school whose name I can never remember. And the cheerleaders kept chanting it incessantly in the halls all day too.

11:05 p.m. I just called Sheeni in Santa Cruz. With any luck, my first paycheck will arrive before the phone bill—thus forestalling the premature termination of my life. By repeating several French phrases that Vijay had written out phonetically, I was able to navigate the Frog-speak barrier and reach The Woman Who Knows How (I hope). I thanked Sheeni for returning our hastily abandoned belongings.

"My pleasure, Nickie. I was concerned that you all might catch colds without your jackets. The postage came to $12.10."

"Uh, I'll send you a check," I said.

"I'd appreciate it, darling. My inadequate monthly allowance seems to evaporate with remarkable celerity. I am all out of eyeliner and simply can't afford to buy any until Father's next check arrives. You have no idea what a handicap this is. Fortunately, Taggarty is generous about sharing hers."

"But, darling," I protested, "you're so beautiful, you don't have to wear make-up."

"Thank you, Nickie. I appreciate the sentiment, however ill-founded. There are a few girls here who eschew cosmetics, but the effect of practiced rusticity they achieve is not something I wish to emulate. Ours is not a Stone Age culture, after all. And how is my darling dog?"

"Uh, he's fine," I said. "Speaking of Stone Age culture, did you hear the big news? Bruno Modjaleski was arrested!"

"You mean Bruno Modjaleski the football player?" she asked, feigning indifference.

"Yes, you know," I repeated. "Bruno!"

"And what did Bruno do, Nickie?"

"He stole a car and stabbed a student in the cafeteria."

"You mean stabbed him with a knife?" asked Sheeni, shocked.

"Not exactly. He used a fork. But there was still lots of blood."

"Well, those football players are a rowdy bunch," she observed calmly. "What else has been going on in town?"

"Sheeni, Bruno may have to forfeit his athletic scholarship. He may even be sent to jail!"

"That's a shame, Nickie," she replied. "I'm sure Candy Pringle must be upset."

"You don't care?" I demanded.

"Well, darling, I am as exorcised as the next person, if not more so, when justice miscarries. Do you believe Bruno to be falsely accused? Are you circulating a petition for redress? I shall sign it, of course."

"Not at all!" I retorted. "I am sure he richly deserves all the punishment meted out and more. I just thought you might be interested in his case, since you and he were . . . were . . ."

"Were what?" she asked.

"Well, you know . . . were lovers."

"What! Nick Twisp, I do not know what sort of person you imagine me to be, but I can assure you that I have never addressed two words to Bruno Modjaleski, let alone had a physical relationship with him."

"But, but, you said you gave up your virginity to a local jock named Bruno. I heard you!"

"I did, perhaps unwisely, divulge that detail of my intimate life to you. But at no point did I link the surname Modjaleski to the given name Bruno. That was your doing, Nick Twisp. I really can't imagine what you must think of me to imagine me capable of selecting that Neanderthal for my initiation into the practice of male/female relations."

"I'm sorry, darling," I protested. "Honestly, I found it very hard to believe myself. I was frankly incredulous. I still am! But there was all this circumstantial evidence. And Bruno is not that common a name. So, I guess it must have been a different Bruno? Huh?"

There was no reply. The Woman of My Dreams had hung up.

I called back immediately, but the Frog-speak barrier had become suddenly impenetrable.

Oh no! All along I've been despising the wrong dumb jock! Who is the rightful Bruno? And how do I get the stolen car rap switched over to him?

FRIDAY, October 19 — I awoke feeling like yesterday's Pampers to find a pair of frightening pink and white dentures soaking in a tray in my bathroom. All the hot water had been exhausted. I took a cold shower, squeezed an erupting zit, shoved the vanity drawer closed on Mr. Ferguson's upper plate (distorting it slightly), then returned it to the soak solution. Bathroom guerilla war has been declared.

After breakfast I sent this telegram (the first of my life) to Sheeni: "Foot extracted from mouth. Patient abject. Call collect. Love, Nick."

Not bad for just ten words.

Later, while pretending to work out on the parallel bars in gym class, I interrogated Fuzzy about alternative Brunos.

"Well," he replied, sucking his teeth, "there was that tennis player named Bruno who graduated last year. I guess you could call a tennis player a jock. I think they do wear them. At least, the guys do."

"What was his last name?" I asked.

"Let's see. What was his name? He was pretty smart. I think he's going to USC now. Oh yeah, I remember. His name's Preston. Bruno Preston."

"Any relation to Trent Preston?" I asked, surprised.

"Yeah, I think they're cousins. But Bruno's better looking."

"Wait a minute," I said, mildly flabbergasted. "You're telling me Bruno Preston is better looking than Trent?"

"Yeah," said Fuzzy, "and taller too. He looks like that new actor they have playing James Bond. What's his name?"

I didn't want to think about it. I wanted to devote all of my cranial capacity to unfettered hatred.

At lunch, I brought up a delicate matter with Vijay and Fuzzy. "Guys, we don't really want to get Bruno in serious trouble do we?"

"Better that fellow than us," replied Vijay in a conspiratorial whisper.

"But what if they convict him?" I said.

"So what?" whispered Fuzzy. "A guy with that many pass interceptions deserves some jail time. We're doing this town a favor. You know who Coach is starting in tonight's game? Rupert Trobilius! All he's supposed to do is hand off to the backs and fall down to get out of the way. They're not even going to let him attempt a forward pass. We're going to get slaughtered. I just hope Heather doesn't get wind of the score down in Santa Cruz."

I ate my peanut butter sandwich and Twinkie in silence. Only Francois, a sociopath untroubled by the qualms of conscience, enjoyed his food.

Work was intolerably tedious until 4:59 when Mr. Preston handed me an envelope. Inside was my first paycheck: $44.12. The total would have been higher except for missing work on Saturday and the exactions of a global superpower. My labors bought three rivets for a Cruise missile and a highball for a colonel in Guam. The balance will go toward my lingering Santa Cruz restaurant debt and monstrous phone bill. I only pray Dad doesn't demand a tithe toward room and board.

Mr. Ferguson was somewhat subdued at dinner. He reported that rumors have been sweeping the picket line that the company may attempt to bring in scabs. To make matters worse, his dentures were giving him trouble.

Fortunately for our houseguest, Mrs. Crampton made salmon croquettes for supper—a dish that could be gummed with comparative ease (except for those excruciating crispy bits).

A momentous day for mail. First, I opened this scented missive:

Dear Nick,

Dearest Lefty asked me to write and let you know he is recovering nicely from his surgery. As you might expect, he is in a great deal of pain, but is bearing it bravely (unlike that big, or should I say, small baby Clive Bosendorf).

I visit Lefty in the hospital as often as I can to help him keep up his spirits. The doctors say that things are healing nicely and that he should come through with all of his faculties intact. Lefty was greatly relieved to hear that, of course. The area is still heavily bandaged and they are giving him drugs to prevent any stimulation from interfering with the healing process.

Lefty is disappointed that he has not yet received a get-well card from you. I trust you will correct this oversight as soon as possible. I am enclosing his hospital address.

I'm sorry things got so far out of hand when I visited you in Ukiah. Nick, I have always liked you as a friend, but I feel I must tell you that my heart belongs to Lefty. Probably it always will. I hope you are not disappointed and will not feel any lesser of me for what happened.

Say hi to Fire Walker for me.

Fondly,

Millie Filbert

P.S. I think it was sweet of you to make up that story about the bulldozer.

Well, I'm happy that everything has worked out for Lefty and Millie. I only hope he is suitably grateful to the resourceful and fast-thinking friend who made it all possible.

Next, I opened this extraordinary note:

Dear Nick,

It was so nice meeting you the other evening. Vijay informs me that you are good friends with Sheeni Saunders down in Santa Cruz. I have a chum in that area also. I wonder if it might be possible for us to get together sometime to discuss this situation?

I am downtown studying in the library most every weekday afternoon from 3:30 to 5. Perhaps you could stop by sometime soon? I would like that very much. By the way, I should appreciate it if you would keep this correspondence confidential.

Sincerely,

Apurva Joshi

The beautiful Apurva wants to have a secret rendezvous with me!

Finally, I opened this welcome but unsettling letter, written in a bizarre, left-slanting scrawl:

Dear Nick,

What a surprise to receive your letter. It's the first I got all term. I almost thought it had been put in my mailbox by mistake. But no, it was addressed to me. Wow!

I did just what you suggested. Tuesday when I was scrubbing the floor in the administration office I sneaked out some of Dean Wilson's stationery. I typed the letter and mailed it that same night. Don't worry, I mentioned the naked stud with the condom and a lot of other stuff you don't know about.

For your information, I saw Trent and Sheeni hanging around outside the Catalyst last night about 10:30. They looked pretty friendly to me. If I were you, though, I'd ask her about a sophomore named Ed Smith from Des Moines. I see them walking to class and eating lunch together all the time. The word around school is that Ed really has the hots for her. It doesn't look to me like she's doing much to discourage him.

In case you're wondering what I was doing scrubbing the floors, that's part of my job as a scholarship student. I also have to wait on all those stuck-up snobs in the dining hall. If you're not rich at this school and don't have nice clothes, no one will give you the time of day. I don't care, they'll all get theirs someday.

If you visit again, stay away from Darlene. She really despises you for touching her precious towel. Thanks for the letter. Feel free to write again. I'll keep you posted on what's going on with little Miss Two-timer.

Regards,

Bernice Lynch

P.S. Why waste your time on Sheeni? You deserve somebody better.

Ed Smith? Ed Smith! Sheeni has a presentiment that she's going to marry an artsy French philosopher named Francois, but in the meantime she's hobnobbing with a sophomoric Iowa hayseed named Ed Smith. Do I really deserve this, God?

Oh well, Sheeni will be a fading memory to Mr. Smith soon enough. I figure Dean Wilson's letter ought to be detonating in her parents' mailbox any time now. Thank you, Bernice. I could (almost) kiss you.

No call from Sheeni. I wonder if I should have had Vijay translate that telegram into French before I sent it?

SATURDAY, October 20 — The phone rang during breakfast.

"Hello, Nickie. How are you?" It was my repulsive, oft-married mother.

"Oh hi, Mom. What's up?"

"Nickie, when we got back last night the house had been broken into! Everything was a mess and the TV and VCR were gone. I feel so violated. They even vandalized Lance's uniforms. And stole my best pair of red pumps."

"That's too bad, Mom," I said, trying to sound sympathetic. "Maybe it was Leon Polsetta again." Leon Polsetta is a popular Oakland hoodlum with an extensive history of burglarizing Mom's house.

"No, Leon's away in the army now. He's training to be a demolitions expert. His mother is so proud. I'm sorry, Nickie, but Lance seems to think you might be involved in this somehow. He says only you would have written that hateful message on the mirror."

"I don't know what you're talking about," I said, affecting my most righteously indignant, earnestly innocent tone. "I haven't been away from here five minutes. You can ask Dad. He's right here. Do you wish to speak to him?"

"No, Nickie, please. I'm upset enough already. I told Lance I didn't think it was possible. I didn't mean to sound like I was accusing you. Everything is in confusion here. We went next door to ask Mr. Ferguson if he'd seen anything, but there was no answer. I was afraid he might be inside paralyzed from a stroke or dead or something, so I had Lance break down the door. The house was empty. Mr. Ferguson is missing!"

"No, he's not," I replied. "He's right here. He's eating oatmeal without his teeth. Boy, I don't think he's going to be happy when he hears about his door. I hope he doesn't press charges against your husband."

"Don't be silly, Nickie. I'm sure he'll understand. What on earth is he doing up there?"

I filled Mom in on Mr. Ferguson's quest for labor justice.

"That sounds nice," she commented. "I just hope he's careful and doesn't get over-excited at his age. Nickie, could you ask him if he saw anything suspicious in the neighborhood while I was away?"

"OK." I held the receiver against my leg and probed my facial epidermis for nascent zits. After an appropriate interval, I reported, "No, Mom. Mr. Ferguson says he didn't notice anything out of the ordinary. Nothing at all. In fact, he said it seemed more than usually quiet for this time of year."

"How peculiar," sighed Mom. "Well, I'm sure Lance will get to the bottom of it. He's at work now with his finger-printing kit. It's quite thrilling to watch." She then chatted on interminably about her wonderful trailer honeymoon in the Nevada desert with just Lance and his sick old mother. Finally, sensing my complete indifference, she stopped.

"Well, Nickie. Study hard. Don't eat too much fried food. And think about maybe spending your Christmas holidays down here with us."

"I'll think about it," I lied.

"I miss you, Nickie."

"Thanks for calling, Mom. It's time for me to go to my job now." *Click.*

We need an answering machine. I have to start screening my calls.

I rode my Warthog downtown and climbed those now familiar creaking, dusty stairs. The office was deserted except for a strikingly elegant older women working on some ledgers in Mr. Preston's office. She greeted me warmly and introduced herself. It was Mrs. Preston, mother of a well-known affected twit, aunt of a despised, cake-eating tennis jock, and wife of a man devoting his life to plywood. Despite these burdens, she radiated a compellingly gracious charm. With her own lovely hands she fixed me a cup of steaming cocoa and interviewed me on company time as if I were Prince Billy Windsor Himself on a royal visit to the hinterlands.

What a handsome, brilliant family. What golden chromosomes! Genes such as theirs should be protected behind glass and heavily insured. Why, I wonder, did Natural Selection progress so forthrightly in their case, yet stagger so drunkenly down a blind alley in the case of the Twisps?

Preoccupied with these imponderables, I set to work arranging the ever-accumulating "P" files in a shiny new plywood filing cabinet. Mr. Preston, it seems, was able to complete his project without further assistance from Dad. Thankfully, the fresh green enamel obscured the blood stains.

While engrossed in these tedious labors, I made an extraordinary discovery. In a file marked "Personal," I found several pages of a rambling, revelatory narration evidently torn in haste from a notebook and then forgotten. The boldly masculine handwriting I recognized at once as that of my affected windsurfing rival. I had stumbled upon nothing less than a fragment of the private journals of Trent Preston!

Heart fibrillating, hands shaking, I read these words:

> ... expression of these perceptions through words must necessarily lessen the experience. That, it seems to me, is the dilemma only the greatest poets (other artists too?) are able to overcome—and then never with any constancy. Words can embrace only a tiny fraction of the infinite jumble we call human consciousness. Plus, there is the whole issue of purely bodily sensations which do not (always? sometimes?) register upon the mind. What is the interplay between words and the body? How does the temperature of the hall, for example, affect an audience's perception during a poetry recital? Should the wise poet, seeking true communication, first seize control of the thermostat? Why cannot I put into words what I experience at every level—consciously, physically, and unconsciously—when I grasp Sheeni's naked breast? Why, when I strive for poetry, do my words read like soft porn?

> Sheeni practically insisted we make love last night. I continue to resist, telling her (and myself) we're too young. Perhaps I am being masochistic—savoring the anticipation of pleasure by denying it in the present. (Admittedly, I was also held back by the lack of appropriate birth control—a complication that didn't seem to deter my partner.) Yet I found last night's crazed naked fondling (for lack of a better term) exquisitely pleasurable in its own right. When we move on (as inevitably we must), shall we ever know such fevers of desire again? Total honesty here: How much of my reluctance stems from resentment of Sheeni's continuing flirtations with Bruno? Do I hold back to punish her for her lack of fidelity? I don't know. Why does the mind have to erect these elaborate screens to hide its hurt?

> I must try to obtain some condoms. This necessarily poses problems in a small town, where everyone minds everyone else's business. Sheeni has volunteered to go on the pill, but I wouldn't want to be within 500 miles of her parents if they found out. Why does this society hold so steadfastly to the fiction that its children are asexual?

> I noticed in the mirror this morning a small red dot on my chin. I am hoping it will develop into a pimple. All the writers I admire were physically unattractive; most were ugly in the extreme. Their art was forged out of rejection, humiliation, and suffering. I've known none of this. Perhaps I should be thankful Sheeni pains me by pursuing my cousin. Why was I cursed with such harmonious features? At least my situation is not as desperate as Bruno's. He will never have to struggle.

He will never know if he owes the admiration of society to his accomplishments or his physical beauty. I wonder if Sheeni has slept with him yet?

I ran into Apurva at the library again this afternoon. Luckily, Sheeni wasn't with me this time. We had a long conversation in the poetry aisle, our hands touching occasionally unconsciously (or consciously). Her pronunciation of "T.S. Eliot" triggered such a rush of desire, I longed to taste her warm, sweet, full lips. Because of our vastly different cultural backgrounds, I can't tell for certain if she has any romantic feelings toward me. Perhaps Indian women just enjoy intellectual conversations about poetry. So I hold back. What if she does like me? Dare I ask her out? Could I ever leave Sheeni? Our hearts have been intertwined so long, sometimes I feel we have merged into one identity. Is there no . . .

What a pretentious, duplicitous, conceited liar! And only one crummy scholarly allusion. How dare he boast of his philandering while libeling The Woman I Love. Sheeni assured me last summer that it was she who was resolutely resisting Trent's boorish advances. As I recall, she stated quite explicitly that she preferred "grand passions in exotic European locales" to "furtive gropings in the California boondocks." How perversely does Trent deceive himself. Only a frighteningly sick person could write such untruths in his own private journal. Not to mention all that bizarre blemish envy. I must protect both Sheeni and Apurva from this deranged young man. Yes, clearly that is my duty.

At 12:30, after making several clandestine copies of the Trent Papers on the office copier, I said goodbye to Mrs. Preston and rode my bicycle over to Fuzzy's house. The place was jammed with grieving relatives laughing, eating, and having a good time. I found Fuzzy and Vijay with their shirts off in the sunshine down by the pool. They were guzzling from soda cans filled with beer. Fuzzy, looking somewhat like an oversized Angora rabbit with sunglasses, handed me a foaming can.

"Eighty-four to two," he said morosely. "A new Redwood Empire Athletic League record."

"Rupert Trobilius didn't rise to the occasion, huh?" I asked, sipping my beer. Yuck. It tasted like warm sock soak.

"He fumbled handing off 16 times," said Fuzzy, shaking his head. "That's a new record too."

"Well, at least we avoided a shutout," Vijay pointed out.

Fuzzy smirked. "You know how we scored? The other team was laughing so hard, they fell down in our end zone with the ball. It was a safety!"

"Does Heather know?" I asked.

"Yeah. She called me this morning in a panic. I told her it wasn't my fault— I was out for the entire game with a groin pull."

"What did she say?" asked Vijay.

"She said she wished she was here. She'd rub it with liniment."

"Rub what?" demanded Vijay.

"My groin, I guess," replied Fuzzy. "I wish someone would rub it. Besides me, I mean. It would make a nice change of pace."

Vijay and I both nodded in agreement.

I pulled off my shirt and relaxed on a lounge chair. Yes, I thought, I could get used to this lifestyle. I swilled the warm beer and looked around: stately poured-concrete and glass mansion, high cement garden walls enclosing vast expanses of concrete patios, concrete pool with cement dive tower and pool cabana, molded concrete birdbaths scattered here and there. Even the chair I was reclining on was immutable concrete under its foam cushions.

"Fuzzy," I remarked, "your parents must crave permanence. This place looks like it was built to survive nuclear attack."

"Yeah," he said. "Dad and Uncle Polly own a concrete company. Whenever a truck doesn't use its full load, they send it here to dump. Dad always has a form set up somewhere. You should see the concrete toys he used to make for me when I was a kid."

"Uh, wait a minute," I said. "Where is this concrete company?"

"Oh, you know it, Nick," interjected Vijay. "You can see the plant from your house."

Startled, I suddenly realized I was hobnobbing with Malefactors of Great Wealth. Mr. Ferguson would not be pleased. "Fuzzy," I said, "aren't your dad's employees out on strike?"

"Yeah," he confessed. "It's a real drag. Dad had to cut my allowance. But things might get better soon. They're thinking of hiring replacement drivers."

"A sensible strategy," commented the alien Republican.

"They'd really hire scabs?" I asked, shocked.

"Not scabs," said Fuzzy. "Replacement drivers. If the other men don't wish to continue working, it's only fair to give the jobs to new people. It helps keep our local economy healthy. We're fighting unemployment."

"But what about the drivers on strike?" I asked.

"They can go do something else," replied Fuzzy. "Maybe get jobs they enjoy more. Would you want to drive a truck all day? Booorrrring! We're doing them a favor."

Yes, I thought, not unlike the favor we're doing Bruno Modjaleski.

On the way to raid the buffet table, we were intercepted by Fuzzy's mom. She was a shapely maturing beauty, keeping time at bay with cosmetics, hair dye, and wire-reinforced undergarments.

"Boys!" she exclaimed, "show some respect for the dead. Go put your shirts on. And who is this young man, Frankie?"

"He's my friend Nick Twisp, Mom," said Fuzzy.

"Hello, Nick," she said. "Glad to meet you."

"Nice to meet you, Mrs. DeFalco. Sorry about your mother-in-law."

"Yes, so sad," she exclaimed happily. "Marie didn't make it to 100 after all!"

When we returned fully garbed, Fuzzy pointed out more relatives across the room. "Dad's the big, balding guy with the five o'clock shadow in the black suit. Uncle Polly is the fat guy next to him crying."

I studied the DeFalco brothers uneasily and decided they were not the sort of men I would choose to confront across a picket line.

We carried our laden plates up to a vast unfinished attic over the four-car garage. Two small windows at each gable end cast a dim light over piles of dusty trunks, boxes, musty garment bags, and discarded furniture. Fuzzy led the way toward a small central clearing containing an elaborate weight bench and a king-size mattress on the floor.

"Have a seat, guys," said our host. "I'll get the wine."

Vijay and I sat gingerly on the heavily stained mattress, as Fuzzy disappeared into the gloom under the eaves. He returned shortly with a dusty bottle wrapped in a woven straw basket.

"Real Dago chianti," he said, attacking the cork with his Swiss Army knife. "I found a whole case of it back there."

"Have you drunk any of it before?" asked Vijay doubtfully.

"Sure," replied Fuzzy. "This is the real stuff—what the Godfather drinks. Well aged too. I think it was my grandpoppa's private stash."

Vijay and I exchanged grim glances.

"Eat guys," said Fuzzy. "This may take me a while. Damn, I wish Uncle Polly had given me a knife with a corkscrew."

I tasted the ravioli. Delicious. "Fuzzy," I said, "I didn't know your name was Frank."

"Yeah, Mom named me after her favorite singer. Believe it or not, my real name is Francis Albert Sinatra DeFalco."

"That's incredible!" I gasped. "He's my favorite singer too!"

"Yeah?" said Fuzzy. "I never cared much for the guy. Too drippy. I prefer the Flesheaters."

"They're totally extreme," confirmed Vijay.

"Though, I'm not so sure I'd want to be named Flesheater DeFalco," admitted Fuzzy. "Gee, Nick, maybe you and my mom should get together. Play a few records, see what develops. I don't think Dad would mind. Rumor is he has a cupcake out at the plant. One of the dispatchers."

"Is she also on strike?" asked Vijay.

"Only for more foreplay," answered Fuzzy, prying out the last chunk of cork. "OK, gentlemen, the wine is served." He took a big gulp from the bottle and passed it to Vijay.

Vijay hesitated. "How is it, Fuzzy?"

"Superb. An excellent vintage."

Vijay sipped, grimaced, and handed the bottle to me. I took a deep, pre-alcoholic's draught. A fetid, sour brackishness washed down my throat.

"A bit medicinal, but pleasant," I lied, passing the bottle to our host. I only hope French wine is more palatable than Italian. I would not wish to embarrass Sheeni in artsy, left-bank cafes by ordering ginger ale.

As the bottle made the rounds, the wine and the conversation mellowed. "You have a tremendous weight bench, Frank," I observed. "Do you aspire to become Mr. Universe?"

"Too much body shaving," replied Fuzzy. "I'm just trying to bulk up for football. It's depressing. I eat like a pig and can't gain an ounce. I just get hairier."

"Puberty will not be denied," slurred Vijay. "It has us in its hot grip."

"Say, want to see my collection of Swedish magazines?" asked Fuzzy. "I found them in Uncle Polly's college trunk."

Fuzzy disappeared again into the gloom and returned with a large stack of glossy, well-thumbed magazines. Inside, handsome, well-endowed Nordic couples in full color were doing far more explicit things to each other than hinted at by the staid men's magazines in my collection.

"These are extremely racy," observed Vijay, slaking with wine his passionate thirst. "Someone must have bribed the censors."

"I don't think they have censorship in Sweden," I said, retrieving the bottle and taking a monumental swig. "They let it all hang out."

"They certainly do," remarked Vijay. "I wish I hung out as prominently as some of these fellows."

Always the proper host, Lefty suggested a circle jerk. Somewhat woozily, we dropped our pants and crouched on our knees in a circle on the mattress, our artillery aimed toward the center. I don't know what Vijay was whining about. In the competition for biggest missile launcher, I was clearly fourth runner-up. Fuzzy placed a styrofoam cup in the center of the mattress and explained the rules.

"OK. Shoot into the cup. Last guy to come has to swallow it all."

Vijay and I nodded, waiting for the signal.

"One, two, three. *Go!*"

Furiously, we pumped away—faces straining in concentration, eyes darting anxiously from groin to groin, chests heaving, abdomens tensing, three hands feverishly stroking three granite obelisks. Six bobbing testicles disappeared in a blur as the crescendo approached. First, Vijay groaned and blasted, then I popped, then Fuzzy squealed and fired.

"Fuck!" exclaimed the laggard, as Vijay and I collapsed on the mattress in hysterics.

"It's not fair," complained Fuzzy. "I'm bigger than you shrimps. Mine has farther to go."

"You made up the rules, Frank," I said. "Be a good boy. Take your medicine!"

Fuzzy picked up the cup with distaste, then broke into a smile. "What a bunch of slobs" he said, turning the cup upside down. "We all missed!"

3:30 p.m. As I pedalled my Warthog homeward, wine continued to sluice from my stomach into my bloodstream. Feeling extremely light-headed, I stopped at Flampert's variety store to buy a get-well card for Lefty. After selecting a tasteful card featuring a 500-pound woman squeezed into an abbreviated nurse's uniform, I encountered Sheeni's prodigal brother Paul in the check-out line. He was buying just the essentials: cigarette papers and *TV Guide*.

"What airline are you flying, Nick?" he inquired.

"Aged chianti," I slurred.

"That stuff will pickle your brain."

"That is my great and earnest hope," I replied.

"Your plan is working, Nick. World War III broke out at 11 this morning."

I wondered if everyone was so transparent to Paul. Or just me. "A letter arrived?" I asked.

"A cunning forgery," he confirmed. "You are playing with fire, Nick."

"Pyromania is my passion," I slurred. "What's new with you, Paul."

"I'm getting my trio back together. Come and hear us rehearse. You'll know where and when."

How can he be so sure?

When I got home, Lacey was in the living room tormenting Dad by performing aerobics in her most curve-hugging body tights. If I were him, I'd bring that foolish quarrel to screeching halt as soon as possible. Dad, though, continues to sulk and play the pain-crippled martyr. I wonder if thumb injuries depress the libido? He's also incensed because Lacey just returned from some morale-boosting cookie-distribution work among the strikers—while wearing those same Incendiary Orange workout togs. She may prove to be the AFL-CIO's ultimate secret weapon.

Lacey interrupted her aerobics for an important bulletin. "Nick, Sheeni called twice. She wants you to call her right away."

"Fine," I mumbled. "Nice. You look nice, Lacey."

I felt like experimenting to see if lying down made the room stop spinning, but instead I stumbled into Dad's bedroom and dialed Santa Cruz. Within moments I was audibly reunited with The Woman Who Owns the Pawn Ticket to My Soul.

"Nickie, where were you? I'm frantic. Have you heard what has happened?"

"I do not believe I have, no," I slurred.

"Somehow Dean Wilson found out about your being discovered in my room. He has written a libelous letter to my parents!"

"How did they react?" I inquired mildly.

"How do you suppose they reacted? You know my parents!"

"All too well."

"They were horrified, shocked, and enraged. I fear there may be no appeasing them. They're on their way here now!"

"They're driving down?" I could scarcely believe the wonderful news.

"That's what I said. Nickie, you sound peculiar. Have you been drinking?"

"I took a little light refreshment at lunch," I confessed. "Nothing I cannot handle."

"You sound totally plastered. I hope you do not intend to abuse alcohol habitually. In that case, I shall have to consider removing Albert from your care."

"The only thing I intend to do habitually is make love to you, darling," slurred Francois. For all his sophistication, he didn't hold his liquor any better than I did.

"That's sweet, Nickie. I'm sorry I hung up on you."

"I'm sorry I implied that you had slept with Bruno Modjaleski. I realize now that was hitting below the belt. I should have known all along it was Bruno Preston."

"How did you know that?" she demanded.

"I am wonderfully resourceful, Sheeni," I replied. "You should know that about me by now."

"I'm pleased to hear it, Nick. And how does your wonderfully resourceful mind propose to placate my parents? If they make me leave school, I shall die!"

"Simple, darling. Tell them you are pregnant and have to get married right away. We'll live in married students' housing and your parents can pay for both of our tuitions."

"Oh, Nickie, it's hopeless talking to you in your present condition. You are no help at all. Call me back when you sober up. And please stay away from my darling dog until you do so. Goodbye!" *Click.*

9:30 p.m. I just awoke with a splitting headache. Inexplicably, I had passed out and slept through dinner. I found this note, written in a nearly illegible scrawl, stuck in my left nostril: "Lier! You do so too slepe! Too bad for you! Mom made hambergars for super! I ate yors! —Dwayne."

My body complains but my spirit soars. Sheeni is coming back to me. But what was Dwayne doing spying on me in my own bedroom? And who unzipped my pants?

SUNDAY, October 21 — Disaster struck at 3:45 this morning. There was a sharp retort, a blinding flash, the acrid smell of burning flesh, and then all-encompassing blackness.

"That was a concussion grenade!" shouted Mr. Ferguson, stumbling about in the dark. "We're under attack! They've killed the power!" He swung his riot shield at a menacing figure advancing toward him from the shadows.

"*Aaaa-iiii-eeyy!*" screeched Dad, as cold steel impacted his bandaged hand.

"Don't come any closer!" screamed Lacey, huddled behind her fabric walls. "I've got a gun!"

"Throw it to me, girl!" yelled Mr. Ferguson, diving toward her linen bedchamber. In one athletic lunge, he yanked down the sheet, screamed in agony, and fell heavily atop the scantily clad occupant.

"Get off!" she screamed.

"I've been shot!" bellowed Mr. Ferguson. "I've been shot! I've taken a slug to the foot!"

"Get off or I'll fire!" screamed Lacey.

"Give me your gun, girl!" pleaded Mr. Ferguson.

"Take our money! But don't kill us!" shouted Dad, diving for the floor.

I got out of bed, put on my robe, found my Cub Scout flashlight, and hurried into the living room. "What's all this commotion?" I demanded, sweeping the room with my powerful three-volt beam.

"Get down, Nick!" hissed Mr. Ferguson. "You're in their line of fire! And turn off that damn light!"

I switched off the beam. Everyone froze and listened intently. The only sound was the wild thumping of four beating hearts.

"Maybe they've gone," whispered Lacey.

"Give me your gun just in case," whispered Mr. Ferguson.

"I haven't got a gun," she replied. "I just said that to scare them."

"Now you tell me!" he sighed.

"Somebody call 911!" hissed Dad.

"Why?" demanded Mr. Ferguson. "It's probably the pigs outside who are shooting at us. Damn, I'm bleeding to death!"

I shone the beam on his foot. "You haven't been shot, Mr. Ferguson," I said. "You have a thumbtack stuck in your big toe. By the way, do you know you forgot your pajamas?"

Lacey pulled a sheet over Mr. Ferguson's hoary nakedness and extracted the tack from his toe. I wonder if this makes them friends for life?

We found the source of the trouble 20 minutes later in the crawl space under the house. Crouching in my pajamas on the damp soil, I shone the rapidly dimming beam of my flashlight on a horrifying scene. Tiring of his innumerable soup bones, Albert had taken to chewing the main power cable from the meter box to the circuit breaker panel. Tonight he had bit through the rubber insulation—propelling himself with great speed and deadly finality into the next world.

Albert's limp body lay near his humble pee-stained bed. He was as ugly in death as he had been in life. He had not been an ideal dog, but he had certainly been a useful one. He was the one living link in the chain of love uniting Sheeni and me. Within hours, she will be home. How can I tell her our love child is no more? She knows I had been drinking. Will she blame me—unjust and irrational though it may be—for his death? Will she seek solace for her loss in the arms of Trent? Or Bruno? Or, God forbid, Ed Smith? Have all my hopes been electrocuted?

9:30 a.m. A dismal morning. Everyone is bleary-eyed and short-tempered from lack of sleep. Despite a grossly swollen toe, Mr. Ferguson was able to crawl under the house and tape the teeth-marked cable. Power has been restored. Dad made me bury Albert before I had a chance to take a shower or eat my breakfast. After age 40 any association with death must come as a terrifying reminder of one's own mortality.

It almost felt like I was digging my own grave. I laid Albert to rest with two of his favorite bones in the back yard behind the metal storage shed. It's shady there and he has a nice view of the concrete plant.

10:15 a.m. Before permitting me to make another telephone call, Dad made me endorse my paycheck over to him. He'll be sorry someday when the courts order him to pay generous rebates to me on all the child-support payments he's saving.

I called Sheeni, but reached Taggarty instead.

"Hello, Nick. What a surprise. Sheeni went out for breakfast with her parents. Quite an extraordinary couple. Have you met them?"

"Yes, I've had the pleasure," I said. "Did Sheeni say when she expected to arrive in Ukiah?"

"Sheeni's not going anywhere, Nick."

"What!"

"Oh, her parents made a fuss, but they came around. It was my argument, I think, that finally persuaded them. I have a great deal of experience in these matters you see."

"What did you say?" I asked, struggling to remain calm.

"Well, I quickly deduced that the primary motivational factor behind their anger was—I'm sorry to have to tell you this—their extreme, nay their overwhelming dislike of you. You really are anathema to them, Nick—at some profoundly visceral level."

"So what did you say?" I repeated.

"Well, I pointed out that if they brought Sheeni back to Ukiah, she would have that many more opportunities to be with you. Whereas, if she remained here under my watchful scrutiny, she would see you seldom if ever. Not only that, here she would, in all probability, soon develop an emotional attachment to someone else far more suitable. Of course, she has also had to promise never to see or speak to you again."

"What!"

"I'm afraid so, Nick. You may be out of her life for good this time. I know it's hard, but look on the bright side. Better now than later. Sheeni is destined to know many men, Nick. You are but an early milestone on a very long journey."

"We'll just see about that," I replied with icy calmness. "Could you have her call me when she gets back?"

"Well, I'll give her the message after her parents leave. But I can't promise she'll call. It was nice meeting you, Nick. Tell Vijay thanks for the picture and to look me up next time he's in Santa Cruz. *Ciao*, Nick. Don't be sad. It really is all for the best."

I hung up. Move over Albert. I may be joining you soon. Right after I assassinate a certain meddlesome roommate.

11:30 a.m. After much maddening badinage with obnoxious French-speakers, I finally succeeded in having Bernice Lynch brought to the phone.

"Hello, Nick," she said breathlessly. "What a surprise. I was just dusting all the second-floor fire extinguishers."

"Bernice, we have a crisis. Taggarty has wrecked our plot to have Sheeni withdrawn from school."

"That interfering bitch! What did she do?"

Briefly, I summarized Taggarty's treacherous machinations.

"I should have expected it," sighed Bernice. "In some ways, Taggarty is almost as bad as Sheeni. What can we do now, Nick?"

"We have to get rid of Taggarty!"

"You want her snuffed!" she whispered. "That's asking a lot, Nick."

"You misunderstand me, Bernice. We have to get Taggarty expelled. As quickly as possible."

"I don't know, Nick. This is a pretty permissive school. I'm not sure you could do anything bad enough to get expelled. It might be simpler just to waste her."

"Think, Bernice. Kids must leave your school for some reason!"

"Well, once in a while a girl gets suspended for being in a family way. I could sneak into Taggarty's room and sabotage her diaphragm. I know where she hides it. I could stab it with a hairpin."

"That'll take too long. It might be months before she's knocked up. We haven't that much time."

"Well, a few kids leave every term because their parents can't pay the tuition. And a few more flunk out. The academics are very demanding. But Taggarty's smart. And her parents are loaded."

I began to see a glimmer of hope. "Bernice, do you still work in the dining hall?"

"Sure, when I'm not swabbing toilets."

"Do you ever serve food to Taggarty?"

"Every day. The bitch digs being waited on. You want me slip some arsenic into her sloppy joe?"

"Not poison exactly. I can't tell you now. These phones may have ears. I'll write to you. Expect a letter soon."

"Great, Nick. I really appreciate the mail."

"Any news of Ed Smith, Bernice?"

"He's working overtime, Nick. He had a date to take Sheeni to some kind of performance art last night, but she had to cancel when her parents showed up. Ed's into theater, you know. He wants to be a stage director, the stuck-up creep."

"What does Mr. Pretentious Aspiring Director look like?" I asked.

"Boring and bland, Nick: six-two, big shoulders, soft blue bedroom eyes. Lots of casually tossed sandy blond hair. Wardrobe of natural fibers in coordinated earth tones. Expensive Italian leather loafers. Some girls find his dimples cute too. Personally, I think he's a real zero. A perfect match for Sheeni."

That's just what I was afraid of. Sheeni must be withdrawn from that corrupting environment as soon as possible.

"OK, Bernice. Thanks for the update. Keep me posted. I really appreciate your help."

"Oh, it's no trouble . . . Nick, you do like me don't you?"

"Oh sure."

"How much?"

"Uh, a lot. You're, uh, neat. I wish I was there, so I could see you more."

"Me too. I like you. Uh, Nick, in your letter, could you write about how much you like me? I never got a love letter before."

"Sure, Bernice. No problem."

"Goodbye . . . sweetheart."

Francois looked at me accusingly. "Hey guy, if you're putting the moves on that chick, I'm parting company, here and now."

"I'm not putting the moves on anyone," I retorted. "I am currying favor with an extremely valuable inside operative."

2:30 p.m. No word yet from Sheeni. Dwayne came over and started blubbering when Lacey informed him of Albert's demise. Worse, he's now refusing to pay the $2 he owes me in accumulated dog-walking fees. He did, however, fork over last night's unswallowed sedative.

"These are quite effective," I informed him. "I was testing one last night when you wrote that rude note."

"Oh, so you wasn't sleepin' 'cause you had to?"

"Of course not. I was conducting an experiment. Tell me, Dwayne, does your mother have many of these capsules?"

"She has a whole big bottle! The doctor doubled my dose 'cause I been stayin' up again. I made it to 3:30 last night and boy am I tired!"

"Good for you, Dwayne. Keep at it. Now, what you must do is bring me about a third of the capsules in that bottle. If we limit our borrowing, your mother likely won't notice the loss."

"What'll you give me if I do?"

"If you do as I say, I won't inform your mother about your violating my privacy while I was drugged."

Dwayne reddened. "I didn't do nothin', Nick. Say, Nick, you think Albert's up in heaven now?"

"Of course not. No one's paid his purgatory fees yet."

"What's that?"

I explained the concept of purgatory to Dwayne, and outlined the typical schedule of fees, interest, and installment payments for deceased canines.

"Wow, it's 'spensive getting into heaven," he exclaimed. "I just thought you had to be good."

"Well, every dollar you pay toward someone's fees is also credited to your own account. It's called the Purgatory Incentive Plan. Now, how much can you afford every week?"

"I guess about $2."

Dwayne handed over his first payment in cash and I wrote out a receipt. "You're doing a very good deed, Dwayne. Albert will appreciate it."

"Thanks, Nick. How much are you paying?"

"Fifty dollars a week."

"Wow, Nick. You must of really loved that dog!"

"We were very close," I lied.

5:15 p.m. Still no call from Sheeni. Surely her parents have left by now. I do not permit myself to imagine she is out with Ed, admiring his corn-fed dimples.

Dwayne returned with 29 purloined capsules. I put them in a small box with the four he had already passed to me and mailed them to Bernice. I also enclosed this tepid mash note:

Dear Bernice,

Here's the plan. You must introduce one of these sedatives into Taggarty's beverage every morning at breakfast. She may be intelligent, but she is not likely to pass her courses when she is falling asleep in class. One capsule should also be administered during the evening meal. This will take the intellectual edge off her homework. Don't worry, I shall be sending you more capsules as I obtain them.

By the way, if Ed Smith should happen to schedule any more dates with Sheeni, please slip him a capsule too.

Since meeting you, I have come to realize my interest in Sheeni was merely a transient adolescent infatuation. I like you more than I can say. I find you as charming as your name. Take courage, my sweet spy. Working together, we shall outsmart all those stuck-up cake eaters.

Affectionately,

Nick

P.S. Please destroy this letter immediately!

I could force my epistolary love-making no further. One can pursue insincerity only so far before the spirit (and Francois) rebel. Damn, I wish I had more pills. I'd put Ed asleep 24 hours a day too. He could become living performance art.

7:45 p.m. Still no call from Sheeni. Mrs. Crampton made grilled porkchops for dinner. Mr. Ferguson had to puree his in a blender and sip it through a straw. Now his bottom plate is giving him trouble too. Fortunately, he has a dental appointment scheduled for tomorrow. Meanwhile, his toe continues to swell to improbable dimensions.

10:15 p.m. Concluding that the wily Taggarty had failed to convey my message to Sheeni, I called My One and Only Love. Macheting my way through thick undergrowths of French, I finally reached my elusive inamorata.

"Nickie, what an emotionally exhausting day! I feel like I just survived the Siege of Leningrad. My parents were worse than I ever imagined possible. And, as you know, I have an extremely agile imagination. For a time, it really seemed this would be my final day in Santa Cruz. I had reached the nadir of despair!"

"Yes, Taggarty told me how she saved the day," I said. "Did she tell you I called?"

"I think she mentioned it. Wasn't she brilliant? Oh, she is such a true friend. I don't know what I would do without her."

But you may soon find out.

Sheeni continued, "Of course, the matron helped also. She assured my parents that except for that one minor lapse my conduct has been above reproach. Thankfully, Dean Wilson was away for the weekend. Odd, the matron insists she never informed on us to the dean. What do you make of that, Nickie?"

I was concerned with more important topics. "Sheeni, what is happening with us? Have you promised never to see or speak to me ever again?"

"I have, Nickie. Fortunately, the moral ambiguities inherent in parental contracts made under duress always permit some amelioration of the terms. But we must be extraordinarily careful. My parents must be given no reason to suspect we have any contact with each other. Absolutely none whatsoever!"

"But we'll still see each other? You still care for me?"

"Of course, darling. You are my one special friend. I'm not going to let my parents separate us. Their intense disapproval of you is one of your most attractive qualities. Besides, there's our love child to consider."

"Our love child?"

"Albert. We are raising him jointly. We must think of his welfare as well as our own. A separation now could be extremely traumatic for a young canine. By the way, how is my darling dog?"

I gulped. "Oh, he's . . . fine."

"Still chewing sweet little bones?"

"Yes, bones and other things."

"Oh, how I miss him, Nickie."

"He misses you too. In the worst way."

"It's late, Nickie. I have to go and collapse now."

"One more thing, Sheeni. I keep forgetting. What grade did Taggarty give Vijay? He's dying to know."

"I believe she gave him an A. It's perhaps uncharitable of me, but I hope that particular talent does not run through his entire family."

"Don't you want Trent to be happy in love?" I asked, playing the devil's advocate.

"I want everyone to be romantically fulfilled. Trent, however, may not be first on my list for such happiness."

"Who is?" I cooed.

"Taggarty I should think," Sheeni replied. "We owe her a tremendous debt, Nickie."

Yes, my darling, I know. I intend to work it off as best I can.

MONDAY, October 22 — Bruno Modjaleski is free again. The Mendocino County jail must be porous in the extreme. He shuffled into wood shop this morning looking decidedly depressed.

"Would you like me to help you sand your project?" I asked, hoping to cheer him up.

"Drop dead, dweeb," he replied.

"Just asking," I said, edging back to my bench. If he's going to adopt that attitude, he can go up river on the car-theft rap for all I care.

At lunch, Vijay was thrilled to hear of his high score. "Taggarty actually gave me a B!" he exclaimed. (To further the cause of humility in my friends, I had altered his grade slightly.) "That must be in the 90th percentile for her."

"I told you she liked you," said Fuzzy. "Why don't you give her a buzz? I talked to Heath for two hours last night."

"Well, I've thought of calling her, but one fact always restrains me."

"What's that?" asked Fuzzy.

"I dislike her intensely," Vijay replied.

"I thought you liked her," I said, surprised.

"I liked sleeping with her, Nick. That was pleasurable in the extreme. But I found her personality quite repellant."

"I could not agree with you more," I replied, shaking his hand.

"Well, I like everything about Heather," announced Fuzzy.

"Frank, what could you two possibly talk about for 120 minutes?" I asked.

"Phone sex," he replied.

Vijay and I looked at each other. "What's that?" we demanded.

"Well, it's not bad. Heath and I get naked and sort of, you know . . . do it, over the telephone."

"How exactly do you do it?" asked Vijay.

"Well, with words. I say I'm sucking your soft pink you know. And she says she's wrapping her warm, wet lips over the head of my big throbbing you know. It's great. We get really turned on."

Vijay and I exchanged glances of wonderment. "Fuzzy," said Vijay, "this development of yours may have possibilities!"

"It's not real pussy," admitted Fuzzy, "but it's the next best thing."

Everyone was on edge at work today. Mr. Preston was mad because some big-shot subscribers have been calling in to complain about outrageous typographical errors in their letters printed in the latest issue. Miss Pliny was upset because Mr. Preston upbraided her for slipshod proofreading. Dad was in a blue funk because his stitches come out tomorrow and he'll soon have to resume actual work. Mr. Rogavere got a splitting headache and went home early after Mr. Preston suggested they change all the headlines to a typeface called "Log Cabin." (The rustic, wood-grained letters appear to have been whittled from pine boughs.) And I was totally pissed because Mr. Preston wouldn't give me permission to leave early to meet Apurva in the library.

Finally, at 4:45 I announced I had caught Mr. Rogavere's migraine and hastily departed before anyone could object. In the library's ornate, pseudo-gothic reading room, I found the beautiful Apurva bent industriously over her homework.

"Good afternoon, Nick. I was afraid you weren't coming. What do you know about algebra?"

"What don't I know about algebra is a better question," I replied, quickly solving for two unknowns and correcting several glaring errors on her worksheet. Her numbers, though incorrect, were decorated charmingly with many cursive loops.

Clearly Apurva was impressed. "Thank you, Nick. I'm afraid I have very little aptitude for this subject. Vijay is the mathematician in the family. I dislike asking him for help, however; he adopts such a supercilious manner."

"I'll help you anytime you like, as humbly as I can," I said, inhaling her delicious scent. She smelled of sandlewood and blackboard chalk.

"Thank you, Nick. You are too kind. How are you enjoying school?"

"It's OK. No worse than lingering paralysis. How's your school?"

"Quite stimulating. It's much better now that the other students are beginning to accept me. It was difficult when I first arrived."

"You don't mind that it's only for chicks, I mean, women?"

"No. I'm used to it. I went to a girls' school in India, you see. I prefer it in fact. You get a much better education at a sex-segregated school. Boys are too much of a distraction in the classroom. Of course, after class they can be quite pleasant to have around. I was fortunate to meet Trent here in this library. We have a mutual interest in poetry. I was even more fortunate when you came along last summer and took Sheeni away from him. You did not know it at the time, but you had a very grateful unknown friend in Ukiah. How surprised I was when Vijay announced he had met you."

"Well, I suppose I should thank you for keeping Trent occupied so well," I said. "Though I wish I could feel more sanguine about his suitability for friendship."

"What do you mean, Nick?" she asked in surprise.

"I happen to know that he has been making false statements about Sheeni."

"What sort of false statements?"

"Libelous ones, I regret to say," I replied. "He has cast aspersions upon her morals."

Apurva bristled. "From what I understand, her conduct has indeed merited censure. And believe me, I have not heard the full story of her misdeeds. Trent has been remarkably discreet. I will not hear him maligned on this matter. His conduct has been above reproach. It is your friend, Nick, whose character should be scrutinized."

"Well," I said, taken aback, "clearly we have a difference of opinion here."

"Yes, we do," she said, calming down. "And I suppose it is likely to persist. We are both in love, Nick. No doubt our feelings rule our judgment. But let us agree to disagree. We can still be friends and work toward our common interests."

"You mean blasting those two out of Santa Cruz?" I asked.

"Yes. The last letter from Trent that escaped Father's detection was devoted almost entirely to encomiums to windsurfing. The ocean is proving a decidedly bad influence. Trent is neglecting his poetry. He must return in-land—before his mind suffers permanent damage."

"Sheeni is befriending farm boys from Iowa," I said. "She talks of nothing but Holsteins and hybrid corn. I must bring her back so that she may resume her intellectual life."

"I have a plan," whispered Apurva, leaning closer.

I leaned forward also. I liked the way soft round forms swelled beneath her clothing. "What is your plan?" I asked.

"We must make them jealous, Nick. We must pretend to be having a torrid affair. I know Trent will come back to me if he believes there is strong competition here. Especially if his rival is someone who has bested him once already."

"That is an excellent plan," I said enthusiastically. "Just last night Sheeni was telling me she wished you were not quite so attractive. I'm sure she will be terribly jealous."

I wasn't sure at all, of course. But I liked the idea of having an affair with Apurva, even if one of us was only pretending.

"There is just one problem," she added.

"What's that, darling?" asked the now unleashed Francois. Conducting torrid affairs was his field of special expertise.

"Well, love of my life," she replied coquettishly, "we must have our wild, passionate, public affair without my father finding out. He'll murder you."

I gulped. "Literally?"

"Perhaps not. But I don't want to find out. Do you?"

"No, darling. We must keep your father in the dark. At all costs."

"Good," said Apurva, gathering up her books. "Now, recite for me your favorite poem."

All I could think of was a poem from the fifth grade. I declaimed:

RAIN
Drops of water fill the sky
Falling hard from up on high;
I ain't been quite this wet
Since I took a bath on a bet.

"What a curious poem," said Apurva. "Who wrote it?"

"I did," I confessed.

"Nick, you are a poet too!" she exclaimed. "Now I am in love with two poets."

"Well, only one," I said, mentally excluding Trent.

"Nick, you are too modest!"

9:30 p.m. Another pleasant evening in the bosom of my family. Lacey is sulking in her bedchamber. Dad is fuming in his bedroom. Mr. Ferguson is soaking his inflamed toe in front of the TV. I am in my room coping with a sudden attack of Persistent Erection Syndrome. I have administered three treatments to my nagging T.E. and each time it springs back for more. I am attributing this sudden libido inflammation to lingering Apurva enchantment in confluence with the full moon. Or perhaps Mrs. Crampton is putting aphro-disiacs in the chicken stew in hopes of prodding Lacey back into Dad's bed.

During dinner Dad hit Lacey with a $45 a month rent increase. He had worked out all the figures on paper based on square footage of occupied floor space and hot water consumption. His girlfriend responded by tossing down her fork and instructing him to do something unpleasant with his calculator, his clipboard, and his modular home.

Just as the shouting was tapering off, the phone rang. Dad took the call and listened with an odd, quizzical expression while the handset squawked non-stop for five minutes. Finally Dad said, "I don't know what you're talking about. Please don't call here again." He slammed down the phone and looked at me accusingly. "You know some girl named Sheeni?"

"I think so," I said noncommittally. "The name sounds familiar."

"That was her father," said Dad. "He was yelling about you corrupting her or something. What's all that about?"

"He's a nut case, Dad. It's a real sad story—in and out of institutions, psychotic episodes, wearing women's clothes. His new medication is working great, but he has bad relapses during full moons."

"Well, stay away from the whole lot of them," instructed Dad. "We don't need any more wackos around here."

You can say that again.

I realize now there is much to be said for parents who are indifferent to your welfare. Sure they don't take much of an interest in you, but they don't snoop too deeply when the shit hits the fan either.

TUESDAY, October 23 — A strange day and getting stranger. Sheeni called me collect before breakfast:

"Nickie, why didn't you tell me about Albert?" she asked brightly.

"Oh, you found out about that, huh?" I said, fighting panic. "It wasn't my fault, Sheeni! I really tried to take good care of that dog."

"Don't worry, Nick. It's all turned out fine anyway." She seemed re-markably cheerful considering the circumstances.

"So you're not upset, Sheeni?"

"No, darling. I'm delighted in fact."

Had I uncovered a new, unanticipated strain of ghoulish sadism in my love? Or was this simply extreme sarcasm brought on by shock?

Sheeni went on, "When did Albert disappear, Nick?"

An odd euphemism, I thought. "He, uh, disappeared early Sunday morn-ing. But don't worry, he didn't suffer."

"Well, I'm sure he must have suffered a little," she said happily.

"Well, possibly. We'll never know for sure."

"I hope you haven't gone to the trouble of putting an ad in the newspaper for him."

"No. We had a simple ceremony. Just the immediate family."

"Nickie, what are you talking about?"

"Uh, what are you talking about, Sheeni?"

"Albert, of course. He's here, Nickie. He turned up on our doorstep last night. The darling dog slept the night on my bed!"

I knocked the phone receiver against the wall. "Bad reception here, Sheeni. What did you say?"

"I said Albert is here. He walked all those miles just to see me. Wasn't that sweet? Although, come to think of it, if he left there on Sunday, he must have gotten a ride or two along the way. Still, it's quite miraculous."

I'll say it is. "Are you sure it's Albert, Sheeni?"

"Of course, I know my own dog. Admit it, Nickie, Albert is not there with you."

"Uh, no. Actually, he's not."

"Well, he will be there shortly. The matron says he absolutely must go today. That sad girl Bernice Lynch is allergic to dogs. So I'm putting him on the bus. You may pick him up at the station late tonight."

"OK, Sheeni. Will do."

"Nickie, you have to promise me you'll be nicer to Albert. I can sense he was not really happy living with you."

"OK, Sheeni. I'll treat him like a prince."

"Do that, Nickie. He has very high expectations. As do I."

"Yes, Sheeni, I know."

"The shipping is going to be $42, Nickie. I'm sending him express."

"OK, Sheeni. I'll send you a check."

So Albert has a twin in Santa Cruz. Thank God Sheeni found him. What's a mere $42 for the safe return of our Love Child? Things are looking up!

5:30 p.m. Well, maybe not. I came home from work to find Lacey and Sheeni's brother Paul sipping herbal tea together in the dining room.

"Oh, hello, Paul," I said, surprised.

"Hi, Nick," he replied. "Sorry your plan didn't work out."

"I'm working on a new one."

"Yes, I know," he said. "She's very beautiful."

"Who's very beautiful?" asked Lacey.

"Nick's friend from India," answered the ever-omniscient Paul.

"Oh, I know her," said Lacey. "She is lovely."

"Not as lovely as you," said Paul, sipping his tea.

Lacey smiled and looked over at me. "Nick, Paul brought us a surprise. Go look in the living room."

I peered through the doorway. A small black ugly dog looked up from a bone he was chewing on the couch. I had met that gaze of canine contempt before. Albert had returned.

"It's your dog, Nick!" said Lacey. "He didn't die."

"But, but I buried him," I protested.

"Well, he must just have been stunned or something," she said. "Then he revived and dug his way out."

From three feet down?

"Uh, Paul, did you by any chance find him near the bus station?" I asked.

"No, Nick. He was sitting on our back porch this morning. Mom pitched a fit when she saw him. So I brought him back." He smiled at Lacey. "And I'm glad I did too."

Lacey returned his smile. "Nick, Paul has his own jazz combo. I'm going to go hear him play Friday night. Would you like to come?"

I gave the desired reply. "No, I have plans that night, Lacey. You'll have to go by yourself."

"OK," she said happily. "Where's your father, Nick?"

"He stopped at the hospital to get his stitches yanked out."

"Good," she said. "I hope they do it without anesthetics. Paul, could I offer you anything? More tea?"

"Of course," he replied, flashing me a lascivious wink.

7:30 p.m. Dwayne was overjoyed to see his exhumed rental dog. Nevertheless, he immediately demanded a refund of all paid-in purgatory fees.

"Sorry," I said, "I already mailed your money to God."

"How do I get it back?" he demanded.

"Pray," I replied.

9:30 p.m. We just received a disturbing call. It was Greyhound Package Express telling us to come down and pick up our dog.

10:15 p.m. We're back. Albert II has just been introduced to Albert I. They don't seem to like each other. I don't blame them. Everyone is confused. Dad is coping with the muddle by yelling profanities at me. Why couldn't Sheeni have liked cats? Or better yet, rabbits? When you have a surplus of them, you can always eat one.

WEDNESDAY, October 24 — The phone rang again before breakfast.

"Nickie, this is your mother."

"Oh. Hi, Mom. What's up? Are you getting a divorce yet?"

"Don't be smart. Lance and I are very happy. I called about your dog."

"What about him?" I asked ominously.

"He's here. He showed up yesterday. I can't keep him. Lance hates dogs."

"It's not my dog, Mom. My dog is right here."

Dogs I and II were on opposite sides of the kitchen growling at each other.

"Don't be silly, Nickie. I know that dog. He was perfectly friendly. He walked right in and went to sleep in his old bed in Jerry's Chevy. I'm sending him back to you."

"Don't send him, Mom!" I implored. "We have too many already."

"Nickie, you're not talking sense. I already sent Lance down to the bus station with him. You can pick him up this afternoon."

"Great! Thanks a pantsfull, Mom."

"Don't speak to me like that, young man. I'm still your mother. That reminds me, I want you to send me a sample of your fingerprints."

"Why?" I demanded. It did not seem like a particularly motherly request to me.

"Lance needs them for his burglary investigation. He's found lots of prints, but he wants yours so he can eliminate them. Don't worry, Nick. He's already fingerprinted me."

"Sounds like the honeymoon is over, Mom," I said.

"Watch your smart mouth!"

I've heard that line before.

More bad news. At lunch, Fuzzy and Vijay nixed my canine adoption proposal.

"But it'd be cool," I pointed out. "We'd all have matching pets."

"Mom won't let me have one," said Fuzzy. "She's afraid it'd give me fleas. Besides, I don't want a little rat dog. I want something cool like a doberman."

"My parents are philosophically opposed to animals kept as pets," said Vijay. "Or so they insist. Actually I think it's just their Brahmin prejudice against unclean beasts. Why don't you put an advertisement in the newspaper to give away your surplus dogs?"

"I'd rather find homes for them with people I know," I replied. "That way, if mine croaks again, I'll still have two in reserve for backup. I need this dog. My relationship with Sheeni depends on it."

"Is that so?" murmured Vijay pensively.

"Nick, how do explain all these dogs showing up?" asked Fuzzy. "I mean, isn't it kind of weird?"

"Frank, how do you explain the late Elvis Presley shopping for underwear in all those K-Marts?" I replied.

"Some matters will always remain beyond the explication of human reason," observed Vijay. "Speaking of which, Nick, my sister wants you to meet her at the library after you get off work."

"Did she tell you about our plan?" I asked.

"Yes," said Vijay. "She has enlisted me as your life insurance policy. I am to act as chaperon on your passionate dates. That way, if Father should happen to hear of your activities, he will assume that you were with me."

"Chaperon?" asked Francois. "Is that really necessary?"

"Well, what is the point of contriving Sheeni's return," asked Vijay, "if you won't be around to see her?"

He had a point there.

At work, Mr. Rogavere showed me how to put melted wax on the back of type galleys and paste them down on the layout boards. This I found slightly less boring than my usual duties of misfiling and mistyping. Somewhat prone to anal-retentiveness, Mr. Rogavere is obsessed that everything should be aligned and absolutely straight. I, on the other hand, feel some measure of typographical kineticism can only be liberating to the prose.

Miss Pliny told me that Mr. Rogavere bluntly informed his employer this morning that "Log Cabin" would be used in the publication only over his "very dead body." After a heated discussion during which an apricot danish was tossed across the conference room, they agreed to an "experimental use" of the typeface in question for one issue on the Editor's Page only. This page contains Mr. Preston's monthly column, featuring his lively personal views and amusing anecdotes from the world of plywood. Needless to say, it is tedious in the extreme. Further use of novelty typefaces, they have agreed, will depend on the reaction of subscribers.

Since Dad theoretically has regained the use of both hands, Mr. Preston sent him home to pack his suitcase. Tomorrow *Progressive Plywood's* star assistant editor leaves on assignment to inspect the waferboard mills of Oregon. Dad is to review the health of the industry and report on new processes and developments. I'll be amazed if he can even find the Oregon border. Best of all, Dad's extensive itinerary will require his absence from home for one entire, glorious week. Except for assorted dogs and Mr. Ferguson, the eager Francois will be alone with Lacey for six sensuous nights. He can hardly wait.

After work Francois found the beautiful Apurva just packing up to leave the library. Since the reading room was crowded with spectators, he greeted his love with a kiss. His boldness took her by surprise, but she recovered in time to respond with no small degree of feigned passion. To Francois' lips, the ersatz variety tasted just as sweet.

"Shall I carry your books, darling?" he asked.

"What a gentleman," she said, handing him the weighty pile.

Not entirely motivated by chivalry, Francois shifted his burden low in the front to conceal a monstrous T.E.

"Would you like to walk to the bus station with me?" I asked.

"Are you expecting visitors?" she asked.

"It's a visitor all right. But I wasn't expecting him."

As we strolled slowly toward the bus station, I explained the sudden and curious multiplicity of canines.

"Have you dug up Albert's grave?" she asked.

"No, and I'm not sure I want to."

"Oh, but Nick, you must. We'll dig it up one week from today."

"Why in one week?" I asked.

"It's Halloween," she replied. "We must have something terrifying planned for Halloween."

"We could make love without a condom," suggested Francois.

Apurva laughed. "Nick, you are so amusing. Why doesn't Trent make me laugh like you do?

"Trent is a serious fellow," I replied. "For him, maneuvering you into bed is an earnest business of intellectual titilation, progressing to strategic fondling, leading to tactical disrobing, culminating in successful organ targeting. Wit has no role in his mission."

"Alas, Nick, your curious theory is belied by the facts," she said. "But perhaps I should hold my tongue."

"Why?" I asked. "There's no one here except the great love of your life."

"Well, Nick, my love, how do you explain that on the two occasions when Trent and I were alone together, it was he who resisted my advances?"

"Easy," I replied, "the guy's brain damaged."

"Not to imply that my behavior was brazen. But, Nick, am I that unattractive?"

"Apurva, you're beautiful!" replied Francois. "So, you and Trent haven't, haven't . . ."

"No. Just a few chaste kisses. Then he transferred to Santa Cruz. You can imagine my despair. I suppose you and Sheeni have been extraordinarily intimate."

"Not as intimate I'd like," I confessed.

"Frankly, Nick, that surprises me—given the reputation of the parties involved. Vijay led me to believe you were quite an experienced man of the world."

"I'm working on it," replied Francois defensively.

"Nick, I think it's very charming. I like you even more now that we've had this chat."

Francois leered seductively.

"Yes," Apurva went on, "I feel a warm, sisterly affection towards you."

When we reached the dingy bus station, Albert III was tethered to a cigarette vending machine in a corner. He curled his ugly lips into a sneer when he saw me, but permitted Apurva to scratch his ears.

"What a delightful dog!" she exclaimed.

"Why not adopt him?" I suggested. "I've got lots."

"My parents don't like pets. They think they're a lower caste, I mean, lower class affectation. Of course, if I were to demonstrate a passionate enthusiasm for a dog, Father might assume I'd lost interest in boys. Under that circumstance, he might let me keep him."

"It's worth a try," I said.

We agreed that Apurva would take Albert III home with her for a trial run.

"Shall we have a date Friday night?" she suggested. "The drama class is doing that Noel Coward play."

"Great idea!" I said. "We can sit in front of Trent's swim team buddies and neck."

"One of them is certain to call Trent with the news," agreed Apurva.

"And he'll tell Sheeni," I said.

Apurva frowned. "You don't suppose they'll just drop us and get back together again themselves?"

"Not a chance. They love us too much."

"How can you be so sure, Nick?"

"Pure logic: you're fabulously beautiful and I'm terribly amusing. We're irresistible."

"Well," said Apurva coyly, "you certainly are."

For that, Francois gave her a goodbye kiss. Eschewing brotherliness, he employed his tongue. She didn't seem to mind.

7:30 p.m. More PES problems. I can't believe Trent could be satisfied with just a kiss from Apurva. To me she's the Snack Food Named Desire: one nibble and you crave the entire package.

Lacey was so thrilled to learn of Dad's trip, she was almost nice to him during dinner. Mrs. Crampton made her famous Mystery Mash—a big mound of mashed potatoes with assorted chopped up leftovers concealed inside. I got the scoop with the sweet pickle—the traditional door prize that entitles its lucky finder to a second dessert. Dwayne was extremely jealous and sulked like a fat, unsportsmanlike child all through the washing up.

To Dad's alarm, Mr. Ferguson's dental apparatus has been restored and he was making up for lost time. Lucky pickle or no, he helped himself to thirds of everything. Mr. Ferguson said his dentist has advised him to stop using his dentures "to pry up railroad spikes."

"How's . . . your toe . . . dear?" asked Mrs. Crampton solicitously.

"It's better since they drained all the pus and mucous out," he replied.

I put down my spoon. My bonus dish of prune whip had lost its appeal.

"How are the boys on the picket line?" asked Lacey.

"Expecting trouble," he said. "Those DeFalco gorillas just came in with the low bid on the cement work for that big sawmill loading dock."

"Will there be violence?" she asked.

"There will if they bring in scabs," he replied.

Damn, and my bedroom window faces the plant. I wonder if the landlord would be amenable to putting in bulletproof glass? Or maybe Dad would like to switch rooms.

8:10 p.m. Dwayne just barged into my room without knocking. Hastily, I fastened my pants.

"I brung the dogs back, Nick. We had a nice walk. Oh, whatcha doin'?"

"I was changing my trousers. Please knock before you enter."

"How come you was changin' 'em at this time o' night?"

"That's my business. Where's my 50 cents?"

"I'll have to pay you when I get my 'lowance," he said, flopping down on my bed. "They're gettin' a little friendlier, Nick. They only had three fights on this walk. I think I like the new dog best. What's his name anyways?"

"I suppose it must be Camus."

"Wow. That's a great name. Kamu the Wonder Dog! If my mom says it's OK, could I 'dopt him?"

"I don't know," I said. "He's an extremely valuable dog. How much money do you have?"

"I got $26 in my college ed'cation fund. Mom might let me take some of that. And God still owes me $2."

"Well, that's a start. And please stay off my bed."

Dwayne reluctantly rolled his flab off the rumpled chenille. "Nick, if you was doin' what I think you was doin', that's OK by me. We could do it together sometime."

"Excuse me, Dwayne," I said, escorting him out the door, "I have homework to do."

"Think about it, Nick," he said. "It's more fun with two."

From the mouths of fools come truisms. Yes, it would be more fun with two. Sheeni and Apurva—singly or jointly—I'm open to proposals.

THURSDAY, October 25 — Albert III is back. The Joshis came downstairs this morning and were shocked to find him in their kitchen lapping up the *nevidya* (food offering) in their *deoghar* (god house). I had neglected to warn Apurva this particular breed has a penchant for defiling religious symbols.

Mr. Joshi brought Albert III back early this morning just as Dad was leaving on his great Expedition to the North. Dew glistened on the trees and all was still except for the sounds of violent oaths being hurled. When I came running out in my bathrobe, negotiations had broken down completely and Dad and Mr. Joshi were circling each other with raised briefcases.

"Nick, tell this maniac that's not our dog!" screamed Dad.

"Nick, explain to this madman you loaned the dog to my daughter!" shouted his adversary.

"Don't you want to keep him, Mr. Joshi?" I pleaded. "He's a great dog."

"He is an ungodly cur! I never wish to cross paths with him again!"

"Just whose fucking dog is this?" demanded Dad, now threatening me with the upraised briefcase.

I only pretended to cower. In my experience Mom is the parent with the proclivity toward violence. Dad is mostly bluster. Besides, I knew the battered attache contained nothing weightier than a peanut-butter sandwich and a road map of Oregon.

"Dad, Mom sent him!" I explained. "Her new husband hates dogs. I've been trying to give him away."

Dad reluctantly lowered his briefcase. "You'll give him away all right, pal. When I get back, all I want to see around here is one fucking dog. Preferably dead!"

"OK, Dad. No problem. Would you like to meet Mr. Joshi?"

Dad eyed Apurva's father suspiciously. "Is he the nut case who wears women's clothes?"

Mr. Joshi bristled. "I do not wish to be insulted any further. Good morning to you all!" Handing me the dog leash, he got into his car and roared off. I didn't know a Plymouth Reliant could peel rubber.

Albert III looked up at me and growled.

"Have a nice trip, Dad," I said, forcing a smile. "Bring me back something nice."

Dad mumbled a reply. I shall not repeat it here. It is not something a son expects to hear from his loving father.

Sheeni called collect just as I was about to leave for school.

"Nickie, did Albert arrive safely?"

"Yes, they all did," I replied.

"What?"

"Everyone on the bus arrived safely, including Albert."

"Are you being extra nice to him?"

"I'm doing my best. I was about to give him a gold-plated steak bone when you called."

"Nickie, your check hasn't arrived yet."

"Well of course it hasn't. I don't get paid until tomorrow."

"Oh," she said darkly. "That puts me in a bit of bind for the weekend."

"Do you have some expensive activities planned?" I asked.

"Oh, nothing special," she replied.

"Well then you'll get along fine," I said cheerfully. "How's dear Taggarty?"

"She's feeling a bit fatigued."

"Overwork?" I asked. "Too many hours of fact cramming?"

"I don't know. She slept most of yesterday. She felt fairly alert at breakfast, but now she's gone back to bed. I think she should see the nurse. It could be incipient encephalitis."

"Anyone else exhibiting the symptoms?" I asked.

"No, just Taggarty. Nickie, do you suppose you could wire the money to me? That way I could get it Friday afternoon."

"I'm sorry, Sheeni. I don't think that will be possible. Well, darling, I don't want to be late for school."

"How about Express Mail?" she asked hopefully.

"Sorry, darling. Goodbye. Thanks for calling." *Click.*

If Sheeni imagines I am going to finance her cultural outings with the Iowan Pretender, she can just think again. My check will be taking the slow route to Santa Cruz—overland by way of Tibet.

I must write another mash note to Bernice expressing my appreciation for her brave resistance work on behalf of the allies. Our plan is working perfectly.

Bruno Modjaleski's long epoch of sanding finally came to a close in wood shop today. He actually applied shellac to his dry sink. Perhaps he is winding up his affairs before departing to take up residence as a guest of the state. His court hearing is set for Monday, Fuzzy informed me at lunch. Miss Wompveldt's sophomore civics class is expected to attend.

This may be Bruno's last weekend as a free jock. I hope he is planning some intense conjugal visitations with Candy Pringle. Yes, Redwood High's Cutest Couple has been reunited. Happily for Bruno, Candy's interlude with Stinky Limbert proved short-lived. She has promised to wait for her man, provided the judge gives him no more than eight months.

At lunch, Vijay handed me this scented note from his lovely sister:

Dear Nick,

I'm so sorry my parents won't accept the dog. I have tried every manner of persuasion to no avail. They are adamant.

Please, Nick, do not give away that dear, precious dog. I should love to come over and visit with him whenever I am able. I shall be very grateful if you can keep him for me. Perhaps I can pay a little towards his upkeep from time to time.

I am looking forward to our date tomorrow. I have choir practice this afternoon, so I won't be able to see you until then. Please let Vijay know if you can keep the dog.

Fondly,

Apurva

P.S. I forgot to ask. What is his name?

What powers of persuasion! I could no more refuse Apurva than I could French-kiss Albert (any of them). Of course, Dad will be livid if he finds out. I must contrive somehow to keep the Alberts apart. If Dad sees them singly, perhaps he will be deluded into thinking he lives in a single-dog household.

Since the late Albert Camus inconveniently achieved existential fame without a middle name, I was obliged to move on to another Frog. I told Vijay to tell Apurva her dog was named Jean Paul.

Vijay made an interesting proposal as we were sharing his vegetarian samosas at the Nerds' table in the cafeteria. (He currently enjoys a nearly insurmountable lead in the race for "Student with the Most Exotic Bagged Lunches.")

"Nick, how would you like to study as an exchange student in my old school in Pune?" he asked. "You could live with my uncle's family."

"Your hard disk has crashed, Vijay," I replied. "You are out of your mind."

"No, listen to what I say. Sheeni's parents want her to stay in Santa Cruz because you are here in Ukiah. Is that not correct?"

"Unfortunately, it is."

"Therefore, if you leave, that impediment to her return will be removed. They will insist she come back."

"Accomplishing precisely what?" I asked. "Sheeni and I are 200 miles apart now. If I went to India, we'd be 20,000 miles apart."

"It's not that far," said Vijay. "More like 12,000 miles."

"Well, it's still a long drive for a weekend," I said. "Besides, I hear India is hot and has a terrible problem with flies."

"It's quite pleasant most of the time," he replied, offended. "Anyway you wouldn't actually go there, you would just give that impression."

"I don't get it."

"Let me explain: you fill out the application, win the scholarship, and then we contrive to have the school newspaper do a big write-up about you. All about this extraordinary honor that has come to Redwood High and how much you will miss everyone during your years abroad. Maybe we could get a story in the town paper too. Anyway, we make sure Sheeni's parents get copies. They'll be overjoyed and decide to bring Sheeni back. Then, right at the last minute, you have a change of heart and decide not to go."

"Won't they change their minds too?" I asked skeptically.

"Not if they don't find out," exclaimed Vijay. "Winning an honor is newsworthy. Turning it down is not. The newspapers won't bother reporting that."

"But I might run into them downtown," I pointed out. "I know for a fact Sheeni's mother shops for magazines at Flampert's variety store."

"Well, you—what is the expression—lay low for a while. Or you wear a disguise. Grow a moustache. Dye your hair."

"It might work," commented Fuzzy.

"How do you know I'll win the scholarship?" I asked.

"Why not? You're intelligent. You get good grades. Besides, no one else has applied. But we'll need your father's signature on the application."

"No problem," I replied. "I've been forging that for years."

8:15 p.m. To celebrate her coming week of carnal license, Lacey gave Mrs. Crampton the day off and took Mr. Ferguson and me out to dinner. Only I ordered steak, so of course there was a vicious dogfight when we got back for possession of the bone. I don't know who won—I haven't a clue which is which. Each Albert exhibits the same out-thrust lower jaw, the same bugged out bloodshot eyes, the same curly pig's tail attached to the same ratty black body besmirched by identically lopsided smears of white muzzle and chest fur. For all I know, they may be harboring matched sets of genetically identical fleas.

The phone rang as we were preparing to sit comatose in front of the TV:

"I hate your slimy guts."

"Hi, Lefty. What's up? Did you get my get-well card?"

"I hate your putrid guts."

"Lefty, what's the matter? Millie said you're healing fine. Did you beat that shoplifting rap?"

"Going to jail is the least of my worries, traitor."

"OK, Lefty. What's bugging you now?"

"They took the bandages off this morning."

"Already, huh? That's a good sign. A very good sign."

"They made me get a hard-on."

"Good. That's progress. How'd you do? Are you straight?"

"I'm straight. Straight as an arrow."

"That's fantastic. Then what's the trouble, dude?"

"I'm three fucking inches shorter!"

I did some quick mental subtraction. Let's see, seven and one-half minus three equals . . . Uh-oh.

"Well, gee, Lefty. That's . . . bad news. Course, you know what they say: size doesn't matter."

"Would you chop off three inches? For $1 million?"

"Well, personally, I wouldn't, but . . ."

"How about for $10 million?" he demanded.

I contemplated life as a well-heeled eunuch. A sumptuous lifestyle to be sure, but what would you do on dates?

"For $10 million, Lefty, I might think seriously about it."

"You might huh? Well, I'm living it right now for free. Or should I say, for $10,000?"

That figure rang an ominous alarm bell in my mind. "What, what do you mean?" I asked nervously.

"You know what I mean. I've had time to think—flat on my back with my mutilated dick in a sling. I figured out what happened to that trailer of your mom's. And that big white Lincoln."

"Lefty, they were stolen!"

"Yeah, by you, traitor. You swiped them while I was upstairs in your room being humiliated by Millie and the cops. You probably planned that too. Admit it. You started that big fire in Berkeley. You're the famous firebug they're calling the 'Griller of the Gourmet Ghetto'."

"Lefty, you're mistaken. I never . . ."

"I got the goods on you, pal. Don't give me any more of your lies. I'm going to turn you in for the reward. Maybe I can use the money for some implants. Maybe I can get fixed up before Millie finds out."

"Oh, don't worry. Millie will find out," I said coolly.

"What do you mean?" he demanded.

"At my arson trial. I'll spill the beans, Lefty. I'll sing like a canary. Oh, you'll have your squealer's money. But your tragic story is going to be headline news. Hell, you might even make *People* magazine. Just think what the kids at school are going to say."

"Nick, you wouldn't do that!"

"Oh, yeah? After you squealed like a rat?"

"I'm not a squealer, Nick. Only you shouldn't have talked me into having that damn operation."

"I'm sorry, Lefty. I truly am. But you have to look on the bright side."

"What fucking bright side?"

"You're still growing, Lefty. Guys don't stop growing until they hit 30. That's why they're always so depressed when that birthday rolls around. OK, so you wind up with ten inches instead of 13. That's not so bad. That's decent. You can still hold up your head in the locker room."

"I did grow over two inches last year," he conceded.

"So you lost a year-and-a-half of pecker progress. Big deal. You got Millie back from Clive didn't you?"

"Yeah, things are great with Millie. But what if she wants to get it on? What if she won't wait four or five years until I get back to normal?"

"Just make sure you keep the lights off. Women are not capable of perceiving physical dimensions without visual clues. Their minds aren't structured for it."

"It's not her mind I'm worried about."

"Don't worry, Lefty. You'll do fine. Just think big."

"Think big," he repeated. "OK, I'll do it, Nick. Gee, that's a relief. I was really worried there for a while."

"Relax, Lefty. Just be thankful you're not crooked any more. Those doctors know what they're doing. They're guys. They wouldn't leave you adrift on a deep river with a short pole."

"The surgeon was a woman, Nick."

"Even more reason for confidence. She's been there. She knows what equipment a guy needs to get the job done."

"You're probably right, Nick. Thanks. I'll keep my lips zipped on the fire."

Whooo. That was a close one. For my sake, 1 hope his doctors are administering massive doses of testosterone. Maybe he could get Millie to steal him some of Clive Bosendorf's growth hormones.

FRIDAY, October 26 — A spectacular day for dating. The planets must be all lined up, spelling "Go for it, Baby!" Even as I write this, I can still taste Apurva's mint-flavored lipstick on the deepest recesses of my tongue. Meanwhile, Lacey is entertaining a local trumpet player in Dad's own private bedroom. Occasionally, the springs pause in their rhythmic song, and the odor of burning hemp wafts out from under the door. Francois is seething with jealousy, but I prefer to dwell on the positive side. Besides being my future brother-in-law, Paul may someday marry my near stepmother. Thus my ties to the Saunders family grow ever more numerous.

I met Vijay and his knock-out sister at 7:45 p.m. in the lobby of the school auditorium. Apurva singed the eyeballs in a mind-numbing red satin dress and my mother's best high-heel shoes. Francois had selected my outfit: black trousers, Dad's grey suede jacket, fluorescent cranberry shirt, and a soft mauve scarf borrowed from Lacey and knotted jauntily at the throat. It was somewhat more flamboyant than my usual dress-for-invisibility costume.

Apurva approved. "Nick, you are sensational. The other girls will be very jealous of me tonight."

"Paroxysms of envy will grip the fellows when they see me with you," I replied. "Your beauty leaves me speechless, my dear."

"How fortuitous for me that it does not," replied Apurva sweetly.

Our chaperon had heard enough. "Let us go now and buy our tickets, please," said Vijay peevishly.

Flush with twenties (I had cashed my paycheck immediately, lest it be seized again by a creditor), I paid for my date's ticket. We chose prime seats in the orchestra—close to the front where we would be seen by the multitudes. I insisted our chaperon sit at least one seat removed. Vijay sighed and scanned the audience for pretty girls.

"How is my essay coming along?" I asked him. The application form for the scholarship, we had discovered to our distress, required a 1,000-word essay on the topic "Why I wish to study in India." Vijay, as the resident Indian expert, had generously volunteered to write it for me.

"It's coming," he said. "My difficulty is in making it illiterate enough so that they will believe it came from the pen of an American."

"Thanks a generous pantsfull," I said. I turned to the more alluring branch of his family. "Apurva, I hope your father was not offended this morning. My dad, I fear, was somewhat rude."

"I'm afraid he came away with a very bad impression. He was not happy to hear that we were going to the theater with you this evening."

"But Vijay is here with us," I pointed out.

"Yes, thank God. He would not have agreed to it otherwise. He is under the impression I came along with Vijay simply out of boredom. Oh, Nick, you can keep my precious Jean Paul—can't you?"

"Certainly," I replied. "Well, I'll try. It may take some artful subterfuge. Fortunately, I have an aptitude for that."

"Good. Also, we must try to improve your standing with my father," she said, looking worried. "It is quite low at the moment."

"What about my applying to study in India?" I demanded. "Surely that must have scored some points with the old boy."

"He said what with communal strife, religious conflict, and political unrest, India has more than enough problems without being burdened with the task of educating you."

As I prepared to reply to this slander, the lights began to dim and the curtain rose.

The play was "Hay Fever." How unfortunate that our laws are so lax in regulating high school dramatic arts. I believe draconian fines should be imposed by statute for such crimes as reckless disregard of the text, willful abuse of comic timing, and falsely impersonating an English accent. In addition, whoever cast the Zit Queen as the breathless ingenue should be barred from the theater for life.

At intermission I took Apurva's warm, wheatish hand and we strolled lovingly among the surprised swim team retinue and their dates.

"I think it is quite good for a school production," commented Apurva. "Don't you, Nick?"

"Possibly," I replied, "for a grammar school."

"Nick, you must not be so severe. These are not trained actors."

"In fact, they are not actors at all," I said. "Shall I buy you some punch?"

"Yes, please," she replied.

But first Francois demanded a kiss. While Apurva was complying enthusiastically, she was addressed by a bronzed, muscular junior named Baborak.

"Hullo, 'Purva," he said. "What you hear from Trent?"

"He's fine," she replied. "He is enjoying his windsurfing. Do you know Nick Twisp?"

"I seen the dweeb around," Baborak replied, cutting me dead and walking away.

Apurva squeezed my hand and whispered into my ear. "Nick, our plan is working. Already Trent's friends dislike you."

I didn't tell her that even when I'm not French-kissing their buddy's girlfriend, guys like Baborak always despise me. It's instinctual with them.

Eventually the curtain came down on the last act. I was sorry that what with all the liberties the thespians were taking with Mr. Coward's story, they hadn't altered the ending. A surprise stabbing of the ingenue would have produced a much more satisfying climax than the author's.

After the show, I squeezed in beside Apurva in her father's rad Reliant for a short cruise down Main Street to the Burger Hovel drive-in. We made Vijay sit in the back and slump down so that he could not be observed by our fellow cruisers.

"How did you like the play?" I asked him.

"I found it quite appalling," replied Vijay's voice from near the floor. "Do they imagine upper-class Brits speak with Cockney accents?"

"You boys are too critical," said Apurva. "I think it requires a great deal of courage to stand up on a stage and perform. I should be petrified with fright."

"Petrification could only be an improvement," said the back-seat critic.

"We should look on the bright side," I pointed out. "At least it wasn't a musical. No one stood up and burst into song."

The restaurant was filling fast with the elite of Ukiah's theater-going community. We claimed the last unoccupied booth in the back.

"I'm going to have a quarter-pounder," announced Apurva, studying the greasy menu.

"Mother won't like it," warned Vijay.

"Mother doesn't have to know," she replied pointedly.

"At least request it well-done," said Vijay. "So the blood doesn't run down your arm."

"Vijay remains a militant vegetarian," commented Apurva. "None of us had ever had meat until we came to the U.S. When we were flying over, the stewardess came around serving cold cuts. I almost vomited from the sight of them. I imagined they were slices of raw flesh!"

We all laughed. "Now the cows run when they see her coming," said Vijay. "They can see the blood-lust in her eyes."

"I eat very little meat," retorted Apurva.

"The animal hardly misses it," countered Vijay.

Something told me they had had this conversation before.

Vijay ordered a double serving of onion rings; I had the house specialty: jumbo chili dog with nachos in a basket.

While we ate, Apurva and Vijay talked about life in Pune.

"You Americans have such crazy impressions of India," complained Vijay. "You think we sleep on beds of nails and spend our time standing on the street corner with our begging bowls."

"You mean you don't?" I asked, feigning surprise.

"We had movies," said Apurva. "We had TV. We'd have our friends over to play records and dance. I made clothes on my sewing machine. Vijay rode his bicycle. Father would go to the country club to play cards."

"Did you have K-Marts and donuts?" I inquired. "How about shopping malls and Rose Bowl parades and hot tubs? Or jacked-up pickup trucks and lowriders and long-haired rednecks and *Mad* magazine? How about Twinkies and jumbo chili dogs?"

"Alas, we have not yet achieved that level of civilization," lamented Apurva wryly.

"But we do have the bomb," boasted Vijay. "And the largest middle class in the world."

How bourgeois, I thought.

Apurva waited until Vijay had finished the last of his onions rings and then said, "You know, of course, those were fried in beef tallow."

"You lie!" he retorted. "It was vegetable oil. I can tell."

"No, I've eaten here before. I asked the waitress. They use beef tallow for additional flavor."

Vijay turned green. "Why didn't you tell me?" he gasped.

"Must have slipped my mind," said Apurva. "I was distracted by my delicious hamburger."

Vijay groaned. "I have rendered cow juices inside me. I'm going to be sick."

As we were leaving, the cast of "Hay Fever" bustled in on a noisy rush of unspent stage adrenalin. "Hi, Vijay!" shouted the Zit Queen. "Did you see the play? Wasn't it wonderful!"

"Most impressive," said Vijay, turning greener and hurrying out.

In the car Vijay ducked scowling into his back-seat hiding place. "That ugly Janice Griffloch is talking to me more and more," he complained. "What do you suppose this means, Nick?"

"Bad news, Vijay," I replied. "It means she likes you." Francois shifted ever closer to his date, seriously impairing her ability to the shift the transmission. She didn't seem to mind.

"How dare she be so presumptuous," the voice said. "I have in no way encouraged such forwardness!"

"Vijay, it is time that you paid more attention to girls," said Apurva. "Why don't you invite her out?"

"Janice Griffloch?" asked Vijay. "I should rather open a vein right here."

"Don't feel bad, Vijay," I said. "All the fat, ugly girls like me."

"Well thank you very much," pouted Apurva.

Francois draped a reassuring arm around his ravishing chauffeurette. "And an occasional beautiful one," he cooed.

A fortuitous red light halted our progress. Francois took advantage of this opportunity to experiment with an automotive kiss. Apurva tasted of virginal desire and well-done hamburger.

"Nick, can you detect meat on my breath?" she inquired.

"Not at all, my love," Francois replied. "Just sweet, innocent vegetables."

"I wish you two *were* in love," said Vijay's voice from the rear. "I am certain you would not be nearly so sickeningly nice to each other."

SATURDAY, October 27 — An entire weekend without Dad. No one to yell at me to mow the lawn or remind us so acutely of the looming disappointments of middle age. What a luxury!

To celebrate, I put on my favorite F.S. album and went back to bed. While Frank crooned softly, I snuggled under the covers and gave free reign to my erotic imagination. As an all-girl team of precision, naked tumblers performed daring sexual acrobatics in my head, a trumpet on the other side of the wall began to play along to Frank. The song was "The Girl Next Door." When the tune ended, the horn accompaniment stopped abruptly and bedsprings began to rock. More bitter regrets for Nick at his misspent youth. Instead of wasting all those years learning harmonica, I should have been studying trumpet. What an aphrodisiac!

A phone call finally got me out of bed. It was Bernice, calling collect with important dispatches from the front:

"Nick honey, Sheeni is going with Ed Smith today to Monterey!"

"What for?" I demanded.

"They're going to visit the Aquarium," she explained.

Oh, yeah? Why this sudden enthusiasm for marine biology? As if either of them had ever shown any interest in a fish that wasn't under a lemon wedge on a plate.

"Did you slip him a capsule?" I asked anxiously.

"I tried to, Nick honey," she replied. "But I, uh, got it in the wrong cup."

"What do you mean?"

"Well, as they were driving off, Sheeni looked a little . . . tired."

"You drugged Sheeni!"

I imagined my Sweet Love regaining consciousness in some tawdry Fisherman's Wharf motel—her clothes awry and a satiated Iowan leering at her unashamed.

"I didn't mean to, Nick honey. It was an accident. Besides, what do you care?"

"Well, Bernice. I, of course, don't mind that much. It's, uh, just that I don't want you to waste the capsules unnecessarily. Do you know when they're coming back?"

"Sheeni's signed out until tomorrow. She told the matron she was going to stay with Darlene at her parents' house in Salinas."

My mind reeled at this grim news. "Bernice, what kind of car does Ed have?"

"He doesn't have a car. I doubt if he even has a license. He's only 15."

What flagrant flouting of California highway laws! As a guest in our state, the fellow should show more respect for our legal institutions.

Bernice continued, "Taggarty loaned them her car. She doesn't need it since she sleeps all the time."

"Good job, Bernice. Now, what kind of car does Taggarty have?"

"It's a red Isuzu Impulse—you know the sports car. She's always bragging guys can't resist the Impulse when they see her."

"Do you by any chance know the license number?" I asked.

"Sure. Are you dumb?"

"Bernice, I was just asking."

"No, Nick honey. That's her licence: R U DUMB. That's the first thing she asks guys when they try to pick her up."

"OK, Bernice. What I want you to do is call up the Santa Cruz police and tell them your red Isuzu was stolen."

"You mean pretend I'm Taggarty?" asked Bernice skeptically. "Gee, Nick, I don't know if I could lie to a cop. What if he asks to see my ID? I could get into big trouble."

She's turning chicken on you, warned Francois. I went to Plan Two. "OK, Bernice. Here's another idea: you call up the Monterey police and tell them your car was stolen in Santa Cruz. Say you've already given a report to the Santa Cruz police, but you have reason to believe the thieves may be headed to Monterey. They'll take the information over the phone."

"Boy, Nick honey, you sure think fast on your feet. I'm impressed."

"We make a good team, Bernice," I lied. "But make sure the real Taggarty stays unconscious so she's out of the picture."

"You don't have to worry about that, Nick."

"Has Taggarty gone to see the nurse yet?"

"Nah, she thinks she's as smart as any doctor. I heard her tell Darlene she's experimenting with herbal remedies for chronic fatigue syndrome."

"Good. If you see her taking any herbs, skip her next pill. That way she'll be encouraged to think her remedies are working."

"Great idea, Nick!" replied Bernice. "Uh, Nick honey, I wanted to ask you one more thing. There was a rumor going around this morning at breakfast. Something about Trent Preston's girlfriend up in Ukiah two-timing him with a stud named Nick Twisp."

"Did Sheeni hear about it?" I asked.

"She did, unless she's deaf. Is it true, Nick?"

"It's more strategy, Bernice. We're conducting this campaign on two fronts. How did Trent look?"

"Like he wanted to strangle his grapefruit. So, Nick, you don't really like that girl?"

"Of course not, Bernice. You know who I like."

"Do you really, Nick honey?"

"You know it, baby," said Francois, stifling a shudder.

As I was leaving for work, Paul—looking somewhat drained—shuffled into the kitchen.

"Good morning, Paul. I enjoyed your trumpet playing."

"Was it acrobatic enough for you?" he asked.

I reddened. What exactly did he mean by that?

Mr. Ferguson must be jealous too. He didn't even offer to shake hands when Paul introduced himself. Perhaps he just didn't want to get out of his chair. He's been moving rather slowly lately. Someone snipped the elastic in his truss.

When I arrived at the office, I was surprised to discover the full staff at work. Due to the vagaries of the Roman calendar, deadline day for the next issue fell on a Saturday. The dress code had been suspended and everyone was modeling their interpretations of casual weekend wear. Miss Pliny had gone all blue and fuzzy in a mohair sweater and matching toreador pants. Mr. Rogavere appeared to be ready to paste up type or dig for clams. Most shocking, Mr. Preston was displaying elderly white executive knees in startling plaid bermuda shorts. I was wearing my usual dress-for-success outfit: tattered jeans and my I'M SINGLE, LET'S MINGLE tee-shirt.

After catching up on my misfiling, I was permitted to do some more free-style paste-up. When he wasn't officiously correcting my column alignment, Mr. Rogavere was excoriating his employer over the photo captions. For typographical balance, our Art Director insists all captions exactly fill the line. He says if *Scientific American* can take the trouble, why can't we? Mr. Preston grumbles, but tries to comply. Thus our captions tend to end abruptly or, more typically, lurch onward in fits of prolixity. An example I noted of the latter tendency: "Large computerized planing mill in Arkansas operates 24 hours a day around the clock (Eastern Standard Time)."

To my surprise, Miss Pliny remains strangely silent about these stylistic outrages. Can it be she finds Mr. Rogavere not entirely unattractive? I would pay in the high one-figures for the full scoop on their respective love lives. Unlike most Ukiahan males, Mr. Rogavere does not drive a pickup truck, own a chainsaw, smoke unfiltered Camels, fart in public, drink until he falls down, or brag about his sexual peccadillos. These qualities make him attractive to a woman of Miss Pliny's breeding, but concomitantly call into question whether there is sufficient overlap in their libidos to hope for love. If Mr. Rogavere fails to notice Miss Pliny in fuzzy tight mohair, yet spots a headline .0001 inch out of level, what does this tell us about his world view?

When I arrived back home, Paul was giving Lacey a foot massage on the couch. Mr. Ferguson was prone on the floor, studying patterns in the shag.

"We saved you some mushrooms," said Lacey dreamily. "Don't tell your father."

"They're powerful," said Paul, handing me a small plastic bag. "Only take two."

I swallowed two of the dry brown pellets and then the reckless Francois gobbled two more. We both shuddered from the vile bitterness. I waited five minutes. Nothing. Waited ten more minutes. Reality clutched defiantly at my mind. Just my luck, I'm immune to psychedelics. I suppose I shall have to experience mind-expanding hallucinations the old-fashioned way—by abusing strong liquor.

I went into my bedroom and noticed for the first time how much my chenille bedspread resembled a medieval tapestry. Every shimmering thread stood out for singular contemplation. Yet, at the same time, I could admire the totality of the weave—while noting every gradation of hue and texture. In a matter of minutes, my aesthetic had accelerated light-years beyond even Mr. Rogavere's. I sat on my bed and examined the hairs on my arm. They formed calligraphic patterns more exquisite than any Chinese brush painting. Aldous Huxley was right. Beyond the narrow doors of perception lies a realm of wide-screen, big-budget Technicolor spectacles. All that was lacking was a Victor Mature in a toga lashed to a marble column.

Hours went by yet the sun refused to set. I strolled into the living room and greeted my precious friends. Kind Lacey generously permitted me to massage her other foot. I rolled her soft pink toes through my fingers like round warm grapes. Each nail was a transparent window on a fascinating three-dimensional universe. A profound revelation came to me: cavemen had no need for television. They must have sat around their primeval campfires and watched the programming in their toes.

I jumped when a carillon rang nearby.

"Nick, get the phone," said Lacey sweetly.

I picked up the sinuously organic sculpture we debase by calling a telephone. "Hello," I whispered.

"Nick, is that you?" spoke a familiar voice.

"I am Nick Twisp," I said. "I am alive. I am a breathing organism."

"Quit fooling around, Nick. This is your dad. Is everything OK there?"

I heard deep pangs of fear in the voice. "Don't be afraid, Dad," I said. "Everything will be all right. You deserve to be loved."

"What the fuck is that supposed to mean? Is Lacey there?"

"Lacey is here. Paul is caressing her toes."

"Paul! Who the hell is Paul?"

"Paul is our friend. He makes beautiful music for the acrobats. They're naked."

"Who's naked? Is Lacey naked?"

I didn't want to talk to this voice about the acrobats. "Don't be afraid, Dad. Goodbye." I hung up and pulled out the cord.

"Dad is afraid," I said.

"He is on the wrong path," said Mr. Ferguson from the floor. "I have felt that for some time."

I want to talk to Sheeni, I thought. I want to touch her. I want to enter her mind and body and find her living soul. I knew with absolute certainly I had never wanted anything so strongly in my life.

SUNDAY, October 28 — A car pulled into the driveway at 3:27 a.m. by the clock. I woke with the mother of all headaches and listened as heavy footsteps approached. No, I could not state with absolute certainty that the front door was locked. Nor did I feel like getting up to secure the bolt. Shoot me in my bed if you must, I thought, at least it will put a merciless end to the hammering in my head.

I heard a key turn in the lock and the door swing open.

"Lacey!" bellowed a voice. It was Dad, returning prematurely from his hegira to the north.

"Nick!" he yodelled into the black night. "What the fuck is going on?"

Three identically pitched dog howls rose from the crawl space below.

I must say Sheeni's brother conducted himself with admirable nonchalance during the ensuing chaos. Paul did not throw on his pants and try to flee out the bedroom window. He got out of bed, slipped on his underwear, and sauntered into the living room to keep Dad at bay while Lacey packed.

As Dad foamed and ranted, Paul suggested in soothing monotones that he think about calming down before the neighbors called the sheriff. He only had to hit my father once, when Dad made a misguided lunge for Lacey as she was retrieving her aerobics tape from the VCR. Paul landed a crisp right to the jaw, dropping Dad like a stone. When he came to, Dad had lost most of his fighting spirit. He let Mr. Ferguson pour him a brandy and pretended to regain his reason.

"Of course you realize you are in serious trouble," said Dad, rubbing his jaw. "Mr. Ferguson is my witness that you assaulted me. And I know for a fact that you two were having naked orgies here involving my son. That child is only 12 years old!"

"I'm 14, Dad," I pointed out.

"Shut up," he replied. "That boy is an under-aged minor. I am going to have you arrested and charged with child molesting."

"Don't be an idiot, George," said Lacey, carrying her suitcase out of the bedroom. "No one was naked and no one was molesting anyone. Isn't that right, Mr. Ferguson?"

"That's right, George," he replied. "I'm surprised you could think such a thing of Lacey."

"When you get out of prison you will both have to register as sex offenders," Dad continued, undeterred by the facts. "You will never be able to get decent jobs again."

"I've never had a decent job," remarked Paul. "I don't think I'd want one."

"Let's go, Paul," said Lacey, pulling on her coat. "George, I'll pick up the rest of my things tomorrow."

"Not until you pay me all the rent money you owe," retorted Dad.

Lacey looked like her headache was approaching the same acute pain stage as mine. "I paid you all your money!" she screamed.

"Not the extra charges," replied Dad.

Lacey bent forward until her beautiful face was one inch from Dad's bloated one. "Fuck ... your ... stinking ... extra ... charges," she hissed.

"Using bad language in front of a minor," said Dad happily. "The judge will hear about that too."

"Dad, shouldn't you be up in Oregon?" I asked.

"Shut your goddam fucking face," he bellowed.

Probably sage counsel under the circumstances. I took four aspirin and went back to bed.

10:30 a.m. When I dragged my post-hallucenogenic carcass out of bed about an hour ago, my headache was better, but the doors of perception had swung firmly closed. Time ticked by at its normal pace, my bedspread had lost its aesthetic fascination, and unalloyed reality was loitering about in its dingiest housedress.

Dad was snoring noisily in his reclaimed bedroom; Mr. Ferguson had left for early morning picketing duty. I made a cup of coffee and plugged in the phone. It rang immediately.

"Nickie, is that you?"

It was my future twice-divorced mother.

"Yes, Mom. Don't you recognize my voice after 14 years?"

"No, I don't. You're beginning to sound just like your father. Nick, why haven't your fingerprints arrived? Lance is livid."

"You know the Postal Service, Mom. I mailed them nearly a week ago," I lied.

"You should have sent them airmail special delivery. Lance thinks you're being deliberately disobedient. And how are things up there with you?"

"OK," I replied. "Dad broke up with his girlfriend."

"He did!" exclaimed Mom. "That's marvelous. Is he taking it badly?"

"Oh, I guess so."

"That's wonderful! Did she ditch him for another guy?"

"You might say that."

"Fantastic! So he's getting a taste of his own medicine. It's about time. I hope he suffers, the heel. Nickie, you've made my day."

"Glad to oblige, Mom."

"Nickie, guess what? I'm beginning to show!"

"Show what?" I asked. Mom had always favored shockingly low necklines and appallingly high hemlines. What was left to bare?

"The baby is beginning to show," she explained. "I'll be in maternity clothes soon."

"That's nice, Mom," I said. "I guess." I tried not to imagine her in a low-cut, mini-skirted maternity frock.

"You're going to have a little brother," she bubbled. "Did I tell you I had amniocentesis? We found out it's a boy and everything's fine. Isn't that exciting?"

"I'm excited, Mom."

"Guess what we're going to name him?"

"John Wilkes Booth," I suggested.

"No, silly. We're going to call him Lance Junior!"

"Great, Mom. You've made my day too."

When I finally hung up, the phone rang promptly again.

"Nick honey, it's Bernice. I've been trying to call you since yesterday. Why didn't you answer?"

"Someone unplugged our phone," I replied. "What's up, Bernice?"

"Plenty. Sheeni and Ed were arrested at a fried clams stand on Cannery Row. The cops made both of them call their parents!"

"That's great! Where are they now? In jail?"

"No, Dean Wilson had to get out of bed last night and drive down to Monterey to pick them up. Boy, was he furious. I got some bad news though, Nick. Dean Wilson recognized Taggarty's Impulse. He made the cops drop the car-theft charges."

"What about driving without a license?" I asked indignantly.

"Oh, Ed's still in big trouble for that," she replied.

"I should hope so. Is he going to be expelled?"

"Maybe. Dean Wilson was totally pissed. He was even yelling in English."

"What about Sheeni?" I asked. "Her parents must have been shocked. Are they going to make her leave school?"

"I don't know, Nick honey. I'm trying to find out, but I have to be, you know, subtle about it."

"I understand," I assured her. "What facts have you discovered?"

"Well, Taggarty was on the phone a long time this morning with her parents."

"Taggarty! She's supposed to be in dreamland!"

"I know, Nick. But you said to skip a pill if I saw her taking some herbs. So I did."

More interference from Taggarty. Maybe Bernice is right. Maybe we should just snuff her.

"OK, Bernice. You're doing fine. Could you leave a message in Sheeni's box? Tell her Nick Twisp phoned and wants her to call him collect."

"OK, Nick honey. I'm sorry about Taggarty. I'll put her back to sleep tonight at dinner."

"Thanks, Bernice. I know I can trust you."

"We're a team, Nick honey."

1:30 p.m. No call from Sheeni. Dad got out of bed at noon and has been stumbling around slamming doors ever since. He's not speaking to me. I don't know if it's because he is acutely embarrassed by his behavior last night or blames me somehow for Lacey's defection. I suppose it's too much to hope for rational conduct from a balding, middle-aged failure who may be facing years of gnawing celibacy.

Dwayne just dropped by in a fat fit of excitement. His mother has yielded to unceasing supplication and agreed to let him keep Kamu the Wonder Dog. But she obstinately refuses to release any hoarded college funds. Unfortunately, even Dwayne could see I was not negotiating from a position of strength.

"I'm doin' you a favor takin' that dog," he pointed out. "Your dad don't want three dogs around. My mom said so."

"Yes, but I can keep one dog and Kamu happens to be my particular favorite. If you can't pay, you'll just have to take Albert."

Dwayne's chin began to quiver. "I don't want Albert. I want Kamu."

"Well I suppose I could arrange an installment purchase plan. How much can you afford every week?"

"Only 15 cents. I got 'spenses. I got to buy dog food. Mom said so."

"Fifteen cents!" I wondered if the young Howard Hughes would have turned his back on this deal. Well, I suppose it was better than nothing. "OK, Dwayne. Fifteen cents it is. But you better pay promptly. And you have to come over and walk the other two dogs too."

"But Nick, I can't 'fford it!" he complained.

"OK, I'll let you walk them for free."

"Gee, Nick. You're a great pal. Can I take Kamu now? Huh? Huh?"

"Take him," I said generously. "Be my guest!"

3:30 p.m. Still no call from Sheeni. Paul and I just tied the last of Lacey's belongings to the roof of her Toyota. Dad saw the happy lovers pull into the driveway and ducked into the bathroom, pretending to take a bath. Jealousy, avarice, and cowardice must have battled for supremacy over his emotions. Not surprisingly, cowardice won.

Lacey gave me a big hug before she left. "Let's not be strangers, Nick. Stop by and see me at the salon."

"I will," I said. I wanted another double-breasted hug, but she had already squeezed into her overladen car.

Miraculously, Paul managed to insert himself beside her. "You're fishing for trouble, Nick," he said.

"What do you mean?" I inquired innocently.

"Fried clams," was his only reply.

5:15 p.m. Apurva just went home crying. Why is the sight of a beautiful woman in distress such a turn-on? I wanted to kiss away her tears while simultaneously removing her sweater. Is this normal? I wish there were books listing appropriate and inappropriate desires for teenage boys.

There has been a nasty dog mix-up. This was revealed when Apurva stopped by unexpectedly with some vegetarian biscuits for her pet.

"But where is Jean Paul?" she asked, alarmed.

I pointed to the two canines autographing the left and right front tires of her father's Reliant. "Take your pick," I said.

"But these are not Jean Paul!" she exclaimed, starting to panic. "What have you done with my dog!"

"Relax," I said. "I know what must have happened. Dwayne wanted Camus.

He probably took Jean Paul home by mistake. No problem. We'll just go over and exchange them."

"I doubt if it was a mistake," grumbled Apurva. "Anyone can see Jean Paul is much superior to these unfortunate animals."

We leashed the surplus dogs and hurried over to the Crampton's littered bungalow. Sprawled topless on the front stoop was Kamu's portly master, eating a fried salami sandwich. Dwayne waved phlegmatically as we approached. I hoped his pendulous pink nudity did not offend my friend's delicate sensibilities. Jean Paul, tied by a dirty rope to a dented 1969 Grand Am, barked with excitement as his rightful mistress approached. Apurva cradled him in her arms and kissed his ugly snout.

"Mumfny bojuum," said Dwayne through a large wad of balloon bread and lunchmeat.

Apurva struggled to untie the grimy rope.

Dwayne swallowed hurriedly. "Hey you!" he yelled. "Don't mess with my dog!"

"Dwayne, there's been a mistake," I said. "You didn't take Camus. That's Jean Paul. I promised I'd keep him for Apurva."

"No way!" said Dwayne, rising and gesticulating with his sandwich. "I know my own dog. That's Kamu."

"It's Jean Paul!" shouted Apurva. "See, he knows me. Nick, tell him whose dog this is."

"Dwayne, if Apurva says it's her dog, then it's her dog."

Dwayne's rubbery masses of rosy flesh began to redden. "Who says?" he demanded. "She ain't got no rights here. This is my prop'rty. She ain't even 'merican. You guys touch my dog, I'll pound ya. I can too!"

Dwayne clenched an immense pink fist under my nose. This uncharacteristic belligerence caught me by surprise. I took several steps back.

"Dwayne," I said, deciding to reason with him, "perhaps you have forgotten, but you have not as yet paid one cent for this dog. Therefore, you do not own him. I own him. And as his rightful owner I say you have to exchange him for one of these other nice dogs."

Dwayne stuffed his sandwich into his pants, freeing both hands for flexing. He advanced and displayed two portly fists under my nose.

"Nick, we made a deal for me to buy that dog. You can't repo'pess him unless I get some a'rears on the payments. That's the law. I know 'cause that's why Monkey Wards ain't took Mom's washin' 'chine yet."

I took two steps back. "I don't want to take your dog, Dwayne. I just want to exchange him."

Dwayne took two steps forward. "I don't want'a pound you, Nick. But I will. Now you guys clear out'a here!"

I retreated, Apurva pleaded, but Dwayne remained half-nakedly but wholeheartedly intractable.

On the walk home, I assured Apurva I would soon find a way to reclaim her precious Jean Paul. "Don't worry," I said. "I have ways of getting around that fat moron."

"Please do it quickly, Nick," she implored, wiping her eyes. "I cannot bear to think of my poor dog living in such squalor!"

6:30 p.m. Speaking of squalid suffering, Dad and I ate a nervous dinner alone together. Both the food and the company could quickly induce ulcers. Mr. Ferguson, whose presence suddenly seems much less objectionable, was out on the town, taking in a movie with Mrs. Crampton. I had volunteered to go with them, but was politely snubbed. It was just Dad, me, and the rapidly emptying zin bottle.

"Are you going back to Oregon, Dad?" I asked.

"Why the fuck should I?" he slurred.

"No special reason," I said hastily.

"Who's this guy Paul?" he demanded. "Where did she meet him?"

"I don't know," I lied.

"What's his last name?"

"Uh, Saunders, I think."

"Saunders, huh? Why does that name sound familiar?" he demanded.

"I don't know, Dad," I lied. "My kindergarten teacher was named Miss Sanders. Remember, you liked her."

Dad had had a brief extra-marital affair with my kindergarten teacher—a source of considerable confusion for me at the time.

"Yeah, I remember that babe. She liked to . . ." Dad paused for another swallow of zin.

I was intrigued. "She liked to what, Dad?"

"None of your fucking business, wise guy."

Someday, when Dad is wasting away from cirrhosis of the liver, I hope his deathbed confession treats in greater detail his relationship with Miss Sanders. Such an unburdening could only be good for his soul.

9:45 p.m. When Dad finally passed out on the couch, I sneaked into his bedroom to call My One and Only Love. After much lingual swordplay, I succeeded in having Sheeni brought to the phone.

"Hello, Nick," she said coldly. "What's up?"

"Sheeni, the person who answered the phone told me you had been arrested!" I exclaimed, employing a small tactical lie to launch the conversation.

"It was just a misunderstanding. Everything's fine."

"They said you were arrested in Monterey. What were you doing down there?"

"Oh, a friend and I went down for the day. We wanted to see the Aquarium."

"Anybody I know?"

"No. Just a friend," she replied laconically.

"So, uh, everything's fine with your parents?"

"Certainly. Taggarty talked to them. She explained it was just an unfortunate misunderstanding. They trust Taggarty, you know."

"She's a wonderful person," I lied. "How's she doing?"

"Well, she felt great today. She really thought she was getting better. But now she's tired again. I had a little touch of it myself yesterday."

"You did?"

"Yes—on the way down to Monterey. It was all I could do to keep my eyes open."

"Perhaps it was the company," I suggested.

"What?"

"Just kidding, Sheeni. Darling, you sound a little, uh, distant."

"Do I? I'm tired. It's been an emotionally fatiguing weekend. My parents are in an uproar over Paul. He's moved some floozie in with him up in the studio over the garage."

"Lacey's not a floozie!" I said indignantly.

"Lacey?" asked Sheeni. "You know her?"

"Of course. She's my dad's girlfriend, well, ex-girlfriend."

"You mean my brother is now living with your father's erstwhile mistress?"

"Yes. Isn't it cool? I think it makes you my stepmother-in-law. Don't worry, sweetheart, we can still get married."

"Oh really?" said Sheeni. "I thought these days you might be more interested in an Asian bride."

"What makes you say that?" I asked.

"Stories get around."

"Yes, well, I hear stories too," I pointed out, losing my cool. "About overnight trips to Monterey with aspiring stage directors!"

"Who told you that?" asked Sheeni indignantly. "Who have you been talking to?"

"Who have you been talking to?" I demanded.

"You seem to know a lot about my personal life, Nick Twisp. I wonder, have your informants also divulged the fact that my friend Ed is gay?"

I gulped. "He is?"

"Yes, not that it is any of your business."

"Why?" I asked. "Is he keeping it a secret?"

"Certainly not. Ed is vice president of the Gay Students Association."

"Oh," I said weakly. This was a monumentally embarrassing intelligence failure worthy of the CIA itself.

"How was the play?" asked Sheeni archly. "'Hay Fever' wasn't it?"

"It wasn't very good," I replied.

"Perhaps you had too many distractions," observed Sheeni. "Perhaps your concentration was impaired."

"I don't think so," I said. "You're the biggest impairment to my concentration, Sheeni. You always will be."

"I wish I could believe that, Nick."

"Sheeni, why don't you come back to Ukiah? We could be together. We could go on double dates with Paul and Lacey. Redwood High's not that bad. I'm learning a lot," I lied.

"Nick, please don't ask that. You know it's impossible. We'll be together."

"When?" I demanded.

"Someday," she replied.

"That's not good enough," I said.

"Then marry Apurva!" she exclaimed. "And live happily ever after in your boring small town!" *Click.*

Well, the good news is I am clearly making Sheeni jealous. The bad news is I feel like hanging myself from the bathroom shower rod with Mr. Ferguson's truss.

MONDAY, October 29 — Bruno Modjaleski pleaded guilty. For his crimes he was fined $2,000 and sentenced to one year in the county jail. Then the criminal-coddling, soft-on-crime liberal judge reduced the fine to $1,000 and suspended the jail sentence, provided Bruno perform 500 hours of community service. He has volunteered to serve as coach in the local pee-wee football league, thus assuring another generation of gridiron mediocrity in the valley.

Although they didn't come out and say so, Vijay and Fuzzy seemed relieved that Bruno was spared the state penitentiary. "He got what he deserved," commented Fuzzy. "Standing up Candy Pringle is a serious offense."

"They are going to let him graduate despite his conviction," observed Vijay. "I hope this ill-considered policy does not inspire any prejudice against Redwood High diplomates by the admissions committee of Stanford University."

"Probably no more than is rightfully merited," I replied.

While I was altering reality through mycelial ingestion last weekend, Vijay had been dutifully applying himself to my essay. The completed work was a masterpiece of obsequious teen Indomania. Reading it, I could almost imagine myself strolling beside the Bay of Bengal with my guru—a scholar I imagined to be 16, female, and comely in the extreme. Perhaps Apurva has a pretty cousin who might consent to serve as my mentor.

"I made an appointment after school to get your photos for the passport application," announced Vijay.

"Why do I need a passport if I'm not actually going?" I asked.

"In case the scholarship committee requests your passport number," he explained. "Besides, you'll need a passport to visit Sheeni and me in Paris next summer."

"You're going to France too?" I asked, shocked.

"Yes, my parents have consented at last," said Vijay. "It was quite a struggle. I had to promise on my honor I would not be seduced by any French girls."

"How did you find out about the summer program?" I asked.

"Sheeni mentioned it the last time we talked."

"You talk to Sheeni?" This was unsettling news.

"Occasionally, on the phone," said Vijay, smiling innocuously. "It is a way of practicing my French. She's making remarkable progress, you know."

It's not her progress I'm worried about.

"The last time I called," remarked Vijay, "Sheeni said Taggarty had awarded me an A. I thought, Nick, you said she gave me a B."

"Perhaps Taggarty altered it upon reflection," I said. "Or perhaps a run of disappointing performances by subsequent lovers raised the curve. Women often change their minds."

"I hope so," said Vijay.

What did he mean by that?

At work, I told Mr. Preston, in answer to his inquiry, that the last I'd heard from Dad he was in Eugene and his research was proving most productive. I told this flagrant lie under orders from you know who. Mr. Preston was so pleased, he graciously permitted me to leave work early.

I rushed over to the photo studio, located on the same downtown commercial block as Heady Triumphs, Ukiah's most *outré* hair salon (workplace of Lacey). After Vijay and I had our photos snapped (he felt his exceptional score merited an up-to-date mug shot for Taggarty's Wall of Fame), we stopped in to see my former stepmistress. She greeted us warmly, but looked worried.

"Paulie's parents are the pits, Nick," she complained. "His mother looks like she was run over by a truck and his dad is this big sleazy lawyer who keeps threatening to get an injunction against me. They're such uptight busybodies. No wonder Paulie disappeared for six years."

"I know, Lacey," I said. "They're the all-time Parents from Hell. They've been plotting like crazed zealots to keep me away from Sheeni."

"And succeeding rather well," noted Vijay.

"Lacey, can't you move away?" I asked.

"Well, we're going to look at places tonight," she replied. "But Paulie doesn't make much money yet from his music. Do you know of any inexpensive rentals?"

We had to admit we did not, but—to assist the cause—we both got haircuts. It was fortunate I had had my passport picture taken first. After Lacey completed her futuristic razor styling, my appearance would have halted my travels at any international checkpoint.

"What shall I tell my parents?" asked Vijay, studying his disquieting reflection in the store windows as we strolled away from the salon. He looked like the son of the Indian from Outer Space.

"Tell them there was an outbreak of head lice at school and we all had to undergo treatment," I replied.

"Oh, that's a good idea," he said. "They'll probably believe that."

Dad did not notice my haircut. Mrs. Crampton said it looked "nice," Dwayne declared it was "totally zinky," and Mr. Ferguson said "you wouldn't have got a scalp job like that back when all the barbers were unionized." He was probably right.

Since Mrs. Crampton knew Dad was upset from his emotional loss, she made her famous "soothing" meal: creamed chicken, macaroni and cheese, ambrosia salad, and corn puffs—followed by warm butterscotch pudding with whipped cream. Not even Dad could resist this culinary equivalent of a return to the womb. He began to mellow slightly (the zin helped too).

"Not a bad meal," he commented.

Mrs. Crampton blushed from this high praise. "Why . . . thank you . . . Mr. Twisp."

"How is Jean Paul?" I asked Dwayne.

"Kamu is fine," he replied, as creamed chicken met its maker in his cavernous maul.

Despite his obstinacy and poor table manners, I invited Dwayne to my Halloween party.

"What party is that?" asked Dad suspiciously.

"Oh, I thought I'd have a few friends over on Wednesday night for donuts and cider. Maybe bob for some apples."

"Who's buying the groceries?" demanded Dad.

"Me," I replied. "Maybe you'd like to charge the guests $5 each for wear and tear on the upholstery?"

"Maybe you'd like to watch your smart mouth," replied Dad.

I've heard that line before.

9:15 p.m. Mr. Ferguson took Dad out to a bar to cheer him up, so I immediately called Bernice. She answered breathlessly as usual.

"Hi, Nick honey," she gasped, "I was up on the sixth floor mopping up a bad hair-dye spill. Did you hear the good news? Taggarty got a D- on her History of the Bourbons test!"

"That's great, Bernice. Listen, I wanted to ask you why you didn't tell me Ed Smith is gay?"

"Who says he's gay?"

"Well, Sheeni told me," I replied.

"And I suppose you believe the lying bitch," sighed Bernice.

"You mean he's not gay?" I asked, shocked. Could My Love actually have uttered an untruth?

"No way," said Bernice. "That stud thinks he's God's gift to women."

"But Sheeni said he was vice president of the Gay Students Association."

"Smoke screen, Nick. She's blowing you a smoke screen and you're swallowing it. We don't have any Gay Students Association. The attitude of the school administration is that sex—in any form—does not exist. And in most cases they're right."

I was virtually speechless. "Bernice, are you sure?"

"Nick honey, if anything I have ever told you is not totally true, may I gain 50 pounds and get pimples for life."

What teen could fail to put his trust in that sacred oath? It was time to face bitter reality: My One and Only Love has deceived me.

TUESDAY, October 30 — Bruno Modjaleski returned to school today. When he arrived, the Student Council went into emergency session and, after heated debate, ruled narrowly that their fallen quarterback possessed sufficient moral character to resume his captaincy of the Marauding Beavers. If only he could be granted sufficient athletic skill by democratic vote.

Nor is Bruno likely to attain eminence as a furniture maker. Mr. Vilprang gave him a D+ on his maple dry sink. He said the joinery was crude, the shellacking blotched, and the lines of the piece were marred by "excessive sanding." By contrast, my Streamline Moderne napkin holder earned a solidly respectable C. Wrote Mr. Vilprang, "Craftsmanship lacking but novelty design shows promise. Shellac blotched."

I think it may be time for the taxpayers of Mendocino County to spring for some new shop supplies. According to the date on the can, our shellac expired when I was eight years old.

At lunch Fuzzy announced that his dad and uncle Polly were now offering $100 finder's fees for names of men willing to earn good pay driving big trucks over angry guys with signs.

"Wow, that's some serious dollars," I exclaimed. "I could use an infusion of cash right now. That passport application wiped me out. I wonder if Paul would be interested in a high-paying job?" It was despicable work to be sure, but the necessity of supporting a beautiful bimbette did provide him with a convenient ethical out.

"I already suggested Paul," said Vijay. "I have dibs on his bonus."

"Paul won't do it anyway," I sniffed. "I have no doubt it would be morally reprehensible to him."

Just then, ugly Janice Griffloch drifted by the Nerds' table. I only pray my zits never reach that state of stupefying repellency. "Hi, Vijay," she cooed. "Love your haircut!"

"Thank you, Janice," he replied coldly.

"Where'd you have it done?" she asked. "It's like totally fashion forward!"

"Heady Triumphs," replied Vijay laconically. "Ask for Lacey."

"Thanks, Vij. I will!" she exclaimed, skipping off.

"You know, Vijay," commented Fuzzy. "She's really not that bad from the neck down. If this was India, and all the girls were wearing veils, we might be walking around thinking Janice Griffloch was hot stuff."

"That's right," I agreed. "Vijay, what would you do if, on the day of your arranged marriage, you raised the veil to kiss the bride and discovered a major temblor like Janice?"

"In the first place," answered Vijay, "Hindu girls don't wear veils. And you always meet to chat a few times with the girl and her family before you agree to the match. But if that were not the case, I would simply halt the proceedings and demand additional dowry."

"Like how much?" asked Fuzzy.

"Like the territories of Kashmir and half of Pakistan."

Nice Miss Pomdreck worked all morning typing my application and took it down to the post office herself to send it off airmail to Pune. Dad and Mom both signed proudly by proxy. Vijay has sent an urgent letter to his uncle asking him to expedite the selection process. "Otherwise," said Vijay, "you might be arriving in my country as a studious pensioner."

At work I announced that Dad had reached the outskirts of Salem and was reporting fresh discoveries of lasting significance. Mr. Preston was so pleased, he excused me early for Halloween costume and party-favor shopping. I made my purchases quickly in Flampert's variety store, then hurried over to the library. In the reading room, I found The World's Second Most Desirable Teen—looking glum.

"Hello, Nick," said Apurva. "Did you have head lice too?"

"Certainly not," I replied. "I paid $20 I could ill afford for this haircut. How do you like it?"

"I like it better than Vijay's," she replied diplomatically. "Oh, Nick, what am I to do?"

"What's wrong, darling?" asked Francois, kissing her mint-flavored lips as a phalanx of prim librarians flashed disapproving frowns.

"I had a long conversation with Trent by telephone," she sighed. "He is most distressed."

"Well, he's jealous. That's good!" I replied.

"Yes, but you see, I love him," she explained. "It pains me more than I can say to cause him any unhappiness."

Why did Apurva's heartfelt vow of love for another man cause her to become even more feverishly desirable in my eyes? Perplexed, Francois put my arm around her.

"I know just how you feel," I said. "Sheeni hung up on me the other night and I've felt like moldy cat vomit ever since."

"Trent hung up on me as well," said Apurva. "You Americans can be so rude at times. I was quite taken aback."

"Hi fellows, having another strategy session?" We looked up in surprise as Vijay sat down opposite us.

"Vijay, have you been spying on me?" demanded Apurva.

"Nothing so tiresome as that," he replied. "I understood this was a public library. I am here looking for books."

"You'll find the Richard Nixon biographies on aisle six," I said, smiling helpfully.

"You might do well to read a few yourself," smiled Vijay in reply. "And I don't think this jealousy plot of yours is going to work."

"Why not?" demanded Apurva.

"I'll tell you why not," he said. "What is every teenager's dream?"

"Being recognized for outstanding academic achievement?" suggested Apurva.

"Having an around-the-clock live-in girlfriend?" ventured Francois.

"No," said Vijay. "It is getting away from your parents. Sheeni and Trent are living the golden life. They can do what they want, wear what they want, go where they want. They're free. They're not going to give that up under any circumstances. The only way they will come back is if they are compelled to return."

Apurva looked even glummer. "You mean I have been risking my reputation kissing Nick all over for nothing?"

"You haven't kissed me all over," I objected. "Only on the lips. And I thought you liked it."

"I do like kissing you, Nick," said Apurva. "But it is not in my nature to be so demonstratively affectionate in public. I do not believe it is proper. Perhaps you could remove your hand?"

Francois reluctantly withdrew the offending limb. I turned to Vijay. "Well, bright guy, what do you suggest?"

"I believe the key here is the parents," said Vijay. "Now, what is every parent's worst fear about their children?"

"That you will marry an American?" suggested Apurva.

"That you will never leave home?" proposed Francois.

"No," replied Vijay, "it is that you will ruin your life and bring disgrace and financial hardship upon the family."

Wow, if that's true I may qualify as my parents' worst nightmare come true.

"That's correct," confirmed Apurva. "Parents have much to worry about. No wonder they age so rapidly. But how do we make Trent's and Sheeni's parents begin to worry?"

"We start a rumor campaign," whispered Vijay. Apurva and I leaned closer.

"What sort of rumor campaign," asked Apurva, intrigued.

Vijay looked around. In his most conspiratorial voice, he said, "We start a rumor that Sheeni and Trent are running drugs from Santa Cruz."

"You mean like cocaine?" I asked.

"No, there's plenty of coke here already. Everyone knows that. I was thinking of something more controversial."

"Like what?" I asked.

"Birth control pills," whispered Vijay. "Bootleg ones."

"But that's absurd," exclaimed Apurva. "Their parents would never believe them capable of that!"

"Sh-sh-sh!" hissed Vijay. "Yes they will. What does history teach us? A mild fabrication may raise suspicion, but a major falsehood invites credulity."

"People do seem regrettably eager to believe the worst of each other," sighed Apurva.

"Facts give substance to a rumor," I said, thinking out loud. "Whom shall we say they are smuggling the pills to?"

"It should be someone we dislike," said Vijay.

We looked at each other.

"Janice Griffloch!"

"How exactly does one spread a rumor?" asked Apurva.

"We must recruit someone who likes to chat and comes in contact with many people," said Vijay.

We looked at each other again.

"Lacey!"

In the end Lacey came around. I knew she would. She resisted Apurva's poetry versus windsurfing argument, she dismissed my evil Iowan influence case, but when Vijay said, "Of course, you realize this will cause considerable distress for Paul's parents," she immediately agreed.

"You know what that woman did last night?" asked Lacey. "She sneaked into our apartment over the garage while we were sleeping and started to pray."

"No!" we exclaimed.

"Yes," said Lacey, "she got down on her old knobby knees right beside the bed and started wailing to God to strike me dead. With a lightning bolt!"

"What did you do?" asked Apurva, appalled.

"I said to Paulie would you *please* ask your mother to respect our privacy. He told her to beat it, but she kept on praying like she didn't hear a word."

"Did she finally leave?" I asked, trying not to imagine Mrs. Saunders bursting in on my honeymoon suite.

"Not 'til Paulie threatened to fornicate right in front of her," replied Lacey. "I wouldn't have done it, of course. Paulie's changing the locks today."

"How's the apartment hunt going?" I asked.

"Too depressing to think about," she said. "In our price range we have a choice between stinky basements, chicken coops, and migrant workers' trailers."

"Lacey, tell Paul to give me a call," said the crassly opportunistic Republican. "I might know of an opening for a position fitting his qualifications."

"Vijay sweetie, if you help Paul find a job," declared Lacey, "I'll give you free haircuts for life!"

It would serve him right too.

WEDNESDAY, October 31 — Halloween. Truly a holiday that separates the men from the boys. The boys get to troop around collecting free sweets from total strangers, while the men have to deplete their meager cash reserves providing high-priced refreshments for free-loading party guests. Oh well, at least the costumes help relieve the tedium.

My theory on costumes is that they provide valuable clues to the personality of the wearer. In the third grade I found the ideal costume for me, and have worn it irreligiously every year since. Yes, I enjoy impersonating a robot. I like walking stiffly, talking like a digital voice synthesizer, and having gears stuck to my chest. It feels right somehow. What does this say about me? What insights into the nature of my being have I gleaned? None, so far. But I do anticipate exploring this rich topic someday with my analyst. At present, the roots of my robot fetish remain obscured. I haven't a clue.

All the teachers at school were encouraged to show up today in costume; I suppose so they might serve as objects of even more intense student derision than usual. Most, lacking imagination, chose to appear as bums, infants, clowns, witches, or obscure historical figures relating in some tiresome way to that day's curriculum. A few isolated pockets of creativity stood out. Miss Pomdreck looked majestically sequoia-like dressed as a redwood tree, which, I learned subsequently, she has worn every Halloween since 1958—letting the seams out now and again to allow for the growth of the annual rings. The chemistry teacher, Mr. Sneelbris, created a sensation in what everyone took to be an immense condom, but which he insisted was a test tube. Top honors, however, must go to Mr. Vilprang, who taught eight shop classes dressed as a Stanley No. 45 hand plane. The shellacking on the wooden parts, I noted enviously, could not be faulted.

The fun continued at work. Mr. Preston conducted the day's business in a dark brown frock, decorated mysteriously with wide vertical stripes.

"Are you Friar Tuck, sir?" I asked.

"Don't be silly," he replied, offended. "Can't you see? I'm three-quarter inch A-C exterior plywood. See, here's my APA stamp." He pointed to what on any other day of the year would have been regarded as approximately my employer's bottom.

"Oh, yes, sir. Very clever."

Reaching for inspiration deep within Great Literature, Miss Pliny smoldered just below the inflammation point of her typing paper as Nana Macquart, a character of prematurely liberated morals in a revered dirty book by famed-Frog Emile Zola. I hadn't seen a neckline that low since Mom stopped going to Tuesday night potlucks at Parents Without Partners.

Giving fresh encouragement to Miss Pliny's flagging hopes, Mr. Rogavere moseyed about the office in the ruggedly manly regalia of an outlaw motorcyclist. More than one cow had been driven down the Chisholm Trail to drape our Art Director's tall frame in chrome-studded black leather. The codpiece alone must have consumed several premium hides.

At 4:15 lovely Mrs. Preston, disguised as a somewhat over-the-hill ballerina, arrived bearing home-baked cookies and sparkling cider. Work was suspended and we all gathered in the coffee room to munch refreshments and look down Miss Pliny's blouse. Everyone stole a peek, even Mr. Rogavere, who creaked noisily with every leathery movement.

"Why aren't you in costume, Nick?" he asked.

"They didn't let us wear them at school," I explained. "Some football players got rowdy last year and set a kid in a paper chicken suit on fire."

"Oh, yes," said the ballerina, shaking her head. "I remember that unfortunate incident. I hope those boys were punished."

"Yes," I replied, "they were required to play all the remaining games of the season."

"Any news from your father?" asked the plywood panel.

"He is on his way home at last," I announced, beaming with filial insincerity. "How we have all missed him!"

10:30 p.m. My Halloween party is over. All the guests have departed, except for Dwayne who lingers in the kitchen laboring over the washing up. That is his excuse. I expect he is also gobbling down the last of the donuts. Thankfully, I had the foresight to secret two choice maple bars for tomorrow's breakfast in the lint basket of the washing machine.

It was a good party, but probably not a great one. It was at times more than weird and, toward the end, nearly frightening. That is, I suppose, the most any reasonable guest can expect on such an occasion—except, of course, for alcoholic beverages, and only Dad and Mr. Ferguson got any of those. Everyone else had to endure the festivities cold sober.

The party was announced as starting at 7. Dwayne showed up prematurely at 7:45. Everyone else drifted in right on time at 8:15.

Dwayne arrived looking like a cannibal's feast, ready for the oven. He had smeared his pink blubber with suggestively mottled dark brown paint and wrapped heavy-duty aluminum foil around his corpulent middle.

"What are you supposed to be, boy?" asked Mr. Ferguson, perplexed. "A vacuum tube?"

"No way," he replied. "I'm a Choc-O-Nougat Nibbler. That's my fav'rite candy bar. I ate six yes'erday. Where's the eats?"

By the time the other guests arrived, Dwayne had made a frightening dent in the buffet. Despite repeated imprecations from his host, he continued to graze relentlessly throughout the evening.

Proving piety could be sexy, Apurva came dressed as a nun. "Sister Brenda at school loaned it to me," she announced. "Wasn't it clever of Father to suggest it? I find the habit most congenial, but pray it won't prove inhibiting to the general merriment."

Uninhibited, Francois lifted his robot's mask and attempted to kiss her. She laughed and pushed me away. "Nick, you forget yourself. Robots don't kiss people."

"Whom do they kiss?" I demanded.

"Other machines, of course," she replied. "The microwave looks lonely. Go kiss it."

"But watch out for jealous toasters," trilled a counterfeit Indian maiden, swaddled in a brilliant green and gold sari. In full make-up, Vijay was almost as drop-dead pulse-quickening as his gorgeous sister. With his well-rouged delicate features and amply padded bust, he could have been a serious contender in any Miss Third World Teen Transvestite competition. His companion in an electric-blue and silver sari posed less of a threat—assuming the judges deducted points for inappropriate body hair.

Mr. Ferguson and Dad did not wear costumes, although the former insisted he was dressed like some guy named Eugene V. Debs, and the latter claimed (to Apurva) he was "an international playboy on the make."

"Any relation to those DeFalco goons over at the cement plant?" Mr. Ferguson asked Fuzzy, after I made the introductions.

"No," diplomatically lied the hairy maiden.

"Come, Meera," said Vijay to Fuzzy, "let us get some refreshments before the pooper scooper eats them all."

"I'm a candy bar!" growled Dwayne with his mouth full. "Anyways, 'mericans always eat first. 'Cause we're Number One."

"Odd, you look more like number two," observed Vijay, helping himself to one of my famous peanut butter and brown sugar-coated celery sticks.

"How are they, Bina?" asked Fuzzy, fluttering his false eyelashes.

"Not as cloying as they appear," she replied, chewing demurely.

While my guests chatted among themselves, Apurva and I dispensed treats to the few tardy trick-or-treaters still straggling up the drive.

"Have you gotten my dog back from your friend?" whispered the nun.

"He's not my friend, Apurva. And don't worry," I replied, "it will all be taken care of shortly. How is the rumor spreading going?"

"Quite well so far," she whispered. "I wrote the libelous accusation on all the restroom stalls at school today. And felt very guilty about it too. I only pray Sister Brenda never finds out it was me."

"Just one crummy piece of bubblegum?" complained a small furry animal, possibly a gopher.

"Oh, all right!" I said, tossing another treat into his overflowing bag.

"What was that?" he demanded.

"It was an individually wrapped dried prune," I replied. "They're good for you."

"Oh Jesus!" he exclaimed, stomping off.

"Ungrateful rodent!" I shouted after him.

"Hey, can we have some better music?" demanded Fuzzy.

"But, Frank, it's Frank," I pointed out. Frank was just then launching into his incomparable rendition of "You Go to My Head."

"Yeah, I know," said Fuzzy. "But couldn't we listen to something from this century?"

"I'm sorry," I replied. "All the music for this party has been carefully programmed in advance. If you wished to make special requests, you should have given them to me earlier."

"I like the music," said Apurva sweetly. "It's very romantic."

At that moment I was swept by a desire to do something extremely sinful with a nun.

After another hour of fatiguing socializing, it was time to adjourn to the back yard. Only guests under the age of 43 were invited to participate in the secret rites of ceremonial exhumation.

A cold, damp wind rustled the brittle trees as we gathered graveside in the deep shadows behind the storage shed. Unseen owls hooted in the distance and a scudding of anxious clouds drifted past the sullen moon. When the blade of my shovel bit into the frigid earth, a shiver ran through the huddled figures—especially those clad in diaphanous silks and aluminum foil.

"Meera, I told you we should have worn our wraps," complained Vijay.

"You said no such thing, Bina," retorted Fuzzy. "You told me it was a fashion faux pas to wear a Forty-Niners jacket over a sari."

"Shh-hhh," I hissed. "Let us show a little respect for the dead. Apurva, shine the flashlight on the hole. Not in my eyes."

When I had excavated to a depth of one foot, the shovel brought up a small cardboard box. Inside was a slip of torn paper.

"What's the writin' say?" asked the candy bar.

Gravely I read the prophetic words, "I am not dead." Handing the paper to Dwayne, I added, "It looks to be written in blood."

"Dog's blood?" asked Dwayne, his voice quaking.

"That, of course, I cannot say," I replied.

I resumed digging. Down six more inches, I found another box with another message: "From one will come three."

"Three what?" gasped Dwayne.

"Dogs, you twit!" said Vijay.

Another half-foot deeper produced a somewhat larger box. The message inside read, "Obey my commands or your fate will be an ulcerous tongue and death by slow starvation."

The candy bar gulped. "That's a nasty way to go," he observed.

Five minutes later and nine inches deeper, the shovel turned up the final box—a small wooden one. I paused to let the suspense build before reading these words: "The wrong must be righted. Kamu is Jean Paul."

"What!" exclaimed Dwayne. "Let me see that!"

I handed him the paper. "There it is in red and white, Dwayne. Albert has spoken."

"His will must be obeyed!" proclaimed the nun.

"Well . . ." said Dwayne, wavering. "If Albert says so . . ."

"Nick, continue your digging," said Vijay. "We haven't come to the body yet."

"Well, it seems to have vanished. And I doubt if . . ." I was interrupted by an unearthly chorus of small ugly dogs, howling from the crawl space.

"Perhaps they want you to keep on digging, Nick," said Apurva.

"But this is as deep as I buried Albert," I objected.

The howling grew louder and the wind increased.

"Get to it, guy!" commanded Fuzzy. "Before we freeze to death."

As I probed reluctantly into undisturbed soil, someone very close barked softly.

"Cut it out, guys," I said.

Everyone denied making a sound.

Another muffled bark.

"It sounds to me like it's coming from the hole," observed Vijay ominously.

"Don't be silly," I said.

Another bark.

"Nick, perhaps we should stop now," ventured the nun. "Father wanted us home early."

"Keep on digging," said Vijay, his black eyes burning with ghoulish curiosity.

I dug. Down three inches, six inches, a foot—as dogs howled, trees writhed, and guests trembled. Then, suddenly, the edge of the shovel clinked against a solid object.

"What is it, Nick?" asked Apurva, wide-eyed.

"I can't see yet. It looks like something metallic."

Ten minutes later a robot, two Indian maidens, and a candy bar—groaning with exertion—pulled a dented old footlocker from the now cavernous hole. A half-dozen blows from the shovel shattered the rusty padlock. As eight eager hands tugged on the lid, the ossified hinges screeched in agony, then snapped. At that moment the winds died and the howling abruptly ceased. All was still.

"Can you tell what it is?" asked Vijay.

"It looks like something electrical," I said, gingerly pushing aside the moldy, foul-smelling excelsior. "Apurva, hold the light steady."

"It's a sign!" exclaimed Fuzzy. "A neon sign! Far out. What does it say?"

I removed the decaying shavings, then traced a finger slowly along the cursive glass tubes. The sinuous letters formed the words: AL'S LIVE BAIT. FISH - PICNIC.

"It must be from some old resort," said Fuzzy.

"Do you suppose it's operable?" asked Vijay. "Old signs can be quite valuable."

"Let's plug the sucker in!" suggested Dwayne.

With much unladylike profanity, Meera and Bina carried the heavy sign into the house and set it down on the kitchen table.

"What the fuck is that?" demanded Dad, pouring himself another highball.

"We found it in the back yard, Dad," I explained. "We're going to see if it works."

"Yeah, well, you electrocute yourself, pal, don't expect any sympathy from me."

"It's a deal, Dad," I said, kneeling beside the wall socket. "OK, Frank, get ready to knock me free in case I get paralyzed by an electrical shock."

Fuzzy nodded nervously. I gulped and pushed in the old-fashioned bakelite plug.

Nothing happened.

"Fuck. Must be busted," sighed Dwayne.

"Wait," said Vijay. "Pull that chain there."

I pulled. The transformer buzzed, the glass tubes flickered, then burst into brilliant crimson light.

"Whoooo!" exclaimed the multitude.

"Hey, all the letters don't light," complained Dwayne.

As illuminated, the sign read: AL'S LIVE BAIT. IS NIC.

"It's almost a message," said Apurva. "It says Al's live bait is nice."

"No, it doesn't," Vijay said. "It says Al's live bait is Nick!"

Everyone looked at me.

What on earth do you suppose that means? Could it be a Sign from The World of the Beyond?

NOVEMBER

THURSDAY, November 1 — Sheeni called collect this morning while I was listlessly masticating a mouthful of Cheerios. To my horror, the eagerly anticipated maple bars had disappeared during the night. I have vowed that Dwayne will suffer cruelly for this latest transgression.

"Nickie, why haven't you called me?" asked my Estranged Sweetheart.

"Well, darling, as I recall, you hung up on me," I explained.

"All the more reason to phone, darling," she replied. "These gestures are a cry for reassurance. I need to feel that you care."

"I love you, Sheeni," I replied matter-of-factly. "I love you every moment of every day. I shall always love you."

"Nickie, you sound somewhat tentative," she complained.

"Sheeni! You are driving me insane!"

Reassured at last, she moved on. "Nickie, how was your Halloween?"

"Oh, fairly uneventful," I lied. "How was yours?"

"We had a boring dorm party. Taggarty had one glass of punch and promptly fell asleep. We're all petrified for her, but she refuses to see the nurse."

"Are her grades suffering?" I asked optimistically.

"Oh, yes, dreadfully. I had to write her last Cartesian Philosophy paper. Fortunately, she got an A on that."

"Is that entirely ethical, darling?" I asked, trying not to let my irritation show.

"Do you mean in Cartesian terms?"

"I mean in absolute terms."

"Nickie, the existence of any absolute is very much in question. I have done what I feel is in the best interests of my friend. I shall continue to assist her any way I can."

"Even if it means putting your own academic career at risk?" I asked.

"How would it do that?"

"Well, suppose the school authorities find out you wrote her paper."

"Oh, I don't think that's likely," she replied. "How would they ever find out?"

I know one way. And I know it absolutely.

"Nickie, where is your check?" demanded Sheeni. "I am completely impoverished. I haven't a sou!"

"Darn, it must have gotten lost in the mail," I replied. "Don't worry, darling. I'll stop payment on it and send you another."

"Hurry, Nickie. I am nearly at the point of having to formulate my own blusher out of native clays—gathered from the river bed and ground between rocks."

"That's a good idea, Sheeni. Very resourceful. You could also color your lips with the juice of wild berries," I suggested.

"Nickie, please!" was her only response.

Following Apurva's industrious example, Vijay, Fuzzy, and I spent most of our lunch period inscribing the walls of Redwood High's restrooms with you know what. Unlike your usual slipshod graffiti perpetrators, we took pains to print legibly, spell the names correctly, and write in indelible ink. If only Bina or Meera had been there to do the ladies' rooms.

"Good party," said Fuzzy, as we finally sat down to bolt our lunches.

"Thanks, Frank," I said. "You looked very nice."

"Thanks, Nick. I was kind of getting into it there for a while. Boy, you should have seen Uncle Polly go wild over Bina."

"I had to threaten to slap him," said Vijay. "You know those Italians and their Roman hands."

"Nick, what are you going to do with your sign?" asked Fuzzy.

"I don't know yet. I put it in my bedroom window for now. Odd thing though."

"What's that?" they asked.

"When I plugged it in this morning, all the letters lit up. And they were green, not red."

"Perhaps you've ceased to be Al's live bait," speculated Vijay. "Although I don't think so. It's still too soon."

Too soon for what?

To my amazement, at work today Dad was even more obnoxiously smug than. Believe it or not, his report on Oregon's waferboard innovations has been greeted by thunderclaps of praise from his employer. Everyone in the office was stupefied by Dad's exhaustive research and incisive prose. Not even Dad's turning in a shocking $300-over-budget expense report dimmed Mr. Preston's enthusiasm. He only chuckled indulgently and had Miss Pliny cut his star Assistant Editor a check on the spot.

With my brown-nosing dad setting such a sterling example, I didn't dare leave work early. I misfiled until precisely 4:59, then raced over to the library. Apurva was just walking down the granite steps when I puffed onto the scene.

"Hello, Nick," she said. "No, you don't have to kiss me in public any more. Remember?"

"Oh right," I muttered, pretending I had puckered my lips for purposes of whistling.

"So you are musical too," exclaimed Apurva. "Nick, you have so many talents. That was extraordinarily clever of you to plant those messages from Albert last night. But I'm still curious—where was your poor deceased dog?"

"Right where I had left him," I replied, "still terminally electrocuted. I dug him up the day before the party. There he was—looking only slightly the worse for wear. Must be all those preservatives they put in dog food. Anyway, I planted him again nearby. I hope the mutt stays buried this time."

"Death usually is so reliably final," sighed Apurva. "Nick, I hope you don't think I'm impossibly dim, but try as I might, I haven't been able to deduce your reasons for burying that neon sign. May I ask what that ingenious ploy was designed to accomplish?"

"Apurva, I didn't bury that sign! I was as surprised as everyone else."

"Oh, I see." she said. "That is a relief. I was beginning to fear you Americans were too labyrinthine for me."

"No, we're generally quite simple-minded," I replied. "Only our mating rituals are complex. How's the rumor mongering going?"

"Sister Brenda was incensed at school today," whispered Apurva, moving pleasantly closer. "At morning prayers she demanded that the party responsible for defacing the restrooms step forward at once and confess her guilt."

"What happened?"

"No one made a sound. I felt terribly self-conscious, of course. My heart was pounding so, I almost imagined Sister Brenda could hear it across the chapel. Then I remembered it was all for the love of my dear Trent and my resolve stiffened. I did not step forward."

"Good for you," I said.

"Sister Brenda became even angrier and ordered a general locker search. She said that any student found in possession of red marking pens or birth control pills would be expelled from school and punished by God. Thankfully, at that moment, I had neither on my person."

"Did they find anything?" I asked.

"Shocking quantities of cigarettes were uncovered, Nick. I don't understand—can't people read the cancer warnings? Oh, and they found a condom in Molly O'Brien's purse. She claimed she didn't know what it was—or how it got there. I hope they don't expel her."

"Looks like you're in the clear," I said.

"Yes, Nick. I hope you won't think ill of me, but I'm rather enjoying all this bad conduct. I just marked up the library ladies' room and experienced a remarkable illicit thrill doing so. Am I becoming a evil person, do you suppose?"

"I hope so," leered Francois. "I can think of several more illicit things we could do together."

"Father's right," laughed Apurva. "Nick, you are a very bad influence!"

When I arrived home, canine triplets were slathering disgusting doggy drool on the blubbery, still-brown-in-spots epidermis of Dwayne, lying motionless in the front yard.

"Are you dead?" I asked, wondering if I dared hope for a coronary thrombosis in one so young.

Still sentient, Dwayne rolled toward me and smiled. "Hi, Nick! I brung Kamu back like Albert says."

"Good," I replied. "Just keep them out of sight. And make sure you take the correct dog home tonight."

"OK, Nick. Guess what?"

"What?"

Dwayne smiled blissfully. "Mom's makin' pizza for supper!"

8:05 p.m. Feeling a bit sluggish, I took a brief post-prandial rest in my room. Say what you might about our housekeeper, but you could never accuse her of being stingy with the pepperoni. When I revived, Dad, Mr. Ferguson, and Mrs. Crampton were chatting in the kitchen, so I sneaked into Dad's bedroom to make a call. After an alarmingly expensive wait, I heard my head spy gasp her customarily breathless "hello."

"Bernice, where were you? Christmas shopping in Carmel?"

"Hi, Nick. Nice to hear from you, honey. I was down in the basement polishing the brass valves on the steam boiler. Nick, I need some more you know whats."

"Don't worry, Bernice. I just put another dozen in the mail for you this morning."

"Oh, good, honey. I knew I could count on you."

"Bernice, what's that strange noise?"

"It's me, honey baby. I was sending you a phone kiss. Could you feel it?"

"Uh, yes. Now, Bernice, listen closely. I have another job for you."

I outlined Sheeni's ethical lapse on behalf of her roommate and pointed out the need to bring this scholastic deception to the attention of the proper authorities.

"You can count on me, Nick honey," said Bernice. "We got the goods on them this time."

"Good. Now, what's been happening with Ed?"

"Ed?"

"You know, Ed Smith," I said. "Sheeni's friend."

"Oh, that Ed. He's gone, Nick honey. Expelled. Dean Wilson canned his butt. Didn't I tell you?"

"No, Bernice, you did not. That's fantastic! You mean the dean expelled him for driving without a license?"

"Not entirely. They also found him up in his room in bed with somebody."

Instant gut-wrenching panic. "Bernice, it wasn't Sheeni, was it?"

"No, Nick. It was some wrestler from Santa Cruz High."

I was confused. "A lady wrestler?"

"Er, not exactly," she admitted.

"Bernice, I thought you told me Ed was straight?"

"Hey, Nick honey. What can I say? I was stunned. We all were."

The untrammeled veracity of My Love has been restored!

"Anyways, Nick," she continued suspiciously, "why would you care if it had been Sheeni?"

"I wouldn't, of course," I lied. "But, Bernice, I want to know I can rely on your information. As I recall, you were quite adamant in proclaiming Ed's enthusiastic heterosexuality."

"Well, I was wrong. I guess I should get fat and have pimples for 50 years. Would that make you happy, Nick honey?"

"Not happy, no," I said. But certainly light-hearted, thought Francois.

When I hung up, throbbing guilt drove me to my checkbook. I just hope tomorrow's paycheck can cover my generous $50 donation to the Sheeni Saunders' Cosmetics Fund. I also enclosed a mash note of such unrestrainedly virulent sentimentality that no rational person could question the author's sincerity.

10:20 p.m. Dad just barged into my room (without knocking) and this shocking conversation ensued:

Dad: "I want you to move all your stuff into half of the room."

Son (alarmed): "Why?"

Dad: "Mrs. Crampton is moving in."

Son (more alarmed): "In with me?"

Dad: "No, moron. Her kid's moving in with you. She's moving in with Mr. Ferguson."

Son (numbly incoherent): "M-M-Mr. Ferguson?"

Dad: "Yeah, they're engaged. Big surprise, huh? Course, she has to divorce her jailbird husband first."

Son (horror dawning): "Me live . . . with . . . Dwayne?"

Dad: "Yeah, now move your ass. They're coming with their stuff tomorrow morning."

Son: "But, Dad. That's impossible!"

Dad: "No arguments, pal. Or it's back to Oakland for you. I have to make up for Lacey's share of the rent. This affluent country lifestyle is a big financial drain."

I need a gun. The NRA is right. If you're not armed to the teeth, people are just going to walk all over you.

FRIDAY, November 2 — I've been Dwayned. A fate patently worse than death because, when you are dead, no matter how many times Dwayne burps or farts or scratches his groin and then sniffs his fingers, YOU ARE COMPLETELY OBLIVIOUS. You are beyond mortal suffering.

Dad made me skip school this morning so I could help them unload. Talk about instant slum. Each new horror off the truck rubbed fresh salt into our bleeding aesthetics. Even Mr. Ferguson looked distressed by his bride-to-be's enthusiasm for particle board disguised as Late Empire and molded styrene masquerading as French Baroque. Nonetheless, he has folded up his humble army cot and tonight will be sleeping (and, God forbid, performing other acts) in an ornate bed of an almost inconceivable ersatz splendor. Not trusting my eyes, I had to look twice. It was true: the gilded cherubs on the headboard are indeed playing electric guitars.

Striving to preserve lebensraum for his BMW, Dad closed all borders to the Crampton's army of dead cars—granting entry only to the still (barely) operating Grand Prix and its tow-mate, the Crampton family camper. This is a tiny decrepit trailer named by its manufacturer, in a moment of sardonic whimsy, Little Caesar. Thank God Francois put his foot down and insisted the mobile eyesore be rolled into the back yard, where it is at least partially hidden from view.

Besides being a disgustingly materialistic pack-rat, my new roommate smells bad. For some reason I never noticed it before. Perhaps I had never before experienced Dwayne in such a concentrated form. After he finished cramming in all his debris, my room looked like a deranged toddler's storeroom and smelled like a gangrene ward.

"Gee, Nick, ain't this great," Dwayne enthused. "You got any games we could play on your 'puter?"

"You touch that computer and you're dead," I replied. "And get your stinking Nintendo games off my bed."

"Don't boss me, Nick. Can I turn on your sign?"

"Don't touch any of my stuff. Ever!"

"Nick, this is gonna be great. Just you wait. I'm so happy. And now I get to live with Kamu too. Nick, are you gonna change your underwear now?"

"Of course not. I just got dressed," I replied. "And what business is it of yours?"

"I was just askin'. Geez, what a grumpy grouch. Nick, you wanna wear any o' my clothes? I got lots."

"No thanks, Dwayne," I said. "Halloween is over."

I arrived at school just in time for lunch. Vijay and Fuzzy were shocked to hear of Dad's latest outrage.

"Gee, Nick," said Fuzzy, "if things get too impossible for you at home, you could come live with me. We have lots of room and I don't think my parents would care."

"Are you serious, Frank?" I asked.

"Sure. I told Mom you liked Frank Sinatra and she about had a cow. She said to invite you over any time. And bring your records."

"Thanks, Frank. That's very generous. Who knows? I might take you up on it."

"Ask your dad tonight," said Fuzzy.

Wow, living in a fabulous mansion with a sexy older woman who dug my taste in music. What an opportunity for spiritual growth.

7:45 p.m. My rotten, so-called father said no.

"Why not?" I demanded. "Think of all the money you'd save."

"Your mother wouldn't like it," he replied.

"Why should Mom care?" I asked.

"That's none of your damn business," he replied.

"Is Mom paying you support money for me?" I demanded.

"Hey, wise guy! That's none of your business either. And when are you getting rid of all those fucking dogs?"

"Uh, soon," I replied noncommittally.

Dad is so transparent. He looks at me and sees dollar signs. I've become a major source of revenue for him. No way he's going to let this gravy train depart the station. My situation is worse than desperate, it's hopeless. The bitter truth cannot be denied: I'm a prisoner in Dwayne Hell.

Can't write any more. Have to leave immediately. Dwayne just passed The Fart That Immolated Fresno.

SATURDAY, November 3 — A rough night. Three cups of black coffee later and I still feel like a sleep deprivation experiment gone awry. At 11:30 last night I locked myself in the bathroom to change into my pajamas. When I subsequently entered the bedroom, my roommate was standing stark, corpulently naked next to his bed with a boner worthy of a Freaks of Nature exhibit. If, as appears to be the case, penis size is inversely proportional to intelligence, why is this critical fact not divulged to pre-schoolers? I'd have happily skipped all those hours of homework, watched a lot of TV, picked my nose, and let nature take its prodigious course.

"Oh hi, Nick," said Dwayne, exhibiting everything except embarrassment. "Whatcha got those 'jams on for?"

"Dwayne! Please cover yourself!"

"Hey, Nick. What's the trouble? We're both guys."

"Dwayne, if you don't put something on immediately, I'm going to yell for your mother."

"Oh, what a sissy," he muttered, reluctantly slipping on a pair of dingy sweat pants. "Hey, Nick. You wanna play Nintendo all night?"

"Of course not. I'm tired. Let's go to sleep."

"But, Nick. You don't sleep! Remember?"

"Oh, yeah. I forgot. OK, I'll read. You go to sleep."

"I ain't tired, Nick. Can I come into your bed?"

"Certainly not."

"Why not? Doncha like me? I like you. A lot."

"Dwayne, you stay in your bed. I'll stay in mine. Cross the space between these beds, pal, and I'll scream bloody murder. Is that clear?"

"Doncha like me, Nick?"

"I like you as a friend, Dwayne. Now, go to sleep."

Suddenly an 8.2 earthquake shook the house.

"That's my mom and Mr. Ferguson," commented Dwayne. "I guess they're doin' it now. Nick, were you 'prised when you heard 'bout sex? I was."

"I don't think I was that surprised. It seemed quite logical to me."

"Have you done it with lots o' folks?"

"That's none of your business, Dwayne. Now go to sleep."

"You have a girlfriend, Nick?"

"I do. Yes."

"Do you do it with her a lot?"

"Quite frequently. Now go to sleep. I'm trying to read."

"If you asked your girlfriend, as a favor, would she do it with me?"

"Dwayne! Don't be ridiculous. Guys don't share their girlfriends."

"Why not?"

"Because, they don't. Men are instinctually competitive. It's so there'll be lots of wars to keep over-population in check."

"Oh, I get ya. You're worried 'cause your girlfriend might get knocked up. What if I pull out, Nick?"

"Dwayne!"

Deep into the night the conversation lurched on. Each time sleep drew me to its warm breast, Dwayne posed a fresh absurdity. Finally, after I pointedly refused to speculate why guys had only two testicles even though they had ten toes and fingers, sleep stilled my loquacious interrogator. But not for long. Just as I was drifting off, someone strangled a moose beside my head. It was Dwayne. My roommate snores like six elephants in heat.

A few moments after my eyelids finally closed, they were flung open in panicked surprise as Mrs. Crampton, wearing a pink plastic hair net and a small flannel circus tent, barged into our room without knocking.

"'Morning, Nick," she said, beginning to shake violently her snoring son. "Did . . . you . . . sleep well?"

"What time is it?" I groaned.

"Six . . . forty . . . five," she replied happily, still shaking. "Time . . . to rise . . . and . . . shine!"

Eventually Dwayne ceased to snore and gave evidence of regaining consciousness. Only when both of his eyes were opened fully did his mother finally desist.

"Where'm I?" he asked sleepily.

"In your . . . new home," she replied. "With . . . your new . . . brother . . . Sorry, Nick . . . to wake you . . . but . . . Doc says Dwayne . . . has to keep . . . reg'lar hours."

"Don't worry 'bout that, Mom," said Dwayne, smiling. "Nick don't sleep. He's 'lergic!"

5:30 p.m. A moment of privacy to catch up on my diary. Dwayne is in the kitchen helping his mother prepare dinner. I smell pork grease frying. Mrs. Crampton, concerned that her betrothed is too thin, has decided to shift the caloric content of her meals into overdrive. Soon, I fear, Dad may have to have the floors reinforced.

Mr. Ferguson had to skip picket duty today. An old Vietnam War peace demonstration injury flared up and kept him flat on his back most of the day. The man does not look at all well.

At work this afternoon Mr. Preston discovered me asleep in the coffee room.

"Nick, what are you doing?" he inquired.

"Uh, examining the table top, sir," I stammered. "Is this walnut veneer plywood?"

"Yes, black walnut over a solid core. Very good, Nick." My employer poured himself a cup of coffee and sat down beside me. "Nick, I wanted to ask you something."

"Yes, Mr. Preston?"

"It's about my son Trent. You know he's away at school in Santa Cruz?"

"Yes, sir."

"Well, I was wondering if you've heard anyone talking about any sort of activities that my son may be involved in?"

"You mean like windsurfing, sir?" I inquired.

"No. Something perhaps less, uh, upstanding as that."

"You mean like belly boarding?"

"No, Nick. I'm not referring to sports at all. Have you heard of my son being involved in anything, well, illegal?"

"Why no, Mr. Preston. That doesn't sound like Trent."

"No, of course not," he replied. "I didn't think so either. Still, if you should happen to hear of anything, Nick, involving my son, I'd appreciate it if you'd let me know."

"Sure, Mr. Preston. Will do."

"I mean it, Nick. And please don't think of it as—well, squealing."

"Oh no, sir," I said, "I wouldn't do that."

"You look tired, Nick. Why don't you take the rest of the day off—with pay."

"Gee thanks, Mr. Preston!"

On my way out, I glanced up at the dusty wooden clock over the door. The big plywood hand had inched to within 12 minutes of quitting time. My employer's magnanimous, morale-boosting gesture had cost him less than a buck. Oh well, at least I know our whisper campaign is beginning to reach the proper ears. I wonder if Sheeni's parents have heard?

Waiting for me at home was a postcard depicting three nubile beach bunnies dressed only in tanned goosebumps and tiny, strategically placed sea shells. This message (lavishly misspelled) was scrawled on the back:

Dear Nick,

Back from recent career-threatening injuries, big league prospect Honus Wagner yesterday scored his first home run. The contest was held at night during a total blackout. Pitching for the home team was the knuckle-baller M. "Babe" Filbert. After a short time-out to check his equipment and change batting gloves, Honus drove another towering long ball deep into center field. "Baseball is a very satisfying sport," he remarked after the game. "I recommend it to all my fans."

Your pal,

Honus

P.S. Your brand of batting gloves sucks the hairy jockstrap. They don't stay on worth beans now either.

Damn, another friend over the top, as it were. Despite his abbreviated manhood, Lefty successfully sleeps with his sexy sweetheart, while I—virtually normal in every way—spend my nights cohabitating with The Roommate from Hell. Is that fair, God?

9:15 p.m. I called Sheeni, Apurva, Vijay, Fuzzy, and Lefty—and found not one of them in. Everyone has a social life except me. Even the three so-called adults I live with are out boozing it up somewhere. Dad put on a tie and had the BMW waxed. This can only mean he is on the prowl for a fresh bimbette. As usual, I pray she is interested in younger as well as older men.

Dwayne's placid nature continues to amaze me. Although just ten minutes ago I excoriated him mercilessly for attempting to insert a Nintendo game cartridge into my computer floppy drive, he has just brought me a cup of hot cocoa. Pretty good too.

Can't write any more. Suddenly swept by a wave of overwhelming fatigue. Must rest immediat. . . .

SUNDAY, November 4 — A strange night. After a frightening nightmare in which I was wrestling for what seemed like hours with an amorous walrus, I awoke this morning with a headache, bruised ribs, and a peculiar stabbing ache in my backside. Oddly, my pajamas, which I remember putting on before I retired, were now on the floor beside my bed. My undershorts had disappeared completely. Putting two and two together, I came up with a disturbingly queer total.

"Dwayne!" I yelled.

Abruptly, the snoring ceased. "Oh . . . 'morning, Nick," yawned my room-mate, broadcasting sour breath throughout the room. "Is it time to get up?"

"It's time to answer some questions," I replied, struggling to remain calm. "What did you put in my cocoa?"

"What cocoa?" he asked innocently.

"Don't lie, you cretin! You put a capsule into it, didn't you?"

"No, I put two in it. What of it?"

"So, I know what else you were doing, you disgusting beast. And I'm going to tell your mother!"

"You snitch on me, Nick," he warned, "and I'll tell your pop 'bout you sendin' those pills down to Santy Cru'."

This threat caused me to pause, but did not long impede the headstrong Francois. "I'm going to get you for this, Dwayne," he replied coolly. "I'm going to make your life a living hell."

"Don't be mad, Nick," pleaded Dwayne. "I like you. You can do it to me too. Anytime. Want to do it now?" He pulled aside the covers, revealing a repellent landscape of rolling pink flab.

Just then, Mrs. Crampton barged into the room. "Boys, time to get— Dwayne! Where's your . . . pajamas?"

"Nick made me take them off, Mom," he said, hastily grabbing for the sheet. "He took his off too."

"You liar!" I screamed.

"Nick!" she cried. "You got . . . your pajamas . . . on?"

"That is none of your business," I replied. "And please knock before you enter."

"You leave . . . my son . . . alone," she said, her voice quaking. "He's . . . a nice . . . boy . . . Don't you go . . . co'rupt him . . . with your . . . nastiness!"

Despite Francois' anger, I felt some parental appeasement was called for. "We weren't doing anything, Mrs. Crampton," I assured her. "It was just hot last night. Must be this Indian summer we're having."

Outside it was gray, 42°, and raining. Nonetheless, Mrs. Crampton seemed willing to accept my explanation. "If you get hot, boys, . . . open a window . . . Don't you go . . . takin' off . . . your pajamas . . . That's nasty."

"OK, Mom," said Dwayne meekly.

"I certainly won't!" I replied, glaring at her son.

"Now get up . . . boys," she said. "I'm makin' . . . hushpuppies . . . for breakfast."

10:15 a.m. I have decided never to speak to Dwayne again. As I silently swallowed my hushpuppies (another misleading euphemism for mush), it suddenly occurred to me that I may no longer be a virgin. I wish there were a board of experts somewhere whose job it was to decide these technicalities for teens. If I were speaking to you know who, I'd ask him if he'd had the forethought to don a condom. Probably not, knowing that cretin. Now, along with all the other teen blights, such as pimples and dancing in public, I have to worry about fatal diseases. Fortunately, my roommate is so monumentally unattractive, his circle of sexual contacts must be necessarily minute.

Dad is still holed up in his bedroom; he did not come out for breakfast. I have looked for all the obvious signs—strange car in the driveway, lipstick-smeared cigarette butts in the ashtrays, unfamiliar lingerie dangling from the lampshades—and have discovered no bimbette evidence. It appears that last night I was the only occupant getting laid. As for our other Don Juan, Mr. Ferguson took his breakfast on a tray in bed. The man looks terrible. He is skipping picket duty again today—a bad sign if you ask me.

11:30 a.m. The phone just rang and D——e handed it to me. After an elaborate display of wiping off the cooties, I said, "Hello?"

"Nickie, is that you?"

It was my trapped-in-a-tragic-marriage mother.

"Oh, hi, Mom. What's up?"

"Nickie, Lance caught the burglar!"

"He did?" I asked, shocked. "Who?"

"It was an Indian cabdriver from San Jose!"

I felt a disturbing quiver at the base of my scrotum. "Uh, Mom. What did he say?"

"Oh, he denied it, of course. But there was my TV and VCR, right in his apartment."

"Is, is he in jail?"

"Oh, no. They deported him immediately."

"They deported him?" I asked, fighting panic.

"Yep. Sent his entire family back in fact. Serves them right too. They were all in this country on expired tourist visas. Can you imagine the gall? Fortunately, the DMV had his fingerprints on file from his chauffeur's license."

"Then I guess the case is closed, huh?" I said, trying to look on the positive side.

"Oh no," she replied, "Lance is still checking some other suspicious prints. He thinks there was more than one crook in the gang. Nickie, how's everything up there? Is your father still miserable?"

"I think so. Probably. Mom, I meant to ask you. Are you paying Dad child support for me?"

"Of course, Nickie. Four-hundred dollars a month. It's all I can afford right now with Lance Jr. on the way."

Four-hundred dollars a month! Dad must be netting at least three-hundred dollars of pure profit on me. That's nearly four grand a year.

"Mom," I said affectionately, "could you possibly make the check payable to me, instead of to Dad?"

"Nickie, don't be silly. I can't do that. Why? Is your father being his usual miserly self?"

"Boy, is he ever," I said.

"Nickie, the arson inspectors haven't come snooping around for a while. It's probably safe for you to come back home now. How about it? Don't you want to be here when your baby brother is born?"

"I'd love to, Mom," I lied. "But I can't leave my classes. I'm studying hard, you know."

"That's nice," she said. "And what sports teams are you going out for?"

"None, Mom," I replied. "I've decided to go straight from the sandlot into the American League."

"Watch your smart mouth," she replied.

I've heard that line before.

After hanging up the phone, I penned this brief note and handed it silently to D——e:

Dear Fat Pervert:

Under the circumstances, I feel it is inadvisable for us to continue cohabitating in the same room. Since it was my bedroom originally and you are the interloper, I believe it is incumbent upon you to move out. As there are at present no other bedrooms available in the house, I suggest you transport your disgusting belongings and repulsive person to your family's camper trailer in the back yard. Please do so by nightfall today if at all humanly possible.

Sincerely loathing you,

Nick Twisp

With much head scratching and lip mumbling, D——e struggled through the note, then said simply, "No way."

Furious, I scribbled another note and thrust it at him.

The illiterate lump plodded through this missive and announced, "I don't care what you say, Nick. I ain't goin' out there an' freeze my balls off. You wanta be a stuck-up snob, you go out an' live in the camper!"

Seething with volcanic rage, I turned to go, then paused as Dad shuffled out of his bedroom. His hair was uncombed, his beard unshaven, and his left eye unopened. All the colors of the rainbow (but with the more ghastly purple hues predominating), it was swollen completely shut.

"Dad," I said, "is it OK if I go live in the Crampton's trailer?"

"I don't give a flying fuck what you do," he replied.

This I interpreted as an assent. "Dad," I continued, "what happened to your eye?"

"None of your fucking goddam business," he answered.

Dad's not talking. Probably he learned the hard way that the bimbettes in the boonies can play rough. Good thing for him she wasn't packing a firearm.

4:30 p.m. I am writing this within a tiny birch-walled cocoon—my new bedroom on wheels. To my surprise, Mrs. Crampton offered not the slightest objection when I proposed moving into her trailer. Perhaps she was still disturbed by the nasty bedroom nudity she observed this morning. She gave her consent eagerly and even found an old electric heater to stave off frostbite. We have plugged the trailer cord into an outlet by the back door. I can turn on the heater and my computer, but the addition of a lamp on the line trips the circuit breaker. Thus, I have a choice: I can write in the warm darkness or the frigid light. Perhaps I'll experiment to see which has the most salubrious effect on my prose.

Trailer life is not as bad as I expected. I have set up my computer on the dinette in the front. I have a little propane stove for preparing tea, a tiny sink for brushing my teeth, a fair-sized closet for my modest wardrobe, two musty drawers for my underwear, a double bed across the aft in case Sheeni should happen to drop by, and—best of all—a stout lock on the door. No toilet though. I have procured a large glass bottle as a substitute. The label says "apple cider" so I can leave it out in public view without embarrassment.

Fuzzy dropped by with some hot gossip as I was putting away the last of my things.

"Hey, this is kinda cool," he observed, ducking his head to come through the Hobbit-sized door.

"Yes, I've decided to think of it as my first efficiency apartment," I replied. "I'm pretending it's an artist's garret in North Beach. Have a seat, Frank."

Due to the shortage of chairs, we both attempted to sit simultaneously on the bed—causing the back of the trailer to dip suddenly and the front to rise up alarmingly. Fuzzy leaped forward to balance the weight and catch my sliding computer.

"Hey, don't you have any jacks under the frame?" he asked.

"No," I replied, "what jacks?"

Fifteen minutes later my tiny dwelling was almost as level as the homes in which the more fortunate reside.

"Thank you, Frank," I said. "You have introduced new stability into my life. Can I offer you some tea?"

"No, but I'll take some juice."

"I recommend the tea," I replied.

"OK," he shrugged. "Say, how does your dad look?"

"Like he forgot to duck," I replied. "How did you know?"

"I heard all about it," said Fuzzy. "From Uncle Polly. He was there."

"Where?"

"The Burl Pit—that's a bar out on Old Redwood Highway. Your dad got decked by one of the musicians."

"Paul?" I asked excitedly.

"Sounds like it," confirmed Fuzzy. "Some chick was biting on his ear too. It might have been Lacey. Uncle Polly said she was built like a brick Space Shuttle."

"That's Lacey all right," I agreed. So that's why Dad's been walking around with his hand over his ear. I thought he was thinking about going into radio announcing.

As we sipped our tea, I told Fuzzy about the news from Oakland this morning.

"Wow, they deported him," he said. "That's bad. I hear those guys keep grudges for a long time. Do you think he'll try to sneak back across the border to find us?"

"Maybe. But he doesn't have much to go on. That's not what's worrying me. Frank, have you ever been fingerprinted?"

"I don't think so," he replied. "They took some prints of my baby toes in the hospital when I was born though."

"That's OK," I said. "As I recall you weren't opening my mom's refrigerator with your feet. Has Vijay ever been fingerprinted?"

"I don't know," said Fuzzy. "Let's go call him."

Dad and Mr. Ferguson, looking like recent hospice admittees, were watching a football game in the living room. I led Fuzzy past them into Dad's bedroom and dialed Vijay's number. After a half-dozen rings, Mr. Joshi answered, sounding annoyed.

"Hi, Mr. Joshi," I said. "Is Vijay there?"

"Young man, what is this I hear about your making advances towards my daughter in the public library?"

"Uh, beg your pardon?"

"You were seen kissing Apurva most licentiously. Is that not so?"

"Apurva?"

"Yes, my daughter. Don't try to deny it. After I received you into my home too. But I am not surprised. Boys like you have no respect. Well, you will never associate with my children again."

"I won't?"

"I have instructed them not to talk to you. Ever again. Now, I have nothing more to say to you. Goodbye!"

"Wait, Mr. Joshi. Can I ask one thing?"

"Well, what is it?" he demanded.

"Has Vijay ever been fingerprinted?"

"Certainly not," he replied. "Except, of course, for his green card application. Now goodbye!" *Click.*

"Bad news?" asked Fuzzy.

"The pits," I replied wearily. "Apurva's now officially off-limits and Vijay may have to apply for a parole before he can enroll at Stanford."

"Should we tell him?" asked Fuzzy.

"Better not," I replied. "We don't want him to panic and do something stupid like confess."

10:30 p.m. As I was preparing for bed, I was startled to hear a rustling noise outside the trailer. Quickly switching off the lamp, I peered out through the tiny porthole over the bed. Peering in through the same round window was a hideous, moon-lit apparition—Dwayne.

Yanking the tattered curtains closed, I screamed "Peeping Tom!" at the top of my lungs.

This brought a muffled curse, followed by rapidly retreating footsteps.

I must borrow a tactic from the Viet Cong and boobie trap my perimeter. I wonder where one obtains stalks of razor-sharp bamboo?

MONDAY, November 5 — Another restless night. The trailer mattress turned out to be profoundly lumpy and smelled heavily of Eau de Dwayne. I must measure to see if the mattress in my bedroom will fit. All the windows sweat from the damp night air, and—even with the anemic heater going full blast— the floor is as chilly as a grave in the morning. I also have reason to believe I am not entirely alone. When I opened my underwear drawer this morning, I found two fresh mouse turds and a newly chewed hole in my best argyles.

But all of this, diary, is just beating around the bush. Yes, disaster has struck again. My eye-blackened, ear-gnawed, mind-addled father has suffered another career setback.

HE'S BEEN CANNED!

Miss Pliny, while fact-checking Dad's Oregon article, came across a listing for a similar report in an obscure Canadian forestry journal. Miraculously retrieving the office copy from the files, she discovered that the pages in question had been mysteriously excised. Smelling a rat, she called the editors in Vancouver and had a duplicate copy faxed immediately. Evidence to sustain a judgment of plagiarism was overwhelming. Except for the misspellings in Dad's version, the two articles coincided word-for-word.

By the time I got to work after school, Dad was gone—already history. His messy desk had been cleaned out, his framed portrait of Ernest Hemingway had been taken away, his neatly stenciled name on the Assistant Editor's parking space had been spray-painted over. All that remained was a heavy atmosphere of lingering outrage and ill-concealed censure.

Quickly I developed a serious case of guilt by association. This must be what is meant by the saying the sins of the fathers are visited upon the sons.

"Shall I resign too?" I meekly asked Mr. Preston.

"That won't be necessary," he replied coldly. "But why did you mislead us by saying your father was in Oregon?"

"He told me to," I answered.

"The plagiarism was bad enough," my employer continued reproachfully, "but the phony expense report was larceny, pure and simple."

"Yes, sir," I replied, studying my shoes.

"But we must not forget, sir, that Nicholas himself has been doing quite well," volunteered Miss Pliny, loyally taking my side.

"I hope so," said Mr. Preston, unconvinced. "I've noticed some strange inconsistencies in the files lately."

"It's my dyslexia, sir," I lied. "I sometimes get my alphabet confused."

"Then why did you take a job as a file clerk?" he demanded.

"My father made me," I confessed.

"Just get on with your work," he replied. "And let us have no further mention of your unfortunate father."

"Yes, sir," I mumbled.

I spent the rest of the afternoon lying low in the deepest thicket of filing cabinets. Mr. Preston is right—the files are a mess.

All of this followed a more than usually stressful day at Redwood High. Vijay, being nobody's fool, demanded at once to know what "this fingerprinting business" was about.

"Why do you fellows care if I've ever been fingerprinted?" he asked Fuzzy suspiciously.

"Yes, Nick. Why do we care?" said Fuzzy, handing the ball off to me.

"Well, er, I just thought maybe we should start wearing rubber gloves when we mark up the restrooms. You know—in case the cops try to take some prints off the walls."

"Nick, that is pure paranoia," replied Vijay. "The authorities are not likely to call in master detectives on a case of misdemeanor restroom vandalism. Besides, there must be 10,000 sets of fingerprints on those walls."

"You're right, of course," I said, quickly changing the subject. "Say, who snitched on Apurva and me to your dad?"

"Who knows?" replied Vijay. "I told you that was high-risk strategy. My sister was crying for hours last night."

How flattering!

"Vijay, you can tell Apurva that I'll miss her too," I said.

He looked at me quizzically. "She wasn't lamenting a separation from you, Nick. She was crying over that dog you keep for her. Father says she can't visit it either."

"Oh," I replied. "That's . . . too bad."

"Yes," continued Vijay, "and, of course, I dare not be seen with you. We must be discreet until such time as Father calms down or Apurva is married off. Fuzzy, you'll have to serve as our go-between outside of school."

"Right," said Fuzzy.

"Any news?" I asked.

Fuzzy looked around and lowered his voice. "I saw Janice Griffloch sitting outside the principal's office this morning."

"How did she look?" asked Vijay.

"Kinda nervous," replied Fuzzy. "And her make-up was all smeared."

"Like she'd been crying?" I asked.

"Well, not exactly," said Fuzzy. "More like she'd had a bad case of the shakes putting it on."

"Good," said Vijay. "That'll teach her."

"Teach her for what?" I inquired.

"Unprincipled opportunism," he replied. "She just joined the campus Young Republican Club. And volunteered to be on my committee!"

9:40 p.m. Damn, wouldn't you know it? My bedroom mattress is four inches too long to fit in Little Caesar. For the foreseeable future, I shall know only lumpy, malodorous rest. I suppose I should be grateful. In a few months I may be sleeping on a urine-stained cot in a homeless shelter.

When I arrived home, my jobless father was deep into his second zin bottle. "Where were you?" he demanded.

"At work," I replied. "Some of us have jobs."

"I don't want you going back there," he slurred. "You tell those bastards you quit."

"But Dad, what'll I do for money?"

"There are other jobs in this town. I'll show them. They can't push us Twisps around. Anyway, I'm suing that asshole."

"For what?" I asked.

"For costing me the use of my hand!" he replied, deftly employing his injured limb to pour another tall tumbler of zin. Dad better pray Mr. Preston's attorneys never plant a video camera in his wine cabinet.

In the kitchen, Mr. Ferguson and D——e were shelling nuts for Mrs. Crampton's famous Bliss Despite Unemployment Pecan Pie.

"Sorry about your dad," croaked Mr. Ferguson wanly.

"He sure can booze it up," commented D——e.

"At least he's not in jail for attempted homicide," Francois said, addressing the refrigerator. "Something I hope no one at school finds out."

D——e swallowed nervously. "If they do, I got some secrets to blab too."

I have counted my wad: $28.12 in cash and $13.63 in the bank. One more measly paycheck and then I am tossed, over-educated and underskilled, onto the rusty barbed wire of the teen job market. I wish now I had not been quite so precipitous in sending that generous check to Sheeni. Damn, too late to stop payment on it. She's probably already converted my hard-earned dollars into cosmetics to make herself even more compellingly attractive to other men.

I do not share Dad's optimism I can find another job. And I refuse to don the pastel polyesters of the exploited fast food worker. I know! I'll put an ad in the newspaper to sell my valuable antique neon sign. It's about time I got back something from that miserable beast Albert. Despite buying strictly freight-damaged, expired-date, bulk generic brands, I've blown a small fortune on dog food. If only dogs ate grass like cows. I'd save a bundle and never have to face the lawnmower again.

11:30 p.m. A blustery rain has begun to pelt Little Caesar's tin roof. It sounds as if I were residing inside a large garbage can. How do people sleep in trailers in damp climates? The din is enough to deafen rock drummers.

TUESDAY, November 6 — I was 45 minutes late for school; my alarm failed to go off. Some vandal unplugged the power cord to the trailer. I suspect a dim donut rustler, who—Francois assures me—is courting swift retribution of the most cataclysmic kind.

Janice Griffloch now has the darkest circles under her eyes of anyone I've ever seen not actively fleeing a major famine. I never imagined becoming a Republican could entail so much inner torment. To compound the anguish, Vijay has assigned her the task of organizing a Republican voter registration drive among the unemployed sawmill workers in town.

I received a nasty shock when I told Fuzzy in gym about Dad's getting the ax. It seems I won't be eligible to receive a $100 signing bonus if I recruit Dad for scab concrete hauling (only a few positions remain unfilled). My so-called best pal Vijay has already claimed it.

"But how did he know my father was fired?" I demanded indignantly.

"He didn't," replied Fuzzy. "He's claimed the bonuses for all our friends' fathers. Older brothers too. If they've got a driver's license, Vijay has his dibs in on them."

"But, Frank, that's not fair!" I complained.

"I know, Nick. But those are the rules. Dibs is dibs. You know that."

I think it's time to call a convention to revise the unwritten code by which American teens conduct their lives. If people from abroad are permitted to exploit unfairly these unfortunate loopholes, our entire way of life will be threatened.

At lunch, Vijay said he was sorry to hear of my family's misfortune and asked if my father would be home this evening. I replied I did not have the slightest idea. Vijay shrugged, dug into his deepest pocket, and handed me this smuggled note from his cloistered sister:

Dear Nick,

By now I'm sure you must have heard the bad news. Father refuses to listen to reason. As a last resort, I told him the truth—that we were simply trying to make dear Trent jealous. That only made him even more furious. He blames you for putting such "unwomanly" notions in my head. As if any sensible girl needs the assistance of a male in such arts!

Father threatens if I ever see you again he will advertise immediately in the local Indian press for a husband. I think he may be serious, so I shall have to be extremely cautious. Nevertheless, I intend to sneak over to see you and Jean Paul as soon as an opportunity arises. In the meantime, I will do the best I can unilaterally to further our plan.

I suppose I should not confide this to you, but Father's reactionary behavior only goads me to further rebellion. I desire to lose my innocence. I want to be bad! Yours affectionately,

Apurva

Thrilled to his marrow, Francois penned this brief reply, sealed it in wood shop with high-strength adhesive, and slipped it to Vijay for delivery:

Dear Apurva,

I feel exactly the same. Let us be bad together. I am now living behind my house in a small, extremely private recreational vehicle. Come to me there as soon you can.

Awaiting your lips,

Nick

P.S. Don't worry, I have some you-know-whats.

Mr. Preston took my resignation like the gentleman he is. He said he understood, excused me from further labors, had my final paycheck prepared, and told Miss Pliny to add $100 as severance. What a nice man! Now I wish I hadn't dispersed all of his business receipts quite so randomly through the files. Fortunately for both of us, tax season is still a long way off.

Clearing out my modest cubicle, I left on the desk a copy of Trent's private journal. I think Mr. Preston may find his son's sentiments interesting—especially those passages dealing with the lack of accessible birth control in Ukiah.

Before departing, I went around and shook everyone's hand. Mr. Rogavere wished me well and said I had nearly a natural talent for paste-up. Miss Pliny said with my spelling abilities I was certain to go far in any profession. Mr. Preston said that "considering my parentage" I was "a remarkably presentable young man." I never imagined quitting your job could deliver such a powerful boost to one's self-esteem. What a step toward positive mental health!

As I trooped, one last time, down those dusty stairs, I felt—not sadness, not financial dread—but an exhilarating sense of relief. I had broken the chains of bondage. I was free!

As a free person in command of his own destiny, I strolled to the bank, deposited my unexpectedly ample check, then walked on to the newspaper office to place my ad. I am asking $500 for the sign, but—if pressed strenu-ously—am prepared to come down to $475.

When I got home, Dad, Mr. Ferguson, and D——e were arrayed zombie-like in front of the TV, watching cartoons. There they remained until Mrs. Crampton called them in for dinner. After gorging themselves on food and drink, they resumed their accustomed places for further video stimulation.

Taking advantage of their preoccupation, Francois slipped into my erst-while bedroom. Following his nose in the darkness, he located D——e's odorous school shoes, pulled back the tongues, and squeezed into each toe a generous dollop of Dentu-Lash, Mr. Ferguson's "miracle formula" denture adhesive.

When Francois returned to the living room, Dad was chatting with some-one on the phone. I couldn't make out exactly what he was saying, but at one point I overheard the word "concrete."

10:20 p.m. A soft knock on my trailer door. My heart leaped! Could it be Apurva so soon? Alas, no. It was just Mrs. Crampton trooping through the rain in an enormous yellow slicker to tell me I had a call. I threw on my robe and finished a surprising second in the 20-yard dash to the back door. For a big woman, Mrs. Crampton possesses blazing speed.

"Nickie, who was that who answered the phone?" It was the Woman Who Commands the Remote Control to My Heart.

"Sheeni, darling, what a pleasant surprise. That was Mrs. Crampton, our housekeeper."

"Are you sure?" asked Sheeni suspiciously. "She has a remarkably sultry voice for a domestic worker. And what is your housekeeper doing there this time of night?"

"She's living here, now," I explained. "Along with her retarded son and elderly fiancé. It's become quite a zoo. My dad lost his job and made me quit mine. I've been ejected from my bedroom and now I'm camping out in a trailer in the back yard."

"That's nice," she replied absently. "Oh, Nickie, I'm so depressed!"

"What's wrong, darling?"

"Taggarty and I were called before the Academic Discipline Committee this morning. Somehow they found out about that paper I wrote for her."

"Oh, no!" I exclaimed, mentally kissing Bernice. (The only form of os-culation I'd care to perform with my spy.)

"Fortunately, since we're good students and it was our first offense, they were persuaded to be lenient. Taggarty's going to be marked down an entire letter grade for the course and we're on probation the rest of the term."

"Oh, I see. So they're not expelling you?"

"Of course not, Nickie."

Now it was my turn to confront black depression.

Sheeni continued, "But we are confined to campus for a week. And we have to work 20 penalty hours in the dining hall. It's almost as bad as being in the army. I hope I don't get dishpan hands."

"You have lovely hands," I sighed.

"Thank you, Nickie. Thank you for the check and the nice letter. Nickie! Did you say your father was fired?"

I related the entire shocking story. Sheeni was clearly appalled.

"Nickie, Trent's father hired your father on my personal recommendation. How do suppose that makes me look now?"

"Well at least you're not walking around with half his chromosomes in your DNA," I replied. "Think how I feel!"

"How is he going to get another job?" she asked. "Mr. Preston will never give him a reference."

"I think he may be contemplating a complete change of careers. An opportunity has come up in the transportation field. How are your parents, by the way?"

"As deranged as ever, I'm afraid. Father called me last night in a panic and asked if I knew anything about birth control."

"He did?" I said, instantly alert. "What did you say?"

"I said I felt my knowledge of the subject was adequate and that he should not be concerned unnecessarily."

"What did he say to that?"

"He asked me some completely absurd questions about selling stolen birth control pills. I don't know where parents get such notions. Probably 60 Minutes ran some sort of tiresome exposé on the subject. I wish reporters would be more responsible. Parents are suspicious enough without all this unnecessary media sensationalism."

"So he's not making you leave school?"

"Nickie, why do you always leap to that same dreadful conclusion? Of course, he isn't! Besides, my parents are entirely preoccupied now with Paul's romantic life. Thank God."

"They haven't warmed up to Lacey yet?"

"Hardly. Mother finally gave up on prayer and tried bribing the woman to leave. She refused. Now Mother wants to have Paul kidnapped and taken to a cult de-programmer. So far, Father's opposing that on legal grounds. It ought to make for a lively Thanksgiving."

"Sheeni! Are you coming home for the holiday?" I asked, not daring to hope for an affirmative.

"Yes, Father insists on it. I hope I can see you, Nickie. It will be difficult. The punishment if my parents find out will be draconian in the extreme."

"We shall find a way!" vowed Francois.

"I hope so. I have a nice surprise for you too, Nickie."

"What's that, darling?"

"Taggarty's agreed to accompany me to Ukiah. Won't that be fun?"

"Yeah, a riot," I muttered. "How is Taggarty?"

"Still disturbingly somnolent. This week she started going to an acupuncturist. She's still sleeping excessively, but she reports her dreams have improved."

"That is something at least," I said.

"Nickie, did you mean all those sweet things you wrote in your letter?"

"Of course, darling. What I lack in material wealth, I make up for in extravagant sincerity."

Sheeni laughed. "Oh, Nickie. You make me feel better. You always do."

Still swaddled in the glow of that loving benediction, I shall now retire to my cozy bed.

I'm back. Someone put a dog turd in my pillowcase!

WEDNESDAY, November 7 — They had to call the fire department to school today. One of the more obese members of my gym class couldn't get his shoes off in the locker room. That will teach the dork not to wear tight loafers without socks. Finally the resourceful fire fighters succeeded in prying him free with the Jaws of Life.

During the tense ordeal, Miss Pomdreck held D——e's hand while pretending to be oblivious to the nudity around her. I have observed she often seems to be bustling through the boys' locker room on one pretext or another. Perhaps she feels adolescent youths in jockstraps are in special need of on-the-spot guidance counseling.

To my surprise, Vijay had no reply for me from his sequestered sister to my brash proposal. Francois feels this is a good sign, but I'm not so sure. He has almost persuaded me to believe we are facing an imminent resolution of our clouded virginity status.

Speaking of reckless optimism, Vijay is convinced he will soon be collecting $100 in blood money from Dad's scab recruitment.

"He wasn't particularly interested at first," admitted Vijay. "He mentioned something about completing an on-going literary project while collecting relief payments from the state. But I pointed out that, according to my father, people who are discharged from their jobs for misconduct are ineligible for the dole. After that, it was merely a matter of enumerating the advantages of the proposed employment."

"Which are precisely what?" I demanded.

"Pleasant outdoor work, fair compensation, exceedingly short commute, no constraints on one's freedom to smoke, and no boss constantly looking over one's shoulder. In addition, I pointed out he would be defending the principles of free enterprise and unfettered competition. I think that may have persuaded him. Your father is a clear-thinking patriot, Nick."

Odd, I thought those qualities were mutually exclusive.

"I also pointed out," continued Vijay, "that in this part of your country, driving a big truck is regarded by a large segment of the female population as an extremely glamorous occupation for a man. That may have carried some weight with him as well. By the end of our conversation, he was talking about turning his experiences on the job into a book."

That's an idea. He could title it: *I Scabbed for Sex.*

After school, with no job to devour my precious free time, I strolled by the library in hopes of bumping into you know who. But instead of beautiful Indian scholars bent—charmingly perplexed—over their algebra, I found only desiccated magazine-crumpling snoozers and scandal-mongering librarians. One of the latter, I feel certain, ratted on us to Apurva's father. To repay them all for their collective treachery, I set them to work researching the origins of the mechanical egg incubator—a subject in which I have not the slightest interest.

As I was leaving, who should walk in but Paul, returning some music scores. He looked tranquil and content—as should any man who spends eight hours a night cohabitating with Lacey.

"Hi, Paul," I said. "Watch out for kidnappers."

"Thanks for the tip, Nick," he replied placidly. "Keep an eye out yourself. Sleeping dogs can still bite."

"Will do, Paul. How's Lacey?"

"Lacey is a divine undulation in the cosmos, Nick. How's Sheeni?"

"Sheeni's fine too," I answered. "She's coming home for Thanksgiving."

"Good. Then consider yourself invited for dinner."

"You mean with you and Lacey?" I asked.

"Sure, us and the entire Saunders clan. It's a family tradition."

"But, Paul," I objected, "your parents despise me."

"All the more reason to come, Nick. Dinner's at two. I hope you like turkey."

"I love it. Should I bring anything?"

"Flowers for Mother, Nick. But you knew that."

"Oh, sure."

Wow! Thanksgiving dinner with the Saunders. Who would ever have guessed?

When I got home, I was startled to find Dad huddled around the kitchen table with Fuzzy's scary father and uncle. In the living room, a purple-faced boarder was being forcibly restrained by his wife-to-be and her shoeless offspring.

"Union busters!" shouted Mr. Ferguson. "Scab bosses! Hoodlum scum!"

"Quiet . . . honey," soothed Mrs. Crampton, neatly pinning him to the sofa. "You're like . . . to have . . . a stroke."

"Nick!" yelled the angry agitator, "your dad's turning traitor! He's selling out to the bosses!"

"I know, Mr. Ferguson," I replied, picking up my mail. "But it's of no concern to me. I don't wish to get involved."

Dumfounded, Mr. Ferguson glared at me. "Where are your principles, boy?"

"I haven't any, Mr. Ferguson," I explained. "Like most of the finer things in life, they are a luxury I cannot afford."

On my way out to Little Caesar, I was detained by Fuzzy's uncle Polly.

"Hey, kid. I hear you got a nifty neon sign for sale. How much you want for it?"

"Five-hundred dollars," I replied. "It's an antique resort sign and it works perfectly."

"I'll give you $40," he said.

"Forty dollars!" scoffed Francois, deeply insulted.

"OK, fifty. That's my final offer."

"Do you have it in cash?" I inquired meekly.

Uncle Polly pulled out a mesmerizing green roll, peeled off a crisp fifty-dollar bill, and slapped it on my out-stretched palm.

"Nice doin' business with you, kid. Where's my sign?"

"Uh, in the bedroom," I mumbled, flabbergasted. Maybe I should forget my aspirations of becoming a writer and go into the cement business instead. That roll contained more than Dad's total lifetime earnings to date.

The mail brought another disturbing mash note from Bernice and my new, official United States of America passport. I wish I didn't look quite so much like a destitute refugee child in the photo. And all those official-looking pages so embarrassingly blank. You'd think they'd start you off with a few nice border stampings just so you wouldn't look like a completely untravelled rube.

A sudden racket outside drew me to my tiny trailer window. My moronic dogs were howling indignantly as Uncle Polly packed away his new purchase in the trunk of his shiny black Caddy. I don't see what those free-loading canines have to complain about. I'll probably blow the entire fifty keeping them in over-priced dog delicacies.

That reminds me, if Apurva drops by for some impromptu lovemaking, I must remember to ask for her dog support payment. She's overdue.

10:05 p.m. Damn. No nocturnal visitations. I had even lit a few romantic candles, brushed my teeth twice, and—to obscure lingering D——e odors—doused the mattress with some of Dad's prestigious cologne (Stampede by Lalph Rauren). All for naught. Oh well, I suppose there's nothing like a nice seductive atmosphere for enhancing the pleasures of auto-eroticism.

Earlier this evening I found my old Cub Scout printing kit and spent a few pleasant hours doctoring my passport. I now have documentary evidence of having traveled to every continent except Antarctica—including several nations usually visited only by second-rate explorers, arms dealers, and TV evangelists.

Speaking of merchants of death, that stool pigeon D——e ratted on me to his mother about the shoe incident. Fortunately, I had preserved last night's offending dog turd as Exhibit A for the defense. So it was the loathsome stoolie, not I, who wound up getting smacked with the yardstick. Serves him right too. Then Mrs. Crampton unilaterally declared a truce and made us shake on it. I hope I don't get leprosy in that hand.

She was not as successful in conflict resolution at the "adult" level. During dinner, Mr. Ferguson vowed his intention of blocking "any and all scab truck movement" by the reckless imposition of his "living and breathing body."

"Just make sure your rent is paid up," replied Dad. "I don't want to have to try and collect it from your estate."

I won't repeat what Mr. Ferguson said to that.

11:35 p.m. Can't sleep. Noxious fumes. I think I overdid it with Dad's cologne. This place smells like a mobile bordello.

THURSDAY, November 8 — Only two weeks until I see The Mother of My Future Gifted Children. Perhaps we'll be able to start practicing some of those tricky conception techniques now while our bodies are still nimble. Beginning a training regimen at this stage, experts say, can avoid those embarrassing fumblings later on when the biological gong is clanging.

I think I'm catching a cold. I had to open all the trailer windows last night to breathe and almost froze to death. At one point, I rose in the frigid blackness and spread all my clean underwear out on the bed for extra warmth. That helped some. I suppose I could have moved the heater under the covers, but since Albert's sudden passing, I found I've developed either a healthy respect or a morbid fear of electricity. I can't decide which.

Still no reply from Apurva. Why are women so curiously noncommunicative after receiving sincere and concrete proposals? Do they, contrary to all reports, place a higher regard on subtlety? Should I instead have invited her over to view my stamp collection?

Dad's scab conversion has had at least one positive result (besides enriching Vijay's bloated wad). It was just the prod Mr. Ferguson needed to rouse him from his pre-marital doldrums. He was up like a shot at dawn and back on the picket line fomenting solidarity.

The scab himself was off the entire day at an undisclosed location receiving instruction from DeFalco subalterns in the operation of a concrete truck. He came home grimy with oil and disillusionment. Dad was surprised to learn that the men were expected not only to transport the concrete to the site, but also to dump it. "Those chutes weigh a ton," he complained, guzzling a beer, blue-collar style, from the can. "And then they expect us to wash the damn things. I don't see why. You just get them all covered with gunk on the next load."

"Was the truck difficult to drive, Dad?" I asked.

"Nah. It has power steering and an automatic transmission. An old lady could drive it. Now a BMW—there's a road machine that rewards your serious driving skill."

I know, Dad. I've got the whiplash to prove it. "When do you start, Dad?" I asked.

He looked around warily. "Where's that nut case commie?"

"Still picketing," I said.

"I'm not allowed to say," replied Dad striving, unsuccessfully, for inscrutability. "It's top secret."

"Fuzzy at school said they were going to fire up the plant tomorrow morning," I pointed out.

"Don't tell that wacko," he warned. "Flora is having him drive her down to San Quentin tomorrow to meet her husband."

"What for?" I asked.

"How should I know? Maybe they want his blessing on their happy union."

"I hope he takes it like a gentleman," I said doubtfully.

"I hope he murders the old commie," replied Dad, swigging his beer. "It'll save me the trouble of running him over."

9:45 p.m. My cold is worse. Kindly Mrs. Crampton gave me her old electric blanket, so perhaps I won't freeze again tonight. The thermostat is broken, but she assures me it still "gets to cookin' real nice."

I just had a long phone conversation with Lefty, my post-virginal pal in Oakland. He reports that he has now done it with Millie Filbert seven times.

"How was it?" I asked enviously.

"Great," he replied. "It was worth all the work."

"Does Millie seem, uh, fulfilled?"

"If she's not, she'd doing an incredible job of faking it," he said. "It's better for me too since I swiped a different brand of condoms."

"Do those stay on?" I asked.

"More or less."

"You mean they sometimes come off?"

"Well, once or twice. Hey, what do you want me to do, staple them on?"

"You have to be careful, Lefty. In 18 years that kid is going to ask you for $100,000 for college."

"Hey, I'm careful. And Millie has me taking lots of hot baths and wearing tight pants. She's really into contraception."

"Don't I know it," I replied ruefully.

"What?"

"Uh, Lefty, where are you two performing the act?"

"Millie's bedroom, believe it or not. She talked her parents into signing up for a Tuesday night group-therapy bowling league. It works out great. While they're out discussing their problems and bowling, we're upstairs balling."

"You keeping the lights off?"

"Like Wrigley Field at midnight. Millie thinks it's cute I'm so shy."

"How's your size?"

"It's been slow, Nick. I think I might've creeped up an eighth of an inch. Depends on where I put the ruler. One good thing, I am solid as a rock. I got one hard stubby pecker."

"Good, Lefty. Women put a great premium on the solidity of the erection. And how's your court case coming along, by the way?"

"Oh, I beat that rap."

"You did!" I exclaimed. "How?"

"That wimp Clive Bosendorf's parents chickened out on pressing charges. Then the judge threw out the shoplifting complaint for lack of evidence. Somebody heisted the goods from the police storage locker."

"Lefty, you're in the clear!"

"Don't I know it, Nick," he replied. "I learned my lesson this time."

"What's that, guy?"

"Crime pays!"

FRIDAY, November 9 — Can't write much. Too sick. Skipping school. Feel like tertiary malaria victim. Had a dream last night I was working as a slave laborer in a ham canning plant. Woke up sweating buckets under the Electric Blanket from Hell. Broken dial stuck on "High." Chest all red. First degree burn?

Lots of sirens, deep booms, and incoherent exhortations through bullhorns from direction of concrete plant. Oops, what was that? Sounded like a howitzer blast.

Can't write any more. Have to go puke.

SATURDAY, November 10 — Praying for recovery or death. Don't care which at this point. Twenty-three strikers arrested, four in hospital, scab concrete now rumbling like clockwork past my sickbed. Strike-breaking Dad earning time-and-a-half for weekend work. Likes job. Says other drivers on road rarely contest right-of-way with big concrete trucks. Mr. Ferguson, back from San Quentin, totally pissed he missed battle. Blames fiancée. Broke off engagement and now bunking with D——e.

SUNDAY, November 11 — Recovery dealt serious blow by dead-of-night tire slasher. Little Caesar now listing ten degrees to starboard. Bed at radical angle. Have to hang on or roll out. Difficult to nap under these circumstances. Dad incensed by vandalism to precious BMW. All vehicles on property struck except Mr. Ferguson's aged Toyota. Dad accused elderly agitator of complicity in deed. Big argument. Dad ordered Mr. Ferguson to move out. He refused unless paid pro rata rent refund. Immediate stalemate. D——e in doghouse for making untoward advances on ex-future stepfather.

MONDAY, November 12 — Have not vomited for six entire hours. Feel corner has been turned. Life may be worth living after all. Vijay called from school with good news. Have won prestigious scholarship to study in India. He has released story and my photo to newspapers. "They sent you a voucher for your ticket," he added. "The program is on-going. Just cable them when you expect to arrive in Bombay." Almost might be persuaded to go if they promised me a level bed. More good news: Ferguson-Crampton engagement back on. Mr. Ferguson off rallying troops for another decorate-your-face-with-tire-tracks plant block-ade. Mrs. Crampton secretly frying resistance meatballs for beleaguered union stalwarts. D——e in doghouse for chronic underwear boycott.

11:30 p.m. Well, it happened. I might as well get the story down on microchip while the wounds are still fresh. As I was doggedly attempting to read *The Old Wives Tale* by Arnold Bennett (having first skimmed unsuccessfully for ribald passages), I heard a gentle tapping on my door. "Come in," I croaked. More soft tapping. "Come in Mrs. Crampton!" I shouted. "You can take my dinner tray away now." The door unlatched and swung slowly open.

"Nick, is that you?" asked a lilting, tentative voice.

Apurva!

Fighting panic, I tossed my book and pulled the covers up over my vomit-specked pajamas. Had it really been three days since my last shower?

"Hi, Apurva," I gasped. "Come in."

The trailer creaked as Apurva climbed in through the narrow doorway and warily looked around. She was in full, no-holds-barred make-up and smelled of flower-strewn Himalayan meadows.

"Nick, it's so small!" she exclaimed. "Is this really where you are staying?"

"For the time being. I don't mind it."

"Oh, Nick. You're in bed! Am I disturbing you?" she asked hesitantly.

"Not at all, Apurva. I was, uh, hoping you'd drop by. Please, take off your coat. What happened to you anyway?"

"I'm sorry, Nick. Father wouldn't let me out of his sight. Fortunately, he was called away unexpectedly on business today. He made me promise I would stay in my room. Of course, he does not realize I am now resolved to be bad. Nick, does the floor always slope at this peculiar angle?"

"Not usually. There's been a sudden deflation of the tires. I was intending to fiddle with the jacks tomorrow."

"I see," she replied. Struggling to maintain her balance, she removed her gloves, scarf, and coat. I was surprised to see her hands were shaking. Francois was thrilled to see she had dressed for the occasion in a ravishing red knit dress that draped every enticing contour without restraint or apology. Since Francois often displays these very same qualities, I decided to let him do the talking.

"Have a seat, darling," he said suavely. "I'd offer you some refreshments, but it's the butler's night off."

"Thank you, Nick. That's all right," said Apurva, sitting at the tiny dinette and struggling—with some difficulty—to keep from sliding off while modestly pulling her dress down over her lovely wheatish knees. "Nick, you don't look at all well," she continued, gripping the door handle for support. "Perhaps I should leave you to rest."

"No! No, Apurva. I'm fine really. Never felt better."

"Are you sure? Forgive me for saying this, but your eyes are watery and your nose appears to be inflamed."

"Hay fever," explained Francois. "Always get it this time of year."

"Oh, that is a shame. Sister Brenda is similarly afflicted. She doesn't mind. She feels harsh nasal discomfort is a worthy penance for her sins. Nick, are you cold? You are all wrapped up in blankets."

"Well, you see, sweetheart," Francois explained, "I don't have much on underneath."

My guest turned scarlet and looked away. "I'm sorry. Perhaps I should leave and let you dress."

"Don't be sorry, darling. I have nothing to hide from you. Do you have anything to hide from me?"

Apurva blushed even deeper and examined the weave of her dress. "I, I don't want to. Not necessarily."

"Would you like to come sit on the bed? It's big enough for two."

"Well, I suppose I could. You're sure you are well enough to receive visitors?"

"Never better," I coughed. "I've never known a sick day in my life."

Apurva edged toward the bed and sat down primly on the lumpy mattress. Only by rigidly bracing her knees was she able to keep from sliding toward the feverish Francois.

"Nick, what is that peculiar odor?"

"Stampede. It's my expensive cologne. Like it?"

"Perhaps—in moderation." She picked up my discarded book. "Oh, what are you reading? I've been reading endlessly since I've been staying home."

Francois plucked the book from her hands and flung it across the trailer. Apurva gave a nervous start. "Let's not discuss literature," he said.

"What, what shall we discuss then?" she asked. "How is my sweet dog?"

"Forget your dog!" he replied. "Let's discuss how that lovely dress unfastens."

Without a word Apurva reached behind her, undid a clasp, and slowly pulled down the zipper. "Do you mind if we turn off the light?" she asked.

"Not at all," said Francois, flipping off the wall lamp while simultaneously shedding his foul pajamas. He reached over and pulled her toward him. She resisted only moderately.

"Are you entirely naked?" she whispered.

"More or less," replied Francois, struggling with her bra snaps in the darkness.

"Please don't do that, Nick," she said, wriggling away. "Let's talk first." But gravity rolled her exquisite body inexorably back toward me. My lips sought out hers and Francois' eager hand found a warm breast clothed in softest wool.

"Oh, Nick. I do like you," she sighed. "But . . .

"But what, darling?" cooed Francois.

"But your nasal discharge is dripping on my cheek."

"Oh, sorry!" I exclaimed, searching among the blankets for my ghastly handkerchief. No luck. Desperate, I used a corner of the sheet.

"Nick, are you quite sure you're all right?"

"Yes, but I'm terribly allergic to wool," lied Francois. "Would you mind removing your dress?"

"I'd like to, Nick. But . . ."

Francois paused in his relentless groping for the elusive bra clasp. "But what, darling?"

"Forgive me for speaking so bluntly, Nick, but the circumstances are not as I imagined them to be."

"Are you uncomfortable?" I asked. "Would you like another pillow? Shall I turn on the electric blanket? We'll be toasty in a jiff."

"Nick, you must realize that when a young woman is growing up, she is naturally curious about, well, these matters and often fantasizes about her first experience of, of lovemaking. Perhaps you have had similar thoughts?"

"They've crossed my mind once or twice," I admitted.

"Naturally, then you can understand why a young woman should desire that her first time be, well . . . as pleasant as possible. She would not wish to have the experience tainted by anything smacking of, well . . . sordidness."

"The mattress is not up to your standards, huh?" I sighed. "I want you to know I am not responsible for that odor. It's an unfortunate legacy of a prior occupant."

"It's not only the bed, Nick," she explained. "This doesn't feel right. It would be disloyal to Trent."

"But Trent never has to know!" argued Francois.

"But I shall know. And you will know. Nick, you must get well, move out of this dreary trailer, and save yourself for Sheeni. Believe me, we shall all be happier in the long run. All four of us—you, me, Trent, and Sheeni."

Yes, but what about Francois? In the short run he has to cope with the T.E. That Wouldn't Die.

At that moment we were startled by the sounds of a violent altercation outside. Apurva leaped from the bed, zipped up her dress, and peered out the window.

"Oh my God!" she exclaimed. "It's Father!"

I groaned and dived under the covers.

"Come quickly, Nick!" shouted Apurva, throwing on her coat. "Your father is murdering him!"

Dad did not murder Mr. Joshi. He just bloodied his nose and tore his suit. In return, Mr. Joshi added a fresh greenish-purple patina to Dad's bar-brawl black eye. This is not to say as they grappled, panting and swearing, in the mud that they did not wish to murder each other. Clearly, homicide was on their minds. But a vigorous knee to the groin, although acutely distracting, is seldom life threatening. Still, for two wimps going at it bare-handed, the combat was surprisingly ferocious. Apurva, for one, was terrified.

"Leave him alone!" she screamed, pounding on Dad's back and sore ear.

"I'll teach you, you communist!" bellowed Dad, gouging his opponent's nose.

"I'll marry you off, you harlot!" gasped Mr. Joshi, presumably addressing his rescuer.

After ten hellish minutes, the combatants had been separated, threats of multi-million dollar lawsuits had been hurled, I had been singled out for a slashing excoriation by you know who, and sweet Apurva had been dragged off and hustled into the Reliant. As Mr. Joshi roared off into the night, Dad clutched his injured eye.

"Did you get the fucking license plate number?" he demanded.

"Uh, no. Sorry."

"Damn! Say, who was that girl?"

"I don't know," I lied. "She said she was selling magazine subscriptions. Why did you attack him, Dad?"

"I spotted the asshole sneaking up the drive toward my car," replied Dad, daubing his eye. "I'll teach those union goons to destroy other people's property!"

I decided under the circumstance it was best not to correct Dad's misapprehension.

"Funny," he continued, "I think I've seen that Mexican son-of-a-bitch somewhere before. And why was he yelling at you?"

"Search me, Dad," I shrugged. "I'm trying to stay neutral in these labor disputes."

TUESDAY, November 13 — Feeling much better, but I decided to stay home from school anyway. I see no point to missing school only on days when you are too miserable to enjoy your idleness. As another labor Armageddon raged in the distance, I spent the morning giving Little Caesar a much-needed fall cleaning. I swept the floor, washed the windows, scrubbed down the walls, scoured the tiny sink, and laundered the diseased sheets. I even dragged out the ancient mattress to "freshen" in the sun—a hygienic practice drilled into me by generations of fastidious Cub Scout camp counselors. I also succeeded in restoring my tiny home to a more or less even keel.

Francois dismissed my frenetic housekeeping as nothing more than sublimated sexual frustration. He's right, of course, but personally I'd rather have an immaculate trailer than a nervous breakdown.

With that accomplished, I rode my bike past the ambulances and sheriff's cars, and treated myself in town to a well-deserved donut break. As usual, I skipped the franchise donut palaces and gave my business to a small place downtown where the only thing older than the aged proprietress is the grease in the blackened deep fryer. Issues of rancidity aside, the donuts are varied, generous-sized, and breathtakingly cheap.

I almost choked on my second maple bar when I opened the newspaper to find a familiar spotted visage beaming out from page five. There, arrayed photographically across three columns, was Ukiah's most distinguished teen— me. I read and reread every glowing word with immense satisfaction. What a lift to the spirits! So what if the article contained a few inaccuracies (I, for one, have never claimed to have an IQ of 195).

I gobbled down my donuts in a fog of pleasure, then raided a newspaper rack for all of its copies. Some I shall give to friends, some I shall put aside for future biographers, and some I shall mail anonymously to girls who have snubbed my overtures over the years. I only wish I could be there to witness their expressions of bitter self-reproach.

I got back home just in time to answer a noon call from Vijay.

"Did you see the article?" he asked excitedly.

"Yes, it was a tremendously flattering write-up," I said. "I appreciate, Vijay, your refusal to be inhibited by the constraints of truth. You have a great future ahead of you in public life."

"I do enjoy misleading the press," he conceded.

"Perhaps this is why you are an active Republican," I noted. "Speaking of reactionary impulses, how is your father?"

"He is quite upset, Nick. Is it true you have slept with my sister?"

"What does she say?"

"She says you were just talking. Father wanted to take her to a hospital last night and have her examined, but Mother finally dissuaded him. Well, go on. Tell me. Confess your crimes. What happened between you two?"

"Vijay, if your sister says we were just talking, I am certainly not going to contradict her. That would be ungentlemanly. How is Apurva, by the way?"

"Quite distraught. Father was threatening to send her back to India. But now that he thinks you're going, he's changed his mind. He says he wouldn't trust his daughter on the same continent with you."

Now it was Francois' turn to feel flattered.

"Tell Apurva I'm sorry that she got in trouble," I said. "And tell her she's welcome to drop by any time," added Francois.

3:30 p.m. I heard a noise like a 747 crashing and rushed into the house. Mrs. Crampton was lying on the kitchen floor in a dead faint. The telephone was off the hook beside her. Putting two and two together, I deduced that she had just received some bad news. Praying some tragedy had befallen her son, I set about reviving her to find out. No such luck. Today's shocking news concerned her other loved one. Mr. Ferguson has been arrested! He's in the county jail charged with inciting a riot, resisting arrest, and assault and battery on an officer.

"It's ... not fair," complained Mrs. Crampton, when she came to. "Now ... both my ... menfolk ... are in prison!"

7:30 p.m. Dad has put his foot down and forbade my studying abroad. He says I am too young and am needed at home. We all know what is really needed at home—Mom's monthly support check. If Dad were still writing those hefty checks, I'd already be working on my Pune tan.

Mrs. Crampton just phoned and asked for a loan of $15,000 for Mr. Ferguson's bail. Dad refused and suggested she call the American Communist Party.

11:30 p.m. We just watched Mr. Ferguson on the local news smack a deputy sheriff over the head with his riot shield. There was also a brief glimpse of Dad scattering some strikers as he roared through the gate with six tons of scab concrete. Everyone made the news except me. Why no mention of important scholarship winners? The press-bashers are right: the media has a deplorable bias against good news.

WEDNESDAY, November 14 — I'm a celebrity at school! Every teacher congratulated me in class, including Mr. Vilprang, who said he hoped I would be able to continue my woodworking studies in India.

Then in study hall I was interviewed for the school paper by a cute junior named Tina Manion. I gave her my entire life story (selectively embellished by Francois), a recent photo, and my phone number. Fuzzy told me later I was fishing out of my depth. He said Tina was going with a college guy and wouldn't be caught dead dating someone from Redwood High—especially a non-athletic, "scum of the earth" freshman. I said it was just that sort of pessimistic attitude that kept him alone on Saturday nights.

"I wasn't alone last Saturday," replied Fuzzy, offended. "I had two hours of hot phone sex with Heather."

I hope all that electronic intercourse doesn't backfire on my friend. He'll be sorry when he grows up and discovers he can't get it on without a handset pressed to his ear.

5:30 p.m. Dad came home whistling suspiciously. I fear he may have flattened his first striker. He also appears to be acquiring some unexpected bulges under his shirt. Can he actually be developing muscles? A Twisp with a physique—what next!

Mr. Ferguson got sprung this afternoon, no thanks to his fellow travelers. He was obliged to put up the deed to his house as security for his bail. Mrs. Crampton has laid down the law: her fiancé has to choose between her and the picket line. What an argument against free will.

7:45 p.m. Dad just got spiffed up and left the house. He has a date. With a woman!

Right after he left, Paul telephoned sounding uncharacteristically nonmellow. He reported that Lacey came out of work today to find that someone had jimmied a window on her Toyota and filled her austere vinyl interior with three cubic yards of rapidly solidifying concrete. She has given a description of Dad to the Ukiah police!

I can't help but wonder if there's some symbolism in this particular act of vandalism. Why concrete, Freudians ask? And what does he really wish to seal up?

10:30 p.m. Sheeni just called in a mild panic.

"Nickie, my parents are totally ecstatic. They say you've won a scholarship to study in India!"

"That's right, darling. You see, you're not the only one interested in exotic foreign cultures."

"But Nickie, you can't go!"

"Why not, darling? I have my passport and everything. I've been granted 10,000 captive rupees as my first year's stipend. It's the first time I've ever had

10,000 of anything—let alone captive rupees."

"But Nickie, if you leave Ukiah my parents will . . . I mean, I'll miss you terribly."

"As usual, Sheeni, the solution is in your hands."

"What do you mean?"

"Leave that school, darling, and I'll repudiate my scholarship—even if it creates an international incident."

"Why don't you turn down your scholarship, Nickie, and I'll think seriously about coming back?"

"Sorry, Sheeni. I need more of a commitment than that. We're at a crossroads, darling. These are momentous, life-altering decisions we're facing. Who knows what wonderful prospects await me in India?"

"When are you leaving?" she asked sullenly.

"I'm not sure," I replied. "Possibly after Thanksgiving dinner at your parents' house."

"Don't be silly, Nickie. I couldn't possibly invite you."

"That's OK, darling. I'm already invited—courtesy of your hospitable brother."

"Nick! My brother is an idiot. You are *not* coming to Thanksgiving dinner!"

"Sorry, Sheeni. I can't refuse now after already accepting. That would be ungracious. Besides, I've promised to bring flowers for your mother."

"Nick, my father has a loaded pistol in the top drawer of his bedroom bureau. He may be capable of extreme violence. I fear he is losing whatever slight grip he had on his reason. He appears to be obsessed with paranoid fantasies involving smuggled birth control aids. He just spent another 45 minutes interrogating me on the subject. Now he claims to have seen some sort of written confession by Trent."

"What did you tell him?" I asked, thrilled.

"I refused to discuss it. I told him to take two aspirin and lie down."

"Good for you, Sheeni. That's the only tack to take with obstreperous parents."

"Nickie, darling," said Sheeni, shifting her magnificent charm into overdrive, "you won't go to India or come to dinner, will you?"

"No, darling," I cooed. "I promise I won't be any more intransigent than you."

"Oh, Nick! You are impossible!" *Click.*

I wonder if Mr. Saunders really has a loaded gun? I must keep my guard up. If he excuses himself to go to his bedroom, I shall exit immediately.

THURSDAY, November 15 — 3:30 a.m. I was just awakened by a rude knocking on my trailer door.

"Who is it?" I demanded.

"Me, Nick," answered D——e.

"Suck the gas pipe!" I replied, rolling over.

"It's your pop!" he called. "He wants you on the phone."

"Oh, all right!"

Expecting the worst, I followed the near-nude emissary back into the house. As usual, Dad did not disappoint.

"Nick," he said, "this is your father."

"Hi, Dad."

"There's been a slight misunderstanding. I'm down here at the police station. I want you to call up your mother and have her arrange for my bail."

"What did you do, Dad?"

"Never mind that now."

"How was your date?" I asked.

"Nick, just call your mother. Tell her I'll pay her back right away."

"OK, Dad. She gets up about seven. I'll call her then."

"Call her now, dammit! I don't want to spend another minute in this stinking hole."

"Oh, all right, Dad," I replied. "Keep your shirt on."

I dialed Mom's number and my worst nightmare came true. Lance answered.

"Hi, Lance," I said, pleasantly businesslike. "This is Nick, your putative stepson. Is Mom there?"

"This better be fucking important, dipshit!" the cop growled.

"Nickie, is that you?" asked Mom, sounding groggily alarmed. "What's wrong? Are you in trouble?"

"Not me, Mom. It's your first husband. He's in jail in Ukiah and wants you to bail him out."

"He does what!"

"He wants you to spring him from the slammer," I said, adopting the appropriate B-movie patois.

"What was the louse arrested for?"

"I'm not sure, but the charge may be malicious mischief. He's allegedly filled his old girlfriend's car with cement."

"Nick, you tell that no-good philandering father of yours that as far as I'm concerned he can rot in jail. I wouldn't spend ten cents bailing him out!"

"That's how I thought you'd feel, Mom," I replied.

"And Nickie, if your father is in serious trouble, you get on the bus to Oakland. I mean it."

"I will, Mom," I lied.

Hanging up the phone, I looked around the kitchen for potential bail donors. I found only three bleary-eyed prospects, none from the affluent classes. One I rejected out of hand on moral grounds. That left two.

"Uh, Mr. Ferguson . . ." I began tactfully.

"Nothing doing, Nick," he stated firmly. "You tell that rotten scab to call the American Nazi Party."

"Mrs. Crampton?" I said hopefully.

"Sorry... Nick," she replied. "I ain't got... but six dollars... to my name... Your dad... owes me... three weeks' back... pay!"

In the end, I had to throw myself on the bristling mercies of my sister Joanie. She bows to no one in her dislike of Dad, but finally agreed to wire a short-term, high-interest loan to save her only brother from Life With Lance.

I fear another financial crisis looms. What will happen to us if Dad gets fired from his scab job? How will I pay my monstrous phone bill?

4:15 p.m. More bad news. Fuzzy took me aside in gym class to relate a shocking story. His mother, purportedly off administering to a sick friend, arrived home in the middle of the night in a Ukiah police car. She had been detained on charges of public inebriation and disorderly conduct, after having been discovered at the Burl Pit tavern in the company of my father.

"Your mother was out with my dad?" I asked, flabbergasted.

"That's what I understood from all the screaming," whispered Fuzzy, earnestly pretending to be performing vigorous sit-ups.

"How in God's pajamas did they meet?" I asked.

"I heard Dad accusing her of hanging around your dad's truck," replied Fuzzy.

"Your Dad was pissed, huh?"

"Totally ballistic."

"Wow, Frank, this is incredible!"

"Yeah, Nick. I guess this almost makes us brothers."

"Yeah, well, at least your side of the family has money," I said bitterly. "Now Dad's sure to be fired!"

7:30 p.m. Or perhaps not. Dad came home from work whistling like he'd just been awarded the Nobel Prize for Truckdriving. I immediately dialed Fuzzy for an update.

"Uncle Polly," he explained. "He's still pissed at Dad for trying to hijack Grandmamma's car. So he went to bat for your dad. He told my dad your father was their best new driver. He also said your dad's cement seatcovers stunt took a lot of balls. But they're docking his pay for the missing concrete."

"So they're not firing him?"

"Firing him? Uncle Polly gave him a raise and a promotion. Dad's still pissed, though."

"How about your mother?"

"She laid down the law at dinner. She said if Dad can diddle the entire dispatching department, she's at least entitled to date one truckdriver."

"You mean they might see each other again?" I asked.

"Could be, Nick. Who knows? But your dad better watch his ass."

"Does your father have any guns, Frank?"

"Any guns!" exclaimed Fuzzy. "Don't spread this around, Nick, but we have a room in the basement that looks like a National Guard armory."

9:45 p.m. I just went into the house to empty my cider bottle, and found Dad lounging in the living room listening to my most prized F.S. album. The front drapes were open, giving any passersby a clear shot at his head.

"Since when are you interested in this kind of music?" I asked. Dad, as a confirmed culture climber, pretends to appreciate only rigorously unmelodious music of the modern Progressive Ennui school.

"I'm not as a rule," he replied, "but a friend of mine claims to dig it. Pretty syrupy in a turgid sort of way, if you ask me."

I, of course, did not. Nor did I close the drapes.

FRIDAY, November 16 — Life is full of surprises. Take, for instance, the phone call I received this afternoon after school.

"I'd like to speak with Nick Twisp, please," said a distinguished masculine voice.

"This is Nick."

"Hello, Nick," said the voice. "We haven't met. This is Trent Preston."

Alarming heart fibrillations.

"Oh. Hello, Trent."

"How are you, Nick?"

"I'm ... fine. How are you?"

"Not so good, Nick."

"Sorry to hear that, Trent. Did you take a bad spill windsurfing?"

Prolonged silence.

"Nick," Trent said finally, "I called to ask you just what you think you are doing?"

"Well, at the moment I imagine I'm talking on the phone," I said, chuckling nervously. I wanted to hand this conversation over to Francois, but he seemed to be off somewhere on an espresso break.

More silence.

"Nick," Trent continued, "my parents are forcing me to withdraw from school."

"Well, the economy certainly is not as robust as one might wish," I said. "Private schools can be quite a hardship for parents. I know—my parents recently found they could no longer financially sustain my private instruction."

"It's not the money, Nick."

"Oh."

"It's all the lies you've been spreading about me. And Sheeni."

"Pardon me, Trent," I said indignantly. "I don't believe I know what you're talking about."

"I think you do, Nick. I think you're deliberately trying to wreak havoc in our lives."

"Why, why would I want to do that?" I asked innocently.

"You tell me, Nick."

More silence.

"No answer. I see. Then tell me this, Nick," he continued. "Do you care anything at all for Apurva?"

"I like her, sure. She's very nice."

"Have you slept with her?"

"Uh, what exactly do you mean?"

"I mean have you callously possessed her body?"

"Not callously, no." I replied. "Have you slept with Sheeni?"

"Yes."

This was not the reply I had anticipated.

"Recently?" I croaked.

"Fairly recently. Two days ago."

Francois muscled the receiver out of my hand. "You're a fucking liar, Trent!" he exclaimed.

"Oh, so now I meet the real Nick Twisp," said Trent.

"You met him, asshole! I'm glad your flunky parents are yanking you out of that cake-eaters' school!" I had seldom seen Francois so inflamed.

"Nick, I've spent the last four months trying to convince myself you're a decent person. I wanted to like you for Sheeni's sake. But now, fella, the gloves are off. Two can play your nasty games, pal."

"It's a fight to the finish," agreed Francois, seizing the gauntlet.

"May the best man win," said Trent.

"Hey, shark bait," added Francois, "suck my surfboard!"

"Kiss my hydraulics, hamster humper," replied my enemy.

SATURDAY, November 17 — More scab overtime for Dad. He left at 6:30 a.m. with Mrs. Crampton's famous Blue-collar Bagged Lunch: one-half fried chicken, three deviled eggs, a danish (for morning break), carrot sticks (for fiber), one pint potato salad, two large homemade brownies, an apple, and a cherry cupcake (for afternoon break). I just hope Dad's fringe benefit package includes an hour off after lunch. He may feel the need for a nap.

Dad won't be running over any elderly boarders today. Mr. Ferguson is spending the day lying on the sofa in a fetal position. You see, he has sacrificed his principles for love.

To distract her fiancé from his ethical qualms, Mrs. Crampton made us all banana waffles for breakfast. I ate mine with yesterday's school newspaper propped in front of me—screening from view a large, unsightly silage grinder named D——e. I also enjoyed rereading the page-one lead story by talented journalist Tina Jade Manion. Her style is a marvel: ungrammatical, as wooden as pine, yet steeped in the warm flush of softly throbbing randiness. As I reviewed her ostensibly straightforward narration of my academic accomplishments, I felt the unmistakable sensation of being covertly, yet brazenly, groped—in newsprint. I have decided to respond by writing a letter to the editor—similarly coded—thanking Ms. Manion for her kind words. I only hope I am up to the task.

11:30 a.m. INCREDIBLE, MIND-JOLTING NEWS!

Sheeni just called in tears. HER PARENTS ARE PULLING THE PLUG!

"Oh, Nickie, it's a tragedy," she cried. "I know I shall forget all my French. I shall never leave Ukiah. I'll be trapped there forever—like a prehistoric fly frozen in amber!"

"At least we'll be together," I said.

"You'll be in India!"

"Oh, right. I forgot." At this delicate stage, I knew I dare not divulge my trip was off. "When are you coming home?" I asked.

"Wednesday is my last day. Trent's too. His parents are being just as unreasonable as mine. Oh, Nickie, I think I'll kill myself!"

"Don't do that, Sheeni!" I said. "Think of me. And Albert. We need you!"

"Yes, at least now I can be with my sweet dog. Has he grown, Nickie?"

"He's tripled in size," I said. "Sheeni, did Trent say anything to you about me?"

"He mentioned he talked to you on the phone yesterday. He didn't say what it was about though. Just that it was a private matter between you two. Oh, Nickie, I'm so distraught!"

"Sheeni, I hate to tell you this, after you've had such an emotional shock, but I have some more bad news. Your friend Trent is spreading disturbing lies about you."

"Like what?" she demanded.

"He said he slept with you. Three days ago!"

"Oh," she said weakly. "He said that, huh?"

"Sheeni, is it true?"

"Of course not, Nick. You must have misunderstood him."

"He said it plain as day, Sheeni. I heard it with my own ears."

"Must you speak in clichés, Nick?" she asked. "You could hardly have heard it with someone else's ears."

"So you haven't been sleeping with anyone?"

"Of course not," she replied. "Have you?"

"Uh, no."

"Good. Then we can all take pride in being equally lonely, miserable, and unloved. I hope you're satisfied, Nick."

"Sheeni, don't be sad. Everything will turn out fine. Trust me."

"I'm not giving up, Nick. Taggarty's still coming for Thanksgiving. I'm hoping she'll be able to persuade my parents to change their minds."

"Oh, that's a thought," I said. "Perhaps I can persuade them too."

"Nick! You are never going to see or talk to my parents. I'm in enough trouble with them already."

"But, darling," I objected, "you said it yourself. We're supposed to be revolting. Remember? Like Jean Paul Belmondo in 'Breathless'."

"Jean Paul Belmondo did not have my parents!" she exclaimed. *Click.*

Our plan worked. Like clockwork. My dear friend Vijay is a genius.

12:15 p.m. I just called Vijay to give him the good news. He sounded nearly as thrilled by today's developments as I am. Then Apurva joined in on the extension to share in the conviviality.

"Oh, Nick!" she bubbled, "my dear Trent is coming home too. He called me last night practically in tears. I was so happy I screamed. I told Father it was Sister Mary Ann, the choir director, checking up on my high C. I'm not certain he believed me."

"Where is your father, by the way?" I asked.

"Oh, don't worry," she replied happily. "He's at the office. Such a workaholic."

"Will you be able to see Trent?" I asked.

"Oh yes, Nick. Don't you worry. We'll find a way. Father won't even know my dear boy is returning from Santa Cruz. Besides, after our night in your trailer, Father naturally considers you the primary threat to my innocence. Perhaps you can call here occasionally to help foster that illusion."

That's not a bad idea.

After reminding Apurva that Jean Paul's support payment was worrisomely overdue, I wished her much happiness in love, hung up, and dialed another number. After 30 rings, someone finally answered.

"The office is closed," announced an exasperated voice. "Call back after 9 a.m. on Monday."

"Wait, Mr. Joshi! Don't hang up," I said. "I wish to speak with you. It's urgent."

"Who is this?"

"It's Nick. Nick Twisp."

"You dare to call me! What is it you want, you unprincipled scoundrel?"

"Mr. Joshi, it's about Apurva."

"You shall never see her again! I'm warning you. I shall prosecute your father for assault!"

"Mr. Joshi, I don't want to see your daughter. It's about her real boyfriend, Trent."

"That pest is in Santa Cruz," he replied. "Thank God."

"No, he's not, Mr. Joshi. He's coming back on Wednesday. For good. Apurva is planning to see him whenever she can."

"How do you know that?" Mr. Joshi asked, clearly shocked.

"She just told me," I confessed.

"Apurva talked to you? That is in direct defiance of my wishes!"

"Mr. Joshi, you can't tell her I told you."

"Why not?" he demanded.

"Because that will tip her off that you know Trent is back. Then they'll be extra cautious. This way, you can watch over her without creating suspicion."

"That is not a bad idea," he admitted. "Why are you telling me this?"

"Because I like your daughter, Mr. Joshi. Just as a friend. And I hate to see her get hurt by a twisted character like Trent Preston."

"I understood he was quite a sober, scholarly young man—for an American."

"I don't wish to alarm you, Mr. Joshi, but the guy is a total sicko. That's why his parents sent him away to school in the first place. They couldn't cope with him any more."

"Then why is he coming back?"

"You don't want to know, Mr. Joshi."

"Please, Nick. Tell me!" he pleaded.

"I'm sorry. I've said too much already. Just be careful. For Apurva's sake."

"Wait, Nick. I want . . ."

But I hung up.

Sit on that one, Trent. And twirl!

4:00 p.m. Too excited to think, read, or concentrate on any meaningful task. So I mowed the yard and bathed all the dogs. Everything must be nice for Sheeni's return. Also took a detailed survey of my zits. Not too bad considering. No more fried foods from now on.

6:45 p.m. Dad is dressing to go out. He had a close call at work today. The mill operator accidentally let fall two tons of gravel just inches from where Dad was unwrapping a cherry cupcake. Dad escaped unscathed, but the cupcake was never found. Uncle Polly stormed up the catwalk and fired the careless operator on the spot. Then Fuzzy's dad immediately reinstated him. So Uncle Polly warned Dad not to loiter under the chutes and to wear his hardhat at all times.

7:00 p.m. I just checked in with Fuzzy.

"Frank, where's your mother?" I asked.

"She's in her bathroom," he reported, "putting on her make-up."

"Where's your dad?"

"He's down in the den, getting plastered."

"Frank, are your parents going out?"

"Not with each other. Where's your dad, Nick?"

"He just left—in his snappiest sport coat."

"You think they're going to get together?" asked Fuzzy.

"Does the Pope swear in Latin?" I replied. "This is their second date, Frank. You know what that means."

"Jesus, Nick. I don't even want to think about it."

"Frank, I'll keep you posted if there's any action at my end. What are your plans?"

"Calling Heather, Nick. So the line may be busy for a while."

"What's on the agenda for tonight?"

"I was thinking of trying something new. Maybe getting into a threesome with the operator. What do you think, Nick?"

"Just don't melt the phone, Frank."

11:30 p.m. A quiet night. Time for bed. No sign of Dad yet. I'm so excited and happy, I don't know if I'll be able to go to sleep. Sheeni is coming back to me! I feel this is a definite turning point in my life. Things are looking up. Dad is in solid at work too. Nothing to face now but a golden future of sun-dappled happiness and prosperity. I may even hear back soon from Tina Manion.

College boyfriend or no, she likes me—Francois can tell. Women are so transparent to him.

SUNDAY, November 18 — 1:05 a.m. Awakened from a troubled sleep by the sound of cars pulling into the drive, I rose and peeked out the window. It was Dad's BMW and a big silver Lincoln. Operation Blood Brother has commenced.

1:10 a.m. The mellifluous, artfully modulated tones of F.S. are now wafting forth from Dad's bedroom window. Frank is singing "Full Moon and Empty Arms"—a ballad I imagine at this point is falling somewhat wide of the mark. There's no moon in sight either.

I'd alert Fuzzy, but the phone is all the way in the house. Dad's brush with celibacy was certainly short-lived. Adults have all the luck.

3:30 a.m. Or do they? A loud tapping on my trailer door abruptly parted the gossamer curtains of sleep.

"Who is it?" I mumbled.

"A nymph," replied a sultry woman's voice.

I was instantly awake.

"Come in," Francois called.

The door opened and Fuzzy's mother, wearing Dad's electric blanket, entered in a clatter of dangling cords and control dials.

"Mrs. DeFalco!" I exclaimed.

"Hello, Nick," she said, smelling of expensive perfume and cheap liquor. "Oh, I'm stuck, honey. Help me with my cords."

"I can't, Mrs. DeFalco."

"Why not?" she demanded, tugging on the dangling power cord snared in the trailer door.

"I can't get out of bed," I explained. "I don't have any pajamas on."

"That's all right, Nick," she giggled. "I don't either. Come on. Help a lady in distress."

I gulped, leaped from my bed, slithered modestly over to the door, freed the cord, then hopped back under the covers.

"Thank you, Nick," she said, gazing about. "I like your little house."

"Shall I turn on a light?"

"Oh, please don't, Nick. My make-up must be a fright." She sat down heavily on the dinette and studied me with interest across the gloom. "Did our music waken you?"

"Yes, Mrs. DeFalco, but I don't mind. I enjoy Frank any time of the day or night."

"That is such a rare quality, Nick. I can sense you are a very special young man."

"Thank you. I do my best."

"Good. I hope so. Now, Nick, what do you have on the premises to offer a lady?"

"How do you mean, Mrs. DeFalco?" Francois asked coyly.

"Do you have anything to drink?"

"Oh," I said. "Just water, I'm afraid, Mrs. DeFalco."

She made a face and rearranged her wrap. "Please, Nick. Call me Nancy."

"OK, Nancy," said Francois. "I like that name."

"So do I," she replied. "I just wish it was mine."

"Are you chilly," I asked. "We could plug in your blanket, if you like."

"Thank you, no. You are so considerate, Nick. Unlike your father."

"Uh, where's Dad?" I asked.

"Your father is asleep," she sniffed. "He passed out. Somewhat prematurely, I might add. Nick, how old are you?"

"Sixteen," Francois lied.

"Your father said you were 12!"

"He's not very good at math," I explained.

"He's not very good at a lot of things," she huffed. "Nick, could I trouble you for a cigarette?"

"I'm sorry, Mrs. DeFalco. I don't smoke."

"Please, it's Nancy. I thought all boys your age smoked. To rebel against authority and appear older."

"I'd like to smoke, Nancy," I explained, "but I don't want to get cancer."

"I hope, Nick, you're not going to turn out to be another one of those perfectly sensible young men. Sometimes I despair for your generation."

"Don't worry, Nancy," said Francois, "I behave quite rashly as a rule."

"Glad to hear it. Now, Nick, since you can't offer me a drink or a smoke, and it's too late for canasta, would you mind terribly if I squeezed myself into your little bed? Feel free to decline if you'd rather not."

"No, Nancy," said Francois, thrilled to his marrow. "There's plenty of room for two."

I pushed over and Mrs. DeFalco slipped under the covers beside me. Her blanket she left behind on the dinette. Radiating waves of perfume-scented heat, she seemed to overwhelm my small bed with extravagant quantities of skin. She draped her warm nakedness against me and giggled. "I'm not squashing you, am I, Nick?"

"No. I'm fine," I said. I marveled at the ampleness of her untethered bosom now enveloping me. "Shall I kiss you, Mrs. DeFalco?"

"That's all right, Nick," she replied. "I've found over the years that kissing has lost much of its appeal. I suppose, though, at your age you still enjoy it."

"From time to time," I admitted. I gave a slight start as a hot hand grasped my T.E. "Shall, shall I get a condom, Nancy?"

"Why? Do you have any major diseases?"

"I don't think so. But what about babies?"

Mrs. DeFalco giggled. "I might get pregnant and have to drop out of high school. No, Nick, I don't think we need worry about that."

With kissing off the menu, I wasn't entirely certain how to proceed. "Would you like some foreplay?" I asked.

"Nick, dear, have you ever done this sort of work before?"

"Oh, sure," lied Francois.

"Then just go about it in your normal fashion—as if I were the girl next door. If you like I can squeal with innocent surprise at the appropriate times."

"That won't be necessary," I said, somewhat offended. I moved to climb aboard her perspiring, indeterminant softness when the flash of a powerful explosion lit up the trailer.

"Oh dear," sighed Mrs. DeFalco, "I was hoping the fireworks would come later."

I disengaged myself from her smoldering limbs, jumped out of bed, and peered out the front window. Fifty feet away, Dad's precious BMW was illuminating the night as a fine German bonfire. It was totally engulfed in flames!

"What is it?" asked Mrs. DeFalco, rising—like a mature Phoenix—from my torrid bed. I liked the way the flickering light bathed her Rubenesque curves in gold. Her nipples, I noted with interest, were nearly as large as saucers.

"Someone's torched Dad's car!" I exclaimed.

"How rude of them," she replied, opening my closet door and calmly donning my bathrobe. "And so inconvenient."

"Where are you going, Mrs. DeFalco?" I asked.

"To call 911, Nick. I suggest you put something on, dear. We mustn't greet the firemen in our birthday suits."

Although the fire fighters arrived promptly, Dad's car was a total loss. He, needless to say, was a total wreck. Mrs. DeFalco comforted him in her arms as he sat slumped—whimpering and moaning—on the front stoop. Fortunately, in all the excitement, no one thought to question why Dad's guest was modeling my robe.

"I bet one of them strikers done it," suggested D——e.

"You . . . just . . . hush!" hissed his mother.

"It was your damn husband!" whined Dad, accusingly to his lover.

Wrong. When I looked out my window, I had caught a brief glimpse of the fleeing suspect—gas can still in hand. But I did not mention this to the fire captain when he interrogated me. No, I have no interest in being a party to the prosecution for arson of my future brother-in-law.

10:30 a.m. A dismal, cold morning. We are deep into late fall—truly the armpit of the year. Fuzzy called me after breakfast and this disquieting conversation ensued:

"Hi, Frank."

"Hi, Nick."

"Where's your mother, Frank?"

"Upstairs in bed. I guess she spent the night with your dad, huh?"

"More or less," I replied. "How's your dad taking it?"

"Pretty bad. He hit the wall."

"He did what?" I asked.

"He hit the wall. With his fist. He does that when he's totally pissed. Mom accused him of torching your dad's car and BAM! He hit the wall."

"Your father must be really strong."

"Yeah. Sometimes he hits a stud and breaks a few fingers. This time, though, he just punched a hole in the plaster board. I think he's memorized now where all the studs are in that wall. Boy, I can't believe it—your dad's made it with my mother. That is so gross."

"Frank, can you keep a secret?"

"Nick, I've got secrets I've been keeping since before kindergarten."

"Frank, nothing happened. My dad passed out—from drinking."

"How do you know that, Nick?"

"Your mom told me."

"She did?"

"Frank, your mom came to my trailer last night."

"She did?"

"Frank, she got into bed with me."

"She did?"

"Frank, we were naked."

"What are you saying, Nick?"

"Frank, your mother tried to seduce me."

"You lie!"

"Frank, it's true."

"You liar! You sick, perverted liar!"

"OK, don't believe me," I said. "Anyway, I shouldn't have told you."

"You repulsive degenerate!" raged Fuzzy. "Eat shit and die, sicko!" *Click.*

Confession may be good for the soul, but it certainly can exact a heavy toll on friendships.

11:15 a.m. TOTAL UNMITIGATED DISASTER! Sheeni just called with dire news.

"Oh, Nick, we're all in a state of shock!" she declared.

"What happened, Sheeni?"

"Well, it was last night at dinner. I was serving my penalty duty in the cafeteria and Trent had very kindly volunteered to assist me at the steam table. The vegetable was brussels sprouts in a cream sauce which can be a handful for one person, as you know. Well, he observed that unfortunate girl Bernice Lynch at the drinks station slip something into Taggarty's cup. Nickie, it was a powerful sedative!"

"How can you be certain?" I asked. "Perhaps it was just a vitamin."

"Nickie, it wasn't a vitamin. That became tragically clear later on."

Once again I felt that familiar, dreaded quivering at the base of my scrotum. "Oh. How so?" I asked weakly.

"Nickie, the dean sent Bernice to her room, pending an investigation, and she swallowed the rest of the pills!"

"She did what?" I gasped.

"She tried to commit suicide!"

"Did, did she succeed?" I asked, not entirely unhopefully.

"No. They found her in time. But she's in a coma. Nickie, she may not live!"

"That's, that's terrible."

"Yes, we're all stunned. Taggarty especially. You should see her back. She looks like a human pin cushion."

"Who? Bernice?" I asked, dazed.

"No, Taggarty. From her acupuncture treatments. Nickie, Taggarty was always extremely pleasant to that girl. No one can conceive of a motive for such a criminal act. Can you imagine—surreptitiously sedating someone for weeks!"

"Uh, well, no. I guess I can't," I admitted. "Sheeni, can you keep me posted? Will you call me if you hear any news?"

"Of course, Nickie," she replied. "You'll be the first to be informed."

That's what I'm afraid of.

4:30 p.m. Too nervous to write. Each time the phone rings I have another debilitating heart seizure. Of course, this *would* be the day every boiler room operation in Northern California calls with news of exciting vinyl siding offers.

Dad just received some bad news from his car insurance agent. He had missed a few too many payments on his policy. It's a good thing he can walk to work.

6:30 p.m. Too scared to eat my dinner. I gave my porkchop to D——e, who devoured it without scruples. Yet, who am I to talk? I wish now I had never befriended Bernice. She's been nothing but bad news. Her last letter was unnerving in the extreme. I should have quashed the scheme right then. Imagine—thinking I'd want to marry her someday and have "four beautiful children: two boys for you and two girls for me." I'm still a kid. Besides, I'm already engaged.

10:00 p.m. So distraught by lack of news, I called Sheeni. Now, I wish I hadn't.

"Any news from the hospital?" I asked.

"No," replied Sheeni frostily, "I said I'd call you."

"What's the matter, Sheeni?"

"I just received a rather disturbing fax," she replied.

"I didn't know you had a fax machine, darling."

"Our school is fully equipped with every modern educational tool. And please don't call me darling. Such endearments reek of hypocrisy."

"What do you mean?" I demanded.

"Shall I read you the fax?"

"OK. Read it."

In her exquisite voice, Sheeni read these alarmingly familiar words: "Dear Apurva, I feel exactly the same. Let us be bad together. I am now living behind my house in a small, extremely private recreational vehicle. Come to me there as soon you can. Awaiting your lips, Nick. P.S. Don't worry, I have some you-know-whats."

"How did you get that?" I demanded.

"It arrived anonymously," she replied.

"It's a forgery, Sheeni!"

"I recognize your affected handwriting, Nick. Don't bother to lie. Your treachery is all too apparent. Goodbye." *Click.*

I can't believe sweet Apurva would stab me in the back like that. I thought she was supposed to be my friend.

11:15 p.m. Dad just barged into my trailer without knocking and accused me of stealing his electric blanket. Since the hot merchandise was right where my visitor had left it, I was hardly in a position to deny the crime.

MONDAY, November 18 — Still no news from Santa Cruz. I haven't been able to eat anything in 24 hours. I wonder if Richard Nixon was this stressed out during Watergate? At least he had all those Secret Service guys and Bebe Reboso to comfort him.

Fuzzy cut me dead in gym class. He chose D——e to be his tumbling partner. Talk about cutting off your nose to spite your face.

Then at lunch Vijay made a shocking announcement. "I've seen the error of my ways," he declared. "After much soul-searching, I've decided to renounce my membership in the Republican Party."

"You have?" I asked, astounded.

"Yes, Nick. Aren't you pleased?" he said cheerily. "I've decided to become a Democrat."

I was not pleased. Suddenly, everything was perfectly clear. Yes, I had been stabbed in the back. But not by Apurva. My assassin was her scheming brother—the "loyal friend" to whom I had foolishly entrusted my most private correspondence. Yes, I had handed him a sword and he had used it against me. Now that he had driven a wedge between me and my love, I realized, he intended to woo my beloved Sheeni under the false cloak of insincere liberality. Was there no limit to his malevolence? Was a committed vegetarian really capable of such deceit?

"Tell me, as one Democrat to another," I said coolly. "Do you, by any chance, have access to a facsimile machine?"

"Yes, my father has one at home," smiled Vijay. "I find it a great convenience at times."

A blatant confession!

"When did you say Sheeni was coming back, Nick?" continued Vijay. "I do so look forward to her return!"

6:30 p.m. No updates on the coma front. I just had this surprisingly productive conversation with an Oakland policeman:

"Your mother's out, dipshit."

"Uh, actually, Lance, I wanted to speak with you."

"So talk, punk. Just don't ask for a handout."

"No, I'm financial fixed at the moment. Actually, I was calling to see how your burglary investigation was proceeding."

"What's it to you, piss ant?"

"I was wondering if you've checked those mystery fingerprints against the INS files?"

"The guy was illegal," replied Lance. "INS didn't even have a record of him."

"Yes, but his accomplices may have been in this country legally."

"Oh, that's possible, I suppose."

"Well, probably it's not worth the trouble to check out," I said.

"Hey, smart ass," replied my loving stepdad, "I'll decide what's proper investigative procedure."

"OK, Lance. I know you'll do your usual splendid job. Say hi to Mom for me."

"Don't tell me what to do, jerk."

A great guy. Maybe Vijay can get a letter of recommendation from him for his Stanford application. Or for his parole hearing.

Dad is working late at the office—the result of a slight mishap. This afternoon, while he was partaking in a union-sanctioned coffee break (always militantly observed by Twisps), his load matured past the point of no return. When he finally went to discharge it, the tank spun industriously but no concrete emerged. Now Dad is deep inside the steel tank, jack-hammering out nine cubic yards of granite-hard cement. Mrs. Crampton packed his dinner in a basket (padlocked to deter tampering) and gave it to D——e to deliver. She also enclosed the eight aspirin Dad requested.

Mr. Ferguson continues his fetus-like absorption in kiddie TV. Even lethargic D——e is showing signs of restiveness under the non-stop bombardment of animated vacuity interspersed with endless toy commercials. I watched for an hour, hoping the therapeutic media violence would relieve my gnawing anxiety, but had to leave when I found myself commenting out loud on the plot to D——e.

Good thing Dad isn't here. Those damn dogs have been barking like Type A hyenas all evening. I shall write D——e a note instructing him to walk them. That reminds me: no Kamu payments have been received. I must begin foreclosure proceedings at once.

10:15 p.m. No news from Santa Cruz. A thought has occurred to me: perhaps Bernice will emerge from her coma an amnesiac. I'll be off the hook and she'll have a nice clean slate on which to construct a fresh, more-appealing personality. Everything could turn out for the best. I must try to find out the common side-effects of massive sedative overdoses.

Dad is back—monumentally fatigued, powdered like a donut with a fine white dust, and deaf as Quasimodo. Just as he emerged from the shower, Mrs. DeFalco telephoned. Dad kept repeating "Say again," until his caller concluded she was being had and hung up. I hope he hasn't cost both of us a pleasant evening's diversion.

TUESDAY, November 19 — ANOTHER CATACLYSMIC DISASTER! What incredibly bad karma. I must have racked up some record-setting penalty points in my previous lives. Who was I anyway—Adolf Hitler's personal attorney?

When I arrived at school this morning, I learned that Fuzzy was absent. I found out in home room it was because a relative had passed away. By gym class I discovered my erstwhile friend was mourning the loss of an uncle. In wood shop my worst fears were confirmed as news reached me that the decedent was indeed Uncle Polly. At lunch I was shocked to learn death resulted from accidental electrocution. But only when I arrived home, was the full, horrifying extent of the tragedy thrust upon. The agent of death, I was informed, was a second-hand neon sign, recently purchased by the victim from the son of a former employee.

"You've been fired, Dad?" I exclaimed.

"What?" he screamed.

"Dad! Have you been fired?" I bellowed.

"Yes, you fuck up!" he replied. "Why do you suppose I'm hitting you?"

There's no need for profanity or sarcasm, Dad. I just like to be in full possession of the facts as I'm being abused.

After Dad finished, I excused myself and called the DeFalcos. Mrs. DeFalco answered, sounding only partially paralyzed with grief.

"Hello, Nick," she said. "I'm annoyed with you, you know."

"It's not my fault, Mrs. DeFalco!"

"Oh? You mean someone else has been tattling on us to my son?"

"Oh," I said, "he told you, huh?"

"Nick, I thought I could trust you to be discreet. I see now my faith was misplaced."

"I'm sorry, Mrs. DeFalco. I'm sorry about your brother-in-law too."

"We're all sorry, Nick. Very sorry. I'm sorry my husband fired your father with such unseemly haste. He might have at least waited until after Polonius was decently buried. And I'm very sorry that he is at this moment downtown talking to his lawyers about bringing suit against your father."

"He is?" I gulped.

"Yes. But perhaps I shouldn't be telling you this. That sign was dangerously defective, Nick."

"I, I could refund the $50," I suggested.

"I expect my husband will want more than that, Nick. Much more. The deputy sheriff found a bare wire exposed on the cord. It appeared to have been chewed—by some animal."

"By a dog?" I asked.

"I don't know," she replied. "Perhaps the detectives will be able to determine that. Do you have any dogs?"

"Yes," I admitted, "three."

"I thought that was a flea bite I received in your trailer," she commented.

"You mustn't let Fuzzy visit you there."

"No, Mrs. Defalco," I replied. "When did Uncle Polly die?"

"Last night. A former girlfriend discovered him floating face down in his hot tub. His pizza was untouched. I tried calling your father when I heard the news, but he suddenly decided to play dumb."

"You mean Uncle Polly kept an electrical appliance next to a hot tub?" I asked.

"Yes. He was under the impression neon lighting created an atmosphere conducive to romance."

"But that wasn't very intelligent, Mrs. DeFalco," I said.

"Perhaps not," she admitted, "but it was very Uncle Polly."

10:30 p.m. I decided not to tell Dad about the potential lawsuit. I think it would be best if the subpoena arrives as a horrifying surprise. Let him retain the shreds of his tattered happiness until then. No need for everyone to feel as miserable as I do.

I realize now I should have suspected something was amiss last night from the peculiar behavior of those damn dogs. Yes, Albert has exacted his revenge. But was Uncle Polly the true intended victim? Or was the sale of the sign unforeseen by my canine adversaries? Did they, in fact, intend that sabotaged wire for me? What have I done, I ask myself, to deserve such opprobrium? Is buying generic that heinous of a crime?

WEDNESDAY, November 20 — 8:30 a.m. Dad and Mr. Ferguson have reconciled. They are sitting together in the living room watching Captain Kangaroo (turned up LOUD for the hearing-impaired). Mrs. Crampton is using the last of the Crisco to fry up some homemade donuts. She has dropped some polite hints to Dad that he consider applying for food stamps. Soon we may be the only family on welfare with a full-time live-in maid.

Thank God Thanksgiving vacation starts today. I have no taste for knowledge at this time. I only hope Mrs. Crampton's donuts give me the courage to call Sheeni. I must know what is happening!

9:45 a.m. As I sat by the phone, disconsolately eating a cruller, it rang. Or, for you doctrinaire grammarians: As I, disconsolately eating a cruller, sat by the phone, it rang.

"I hate your slimy guts!" said a familiar voice.

"I'm sorry, Lefty," I replied. "You'll have to wait your turn."

"I hate your putrid guts!"

"Sorry, pal," I said. "My abuse quota is all filled up. I suggest you call back after the new year."

"You're going to be sorry you were ever born!"

"OK, Lefty. It can't wait, huh? What's up now?"

"I had a date last night with Millie."

"I know. It was bowling night. Did you roll any strikes?"

"We went up to her room and turned out all the lights."

"Good work, guy. I wish I could have been there to study your technique."

"Millie had a surprise waiting for me."

"Like what? Spearmint-flavored condoms? Norwegian sex novelties? Edible panties?"

"No, asshole," replied Lefty, "glow in the dark sheets!"

"Oh," I said darkly. "Uh, how bright did they glow?"

"Very bright. She said she got them so she could see my scar. She saw all right!"

"Er, what did she say?" I asked, dreading the reply.

"She said a guy's equipment doesn't keep on growing until he's 30! She said this is all as big as I can expect to get! She says you're a dirty rotten liar!"

"Difference of opinion, Lefty," I replied evenly. "What we've got here are two divergent interpretations of available medical data."

"What we've got here," he replied, "is a traitor who deserves to fry for arson."

"Lefty!" I implored, "you wouldn't do that to a pal!"

"Maybe not," he conceded. "I promised you I wouldn't."

"That's right," I reminded him.

"So I told Millie. She's going to turn you in and we're going to split the $10,000 reward."

"Lefty, you can't do that! I'm in enough trouble here as it is."

"Too bad, back stabber."

"Lefty! Where's Millie now? I need to talk to her."

"Call the Berkeley Police, traitor. That's where she just left for."

"Thanks a pantsfull, pal," I sighed.

"Don't mention it, Nick. And thanks for the $5,000."

"OK. Spend your blood money," I said. "But just remember one thing."

"What's that?" asked Lefty.

"You're still a shrimp."

I won't repeat what Lefty said. It would only further confirm his regrettable paucity of imagination.

11:45 a.m. Palms sweating, eyelids twitching, spleen fluttering, I finally worked up the courage to dial Sheeni's number. After wading through deep quagmires of Frog-speak, I reached my Re-estranged Sweetheart.

"Hello, Dolores," she said frigidly. "What a surprise."

"Sheeni, darling, are your parents there?"

"Yes, Dolores. They've come to take me home. What do you want? I'm in a bit of a rush."

"Sheeni, how is Bernice?"

"No change, Dolores. There has been one strange development though."

"What's that, darling?"

"Do you remember the last letter you wrote to me?"

"Of course, darling. I remember it distinctly. I wrote, among other things, that as I exhaled my last human breath, your name would be upon my lips."

"Yes, Dolores. How ironic that seems now."

"Sheeni, I meant every word!"

"Yes, Dolores. You certainly can't trust everyone you meet on summer vacations."

"Sheeni, what about the letter?"

"The authorities discovered it in Bernice's room—when they were searching for suicide notes."

"They did!" I exclaimed. "How did she get hold of it?"

"She must have taken it when she emptied my wastebasket."

"Sheeni! You mean you haven't been saving my letters?"

"No, Dolores. I am committed to resource recycling, as you know. Besides, they have no value to me now."

"Darling, don't say that!"

"Of course, Dolores, I am a realist. We all must be."

"Sheeni, have some compassion! Consider our time of life. During these trying years one's hormones can sometimes overpower one's moral judgment. These slight missteps should not necessarily be construed as infidelity."

"Yes, Dolores. We all recognize facile exculpations when we hear them. Well, I mustn't keep my parents waiting."

"Sheeni, one more thing. Did they find a suicide note?"

"No, Dolores. Few teens have the time or aptitude for composition these days. Ours is not a literarily inclined generation."

Thank God for that, I thought. "Well, have a good trip home, darling," I said. "I look forward to seeing you tomorrow."

"Dolores, you must dismiss that notion from your head. I remain firm on that issue."

"Sheeni, we've been through this before," I replied, just as firmly.

"If you persist, Dolores, I shall have no choice but to invite dear Trent as well. How would you like that?"

I wouldn't like it at all, I thought. I said, "I'm not squeamish, Sheeni. If you can tolerate his loutish company, so can I."

For being one of the sweetest, kindest persons I've ever known, Sheeni can be remarkably hard-assed at times. I'd better bring her flowers tomorrow too. Something flamboyantly expensive, I fear.

More guilt for Nick. If Bernice succumbs, I shall have two deaths on my conscience. (Three if you count Albert.) I must make amends by leading an exemplary life from now on. I shall begin by forgiving Dwayne. He deserves understanding as much as any of us. He can't help it that he's an obnoxious cretin.

1:15 p.m. (written in pencil). After a nice lunch, I invited dear Dwayne in to play computer games on my AT clone. Now he is banging away on my fragile, bargain-brand keyboard as happy as a four-year-old (his approximate mental age).

Dad and Mr. Ferguson have gone into town to meet with their respective lawyers. I look forward to their upcoming trials. They should offer valuable lessons in the operation of our judicial system. I hope neither defendant is persuaded to plead guilty. That seems like such an ethical copout.

Can't write any more. I have to go prepare my chum Dwayne a snack.

2:30 p.m. A man with "process server" written all over his suspicious face and thrift-shop suit just came snooping around asking for Dad. I told him a Mr. George F. Twisp used to live here, but had moved to Missoula, Montana recently to find work as a TV weatherman. The guy left, but I'm not sure he believed me. Mr. DeFalco's vengeful lawyers sure work fast.

4:05 p.m. Candy Pringle and some other do-gooder seniors from my high school just dropped by with a frozen turkey and a big bag of canned goods. Mrs. Crampton was so grateful she started blubbering. I have never been so embarrassed in my entire life.

5:30 p.m. I just blew $43.27 on two large bouquets of assorted over-priced holiday flowers. I had to sneak them into Little Caesar lest Mrs. Crampton conclude they were for her, setting off another crying jag. I'd put them in water, but they're wrapped in festive, high-priced paper. I am keeping them moist by spritzing them periodically with my deodorant.

7:30 p.m. Hard times are here. For dinner we had canned wax beans, canned creamed hominy on toast, and canned smoked oysters—washed down with reconstituted powdered milk. Canned kiwi cocktail for dessert. Needless to say, I only picked at my food. Mrs. Crampton is husbanding the less esoteric canned goods for tomorrow's festive dinner of thanksgiving. I have never had such a gloomy meal. It did not help that Dad is down to his last half-bottle of zin and is irritable in the extreme. His lawyer was not encouraging. The Ukiah police took a remarkably clear set of his prints off Lacey's jimmied window.

10:45 p.m. I have pressed my brown flannel trousers, brushed my tweed coat, and successfully pilfered Dad's best knit tie. In less than 24 hours I shall be eating turkey and all the trimmings with The Woman Who Makes Me Thankful for the Human Sex Drive. But will she be thankful to see me?

I believe she will. That is the thought that sustains me as I, a disadvantaged American youth, go to bed hungry.

THURSDAY, November 20 — Happy Thanksgiving to me. The day has not started well. I awoke to discover that sometime during the night my extortionate bouquets had violently transmogrified. They now resemble some grim floral vestige of a post-holocaust nuclear winter. Oh well, I have no choice. I shall take them anyway. As the Florists Marketing Council reminds us: it's the thought that counts.

11:45 a.m. (written in pencil). I'm composing this in the back booth of the donut shop to calm my nerves. The maple bars are helping too.

It all started before breakfast as I was peacefully sitting in my tiny home polishing my dress shoes. Dwayne knocked on the door to tell me I was wanted on the phone.

"Who is it?" I asked him warily.

"Some for'ner," he replied, with evident distaste.

"Man or woman?"

"Girl, Nick. I think it's that one what tried to swipe Kamu from me."

My sweet, lovely Apurva! I greeted her warmly.

"Nick, something terrible has happened!" she said, alarm adding to the poignancy of her unflagging charm.

"Your father hasn't married you off?" I asked.

"No, thank God. But he has been acting most suspiciously the last few days. I'm afraid he may be plotting the ruination of my hopes. No, I'm calling about another emergency. Vijay has just been arrested!"

"What a surprise," I said, not at all surprised. "What is the charge?"

"Breaking and entering, malicious mischief, and grand theft. Two nice Ukiah officers and a rude policemen from Oakland have taken him away. Nick, they confiscated a pair of my shoes. My nice red pumps!"

"What did Vijay say?"

"He assured my parents it was all a misunderstanding. That's why they're all going over to talk to you."

"They're coming over here?" I asked, alarmed. "Why? I don't know anything!"

"Well, Vijay thought you might."

"Apurva, I've got to go. Thanks for calling. Remember, no matter what you hear, I'm innocent. Totally innocent!"

"Of course, Nick. I never imagined that you . . ."

Rudely, I hung up and raced out to Little Caesar. Dressing hurriedly, I was interrupted by another knock on the door. My blood froze.

"Who is it?"

"It's me," said Dwayne. "'Nother call, Nick. It's your ma."

"Tell her I'm too busy to talk now!"

"She says it's a 'mergency, Nick."

"Damn!"

I grabbed the flowers, my bankbook, a few other vital necessities, and hurtled past Dwayne toward the house. No sign of approaching police cars. So far so good.

"Hi, Mom. What's up?" I gasped.

"Nickie, I have some bad news!" she exclaimed.

"OK. I'm ready. What is it?"

"Nickie, you don't sound well."

"TELL ME THE BAD NEWS, MOM!"

"The Berkeley police were just here. They know you started the fire. Oh, I wish Lance hadn't left in such a big hurry early this morning. They made me tell them where you live. Nickie, they're on their way up there!"

"They're coming here?" I exclaimed, with a distinct sense of déjà vu.

"Yes. They're driving to Ukiah to arrest you!"

No longer merely quivering, my testicles were dancing a rhumba in my pants. I slammed down the phone and fled out the front door, nearly flattening a low-life process server.

"I've called every TV station in Montana," he announced snottily. "I think you're lying!"

"So sue me!" I replied, scurrying past him. I stopped abruptly as a black and white car crested the hill in the distance. As I turned to retreat, the loathsome court lackey blocked my way.

"Where's George F. Twisp?" he demanded.

"Inside in bed!" I replied. "Go in if you want! Tell him Nick sent you!"

As I fled toward the welcome cover of distant trees, a blood-curdling scream rose from the house. Dad was having a bad morning too.

1:30 p.m. I am lurking in some bushes one block from Sheeni's house. I hope I don't get my trousers soiled. I have picked some municipal flowers to flesh out my diseased bouquets. I am extremely nervous and growing more so by the minute. Where did I go wrong?

5:30 p.m. (written in pencil under a bridge on the outskirts of Ukiah). Well, Thanksgiving dinner is over. I didn't stay for dessert.

I rang the ornate Victorian doorbell precisely at 1:59. After an ominously long interval, Paul—wearing an apron and grasping a large turkey baster—opened the front door.

"Hello, Nick. Right on time. Come in."

"Happy Thanksgiving," I said, cautiously entering the dark-paneled foyer as Lacey, smiling beneficently, floated toward me in a golden fog of hormone-wrenching pulchritude.

Pressing me forcefully against her as if taking an impression for a custom-made brassiere, she exclaimed, "Oh, what interesting flowers, Nick. Who are they for?"

"Uh, Mrs. Saunders and, uh, you, I guess," I stammered.

"Oh, thank you, Nick," she said. "Come, let us show them to Mother Saunders."

Every nerve cell madly palpitating, I followed my host and hostess into the chintz-bedecked parlour. Dressed in their best holiday finery, Sheeni's larger-than-life father and 5,000-year-old mother were sitting cross-legged on the floor—running their ancient, liver-spotted fingers over the hooked rug. Had someone lost a contact?

"Mr. and Mrs. Saunders," said Lacey gaily, "you remember Nick Twisp, don't you? Look, Mother Saunders, he's brought you some flowers."

No one rose in welcome. Mr. Saunders looked up and squinted myopically at me. Mrs. Saunders cut me dead and pretended to be completely absorbed in admiring my splendid gift. Hey lady, I thought, sticks and stones may break my bones, but sarcasm will never hurt me.

"You are very, very tall," gurgled Sheeni's father, staring intently at me. More sarcasm!

"No, he's not, Dad," corrected Paul. "He only appears to be tall, because you are seated on the floor."

At that moment, I noticed, Mrs. Saunders was tentatively biting into one of my deodorant-blighted chrysanthemums.

"I feel the power of the floor pushing against me," noted Mr. Saunders. "Do you feel it too, tall youth?"

"Sometimes," I replied, glancing quizzically at my hosts.

"Paul served his parents an appetizer earlier," said Lacey, beaming.

"Yes," said Paul, "it's a recipe I picked up in the Southwest. Stuffed mushrooms."

"Now remember, Paul," declared a voice that could grate parmesan. "You promised you'd let me sample some later!"

As the speaker desired, we all turned to watch as she continued her entrance down the stairs. Taggarty had dressed for the occasion in a bizarre green cape that was either fashionable art-to-wear or a fragment of an asbestos theater curtain.

"Hello, Nick!" she said, walking over and greeting me, New York-style, with a wet, casually intimate kiss full upon the lips. "How's the star-crossed, persistent lover?"

"OK, I guess," I said, wiping off her saliva. "How are you, Taggarty?"

"Glorious, as usual," she replied. "Oh, Lacey, what remarkable flowers. I bet Nick brought those!"

"All the flower shops are closed today," I said coldly. "I had to buy them yesterday."

"Well, Mrs. Saunders is certainly enjoying hers," she replied.

Sheeni's mother, now humming softly, had inserted her face deep into her bouquet. The tune I recognized as "Anchors Away." Still studying me intently, Sheeni's father began to whistle along.

"Well, I'd better put these flowers in water," said Lacey. "We'll let Mother Saunders keep hers for the time being."

"Nick, you look parched," said Paul. "Running is thirsty work. What can I get you to drink?"

"Uh, ginger ale for me," I said uneasily.

"I'll have some sherry," said Taggarty, eyeing me languidly.

"Right," said Paul. He escorted Lacey back toward the kitchen, leaving me to converse with my caped adversary.

"Are you a jogger, Nick?" asked Taggarty.

"Only when events demand it," I replied cryptically. "How was your trip?"

"Not bad," replied Taggarty. "I never realized Sheeni's home town was so extraordinarily far into the hinterlands. How ever do you cope?"

"We have cable TV," I said.

The martial humming and whistling grew louder.

"Sheeni's parents are certainly quite musical," observed Taggarty, turning up the volume on her grating voice. "Perhaps we can have a sing-along around the piano later. Isn't that what you people in small, isolated hamlets do in the evenings?"

"When we're not interbreeding," I replied. "Where is Sheeni by the way?"

"Upstairs, Nick. She saw you coming up the walk and locked herself in the bathroom."

"Is she crying?"

"Don't flatter yourself, Nick. More likely she is laughing hysterically."

"Did she invite Trent?" I asked, ignoring the gibe.

"Of course, Nick. He's one of her dearest friends. But he just called to say that he may be arriving late. He's looking forward to meeting you."

"Same here," I lied.

Thankfully, at that moment Paul returned. "Mom, Dad!" he shouted, handing us our drinks. "Let's use our noses. Hmmmmm. What is that aroma?"

Following their son's example, Mr. and Mrs. Saunders paused in their song and began to sniff the air.

"Turkey," croaked Sheeni's craggy mother.

"Big turkey," added her husband. "Big, big turkey."

"The turkey smells so marvelously . . . rustic," commented Taggarty, swigging her sherry like a lapsed twelve-stepper.

"Thanks," said Paul. "Lacey reports it's almost ready to come out of the oven."

"I thought you might be barbecuing it, Paul," I said. "I know how much you like to roast things outdoors."

Paul flashed me a wry grin. "Only after dark, Nick. And only when coached by a beautiful woman. Now, where's my baby sister? Nick, why don't you go upstairs and see if you can hurry her up?"

I found Sheeni lying on her bed reading a book. Her bedroom was charmingly decorated in shades of virginal white.

"Hello, Sheeni," I said. "Dinner is almost ready."

"Hello, Nick," she replied, not looking up. "I do not intend to be a party to my brother's absurdities. He has invited you and drugged my parents."

"Yes, I know," I said. "But I think your parents may be deriving some good from the experience. You yourself have observed on numerous occasions that they are excessively strait-laced. Perhaps this brief psychedelic interlude will broaden their horizons. I know it did mine."

"Yes, it certainly seems to have expanded your vistas to the east."

"I repeat, Sheeni. I have never slept with Apurva Joshi. I am willing to submit to a polygraph test, should you desire it."

Sheeni looked up from her book. "How is my dog?"

"Excellent," I said. "He should be coming out of the oven right about now."

I ducked to dodge a flying book.

"I hate you, Nickie!" said Sheeni, leaping from the bed.

"I hate you too," I said, taking her in my arms.

We had a long, slow, intense kiss such as the kind teens are warned can lead inexorably to pre-marital sex.

"Nickie," observed Sheeni, when we came up for air. "There's a disgusting protrusion in your trousers."

"It is a revolver, darling," I lied. "In case your father demands a duel after dinner."

"Then you are not happy to see me?" she asked.

I replied with a kiss. An extremely passionate one.

We all sat down to dinner a few minutes later. Trent was still happily delayed. With much coaxing from Lacey, Mr. and Mrs. Saunders moved from the living room floor to the dining room table. Thankfully, my considerate hostess seated Mrs. Saunders and her flowers at the opposite end of the polished mahogany table from Sheeni and me. Lacey did, however, commit the social gaffe of placing Sheeni's father to my immediate left. Following the first law of etiquette, I ignored him as much as possible. Opposite me sat Taggarty—fortunately partially screened by the turkey carcass.

Lacey led us in prayer: "Dear Lord. Thank Thee for Thy bounty which we are to receive. Help us be tolerant and accepting of others—especially the boyfriends and girlfriends of our immediate relations. Thank Thee also for sending us the company of Taggarty and Nick and Trent who has been slightly delayed. Amen."

"Amen," we echoed.

First course was a hearty consomme—steaming, bracing to the palate, with a delicate aftertaste of metallic can coating.

"Lacey made the soup," announced Paul proudly.

"The instructions said to warm it in a pan, but I microwaved it instead," she noted.

"Delicious," I lied.

"It swims on my tongue, tall youth," said my table companion.

"Yes, sir," I replied, noticing for the first time that my future father-in-law was raising a remarkable crop of white hair in his ears. I pray Sheeni has not inherited this tendency.

"How are you feeling, Taggarty?" Sheeni asked her friend, who appeared to be boycotting the soup.

"Fine, Sheeni. I'm afraid I've lost my taste for hot liquids. It's irrational I know, but somehow I still fear they might contain drugs."

Damn, I thought. I should have smuggled in a capsule or two.

"I understand perfectly," replied Sheeni. "You've been through a terrifying ordeal."

"Not as terrifying as our friend's," I said, pointing to the main course.

Only Sheeni's mother laughed. I hope at future family get-togethers she continues to find my jests amusing.

The roasted turkey was served with sage stuffing, candied yams, mashed potatoes and gravy, buttered noodles, cranberry sauce, individual molded salads, hot rolls and muffins, and mixed steamed autumn vegetables. To my amazement, everything was delicious.

"Paulie made the rest of the meal," confessed Lacey. "He likes all the traditional Thanksgiving foods."

"What is Thanksgiving without traditions?" he asked. "Sister dear, how long has it been since we all gathered 'round this groaning board to observe the rituals of thanksgiving?"

"Not long enough, Paul," Sheeni replied.

"I hope it's the first of many such occasions for me," I said, giving a start as Sheeni tweaked my white meat under the table.

"Don't push your luck, pal," she whispered coyly.

Mr. Saunders put down his fork and stared intently at my jacket. "Fascinating weave," he remarked.

"Genuine Harris Tweed," I replied. "Hand-woven on the Outer Hebrides—wherever that may be."

"I believe they are small islands off the west coast of Scotland," replied my encyclopedic inamorata.

Just as my hunger asserted itself and I began to eat in earnest, the doorbell rang. My stomach convulsed anew in a fresh spasm of anxiety.

"That must be Trent," said Sheeni, jumping up and hurrying toward the door.

"Fascinating weave," repeated my seatmate, still engrossed in my outerwear.

And then, eight seconds later, my enemy walked into the room. Imagine, if you can, a young Laurence Olivier with a tall, lithe swimmer's body and a California tan. Imagine a chiseled, noble profile—like a Roman coin come to life. Imagine golden lashes curling over smoke-blue eyes that seem to flash—like subliminal neon—"Bedroom. Come with me to the bedroom. Now." Imagine all that and then know this: words alone cannot begin to limn the formidability of my adversary.

Trent turned toward me. Smoke-blue eyes locked onto Francois' dingy brown ones.

"Oh, Trent, darling," said Sheeni, "this is Lacey, Paul's friend."

Trent broke my gaze and turned, radiating charm like an illicit plutonium broker, toward his hostess. "Oh, yes," he said. "We've met—at my dad's office. Hello, Lacey."

"Hello, Trent," said Lacey, barely controlling an impulse to swoon.

"And this is my friend Nick," said Sheeni.

Trent swiveled around slowly and looked again into my eyes. I gazed back, probing for weakness, but meeting only stout walls, thick armor, and endless ranks of heavy cannon. "Hello, Nick," said Trent, extending his hand.

"Hello, Trent," I said, briefly grasping his dry, patrician warmth with my arctic clamminess.

"Fascinating weave," repeated a voice.

"Do sit down, Trent," said Sheeni. "We've just begun to eat. Paul's dinner has turned out improbably toothsome."

"I'm sorry, Sheeni, I regret to say I can't," apologized Trent, gazing steadily at me. "There's been a new development in the Bernice Lynch case. It demands our immediate attention. Taggarty, this concerns you as well."

"What is it, Paul?" she asked, obviously thrilled.

"Before I left school, I searched Bernice's room," he declared, still looking at me. "Thoroughly. From top to bottom."

"Did you obtain proper authorization from school officials before doing so?" Francois demanded.

"No, Nick. I acted on my own initiative. In Bernice's closet, hidden inside a can of brass polish concealed under a large bag of soiled laundry, I found this cache of letters," he said, dramatically extracting several familiar-looking envelopes from his jacket pocket.

"Who are the letters from?" asked Sheeni.

"Someone sitting at this very table," replied Trent, stooping shamelessly to melodrama.

Everyone except Mr. Saunders gazed curiously about the circle of tense faces.

"Fascinating weave," he said.

"Who was it?" demanded Taggarty.

"In the letters," continued Trent, ignoring the question, "the writer expressed a strong affection for Bernice. And instructed her to begin a program of sedating Taggarty with the drugs he himself supplied."

"Nickie, you didn't!" screamed Sheeni, recoiling in horror.

"Well, you see," I stammered. "There's a simple, logical explanation . . ."

"Nick, you could have killed me!" shouted Taggarty, overplaying her emotional hand as usual.

"As it is," interrupted Trent, not raising his voice, "if Bernice should die, he may well be an accomplice to homicide."

"Oh, Nickie!" exclaimed Lacey, obviously disappointed.

"Bad break, Nick," said Paul sympathetically.

"Who died?" demanded Sheeni's mother.

"No one yet, Mrs. Saunders," replied Trent.

"Arrest him!" screamed my future mother-in-law, pointing a dead geranium at me.

"I can't arrest him," said Trent. "But I have called the Santa Cruz police. They are on their way here now."

"Fascinating weave," droned the voice.

More alarming déjà vu for Nick. Hands shaking, I placed my napkin beside my plate. "Well, I shall be going now. Please continue on without me."

"Nick, I would advise you to remain here," said Trent. "And face the consequences of your actions like a man."

"Thank you for that unsolicited counsel, Trent," I replied. "And please, do drop dead."

To a clamor of remonstrances, imprecations, and violent condemnations, I resumed my long walk to the front door.

"Goodbye, Sheeni," I said, turning to face my accusers. "I did it all for you."

"You are completely contemptible," declared My Love. "I never wish to see you—ever again!"

With that dreadful proclamation ringing in my ears, I left the house.

Not quite the festive holiday celebration I had been anticipating.

Now what do I do?

Sitting here in the trash-strewn gloom as cars and trucks roar by overhead, I see only two ways out: suicide or India.

I'm leaning toward the former, but Francois suggests I try the latter first. Then, if that doesn't work out, I can kill myself with a clear conscience. There is some logic to that.

I have my passport and ticket voucher. On the other side of the world wait new friends, new experiences, and 10,000 captive rupees.

Now, how do I get to San Francisco airport?

More to the point: How do I get past all the police roadblocks?

Book III

YOUTH IN EXILE

NOVEMBER

FRIDAY, November 21 — Well, what would you do in my place? You're a 14-year-old intellectual minor, reviled by all of your former friends, relentlessly pursued by three police jurisdictions, and stranded in the boonies 100 miles from the airport that offers your only hope of escape.

Faced with that dilemma yesterday, I did the only sensible thing. I turned the problem over to Francois Dillinger, my always-resourceful, ever-sociopathic alter ego.

"Give me 20 cents," he said brusquely, wiping his hand over his sensual mouth like Jean Paul Belmondo.

Francois took the proffered dimes and deposited them in the slot of a grimy payphone next to the beef jerky and belt buckle displays in Irma's Fast Gas, just outside the dusty city limits of Ukiah, California. He adjusted his crotch and dialed a number.

"Hello," said Francois, "let me speak to Tina Manion. This is Nick, Nick Twisp. A friend of hers from school."

Forty minutes later we were hurtling south through the black night on Highway 101. Tina drove the big Buick stationwagon like she wrote news articles for the high school paper: badly, but with a curious erotic intensity. She has fiery dark eyes, smooth olive skin, interestingly upturned nose, and an artfully composed journalist's body.

"Sure you don't want me to take you all the way to San Francisco, Nick?" she asked.

"No thanks, Tina. I can catch the airport van in Santa Rosa. I really appreciate your coming out on Thanksgiving to help me out."

"Holidays bore me to tears," she replied. "Besides, I need more practice driving at night. I just got my license last month. How come those cars keep flashing their lights like that?"

"Uh, Tina, I think you're supposed to dim your brights for on-coming traffic."

"No way, Nick. I can't see a damn thing out there as it is."

"Oh," I replied, casually bracing my knees against the dashboard as fog-shrouded redwoods whizzed by.

"Nick, you're a lucky guy. Traveling to India to study. How long are you going to be there?"

"Oh, eight or nine years, I expect."

"Wow! And you're not even taking a suitcase."

"Uh, no. I'll be buying everything I need in Pune. With my 10,000 captive rupees."

"Redwood High will miss you, Nick."

"Thanks, Tina," said Francois, unlocking my rigid knees and sliding closer to our alluring driver. "You know, Tina, you're probably the last American girl I'll ever see during my teenaged years."

"Really, Nick?"

"That's right," Francois confirmed. "And I'm glad it's you."

"Why, Nick?" she asked, the softness of her voice contrasting with the firmness of her foot upon the accelerator.

"Because you're a special person."

"Oh, I'm not so special."

"Yes, you are," said Francois. "You're intelligent, beautiful, and a great writer."

"You really think I can write, Nick?"

"You're a natural, Tina. That interview you did with me after I won the scholarship captured the essence of my being."

"Mr. Perkins says my sentence structure needs work."

"Your sentences are perfect, Tina," said Francois. "All your structures are perfect."

"Nick, what time did you say your plane leaves?"

"Not 'til 7:05 a.m.," replied Francois.

Five minutes later we were parked behind a used tire rack at a darkened gas station, our eager tongues exchanging the lingering flavors of cranberry sauce and sage stuffing. As I reached for the enticing convexities inside her blouse, I felt a hand slowly pull down the zipper over my throbbing T.E. (Thunderous Erection).

"Nick," whispered Tina, "here's a going-away present from the women of America."

Three minutes later, 14 years of dangerously compressed libido gushed into the enveloping warmth of Tina Manion's inquisitive mouth. She didn't seem to mind.

Francois, still inflamed, wanted more. "Tina," he implored through the mind-fog of ecstasy, "let's do it!"

"Sorry, Nick," she said, straightening her clothes and starting the engine. "I have to be faithful to my boyfriend."

Twenty-two hours later, as the world continues to heave and lurch around me, I savor those few minutes alone in the dark with Tina. Clearly, God invented this diversion as an incentive to keep us plodding on doggedly through darkest adolescence. It is the light at the end of the tunnel—a tunnel you don't have to be Sigmund Freud to identify.

Yes, I made it on the plane to Bombay.

No, I'm not in India.

At the last minute, I slipped off the plane in Los Angeles. No way I could live 12,000 miles from Sheeni Saunders. Even if she does (temporarily, I hope) despise the very smog I breathe. It also helped that my seatmate, an enterprising Pakistani fellow, offered me $150 in cash for my ticket. And chipped in another C-note for my passport!

SATURDAY, November 22 — My second day in Los Angeles. So far at least, I have not had to become a street person. I'm staying in my sister Joanie's tiny condo in Marina del Rey. It's not as cramped as you might suppose; Joanie is presently out-of-state slinging airline hash. Kimberly, her cute but suspicious roommate, reluctantly let me in after I divulged a few intimate details about Joanie only a close family member (or IRS extortionist) could know.

Still suspicious, Kimberly has refused to lend me a door key, so I haven't dared leave the apartment. To distract my feverish mind from my desperate situation, I've been watching TV and snacking from Joanie's meager food stocks (all their kitchen stores are rigorously labeled as to ownership). Kimberly has consented to sell me two cans of Diet Pepsi—at somewhat above the normal retail markup. She's studying for her MBA at USC and therefore, I expect, has been trained to see in my unexpected arrival an entrepreneurial opportunity. If I didn't need to husband my cash reserves, I'd offer to lease a door key from her.

Every few hours I have to erase all the frightening messages from police detectives that have accumulated on Joanie's answering machine. I don't know why they imagine my sister is so well informed as to my whereabouts. We see each other no more than twice a year. And hardly ever talk on the phone. (In truth, no one in my family likes his or her relations very much. This entrenched dislike may be our strongest familial bond.)

In clearing the tape, I've also been wiping out some sappy messages from "Philip," presumably Joanie's respectably married physicist boyfriend in Santa Monica. He calls at least once an hour in a cultured but panicky voice to demand Joanie "quite fooling around and not do anything desperate." I don't know what that's all about, but I'm hoping it's sufficiently serious to give me some leverage over Joanie in my time of need. I asked Kimberly if my sister was having any problems, but she went off on an indignant tangent about three missing Oreo cookies and an unexplained shortfall in her skim milk carton. As usual Francois has denied any knowledge of the affair.

2:30 p.m. Nothing on TV except USC football. I am watching for the sake of my former friend Fuzzy, the aspiring jock whose sexy mother recently tried to seduce me. I wonder if Dad will be asking her out again, despite her husband's lawsuit against him. Dad just left a message for Joanie in which he expressed a desire to strangle me with his bare hands. Maybe Mom informed him she was cutting off my child-support payments. It's a good thing Dad may be going to prison soon for filling his former girlfriend's car with cement. An enforced confinement should give him plenty of time to cool off.

3:30 p.m. Halftime. USC is ahead 62-14. Still the crowd is screaming for more blood. I wonder if Bruno Preston, Sheeni's inaugural lover, is in the stands. Perhaps there will be a stampede and he will be crushed to death. Not likely, given my present string of bad luck. One of the Trojan cheerleaders looks just like my former friend Lefty's treacherous girlfriend Millie Filbert, who ratted on me to collect a $10,000 reward from Berkeley arson investigators. Francois hates her, but deep-down I wonder if I wouldn't have done the same thing in her place. In these times, who wouldn't betray their friends for a nice cash windfall?

I just called the hospital in Santa Cruz. Bernice Lynch has emerged from her sedative-induced coma and is expected to recover fully. What a weight off my conscience. Not to imply, as Francois points out, that I was in any way responsible for her swallowing those pills. If I were as unpopular and unhappy as she, I'd probably want to get it over with too. In fact, the idea doesn't sound so bad right now. Except I want to see how many points USC pours on in the second half.

5:15 p.m. Final score: 83-17. Mom just left a phone message telling Joanie to call, adding, "If your no-good brother took that plane to India, I hope he stays there and is never heard from again!" I wonder if a psychologist would conclude I am receiving powerful "don't exist" messages from my parents?

On this date they shot Kennedy all those years ago. I think I know now how he must have felt.

SUNDAY, November 23 — Joanie is back. She stumbled in at 1:30 this morning looking like something the cat dragged in: hair a mess, make-up smeared, dark circles under her eyes. Finding me asleep in her single career woman's queen-size bed did not improve her mood.

"What the fuck are you doing here?" she demanded, snapping on the light and dumping her airline travel bag on the floor.

"Oh, hi, Joanie," I mumbled, rubbing my eyes. "Did you have a difficult flight?"

"I repeat, what the fuck are you doing here? Nick, are you in trouble again?"

"Well," I sighed, "there have been a few misunderstandings with the police. But it's OK. Everybody thinks I'm in India now."

"Oh my God!" she exclaimed, slumping into a chair. "This is all I need. On top of everything else!"

"What's the matter, Joanie?" I asked. "Philip keeps calling and leaving messages for you not to do anything desperate."

"I don't wish to speak to that man!" she screamed. "If he calls here again, tell him he's going to be sorry. Very sorry!"

"What's wrong, Joanie?"

"None of your business. Nick, you can't stay here. You've got to leave!"

I gulped. "Now? It's the middle of the night."

"OK. You can leave tomorrow. But get out of my bed. I need to be alone. You can go sleep on the sofa in the living room."

"No, I can't. Kimberly says it's her sofa and she doesn't want people ruining the upholstery by camping out on it. That's why I moved in here."

"Well, then go sleep on the floor. The living room carpet's nice and soft."

My sister lied. The thin beige pile offered all the resiliency of a rock maple bowling alley. Every ten minutes I had to shift positions to relieve the excruciating pressure on my skeletal promontories. I rose at 7:05 feeling like I had spend the night tumbling in an industrial-size clothes dryer.

As I was climbing back into my one change of clothes (and the same four-day-old socks and underwear!), a strange man dressed in coordinated jogging togs emerged stealthily from Kimberly's bedroom. He was in his early twenties, about five-eleven, deeply tanned, with eroding black hair, and dark eyes that blinked at an accelerated frequency.

"You must be Nick," he said, blinking.

"You must be the Westside Strangler," I replied.

He smiled. "No, I'm Mario, a friend of Kimberly's. I arrive late and leave early. I'm a busy guy." He looked at his watch, then consulted a second timepiece on his other arm. "Damn, I'm late for my run. Got to go."

In a flash, he was out the door.

Wow, Kimberly has a boyfriend. I wonder how much she charges for that?

2:10 p.m. At 11:30, my sister finally emerged from her bedroom. Dressed in sweat pants and a ratty sweater, she looked as rested as I felt.

"You still here?" she asked.

"Uh-huh," I replied.

"You have any breakfast?"

"No."

"You want to go out?" she asked.

"OK."

Although the coffee shop on Venice Boulevard was less than a quarter-mile away, Joanie drove there in her old brown Honda Civic. Once a Twisp, always a Twisp. I rolled down the window and inhaled the warm breezes off the ocean. Late November and it was still like summer here. No wonder people were shoving in by the millions.

Joanie waited until I had wolfed down my pecan waffles before she began the third degree.

"OK, let's hear the whole ugly story," she sighed, gulping her sixth coffee refill. Her untouched omelet lay congealing on her plate.

"Aren't you going to eat your eggs?"

"No, Nick. You can have them. I'll just throw them up."

As I reached for her plate, a familiar alarm bell rang in my head. "Joanie, you're not . . . not expecting anything are you?" Next to my mother, Joanie is the least likely candidate for motherhood I know. And my mother, let us not forget, is currently modeling the latest in low-cut maternity frocks.

"That's none of your business," she replied peevishly. "A woman's reproductive system is no one's concern but her own. Other people should just butt out."

"Other people like Philip?" I asked.

"Especially that lying degenerate asshole," replied Joanie. "Now, why are you in trouble with the cops?"

Since Joanie can see through me like a fluoroscope, I was obliged to give a relatively candid and thorough review of the events of the past week. She listened gravely, shaking her head now and then during the most gruesome parts.

"Nick," she said, when I had finished, "six months ago you were just another brown-nosing honor student. What happened?"

"I'm not sure exactly," I replied pensively. "I fell in love with Sheeni. All I want is to be together with her. The rest is all a big misunderstanding."

"Some misunderstanding. Maybe you should just turn yourself in and face the consequences."

"Joanie, I can't do that! I don't want to go to jail. How will I ever get into a decent college?"

Joanie sighed and drank her coffee. If she *were* pregnant, I figured the kid must be doing cartwheels by now from the massive caffeine overdose.

"So everyone thinks you're in India?" she asked.

"Right. No one will be looking for me here."

"But they'll find out soon enough that you never showed up at that Indian school."

"Yes, but fortunately India is a very big country. They could be looking there for me for years. By then I might have a full scholarship and be attending Stanford under an assumed name. Mom and Dad don't care. They're glad to be rid of me. They said so on your answering machine."

"What happened to my messages?" demanded Joanie. "The tape was empty."

"Really?" I replied innocently. "I must have erased it by mistake."

"Well, our jerk of a father probably won't miss you. I don't know about Mom. Now I wish I hadn't loaned him that money for his bail. I'll probably never see it again. And I was counting on it for . . . for my, uh, expenses."

"Dad is a mess," I agreed. "He's the last person I'd ever loan money to."

"I only did it for you, Nick! So you wouldn't have to go live with Mom and Lance."

"I know, Joanie. I really appreciate it. I guess I've messed up your life too."

"Don't worry," sighed Joanie. "It was already messed up. By a real professional."

"Joanie," I implored, "can I stay with you for a few days? Until I get a job and my own apartment?"

"Nick, you're only 14 years old!"

"I know," I replied, "but I'm a mature 14."

Joanie groaned. "I think I'm going to kill myself. Sometimes I think that's the only sensible way out."

"Really?" I asked, intrigued. "I often think that too."

"I was strongly suicidal in high school," confided Joanie.

"Is that why you went out with all those industrial arts majors?"

"Watch your smart mouth!" she replied.

I've heard that line before.

6:30 p.m. Joanie finally relented and gave me a spare key, saying I could stay "for just a few more days." She also told a Berkeley police detective who phoned this afternoon that she hadn't seen me in months and thought it likely "my brother at this moment is somewhere in India. We're all very concerned about his welfare."

"There, I hope you're satisfied," she said, hanging up the phone. "I have just laid myself open to charges of obstruction of justice and harboring a fugitive."

"Thanks, Joanie," I said. "I hope I can do the same for you someday."

"What's that supposed to mean?"

"It means I'm very grateful, Joanie. If it weren't for you, I'd be out on the streets."

"Well, you may be out there soon enough," she replied grimly. "I repeat, Nick, you are not my responsibility. I have problems of my own."

To lend tangibility to my gratitude, I vacuumed the apartment, shopped for groceries (with my own money!), and cooked a gourmet dinner (Mrs. Crampton's famous cheese-and-pimento-stuffed porkchops). I even invited Kimberly, who hadn't looked especially pleased to hear I would be hanging around awhile.

Right before dinner Joanie had a screaming argument in the privacy of her bedroom with someone on the telephone (my guess Philip). This fresh emotional turmoil appeared to take the edge off her appetite. (I hope the kid had the foresight to set aside a few calories for those lean days.) While Joanie picked at her food, Kimberly ate like the cute, but voracious Republican she revealed herself to be. She said she and Mario recently toured the new Ronald Reagan Presidential Library and found it "profoundly inspiring." Since I was at that moment harboring designs on her sofa, I was forced to listen with a pretence of interest. Over dessert (pumpkin pie, for which I've had a curious craving ever since circumstances deprived me of it on Thanksgiving), Kimberly rattled on about her "marvelous marketing" courses at USC.

This was my opportunity. "Speaking of marketing, Kimberly," I said, "I was wondering if you would be interested in renting me your couch. Say between the hours of 11 p.m. and 8 a.m.?"

"For what purpose?" she asked, brazenly helping herself to the last piece of my pie.

I reminded myself that Republicans always expect to receive the largest slice of the pie. "I thought I might sleep on it," I said. "The wear and tear should be minimal. I only weigh 132 pounds."

"How much are you prepared to pay?" she asked, pushing up her glasses. She wears expensive tortoise shell glasses that lend a false front of aristocratic intelligence to her sparkling blue eyes.

"How about a dollar a night?"

Kimberly frowned. "I couldn't possibly let it go that low, Nick. I think $5 a night is closer to the market rate."

We settled on $3 a night, with the stipulation that at all times I was to maintain at least one layer of bedsheet between my actual body and the leased upholstery. Joanie distractedly agreed to lend me (at no charge) the specified linen. The deal done, I paid Kimberly for five nights in advance. She happily pocketed the greenbacks and retreated to her bedroom, leaving me to do the washing up.

And she thinks she's a skilled negotiator. Hell, even on my limited income, to escape that punishing carpet I'd have gone as high as $10 a night. Maybe more.

10:15 p.m. Someone just buzzed from the lobby, and Joanie told them over the intercom "to take a flying fucking leap off the Santa Monica Pier." I think they went away.

11:30 p.m. Mario just slipped in for his nightly you know what.

"Hi, Mario," I said.

"Oh, hi, Nick. You allowed on that couch?"

"Kimberly leased it to me," I replied.

"Yeah, I'll bet she did," he said, blinking and checking his watches. "Damn, I'm late." He turned and slipped silently into his mistress's bedroom.

I'm beginning to experience couch-renter's remorse. Besides offering all the support of a melted marshmallow, Kimberly's sofa is at least a half-foot shorter than my body.

Speaking of acute pain, I wonder where Sheeni is at this moment? I wonder if she is worried how I am getting along in faraway, exotic India? Listen, darling, wherever you are, here is a telepathic love message: "We will be together again. Soon! I shall find a way!"

MONDAY, November 24 — I'm growing a moustache. I haven't shaved since Thursday and a darkening shadow is closing over my upper lip. I am hoping it will make me appear old enough to be legally exempt from all compulsory school attendance laws.

I have decided to take a brief sabbatical from my education while I try to sort out the debris of my life. In my present emotional state I feel I would be ill-advised to venture into a third second-rate public school this term. Besides, I just read in the *Los Angeles Times* that the city's teachers are agitating for a strike. It sounds like the schools are in even more chaos than usual. Fortunately, Joanie always hated school and is unlikely to insist that I knuckle under soon to its tyranny.

After breakfast (I found a good donut shop just a block away), I took a stroll around Marina del Rey. Lots of high-priced yachts in the marina, but who let them jam in so many ugly condos? Joanie's building is a particular eyesore. It's a big orange stucco box with fake midget balconies stuck under the windows here and there. The upper floors probably have views of the water, but Joanie's unit looks out on the gray stucco of the condo next door. Oh well, at least the developer probably made a pile and is enjoying an active sex life.

After my tour, I rode the bus into Santa Monica for some emergency wardrobe shopping. On the downtown mall, workmen were stringing Christmas tinsel and lights on the lamp poles, lending a festive touch to the vernal scene. After salivating over the latest laptops in a computer store, I located a thrift store on Lincoln Boulevard having a gala post-Thanksgiving sale. I bought six changes of used underwear, eight pairs of mostly-matching socks (no holes), two pairs of jeans, five shirts, a pair of almost-new running shoes, and a somewhat scratched Ravi Shamar album. The total came to $46.12, and the nice old lady at the cash register knocked off the sales tax when Francois told her he was homeless. Next, I went to a discount drug store and bought a toothbrush (I'd been using Joanie's), razor (ditto), deodorant, foot powder, notebook (for my, *groan*, hand-written journal), acne salve, and three-pak of condoms (just in case something comes up). The bill came to $21.08. Boy, have I learned my lesson. In the future I shall always keep a packed suitcase in reserve for emergencies. I believe every teen would be wise to take this precaution.

When I got back to the condo (deserted), I changed out of my crusty clothes (what a relief!), and checked out Kimberly's messy bedroom. On the unpainted pine desk were piles of boring marketing textbooks and an old IBM PC (not even an XT, talk about stone-age computing). I discovered more of interest in the drawer of her nightstand: a box of Sheiks, three copies of *Playgirl* (well thumbed), and a large battery-powered vibrator (smelling faintly of you know what).

I checked out the guys in *Playgirl*. "Not such a big deal," muttered Francois. I did not point out that these fellows, unlike my alter ego, were all in a state of repose. I found Kimberly's bank book in a bureau drawer under a pair of red lace panties. I gasped when I read her savings balance. Even though she is presently sitting on interest-earning cash reserves of $48,729.71, Kimberly finds it necessary to charge me $3 a night to sleep on her crummy sofa. To repay her for her compassion, I found a pin and poked a tiny hole through each foil condom package. I also unscrewed the vibrator and shorted out the batteries. Thus commences every Republican's worst dread: class warfare.

7:00 p.m. Joanie came back from a session with her therapist this afternoon feeling a little better. She tore up a Mailgram (from Philip?) without reading it, and took me out to dinner at a Mexican restaurant on the boardwalk in Venice. To the kid's probable relief, she even ate most of her enchilada. But I wonder if the two strawberry margaritas were such a good idea.

Joanie said my moustache makes me look like "some would-be, under-aged gigolo." I'm not sure, but I think I'm flattered. While finishing up my flan (egg custard with a Latin disguise), I heard some men at an adjoining table discussing "residual rights." I think they may be connected in some way with the movie business. Maybe they're high-powered agents. They were certainly chugging down the cocktails like mega-buck deal-makers. Three days in this town and I've yet to spot a single star. I must undertake a pilgrimage soon to Hollywood.

11:30 p.m. No sign of Mario. Like me, Kimberly will be retiring for the night with only the cold embrace of sexual frustration for company. At least she has a comfortable bed. I think I just heard my spine snap.

TUESDAY, November 25 — This morning as Joanie was getting ready to leave for her flight hostessing duties, our cop-cohabitating mother called. I listened in on the extension in the living room.

"Joanie, why didn't you return my calls?" demanded Mom.

"Sorry, Mother. Things have been hectic here."

"Your brother will be the death of me. He's disappeared! And those impossible people at the Indian Consulate are so rude. Worse, your father and I may be sued by the insurance companies for the Berkeley fire damages."

"I'm sorry, Mother. How can I help you?"

"Joanie dear, can you use your free travel privileges to fly to Bombay and look for Nick?"

"What!" exclaimed Joanie.

"He hasn't shown up at that school in Pune." (Mom pronounced it Pun-ee, rhymes with funny.) "I asked Lance, but he refuses to go. He says good riddance to bad rubbish."

I like you too Lance!

"How do you know Nick's in India?" asked Joanie. "He might be, be . . . still in California somewhere."

"No, he went through customs in Bombay. I did find that out. They recorded his passport number when they issued him a visa."

"Well, Mother, I can't go to India. I . . . I don't have the time. Nick will be all right. I'm sure he'll get in touch with you soon."

"Joanie, he's your only brother!"

"I'm sorry, Mother. Don't worry about Nick. I'm late for work. I have to hang up now."

"OK, I guess I'll just have to go to India myself," declared Mom.

"Mother!" exclaimed Joanie, "you can't possibly undertake a strenuous journey in your condition—at your age. You need to rest."

"There's no one else, Joanie."

"Mother, don't do anything at the moment. Promise me you won't. I'm sure Nick will contact you soon. Very soon!"

"Well, all right," Mom said weakly. "I'll wait a little bit. I should never have let him go live with his deadbeat father. He tried to poison some innocent girl in Santa Cruz. And it was Nick who broke into my house and wrote that horrible message on the mirror. Lance feels he should be institutionalized—until the age of 24 at least. I'm inclined to agree. What do you think, Joanie?"

"Nick's just . . . just misguided, Mother. He's had a difficult emotional time with the . . . the divorce and all."

"Oh, I suppose it's all my fault!" screamed Mom. "It's always the parents' fault!"

Wow, she's finally beginning to see the light.

"Mother, don't worry. Nick will contact you soon. I have to go. Goodbye."

Joanie walked out of the bedroom and glared at me. "You call Mother today!"

"OK," I said nonchalantly. "I was going to anyway."

Joanie picked up her airline coat and travel bag. She looked surprisingly attractive in her trim blue uniform. Expertly applied make-up had camouflaged the dark circles under her eyes.

"I'll be back Friday night," she said. "Try not to get into any more trouble."

"OK."

"If a man named Philip Dindy calls for me, you can tell him I do not wish to speak to him. Ever again. And tell him he can stop worrying, I'm not going to say anything to his wife."

"Say anything about what?" I asked.

"None of your business, smart guy." She opened the door, then stopped. "Do you have any money?"

"About $10," I lied.

Joanie opened her purse and fished out two twenties. "This is all I can afford. You're not my responsibility, Nick."

"Thanks, Joanie," I said gratefully. "Sorry to be a burden. Have a nice trip."

"Goodbye, Nick. Oh, and stay out of my bedroom. I know how much you like to snoop."

"I do not," I said, offended.

Wow, three days of total freedom on someone else's money! I wonder if I should unleash Francois to put the moves on Kimberly?

11:00 a.m. When I returned from donut gorging, my cute Republican roommate had left for school. "Well, let's get this over with," I said to Francois. I put my Ravi Shamar record on the stereo and dialed Mom's number in Oakland. She answered on the second ring.

"Nick! Is that you?"

"It's me, Mom."

"Where are you!?"

"I'm in India, Mom. I'm calling international long distance."

"Nick, you come home right this minute!"

"Sorry, Mom. I think it would be better for everyone if I stayed here for a while. I'm sorry I caused you so much grief."

"Where are you, Nick? How are you living?"

"Don't worry, Mom. Everything's working out. I got a job with a nice family as a math tutor."

"What family? Where?" she demanded.

"I can't tell you that, Mom, but they're really nice and rich. It's a wealthy businessman. I met him on the plane. We had a nice long talk. His kids were all flunking algebra so he invited me to come and live in his mansion and give them private lessons. It's great. I even have my own servant, Ravi. No thanks, Ravi, I don't care for any more somosas right now."

"Nick, are you lying to me?"

"No, Mom. Honest. I'm really happy. And safe. I'm learning how to play the sitar. My instructor is here now warming up for my lesson. The father says he's going to send me to a good private school to become an educated gentleman. They really like me here."

"How old are the children?" she demanded. "Are they boys or girls?"

"Uh, both. There are lots of them. About 12, I'd say. All ages."

"Does the man have a wife?" she asked suspiciously. "He isn't . . . he isn't . . ."

"No, Mom. He's married. In fact he has three wives. They get along fine though. Well, Mom, these international calls cost 95 rupees a minute."

"Nickie, what's your address? How can I write to you? What's the phone number there?"

"Sorry, Mom. It would be better if I called you. Don't worry, I'll phone as often as I can."

"Nickie, wash all your food before you eat it. They've got terrible diseases there. If you get sick, call me right away."

"OK, Mom. Don't worry about me. Say hi to Lance for me. And happy birthday."

"Nickie," said Mom, starting to blubber, "you remembered."

"'Bye, Mom." *Click.*

"She bought it," said Francois.

"Hook, line, and sinker," I replied.

1:20 p.m. A knock on the door startled me as I snooped through Joanie's bank statements. Her finances, alas, are in as wretched a condition as her personal life. Quickly, I closed the drawer, walked silently over to the door, and peered out through the peep-hole viewer. In the fluorescent-lit hallway a 105-year-old woman leaned heavily on an aluminum walker. Cautiously, I opened the door a crack.

"Yes?" I said.

"Who are you?" she demanded.

"I'm, uh, Francois, I mean Frank Dillinger," I replied, remembering not to give my real name. "A friend of Joanie's. Who are you?"

"I'm Bertha Ulansky from across the hall. I'm ready for my videos." Despite her great age, her face was elaborately made up. Thin eyebrows had been penciled in, and black mascara, applied thickly to her false eyelashes, fell like polluted snow on her rouged cheeks.

I was confused. "Excuse me?"

"My videos. My videos," she insisted. "Joan always goes and gets my videos for me. I got my list ready."

"Uh, Joanie isn't here right now. She's gone to work, Mrs. Ulansky."

"It's Miss Ulansky, young man," she huffed. "I never took my late husband's name—for professional reasons." The old lady looked down at my feet. "Are your legs broken?"

"Er, no," I admitted.

"Then get a move on it, Frank. You gotta get there before two to get the senior citizen discount!"

4:10 p.m. When I returned from the video store, my elderly neighbor invited me in to watch the film with her. Believe it or not, my sister lives right across the hall from an actual retired movie actress. Miss Ulansky starred as a professional extra in over 400 films—starting as a cabaret floozie in "Morocco" in 1930.

"Joseph von Sternberg made that picture with Gary Cooper and Marlene Dietrich," she observed, shifting her aged amorphous bulk painfully from the walker to a pink velour recliner facing the largest TV I'd ever seen outside of a pizza parlour.

"Wow, Gary Cooper!" I exclaimed. "Did you get to meet him?"

"Of course," she sniffed. "Frank, you fans don't seem to realize it, but the extras are just as important to a film as the featured players. We provide the context to make the drama believable. Nowadays, the producers try to scrimp and shoot out on the street with non-professionals. Hell, half the ninnies in the crowd are looking straight at the camera. There goes your realism right out the window. If we dared look at the camera, we'd have been fired on the spot. Of course, we were professionals. We knew better."

"What was Gary Cooper like?" I asked excitedly.

"He was quite a presentable young man," she replied. "At least back then. All of his teeth were false you know. His toupee cost over $5,000—that was a fortune back then, believe me. The hair, I heard, was gathered strand by strand from one particular family in rural Finland."

"Gary Cooper wore a toupee?" I exclaimed.

"Certainly," she replied. "They had to use a special glue to hold it on during westerns. Made his scalp break out terribly, poor thing."

Today's film was "You Were Never Lovelier," a 1942 musical starring Fred Astaire, Rita Hayworth, and Bertha Ulansky as a sybarite party-goer. Miss Ulansky pushed the freeze-frame button on her remote control when she made her grand entrance.

"See, there I am in the crepe de Chine ball gown back by the potted palm," she said proudly.

On the giant TV screen, suave millionaire Adolphe Menjou was hosting an elegant party in his South American mansion. Among the motionless party guests, frozen in shimmering black and white, I recognized my hostess—much thinner, with a half-century fewer wrinkles.

"Miss Ulansky, you were very pretty," I commented.

"No, I wasn't," she said matter-of-factly, pushing the play button. "I had a nice ordinary face. They didn't want the girls or the fellas to be too good looking. 'Cause naturally they didn't want the extras upstaging the stars. Watch, though, I'm a pretty fair dancer. That's a fox trot. Bill Selter had us do 14 takes of that scene. Boy, were my feet killing me."

"Who was your partner?" I asked.

"A fella named Doakes Farley," she said. "He's a good dancer, but he has a bad case of B.O. He's dead now, of course. That's his boyfriend Jim who Evelyn is dancing with. I roomed with her for a while out in the valley before I met my husband Tom."

"Was he an extra too?" I asked.

"No, Tom isn't in the entertainment industry. He's an accountant. He passed on in 1972. Heart attack."

"Boy, Rita Hayworth was certainly beautiful," I observed.

"She wasn't so gorgeous when she was Rita Cansino," Miss Ulansky replied. "They used electrolysis on her to alter her hairline. She looked like a Mexican peasant girl before."

"Wow, you don't say. What was she like?"

Miss Ulansky looked around and lowered her voice. "Obsessed."

"Really?" I gasped.

"Obsessed," she repeated. "That's why Orson had to divorce her. 'Course he is known to be very cerebral. Rita eats like a horse too. She's always had a bad weight problem."

"Uh, Miss Ulansky," I said. "I think they're dead now."

"I know that," she replied, offended. "I still read the trades."

Miss Ulansky, I concluded, preferred a freestyle mix of her tenses. As we watched the rest of the film, she froze the action now and then to identify her extra friends and divulge more of her valuable insider movie lore.

She sighed when "The End" appeared on the screen. "I always liked that picture," she said, pushing the rewind button. "'Course, Jerome Kern never wrote a bad song."

"What was Fred Astaire like?" I asked. "He's one of my favorite movie stars."

"I like Fred," she replied pensively. "Not funny either, if you catch my drift. Not, at least, that I ever heard. Now that's a rarity in his profession. 'Course, his toupee is pretty obvious. And he is very short."

"Fred Astaire was short?" I asked, surprised.

"Practically a midget. For all of his love scenes with Rita the director had him standing on a stepladder. Back in the '30s RKO had to give Fred secret lessons to teach him to dance in elevator shoes. First they tried him on stilts but the planks showed under his trousers."

"I didn't know that!"

"Yes, and you know all that precision tap dancing he did in his films?"

"Sure. He was great."

"It wasn't him," she whispered.

"It wasn't?" I whispered back.

"No. It was a negro they used to fly in secretly from Harlem just for those numbers. Then they matted in Fred's head. It was all very hush-hush. Not even Ginger was in on it."

"That's incredible!" I exclaimed.

"Better keep it under your hat, Frank," she said. "The studios still have goons on the payroll to keep a lid on explosive information like that."

When I returned to the apartment, I discovered this message from Mom on Joanie's answering machine: "Good news, Joanie. We don't have to worry any more. I just spoke to Nick in India. He's living with a nice family, who may teach him some manners and sense. What a miracle that would be. Lance says as long as Nick's not here to be prosecuted, we can't be held legally liable for the fire damages. And that girl who snitched on him won't be collecting any reward either. So Nick running away to India may be a blessing in disguise. I certainly don't mind having him out of my hair for a while. Oh, and your miserable father is being sued for $3.5 million for some dangerous neon sign Nick found and sold to a man which electrocuted him—the man I mean. Fortunately that is of no concern to me. Personally, I wish the man's family the best of luck. I only wish they'd asked for more! Well, got to go. Lance is taking me out tonight to celebrate my birthday—not that that is apparently of much concern to you."

Three-and-a-half-million dollars! That is pure pie in the sky. From my unemployed deadbeat father Fuzzy's family would be fortunate to collect $3.50. Which, I'm happy to say, is more loot than that pair of traitorous back-stabbers, Lefty and Millie, will be getting their greasy mitts on.

6:30 p.m. Kimberly just returned from a hard day of business theory ingestion.

"Good news, Kimberly," I said. "Joanie said I could sleep in her bed while she's away, so I won't be needing your couch for a few days."

Kimberly shrugged with feigned indifference, but I could tell she was mentally calculating this unexpected assault on her net worth.

"Is Mario dropping by tonight?" asked Francois.

"I don't know," she said, flipping through her mail. "Why do you ask?"

"Oh, I thought maybe we could go to a movie or something," said Francois.

"Who? You and Mario?"

"Er, no. You and me," said Francois. "I'll pay."

"Sorry, Nick. I have to work on my marketing plan."

"I could pay for the popcorn too," persisted Francois.

"Sorry, Nick," said Kimberly, walking toward her bedroom. "Maybe some other time."

She went into her room and closed the door.

"She likes me. I can tell," observed Francois.

"Then why did she lock the door?" I asked.

"Temptation," he replied. "She's trying to resist temptation."

WEDNESDAY, November 26 — This afternoon's movie was a 1942 black and white comedy, "The Talk of the Town," starring Ronald Coleman, Jean Arthur, Cary Grant, and Bertha Ulansky as an irate townsperson. Cary played (none too convincingly) a blue-collar labor radical wrongly accused of arson. Perhaps John Garfield had a scheduling conflict that month.

After the film Miss Ulansky filled me in on all the inside dope.

"Cary Grant and Ronald Coleman hate each other you know," she said. "They're both English. All the English actors in Hollywood hate each other."

"Why?"

"Because they're rivals for the same parts. Everyone would test for a part and then Leslie Howard would get it. He was especially despised. I've heard rumors his death was not by natural causes."

"Wow," I exclaimed, eager for more. "What was Ronald Coleman like?"

"Self-absorbed. Very self-absorbed," she said. "That velvety voice of his is all fake. To hear him talk on the set, you'd think he was one of the grips. His accent is quite coarse and his natural speaking voice is a high falsetto. And he is very short."

"Ronald Coleman was short?" I asked.

"Dreadfully short. Practically a midget," she said. "He refused to use an American stepladder for his love scenes. They had to import one from England with the rungs on the left side."

"Was Cary Grant short?" I asked.

"Yes, quite charmingly diminutive," she replied. "Standing next to Ronnie Coleman, they looked like two jockeys at the track."

"What was Jean Arthur like?"

"Vain. Terribly vain. She insists they only shoot her from her left side. Or was it her right side? I forget now. She used to drive the directors crazy. And she is obsessed, of course."

"Really?" I exclaimed. "She didn't give that impression on screen."

"Obsessed," repeated Miss Ulansky. "I can say no more than that."

I wonder if the Hollywood community continues to be plagued by this phenomenon? I must send Francois there soon to investigate.

6:30 p.m. When I returned from next door, Kimberly was microwaving dinner for Mario, who sat at the table blinking impatiently. I loitered about hoping to be invited, but the cook successfully resisted all impulses toward gracious hospitality. So I walked the eight blocks to McDanold's. When I returned, Kimberly was watching TV on my rental couch while Mario was washing up in the kitchenette.

"Say, Nick, how old are you?" she asked, flipping off "The Nightly Business Report" with the remote control.

"Nineteen," I lied.

"More like 14 or 15, I'd expect," she replied. "Would you like to answer some questions for our survey?"

"What kind of survey is it?" I asked warily.

"It's a marketing survey," she explained. "Mario and I are thinking of starting a company to market unique, fashion-forward products to younger consumers."

Mario looked over from his dishpan. "Nick, you American teenagers have an annual disposable income in excess of $80 billion."

Eighty-billion dollars! Boy, am I missing out on my fair share.

"OK," I said. "I'll answer your questions. Fire away."

Kimberly picked up her clipboard and asked me a long series of exhaustively thorough, boringly repetitious questions about my expendable income, purchasing habits, and tastes in clothing, with a particular emphasis on footwear. Except for the income questions, I answered as honestly as I was able. Kimberly seemed pleased with my responses.

"Well, aren't you going to ask me one more question?" I inquired, when she had finished.

"What's that, Nick?" she asked.

"Aren't you going to ask me if I would consider buying polka dot running shoes?"

Kimberly gasped. Mario nearly dropped a plate. "How did you know that?" they demanded.

"Well, it was obvious from your questions," I explained. "You intend to sell running shoes with fluorescent orange or purple polka dots. Right?"

"No comment," replied Kimberly.

"Certainly not," said Mario, blinking even faster than usual.

"Good," I replied. "Because I wouldn't buy a pair of shoes like that in ten million years. And neither would my friends."

"That's just your opinion," sniffed Kimberly.

"Well I thought that's what you wanted," I said. "I thought that was the reason for conducting marketing surveys."

"He's right, Kimmy," said Mario, blinking glumly.

"Yes, but look at him, Mario," she replied. "He hardly qualifies as a member of our high-income, fashion-conscious target stratum."

I chose to overlook that slander. "Now I have an idea for a product that I think a lot of teens would buy," I said.

"What's that, Nick?" asked Mario, blinking eagerly.

"I'll tell you," I replied. "But I want a third of all the profits—in writing."

After 15 minutes of fierce, no-holds-barred negotiating, my new partners signed a contract agreeing to pay me 19.6 percent of all net profits (after taxes) accruing from my proposal.

"Now what is it?" demanded Kimberly skeptically.

"OK, picture this," I said. "Running shoes . . . shaped like . . . sports cars! With headlights and taillights molded into the soles. That actually light! And little license plates on the chromed rubber bumpers that kids can personalize with stick-on letters. I even have the perfect name: Roadsters."

Mario and Kimberly exchanged glances.

"That idea sucks," declared the latter.

"Where would you put the batteries?" demanded Mario.

"Lights on shoes," scoffed Kimberly. "What nonsense!"

"OK," I said. "You don't like that idea. Fine. I've got another one."

"I don't want to hear it," said Kimberly.

"What is it?" asked Mario.

"Same terms?" I asked.

"OK, same terms," he replied, blinking doubtfully.

"All right," I said, "this one's a watch. Now, there are thousands of nice-looking watches on the market. Right?"

"Sure," they agreed.

"But what about all those millions of kids who aren't interested in dressing to look nice? Who, in fact, try at all times to look as offensive as possible. How about a seriously ugly watch? The dial could look rusty and broken—maybe with a fake bullet hole through it. And you could have a disgusting flesh-colored plastic band with scars, tattoos, and a big, gross, hairy wart on it. In fact, that would make a great name: the Wart Watch."

I paused and gazed at them expectantly.

Mario sighed. Kimberly got up to leave.

"Well, what's wrong with that idea?" I demanded.

"It sucks," said Kimberly.

"Could you possibly be a little more specific?" I asked.

"Nick," said Mario, "there's one major problem I see with your idea."

"What's that?"

"Kids who want to dress like that don't care what time it is."

Oh. He had a point there.

"And what little disposable income those creatures have," added his business partner, "they spend entirely on drugs and heavy metal albums."

She had a point there too.

Oh well, like countless impoverished Twisps before me, I never aspired to success in business. Ours is a family devoting itself to the arts.

THURSDAY, November 27 — It's been one week since I last held Sheeni Saunders in my arms. It feels like an eternity. How unbearable to be estranged from your beloved during the holiday season. Each romantic, soft-focus perfume commercial on TV plunges me deeper into despair. Perhaps I should mail her a nice expensive bottle anonymously. No, she might sprinkle it on for her dates with that traitor Vijay Joshi.

4:05 p.m. I decided to skip today's movie: "The Philadelphia Story," starring Cary Grant, Katherine Hepburn, James Stewart, and Bertha Ulansky as a Main Line society matron. I'd seen it before. Besides, I didn't particularly want to learn that Jimmy Stewart was only four-and-a-half feet tall and Katie Hepburn was obsessed with you know what. So I rode the bus (90 minutes each way) across the vast, car-clogged L.A. basin to the magic dream emporium itself: HOLLYWOOD!

What a dump. The entertainment capital of the world, I discovered, looks like Duluth with palm trees. Endless streets of seedy bungalows, cheap motels, and tawdry shops. The sound stages were still there lining Gower Gulch, but now they echoed—not to the cries of "Action," "Cut," "Print it!"—but to the *plonk, plonk, plonk* of yuppies playing racquetball. I did experience one momentary thrill when I happened to look down and discovered, purely by chance, I was standing on the Walk of Fame star for Frank Sinatra. Reverently, I touched the well-trod brass letters, gazed around, and realized the Golden Age was over. As usual, I was 50 years too late. And why were all those tough-looking kids loitering about on street corners? Shouldn't they be in school?

6:20 p.m. No sign of Kimberly and Mario. There was another panicky message from Philip on the answering machine. The guy sounds like a real mess. I decided to show some compassion and put him out of his misery. I found a listing for Philip Dindy, PhD in Santa Monica and dialed the number. A woman answered.

"Is this Mrs. Dindy?" I asked, in my most lyrical Bombay accent.

"Yes, it is."

"Mrs. Dindy, I believe you would do well to ask your husband about the lovely young flight attendant in Marina del Rey."

"What flight attendant?" she demanded.

"The one who is expecting his child!"

Having done my good deed of the day, I hung up quickly and went out for dinner. Tonight I thought I'd try Taco Bomb.

8:40 p.m. Four beef burritos, a new record for me. While recovering, I decided to gather intelligence on the unfolding situation up in Ukiah. I put on my Ravi Shamar record and dialed Fuzzy DeFalco's number. Fortunately, the hirsute teen himself answered my call.

"Nick! Where are you?"

"I'm in Bombay, India. I'm calling international long distance."

"Really? It sounds like you're right next door."

"Frank, I'm sorry I made up that story about your mom and me in bed together. I guess it was a pretty lousy joke."

"That's OK, Nick. No hard feelings. Mom told me it wasn't true. I figured you must have been stressed out. Wow, I can't believe you're in India. What's it like? Is it hot?"

"Pretty hot, Frank. About 112° in the shade. But they're forecasting a monsoon for this afternoon which should cool things off."

"Neat! A monsoon!" he exclaimed. "Nick, how are you getting by? Do you have a place to live?"

"Yeah, a great place. I met a stewardess for Air India on the plane. I'm staying at her penthouse apartment."

"You're staying with a real live stewardess! Is she cute?"

"Gorgeous. She looks just like Merle Oberon."

"Who did you say?" asked Fuzzy. "Merle Haggard?"

"No, Merle Oberon. She was a famous movie star. Rava's thinking of going into films here when she gets tired of flight attending. That's her playing the sitar."

"Is that what that is?" commented Fuzzy. "I thought maybe it was a bad connection."

"Frank, what's happening there?"

"Oh man, Nick. You cut out just in time. I guess the cops traced Vijay's fingerprints. They grabbed him and the fink ratted on all of us. I thought my parents were going to kill me for sure when they found out we were the ones who swiped Grandmamma's car. My dad hit the wall again."

"Did he miss the stud?"

"Yeah, thank God. But he went clear through both layers of plaster board. I'm grounded 'til Christmas. And they're limiting my calls to Heather to five minutes a week. Boy, am I horny."

"Too bad, Frank," I said. "What happened to Vijay?"

"The cops didn't arrest him. They're a lot more interested in finding you, Nick. Boy, I don't think I've ever heard of a kid in as much trouble as you are. It's a good thing you had that plane ticket to get out of the country. You'd be dead meat for sure here."

"Possibly," I conceded, not wishing to dwell on the negative. "Frank, what did Vijay's parents do?"

"They yelled at him a lot, I guess. I'm not talking to that stool pigeon any more. Nick, he told Sheeni you were the one who spread all those rumors about her and Trent smuggling birth control pills."

More grim news.

"Is he putting the moves on Sheeni?" I asked, fearing the worst.

"He's doing his best. They had lunch together today in the cafeteria. They were talking in French, the stuck up creeps."

"How does Sheeni look?" I asked.

"Kind of sad. I don't think she's that thrilled to be back in Redwood High. She kept correctly Mr. Perkins in English today, and she wasn't even polite about it like she used to be. I bet a lot of the teachers would be willing to chip in and buy her a bus ticket back to Santa Cruz."

"Is she hanging around Trent?"

"No, I see her more with Vijay, Nick."

"Are they holding hands?"

"Not yet, Nick. But what do you care? You've got Merle your sexy stewardess."

"Her name is Rava," I corrected him. "And whatever you do, don't tell Sheeni about her. In fact, I'd appreciate it if you wouldn't tell anyone you'd talked to me."

"OK, Nick. I understand. I'm zipped."

"Frank, your mother isn't going out with my dad any more is she?"

"They had a date last night, Nick. It's so gross. I don't see what she sees in the creep. No offense."

"No offense taken."

"I mean, especially since we're suing his ass for so much money. I hope, Nick, our cleaning out your dad won't affect your finances for college."

"That's OK, Frank. Dad wasn't saving a cent for my college education anyway. He prefers to spend his money on bimbos."

"You talking about my mother?" demanded Fuzzy, offended.

"No, Frank. I meant his previous under-age girlfriends like Lacey. Your mother is a very fine person."

"Well, I don't know if I'd go that far," he replied.

The needle, I noticed, had become lodged in a groove on the record. Fortunately, with sitar music it was difficult to tell the difference.

"Well, Frank, I better go. These international calls cost 200 rupees a minute."

"Boy, Merle must be loaded to let you make such expensive calls."

"She's very generous, Frank. With everything."

"I hope that means what I think it means, Nick."

"I can say no more, Frank. Well, see you. I'll keep in touch."

Francois is furious. He wants to recruit a skinhead to deal with Vijay. He believes the cops will view the assault as another case of random, unprovoked immigrant bashing.

But where do you find a skinhead? And do any of them offer budget rates?

FRIDAY, November 28 — Joanie's condo is getting crowded. Dr. Philip Dindy showed up at 1:30 this morning with two suitcases, his squash racquet, and an extremely attractive 586 laptop—the first I'd ever seen outside of a magazine.

"Who are you?" he demanded, after I crawled sleepily out of Joanie's bed and let him in.

"I'm Frank Dillinger," I yawned. "A friend of Joanie's. An old family friend."

Philip studied me suspiciously through his thick glasses. I was clad only in my thrift-shop underwear. "Joanie never mentioned a friend named Frank."

He was, as Miss Ulansky would say, dreadfully short, practically a midget. He had wild red hair, freckles, a prominent nose, no chin, and a paunch. Not exactly the over-educated stud I had been anticipating.

"Well, Joanie *did* mention you to me," I replied. "But she didn't say anything about expecting you tonight."

"I, I've had to move on short notice," he said, still suspicious. "Where's Joanie?"

"She's off attending flights," I replied. "She won't be back until tonight."

Philip gave the living room a quick, shifty-eyed scan. "Are you staying in Kimberly's room?" he asked.

"No, I'm borrowing Joanie's bed," I said. "Feel free to camp out on the carpet here if you like. It's nice and soft."

Philip had other ideas. Obstinately asserting his territorial rights, he barged into Joanie's bedroom, bouncing me back onto the Couch from Hell.

"You'll regret this, Dr. Dimby," I said, making up my tortuous bed. "I know for a fact Joanie will be furious."

"It's Dindy," he said. "With two 'd's and one 'n'."

"It's the middle of the night," I snapped. "I am not interested in a spelling bee at this hour. Good night!"

"Up yours," he said, slamming and locking the bedroom door.

Boy, Joanie can sure pick them, I thought, settling into my bed of horrors. Nice expensive new chest implants and all she can attract is the Creature from the Atomic Accelerator.

10:30 a.m. Philip was a little friendlier this morning. He wanted something.

"Uh, what did you say your name was?" he asked.

"Frank Dillinger."

"Uh, Frank, do you know if Joanie has a spare door key around?"

"No, Dr. Dimby, I don't believe she does," I answered coldly, pretending to scan the job ads in the *Los Angeles Times*.

"Uh, Frank, will you be here this afternoon, say around four, to let me back in?"

"I don't think so," I replied. "I don't think I should have let you in in the first place. Joanie told me explicitly she never wanted to see you again."

"Joanie will want to see me now," he said confidently. "I've left my wife."

"How fortunate for her," said Francois. "Your wife, I mean."

11:45 a.m. After the runty physicist departed for his lab, I sent Francois into Joanie's room to snoop through his stuff. His bags appeared to have been packed in considerable haste. Among the tumult of preppy knit shirts (size small), chino slacks, argyle socks (some with holes), and Kevin Clein bikini briefs (ditto), I found a checkbook (balance of $273.12), a framed photo of a chihuahua-like woman surrounded by three be-freckled children (the Dindy clan?), crumpled reprints of a dozen boring monographs on particle physics by you know who, and a box of Trojans.

"Looks like Dr. Dimby intends to lock the barn after the bun is in the oven," observed Francois, mixing his metaphors.

Next Francois turned his attention to the gleaming, state-of-the-art laptop. He switched it on and watched in awe as the powerful 586 CPU hurtled through its self test.

"I wonder how big the hard drive is?" said Francois, calling up its directory. "Holy shit, 385 mega-bytes! And nearly full of programs."

Francois typed "Format C:."

"Uh, Francois," I said nervously. "Do you really want to do that?"

"Did you enjoy sleeping on the couch last night?" he asked. Francois hit several keys, and the hard disk began to spin, industriously performing a form of electronic house cleaning. After ten minutes, the whirling stopped.

Joanie's apartment may be crowded, but Dr. Dimby's hard disk is as desolate as Francois' conscience.

3:45 p.m. Today's movie was "My Man Godfrey," a 1936 comedy starring William Powell, Carole Lombard, and Bertha Ulansky as a jaded parasitic socialite. I'd seen it before, but enjoyed watching it again on Miss Ulansky's giant screen. This time I watched carefully and noted that in several scenes suave Boston-Brahmin-in-disguise William Powell was shown full length against common objects of a known size. No way that great star was a midget.

"He may be of average height, possibly less," conceded Miss Ulansky, "but he wears a toupee. The man is as bald as a monkey's butt."

"Did Carole Lombard have a bad reputation?" I asked.

"Terrible," confirmed by hostess. "She has the foulest mouth in town. And after she was married to Gable, she had the gall to complain about his performance in the sack. That's being pretty damn particular if you ask me. You know she was married to Powell too."

"Really?" I said. "I didn't know that."

"Oh yeah. For a couple of years. They got divorced about four years before they made that picture."

"That's amazing," I said. "They seemed so loving on the screen."

"Just an act," she replied. "They hated each other."

I tried to imagine Mom and Dad coming together to do a love scene four years after their divorce. Not for $10 million in cash could they make that drama convincing. Of course, Mom is no Carole Lombard. And Dad hardly qualifies for the role of William Powell's toupee attendant.

7:30 p.m. The dingy Dr. Dindy returned right on time this afternoon, but unfortunately Kimberly was here to let him in. Cutting me dead, he changed into one of his innumerable polo shirts and called his wife for some aerobic telephone shouting. I predict their divorce will be ugly in the extreme. Like many men of science, Philip is obsessively rational about all matters except his private life. Only within this sphere can he let down his hair to revel in primitive emotions, unprincipled manipulativeness, and unrestrained vindictiveness.

Just as he slammed down the phone (I could hear his wife's violent sobs), Joanie arrived home from her stratospheric hostessing.

"Philip!" she shrieked.

"Joanie, darling," he said, smiling lovingly, "I've left Caitlin."

"Oh, Philip!" she exclaimed, falling into his freckled arms.

They embraced, kissed, and groped each other. Embarrassed, I pretended to read my book (*Superstar Los Angeles on a Depression Budget*).

The groping grew more flagrant. I wondered if silicone was formulated to withstand that sort of handling.

"Uh, Philip honey," whispered Joanie, "maybe we should go into the bedroom."

Still joined passionately, they moved as one toward the sanctuary of the bedroom.

Joanie paused. "Philip honey, have you met my brother Nick?"

"He's your brother?" asked Philip. "He told me his name was Frank Dillinger."

"Nickie Twisp," called Joanie, drunk with happiness. "Why did you tell Phillie your name was Frankie Dillinger?"

"I forget," I replied.

"Is he staying here long?" demanded the lipstick-smeared swain.

"Oh, no," replied Joanie. "He's going soon!"

"We must have our privacy," he insisted.

"We will, honey," she said, as they disappeared into the bedroom.

"Call 911," suggested Francois. "Tell them a short rapist with freckles is attacking your sister."

I thought about it, then remembered. I can't call the cops. I'm a fugitive from justice!

SATURDAY, November 29 — This morning Joanie telephoned out and had bagels and lox delivered (she paid). Everyone gathered around the table for a celebratory feast—the two roommates, both boyfriends, and me. Nearly everyone looked well rested and sexually fulfilled.

"I never thought you'd leave your wife," observed Kimberly, biting into her third bagel.

"I had a little help," confessed Philip. "I think one of my Pakistani grad students told her about Joan."

"I'm glad he did," declared Joanie happily.

"Me too," said Philip, draping a freckled paw over her shoulder. "But it was still none of his business. Next spring the guy comes before me for his orals. I can't wait. I'm going to tandoori his skinny brown ass."

"That doesn't sound very ethical," commented Francois. "To ruin a man professionally because of a personal vendetta."

"What's it to you?" demanded Philip, glaring at me over his lox-laden bagel. "What business is it of yours, kid?"

"Ethics are everyone's concern," replied Francois with conviction. "Or should be."

10:45 a.m. Joanie made us all talk in hushed tones and walk around on tiptoes after Philip retired to the bedroom to work on his "important new book." Five minutes later, we were startled by a blood-curdling scream. Moments later, Philip—looking more than usually deranged—burst through the doorway.

"It's gone!" he gasped. "My entire manuscript! Three years' work totally evaporated!"

That will teach the twit to back-up his files. As a scientist, he should know the infallibility of technology is a cruel myth.

4:30 p.m. Before today's movie ("The Long, Long Trailer," starring Lucille Ball, Dezi Arnez, and Bertha Ulansky as a gregarious trailer court resident), Francois asked our hostess if she would like to have a live-in caretaker companion.

"You mean you, Frank?" she asked doubtfully.

"Well, yes," I replied. "I could get you videos whenever you want. And I'm a pretty fair cook. You could cancel your Meals on Wheels."

"But Frank," she replied, blushing under her rouge, "you're a man."

"So?"

"Well, whatever would people think?" she asked, her penciled eyebrows arching far into her wrinkled forehead.

"But I'm only 14," I said. "You're much, much . . . more mature."

"Frank, I'm afraid you've been watching too many of those filthy new movies," she said, pressing the play button on her remote. "I do not share the industry's present obsession with sex. This picture we made at Metro in 1954. I suggest you study it well. You'll see Lucy and Dezi don't spend a single night together in the trailer until they are married."

She was right. In fact, thanks to chronic road fatigue and a bad case of twin beds, they didn't seem to spend any nights together after the wedding either. What a tense movie! Lucy and Dezi hauling a block-long trailer through the mud and over the Sierras. It was like one continuous Technicolor anxiety dream. Still, it made me homesick for the cozy comforts of Little Caesar, my erstwhile trailer-home/lovenest in distant Ukiah.

"Was Dezi short?" I asked dutifully, as Miss Ulansky was rewinding.

"Yes, dreadfully," she replied. "Practically a midget. Of course, that doesn't stop him from carrying on. The man is obsessed."

A new development. I hadn't realized male actors were prone to this trait as well.

"Was his wife obsessed too?" I inquired. It seemed to me having that bond in common could bring great stability to a marriage. In fact, I believe this will be the bedrock upon which Sheeni and I construct our happy union.

"They're all obsessed, Nick," Miss Ulansky replied. "Believe me, you don't know the half of it. Now, you take Lucy. That woman saves every penny she's ever made. That's how they bought RKO. She paid for it out of her grocery money. The day they made that deal, this town was in a state of shock. I wish she'd lived a few years longer. With the Japanese over here buying up every studio, Lucy could have quietly purchased Tokyo. Would have served the bastards right."

Francois had one more ace up his sleeve. "Miss Ulansky," he suddenly blurted out, "will you marry me?"

"Why, Frank, this is so unexpected," she replied, smiling coquettishly. "I shall, of course, have to think about it."

"Please do," he said.

"This is the sixth proposal of marriage I have received," she observed pensively. "There were four young men before my husband Tom. I feel you should know that, Frank."

"I appreciate your candor, Miss Ulansky."

"Not to imply, of course," she added, "that there was ever any hint of promiscuity on my part. I was quite innocent when I married."

"I could never believe otherwise," Francois answered. "I feel you should know, Miss Ulansky, that this is my second proposal of marriage."

"The first young woman declined?"

"Yes, she wanted to finish high school."

"The course of love is never easy," Miss Ulansky observed. "Or so 10,000 screenwriters would have us believe."

7:35 p.m. When I returned, Kimberly was microwaving dinner for Mario; Joanie and Dr. Dinge were cuddling on the couch. They were eating with chopsticks out of a Chinese take-out food container. It was fortunate I had accepted Miss Ulansky's offer to share her Meals on Wheels mystery food substances. (She claimed it was Swiss steak; I argued it was loin of pork.)

"Oh, Nick," said Kimberly, "before I forget, I've got something for you."

I prayed it required turning out all the lights and removing her USC sweatshirt. As usual, my prayers went unanswered. Kimberly wiped her hands on a towel, dug into her skin-tight jeans, and handed me three one-dollar bills.

"What's this?" I asked.

"It's a refund," she explained. "I got a better offer on the couch."

"Like what?" I asked, shocked.

"One-hundred dollars!" she beamed. "From Philip. He's renting it for a month."

I turned to face the chinless chow mein-gobbling runt. "What do you want it for?" I demanded.

"I forget," he replied, smiling innocently. "But you can camp out on the carpet, Frank. It's nice and soft."

It was all I could do to keep Francois restrained.

MONDAY, November 30 — 2:45 a.m. Can't sleep on this killing floor. My body feels like I went skydiving and forgot the parachute. Francois has put his foot down and refuses to spend another night like this. I'd sneak up on the couch, but Dr. Dinge has removed the cushions to Joanie's bedroom for safekeeping.

8:20 a.m. A miserable morning. Grey and cold. Yes, Los Angeles has winter too—something the Tourist Bureau does its best to conceal. I am writing this in the relative warmth and comfort of the local donut shop. I have just consumed

eight large buttermilk bars still warm from the grease. I feel much better—
except for a throbbing headache from the sugar rush.

9:55 a.m. I am now batting zero-for-two in marriage proposals. After a
restless night, Miss Ulansky turned me down. She said that try as she might,
she could not excuse the fact that I did not have wavy hair.

"Call me superficial, Frank," she said. "I don't know why it is, but I never
could warm up to men with straight hair. My husband Tom had the loveliest
wavy brown hair. Until he went bald, of course."

"I could have my hair curled," suggested Francois.

"Sorry, Frank. It wouldn't be the same. I'd know, you see."

"I understand, Miss Ulansky," I said. "Well, thanks anyway."

"Thank you, Frank," she replied, patting my hand. "I want you to know I'm
extremely flattered that you asked."

10:45 a.m. Securing the number from long-distance information, I called
Redwood High School in Ukiah and asked to speak with ninth-grader Frank
DeFalco.

"It's an emergency," I told the suspicious secretary. "There's been a plane
crash."

After several interminable minutes, Fuzzy, sounding scared, came on the
line.

"Nick! What happened? Did Merle's plane crash?"

"No. Listen, Frank, the monsoon was bad. Our penthouse was wrecked.
Cholera is breaking out all over. I'm thinking of coming back."

"You can't come back, Nick. I just heard the FBI is looking for you now."

"Frank, I'm coming back. Can you hide me out in your room over the
garage?"

"I don't know, Nick. Mom likes to go up there sometimes and scream and
beat the mattress with a tennis racket. She says it helps relieve stress."

"Do you have any other place you could hide me? Frank, I'm desperate."

"Well, there's Grandmamma's house. No one's living there. I guess I could
sneak the key."

"Great! What's the address? I'll meet you there tonight around eight."

"Can't, Nick. I'm grounded. But I could drop the key off on my way to school
tomorrow. There's a grape arbor in the back yard you can hide in until I get
there. The address is 507 Cripton Street. It's a little green house with pink
shutters."

"Thanks, Frank. I really appreciate it. I'll see you tomorrow."

"Wait, Nick! Whose plane crashed?"

"Buddy Holly's," I replied sadly. "He'll never sing another note."

2:15 p.m. Riding the bus to Ukiah. Three hours ago I packed my meager
thrift-store possessions in a brown paper sack and left this note for my sister:

Dear Joanie,

    Thank you for your hospitality. I can see it was time for me to leave. I hope in spite of his many faults you are happy with Philip. If you should happen to be in the family way, I hope that turns out OK too. For your sake, I hope the kid doesn't come out with freckles and a weak chin.

Do not look for me. I am changing my name and melting into the vast anonymous expanses of America, Europe, and/or Asia. Someday, if you should happen to see my photo in *The New York Review of Books*, please feel free to look me up. I suggest you write to me at that time in care of my publisher.

Goodbye for now. Tell Mom not to worry.

Regards,

Nick

P.S. Miss Ulansky requests "You Can't Take it with You." Try to get to the video store before two.

A grey rain is falling on the desolate cotton fields of the Central Valley. What a blow to my hopes. Frankly, I had expected more from my sojourn to Los Angeles. I imagined glamorous parties beside the pool, stimulating conversations with Nobel Prize for Literature winners in town for a fast buck, exciting evenings with nubile starlets desperate for career advancement. Oh well, at least I shall soon be breathing the same dusty rural air as My Beloved.

The overpriced bus ticket dealt a crippling blow to my finances. I have $68.12 to my name.

6:30 p.m. A two-hour layover in downtown Sacramento's fashionable skid row area. I am gripped by insecurities. Should I turn myself in? No way. Lance would have me sent up-river for a ten-year stretch. Being an uneducated ex-convict virgin at age 25 is not in my plans. Sheeni wouldn't wait for me either, that I know.

10:15 p.m. Can't write much. Too cold. No light. Bus pulled into Ukiah about an hour ago. Fortunately, streets downtown deserted. No one noticed me. Glad I have moustache for disguise. Found Fuzzy's grandmother's house. Only two blocks from Sheeni's! Now in dank grape arbor. Sharing old wooden lounge chair with 89 hairy black spiders. Please, God, don't let it rain.

DECEMBER

TUESDAY, December 1 — 12:45 a.m. God not listening as usual. Icy rain falling. Getting soaked through. No shelter. Teeth chattering. Spirits sinking.

2:30 a.m. Rain still falling. Fear onset of hypothermia. Will this night of hell never end?

4:45 a.m. Starting to thaw. Forced to abandon grape arbor. Found laundromat open 24 hours. Deserted except for one scary-looking guy washing oddly spotted blankets. Look suspiciously like blood stains. Certain there's a logical explanation. Probably shot a deer and had to bring carcass home in double bed of his Winnebago.

5:30 a.m. Grizzled, shifty-eyed deer hunter finally left. Removed most of my clothes and put in dryer. Damn! Was that a police car that just cruised by?

6:45 a.m. Getting light. Still raining. Extremely fatigued. Have to leave. Can't risk being seen on streets in daylight.

7:45 a.m. Back in dripping arbor. Just as wet as before. Pray Fuzzy comes soon.

8:30 a.m. Where is that hairy scum bag?!!!!

9:10 a.m. Fuzzy finally showed. Opened back door. Going to bed now.

7:30 p.m. I awoke at twilight after an intense, leaden, dreamless sleep. I yawned, stretched, and looked around: pink rose wallpaper, flowered drapes, rag rugs, dark ornately carved furniture, framed photos of swarthy people in old-fashioned clothes, large disturbing crucifix over the heavy walnut bed, faded black housedress hanging from a peg on the back of the dark-stained paneled door.

"Well," said Francois, scratching our balls under the musty-smelling quilt, "you were the guy always saying you were born 50 years too late. Welcome to Little Italy, circa 1943."

"I wonder if the utilities are still on?" I said.

"I'd kill for a hot shower right now," he growled.

On the way to the bathroom I paused to examine my nascent moustache in the bureau mirror. Quite continental if you ask me. I look like a young Errol Flynn with zits.

Francois had to settle for a hot bath. The immense claw-foot tub in the black and pink tiled bathroom lacked a shower. But the water poured out steaming hot from the tarnished brass tap. I settled back in the luxurious warmth and lathered up. The big square cake of soap smelled of violets.

Later, as I was toweling off in the gloom, someone switched on a light in the living room. I froze. Suddenly a clangorous ringing broke out. Heart thumping wildly, I stood motionless, waiting for the intruder to answer the telephone. After 13 terrifying rings, the phone fell silent. I listened intently. Absolute silence. Still clutching the towel, I peered around the doorway into the old-fashioned living room. No one in sight. But the lamp by the front window was now lit. As I pondered this mystery, the phone rang again. After several moments of indecisiveness, I picked up the ancient black handset.

"Who is this?" demanded Fuzzy.

"Who do you think it is?" I whispered, sighing with relief.

"How you doin', guy?" asked Fuzzy. "How come you didn't answer the first time I called?"

"Frank! Someone's here! They turned on a lamp in the living room."

"Oh, I forgot to tell you, Nick. That lamp's on a timer. So the house looks lived in."

"Now you tell me! I almost had a heart attack."

"You OK, Nick? You looked pretty awful this morning."

"Not bad," I replied. "No signs of pneumonia yet. How do you turn the heat on? This place is like a crypt."

"The thermostat is on the wall in the living room next to the picture of the Last Supper. Make sure you keep the drapes closed."

"I know that," I said. "Can I turn on lights in other rooms?"

"Sure. The yard's such a jungle, people can't see the house except from the front. Just don't mess with the lamp on the timer."

"OK."

"I came by after school today," said Fuzzy. "You were still sleeping. I put some food in the fridge."

"Thanks, Frank. You're a life saver."

"How's Merle?"

"Who?"

"Your girlfriend, the stewardess."

"Oh, uh. She died. Cholera."

"Man, Nick, that's tough!"

"Yeah, it's been a pretty rough week. Say, Frank, how come your parents are leaving this house empty with all your grandmother's stuff in it? Are they anticipating her return as a ghost?"

"Dad says he's too busy to deal with it right now. What with the strike, and Uncle Polly passing away, and Mom having an affair with your dad. They haven't done anything with Uncle Polly's house either. But I didn't think you'd want to stay there. I mean, since it was your neon sign that, that . . ."

"I know what you mean," I said. "Frank, what's happening at school?"

"Bad news. We lost the last game of the season, 57 to 3. Bruno threw four interceptions."

"I mean with Sheeni," I said. "What's happening with Sheeni?"

"Not much, Nick, that I can see. Looking good, as usual. Still educating the teaching staff. Oh, and she had lunch again with Vijay."

"Are they holding hands?"

"Nah. I think the shrimp's too chicken. Looks like he's trying to soften her up first with his French. Well, Gary, I better go now. Mom doesn't want me to use the phone much since I'm grounded."

"She came into the room?" I asked.

"Yes, Gary. The offense looks pretty strong too." *Click.*

I found the thermostat and turned it up to a semi-tropical 82. Now to raid the refrigerator. I'm famished!

9:45 p.m. Gathered in a lonely clump in the elderly yellow refrigerator were a quart of low-fat milk, a loaf of white balloon bread, a jar of sliced sweet pickles, and a shrink-wrapped package of sliced bologna. The four basic food groups as interpreted by Frank Sinatra DeFalco. Sighing, I prepared a fast bologna sandwich and checked out the kitchen.

This was obviously the atelier of a serious cook: big double-oven chrome-top range (also yellow), arsenal of iron and copper pots hanging from hooks in orderly rows, cupboards stacked high with dishes and glassware, drawers stuffed with every imaginable utensil (including several mystery gadgets whose purpose I could not begin to fathom). Everything was at least 40 years old and shone like new. Here in a state of near perfect preservation was a fully intact time capsule of 1950s cookery. Even the green-and-cream tile counters and swirling greenish-purple linoleum were classics of that era. (Someday I hope to have an opportunity to experience that linoleum on mushrooms.)

I hit the jackpot when I opened the door to the pantry: row on row of big glass jars filled with flour, sugar, beans, lentils, and every imaginable form of pasta. Dozens of smaller jars filled with spices. Large tins of olive oil and more baking supplies in neat formations. And an entire canned goods section of a large supermarket.

"Holy shit," said Francois, surveying the mountain of tin. "Why would anyone need 48 cans of garbanzo beans?"

I decided cream of mushroom soup would make a nice complement to bologna. Thirty-five maddening minutes later I found the can opener (a big chrome hand-crank model clandestinely mounted to the back of the pantry door). I warmed the soup on the gas range, laid out a setting for one on the yellow chrome dinette, poured a glass of red wine (from a dusty jug discovered on the floor of the pantry), and sat down for my first meal in my new home.

Francois proposed a toast: "Live fast. Play hard. Death to Vijay Joshi."

"Here, here," I said, taking an experimental sip of wine.

The flavors were complex: peppery cherry, blanched oak, sunny wild-flowers, post-game jockstrap, dead skunk, battery acid, toxic waste. The first glass was a struggle. The second slithered down somewhat easier. The third was a total breeze.

WEDNESDAY, December 2 — 9:25 a.m. The rain stopped. Now, if only the pounding in my head would cease, I might feel positively non-suicidal.

Fuzzy stopped by on his way to school to say hi and yell at me for leaving dishes in the sink.

"Nick, you have to keep a low profile here," he said.

"Why?" I demanded, listlessly eating my breakfast of toasted balloon bread with a side order of fried bologna.

"Well, what if my mom or dad should happen to drop by?"

"Frank, I thought you said they never came here?"

"They don't, Nick. As a rule. But they might check on things once in a while."

"OK," I said. "I'll lay low. Say, how do you like my moustache?"

"Is that what you call it?"

That Fuzzy brought a certain braggadocio to discussions of facial hair I felt was understandable.

"Yes, Frank. Now here is my question. Suppose you were to run into me on the street. Does my new moustache so alter my appearance that you would be unable to recognize me?"

"Sure," he replied, "if I was blind."

"It doesn't, huh?"

"No way. You look like Nick Twisp with something on your upper lip. Maybe a dust ball."

"Damn," I sighed. "I guess I'm stuck in this house. At least in the daytime. Frank, can you get me a few groceries? I made a list."

Fuzzy scanned my list with alarm. "Nick, this is like $20 worth of stuff. I haven't got that kind of bread."

I took out my wallet and handed him one of my precious twenties. "Buy generic if you can," I implored. "And please bring me the change."

3:30 p.m. Medical tip: If you keep swallowing aspirin, any headache—no matter how excruciating—eventually goes away. And the lingering numbness can be mildly exhilarating.

I revived enough to spend a pleasant day snooping through the late Mrs. DeFalco's closets and drawers. What a pack rat. I found programs from World War II USO dances at the Ukiah Grange, souvenirs of the 1939 World's Fair (on Treasure Island in San Francisco Bay), old Parchessi sets, bundles of letters in fading blue flowery-script Italian, cardboard pictures of saints lithographed in ethereal colors, an owner's manual for a 1952 Hudson Hornet, bizarre hats and costume jewelry, a dozen pairs of white gloves, ornately engraved United States of America Certificates of Naturalization, ancient cigars, rusty iceskates, tins full of buttons, strange garter belts, odd medical appliances, and thousands of other fascinating relics of an alien era.

Grandmother DeFalco's tastes in clothes were similarly eccentric. Hanging in her bedroom closet were dozens of nearly identical dresses: all old, all neatly pressed, all in shades of black. Along the floor were ranks of old lady's shoes: all nicely polished, all black.

"Who died?" asked Francois, surveying the morbid scene.

"Maybe her hobby was attending funerals," I replied.

"You know," said Francois, "she might have been one of those seriously wacky types who liked to stash small fortunes in cash around the home."

I searched all the conventional hiding places: under the mattress, in the cookie jar, in the toilet tank, in the freezer compartment, behind the water heater, inside the furnace, under the bureau drawers and couch cushions, behind the pictures on the walls, in the Brillo box under the sink. Total haul: $1.73 in coins and 12 lira in greasy Italian currency. I was checking the laundry room for loose floorboards when Fuzzy arrived with the groceries.

"Hi, Nick. Whatcha doing?"

"Uh, looking for dry rot. The washing machine hose has a small leak."

"Don't sweat it, Nick. This dump is falling down anyway. I got your stuff. You owe me $1.28 more."

"Thanks, Frank."

I paid him from my treasure haul; he refused the lira notes.

"How was school?" I asked, putting away the groceries.

"Boring. Oh, I found out something interesting in gym class from Dwayne."

I was immediately intrigued. "What, Frank?"

"You know your ugly dogs, Nick?"

"Of course. I've got three of them."

"Not any more. Trent Preston came by yesterday and took two. Boy, was your dad thrilled. Trent's keeping them for Sheeni and his girlfriend Apurva."

TRENT PRESTON HAS OUR LOVE CHILD! MY ONE INFRANGIBLE LINK WITH SHEENI SAUNDERS. NOW IN ENEMY HANDS! THAT IS THE FINAL, FINAL STRAW!

"What's the matter, Nick. You look kind of sick."

"Uh, nothing. Say, Frank, could you sneak me out a gun?"

"Sorry, Nick. Dad keeps the gun room locked up tight. I think he's afraid Mom'll turn on him. What do you want a gun for?"

"Uh, protection. In case somebody tries to break in."

"I wouldn't worry about that, Nick. This neighborhood is pretty peaceful."

It won't be for long if Francois has his way.

10:40 p.m. After dinner (rigatoni with clam sauce, butter lettuce with marinated garbanzo beans, French bread, no wine), I sneaked out the back door, ducked around the padlocked garage (still sheltering a choice low-mileage Falcon), and walked up the dark alley to the street. Pulling up my collar to conceal my face, I strolled south one block, turned the corner, and sauntered toward Sheeni's house. My heart began to beat irregularly as I approached the stately moon-lit Victorian. Sheeni's bedroom window was alight! I glanced up as I walked slowly past the wrought iron fence and gate. I saw lace curtains, part of a frilly lampshade, a section of virginal white ceiling, but alas, no sign of the room's lovely occupant. Doubtless she was bent over her books, adding to her already prodigious stores of knowledge.

"I love you, Sheeni," I whispered, as I walked by. "*Je t'aime,*" added Francois.

Five minutes later, I approached a more imposing brick residence, set back from the street behind a tall, impenetrable hedge. This, according to the Ukiah phone directory, was the privileged home of affected twit Trent Preston and my hostage love child. From somewhere behind the structure rose a chorus of indignant barks. There was no mistaking those particularly grating sonorities. It was Albert and Jean Paul, yearning to be free.

But how to do the job? The property looked as impregnable as the Kremlin. Even Francois had to admit his Molotov cocktail proposal would require more study and planning.

"I hate you, Trent," I whispered as I walked by. I can't report what Francois said. It would be too incriminating should this journal ever fall into the hands of the authorities.

THURSDAY, December 3 — I fear the imminent onset of cabin fever. There is only so much stimulation a modern teen can derive from extended confinement in the modest stucco bungalow of a deceased elderly Italian widow. No video games, no racy novels, no billiards, no ping pong, no Danish sex magazines, no VCR, no swimming pool. In short, none of the technological advances devised by man to fill up the countless hours between birth and death. I did find a stack of old 78 RPM records to play on Mrs. DeFalco's Crosley hi-fi/TV console. But how many hours can you spend listening to Nelson Eddy warble "Stout Hearted Men?"

So I watched TV (in fuzzy black and white). I watched Opra and Phil and Geraldo. I watched cooking shows and game shows. I watched reruns of programs my dad first watched back when he was a bored teenager. I watched commercials for truckdriving schools and welding schools and electronics schools and meat cutting schools and radio announcing schools. (They must imagine their audience is sitting around bored and unemployed.) I watched kiddie cartoons and the CBS evening news. I watched TV until my eyeballs fried and my mind turned to mush. Then I watched TV some more.

And why, I wondered indignantly, didn't Fuzzy drop by after school? Twenty-four hours have passed and my only human connection has been to Geraldo Rivera. No wonder I am filled with self-loathing.

FRIDAY, December 4 — Fuzzy got a surprise when he stopped by after school today. Seated on the be-doilied chintz sofa, applying red polish to her nails, was a strange woman.

"Hello, young man," she said.

"Oh, uh, hi," he stammered. "I was looking for . . . somebody else. Who are you?"

"I'm the Avon lady," she replied, displaying five crimson fingertips. "This shade is called Sophomoric Passion. Do you like it?"

"Yeah, I guess so. You know, uh, my grandmother died."

"Did she? I didn't know that. We have some lovely shades to coordinate with all the popular casket linings. Has she selected her make-up for the funeral?"

"She's buried already."

"Oh, dear. That does seem precipitous. I should really have been consulted first, you know."

"Uh, have you seen a guy named Nick?"

"Is he a good-looking fellow with a moustache?"

"Well he has a moustache. Sort of."

"Yes, I saw him. He was telling me about you in fact."

"He was?"

"Yes. He said you had a girlfriend in Santa Cruz named Heather. He said you two had been apart now for some time and consequently were horny in the extreme. Is that true?"

"Nick told you that?" asked Fuzzy, shocked.

"Oh, yes," she replied. "That and more. He said you have a secret stash of dirty magazines over your garage and you invite friends over for orgies of competitive self-abuse."

"I never!" exclaimed Fuzzy.

"Don't lie to me, young man. I know for a fact it's true."

"How?" he demanded.

"I was there," she replied. "I came in second."

"Nick! Is that you?"

"Of course it's me," I said in my natural voice. "How do you like my new look?"

"Nick, I think the pressure's got to you. You've completely flipped out."

"Not at all, Frank. You yourself pointed out my moustache was not making it as a disguise. So I shaved it off and tried on your late granny's clothes. They fit me perfectly. Even the shoes." I thrust out a foot garbed in gleaming black orthopedic lace-ups. "Your grandmother must have had quite large feet."

"Not that big," he replied defensively.

"I also shaved my legs and my armpits. I never realized being a woman entailed so much work in performing one's toilette."

"Nick, what are you using for boobs?"

"Oranges for now. The firmness is commendable, but they are inclined to droop unattractively. Tomorrow I'm going down to Flampert's variety store and buy a nice padded brassiere."

"That I got to see."

I stood up and modeled Mrs. DeFalco's black rayon dress and bouffant miracle-fiber wig. "Well, Frank, how do I look?"

"Like an ugly chick with pimples. And really rotten taste in clothes."

I appreciated Fuzzy's honesty. "I don't look like Nick Twisp?"

"Not at all. It's amazing. Grandmamma's glasses help a lot. Can you see out of them?"

"Unfortunately no. Everything's a nebulous blur. I'll have to pick up some neutral reading glasses at Flampert's."

"The voice is great too. Say something again, Nick."

"Hello, Frankie darling. Would you like to caress my nubile body?"

Fuzzy laughed. "I don't believe it, Nick. I'd swear you were a girl. The make-up job is really professional too."

"Thanks, Frank. I used to watch Mom layer it on when she was trying to reinvigorate Dad."

"My mom does the same thing."

"For the same man," I pointed out.

"Yeah, Nick, don't remind me. Well, what should I call the new you?"

"The name's Carlotta," I replied, "Carlotta Ulansky. My mother is a famous obscure film personality."

"Who's your father?"

"Another Hollywood great," Carlotta replied. "The late William Powell's personal valet!"

9:10 p.m. Despite Carlotta's seriously impaired vision, I decided to take her out for a preliminary field trial to the Golden Carp, Ukiah's budget-conscious Chinese restaurant. Strolling toward downtown in the late afternoon twilight, she was the object of much probing scrutiny by curious passersby. Carlotta gripped her black shawl and walked resolutely on, pausing only to feel her way around obstacles. On Main Street near the restaurant, she walked straight into a poorly illuminated fire hydrant, suffering a nasty knock to her right shin and tearing her hosiery.

"Fuck!" she exclaimed, startling an elderly couple walking nearby. As she bent over to attend to the injured limb, an orange tumbled out of her dress and bounced into the gutter. "Hot fucking damn!" she muttered. The couple paused to stare as she felt around under a parked car for the errant citrus.

"I think you dropped this, ma'am," said the man, picking up the body-temperature orange and offering it to her.

"Many thanks," replied Carlotta.

The man and his wife glanced questioningly at her lopsided chest. Carlotta pulled her shawl tightly around her.

"I do like a nice piece of fruit when I'm out for a stroll," Carlotta remarked. "It can be so . . . so refreshing!"

The couple edged away and crossed the street. Thank God they weren't out on a mission for Chinese food.

In the restaurant Carlotta held up her menu as a screen and discreetly rearranged her charms. That accomplished, she ordered the Economy Dinner for one: egg roll, pork fried rice, prawns with vegetables, champagne sherbet, fortune cookie, and tea. All that and an exotic foreign ambience for just $3.95.

Later as she was nibbling the tail of her final delectable prawn, she was alarmed to observe Steve the waiter lead a familiar couple to a table across the room. It was Sheeni's trumpet-playing brother Paul and his love goddess girlfriend (and Dad's former bimbette) Lacey.

As Carlotta hurriedly gulped her sherbet, Paul stopped beside her table on his way to the restroom.

"Hi," he said, smiling.

"Er, hello," she replied nervously. "Do I know you?"

Paul chose to ignore the question. "Did you hear?" he asked, "Bernice Lynch is going to be OK. She's out of the hospital now."

"Yes, I had heard that."

"She told the police everything though. I think her mother's going to sue Nick's parents."

"Well, they're certainly used to it," Carlotta sighed.

"Your fortune cookie may have some good news," he added.

"I could use some," she replied. "You won't, uh, mention to anyone you've seen me?"

"I didn't see anything. Nice dress. Very becoming . . . Carlotta."

"Thanks, Paul," she said, impressed as usual by his omniscience.

After he left, Carlotta cracked open the cookie. Her fortune read: "Despair not. An unexpected windfall awaits."

All right!

11:30 p.m. No windfall yet. Going to bed. Today I dressed as a woman and thoroughly enjoyed it. In fact, I developed a fairly spectacular T.E. just now while Carlotta was disrobing. I wish I could afford psychoanalysis to find out what precisely this means. Do you suppose there's any cause for concern?

SATURDAY, December 5 — I'M RICH! I'm in the chips. My ship has come in. I'm rolling in it. I have acquired some tall paper. I'm a member of the affluent classes. Bodybuilders could develop powerful muscles hoisting my wallet. In short, I'm loaded.

Francois was right. Why didn't I pay more attention to him? Unscrupulous people always know best.

This morning as Carlotta was preparing to go out, she opened Mrs. DeFalco's underwear drawer. As she was rummaging about for a fresh pair of black hose, she felt a curious lump in a repulsive-looking garment she took to be a girdle. Her curiosity piqued, she overcame her revulsion, reached inside the shriveled Spandex, and pulled out an immense roll of U.S. government currency (yes, the genuine green variety, in startlingly large denominations).

All plans were put on hold as she unrolled the giant wad and counted the awesome cash cache.

$2,385!

More actual money than I'd ever seen before. Five lifetimes of my erstwhile meager weekly allowance.

I could buy a near state-of-the-art computer, thought Nick. I could buy a large-caliber revolver, ruminated Francois. I could buy modern pantyhose, speculated Carlotta. Or, pointed out Nick's practical side, I could buy food. I could actually postpone disagreeable starvation for many months. For a change, all my choices were pleasant ones. Such is the awesome power of money. Francois is convinced wealth is the ultimate aphrodisiac. That's why Republicans are so conservative. Sexual satiety naturally stunts the social conscience.

4:30 p.m. I'm back. What a glorious day. Carlotta, I discovered, was born to shop. Money flows from her hands like drool from a toddler. Of course, it helped that all the stores downtown were piping in festive holiday music. Swept up in the spirit of the season, Carlotta indulged her every whim.

She began with a mid-morning snack of six maple bars in her favorite donut shop. Then it was on to Flampert's for lingerie shopping. Disappointed by the thinness of the foam in the padded brassieres (why such deplorable timidity on the part of the undergarment industry?), she had to augment her purchase by stuffing in two large shoulder pads from the notions counter. Then she bought eyeliner, mascara, blusher, lipstick (color: Carmine Swoon), perfume (Writhe by Kevin Clein), six pairs of black pantyhose (no more outmoded garter belts), and a nice pair of rhinestone-studded reading glasses.

From Flampert's, she proceeded on to an electronics store, where she purchased an expensive AM/FM stereo walkabout tape player with inconspicuous bud earphones. Unfortunately, neither her dress nor her shawl was equipped with pockets. After some experimentation, she discovered her personal stereo system would nestle conveniently between the shoulder pads in her bra (although adjusting the controls tended to attract unwelcome stares from fellow shoppers).

Next, at the local record shop, she purchased two Frank Sinatra tapes (the store's entire meager selection), and cassettes by Artie Shaw, Duke Ellington, Jeri Southern, Karen Akers, Ella Fitzgerald, and Mildred Bailey.

"You're losing something, lady," said the clerk listlessly.

I interpreted this remark as a comment on my musical tastes. Apparently this strung-out young woman with purple hair felt I was missing out by not purchasing the newest mind-rotting heavy metal releases.

"They're for my aunt in Cleveland," apologized Carlotta. "Her tastes are quite conservative."

"You're losing something," repeated the phlegmatic clerk, pointing casually to her Young Dickheads sweatshirt.

My god, I thought, this woman is completely stoned. They must let them do dope right here at the cash register. I only hope she hands over an extra ten with my change.

Then Carlotta glanced down at her dress. An earbud cord had become tangled in a shoulder pad and dislodged it. Several inches of white pad were visible above her heaving bodice. Blushing, Carlotta fumbled to free the cord, then hurriedly stuffed the pad back into place.

"Perfume blotters," explained Carlotta. "They're the newest sensation over at Flampert's."

"I never shop there," huffed the clerk, handing me the correct change. "They sell *Hustler* magazine."

Damn. I knew I'd forgotten something.

After a pleasant lunch at the Golden Carp, a heavily laden Carlotta crept back up the alley toward home. As she was about to duck behind the garage, a gate opened across the alley and out bounced a large garbage can gripped in the powerful but uncoordinated arms of Bruno Modjaleski, Redwood High's most celebrated gridiron mediocrity.

"Oh, hello," guiltily gasped a startled Carlotta. I still suffer qualms of conscience for nearly sending Bruno up-river for car theft.

"'Lo," he replied shyly, but with evident curiosity. "Need some help with your packages?"

With Frank crooning in both ears, Carlotta missed the question. She turned down her stereo—an operation Bruno observed with much interest. "Beg your pardon?" she asked.

"Your packages," repeated Bruno. "Need any help carrying them?"

"Oh uh, no, thank you. I can manage."

"You're stayin' at Mrs. DeFalco's, huh?" he asked.

"Uh, am I?" I replied uncertainly.

"I seen you goin' in and out of the bushes there."

"Uh, yes. It's a handy shortcut. Well, good day."

"'Bye," he said with a stare that suggested he could be devoting some of his limited cranial capacity to the act of mentally undressing me.

Carlotta hurried into the house and dumped her packages. Damn. That alley is not as deserted as I had supposed. I just hope Bruno can keep his big fat mouth shut. I wonder if football players are prone to gossip?

2:15 p.m. Four-dozen peanut butter cookies—fresh from the oven. I hope they do the trick.

8:15 p.m. I just counted my wad. Carlotta managed to spend nearly $300 today. At this rate, my windfall will be exhausted in less than a week. I am resolved to begin a regimen of strict economy. Tonight for dinner I had reheated Chinese food with garbanzo beans mixed in for supplemental protein. A thrifty, filling meal that left me feeling only moderately suicidal.

Saturday night in front of the TV. I wonder what Sheeni is doing tonight? I wonder if she has a date with someone? I wonder if garbanzo beans are a depressive? I feel totally paralyzed with a leaden black angst. Why is the exhilaration of sudden wealth so short-lived? Now my wonderful new tape player seems like a needless, frivolous expense.

Francois reminds me to accentuate the positive. At least I am enjoying my new pantyhose. It's true: I get a curious thrill every time I slip them on.

SUNDAY, December 6 — I JUST SAW SHEENI SAUNDERS! I ACTUALLY SPOKE TO HER!

The good news is she's even more achingly lovely than I remembered. The bad news is she was on her way to meet loathsome Trent Preston. They are going on a long, intimate walk—just the six of them (Sheeni, Trent, Apurva,

Vijay, Albert, and Jean Paul.) If you ask me, it all sounds suspiciously like a double date with dogs.

Carlotta was about to dive into her usual donut assortment, when into the shop walked Sheeni carrying the Sunday *New York Times*. As Carlotta watched transfixed, Sheeni ordered three orange-glazed cake donuts and a large coffee, then carried them over to THE TABLE NEXT TO MINE. Gripped by a sudden disquietude, Carlotta concealed her tremulous hands under the brown Formica table. Sheeni was on her second donut and well into the Book Review section before Carlotta worked up the nerve to speak.

"Miss, could you possibly pass me the cream?" she asked.

Sheeni looked up and focused her beautiful blue eyes on my rouged countenance. She examined Carlotta with some interest. "I'm afraid my cream is curdled," she replied.

"That's all right," said Carlotta. "No matter. I see now I've finished my coffee after all. Silly me."

Sheeni resumed her reading.

Carlotta cleared her throat. "Miss, can you tell me where one obtains the *New York Times* in this town? I am new here, you see."

Sheeni marked her place with a lovely finger and looked up. "There's a newsrack in front of Flampert's. Down the street."

"Thank you. I want to see if my mother's new film is reviewed in the entertainment section."

Sheeni looked at Carlotta with new interest. "Your mother is in films?" she asked.

"Yes, she's an actress. Bertha Ulansky. Perhaps you've heard of her?"

"I don't think so. What films has she been in?"

"Oh dozens. Primarily character roles now, of course. She played the mother in 'After Hours,' if you recall that picture."

"I do, yes. But I don't remember a mother character."

"Well, it was a small part. She did it to work with Ridley Scott. The man is a genius."

"He is gifted," agreed Sheeni. "But wasn't 'After Hours' directed by Martin Scorsese?"

"Possibly," admitted Carlotta. "Mother gets confused at times. It's all that rich food at Spago. I tell her to go easy at her age. By the way, my name is Carlotta Ulansky."

"I'm Sheeni Saunders," she said, extending a lovely hand.

Struggling to hold her tremor in check, Carlotta grasped the familiar hand and squeezed it gently. At least one of the parties felt an electric thrill at the moment of contact.

"Have you lived in Ukiah long, Sheeni?" inquired Carlotta.

"Unfortunately yes, Carlotta. I enjoyed a brief escape to Santa Cruz recently. But now I'm back. Thanks to the treachery of a former friend."

"How unpleasant for you," gulped Carlotta. "Is your friend entirely beyond forgiveness?"

"I never want to see him again. He revealed himself to be a liar and a cheat."

"Surely, Sheeni, there are some small extenuating circumstances. Few of us are entirely evil."

"I should like to think he did what he did out of some sort of affection for me—twisted as it may have been. But that hardly excuses his behavior."

"Doesn't it?" asked Carlotta. "Love compels us to desperate acts. People cannot always act rationally. The greater the love, the stronger the passions, the more reckless the crimes. Love is not an emotion that conduces sensibility. Especially if your friend possessed a fiery, artistic temperament. Did he?"

"Not so fiery, but possibly artistic," Sheeni admitted. "He was certainly not your ordinary teen."

"Where is he now?" Carlotta asked.

"Somewhere in India. The FBI is looking for him."

"How extraordinarily romantic! He sounds to me like quite an exceptional young man. Rather in the rebellious traditions of Errol Flynn or James Dean or—to cross the pond—Jean Paul Belmondo."

Sheeni gave a start. "Whom did you say?"

"Jean Paul Belmondo," repeated Carlotta. "He's a French actor."

"I know who he is!" she affirmed.

"Mother had a small role in one of his pictures, a film called 'Breathless.' But I don't suppose you've seen it."

"It's my favorite film!" declared Sheeni. "What did she play?"

"Er, she played the street car conductoress."

Sheeni looked perplexed. "I don't remember any scenes on a street car."

"Well, it was a small role. They may have cut those scenes from the American prints. Too bad too. Mother was quite a sensation in France."

Sheeni and Carlotta chatted on happily for another half hour, until the former excused herself to go meet her loathsome friends (excluding from that adjective only the lovely Apurva).

"It was nice meeting you, Carlotta," said Sheeni, gathering up her newspaper.

"Oh, Sheeni, the pleasure was entirely mine," replied Carlotta, extending her hand for another thrilling touch. "It's nice to encounter a person of intelligence and culture in this town."

"I agree, Carlotta. Well, perhaps we'll see each other again."

I have no doubt of that, Sheeni darling. And our reunion will occur much sooner than you imagine.

1:25 p.m. As Carlotta sneaked up the alley toward home, Bruno and garbage can emerged from the gate.

"Hi, Carly," he said, smilingly indifferent to the deafening din as he cheerfully dropped the can.

"Hello, Bruno."

"I'm enjoying the cookies, Carly. The season's over so I can eat as many as I want."

"Good for you, Bruno. I appreciate a man with a hearty appetite."

"Candy gets on my case when I pig out," he complained. Head cheerleader Candy Pringle was Bruno's alluring inamorata.

"You must stand up to her, Bruno," said Carlotta. "That's what women like."

"I'm no wimp," he said darkly.

"Good, Bruno. Well, thank you for your continued discretion."

"Huh?"

"About my presence here," Carlotta reminded him. "My uncle, Mr. DeFalco, wants me to keep a low profile. For tax reasons."

"No problem, Carly. You want me, uh, come over sometime?"

"Uh, we'll see," she replied, hurrying away.

I don't care for that peculiar glint in Bruno's eyes when he checks out Carlotta's legs. Maybe she should switch to a less provocative shade of lipstick. And go a little easier on the perfume.

3:40 p.m. After prolonged reflection, I decided one source of my lingering malaise is computer deprivation. A writer should not be so long separated from his word processor. I am resolved to rescue my precious PC clone and other important personal effects left behind in Little Caesar, still parked (I hope) behind Dad's rented modular home. Fuzzy has agreed to defy parental grounding edicts and sneak out tonight to assist Carlotta with the burgle.

11:30 p.m. Disaster! Carlotta and Fuzzy received the full, shocking story when they were surprised in the act of ransacking Little Caesar by Dwayne, the moronic son of Dad's welfare maid.

"Who's there?" he demanded, shining the beam of *my* Cub Scout flashlight into the darkened trailer.

"Dwayne, it's me," hissed Fuzzy. "Turn out that damn light."

Dwayne dutifully complied and introduced his odorous, ungainly bulk through the narrow trailer doorway. "Hi, Fuzzy," he whispered in the musty darkness. "Whacha doin'? Who's the zinky chick?"

"This is my friend, uh, Carlotta," answered Fuzzy. "We're . . . we're . . ."

"Actually, we were hoping to find some privacy," volunteered Carlotta sultrily. "Fuzzy mentioned this trailer had a nice double bed."

"I did?" asked Fuzzy.

"Go on ahead, Fuz," said Dwayne. "But can I stay and watch? Can I, huh?"

"Certainly not," replied Carlotta.

"Then how 'bout I join in?" he suggested.

"No thank you, young man," replied Carlotta, shuddering. "If you leave us and go into the house, Fuzzy will tell you all about it tomorrow at school. In explicit detail."

"I will?" asked Fuzzy.

"No way," stated Dwayne obstinately. "This is my mom's trailer. If I can't do it too, I'm gonna tell you're out here. Mr. Twisp'll call the cops."

"Try it, buster," hissed Carlotta, "and before the week is out your dog will be munching an arsenic burger."

"Not Kamu the Wonder Dog!" gasped Dwayne.

"The very same," said Carlotta, poking Fuzzy in the ribs.

"Er, Dwayne," said Fuzzy. "What happened to Nick's computer? We noticed it's not on the dinette any more."

"Mr. Twisp took it. He needs it for his new job."

"What new job?" demanded Carlotta.

"It's with a big lumber company," explained Dwayne. "He does, whachermercallit, public relations."

My father progresses from pesticide ad-writer to strike-breaking scab to paid flack for the despoilers of the forest. Talk about a career track to infamy.

"What does he use the computer for?" asked Carlotta.

"Writin' stuff, I guess," replied Dwayne. "Boy was he burned, too. He found a whole bunch o' nasty stuff Nick wrote."

My private journal!

"A lot of it was real insultin' to him too," continued Dwayne. "And to me. I almost got into some deep shit, on account of some lies Nick wrote about me molestin' him. I denied it though. Boy, and I was always real nice to him too."

Liar!

"Mr. Twisp looked at Nick's private journal?" asked Fuzzy.

"Ain't that's what I been sayin'?" said Dwayne. "Yeah, and Nick wrote some real nasty stuff about your mom, Fuz. Mr. Twisp, he turned some of it over to his lawyer."

"Why?" demanded Carlotta. Could my doting dad actually be contemplating bringing suit against his own son for libel?

"'Cause there was a part where Nick said Paul and Lacey gave him some drugs," explained Dwayne. "Nick had this weird trip where he went crazy for his bedspread. The lawyer showed it to Lacey, and she had to quit prosecutin' Mr. Twisp for fillin' up her car with cee-ment."

My dad beat the rap!

"What did Nick say about my mom?" demanded Fuzzy.

"Uh, Fuzzy," cooed Carlotta. "It's late. We better be going now. You'll excuse us, young man?"

"Sure," he replied. "Come by anytime. How 'bout tomorrow night? By yourself."

Carlotta stifled a shudder. "What an attractive invitation. I shall certain consider it."

My felonious father has electronically accessed, snooped through, and possibly erased my personal journal! I feel as if my most private thoughts have been invaded and defiled. I see now I should have locked my personal files behind a coded password. All those years spent in the custody of my computer-illiterate mother tragically lulled me into a false sense of security.

I feel lost in a state of computerless nakedness. Another wrong to be avenged. I must unleash Francois and damn the consequences!

MONDAY, December 7 — Today I experienced my third first day as a new student in a second-rate public high school. At least this time I arrived already acquainted with many of my new teachers and fellow students—even if they were unaware they knew me.

Since Carlotta arrived sans transcript, Miss Pomdreck, my aged guidance counselor, was faced with a familiar dilemma.

"I don't know," she said doubtfully. "The last student I admitted without papers caused the worst scandal in the history of the school. The FBI is still looking for him."

Carlotta gulped. "I'm certain my transcript will arrive soon, Miss Pomdreck. I fear it must have been delayed by the crush of holiday mail. Of course, it has to come all the way from Switzerland."

"You say you were attending a private finishing school there?" she asked, studying my black dress and shawl with evident unease.

"That's right. In the mountains near Geneva."

"Well, my dear. You are obviously an intelligent girl. But I must tell you, most of our tracked classes are filled now. You will have to make do with what's available this semester."

"That's fine," replied Carlotta. "Oh, I should also mention I have a congenital bone condition. Ossifidusbrittalus syndrome. I'll have to be excused from gym class."

"May I see the note from your physician?"

"Oh. You need a note?"

"Of course, my dear. Otherwise, our gym classes would be quite deserted."

"I'll bring you a note as soon as I can," promised Carlotta.

"I'll need it by Friday," Miss Pomdreck replied, beginning to fill out my registration forms. "Or I'll have to put you in gym next week. I can only bend the rules so far."

Twenty minutes later, I left Miss Pomdreck's cluttered office with this stimulating schedule in hand: typing, physics, world cultures, clothing technology I, lunch, business math, study hall (or girls' gym!), art, and health issues.

Having missed the first period, I was walking to physics class when I felt a hairy hand upon my shoulder.

"Nic . . . I mean, Carlotta!" hissed Fuzzy. "What the fuck are you doing here?"

"Hi, Frank," I replied. "I'm pursuing what passes for an education in this school."

"Carlotta, are you bonkers? You'll never get away with it!"

"Don't worry, Frank," I whispered. "I'm going to be one of those shy, wallflower girls who no one pays the slightest attention to. I intend to disappear into the institutional woodwork, as it were."

In physics class, Carlotta slipped into the desk immediately behind My Beloved, just acing out traitorous Vijay. The vile alien took the next desk across the aisle and studied me with obvious interest. Cutting him dead, I lightly tapped Sheeni on her lovely shoulder. She turned and smiled in ill-concealed amazement.

"Carlotta!" exclaimed my future life partner. "What are you doing here?"

"Hello, Sheeni. I'm going to be attending your school. I just received my schedule from nice Miss Pomdreck."

"You are! That's marvelous, Carlotta. But somehow I thought you were, uh, older."

"Everyone makes that assumption. It must have been all those years I spent at finishing school in Switzerland. No, I am a mere teen."

"Carlotta, this is my friend Vijay Joshi," said Sheeni. "Vijay, this is Carlotta Ulansky. Her mother is a famous actress."

Vijay smiled a warm, although transparently insincere greeting. Carlotta nodded coldly. She did not extend her hand. Embarrassed, Vijay withdrew his.

When the class began, Mr. Tratinni, as was his custom, asked the new student to stand and introduce herself. Not wishing to draw undue attention to herself, Carlotta kept her remarks brief.

"I'm Carlotta Ulansky," I said. "I just moved here from Los Angeles. Thank you." I sat down and devoted myself to my textbook, ignoring the curious stares of my classmates. I was two weeks behind and determined to reassert my academic hegemony.

After physics, Carlotta bid adieu to My Beloved and left the track to disappear among the teeming masses of Redwood High's scholastic underachievers. First stop was Miss Najflempt's world cultures class, where, in a room palpitating with subnormal IQs, Carlotta found herself seated in front of the dimmest light of them all: Dwayne Crampton.

"Hi, Carlotta," he said, poking me in the shoulder. "Guess what?"

"What?" she asked indifferently.

"I ain't wearin' no underwear," he whispered.

"Good for you, Dwayne."

"Are you comin' by the trailer tonight?"

"Certainly not."

"How come not?"

"I heard something troubling about you from Vijay Joshi."

"What'd that spic say?" demanded Dwayne.

"He said some guy named Nick told him you were queer. That you forced yourself on him."

"Liar!" hissed Dwayne, reddening.

"Take it up with Vijay," sniffed Carlotta. "I understand he's telling it to everyone in school."

Dwayne was interested in pursuing the topic further, but at that moment Carlotta was called upon for some extemporaneous autobiographical remarks.

She kept them brief. After that, in honor of the anniversary of the Japanese attack on Pearl Harbor, Miss Najflempt showed a boring video on the Burakumen—Japan's oppressed untouchables caste. This "unclean" minority looks, talks, and acts like everyone else. Being a bigot must be a tricky business in Japan.

Next stop was clothing technology I, where Mrs. Dergeltry is teaching 24 young women, Carlotta, and a sophomore named Gary to transform raw cloth into sophisticated, fashion-forward garments. I may enjoy this class once I figure out how to adjust the tension on my sewing machine. (Carlotta is desperately behind the others, who are already up to interfacing, whatever that is.) Despite the presence of Gary (or because of it?), there seems to be considerable casual disrobing among my fellow sewers as they try things on. Even Mrs. Dergeltry removed her blouse briefly to test a dart. With a build like hers, the position and load capacity of such darts must be carefully engineered.

Lunch came next. As her customary lunchmate was away being treated by the school nurse for a cut lip and swollen eye, Sheeni was free to dine with Carlotta. We found two seats together at the Scholarly Elites' table. Across the room, I noticed, my despised adversary Trent Preston was chowing down at the Varsity Jocks' table.

"Vijay was just attacked by that horrible boy Dwayne," Sheeni announced, removing the neatly wrapped contents of her bagged lunch and arranging them carefully on the scarred table. Carlotta did the same, hoping the rapidity of her movements would conceal the tremor in her hands. An intimate cafeteria lunch with Sheeni! Within the very sight of Trent! Almost more than I had ever dared hope.

"Boys are so aggressively combative," sighed Carlotta philosophically. "It's the testosterone, you know."

"Speaking of elevated testosterone, Carlotta," said Sheeni, "that boy they call Fuzzy seems to be watching you."

Carlotta looked up and directed a cautionary glance at Fuzzy, dining at the Wanna-Be Jocks' table not far (except in the social hierarchy) from Trent and his buddies.

"Perhaps he likes you," suggested Sheeni. "Do you know him?"

"We've met," Carlotta replied noncommittally.

"No spark of passion?"

Carlotta reddened. "Hardly, Sheeni. How about you? Is Vijay your boyfriend?"

"Not exactly, Carlotta."

What's that supposed to mean!

Sheeni bit into her sandwich, masticated pensively, then continued. "He's a nice boy. Very intelligent. I think he likes me. But I don't know if I'm fully over my last boyfriend yet."

A wave of rapture swept over me. "You mean the fellow in India?" asked Carlotta.

"Him too. I was referring to Trent Preston. He's the godlike person over there with the blue shirt and deep tan. No, Carlotta, don't look at him. I don't want him to think we're talking about him. He's going out now with Vijay's sister Apurva. I feel so torn when I see them together."

Carlotta prayed her thick layer of rouge concealed my profound emotional distress. "You're, you're still in love with Trent?"

"I honestly don't know, Carlotta. I thought I was over him. Then a friend of mine visiting from school last month made a big play for him. I got insanely jealous and told her to leave."

"Oh, who was that?" asked Carlotta casually.

"My former roommate, a girl from New York named Taggarty. I feel she betrayed our friendship. Do you think I'm being petty, Carlotta?"

"Oh no! No, Sheeni, no. Definitely not." Carlotta was nothing if not emphatic on this point.

Another despised Nick Twisp adversary shot down in flames. Rest in peace, Taggarty!

"But you still care a little for the boy in India?" Carlotta persisted.

"His name is Nick, Carlotta. Nick Twisp. At least, I think it is. That's what he told me, at any rate. I've learned with Nick never to trust entirely what he says. It was a painful lesson. For example, I learned from Vijay that he killed my dog through gross negligence, then lied to cover up his carelessness. Fortunately, darling Albert has returned in another, quite similar form. Although I wish he hadn't parcelled himself out to Apurva as well. Am I confusing you, Carlotta?"

"Er, not at all, Sheeni. And you, you never told any untruths to Nick? You were always completely honest?"

"Not exactly," she replied, flushing slightly. "I knew for weeks last summer that I might be transferring to Santa Cruz, but never told Nick. I didn't want to upset him. And when he got that scholarship to India, I tried to persuade him to turn it down. I knew as long as Nick remained in Ukiah my parents would have a powerful incentive to keep me in Santa Cruz. Then, there was my affair with Ed."

"Ed?" piped Carlotta, startling her lunchmate.

"Yes. Ed Smith. A sweet guy from Iowa I met at school. You see, Carlotta, it was his first time away from Des Moines and naturally he was in sexual crisis. We were driving to a motel in Monterey to help determine his, uh, orientation when we were arrested in error. I think Nick got wind of it somehow."

So they weren't on an innocent sightseeing trip to the damn Aquarium! I knew it all along!

"And were you, uh, ever able to assist Ed with his, uh difficulty?" asked Carlotta, dreading the reply.

"I did all I could, Carlotta. The boy had deep problems. I think it may have been his repressive Midwestern upbringing. I concluded eventually he was polymorphous-perverse. He wanted to put it in anything warm that moved. He

certainly put it in every place he could find on me."
AUUUUGGGGHHHHH!!!!!!!!

Somehow I got through lunch and the rest of the school day. I trooped through business math, study hall, art (with Trent at the next easel!), and health issues in black despair—the cool compress of boredom providing the only solace to my hemorrhaging heart. My One and Only Love has betrayed me. My last reason to live is gone.

TUESDAY, December 8 — I'm still alive. After a dismal, sleepless night, I decided to forgive Sheeni. I see now her actions were prompted by beneficence. She did what she did with Ed out of a commendable desire to help a fellow human being. The deed was unfortunate, but not strictly censurable. Nevertheless, I shall strive with unflagging vigilance to prevent a recurrence. Sheeni's generous nature must be redirected into more positive channels—such as pining for the absent Nick Twisp.

As Carlotta sneaked into the alley this morning on her way to school, Bruno Modjaleski bounded athletically through the gate. He was wearing his varsity football jacket and carrying a wood technology textbook.

"Good morning, Carly," he called.

"Oh, good morning, Bruno. You startled me."

"I seen you in the halls yesterday, Carly. Are you like student teaching or something?"

"Hardly, Bruno. I am a matriculated student."

Bruno looked impressed. "Congratulations, Carly. Would you like me to carry your books?"

"No, thank you, Bruno. I can manage." I had enough enemies without adding a jealous Candy Pringle to the list.

"I usually ride my chopper to school," apologized Bruno, "but I blew a head gasket last Saturday night cruisin' down Main Street at 110 miles per hour."

"I trust, Bruno, you were wearing a helmet at the time."

Bruno scoffed. "A guy like me don't need to wear no helmet, Carly. Hell, I wouldn't wear one playin' football, 'cept Coach makes me."

"Oh, do you play football, Bruno?"

"Damn, Carly! I'm the quarterback!"

"Oh, then you must be that fellow they call the Fumbler Bumbler of Redwood High."

"Who calls me that?" demanded Bruno, flexing his great ham-like hands.

"I believe he's a freshman," replied Carlotta. "A short Indian student named Vijay Joshi. Do you know him?"

"No," growled Bruno. "But I'll find him!"

In home room, Carlotta sat next to Fuzzy, who seemed more than usually dispirited.

"My mom stayed out all last night," he said accusingly. "This morning I had to fix my own breakfast and pack my own lunch. Your dad is really cruising for a bruising, Carlotta."

"Sorry, Frank. Knowing Dad, he's probably dating your mom as a bargaining chip. I imagine he'd lay off your mom if your dad dropped his lawsuit."

"Not a chance of that," said Fuzzy gloomily. "I think Dad's counting on some of that $3.5 million to help cover the strike losses. Now that damn Mr. Ferguson has got the scabs out on strike too."

"Sorry, Frank," Carlotta repeated. "I'm truly grateful for all you've done to help me out. I feel terrible about my dad and his roommate wrecking your homelife. "

"That's OK, Carlotta. I guess it's not your fault your dad is a repulsive creep."

"Tell you what, Frank. Maybe I can do something about breaking them up. Would you like that?"

"Could you really, Carlotta?" he asked, brightening.

"I can try, Frank. But I may need your help."

"You got it, Carlotta!"

"Of course, I may also need a favor or two in return."

"Like what?" he asked suspiciously.

"I'll let you know, Frank," I replied coyly, "when the time comes."

After 45 stimulating minutes in typing class, Carlotta was ready to be reunited with my love. Once again, I arrived in physics class just ahead of the loathsome alien. I claimed the choice seat behind Sheeni, forcing Vijay to settle for second best across the aisle. He scowled at Carlotta through his colorful black eye and nicely swollen lip. Pointedly ignoring him, Carlotta conversed with her special friend.

"Sheeni, I've made a remarkable discovery about your name."

"What's that, Carlotta?" she asked. Sheeni was wearing a stunning magenta outfit that coordinated nicely, I thought, with my sophisticated black ensemble.

"Can't tell you now, Sheeni," replied Carlotta mysteriously. "Let's do lunch."

"Oh, Carlotta, I can't today. I promised I'd have lunch with Vijay."

Vijay flashed a repellent smile in my direction.

"Er, that's fine, Sheeni. It can wait until tomorrow."

In world cultures class, Dwayne Crampton experimented with new ways to relieve tedium through boorishness. As we viewed a video on the downtrodden but culturally rich indigenous peoples of Bolivia, Dwayne punctuated the action by reaching forward and fiddling with Carlotta's buttons. When that amusement lost its novelty, he began snapping her bra straps. Not wishing to attract undue attention to herself, Carlotta resisted silently with mouthed imprecations and menacing glances.

Lunch brought a welcome change of plans. Sheeni's date had to cancel when he was forced to make another unscheduled trip to the nurse's office.

"The outrages continue, Carlotta," lamented Sheeni, opening her tidy lunch bag. We were seated again at the summit of cafeteria society; her position claimed by divine right, mine secured by our glittering friendship. I noticed Sheeni was having tuna salad for a second day. The Woman of My Dreams likes tuna fish. What an interesting fact to discover. "Vijay has been set upon by hooligans again!" she continued. "This time it was that neanderthal Bruno Modjaleski. I am considering notifying the ACLU."

"Such violence is deplorable," agreed Carlotta, unfolding her black paper napkin.

"Tuna again!" complained Sheeni. "I hate tuna salad!"

"I seldom touch it myself," replied Carlotta, revising her previous mental note. "But here. Would you like to trade? I'm having mashed garbanzo beans on pumpernickel."

"No, thank you, Carlotta. I shall make do with my fish. Now, what did you wish to tell me about my name?"

"Sheeni, I think it was definitely propitious that you left that school in Santa Cruz. In fact, perhaps you should be grateful to your friend Nick. Rearranged, the letters in your name, Sheeni Saunders, spell SEASIDE SHUNNER!"

"Oh, do you like anagrams, Carlotta? How interesting. So do I. Seaside shunner, yes, you're correct. Of course, 'seaside' has the same letters as 'disease.' You could just as well say I'm a disease shunner, which seems the more applicable to me."

I hope this means that Sheeni forced the confused Iowan to don a condom before submitting to his free-style orifice-probing.

"Both have a great relevance," insisted Carlotta. "Names are cosmically significant."

"Have you found any other anagrams in my name?" inquired Sheeni.

"Yes," admitted Carlotta, blushing. "The letters also spell A NEEDINESS RUSH and DEARNESS IN HUES." These discoveries had come to me at four this morning after hours of feverish paperwork. I took them as a sign from God.

"How interesting. Of course, there are many others," said Sheeni, thinking our loud. "For example, DUENNA'S HEIRESS or A SUNNED HEIRESS or AN HEIRESS'S NUDE Although, I'm hardly an heiress. Let's see, HE UNDRESSES IAN. Rather cryptic, as is AH RUE SNIDENESS and HERD UNEASINESS. Of course, there's also I SHUN SERENADES and I SHARE NUDENESS. I suppose both could be true under the proper circumstances."

Carlotta was flabbergasted. "Sheeni, how did you do that?"

"It's easy, Carlotta. You just visualize the letters and shuffle them about in your head. Let's see, Carlotta Ulansky, does 'Ulansky' have one l or two?"

"One."

"Oh, too bad. If there were two, one could make UNCLOAK'T ASTRALLY. Interesting, don't you think?"

Carlotta nodded uneasily.

Sheeni went on. "But only one l. OK, let's see. There is STARK UNLOYAL ACT and SOCK A TRUANT ALLY. Rather negative, aren't they? How about ATTACK ONLY

A SLUR or OK ALL RACY TAUNTS or ROT KLAN CASUALTY or A CUR SANK TOTALLY. Not very flattering, Carlotta. I'm sorry."

"That's all right, Sheeni," she said, marvelling. "You did those in your head? You must be incredible at Scrabble."

"I have enjoyed some small triumphs in that game," admitted Sheeni modestly.

At that moment, ugly Janice Griffloch approached the Scholarly Elites' table, clearly a serious act of trespass. Time had not tempered the virulence of her acne.

"Vijay's been hurt again," she said accusingly to Sheeni. "He may have a broken arm! It's all your fault!"

"Don't be preposterous, Janice," replied Sheeni indignantly. "I am just as upset about these attacks as you are."

"Liar!" she screamed. "You don't care anything about Vijay. You're just toying with him."

"Perhaps you should go somewhere and calm down," suggested Carlotta.

Janice turned on me angrily. "I'm not talking to you! Who are you anyway, some exchange student from Bulgaria?"

"I am new at this school," replied Carlotta icily. "But I have been here long enough to hear Vijay declare that you are the last person on earth he would ever go out with."

"He never did!"

"Ask him yourself."

"I will!" she said, stomping off.

"What an unhappy girl," said Sheeni. "How unfortunate to like someone when the affection is not returned."

Tell me about it Sheeni!

"I've thought of another anagram for your name, Carlotta," continued Sheeni. "A particularly curious one: OUTTASK CARNALLY. What do you suppose is the significance of that?"

I'm sure I don't know. I was beginning to wish I had never brought up the topic.

I should never have gulped down that second orange soda at lunch. By seventh period my throbbing bladder could no longer be ignored. For the first time Carlotta was compelled to enter a Redwood High girls' bathroom. She darted in, eyes straight ahead, entered a stall, and quickly closed the door. Secondhand cigarette smoke swirled about in dark, mephitic clouds, but she gave thanks for the door. To discourage the temptations of excessive privacy, school authorities had long since expunged the stall doors from the boys' bathrooms.

Sitting uneasily, I was amazed to discover my alter ego was now the target of cruel restroom graffiti. Some of the more libelous I copied down word-for-word in my notebook:

Beauty and the beast—
Sheeni and Carlotta eating lunch together.
Wrong! They're both beasts!
Keepin' score on Carlotta:
Buys her makeup at Texaco.
Gets her hair done at Pizza Hut.
And asks for extra grease!
Dresses like that cause one of her pimples died.
What do you mean? She's well dressed for Willits!
Whispers in study hall with the Fuzz.
Hair envy?
No, the girl wants it bad.
But first she has to find it!
Plays with her tits in study hall.
Yeah, I saw Bruno watching.

I was not playing with my tits, I was adjusting my brassiere. I felt like noting this on the wall, but instead wrote:

Are any of us so perfect that we cannot extend a gracious welcome to a lonely stranger?

Later in art class, artsy Mr. Thorne demonstrated the rudiments of water-color painting, then suggested we let our "creativity flower" (his phrase). Trent painted a view of some seaside cliffs at Santa Cruz that was clearly inferior to the mature work of Cezanne. Carlotta painted some daringly muddied orange and brown splotches.

"I wish I could paint abstractly like you," commented Trent, glancing over at my work. "My mind is stuck in a pictorial rut."

"It's not abstract," replied Carlotta, offended. "It's a view of the Matterhorn in autumn."

"Ah, yes, I see that now," replied Trent, smiling. His teeth, I noticed, were absolutely straight and dazzlingly white. "Very well done, Carlotta."

"Thank you, Trent," she answered, so needy of praise even insincere compliments from sworn enemies were welcome. Besides, Carlotta enjoyed the looks of hatred from the other girls as she occupied the attention of the best-looking fellow in school.

6:15 p.m. After school, Carlotta strolled to the library for some emergency research. She found what she was looking for in the back pages of the *Journal of the American Medical Association*: a small ad for mail-order physicians' stationery. Carlotta called the 800 number from the library payphone and requested they rush the sample kit to her by overnight express.

Returning to the reading room, Carlotta spotted the beautiful Apurva Joshi, seated at her usual table and gazing in endearing puzzlement at a book open before her. Carlotta walked over and sat down quietly in the chair opposite her. Apurva did not look up.

Carlotta cleared her throat. "You look a little confused. Perhaps I can help."

Apurva looked up with a start, closed the book hurriedly, and flushed a remarkable shade of wheatish crimson. Surprised by her reaction, I stole a glance at the cover. It was not, as I had supposed, her textbook on algebra. Now it was Carlotta's turn to blush. The book was titled, *Sexual Technique in Marriage.*

"I, I," stammered Apurva guiltily. "I didn't . . . I mean, the book was on the open shelf. I thought anyone could . . . Are you the librarian?"

"Of course not, my dear," Carlotta assured her. "You have a perfect right to read any book you like. I myself have read many such books. As women, we should all be as well informed on that subject as possible. Don't you agree?"

"I do, yes," she replied with conviction. "One feels so ignorant sometimes. Thank God this is America where one has at least some access to information."

"You are not from this country?"

"No, I'm from Pune. That's a city in India. Near Bombay. My name is Apurva, Apurva Joshi."

"Nice to meet you, Apurva. My name is Carlotta Ulansky. I am a newcomer to this town myself."

"Are you by any chance a recent immigrant from Eastern Europe?" asked Apurva, studying my dress. I prayed my shoulder pads passed her close inspection. As usual, Apurva's certainly did mine.

"No, Southern California," I replied self-consciously. "My mother is a prominent member of the film colony there."

We chatted on for some time about the Hollywood scene, then—at Carlotta's suggestion—adjourned to the lunch counter of Flampert's variety store for cups of tepid tea, slices of indifferent pie, and more stimulating girl talk.

"I can't tell you what a pleasure it is meeting you," said Apurva. "I almost feel as if I've known you for some time, Carlotta."

"I feel exactly the same, Apurva. We are, in our different ways, both outsiders here. Perhaps this has brought us together. Now, tell me about the book you were reading."

Apurva blushed and sipped her tea.

Carlotta was insistent. "Now don't be bashful, Apurva. It's just us girls here. I've had lots of experience at these affairs. What's up?"

"It's, it's my boyfriend," stammered Apurva, leaning pleasantly closer.

"Well, that sounds like good news."

"I beg your pardon, Carlotta?"

"Your boyfriend, Apurva. You were telling me about your boyfriend."

"Yes, Carlotta. His name is Trent. I love him urgently, desperately."

"You're obsessed?"

"Oh yes, Carlotta. Completely!"

"Sounds normal so far. So what's the problem?"

"Well," she whispered, leaning even closer, "last Friday night I went over to his house. His parents were away at a plywood convention in Portland. I had told my parents I was going to a choral recital in Willits."

"Lying to your parents, Apurva. Good. That shows a commendable independence of spirit. So you're all alone with Trent. What happened?"

"Well, after a while we went up to his bedroom. We got into his bed. We read some poetry."

"That's all?" I asked.

"Well, then we removed our clothes."

"All of them?"

"Eventually. We were quite nude after a time. It was the first time I had ever been in such a situation with a boy. I was quite aroused."

"Uh-huh," said Carlotta, her voice unexpectedly deepening. "Then what happened?"

"Then he touched me. Down there. It was like an electric shock. My whole body convulsed."

"You didn't like it?"

"Oh, no. It was wonderful. I never imagined I could be capable of such passions. Then, then I touched him."

"Down there?"

"Yes," she whispered. "I grasped his, uh, private area and told him I, I wanted him."

Carlotta shifted on her stool. She felt a sudden hot flash as rivulets of perspiration ran down her back. "And, Apurva," she said, mopping her brow with her paper napkin, "did he, uh, oblige?"

"No, Carlotta," she sighed, "he did not."

"He wasn't, uh, turned on?" I asked, incredulous.

"Oh no. Believe me, that wasn't the problem. In fact, to tell you the truth, Carlotta, he was larger than I had been led to expect from the diagrams. Considerably larger. But I was willing to accept some small measure of discomfort to achieve union with my love."

"Then what was the problem?"

"I don't know. That's why I was reading the book. I think I must have done something wrong. He wouldn't go through with it. We had the prophylactic on and everything. He just rolled off me and said it would be better if we resumed our poetry reading. I can't believe I'm telling you this. But it's such a relief to talk to someone about it. What did I do wrong, Carlotta? Tell me. You know. What do boys expect?"

Carlotta sighed. More evidence confirming Trent's profoundly disturbed state, yet her misguided friend clings to him ever tighter. Poor Apurva, how love has anesthetized her reason. Fortunately, Carlotta had a plan to effect a gradual disunion. "Apurva, my dear, you mustn't give in so easily. You are denying Trent the pleasures of the chase."

"But I thought American boys expected sex immediately."

"They just think they do, Apurva. In fact, they're extremely disappointed if it happens too soon. Often, as in Trent's case, the shock of premature intimacy renders them incapable of functioning. No, you must retreat from the brink."

"I should resist Trent's advances, Carlotta?"

"At all costs, Apurva. You must refuse his embraces, snub his kisses, and repel his probing hand. Make him think you're guarding your virginity like the Hope Diamond. It will drive him wild."

"Play hard to get, I see," said Apurva pensively. "But, Carlotta, I thought that was an essentially outmoded concept."

"Dating fashions come and go, Apurva, but the smart girls know the eternal verities never change. Love is like football, my friend. Guys expect to play four full quarters, not score a touchdown on the first play from scrimmage."

"American football is also a complete mystery to me," confessed Apurva, sipping the last of her tea. "I suppose I must read up on that too. Dear Trent often speaks enthusiastically of something called the Forty-Niners."

"That is your clue to his desires, Apurva. When he tries to kiss you, you must say: 'How about those Forty-Niners'!"

"How about those Forty-Niners!" repeated Apurva. "Oh, Carlotta, I can't thank you enough. I think God must have sent you to me."

That seemed as likely an explanation as any.

After exchanging our phone numbers and a warmly affectionate (and wildly erotic) hug, we paid our separate checks and went our separate ways.

8:30 p.m. Just did my laundry, and—taking the restroom barbs to heart— tossed in Carlotta's wig. Can I help it if Redwood High is so overheated those damn miracle fibers make me sweat like a pig?

9:45 p.m. Francois is not speaking to me. He is sulking because I continue to veto his plans for liberating Albert, our captive canine love child. Each new scheme he cooks up is, needless to say, more reckless than the last. At this point, I simply can't risk another arrest. Besides, where would I keep the damn ungrateful beast?

11:15 p.m. I just saw my father! On the local TV news! He's gained at least 20 pounds and now has a pronounced double chin. Life with Mrs. Crampton's cooking must continue calorically stimulating. Dad was being interviewed in connection with a flaming controversy over a new sawmill opening in Costa Rica. Local logs will now be sent down there for processing into finished lumber, but, according to Dad, "This will not result in the loss of any local jobs."

I recognized his facial expression. It was the same one of heartfelt sincerity he once employed with Mom while assuring her he had absolutely no interest of any sort in Miss Radmilla Sanders, my preternaturally ripe kindergarten teacher.

WEDNESDAY, December 9 — Bruno Modjaleski did not walk me to school today. He burst through the gate, savaging again Carlotta's stressed-out nervous system, and explained he had been suspended from school for 24 hours.

"That kid denied what you said, but I pounded him anyway," said Bruno, studying Carlotta's chest.

She anxiously reached up to adjust her bra, then thought better of it. "Violence is never the solution to a problem," counseled Carlotta.

"Oh yeah?" said Bruno."How about when it's third down and goal-to-go?"

"No," replied Carlotta severely.

"OK, say it's the fourth quarter, you're down three points, and it's the championship game?"

"No, Bruno. That is mere sophistry."

"The championship of the world!"

"Not even then!" she retorted, walking away.

Bruno blew a fierce wolf whistle. "Carly!" he called, "I like the way your butt moves when you walk."

What a louse! Carlotta, feeling not unlike a piece of meat, hurried down the alley.

In home room, Fuzzy, looking alarmed, leaned over to whisper, "Carlotta, what's wrong with your hair?"

"Why? What's the matter?" I whispered, self-consciously patting my coiffure.

"It looks like some kind of strange Afro. What happened?"

"Well, Frank, I washed it. And now I can't do a damn thing with it. Does it look that bad?"

"Like you just joined the Rastafarians."

"Fuck! Well, I'll just have to retreat deeper into the woodwork. Maybe no one will notice."

A good plan, but not a perfect one. As Carlotta walked through the halls, I felt many curious eyes upon me. After typing class, I ducked into a bathroom and managed to borrow a spritz of hairspray from a Chicana girl with eight inches of teased hair towering above her plucked eyebrows. This delay cost me the precious desk behind Sheeni's in physics class. I arrived to find it occupied by a much battered Vijay, his left arm nicely confined in a sling and his nose pleasantly buried in a bloody handkerchief. Carlotta sat down in the runners-up seat and smiled warmly at her dearest friend, who, she noticed, was making a polite effort not to stare at my hair.

"Good morning, Carlotta," said Sheeni. "Vijay was just attacked by Janice Griffloch. It's an outrage!"

"That girl is a hysterical ruffian," complained Vijay nasally. "She ought to be expelled."

"It's love, I expect," commiserated Carlotta. "When the love object does not respond, thwarted desires can lead to desperate acts. I've seen it happen before. Often the violence becomes habitual. My advice, Vijay, is to learn karate or withdraw from school."

"I did not ask you for your damn advice!" he sneered.

Despite Vijay's loutish behavior, Sheeni felt a social obligation to keep her oft-postponed luncheon appointment with him. Seething with jealousy, Carlotta dined at noon with Fuzzy as his guest at the Wanna-Be Jocks' table. She chewed her sandwich phlegmatically, and tried to ignore the tête-à-tête across the cafeteria.

"I'm making a nice A-line skirt in sewing class, Frank," I remarked, stirring from my lassitude.

"That's nice, Carlotta," he said. "What color is it?"

"Black."

"Oh."

"If you like, I'll model it for you when it's finished."

"OK, Carlotta. Oh, by the way, how are you coming along with your plan to get your dad to lay off my mom? I know for a fact she hasn't bought a single Christmas present for me yet."

"I'm working on it, Frank," I snapped, cringing as Vijay rested a disgusting mitt on Sheeni's bare arm. Carlotta will just have to get Bruno to break that arm too!

"Not a single present," repeated Fuzzy. "She's too busy sneaking around with your dad, the fat jerk."

Carlotta writhed in her seat. Now Sheeni was resting a delicate arm on Vijay's repellent shoulder.

"Shoot the guy," hissed Francois. "You know how to get hold of your father's guns, Frank. Plug the sucker."

"But, Carlotta," said Fuzzy, shocked. "He's your dad!"

"OK, then stop complaining and let me handle it."

"Boy, what a grouchy chick," said Fuzzy. "What's the matter, Carlotta? Getting your period?"

"Up yours, sexist pig!"

Distracted by homicidal ruminations, Carlotta later found herself cornered by Miss Pomdreck in a blind corner outside art class.

"Carlotta," said my guidance counselor severely, "neither your transcripts nor your physician's note has arrived."

"I'm sorry, Miss Pomdreck. I'm sure the delay stems from egregious Postal Service lapses."

"Well, I must have the doctor's note by Friday. Already Miss Arbulash is making inquiries about your absence from gym."

Miss Abulash was Redwood High's celebrated lady-bodybuilder girls' gym teacher.

"You'll have the note by Friday, Miss Pomdreck. I promise."

"Good. Oh, and Carlotta, you will have to alter your hairdo. According to the school dress code, dreadlocks are not permitted."

"Yes, Miss Pomdreck."

"And I must tell you that I am surprised that a girl of your character and breeding would adopt such an extreme and unbecoming hair style."

That makes two of us, lady.

In art class, Trent painted a Winslow-Homer-on-an-off-day watercolor of windsurfers skimming across sun-dappled waters off the Santa Cruz pier. Carlotta painted a vigorous smear of purples, greens, and blacks.

"You bring such energy to your compositions, Carlotta," commented Trent, smiling his disarming smile.

"Thank you, Trent," I smiled back. "But I am merely a conduit. The kineticism is in my subject."

"Which is?"

"The gas works at Hamburg. The broad aquatic swath in the foreground is the Rhine."

"Marvelous, Carlotta. And so imaginative. My subjects, by comparison, are so mundane."

"Yes, they are," I agreed. "But don't let that discourage you."

Perhaps Trent is so filled with innate charm he has to dribble small amounts continuously, lest the pressure build to dangerous levels—just as, analogously, the build-up of sperm in the sexually inert is relieved by a therapeutic wet dream. How else to explain Trent's smarmy art-class overtures?

7:15 p.m. After school Carlotta headed straight for Flampert's variety store, strode resolutely to the wig counter, and purchased a medium-brown modified-flip with frosted highlights for $13.99. Of course, she didn't dare try it on in the store. But later, in the privacy of her borrowed home, she was pleased to discover it flattered her features far more than Mrs. DeFalco's ratty hand-me-down. And this one, thank God, came with laundering instructions.

What a relief to take off my dress, wipe off my make-up, and just be Nick Twisp, runaway youth again. Peering out the front window, I was pleased to spy a Federal Express package waiting for me on the porch. I sneaked it inside, tore open the box, and found page after page of expensively engraved, obviously genuine physicians' stationery. Unhappily, across each sheet some officious meddler had caused to be printed, in giant letters, in shocking red (indelible?) ink, the word SAMPLE.

8:55 p.m. Kerosene, gasoline, lighter fluid, spot remover, fingernail polish remover, acetone, Windex, zit cream, lemon juice, vinegar, toothpaste, human spit, Right Guard, turpentine, chianti, hair spray, bag balm, Clorox. The damn red ink defied them all.

9:45 p.m. Eureka! Just as I was about to resign myself to keeping a firm grip on my towel (and on my erectile response) in Miss Arbulash's locker room, I discovered the life-saving solvent. All along the solution was right under my ears. I should have used my nose. What dissolves red ink? The same remarkable formula that dissolves inhibitions as it inflames the libido—Carlotta's perfume of choice: Writhe by Kevin Clein.

THURSDAY, December 10 — Carlotta's new hairstyle was a great success. The unsuspended Bruno redoubled his coarse alley blandishments, Fuzzy in home room was lavish in his compliments, Miss Pomdreck nodded approvingly from across the corridor as she disappeared into the boys' locker room on a counseling errand, and dearest Sheeni in physics class was unstinting (for her) in her praise.

"Carlotta, I like what you did with your hair," she exclaimed. "Vijay, doesn't Carlotta look nice today?"

The bruised alien sat in the runner's-up desk and endeavored to cut me dead while responding with polite neutrality to Sheeni's question. Of course, he only succeeded in appearing ridiculous. Carlotta ignored him.

"I should never have had my hair done at Heady Triumphs," sighed Carlotta. "That woman Lacey has some peculiar notions about styling." A bad case of scapegoating, I admit, but Carlotta felt some explanation should be offered for yesterday's aberrant coiffure.

"She's actually the girlfriend of my brother Paul," confided Sheeni. "Remember my roommate Taggarty I was telling you about? Well, after Taggarty threw herself at Trent, I suggested she let Lacey cut her hair. She went back to Santa Cruz in tears, poor thing. I suppose it must be growing out by now."

"Lacey cut my hair once also," interrupted Vijay. "It was that hooligan Nick Twisp's idea. He liked her, you see."

Carlotta glanced over at the traitorous slimebag. "And you didn't find Lacey at all attractive?" she asked icily.

"Not in the slightest," Vijay replied scornfully.

Liar! It was all he could do to keep the drool in check.

"How about Taggarty, Vijay?" asked Carlotta pleasantly. "Did you ever get a chance to meet her?"

Vijay shifted uneasily on his bruises. "Only once, briefly," he grunted. "I didn't like her very much."

"Really?" said Sheeni. "I should have thought you did, Vijay. The evidence at the time seemed to point in that direction."

Vijay was about to reply, but fortunately for him Mr. Tratinni rapped for order.

In sewing class, after four failed attempts, Carlotta succeeded in transplanting a zipper into her A-line skirt. To mark the occasion, Mrs. Dergeltry took off her blouse and cute Ambrosia Krinkler removed her dress. The latter exhibited a remarkable pair of sheer bikini panties, which required Carlotta to remain seated at her machine for some time. They appeared, however, to have no noticeable effect on Gary, who roamed about biologically unhindered.

Once again, Carlotta and Sheeni dined apart. Today Redwood High's newest student was the subject of a lunchtime interview in a private corner of the cafeteria by ace reporter Tina Manion.

"Really, I've led such a boring life," confessed Carlotta. "I can't imagine why you'd want to interview me."

Tina bit provocatively into a potato chip, and gazed abstractly at my chest. Carlotta did the same to hers, trying not to recall other tuberosities those luscious lips had nibbled.

"You are too modest, Carlotta. I understand your mother is a famous actress."

"Well, Mother has acted, uh, somewhat anonymously, in many films. She prefers those small, meaty parts," said Carlotta, suddenly coloring.

"What sort of parts?" asked Tina, flicking potato chip crumbs from her blouse onto my skirt. I wondered if this was some form of subliminal communication.

"Character roles," explained Carlotta. "My mother often plays those small, but demanding character roles. For example, she appeared as the gypsy fortune teller in 'Terminator 2'."

"Oh, I saw that movie. But I don't remember a gypsy fortune teller."

"Mother would be flattered to hear that. She believes great actors identify so completely with their characters they disappear in the *mise en scène*. I had to watch the film three times before I noticed Mother. And I, of course, was looking for her."

"That's amazing, Carlotta. What other movies has she been in?"

"Oh, well, you name it: 'Dr. Strangelove,' 'Cleopatra'—she played Liz Taylor's big sister in that one, 'Lawrence of Arabia,' 'Son of Flubber,' 'Harold and Maude,' 'Rebel without a Cause'."

"Carlotta!" exclaimed Tina, "your mother made a movie with James Dean. Did she know him?"

"Of course, Tina. Mother knew all the greats of Hollywood. Jimmy used to come over to use our pool sometimes when his was being treated for that bad algae inflammation they had back in '55. Of course, that was way before my time. Mother was just a girl then herself."

"I wonder if they had an affair?" whispered Tina, leaning closer and resting a warm hand familiarly on Carlotta's leg. She didn't mind.

"Knowing Mother, Tina, I'd say that was a definite possibility."

"Your mother got it on with lots of movie stars?"

"Everyone did, Tina. It was the winds, you see. Hot, dry winds off the desert. Santa Ana winds we called them. Sweeping down the San Fernando Valley, the desert winds would pick up the scent of orange blossoms and blow a hot, concentrated perfume over the Cahuenga Pass into Hollywood. It drove the actors wild. When conditions got really bad, the studios would have to shut down production. The actors couldn't keep their hands off each other. Expensive costumes would be ripped in frenzies of meteorological desire."

"Oh, my God," said Tina, squeezing my leg. "That's incredible!"

"I believe it was, uh, quite stimulating. Of course, nowadays smog has mostly put an end to that particular problem."

"Who else did your mother have affairs with, Carlotta?"

"Oh, I couldn't possibly tell you that. Mother would be furious. She's always hanging up angrily on the *National Enquirer*. No, Tina, my lips are sealed."

"Please, Carlotta," she implored, tightening her grip. "Off the record?"

"I can only say that they were all major stars—many, in fact, Academy Award winners."

"That's incredible!" repeated Tina, at last releasing Carlotta's leg.

I made a mental note to check later for bruises.

"What was it like, Carlotta, growing up in such a rich cultural scene?"

"Nothing special," sniffed Carlotta. "One gets used to it. You come downstairs in the morning and there's William Holden passed out on the sofa. You don't make a big deal out of it. You fix Bill a bloody mary, tell him you admired his work in 'Network,' and hurry off to school. It all seemed quite normal to me."

"And your father, Carlotta? Was he in the movie business as well?"

"Er, possibly. I, uh, I'm not sure."

"You're not sure?" asked Tina, journalistic confusion adding another enticing layer to her allure.

"You see, Tina. I don't know who my father is. Mother is acquainted with all the candidates, presumably, but she refuses to discuss the issue. She claims it's none of my business."

"None of your business! Who your own father is! Why, it could be . . . It could be . . . Steve McQueen!"

"I don't think so, Tina. Mother prefers tall men. Steve McQueen was short."

"Steve McQueen was short?" she asked, shocked.

"Dreadfully short," Carlotta shuddered. "Practically a midget."

"That's amazing," said Tina, peering intently into Carlotta's face.

I shifted uneasily in my chair. "Is, is something wrong, Tina? Is my lipstick smeared?"

"No, Carlotta. I'm just trying to see if you look like anybody famous."

"Oh. Do I?"

Tina studied Carlotta's face for some moments before replying. "Well, you look like somebody I've seen before. I just can't quite put my finger on who."

"Actually, I look just like Mother," I said, endeavoring to throw her off the scent. "The genetic contributions of my father, such as they were, must have been entirely recessive. I seriously question whether such a self-effacing person could have been an actor at all."

"Then who could he have been?" insisted Tina.

"Perhaps a screenwriter," Carlotta speculated. "You know, one of those weak, alcoholic types with the nicotine breath and typewriter pallor. Mother is always summoning them to her trailer and demanding rewrites. Perhaps some late-night story conference got out of hand."

"And nine months later out popped the surprise ending," added Tina.

"It's possible," agreed Carlotta. "I do have a pronounced literary inclination. Of course, that wouldn't necessarily point to a screenwriter."

"I could swear you look familiar though, Carlotta. Are there any famous screenwriters?"

"Alas no, Tina. It's an entirely anonymous profession."

"I know what," said Tina, "give me your phone number. If I think of who you remind me of, I'll call you." After recording my number on her steno pad, Tina had one final question. "Well, Carlotta, as a new student here, what are your impressions of Redwood High?"

"It's not a bad place," Carlotta replied magnanimously. "A bit provincial, of course. That's to be expected. And the fashion of dress among the student body is so amusingly antiquated. I almost feel as if I've traveled back in time."

Tina bristled. "I don't mean to be unkind, Carlotta. But one could say the same thing about your choice of outfits."

"People have, Tina. In fact, they're probably scrawling it on the restroom walls as we speak. The poor misguided dears."

"What do you mean?" she asked uneasily.

"Tina darling, to be perfectly blunt, in case you don't know it, my current ensemble is the *dernier cri* in Beverly Hills."

"It is?" she gasped.

"Of course. The color is black and the cut is pre-war Italian. It's the Mussolini Revival."

"But, Carlotta, I haven't seen it in any of the magazines."

"Time lag, Tina," explained Carlotta, adjusting her shawl. "Those magazines are printed months in advance. The Il Duce sirocco just swept up Rodeo Drive last week."

"It did?"

"Yes, but I'm resisting some of the more extreme trends."

"Like what?" she asked.

"Like not shaving your legs," whispered Carlotta. "Tina, razor sales are plummeting in Brentwood and Bel Air. The shaggy look is in."

"Oh my God!" exclaimed Tina, horrified.

"Of course, it may be some time before it reaches Ukiah," Carlotta added consolingly.

Reporters are all alike, thought Carlotta later, walking slowly toward the soporific quagmire of business math class. So inspiringly gullible. Especially the cute ones.

After school Carlotta headed downtown to the library to use its battered rental typewriter. Since the dissolved red ink had tinted my medical stationery pink, to allay suspicion I decided to employ the letterhead of a female physician. In 15 minutes, I had produced this sterling counterfeit:

Hilary Doctor, M.D.
123 Elm Street
Anytown, Massachusetts 02167

To whom it may concern:

After duly examining my patient, Carlotta Ulansky, it is my diagnosis that she is suffering from a transparently obvious case of Ossifidusbrittalus syndrome.

This unfortunate condition is characterized by precalcification of the skeletal mass leading to a chronic reduction in bone tensile strength. Therefore, Miss Ulansky must be excused from any vigorous physical exertion, including, but not necessarily limited to: shoveling snow, mowing the grass, mopping floors, dusting, picking cotton, and, most important of all, gym class. On this last point, I must remain firm.

I wish Miss Ulansky all the best in her struggle against this dreaded, but thankfully rare disease.

Yours sincerely,

Hilary Doctor, M.D.

Very professional, I'd say. Indeed, I wonder if Hilary herself, with all her years of medical training, could have done any better.

On my way out, I heard a soft "How about those Forty-Niners!" gasped lyrically from the poetry stacks. I stopped and peered down the dimly lit row. In the gloom under Twentieth Century Poetry, Trent Preston was being repulsed in his attempts to nuzzle Apurva Joshi. Decisively removing his hand from her sweater, she glanced up, saw Carlotta, and smiled a warm greeting.

"Oh, hello, Carlotta. How nice to see you again. Trent darling, this is my friend Carlotta."

"Carlotta and I have met," said Trent affably. "Apurva, Carlotta and I are in art class together. But I didn't know you two knew each other."

"We're old friends," said Apurva. "I was hoping I'd see you, Carlotta. It would please me very much if you could come to dinner tomorrow night."

Carlotta forced a smile. "You mean with your family, Apurva?"

"Yes. My mother is an excellent cook."

Dinner with Vijay and the stern Mr. Joshi. What an assault on the digestion. "I've got a better idea, Apurva. Let's go out for dinner tomorrow night. Just the two of us. It'll be my treat. Say 7 p.m. at the Golden Carp?"

"Well yes, fine, Carlotta. If that's what you'd prefer. Do they have vegetarian dishes?"

"Oh, yes. They have an extensive vegetarian menu. The kung pao tofu, I'm told, is to die for."

"Good. I don't care myself, but Mother will want to know."

"Darling, why don't I ever get invited to dinner at your house?" pouted Trent.

"Because my father would delight in poisoning you," replied Apurva.

That makes two of us, thought Carlotta, smiling benignly at the happy couple.

9:45 p.m. Washing the dinner dishes, I was startled by a knock on the back door. Hurriedly flipping out the light, I peered out through the old lace curtain.

"Nick, it's me," said a shadowy figure on the back porch. "Let me in."

"Hi, Frank," I said, opening the door. "What a surprise. I thought you were grounded."

"I am," Fuzzy replied, coming in and shedding his heavy parka. "But my theory on grounding is if you just ignore it, eventually it goes away. Anyway, my parents are too busy hating each other right now to pay much attention to me."

"I know the feeling, Frank. Want some wine? I got a jug of rotgut your granny left behind."

"Lay it on me, guy."

I poured two generous tumblers of the vile red swill.

"To the indifference of parents," I said, holding my glass aloft.

"I'll drink to that," said Fuzzy, clinking his glass against mine and tossing back a chug.

I took a tentative sip, fought an impulse to gag, and—overruling the well-founded objections of my palate—swallowed. Fuzzy gave signs of struggling similarly.

"Tastes a bit off," he admitted. "But it gets the job done."

"Let's hope so," I said.

I found a dusty can of mixed salted nuts in the pantry. We sat at the kitchen table and sampled the refreshments. The rancidity of the nuts, I observed, complimented the brackishness of the wine. Fuzzy belched in agreement.

"It's good to see you again, Nick." he said. "I was starting to think of you as a girl."

"Sometimes I'm almost beginning to feel like one," I conceded.

"I don't know, Nick. It may not be so healthy dressing up like a chick all the time. You could get, you know, warped."

"I don't feel particularly warped yet, Frank."

"Well, watch out, Nick. It could sneak up on you."

"One thing, Frank, I do have a new appreciation for what women go through. Take my word for it, being a chick isn't easy."

"Are you sure, Nick? Maybe it's just not easy being a chick when you're a guy."

"I don't think so, Frank. I mean, just preparing to go out the door in the morning. It's more work than guys have getting ready for a wrestling match and the senior prom put together. And then there's the constant worry during the day if your make-up and hair are all right. Not to mention the harassment."

"What harassment, Nick?"

"Bruno and Dwayne, Frank. They've got the hots for Carlotta."

"You're kidding, Nick."

"No lie. And, if you ask me, Trent's being awfully chummy too. I know for a fact something is holding that guy back from getting it on with Apurva."

"But, Nick, compared to Apurva, Carlotta is dog meat on the hoof. Er, no offense."

"Well, God knows I try," I replied, offended. "Besides, buster, beauty is in the eye of the beholder."

"Carlotta *is* a popular chick," conceded Fuzzy. "You should see what they're writing about her in the boys' room at school. Have you been in there lately?"

"Of course not. I use the girls' bathroom."

"Is that legal, Nick?"

"There are no signs posted against it, Frank."

"What goes on in there, Nick? I never been in a girls' restroom."

"Well I should hope not. It's nothing special. Just the usual: smoking, swearing, gossiping, extorting petty cash from the meek, forming cabals. Oh, and a great deal of competitive primping. If the cigarette smoke doesn't kill you, the hairspray will."

"Do the chicks like take their clothes off?" leered Fuzzy.

"Why would they, Frank? Do guys take off their clothes in the boys' restroom?"

"Just Malcolm Deslumptner."

Malcolm Deslumptner was the junior class' famous exhibitionistic masturbator. He did it everywhere: in restrooms, into a beaker in chem lab, behind the auditorium curtain during an Honor Society induction (you could see the red velvet moving rhythmically), on the bus during a debate team outing, and once in the stands during a pep rally in full view of the varsity cheerleaders (who shouted Go! Go! Go! as Malcolm went, went, went).

"That guy is a total sicko," observed Fuzzy.

"He just craves attention," I replied. "We all do in our own way. Speaking of which, what are they writing about Carlotta in the boys' restroom?"

"Nasty stuff, Nick, I'm sorry to say. Someone's been writing that Carlotta has the hots for Sheeni. They're calling you a lesbian, Nick."

"Of all the nerve! Did the handwriting look anything like Vijay's?"

"You know it might have, Nick. Come to think of it."

"I'm not surprised, Frank. The guy is desperate. He can see he can't even compete with a woman for Sheeni's affections."

"Well, he's taking her to the Christmas dance."

I slammed down my glass, splashing the late Mrs. DeFalco's aged rotgut on the flowered wallpaper. "What!"

"Yeah, Nick. I got the word from Dwayne in gym today. It's all over the school. Vijay asked and Sheeni accepted."

Grim, grim news. I struggled to remain calm.

"Fuck!" I said softly. "How can he go to a dance? He's got a broken arm!"

"Just a bad sprain, Nick. The cast comes off next week."

Great job, Bruno! See if I ever bake you another cookie!

"What are you going to do, Nick?"

"I'll think of something, Frank. Vijay will get his."

"While you're at it, Nick, don't forget to do something about your dad."

"Don't worry, Frank. I got a plan for that."

"Oh, yeah?" said Fuzzy, interested. "What?"

"I decided to fix Dad up with someone younger and prettier than your mom. It's the least I can do."

"Do for what?" asked Fuzzy.

"For not looking too hard for me," I replied. "Lots of parents would be leafletting Seven-Elevens and going on TV with urgent appeals. Dad's just playing it cool—working at his misinformation job, piling on the blubber, and dating your mom."

"You don't mind, Nick?"

"Nah."

"Isn't it scary being away from your parents? Not having, you know, security?"

"Sometimes it's scary. But to tell you the truth, Frank, security seemed in pretty short supply even when I lived with my parents. At least now I don't have them telling me what to do."

"You're lucky, Nick."

"Let's face it, Frank. Monetary considerations aside, once you hit your teen years, parents exist only as two grotesque carbuncles on your life."

"I'll drink to that," said Fuzzy. We hoisted our glasses.

"Me," I said, gulping a handful of nuts to obscure the taste of the wine, "I just had my surgery early."

"What surgery was that?" inquired Fuzzy.

"My carbunclectomy!"

11:30 p.m. I was roused from a drunken slumber by the ringing telephone.

"Hello," I mumbled into the receiver.

"May I speak to Carlotta, please."

"Oh, hi, Tina," said Carlotta, awake now, but still thick of tongue.

"Hi, Carlotta. I didn't recognize your voice at first. Guess what? I thought of a writer you look like."

"Who?" inquired Carlotta.

"Truman Capote."

"Truman Capote!"

"There's definitely a resemblance, Carlotta. Did your Mom know him?"

"Not in any sense of the word, Tina. I assure you of that. Now, good night."

"Wait, Carlotta! Did you ever have a lisp? Maybe when you were younger?"

"Good night, Tina!" *Click.*

The nerve of some people! I'm sure I don't look anything at all like the late Truman Capote. And I'm much taller too.

FRIDAY, December 11 — Another busy day, diary. What I really need is a full-time stenographer to take down all the details of my stimulating life.

This morning, in a momentary lapse of judgment, I let Bruno browbeat Carlotta into accompanying him to school on his chopper. My body was still shaking uncontrollably well into fourth period. Every few seconds in sewing class, a fresh spasm of lingering terror would vibrate down my right leg, stomping my foot on the sewing machine pedal, and sending yards of black cloth hurtling under the needle. I fear the hem of my unfortunate A-line skirt may never pass Mrs. Dergeltry's rigorous scrutiny.

I began the school day in Miss Pomdreck's office, where my aged guidance counselor was relieved to receive at last Carlotta's physician's excuse.

"A doctor named Doctor," she mused. "How appropriate indeed. She apparently was the recipient of very sound career counseling. I only wish my own cases were all so simple. And where is Anytown, Carlotta?"

"Er, near Watertown, Miss Pomdreck. It was named for Matthew Any, the great abolitionist."

"Ah yes, a notable figure in our history. Well, everything looks in order. I shall put a copy of your letter in Miss Arbulash's box. She, of course, will be disappointed not to have you in her class. She was just mentioning yesterday how much she looked forward to getting you started on the stair-climber machine. And I'm sorry about your affliction. I notice your hands are trembling. Are you in great pain, my dear?"

"Not too unbearable," winced Carlotta.

"Well, don't overexert yourself, Carlotta. If you ever feel ill or in pain, you may go rest in Nurse Filmore's office. Or, if you prefer, you may go home."

Wow, a license to cut class. Every teen's dream!

A few moments later in home room, Fuzzy handed me a bombshell.

"Check this out, Carlotta," he whispered, pointing to the front-page headline of today's newspaper. Bold black type screamed: "Runaway Empire Youth Held in Huge Drug Haul."

Shocked, I scanned the inflammatory news article.

"Carlotta," whispered Fuzzy, "it says there they busted Nick Twisp in Seattle with $4 million of cocaine in his raincoat. How exactly is that possible?"

"It's not," I whispered, stunned. "Nick doesn't have a raincoat. And he's never been to Seattle. And he certainly never arrived there yesterday on a flight from Islamabad."

"Where's that?" asked Fuzzy.

"Er, Pakistan, I think," I replied, suddenly recalling the pleasant Pakistani fellow I had met on the plane to Los Angeles.

"That's near India, I think," whispered Fuzzy. "Carlotta, do you suppose Vijay is behind this?"

"Possibly, Frank. But not likely."

"Carlotta, they got a quote in that article from your dad."

"Where?"

"On the inside page. At the bottom of the story."

I located the paragraph in question. It read:

Reached at his corporate office, timber company information officer George W. Twisp, father of the alleged drug smuggler, said he deplored the actions of his son. "The boy is bad, plain bad. We did all we could for him—sending him to expensive private schools, buying him nice clothes and a high-priced computer—but he was incorrigible. I just hope prison straightens the kid out. Nick has been a great disappointment to his mother and I."

The feeling is mutual, Dad. I only pray the sentiments I express are grammatically correct.

By the time Carlotta reached physics class everyone was bent over newspapers—even Mr. Tratinni.

"Carlotta! Have you heard the news?" asked Sheeni. "Nick has been arrested!"

"I know," I replied. "It's a dreadful shock."

"I'm not surprised at all," averred Vijay, his bruises showing alarming signs of fading. "That Nick Twisp is an unprincipled ruffian. No depraved act by his hands would surprise me!"

Oh yeah? How about the strangulation of a traitorous classmate?

"In some ways I blame myself," said Sheeni, sadly shaking her head. "I encouraged Nick to loosen up and not be so tediously good. I never imagined he would take my advice so much to heart."

"Women can exert a profound moral influence over men," affirmed Carlotta.

"It was nothing you said or did, Sheeni," said Vijay. "His father is right. Nick is an innately evil person. I knew it when he used to lie to you, Sheeni, about performing well in French class. His French was abysmal!"

"But I understand he did quite well in physics," hissed Carlotta.

"Almost as well as you, Carlotta," remarked Sheeni, smiling. "Did you know you received the highest grade in the class on yesterday's test?"

"Just beginner's luck," said Carlotta modestly.

"That was doubtless the case," scowled Vijay.

Fighting an impulse toward mayhem, Carlotta turned to My Beloved. "Sheeni, what's this I hear about your going to the Christmas dance?"

"Yes, kind Vijay has consented to be my escort."

"That's so sweet," smiled Carlotta. "I'm so happy you two are not permitting your extreme disparity in heights to deter your enjoyment of these social functions."

"I am nearly as tall as she is!" spat out the diminutive alien.

"Of course you are," smiled Carlotta. "Sheeni, I hope you're planning on wearing your flats. Heels, I believe, would be a mistake."

"I hadn't given it much thought, Carlotta. But that is a good suggestion."

"And who is taking the lovely Carlotta to the dance?" inquired Vijay.

Before I could deliver a withering reply, Mr. Tratinni rapped for order.

Taking advantage of my new freedom, at lunchtime I brazenly left the building and hurried home to call Joanie long distance. My sister, sounding more than usually harassed, answered on the fifth ring.

"Nick! Are they letting you make phone calls?"

"Are who letting me?" I asked, confused.

"The cops," said Joanie, "in Seattle."

"That's what I'm calling to clear up, Joanie. There's been a slight mistake. I don't know who they arrested, but it wasn't me."

"It wasn't you?"

"Of course not."

"Boy, Nick, Mom's not going to like that. She just put Lance on the plane to Seattle."

"Good. I hope the lump falls off the Space Needle."

"Nick, where are you?"

"Oh, here and there. Don't worry, Joanie. I'm OK. I'm not smuggling drugs. I'm living OK. I'm even going to school."

"Nick, you can't keep this up. You're driving us all nuts."

"Joanie, I'm OK! Don't worry. What's all the commotion there?"

I could hear loud voices in the background.

"It's the men from the coroner's office," she replied cryptically.

My mind raced. I imagined Dr. Dimby slumped dead over his laptop—felled in his prime by the pressures of academia and unforeseen middle-aged fatherhood.

"Joanie," I gasped, "who died?"

"My neighbor, Nick. Miss Ulansky. The Meals on Wheels guys found her about a half-hour ago. Looks like she passed away quietly while watching a video."

"That's too bad," I said. "What was the film?"

"Nick, don't be morbid."

"I'm not being morbid. Films meant a lot to her. What was the movie?"

"'The Ten Commandments.' Why?"

"She's in the arms of God now," I said somberly. "Or, at least Charleton Heston's."

"Nick, how did you get to be so warped?"

"Bad home life."

"Well, you better call Mother. She thinks you were running drugs because you were kidnapped by gangsters."

"Wow. Sounds like Mom's starting to give me the benefit of the doubt. That's progress. No, Joanie, you call her. Tell her I'm OK. Tell her I'll look her up someday when I'm grown up."

"Nick, I can't tell her that. You call her."

"I'll think about it."

"Well, call me then. Stay in touch."

"OK, Joanie. How's Dr. Dimby?

"It's Dindy, Nick. He's fine. Kimberly moved out, so we have plenty of room now for the . . ." She paused. "For us."

"That's nice. I hope all two of you will be very happy."

Carlotta's spiritual mother is deceased. How sad. How fortunate the younger Miss Ulansky is so well-equipped to dress for mourning. I wonder how old Bertha Ulansky was at the end? Not a day younger than 90, I'd estimate. Once she was Carlotta's age, with her whole life ahead of her. Now she's a disturbing interruption to her neighbors, an everyday inconvenience for the coroner. At least she will live on anonymously in her 400 films. Death: the final censor. He waits for us all with his editing shears—as our colors fade and our celluloid slowly dissolves.

Bummed out by the transience of life, I resolved to take the afternoon off from school and savor every golden, fleeting moment. Twenty minutes later, tiring of living life to the fullest, I picked up a *Penthouse*, leafed through it for a while, dealt peremptorily with a sudden T.E., squeezed several erupting zits, then took a nap. Life, I decided as time dissolved into clockless unconsciousness, must go on.

5:45 p.m. I awoke from my nap and hurriedly phoned Fuzzy.

"Frank," I said cheerfully, "you know that favor you owe me?"

"What favor?" he demanded.

"You know: for breaking up your mom and my dad."

"Some breakup, Nick. I think Mom has a date with the creep tonight. She just got her hair done and her legs waxed."

"Don't worry, Frank. The deed is practically done. Now for the favor: you know the Christmas dance?"

"Yeah. What about it?"

"You asked anybody yet?"

"Who can I ask, Nick? Heather's in Santa Cruz."

"Good. Frank, I want you to take Carlotta."

"What!"

"Frank, you don't have a date. Carlotta doesn't have a date. It's a perfect match."

"Nick, you're out of your mind. I'm not taking no guy to no dance!"

"Frank, I promise Carlotta will look nice. And feminine. No one will ever know."

"Nix, Nick. That's final."

"OK, Frank. Have a nice Christmas with your mom. And my dad."

"Do I have to dance with you, Nick? I'm not dancing no slow dances with you."

"OK, Frank. No slow dances."

"I'm not holding hands either."

"OK, Frank. No public displays of affection. But I *will* expect a nice corsage."

"OK, Nick. But if it ever gets out that Carlotta's a guy, you're dead meat."

"Fair enough, Frank. See you this weekend?"

"I'll probably drop by."

"You want to go shopping with Carlotta to pick out her dress?"

"You want to suck my big royal Canadian?"

"Just thought I'd ask, Frank. What color suit will you be wearing to the dance?"

"How about pink?"

"Frank!"

"OK, Nick. Blue, I guess."

"To match your attitude, I suppose."

"Yeah," he growled. "Well, Nick, I guess I better go pluck my eyebrows."

My first high school dance! Not the partner of my desires, but at least I'll have the consolation of loitering in the general vicinity of that dear person. I wonder if Carlotta could conceal a cattle prod in her gown for use against amorous Indians?

How time flies. Carlotta must rush. She has to get ready for her dinner engagement with lovely Apurva.

11:30 p.m. I'm back. What a night. One plans a quiet evening with a close friend and winds up huddled under a juniper bush in the frigid darkness. Such are the vicissitudes of adolescent homelessness.

As is her custom, Carlotta arrived at the Golden Carp ten minutes early. Seated by Steve, the balding Chinese waiter, at a choice table under a carved rosewood pagoda, she sipped her tea and waited. 7 p.m., 7:15, 7:30. No Apurva. At 8:10 p.m., just as the now ravenous Carlotta was about to order the lonely budget dinner for one, the door opened and in rushed Sheeni Saunders—breathlessly aglow and achingly beautiful. My heart thumped in delighted surprise as My One and Only Love hurried over to my table.

"Oh, Carlotta, you're still here," said Sheeni. "I hope you haven't been waiting long."

Carlotta smiled warmly to hide her confusion. Had she somehow confused darling Sheeni with dear Apurva? Did wanton application of Writhe cause memory loss?

"Er, no, Sheeni," stammered Carlotta. "Please, sit down. You're right on time."

Now it was Sheeni's turn to appear confused. She paused in the act of hanging up her coat.

"On time for what, Carlotta?"

"Uh, whatever you like. Dinner, for example?"

"Oh, I've already eaten," said Sheeni, sliding into the chair next to mine and removing her gloves. "Hours ago. But please, go ahead and order. Apurva won't be coming."

"She won't?" Carlotta asked, at once relieved, disappointed, and excited.

"No. Sweet Vijay just called me with the bad news. Apurva's being confined by her parents. She couldn't reach you, so she asked Vijay to come here and tell you. He telephoned me instead."

"Oh, I see," said Carlotta, beckoning to Steve and ordering the Economy Dinner for one. Sheeni surveyed the menu and ordered a cappucino—something cautious Nick would never have done in a Chinese restaurant. But he liked a woman who lived dangerously.

"I didn't realize you were acquainted with Apurva," said Sheeni.

"Oh, we happened to meet recently, Sheeni. It's a small town you know."

"Yes, distressingly small, Carlotta."

"I'm sorry to hear about Apurva and her parents. Do you know what the difficulty is?"

"I received a brief summary from Vijay. Apurva told her parents last week that she was going to a choral recital in Willits, then spent the evening alone with Trent Preston. Somehow they found out."

Ever alert to treachery, Carlotta smelled a rat. "How did they find out?"

Sheeni casually examined the immense rosewood temple looming overhead. "Don't they ever dust that thing?" she asked.

"How did they find out?" Carlotta repeated.

"A letter detailing the alleged incident arrived in the mail today. It was unsigned."

"The allegations could have been false," Carlotta pointed out.

"Mr. Joshi called Trent's parents and confirmed they were out of town at a convention on the evening in question. He also checked with Apurva's choir director. She reported Apurva had excused herself from the concert that evening for reasons of health. Confronted with this evident, Apurva confessed."

"Poor Apurva," sighed Carlotta. "She would do something silly like that."

"Yes," said Sheeni, "and now unfortunately she's had to miss your nice engagement."

"Who do you suppose sent the letter?" Carlotta asked. "Not many people could have known of the affair."

"Just a handful, I presume."

"Did you know about it, Sheeni?" Carlotta inquired casually.

"I might have," Sheeni replied, just as casually. "I think Vijay mentioned something about it."

At last, Carlotta's long-delayed pork fried rice arrived, but my hunger had evaporated. The situation was painfully clear. Sheeni had sent the letter. She was still adamantly in love with Trent and wanted Apurva out of his life. Foolishly, I had abetted her schemes. Instead of counseling virginal restraint, I should have encouraged Apurva to demand what is rightfully hers: immediate, passionate possession by Trent Preston. As long as that deranged poet wavers on the brink, I shall know no peace. I must convince My Love that Trent is now and forever out of reach.

While Carlotta ruminated, Sheeni sent back her cappucino. Then sent it back again.

"I recommend the tea," said Carlotta, lifting her cup. "The Chinese have had more experience with this beverage."

"I shouldn't call that tannic swill tea," answered Sheeni, eyeing my plate. "Carlotta, aren't you going to eat your eggroll?"

"No. I'm not very hungry. You have it, Sheeni."

Sheeni ate the eggroll, most of my pork fried rice, and a considerable portion of my prawns with vegetables. This drew frowns from Steve, still smarting from the rejection of his cappucino. The menu stated clearly in small print that the Economy Dinner for one was *not* to be shared. Steve, I knew, took these issues seriously. He worked 18 hours a day, seven days a week, and consequently saw life as a grim struggle for existence. Oddly, I hardly work at all, yet share a similar philosophy.

Ignoring Steve's sighs of outrage, Sheeni asked Carlotta about her school life in Switzerland. "Carlotta, was your finishing school in the French, German, or Italian-speaking region of Switzerland?"

No way I was going to step into that trap. "It was in the English-speaking region, Sheeni," Carlotta replied.

Sheeni put down her chopsticks. "The English-speaking region?"

"That is to say, the main focus of the school was inculcating students with a knowledge of English. That was the only language permitted on campus, and, indeed, in the surrounding countryside."

"Then you weren't afforded the opportunity of learning a foreign language?"

"No, I learned only English spoken haltingly by non-native speakers. I picked up a dreadful accent, or so Mother used to tell me."

"How is your mother?" asked Sheeni, helping herself to my champagne sherbet.

"Very well, thank you," Carlotta lied. Under the circumstances, she did not feel she could share her grief with her friend.

We chatted on another half hour—Sheeni wanting to know about my glamorous life in Hollywood, angry Steve wanting us to pay the damn bill and leave, lovesick Carlotta wanting only to grab her dinner companion and ravish her on the moldering red carpet. Finally, one of us satiated, we rose from the table and Carlotta paid the bill. She noticed with surprise that Steve had tacked on $2 for the rejected cappucino and another $2 for "extra plate." The latter charge she protested silently by leaving a more than usually niggardly tip.

"Thank you very much for the cappucino," said Sheeni, as we walked out into the freezing darkness.

"My pleasure," replied Carlotta, shivering in the icy wind. "Shall I walk you home, Sheeni?"

"No, thank you, Carlotta, I'm not going home."

"Oh? Where are you off to on such a dismal night?" Carlotta asked with all the feigned casualness she could muster.

"I'm going to Vijay's. He's rented a French film. We're going to watch it together on his VCR."

"Really?" said Carlotta, through fiercely clenched teeth. "Isn't it a bit late for movie watching?"

"Of course not, Carlotta," she laughed. "It's only 9:30. Don't be such a stick in the mud."

"And what film are you seeing, Sheeni?"

"Oh, something by Truffaut. 'Stolen Kisses' I believe."

Carlotta lurched backward from this grievous blow. "Well," she croaked, "have a nice time."

"I'll do my best," replied My Love cheerfully. "Do you have any messages for poor Apurva?"

"Yes, tell her not to despair. And tell her love will prevail. She and Trent will be together soon, I am certain of that."

The light went out of Sheeni's smile. "Such confidence may be misplaced, Carlotta. But I shall convey the sentiment, if an opportunity arises. Good night."

"Good night, Sheeni."

Separating from the source of her pain, Carlotta trooped homeward in black despair. A private dinner with The Woman I Love, and all I had to show for it was gastric distress, acute heartache, and a serious case of homicidal rage. My mood did not improve when—sneaking around the garage from the alley—Carlotta found a large silver Lincoln parked in the late Mrs. DeFalco's driveway.

"Fucking hell!" muttered Carlotta. "It's Frank's mother's car!"

And where one encounters the underwired and over-sexed Nancy DeFalco, can my home-wrecking dad be far away?

Infiltrating the bushes alongside the house, Carlotta spotted a light in a window, hoisted herself up by her fingertips, and peered in through the narrow opening. Six feet away, two walruses were wrestling under an antique quilt. It was the adulterous couple, humping away in my bed.

"Damn!" muttered Carlotta, releasing her grip and slumping down into the prickly blackness. "The nerve of some people!"

Huddled against the icy stucco, Carlotta listened with appalled fascination to the grunts, salacious moans, and sloppy thumps of middle-aged lovemaking. "Goodness," she observed to herself, "it's just like being in the pig barn at the county fair."

As the grunting intensified, I realized the gravity of the situation. Dressed as a woman, I was eavesdropping on my father making love to my best friend's mother who had once tried to seduce me. What a field day my future analyst will have with this episode. Even now, as I write this, I can feel fresh stalactites of neuroses erupting on my twisted psyche.

Shortly after the traumatic climax, the phone rang.

"Who on earth could that be?" I heard Nancy ask.

"I'm not here!" said Dad, evidently lighting a cigar. (More grist for my analyst!)

"Hello?" said Nancy. "No, I'm sorry, there's no one here by that name. Who? She looks like what? No, certainly not. You must have the wrong number. That's all right. Goodbye."

"Who was that?" asked Dad.

"Somebody wanting somebody named Carlotta."

"Carlotta who?" he asked.

"I don't know. She said she had an important message. She had to tell Carlotta that she looked like Liberace."

Thanks a pantsfull, Tina!

"Liberace, the piano player?" inquired Dad.

"What other Liberaces are there?" she replied.

"If she looks like Liberace," commented Dad, "this Carlotta must be one *ug-g-gly* chick."

A second overflowing pantsfull for Dad!

"You know, George," she said, "you look a little like Liberace yourself."

"Get out a here!" he replied.

"No, you do. Just a little—around the eyes especially. Too bad you don't have his musical talent."

"That swish was as flaky as a three-dollar bill," replied my tolerant father.

"He had more soul than some people I could mention," said Nancy. "And more money."

"What's that supposed to mean?" demanded Dad.

"Figure it out yourself, George. And put out that damn stinky cigar!"

Many arctic minutes later, as they were climbing back into their passion-rent garments, I heard Nancy shout, "That lousy rat!"

"What's the matter, Irene?" asked Dad, apparently confusing the name of his date.

"It's gone!" she replied. "The money!"

"What money?" asked Dad, his curiosity naturally piqued.

"Polly's money! Over $2,000! I took it from his pants when the cops were hauling him out of the hot tub. I hid it here in this drawer. Fuck!"

"What happened to it?" Dad demanded.

I could hear sounds of drawers being violently rifled and Carlotta's delicate underthings being strewn about savagely.

"It's gone," said Nancy. "The rat got my money."

"What rat?" demanded Dad.

"The slimy, sneaky rat I'm married to," she replied. "He's got the only other key."

"Shit!" exclaimed Dad, clearly distraught over this sudden loss of vicarious wealth.

"He's probably been bringing his bimbos here," she continued. "The towels in the bathroom are damp, there's a ring around the tub, and I saw three empty garbanzo bean cans in the trash."

"So?" asked Dad.

"So Dom loves garbanzo beans. I refuse to serve them because he stinks up the house for days. But his mother used to buy them by the case. He probably screws his bimbos right here in his mother's bed."

"What a rat!" said Dad, probably contemplating the scene of his own recent debaucheries.

"Only one thing doesn't figure," she added.

"What's that?"

"The bathtub," said Nancy. "The dirty rat hates to take baths."

Twenty minutes later, after the big Lincoln finally pulled away, a nearly hypothermic Carlotta stumbled into the house and gazed in profound dismay at her violated bedroom: clothing scattered everywhere, expensive hosiery dangling from the overhead lamp, bed torn apart, mattress askew, pillows and blankets in disarray, large odorous wet spot despoiling the center of the once-virginal sheet. And a dead cigar snubbed out in my hot-water bottle.

Too tired to clean up the mess, I am going to retire on the couch. At least I still have my money and a designated patsy to take the rap for grand theft. I suppose the Frog movie must be over by now. 'Stolen Kisses.' Perhaps it's a crime film, and not—as I fear—a libido-inflaming romance. Damn those French. Damn Vijay. Damn them all!

SATURDAY, December 12 — 2:47 a.m. Waking from a bad dream, I just had one of those ugly revelations that come—as Frank puts it—in the wee small hours of the morning. Nancy was right: Dad does look like Liberace.

Especially around the eyes.

9:52 a.m. A hard night on a soft couch. To cheer myself up, Carlotta bought a newspaper and went out to her usual hole-in-the-wall (and in-the-food) breakfast place.

Gulping down a double order of my usual assortment, Carlotta read with interest the latest developments in the big Seattle drug haul. It seems a special agent from the Oakland PD had arrived and, much to everyone's annoyance, identified the suspect as a Nick Twisp impostor. It was also disclosed that the suspect might have passed unscathed into the country had it not been for some suspicious, obviously forged custom stamps in his passport. (I hope the Cub Scouts don't insist I return my printing badge.)

The article went on to say that authorities now fear the rightful Twisp may have been the victim of foul play in Asia. According to the Associated Press, I could be a deceased murder victim! I wonder if Sheeni has hear the news?

Five minutes later, I had a chance to pose this question myself, when My One and Only Love entered for her morning cappucino.

"Sheeni, have you heard the news?" asked Carlotta. "That wasn't your friend Nick they arrested in Seattle!"

Sheeni, looking radiant (from anxiety?), sat down at the chair opposite me with her double cappuccino and triple maple bars. Clearly, grief had not paralyzed her appetite. "I never imagined it was," she replied calmly. "I don't believe Nick has an aptitude for international drug smuggling. And how are you this morning, Carlotta?"

"Frankly, Sheeni, I'm worried. The newspapers are saying your friend could be the victim of foul play. Aren't you concerned?"

"Not particularly," replied Sheeni, sipping her foamy beverage.

"Why not?" demanded Carlotta, shocked.

"It is idle speculation without foundation in fact. Nick probably had his pocket picked. I'm told such petty thefts are common in the Third World. U.S.

passports are a special target of thieves. No, I'm confident Nick was simply inattentive and lost his passport."

"That sounds very much like blaming the victim, Sheeni," said Carlotta severely. "If Nick is OK, why hasn't he tried to contact you?"

"Oh, but he has, Carlotta," replied Sheeni.

"He has?" Carlotta exclaimed, incredulous.

"Yes, I received a letter from him a few days ago."

I wondered if the caffeine and sugar rushes were affecting my hearing. "Sheeni, are you telling me that you have received a letter from Nick?"

"Yes, Carlotta. Is that so surprising?"

"Er, I suppose not. And what, exactly, did he say?"

"Here, read the letter if you like."

Sheeni removed an ordinary white business envelope from her purse and handed it to Carlotta. The envelope, I noted with surprise, bore several authentic Indian airmail stamps and an apparently genuine Pune postmark. Inside was one thin sheet of bond paper bearing this extraordinary typed message:

Dear Sheeni:

I have arrived safely in Pune and will start classes tomorrow. I am staying with a nice family in their digs across the river in the Deccan Gymkahana district. They have a daughter near my age who has been most attentive in showing me the sights of her great city. She is keen on literature and we have been having stimulating discussions far into the night. I cannot recall ever meeting such an intellectually gifted young person. Nayana is also very beautiful and homely.

Sheeni, I am falling in love with this wonderful country and its friendly peoples. I think I shall be staying here for many years. If we never meet again, remember me kindly and know that I am happy. I pray you have a good life in the U.S. or your beloved France, and marry a proper boy who will make you a dutiful husband. Goodbye and good fortune to you.

Regards,

Nick Twisp

"A curious letter," commented Carlotta, seething inwardly. "How, I wonder, does one contrive to be simultaneously beautiful and homely?"

"Oh, Vijay explained that to me," replied Sheeni, taking back her letter. "In India they use the word 'homely' to mean devoted to the home and possessing desirable homemaker skills. Thus, it is unlikely I shall ever be described as homely."

"It certainly is," agreed Carlotta. "But Sheeni, don't you think it's odd that Nick should employ an obscure Indian usage so soon after arriving in that country?"

"It's not so odd," replied Sheeni. "Perhaps intellectually gifted Nayana has been boasting of her homeliness—far into the night."

"Sheeni, did Nick normally type his letters and sign them 'regards'?"

"No. His customary practice was to write them in his affected handwriting and close with a gushing declaration of eternal devotion. Now that you mention it, the prose does not exhibit Nick's usual sesquipedalian effulgence. But perhaps we can attribute that to a slight maturation of style."

"Sheeni, notice that even the signature is typed. Who would send a letter to a close friend without at least signing their name?"

"What are you suggesting, Carlotta?"

"Just that it is my professional opinion that your letter is a forgery."

"Oh, Carlotta," she scoffed, "you've been reading too many spy novels. Who would want to counterfeit a letter from Nick?"

"A rival in love," proposed Carlotta. "Someone with friends or relatives in Pune who could forward the letter so that the postmark would be genuine. Someone who would unknowingly employ a foreign word usage because he himself is an alien in this country."

"Vijay would never do such a thing," insisted Sheeni. "He is far too honorable. I should much sooner expect such underhanded machinations from Nick."

Carlotta chose to overlook that slur. "Speaking of your honorable Indian friend, how was the film last night?"

"A tremendous disappointment, I'm afraid. The print turned out to be dubbed. Two hours of Jean-Pierre Leaud pursuing endearing fecklessness with an American twang. I was sickened."

"Oh dear," said Carlotta. "Was the gratuitous violence that excessive?"

"You misunderstand me, Carlotta. I was sickened by the callousness with which an important film is butchered to make it palatable to Americans. It is not violent at all. It's one of the ground-breaking lyrical romances of the French New Wave."

More dire news.

"And how did Apurva and Mr. and Mrs. Joshi enjoy the film?" asked Carlotta, hoping for the best.

Sheeni gave me a quizzical look. "They were in bed, Carlotta."

"All of them?" she asked weakly.

"Well, Apurva wandered out from her room once for a glass of water. That girl does not look well."

"I hope she didn't interrupt anything," said Carlotta.

"No," replied Sheeni cryptically. "The film had just started."

For the sake of my remaining sanity, I am choosing to interpret that remark narrowly.

10:45 a.m. On my way home from the donut shop, Carlotta ran into Fuzzy, who was loitering about in front of the courthouse with the usual Saturday throng of disaffected youth.

"Hi, Carlotta," he called.

"Hi, Frank," she replied, distracted. "Say, Frank, what's a good way to dispose of a body?"

"A dead one?" he asked.

"Of course."

"Take it up to the woods and bury it. Deep though, so the wild pigs don't root it up. Or dump it in the chipper out at the waferboard plant. That's riskier though."

"What about burying it in concrete?"

"That's an option too. Compact it in gravel, then pour a slab over it. Maybe make a nice patio out of the project. Whatcha got in mind, Carlotta?"

"Oh, just thinking. Frank, is your dad's concrete plant working?"

"Nope. Shut down by those flunky strikers. Thanks to your fat dad's old commie roomie."

"Damn! Oh well, strikes can't go on forever."

"This one might," said Fuzzy gloomily.

"Say, Frank, what time did your mom get home last night?"

"Late, Carlotta. And boy were there fireworks. I came down this morning and found two fresh holes in the plaster board. That's when I decided I better lay low for the day."

"Sorry to hear that, Frank. What were they fighting about?"

"The usual, I guess. Money and sex."

"Frank, your mom and my dad came to your grandmother's house last night."

"They did?" said Fuzzy, alarmed. "Where were you, Carlotta?"

"Outside in the bushes, freezing my balls off."

"So they didn't see you?"

"I don't think so, Frank."

"Good. What were they doing?"

"What do you think they were doing? And in your dead grandmother's bed too."

"Fuck!" said Fuzzy. "That is so gross. You saw them?"

"Heard them mostly."

"God, that's gross," he shuddered. "Carlotta, is it your dad you want to bump off? If so, you can count me in."

"No, Frank. Believe me. Dad is taken care of. He won't be molesting Nancy for long."

"Who's Nancy?"

"Isn't Nancy your mother's name?"

"Hell, no. Her name's Irene. Why? Was the woman named Nancy? Maybe it wasn't really my mom!"

"Frank, it was your mom. Believe me, I recognized the car." (And the bustline.)

"My mom doing it with your dad. I can't believe it. Carlotta, this is weirding me out."

"Welcome to the club, Frank," I said, adjusting my brassiere.

12:45 p.m. I just called Miss Sanders, my old kindergarten teacher in Oakland. Her number was listed—perhaps so concerned parents can reach her any time of the day and night to complain about the progress of their children.

As I dialed the number, I was surprised to see my hand was shaking. Like it or not, back when I was learning to take naps on cue, Miss Sanders was extremely hot stuff in my life. I continue to be strongly attracted to women who can read upside down. When she answered, I disguised my voice.

"Hi, Radmilla. This is George Twisp."

"Who?"

"George Twisp. You remember, you taught my son Nick."

"Oh, yeah," she said, holding her enthusiasm in check. "Hello, George. What a surprise. It must be what? Ten years?"

"Oh, not that long, Radmilla. More like nine."

"I'm sorry about your son turning bad, George. I read about him in the papers here. I hope you don't blame me, George. I did all I could for the little squirt."

"Uh, I'm sure you did your best, Radmilla."

"How's your novel coming, George?"

"Great. I'm on page 12."

"You were on page 12 nine years ago!"

"Yes, but I've done some extensive revisions."

"That's nice, George. How's your lovely wife?"

"I got a divorce, Radmilla. We were incompatible."

"Well, you were certainly incompatible with monogamy, George."

"Are you married, Radmilla?"

"I was, George. He was incompatible with monogamy too. I've been divorced now for three years."

"Radmilla, I've never forgotten you!"

"Well, George, I suppose I haven't forgotten you either. I've tried, God knows, but evidently I failed. What's on your mind?"

"Radmilla, have you ever been to Ukiah?"

"I think I stopped there once. I was on a field trip by bus with 32 six-year-olds to tour a sawmill in Willits. It was a mistake, as I recall, a bad one. Why do you ask?"

"Radmilla, I'm living here in Ukiah now."

"Back to the land, huh, George? Odd, you never impressed me as the hippie type."

"It's quite a cosmopolitan city, Radmilla. I think you'd like it here."

"OK, George, what are you selling? Tour packages? Condos? Mountain cabin time-shares?"

"Radmilla, I'm trying to tell you that I still feel deeply for you."

"You do? I didn't know you felt deeply in the first place, George. You never mentioned it at the time."

"Well, I did and I do. Radmilla, do you have any plans for your Christmas vacation?"

"Well, I thought I'd smoke too much and drink more than I should. Why?"

"Radmilla, darling, would you like to come up here and stay with me? We can get to know each other again."

"And I know exactly how you mean, George."

"We, we don't have to sleep together, Radmilla. Not if you don't want to. At least, not right away."

"Thank you for the offer, George. It's by far the best one I've received all morning."

"Then you'll come?"

"No, George. I don't think so."

"Why not?"

"Have you forgotten the incident in the restaurant? I haven't."

Jesus, I wonder what Dad did!

"Er, Radmilla, I'm, uh, sorry about that. I guess I must have been, uh drunk."

"You were plastered, George. But that's no excuse for bestiality."

"No, I suppose not. But Radmilla, let me tell you, I've never forgotten how wrong I was. I've been tormented by the memory of that night for nine long years."

"It was morning, George. We were having breakfast."

"I've never enjoyed my ham and eggs since, Radmilla."

"Uh-huh. Well, George, I have to go. It was nice talking to you."

"Radmilla, please reconsider. We had something precious once. We can have it again."

"I had the chicken pox once too, George. I don't necessarily want it again though. Have a nice holiday, George. I hope they find your kid."

"I'm in the phone book here, Radmilla, if you change your mind. Don't spend Christmas alone!"

"OK, George. If I get desperate, I'll give you a call. Goodbye." *Click.*

Damn, so much for that plan. I never realized Miss Sanders was so steeped in cynicism. She always brought such wholesome enthusiasm to story hour.

5:37 p.m. I'm back! Four grueling hours of non-stop dress shopping, and nothing to show for it except Carlotta's massively bruised ego. It's hopeless. All the long dresses in my size in Ukiah are strapless, low-cut, or strapless and low-cut. No way I can show up at the Christmas dance in a number like that. I haven't got the build for it. Perhaps Carlotta will have to swallow her pride, bite the sartorial bullet, and go to the ball in a Granny DeFalco hand-me-down.

6:10 p.m. A glimmer of hope. Carlotta called Sheeni for advice and was invited to accompany My Love on a gown-shopping expedition tomorrow to the fashionable boutiques of Santa Rosa. That's the good news. The bad news is we're going with Sheeni's 5,000-year-old mother—who, Sheeni reports, is dying to meet me!

10:05 p.m. Boy, what a night. Never open your door when you're feeling emotionally vulnerable.

While engrossed in post-prandial nail polishing, Carlotta was startled by a knock on the back door. She straightened her dress, donned her wig, touched up her lipstick, and went to investigate.

"Who is it?" she called.

"It's me," replied a familiar voice.

Carlotta opened the door a crack. "Oh, hello, Bruno. What can I do for you?"

Interpreting this question as an invitation, Bruno pushed his way into the kitchen.

"Hi, Carly," he said. "What's up, girl?"

"Up?"

"What's cookin'? What's a hot babe like you doin' all alone on Saturday night?"

"I'm not alone, Bruno," replied Carlotta nervously. "Mom and Dad just stepped out. They went to buy a magazine, *Atlantic Monthly* I believe they said. I expect them back any minute."

"I ain't seen any cars go in and out, Carly. Except for that big Lincoln last night."

"That's, that's my father's car. I expect him back soon, Bruno. You better go. Dad doesn't like me to associate with older men."

Bruno pulled out a chair and sat down at the dinette. "I'll wait, Carly. I ain't got nothing to do. I been wantin' to meet your folks, since we're neighbors and all. What you wavin' your hands around like that for?"

"I'm drying my nails, Bruno."

"What color is that?"

"Hedonistic Folly. Do you like it?"

"It's OK. Looks like red to me. You got any beer, Carly?"

"Fresh out, Bruno. Sorry."

"How about some wine?"

"OK, but you won't like it."

Carlotta poured her uninvited guest a small glass of oxidated rotgut. He gulped it down, smiled, and held out the glass for more.

"Pour me a tall one this time, Carly. This stuff is great. Don't be so stingy."

I complied reluctantly, then poured a glass for myself. Bruno hoisted his tumbler.

"Here's to the girl next door," he said.

We clinked. "Whoever she may be," added Carlotta, swallowing with a shudder.

Bruno took another gulp and stared at my chest.

"How, how's Candy?" Carlotta inquired.

"Don't know," said Bruno, belching. "I dumped the bitch."

"You broke up with Candy?" Carlotta asked, flabbergasted.

"I cut her loose. Told her to peddle her ass somewheres else."

"Why, Bruno? Candy Pringle is gorgeous!"

"That don't make her good in bed," he replied, eyeing Carlotta's charms hungrily. "Besides, the bitch is really stuck up."

"I'm sorry to hear that," I said.

You don't know how sorry!

"It don't bother me none, Carly," he said, drowning his disavowed sorrows in cheap wine.

"Bruno, Candy is the queen of the Christmas dance. Aren't you taking her?"

"The bitch is going with Stinky Limbert. If he lives 'til Friday."

"Stinky Limbert?"

"Stinky Limbert," confirmed Bruno. "A guy who never threw for a touchdown in his whole life. His short life."

"I'm really sorry," repeated Carlotta.

"Don't bother me none," repeated Bruno. "Carly, you want to go to the dance with me?"

I sat back in my chair in stunned surprise. "Sorry, Bruno," I stammered. "I already have a date."

"With who?" he demanded.

"Fuzzy DeFalco."

"Fuzzy DeFalco!" exclaimed Bruno. "You mean that fur-ball manager of the football team?"

"He's a very nice boy, Bruno."

"Carly, that hairy twerp's a worse case than Stinky. He didn't even make the football team for chrissake."

"Bruno, I don't necessarily evaluate my potential escorts solely on the basis of their perceived athletic prowess."

"What'd you say, Carly?"

"Bruno, I don't care that Fuzzy is lousy at sports."

"Well, he ain't pop'lar neither. He ain't no brain trust. He ain't even good lookin'. Why you want to go to the dance with him?"

"Because he asked me and I said I would."

"He could change his mind kinda sudden. Maybe pull a muscle in gym."

"Bruno! Don't you dare do anything to Fuzzy! If I can't go to the dance with him, I'll stay home. And never speak to you again!"

"OK, Carly. Keep your shirt on. Or," he leered, "take it off if you're hot."

"No thank you, Bruno. Please drink your wine and go."

"Carly, are you and this Fuzzy gettin' it on?"

"That is none of your business, Bruno."

"Come to think of it, I seen that punk sneakin' around here. I bet he makes you turn off all the lights too. Carly, you want to know what that guy looks like nekkid? Like a giant pad of rusty steel wool!"

"Bruno, you are insufferable. Please go."

"What'll you do if I don't?" he asked, his voice beginning to slur.

"Bruno, please be a gentleman."

"I want some more wine."

"If I give you more wine, will you go?"

"OK," he replied. "It's a deal. But I'm tired. Let's go finish our wine in the bedroom."

"No, Bruno. We're staying here."

"Come on, Carly," he said, standing up and grabbing my arm. "Let's take a time out in the old locker room."

I pushed the drunken brute away, sending him staggering against the stove.

"Boy, Carly," he said, surprised, "you're pretty strong for a chick. Wanna wrestle?"

I grabbed a bread knife off the drainboard. "Hit the road, Bruno," said Carlotta, standing her ground.

"Is that thing loaded?" asked Bruno, eyeing the foot-long serrated blade.

"Yes, and I'm prepared to use it."

"Carly, I like you," he whined. "Didn't I give you a nice ride on my Harley?"

Bruno piloted a Honda, but I thought it wise to overlook that point.

"I appreciated your thoughtfulness, Bruno. But I don't appreciate rude behavior like this."

"I'm sorry, Carly," he said, rubbing his ham-like hand over his oft-dislocated face. "I, I just like you so much, I want to prove it. The only way a man can!"

I wondered if that was the line that conquered Candy.

"Bruno, the best way you can show your regard for me is to treat me with respect. And leave. Now!"

"OK, OK, Carly. I'm going." He drifted toward the door. "Sorry, if I offended you. Some chicks go for the rough stuff."

"Well, I don't!" declared Carlotta, still clutching the knife.

"Are we still friends, Carly?"

"I guess so, Bruno."

"Then how about a friendly good night kiss?"

"I can't, Bruno."

"Why not?"

"Er, Fuzzy wouldn't like it."

"Fuck Fuzzy!" he said, an unnerving edge of belligerence creeping back into his voice. "I ain't leavin' 'til I get a kiss!"

"That's impossible, Bruno."

"Why?"

"I've, I've got VD."

"No, you don't. Besides, you can't catch the clap from kissin'. Coach said so. So pucker up, Carly. 'Les you want to stand there all night with a knife in your hand."

At that point, diary, I concede I was desperate.

"OK, Bruno. I'll give you a kiss. But I'm keeping the knife. So don't try anything."

"It's a deal. Come here, baby."

Reluctantly, Carlotta walked over to Bruno until they were separated only by the width of a knife blade. Gingerly, conscious of the cutlery between them, Bruno put an immense arm around her shoulder and pulled her to his coarse lips. They kissed. Fireworks on one side (I presume), extreme revulsion on the other. It wasn't so bad after he stopped trying to pry my teeth open with his tongue. Eventually, like root canal surgery or junior high school, it was over.

"Thanks, baby," he said, savoring the salivary aftertastes. "That was nice. Change your mind about the dance?"

"No, Bruno. I promised Fuzzy."

"Too bad. I guess I'll just have to murder Stinky and take Candy."

"You do that, Bruno," Carlotta said. "It sounds to me like an excellent plan. Good night."

"'Night, Carly. Thanks for the wine."

Then, miraculously, he was outside and the deadbolt was clicked safely closed.

And Frank complains that Saturday night is the loneliest night of the week. Sometimes a guy doesn't know when he's well off!

SUNDAY, December 13 — As arranged, Fuzzy dropped by early for a morale-boosting breakfast. We both needed it. Over sweet rolls and coffee cake, I told him about the incident with Bruno.

"Wow, Nick," exclaimed Fuzzy, "I can't believe you actually kissed Bruno Modjaleski on the lips!"

"Frank, I had no choice. It was either that or get dragged kicking and screaming into the bedroom."

"You really think Bruno was ready to rape you, Nick?"

"More than ready, Frank. I guess it's true what the feminists say. Any man is capable of rape, given the opportunity."

"Boy, Bruno would have been in for a real surprise, if he'd tried it. I'd have paid a hundred bucks to see the expression on his dumb face when he got Carlotta's dress off."

"And I'd have paid a thousand dollars not to," I replied. "I'm sure he would have murdered me."

"Nick, do you have a thousand bucks?"

"Of course not, Frank," I replied hastily. "That was merely a figure of speech."

Fuzzy leaned closer over the table. "So, Nick, what was it like?"

"What?"

"Making out with Bruno."

"Pretty damn revolting, if you must know."

"That is so gross, Nick. But hey, if the dude's set on taking you to the dance, I won't stand in your way."

"Forget it, Frank. You're my insurance policy now. You have to take me. And don't let Bruno try to cut in on us on the dance floor."

"He's a big guy, Nick. How am I going to stop him?"

"Frank, I am relying on you to defend Carlotta's honor. That is your role as a guy."

"Not when I'm taking another guy it's not."

"Carlotta is not a guy."

"Hey, Nick. Wake up! Smell the coffee, dude. I swear you and Carlotta are going off the deep end together. Nick, Carlotta is you. She's not a chick."

"I know that," I replied defensively. "I'm not crazy."

"Good, Nick. Glad to hear it. Sometimes I worry. Sometimes Carlotta seems so real even I forget she's you."

"I have to make Carlotta convincing, Frank. She's all that stands between me and ten years in the custody of the California Youth Authority."

"Don't I know it, Nick. That's why I'm sticking my neck out for you."

"I appreciate it, Frank."

"So how's the plan going, Nick?"

"What plan is that?"

"The most important plan: breaking up my mom and your dad."

"Oh. There's been a minor setback, Frank. Turns out the younger and prettier chick I had lined up for Dad wasn't interested in the job. So, I have to go to Plan Two."

"When does Plan Two kick in, Nick? There's still not single Christmas present for me in Mom's hiding place."

"Soon, Frank."

As soon as I figure out what Plan Two is.

"It'd better, Nick. If Mom waits any more, the stores are going to be all cleaned out. I don't want to get up Christmas morning and find a bunch of pawed over junk."

Which is more than I'll find under my nonexistent tree. That reminds me, I haven't bought Sheeni's present yet.

"Don't worry, Frank," I said reassuringly.

"You're the guy with the worries, Nick."

"Why's that?"

"Bruno. If he ever gets the scoop on Carlotta, he'll know he was making out with a guy. Jocks like him don't laugh that stuff off. You'd be dead meat for sure."

"Well, it was his idea!"

"I don't think he'll see it that way, Nick."

Fuzzy had a point there.

"Well, Bruno's not going to find out," I declared.

"I hope not, Nick. You better pull the blinds down when you take a bath. Just to be on the safe side."

Good advice. It would be just like that no-neck Peeping Tom to start loitering about in the shrubbery.

7:45 p.m. I'm back from the big city. What a delightful day! We went to the downtown Santa Rosa mall, another big mall, plus the fashionable east-side shopping center. After approaching a state of near despair, Carlotta found a lovely azure chiffon dress with three-quarter-length sleeves, beaded bodice with high lace collar, and a daringly scooped out back. I was hesitant at first, but Sheeni insisted it was "perfection personified." A brassiere will be impossible, of course, so I'm not exactly sure yet how I'll work out Carlotta's figure. I may have to strap things on with duct tape. Dress, gloves, and shoes (high heels!) came to $368.17. Being a young woman in the social whirl certainly runs into some tall paper. I wish I had rich parents like Sheeni.

I also had to kick in another $43.89 for a completely useless clutch purse. I may be able to cram in a lipstick, eye shadow, and eyebrow pencil, but what will I do with my blusher and breath mints? Fuzzy may have to lug those. Thank God I don't have to worry about tampons. I'd have to decorate them with rhinestones and wear them as earrings.

That reminds me. Sheeni is insisting I get my ears pierced. Another painful sacrifice for love and I'm still only 14. When will it all end?

For being an ancient wacko religious zealot, Sheeni's mother can let her hair down and be surprisingly pleasant to be around. Of course, long years of intensive practice have made Sheeni a master at maternal manipulation. Under her daughter's skillful cajolery, Mrs. Saunders drove over 150 miles through heavy holiday-shopping traffic, bought us all a nice lunch, and wrote out checks totalling nearly $700 for Sheeni's ball finery.

As for Carlotta and Mrs. Saunders, they got on like two cross-generational soulmates. I think Sheeni's mother approves of Carlotta as a companion for her daughter because she dresses conservatively, is respectful of her elders, and acts like a lady. I also told her at lunch that I was thinking of going into missionary work when I graduated from college. She was thrilled and invited me to attend church with them next Sunday. I also agreed I would help pray for her son's release from the temptations of mortal flesh (Lacey).

Carlotta had some first-hand experience of this herself as she was helping her friend try on dresses. Just the two of us together in nearly a dozen intimate dressing rooms. What a shock when Sheeni prepared to squeeze into that first fuchsia gown.

"Goodness, Sheeni," remarked Carlotta, "you're not wearing a bra."

"Well, I'm looking for something strapless," she replied, tugging up the skin-tight satin. "So I thought I'd better not wear one today. I hope you're not offended."

"Uh, not at all," said Carlotta, sitting down and struggling to think about the stock market. "It's just us girls here."

Carlotta was more modest. She went into dressing rooms alone and obdurately declined her friend's gracious offers of assistance. These brief interludes of solitude also served as welcome cooling off periods for my flagrantly overstimulated nervous system.

"Mutual funds," repeated Carlotta to herself as she struggled into silks, satins, velvets, and chiffons. "Stock mutuals versus bond funds. Which, do you suppose, offers the best opportunity for long-term capital growth and tax-sheltered income? Nope, not this dress. I look like I'm testing for the remake of 'Bride of Frankenstein'."

Despite Sheeni's entreaties, Mrs. Saunders resolutely vetoed every strapless design, finally consenting to a moss green silk dress with spaghetti straps. Still, no one could describe this compromise gown as conservative. Going on, on, and coming off, it registered a cumulative 9.2 on my Richter scale.

To spite Vijay, Carlotta had a change of heart and talked her friend into buying the highest pair of heels in Northern California. I only hope you-know-what doesn't wind up at her escort's eye level.

10:12 p.m. Two hours of labored practice and I can now walk slowly almost ten feet in my high heels before falling on my face. God, how will I ever dance in them? Master that, and I'll be ready to join the Flying Wallendas. I wonder how Fuzzy would react if I told him Carlotta was only capable of slow dancing? It's not like I would insist it be cheek-to-cheek.

10:51 p.m. I just heard some rustling noises outside in the bushes. Lovesick Bruno must be on the prowl. I have double-checked all the doors and windows. Every lock is securely bolted; all blinds are closed against prying eyes. The phone is at hand should I have the need to dial 911. I am going to bed, where I shall not ponder investment alternatives, but shall reflect freely on my impressions of the day. I have several powerful ones in urgent need of vigorous contemplation.

MONDAY, December 14 — No news in today's paper about the mysterious Nick Twisp disappearance. Good. I hope the FBI loses interest and goes back to wiretapping Teamsters and harassing environmentalists.

As expected, Bruno was waiting for Carlotta this morning in the alley.

"How about another kiss, baby?" he cooed.

"I'm not your baby," replied Carlotta coldly. "And I feel my herpes flaring up again. I'm getting another ugly chancre on my lip."

"Where?" he demanded.

"I've covered it over with lipstick, Bruno. I had to. The pus was beginning to drain."

That cooled his ardor in a hurry.

In sewing class, Mrs. Dergeltry gave Carlotta a C- on my skirt. She said the seams were uneven, the zipper was crooked, and the level of the hem "varied more than three inches across the garment." Well, what does she expect from an amateur? I say if you want a decent skirt, go buy one in a store. It's those ladies in the Hong Kong sweatshops who really know how to sew. Of course, Gary got an A on his bolero pants, which I dare him to wear to school. One step inside the front doors and he'd be another victim of the whims of fashion.

My next sewing project is a blouse to match my skirt. After anxious contemplation of the pattern, I have concluded it is a technical impossibility. Darts! Buttonholes! Seams that curve! What a nightmare! Why not a few nice handkerchiefs or a scarf instead? I wonder if it's too late to wrangle a transfer back to woodshop?

Then, in world cultures class, Dwayne took a break from snapping Carlotta's bra straps to invite her to be his date for the Christmas dance. In this instance, I felt tact was uncalled for.

"Dwayne," declared Carlotta, "I wouldn't go with you to a dogfight in Tijuana."

Dwayne looked intrigued. "I ain't heard about that, Carlotta. Who's arrangin' it? Maybe I could enter Kamu, my wonder dog."

"Why don't you," replied Carlotta, sensing an entrepreneurial opportunity. "The entrance fee is only $25. Payable to me."

"That's a lot of money," he said doubtfully.

"Yes, but the grand prize is $5,000."

"OK, I'll ask my mom. So you wanna go to the dance with me, Carlotta? Huh? Huh?"

"No thanks, Dwayne. I'm already spoken for. I'm going with Fuzzy DeFalco."

"Fuzzy, huh?" said Dwayne, obviously disappointed. "Then who should I ask, Carlotta?"

"Why not Janice Griffloch?"

"She the girl what beat up that spic Vijay?"

"That's her. Why not ask her? I hear she has the hots for you."

"OK," said Dwayne, "I will!"

At lunch, hurrying to commandeer a vacant chair beside Sheeni, Carlotta was amazed to encounter her sartorial mirror image.

"Tina," said Carlotta, "where did you get that lovely outfit?"

"Like it, Carlotta?" Tina Manion asked, twirling around. "It's the Mussolini Revival!"

"It's a breath of fresh, fashion-conscious air," I replied.

"Carlotta," said Tina, gripping her shawl, "I've been trying to reach you all weekend. I figured out who your father is. He wasn't a writer at all!"

"I know," I said, interrupting her. "Inspired by your interest, I put the question directly to Mother. She broke down and told me everything. My dad was Adolf, her Rumanian masseur."

"Oh, dear," said Tina. "Are you sure?"

"Positive. Mother finally produced the missing birth certificate. What a shock to discover one is half Rumanian. But what a rich heritage to explore. Would you like a massage sometime, Tina?"

"Oh dear," she replied anxiously. "I hope there's time to change my news article."

"Why, what's the problem?"

But my fashion double had abruptly fled.

Carlotta also missed a deadline. When she arrived at the Scholarly Elites' table, her chair was occupied by a dwarfish Indian speaking French. Seething inwardly, I dined at the Shunned Loners' table, from which seat I was able to observe zit-plagued Janice Griffloch administer a sharp rebuke to the jaw of a despised bra-strap snapper.

Carlotta received her second dance invitation of the day after school at the lunch counter of Flampert's variety store. The assignation was made hurriedly during art class, at the request of you know who. Though surprised, Carlotta agreed. I assumed Trent wished to discuss his situation with Apurva. His actual intention, when haltingly but charmingly expressed, nearly knocked me off my stool.

"You want me to go to the dance with you?" asked Carlotta, dumfounded.

"Yes," replied Trent softly. "If you'd like to, Carlotta."

"But Trent, what about Apurva?"

"Apurva's been banned from my life, Carlotta. Her parents found out about us."

"So?"

"Well, so I can't see her any more."

"Why not?" Carlotta demanded.

"What do you want me to do, Carlotta? Sneak around?"

"That's a good place to start. Apurva loves you, Trent. Who cares what her parents say?"

"I do. I think we should respect their cultural traditions."

"Even if their tradition is dogmatic parental fascism?"

"That's our interpretation of it, Carlotta, as Americans. To us, raised in our cultural milieu, their actions seem unfair and heavy-handed."

"They are!"

"Not necessarily, Carlotta. Not in the context of their social structure."

"Is that why you wouldn't sleep with Apurva?" I asked.

"Who told you that?" he demanded, shocked.

"Trent, between Apurva and me, there are no secrets," I lied.

"Well," he conceded, "that's part of it. Her culture believes brides should come to the marriage bed as virgins."

"Her culture also occasionally burns brides when their dowries prove inadequate," I pointed out. "Do you condone that practice as well?"

"Of course not, Carlotta. Why are you getting so upset?"

I ignored the question. "OK, besides cultural qualms, what else is holding you back?"

"You'll misinterpret what I say."

"Try me, Trent."

"Carlotta, Apurva is a very beautiful girl, I mean, woman."

"That's a fair statement," I conceded.

"How do I know I love Apurva? I mean intellectually. How do I know I'm not just entranced by her physical beauty?"

"What difference does it make?"

"It means a great deal to me."

"I see, Trent. So you thought you'd ask out somebody less attractive to see if you can divorce aesthetics from love."

"That wasn't the only reason, Carlotta. I do like you. You're very... offbeat."

"Trent, you don't love someone intellectually. You love them with your body. Physical appearance is a powerful source of desire. Believe me, I know."

"Beauty is an accident of genetics and societal conventions," he retorted. "What about the unlucky people? Don't they have an equal right to be loved?"

"Sure. And they are—by other ugly people."

"I wish I were ugly," he said, sipping his coffee. "Then if someone said they cared for me, I'd know they were sincere."

"Yes, unless you were rich or well-connected or sang rap songs or juggled flaming torches or distinguished yourself in a thousand other ways. There's always room for doubt, Trent, if you want to play those games."

"I do feel strongly for Apurva," he admitted. "I think about her incessantly. Especially when I walk her dog."

"Then make love to her, Trent. She wants you to, quite badly."

"You've spoken to her on this topic, Carlotta?"

"At length, Trent. Believe me, she's made up her mind. Taking her to bed would not be an act of cultural imperialism."

"I'm too young for marriage, Carlotta."

"Apurva does not expect marriage, Trent. She's a modern woman living in a global culture. She realizes young love can be transitory."

"Thank you, Carlotta. You've given me much to think about."

"Don't think, Trent. Act!"

"I'll try, Carlotta. If I require assistance, can you serve as our go-between? Apurva's parents aren't likely to suspect you."

"I'd be glad to, Trent."

"That still doesn't give me a date for the dance. Apurva could never get permission. Are you available, Carlotta?"

"Sorry, Trent. I'm spoken for. But I have a suggestion."

"What's that?"

"If you're really serious about separating aesthetics from love, ask Janice Griffloch."

Trent paled under his perfect tan. "Janice Griffloch. Yes, that is a suggestion worth considering."

Carlotta ordered another piece of pie. This day she could afford to indulge her sweet tooth. Trent was picking up the tab.

When I got home, Carlotta phoned Sheeni immediately. After a warm exchange of pleasantries with Mrs. Saunders, I was connected with My Love.

"Sheeni, I wanted to tell you, before you heard it from someone else: Trent Preston just asked me to the Christmas dance, 40 minutes ago in Flampert's variety store."

"You're kidding, Carlotta."

"No, and I want you to know I refused him. Out of loyalty to you."

"I appreciate that, Carlotta. But hadn't you already promised to go with Fuzzy?"

"Fuzzy would have released me from that obligation. He is more flexible, Sheeni, than you imagine."

"What did Trent say when you turned him down?"

"He was disappointed, of course. I suggested someone else. Someone I think you may approve of."

"Not Apurva?" asked Sheeni suspiciously.

"No. Janice Griffloch."

"Oh, Trent would never ask her, Carlotta."

"I think he may be seriously considering it."

"But why?" Sheeni demanded.

"He wants to separate beauty from affection."

"Well, in that case Janice Griffloch would be an appropriate place to start. Well, Carlotta, now we have another reason to look forward to Friday night."

"It should be quite exciting," I agreed.

"At my suggestion, my brother's volunteered to drive us all to the dance, Carlotta. It's such an inconvenience that Vijay and Fuzzy don't have their licenses."

"Your brother Paul?" I asked doubtfully.

"Yes. He says he's looking forward to seeing you in your ball gown, Carlotta."

I'll bet he is.

"Oh, and Carlotta," she continued, "I've made an appointment for you to get your ears pierced tomorrow after dinner."

"Sheeni, I think I should mention there's a history of hemophilia in my family—on the Rumanian side."

"Hemophilia only affects males, Carlotta. Don't be a coward. We all have to make sacrifices for beauty. Don't you want to look your best for Fuzzy?"

"Yes," I lied.

"I'm going to loan you my blue sapphire studs, Carlotta. They'll go nicely with your dress. That is, if you're healing properly."

I think I'm going to be sick.

8:20 p.m. The phone just rang as I was working on my physics problems. It was Fuzzy, calling in a state of extreme excitement.

"Hi, Nick," he said. "I've got some amazing news."

"Me too, Frank. You're never going to believe this. Trent just asked Carlotta to the dance."

"Really? Man, Carlotta must be foxier that she looks. That's going to work out perfectly."

"What do you mean?" I asked suspiciously.

"I just talked to Heather. And guess what?"

"She's pregnant from unprotected phone sex?"

"No, Nick. She's coming here! For a visit!"

"That's nice, Frank. Your parents said it was OK?"

"Are you nuts, Nick? The parents are out of the loop. Hers and mine. She's telling her parents she's visiting Darlene in Salinas."

"But where will she stay?" I asked, as a dreadful realization dawned. "Forget it, Frank. No way is she staying here."

"But why not, Nick? You've got lots of room. She can take the bed and Carlotta can camp out on the sofa. It's nice and soft."

"I've already slept on that couch, Frank. It's registered with the torture committee of Amnesty International."

"OK, Nick. Heather and I can take the couch."

"Frank, if Heather stays here, I'll have to be Carlotta 24 hours a day!"

"Aw, we can tell Heather."

"No way, Frank. If she blabs to anyone at her school, and you know she will, chicks always do, Bernice's parents will nail my scalp to their living room wall. I have a better idea. Why not stay at your Uncle Polly's house? He has a hot tub."

"It's way out in the boondocks, Nick. Besides, who wants to get in a hot tub your uncle croaked in—even with Heather? That is so gross."

"Well, it's your grandmother's house, Frank. I suppose I can't refuse. When is Heather arriving?"

"That's what's so great, Nick. She's coming on the bus Thursday night. So we can go to the Christmas dance. I can go with Heather and Carlotta can go with Trent."

"No way, buster. I turned Trent down. You have a date with me, remember?"

"But, Nick, Trent is better looking than me. And more popular too."

"I agree, Frank, but you have one sterling quality in your favor."

"What?"

"You're not interested in getting into my pants."

"Trent might not try anything, Nick. Not on a first date."

"I can't take that chance, Frank. No, it's you and me, kid. Heather can stay home and watch TV."

"Wait, I know, Nick. All three of us can go. I can dance with Heather for the slow dances and with Carlotta for the fast ones."

"Not the really fast ones, Frank. Carlotta may have to sit those out. But how do you propose to explain this terpsichorean *ménage à trois* to Heather?"

"I'll just say Carlotta's my cousin. My homely cousin I promised to take to the dance 'cause nobody would invite her. Heather will understand."

"Frank, Carlotta has had three legitimate offers. She's very popular."

"I know, Nick. Don't get sore. Carlotta is quite a babe, for a guy."

"When did you say Heather was arriving?"

"Thursday night. She's coming by bus. One more thing, Nick."

"What?"

"While Heather's staying there with you, you have to promise me you'll keep your filthy mitts off her."

"Frank, I'm going to be dressed like a chick the whole time! How can I put the moves on her?"

"Yeah, that's a point. I guess I don't have to worry about Carlotta getting the hots for Heather."

"Nope, just Heather getting the hots for Carlotta."

"What are you saying?" he demanded.

"I'm just saying I won't be held responsible. Lately Carlotta seems to be pretty irresistible. She has tremendous animal magnetism."

"Yeah, well just keep it in your pants, guy."

"Where are you going to be keeping it, Fuzzy?"

"You know where, Nick. As often as possible!"

Some guys have all the luck. Fuzzy gets sex on demand, and I get 24 hours a day of uninterrupted brassieres, panty hose, Writhe, and face powder. I hope my skin doesn't become saturated with cosmetics and break out even more.

Can't write any more. I have to go practice walking in high heels. Maybe I'll put a few Nelson Eddy records on the gramophone and see if I can stumble around to the beat. I realize now how unfair life can be. Fred got all the glory, but it was Ginger who was doing all the work.

TUESDAY, December 15 — In homeroom this morning Janice Griffloch floated about looking as if she had just won the state lottery, received a full scholarship to Stanford, and been canonized by the Pope. This week will probably go down as the high point of her dreary life. I wonder if she realizes she owes all this improbable happiness to me?

Vijay came to physics class looking strangely incomplete. He was missing his nice cast. If only he'd catch the bad flu that's going around. I wonder if multiple contusions and a sprained arm weaken the immune system? They certain haven't impaired the large portion of his brain devoted to bad-mouthing Nick Twisp. And Carlotta only catches the comments in English. God knows what vile slander the turncoat Republican's been spreading in French.

As Miss Najflempt warmed up the VCR in world cultures class, Dwayne slipped Carlotta $5 as a down payment on his dogfight entry fees. His mother vetoed his budget request, so he is forced to pay on the installment plan. Carlotta agreed, but stipulated that button-fumbling and bra-strap snapping must cease.

"Aw, I only do it 'cause I like you," Dwayne complained.

"Well, I don't appreciate it one bit," replied Carlotta. "How would you like it if I snapped your athletic supporter straps?"

Dwayne leered. "Would you really do it, Carlotta? Huh? Huh?"

"Certainly not," she sniffed.

Believe it or not, Dwayne has a date for the dance. He will be escorting Sonya "The Refrigerator" Klummplatz, a sweet girl I know from sewing class. Sonya and Carlotta have become fast friends, perhaps because they both bear scars from the stinging barbs of cruel restroom graffiti. Sonya, for one, doesn't turn the other cheek. She makes a regular tour of the facilities, scrawling under every derogatory allusion to her weight, "Up yours, twinky!" in vivid purple ink.

"Sonya," inquired Carlotta in sewing class, "is it true you and Dwayne Crampton are now an item?"

"I guess a tiny one," she replied, taking straight pins out of her mouth. "I said I'd go to the dance with the guy."

"When did he ask you?"

"He didn't, Carlotta. His mom called my mom last night. I guess the boob was too shy to ask me."

"Boys can be reserved at times. Do you like him?"

"I think he's a creep. But he's my ticket to the dance."

"Watch the guy," confided Carlotta. "He may try something."

"I hope so," whispered Sonya. "I don't know about you, Carlotta, but I'm ready to lose my girlish reserve. In a big way."

"You don't care who the guy is?" I asked, shocked.

"Well, I'd prefer it was someone like Trent Preston. But he hasn't been pestering me for dates lately."

"Damn, Sonya," said Carlotta, "you should have said something yesterday. I could have fixed you up!"

Lunch was another nightmare of Sheeni monopolization by my dwarfish rival. Carlotta sat, somewhat self-consciously, with Sonya at the Zaftigs' table. We munched our sandwiches and studied Trent, dining in aesthetic disquietude two tables away with Janice Griffloch.

"He's not smiling," observed Sonya.

"He's trying to," Carlotta replied. "He's looking at her with interest."

"He's counting her pimples, Carlotta."

"Look, Sonya. He's sort of smiling now."

"He's come up with the grand total: 512, not counting the cherry bomb on her nose."

"Oops, he stopped smiling."

"Maybe she goosed him under the table. God, Carlotta, hide me! Dwayne's coming this way."

Sonya tossed her sandwich and struggled, against all odds, to make herself inconspicuous.

"No he isn't, Sonya. Look, he's turning the other way."

Across the room, Dwayne lurched off toward the candy bar machine.

"Coward," huffed Sonya. "I bet the creep ignores me until the dance. And to think I could have been going with Trent."

"Sorry, Sonya," said Carlotta, "I wasn't thinking."

"I may be heavy," she conceded, "but my skin's OK."

"You have a wonderful complexion," I assured her. "It's just like peaches and cream."

"Stop it, Carlotta," giggled Sonya, flattered. "You're making me hungry."

After lunch, Carlotta cut business math, found a payphone off-campus, and called Miss Penelope Pliny, the secretary at Dad's (and my) former place of employment.

"Progressive Plywood. How may I help you?" answered Miss Pliny in her prim and characteristically business-like manner.

"Hi, Penelope," I said, disguising my voice. "This is George."

"George who?"

"George Twisp. We used to work together."

"Well, one of us worked, George. Have they located your son yet?"

"No. Nick is still away. We're all very concerned."

"You did not sound much like it in the newspaper, George."

"I was misquoted, Penelope. You know how the press is."

"I know, George. All of us here are very sorry to hear of Nicholas' difficulties. Mr. Rogavere is quite alarmed. He has an airline steward friend who is putting up flyers in India."

"Well, tell Roger not to go to any special trouble. I'm sure Nick will turn up one of these days."

"I shall inform him of your lack of concern, George. I do not believe it will surprise him. Nor alter his efforts."

"How is Roger, Penelope?"

"Very well, it would appear, for a single man living alone. He is at present devoting much of his spare time to experimenting with the regional cuisines of Portugal."

"And you, Penelope, how are you?"

"I am well enough, George. Why do you inquire?"

"Penelope, I don't know if you were aware of it at the time, but you made an extraordinarily powerful impression on me."

"I can assure you, George, that was not my intention."

"Perhaps not, Penelope. But you have captured my heart."

"You may consider it returned, George. I have no use for the affections of a plagiarist."

"Penelope, try to understand. I had to terminate that business trip to Oregon. I discovered people were administering hallucinogenics to my son. Desperation drove me to an unspeakable act. Is there no way I can regain your esteem?"

"On the contrary, George, the incident to which you allude produced no diminution in my regard for you. It merely confirmed the correctness of my initial impressions of your character. I am sorry, George, this call appears to be one of a personal nature. Mr. Preston requests that this line be reserved for business matters. I must go."

"Penelope, may I call you at home?"

"For what purpose?"

"Penelope, Nick needs a mother. I believe you are that woman!"

"I believe you are mistaken, George. If Nicholas is in need of a parent, it is a father that he wants. Goodbye."

"But, Penelope, wait . . ."

Click.

Damn. Another strikeout for Dad. Miss Pliny wouldn't touch my father with a ten-foot pole, and she's in the statistically desperate age group too. No, if I am to fix up Dad with someone younger and prettier, it will have to be with someone he has never met. I wonder how much an emergency personals ad campaign would cost?

In art class Trent Preston painted a disturbing, Rhyderesque view of a fierce winter gale assaulting the Santa Cruz coast. In the foreground a fallen windsurfer floated lifeless in the churning seas.

"Is that you by any chance?" asked Carlotta solicitously.

"It is my rapacious, overweening ego," replied the painter darkly.

"I see, Trent. And how are things with Janice?"

"Fine, Carlotta," he muttered. "I'm beginning to get in touch with her pain."

"Splendid," replied Carlotta. "The heart beats when the spirit bleeds."

"Life is eternal misery," he declared.

"And then you die," pointed out Carlotta.

"From nothing to nothingness," he said.

"Oblivion, the final frontier," Carlotta added.

"Every breath is a foretaste of death," he observed.

At that point Carlotta desisted. One cannot hope to compete in nihilism with someone dating Janice Griffloch.

After school I hurried to the library, where I found Apurva in her usual spot—now under the watchful supervision of her mother. Apurva greeted me with affection, introduced Carlotta to Mrs. Joshi, and asked if we might be permitted to chat privately.

"You must first promise me that you won't discuss that boy," said Mrs. Joshi severely.

"I promise, Mother," replied Apurva.

After her mother moved reluctantly to a table across the room, Apurva turned eagerly to Carlotta. "And how is my dear Trent?"

"Apurva, I thought you promised not to speak of him?"

"I am keeping my promise, Carlotta. Mother did not specify the boy. I am not speaking of a great many boys."

"That's true, Apurva. Your Jesuit training is beginning to serve you well. I have spoken to Trent. He loves you."

"And I him. More than ever. What news do you bring of him?"

"He wants to get together with you."

"Not to read poetry, I hope? I enjoy poetry, Carlotta. But I feel I've had a sufficiency of verse."

"No, Apurva. Trent is resolved to make love to you."

"When?" she asked urgently.

"Whenever you are able."

"They cannot watch me forever. I shall get away—as soon as I can."

"Good, Apurva. In the meantime, to divert suspicion, Trent has asked Janice Griffloch to the Christmas dance."

"He has what!?" she demanded.

Across the room, Mrs. Joshi looked up in surprise. Carlotta motioned to her friend for caution.

"Don't be alarmed, Apurva. Trent has taken this unpleasant step at my suggestion."

"But why? Who is this Janice person? What does she look like?"

"Don't worry, Apurva. She is reliably unattractive. I can assure you Trent has no feelings for her."

"But why is he taking her to the dance?"

"Because, Apurva, you are unavailable."

"Then why doesn't he simply stay home?"

"He can't do that, Apurva. He has a social obligation. He's the best-looking and most popular boy in the school."

"I shall never understand you Americans. In India, such a step by Trent would be an unforgivable act of infidelity."

"Well, Apurva, in this country it is a selfless act of devotion. Trent must endure Janice because he has given his heart to you."

"The dear, darling boy," sighed Apurva. "I must try to curb my feelings of jealousy and be more understanding."

"Yes, and some of our redwood trees are many centuries old," said Carlotta, noting Mrs. Joshi's approach.

"Apurva," she said, "it is time to go. Your father will be returning from his office soon."

"Yes, Mother. Thank you, Carlotta. I found our chat most valuable. I do so love the forest."

"The forest has much to give," noted Carlotta, "if you are open to its embrace."

"I am," replied Apurva, with conviction. "Be assured of that!"

8:10 p.m. Can't write much. In desperate agony. Two heavy slugs of metal have brutally pierced my body. I feel like John Dillinger five minutes after the movie ended. With every beat of my heart, twin throbs of stereo pain stab into my being. Now I know why women get their ears pierced. Once they've survived this ordeal of mutilation, they can face the discomforts of childbirth with equanimity.

Ours is a barbaric species. We rend our bodies to adorn ourselves with hoops of gold. Bernice Lynch had six perforations in each lobe. No wonder she was mentally unstable; the torment must have unhinged her reason.

I have been gulping aspirin non-stop for 90 minutes. No relief in sight. Should I dial 911? Clearly, morphine must be administered soon.

9:15 p.m. Just found bottle of mystery pills in back of medicine cabinet. Label says "analgesic." Looked it up, means "relieves pain." Expiration date is June, 1974. Have swallowed four anyway. Hoping for the best. Ears feel like pack of angry pitbulls are clamped to them.

10:05 p.m. Dogs have released their grip. Mellowness has been achieved. Have been admiring my new gold posts in the bathroom mirror. Sheeni's right. They produce a remarkable alteration in one's appearance. Left one is oozing a drop of blood now and then. Makes for an eye-catching effect. Be a hit at vampire parties.

Numbness is exquisite. How much better life would be if the human nervous system were equipped with an on/off switch. Have stumbled upon a wonderful, fabulous drug. Only 19 precious pills remaining in bottle. Wonder if it's too late to get the prescription refilled? Wonder how many cases of drug addiction result every year from unregulated teen ear-piercing?

WEDNESDAY, December 16, 4:52 a.m. — Dogs are back, angrier than ever. Swallowed two more pills. Ugly scab on left ear. Both lobes turning odd shade of green-orange. Wonder if that clerk knew what she was doing? Perhaps we shouldn't have had such a major operation performed in a discount jewelry store. Not a single trained medical doctor on the premises. Wonder if they do abortions in the back room? What if both ears turn black and fall off? No way Fuzzy would take Carlotta to the dance in that case. Lonely, unloved, and earless—what a blow to one's social hopes.

7:28 p.m. High school on powerful narcotics. A profoundly mellow experience. The struggle for status now suspended. Pressures to conform on hold, academic competition in abeyance, sexual anxieties at rest, even corrosive boredom dissolved in the warm puddle of frivolous time.

Carlotta had a wonderful day. Rode to school with kind Bruno on his motorcycle and enjoyed it immensely. Pleasant hullabaloo in homeroom as school newspaper was distributed. Flattering front-page profile of yours truly by lovely and talented Tina Manion. Curious blank spaces in headline and story where text had been excised by emergency application of acid to printing plate (process explained by apologetic author in chance hallway encounter; I assured her deletions were of no consequence to me). Much comment in classes throughout day on Manion revelations. Student body abuzz with speculation about matters relating to my feminine alter ego's ancestry. Carlotta chose to remain above the fray. Was assured by Sheeni in physics class that my ears were progressing normally. A great relief. At lunch Fuzzy DeFalco posed several pointed questions regarding missing avuncular cash wad and recent Carlotta extravagances. She preferred to discuss therapeutic effects of a remarkable wonder drug. Gave two tablets to Fuzzy; he quickly dropped interest in errant cash. Later, Carlotta for first time entered into the spirit of business math class. Enjoyed learning about percent mark-ups and mark-downs. Spent study hall with Sonya writing "Fat Power!" on walls of girls' bathrooms (and boys' too?). Slipped two pills to Trent in art class. He painted anguished nude self-portrait, attracting much interest from classmates and a cautionary lecture from Mr. Thorne. In health class, watched a video on the evils of drug abuse. Felt the film was sensationalist and one-sided. Rode home with Bruno and possibly kissed him in the alley. Just swallowed final three pills. Feel sleepy. Think I'll hit the sack early tonight.

THURSDAY, December 17 — I seem to have lost a day of my life. All I have to show for yesterday is a wretched hangover, strange gaps in my memory, and some cryptic entries in my journal. At least my ear crisis seems to have passed. The swelling is starting to go down, and the angry pitbulls have given way to petulant chihuahuas.

Carlotta had a trying day at school. If she ever learns how to write, Tina Manion will have a great future ahead of her in tabloid journalism. Her error-riddled article, made even more inflammatory by titillative censorship, could not have been more recklessly sensationalist. It postulated that Carlotta was the offspring of a famous celebrity, then teasingly, maddeningly withheld the name. When pressed, when pestered, when harangued by curious classmates, Carlotta could only smile wanly and deny any knowledge of the affair. She did characterize as false the reported claims that her mother had won an Academy Award and had spurned an offer of marriage from James Dean, breaking his heart with tragic consequences.

"It's all a mistake," became modest Carlotta's standard reply to queries. "I think they must have me confused with someone else. No, I have no intention of going into films myself. Yes, the Mussolini Revival is all the rage in Hollywood now. Why else do you suppose I dress like this?"

Even Sheeni took advantage of our friendship to make her own discreet inquiries into Carlotta's parentage.

"My father was Rumanian," Carlotta replied. "With marvelous hands. He wanted to be a concert pianist, but the Depression intervened, so he became a masseur instead. He died when I was a baby."

"I'm sorry, Carlotta," said Sheeni. "What did he die of?"

"Acute liniment poisoning. It was a common occupational hazard at the time."

"So you never really knew him?"

"No, but people tell me I've inherited his touch. Would you like a massage sometime?"

"Possibly," replied Sheeni noncommittally. "We'll see."

Boy, some people charge big money for massages. I can't even give them away.

6:35 p.m. Carlotta has eaten my lonely dinner and is awaiting the arrival of Fuzzy and Heather. My lipstick is freshened, my wig is combed, and my bust is situated precisely where nature might have placed it. I have been instructed by my friend to say a few words of greeting, then immediately excuse myself for several hours. Fortunately, the library is open late tonight. Otherwise, I'd have to freeze to death outside while Fuzzy undertakes his grueling ascent of the Orgasm Pass.

7:20 p.m. A slow night at the library. Literature, I fear, is on the wane. Perhaps I should reconsider my vocational aspirations. If I abandon writing, what can I do instead? Being a psychologist has a certain appeal. You get paid extravagantly well to sit around and listen to the most intimate dirt. The hours are good and you can ask attractive women, in your soberest professional manner, what really turns them on. I'm told you also get an invaluable perspective on your own neuroses.

Heather looked rosily robust from her walk through the night air from the bus station. I had forgotten she was so athletically statuesque. I wonder if she often wears sweaters that tight? When she removed her coat, one could almost sense a sudden tension grip the room. I knew then one of us would have to leave. Too bad it turned out to be Carlotta.

10:05 p.m. Fuzzy just said his farewells to Heather and departed, reluctantly, for home. He will have to hurry if he is to avoid parental censure. He looked fatigued but fulfilled, which, from the condition of my bedroom and his guest, I believe him to be. Heather is now taking a bath in the bathroom with the door ajar. This could be a strenuous weekend for us all.

11:10 p.m. Five minutes until lights out. I am in my disheveled room; Heather is bedded down, in a state of advanced nudity, on the sofa in the living room. We had a nice chat earlier when she emerged—pink, steaming, and naked—from the bath.

"Oh, hello," said Carlotta, her glasses suddenly fogging. "Would, would you like a robe?"

"That's OK," replied Heather, bending over to rifle her bag beside the sofa. "You keep it nice and toasty in here." She brought out a brush and began to comb the long wet tresses that fell in brown cascades over her gleaming chest.

"I do like a warm house," observed Carlotta, hastily wiping her glasses. "Did, did you have a nice bath?"

"Scrumptious, Carlotta. I'm so relaxed. I'll sleep like a baby tonight."

Well, that makes one of us, I mumbled under my breath.

"What did you say, Carlotta?"

"Oh, nothing, Heather. I was just thinking about the stock market. How, how do you stay in such marvelous shape?"

"B-ball," she replied. "I scored 32 points against Holy Names Academy last weekend. We murdered those weinies. Do you play, Carlotta?"

"Uh, no. Not much. Sports are not my thing."

"Too bad," she replied. "You really ought to give it a try, Carlotta. Fuzzy and I are totally committed to athletics. That's why I love the furry critter. 'Course, I'm a little top-heavy for basketball, but he gets a kick out of it."

Yes, I could see where he might.

"So you're Fuzzy's cousin," she continued. "Funny, you don't look anything like him. You don't even look Italian."

"I'm from the Rumanian side of the family," I explained. "We're more intellectual and less hairy."

"Bet you're glad of that, Carlotta. Fuzzy's the hairiest guy I ever met. I'm ticklish too, so we have to be careful when we get it on."

"Why's that?" I asked.

"If we get too close, I start laughing hysterically."

"How do you manage, Heather?"

"Oh, we do somehow. Where there's a will, there's a way."

Carlotta smiled, but could put no faith in the veracity of that aphorism. I often have the will, yet find the way impeded at every turn. At the moment, I am in the grip of a particularly powerful will, but must lie here in my lonely room and stifle it.

In case of emergency visitations from my guest, Carlotta has retired to bed in her wig, glasses, make-up, nightgown, and brassiere. When you're not used to it, sleeping in a brassiere seems extremely strange. I am trying to keep the lid closed on that can of worms. If I permitted myself to dwell on it, many aspects of my present life might begin to seem peculiar.

FRIDAY, December 18 — The day of the big dance. The last day of school before Christmas vacation. The first day of the rest of my life. And, if memory serves me correct, Dad's 45th birthday. I think I may have a plan for celebrating that grim milestone of middle age.

My houseguest continues to be comfortable in her body. While Carlotta munched her toast and looked on enviously, Heather cleared a space in the living room and performed 15 minutes of vigorous nude aerobics—elevating her pulse rate and nearly quadrupling mine. The leg extensions, I observed, were particularly invigorating.

"Come on, Carlotta," invited Heather, not pausing. "Join in."

"Sorry, I can't," I replied, thankful again for the fullness of my skirt. "I'm don't want to be late for school. What will you do today, Heather?"

"Fuzzy's cutting school," she replied, touching her toes. "He's coming over."

"I'll bet he is," muttered Carlotta ruefully.

"Look, Carlotta. I can touch the floor with the palms of my hands."

Carlotta looked. It was a remarkable sight.

In the alley, Bruno blocked Carlotta's way and demanded a kiss.

"Sorry, Bruno. I just came from my doctor."

"What's the trouble, Carly? Knocked up?"

"They think it might be leprosy. I have to start radiation treatments tomorrow."

Bruno took two anxious steps backward.

"Too bad, Carly. Hey, who's that chick staying with you?"

"God, Bruno! Can't a girl have any privacy at all?"

"She's cute. Who is she?"

"If you must know, she's my married sister from Boise."

"Does she have a date for the dance?"

"Bruno, I told you she was married."

"That's fine with me. I ain't lookin' for a steady thing."

"Forget it, Bruno," said Carlotta, hurrying on. "Murder Stinky and go back to Candy. I still think that's your only viable option."

Bruno struggled to think. "Yeah, Carly. You might be right."

The Mussolini Revival is starting to catch on. I noticed two more Carlotta clones in the corridors today. Such is the awesome power of the media to mold public tastes.

In physics class, Sheeni slipped Carlotta a small velvet box.

"For the dance," she whispered. "They're my sapphire studs. Guard them with your life."

"Thanks, Sheeni," I whispered, carefully depositing the precious jewels in my purse. "What will you be wearing?"

"I'm borrowing Mother's diamonds. What time is your hair appointment?"

"My what?"

"Your hair appointment," repeated Sheeni, slightly louder. "Aren't you getting your hair done?"

"Why no," Carlotta said. "Do you think I should?"

"Perhaps we can let the class decide," said Mr. Tratinni, turning around from the blackboard. "Well, what do you say, Carlotta? Shall we take a vote on it?"

"No, sir," I replied, coloring.

I hate it when teachers try to be sarcastic. It's so pathetically inappropriate. Besides, he knew as well as anyone we were only going through the motions today. Education, such as it is, was on hold. The student body was in attendance, but our minds were already on vacation.

At lunchtime Sonya and Carlotta sneaked off campus to the Burger Hovel. While my companion ordered a double chili-cheeseburger, large fries, and a diet rootbeer, I called Fuzzy's house from the parking lot payphone. After three rings Mrs. DeFalco answered. As usual I disguised my voice.

"Uh, you don't know me, Irene. I met a friend of yours at a bar last night. Guy named George."

"George Twisp?"

"I think so. He looked a little like Liberace."

"That's him," she confirmed.

"Yeah, I got to talkin' to ol' George. He just come into some money. Big money. He was buyin' drinks for the house."

"Oh, that's odd. Did he say where he got the money?"

"No, he just said he found a big stash. And wanted to spend it before his ol' lady found out."

"He said that?" she demanded.

"Yeah, something like that. Anyway, he told me about the tapes. And I'm interested."

"What tapes?"

"The video tapes of you and George. He said he had a camera hidden at this house where he found the money. I distribute those kind of tapes, Irene. I can cut you in for some nice cash royalties. What do you say, babe?"

No reply, just the sound of a cigarette being lighted violently.

"Irene, are you there?"

"If you see that lying degenerate," she said, exhaling fiercely. "Tell him I won't forget this!" *Click.*

Sorry to have to go to Plan Three on your birthday, Dad. But I couldn't let you spoil my best pal's holiday.

"Who were you talking to?" asked Sonya, when Carlotta returned and slid into the booth beside her.

"Uh, my broker," I lied. "Sonya, are you getting your hair done this afternoon?"

"Of course, Carlotta," she replied, munching the last of her French fries. "You don't think I'd go to a dance looking like this, do you?"

"I suppose not."

"Why?" she asked defensively. "What's wrong with my hair?"

"Nothing, Sonya. It's absolutely perfect. Going to a hair stylist would be a complete waste of time and money."

"Boy, Carlotta, what's eating you?"

What was eating me? A serious case of Christmas dance cold feet, that's what. Why should I humiliate myself just so I can watch a despised rival dance cheek-to-cheek with The Woman I Love? Of course, I'd probably be even more miserable staying home and imagining it all.

By seventh period, Redwood High was beginning to take on the appearance of a rigorously non-elitist boys' school. Most of the female students had quietly slipped away. How, I wondered could so many clients be accommodated? Were they busing up hairdressers from San Francisco? Not wishing to appear conspicuous or impede the male bonding, Carlotta decided to bail out as well.

When I arrived home, Fuzzy was stretched out prone on the sofa.

"Hi, Carlotta," he said listlessly.

"Hi, Frank. Where's Heather?"

"Downtown getting her hair done."

"Really?" I said, mildly shocked.

"Carlotta, guess what?"

"What Frank?"

"I did it four times today."

"I hope you didn't overdo it, Frank. You don't look very fresh for the dance tonight."

"Why is sex so great, Carlotta?"

"I'm sure I wouldn't know. I think it has to do with enzymes in the brain."

Fuzzy sat up quickly. "That reminds me, Carlotta. What's this I hear about you offering to give Heather a massage?"

"I might have, Frank. I was just trying to be sociable. She looked sort of tense."

"Well, she isn't. So keep your mitts off her."

"Frank, shouldn't you be out picking up my expensive corsage?"

"Yeah, I suppose so," he said, rising heavily from the sofa. "Boy, I feel like I just ran the Boston Marathon—with a brick strapped to my balls."

I pushed the sluggard toward the back door. "Step on it, Frank. Carlotta wants to take a bath before your love slave returns."

"I like your earrings, Nick," he said, grinning. "Have I told you that? They really do a lot for you, guy."

"Thanks, Frank. And suck my girdle snaps."

"Why not?" he said agreeably. "I've sucked everything else today!"

5:20 p.m. Carlotta is ready. She has been washed, shaved, plucked, sprayed with antiperspirants, powdered, perfumed, strapped into exotic undergarments, dressed, and mounted precariously on spike heels. An artificial foam bosom has been affixed with industrial-grade adhesive. Camouflaging cream has been applied to bare, prominently showcased back and shoulder zits. Sprigs of baby's breath, thoughtfully provided by Heather, have been woven artfully into her manmade hair. Sparkling blue sapphires have been inserted through still-raw ear wounds. Cheeks have been rouged, lips chromatically highlighted, eyes outlined in fanciful hues, nails painted, breath chemically freshened.

How does she look? Pretty damn good, if the evidence of Mrs. DeFalco's kitchen mirror is to be believed.

Can't write any more. I have to go hand Heather a towel.

6:20 p.m. Heather is ready, more or less. She has completed the tertiary stages of make-up application, and is now in the anxious touch-up mode. I hope she stops soon. Any more mascara will raise fears of an avalanche. With my ungrudging assistance, she has been encapsulated in a sequined gown the color of highway danger signs (fluorescent cautionary yellow). In front, a daring cantilever obviates the need for straps. No wonder American industry can't compete with the Japanese. The cream of our engineering talent is going into dress design.

Heather and Carlotta have remarked to each other how nice they look 16 times. From repetition comes conviction. Or does it? Oops, I hear a car in the driveway. This is it, kids. Wish me luck.

SATURDAY, December 19, 12:45 a.m. — I'm back. Too wired to sleep. What a night!

Sheeni in her soft jade gown, diamonds glittering, her hair pinned up in bronzed, undulating folds, was a vision: an absolute, heart-stopping black hole of orchid-bedecked pulchritude. In her presence, no light reached the human eye from the feeble radiances of Heather and Carlotta. We might as well have dressed from the castoffs box at the local homeless mission.

As Paul opened the car door for us, Sheeni—arrayed regally on the front seat beside loathsome Vijay—made the introductions.

"Heather, what a surprise. Carlotta didn't tell me you were coming too. How nice you both look. This is my brother Paul."

"It's a pleasure to meet two such charming and lovely ladies," said Paul, smiling at Heather and winking slyly at me.

"How you doin'?" said Heather, indifferent to the tumultuous heaves of her bodice as she dived athletically into the back seat. I nodded shyly and slid sedately in beside her.

"I'm just along for the ride," announced Heather graciously. "Carlotta has first dibs on my guy."

"No, Heather," I insisted, "we're sharing Fuzzy equally. Yours is the prior claim."

"This Fuzzy must be quite a guy," said Paul, starting the engine.

"He's the sparkplug of our team," noted Heather proudly.

Soon we were on our way to pick up our communal escort.

"Carlotta, are your shoes pinching?" inquired Sheeni solicitously. "You appeared to be having difficulty walking."

"Not at all," I replied. "I'm not accustomed to heels this low. Normally, I prefer them much higher."

"I feel like I'm on stilts," said Sheeni. "Vijay, do you mind terribly?"

"Mind what, darling?" he asked presumptuously.

"That I'm wearing high heels."

"Of course not. I believe they are an appropriate pedestal for your beauty."

At that point Carlotta wished she had thought to bring along a blunt instrument.

"Hey, Vijay," said Heather, leaning recklessly forward, "Taggarty told me to tell you she wants you to call her."

"I have nothing to say to that person," replied the two-faced snob, inspecting my companion's décolletage.

"Well, if you do talk to her, tell her I delivered the message," said Heather. "I don't want Miss Bossy Boots on my back all next semester."

"Heather, how is that poor girl Bernice Lynch?" asked Sheeni.

"A lot better, Sheeni. They made her get counseling. She's starting to come out of her shell. She's still obnoxious, but you can say that about a lot of the girls at school. Bernice has this incredible energy now. She's totally committed to her cause."

"What cause is that?" inquired Carlotta.

"Bringing this guy Nick Twisp to justice," replied Heather. "She's always calling the FBI with suggestions."

"Oh," I said weakly, "that's nice."

"I'm certain they'll apprehend him soon," said Vijay. "Criminals always trip up somehow."

I should have filled my clutch purse with ball bearings. Carlotta could have used it as a sap.

Fuzzy was waiting for us on the concrete piazza of his imposing mansion. He got into the back seat, exchanged greetings with the multitude, and handed ribbon-tied boxes to his two dates. Heather opened hers and found a lovely orchid corsage; I opened mine and found a truncated gladiolus with a safety pin stuck through its sawed-off (with a dull machete?) stem.

"Oh, Fuzzy, it's beautiful!" exclaimed Heather.

"Oh, Fuzzy, it's plant material," echoed Carlotta.

Fuzzy copped a nice feel helping Heather attach her flowers to her cantilever. The effect, I felt, was somewhat obscene. And I wondered if the engineers had made allowances in their calculations for the additional strain. Unassisted, Carlotta pinned her pink specimen to her blue dress and examined the result in the mirror of her compact. Just as I expected: I looked like a delegate at a botanists' convention.

"Good news, Carlotta," whispered Fuzzy. "My mom cancelled her date tonight."

"I thought somehow she might," I replied.

Dropping us off at the curb in front of the high school, Paul promised to return promptly at midnight. By hanging onto her date and treading carefully, Carlotta crossed the vast quadrangle without major incident. Sheeni was only slightly more sure-footed, finding it necessarily to grasp Vijay's reptilian hand for stability.

Three senior girls, dateless by reason of appearance, sat behind a table outside the boys' gym and took our tickets. Miss Pomdreck, garbed in a gray, government-issue chaperon's gown, hovered nearby to intercept underage gate-crashers, gang members, stimulant abusers, and trespassers against taste or decency.

"Miss," she said severely to Heather, "please pull up your dress."

Heather gave a half-hearted tug. "It is pulled up," she replied.

Miss Pomdreck frowned, but permitted her to pass. "You look very nice, Carlotta," she said. "How are you feeling?"

"I'm coping," I replied.

"Is that a gladiolus?" she asked.

"No," Carlotta replied, following her companions, "it is an extremely rare species of orchid."

What a transformation! Instead of the dreary, fluorescent-lit scene of countless hoop humiliations, the gym was now a magical fairyland of romantic colored lights, glittering white sand, imitation torches, faux coconuts, artificial starfish, and giant cardboard palm trees. A large computer-printed banner proclaimed the theme: "Christmas in the Islands."

"Isn't this festive!" exclaimed Sheeni, as a freckled junior in a grass skirt hung a tissue-paper lei around her neck. Soon, the wanna-be wahine had graced us all with leis; and Fuzzy, cued by the muse of adolescent humor, had made the obligatory allusion to "getting leied."

"Well, it looks like Hawaii," remarked Vijay, wrinkling his tiny nose. "But it smells like Christmas in the locker room."

"I don't smell anything," replied Carlotta. "Perhaps it's you."

The implacable adversaries exchanged daggerlike glances.

After we greeted our many friends, found a table, sorted ourselves out, and sat down, the women promptly excused themselves to dash to the powder room. Unquestionably, this room smelled like a locker room. It was one. More than once I had showered, stark naked, within its musty walls.

"Oh look," said Heather, as we muscled our way in among the strapless throngs, "they've covered up the urinals. Isn't that cute?"

It was true. Someone had taped a modesty sheet over the ranks of hygienic porcelain.

"Why do you suppose they did that?" asked Carlotta.

"For historical authenticity," replied Sheeni. "They didn't have urinals in colonial Hawaii."

Despite the press of humanity in front of the tiny mirrors, we were able eventually to effect our facial tuneups and return, our allure refreshed, to our impatient escorts.

Hopelessly deadlocked (as usual) over choice of bands, the dance committee had opted to hire an African-American DJ from Oakland. "Are you ready to blast off?" he asked over his powerful sound system from behind his lavish electronic bunker.

"Yes!" roared the crowd.

Very likely not, thought Carlotta.

Throbbing thumps and rumbles. Toxic banging. Nerve-pummeling screeches.

"Carlotta, it's a fast dance," yelled Fuzzy over the din. "You wanna go for it?"

"OK," I said meekly.

Following my date, I tottered toward the dance floor, and—getting into the spirit of the music—began to gyrate spasmodically. I soon discovered that if I didn't actually move my feet, I was able to remain relatively upright. Not too bad, I thought, as I thrashed my arms in time with my rattling eardrums. Probably no worse than Marine boot camp. Nearby, Sheeni and Vijay gyrated similarly in paired apartness. He dances like a girl, thought Carlotta. And where does he get off with those suggestive gestures? Oh, and look. There's Trent and Janice. My God, she looks ghastly. She shouldn't toss her head like that. Her make-up could peel off in a sheet and kill someone. God, when is this dance going to end?

Eventually the tortured rumblings ceased and Fuzzy happily traded in his partner for the preferred model. Carlotta sat on the sidelines and watched Sheeni and Vijay, Fuzzy and Heather, Trent and Janice, Tina and her college stud boyfriend, and Candy and Stinky (among others) drift across the scarred maple like coupled bumper cars. I noted with satisfaction that Sheeni was not permitting the slowness of the tempo to lead to excessive bodily contact. I prayed her commendable restraint stemmed from a distaste for her partner, rather than a desire to preserve the integrity of her corsage.

"Hi, Carlotta," said a voice.

I looked up into a vast cloud of lavender chiffon.

"Sonya, you look great!"

"Carlotta, be honest. Do you think the purple lipstick and eyeshadow was a mistake?"

"Not at all, Sonya. Your imaginative coordination of hues achieves a remarkable chromatic unity. Where's Dwayne?"

"I can't pry the boob away from the refreshment tables. What should I do, Carlotta?"

"Leave it to me. I know how to handle cases like this."

We marched across the floor, turned right at the snow-capped papier-mâché volcano, and entered the luau area. Squeezed into a baby-blue linen suit, Dwayne had stalled beside a large bowl of corn chips and bean dip.

"There you are, Dwayne," I said.

"Hi, Carlotta," he replied, bean dip dribbling down his chins, "what's up?"

"Your snack time, Dwayne. Sonya wants this dance."

"I'm still hungry."

"Dance, Dwayne," I said severely. "Or you forfeit all Tijuana entry fees."

"Oh, all right!" he replied testily. "Just don't boss me!"

Dwayne stuffed in a handful of chips for the road, then let Sonya take his hand and lead him away.

"Hi, Carly," said a large brown Hawaiian with beer on his breath. Garbed only in a loincloth, daubed head-to-toe with fierce war paint, the burly native was brandishing a long, lethal-looking spear.

"Bruno, is that you?"

"It's me, babe. Don't you recognize my pecs?"

"Bruno, what are you doing?" I asked, ignoring his lascivious query.

"They think I'm playing King Kamiwhatshisface in the coronation ceremonies," he whispered. "But I got a different plan. It's time for a human sacrifice, Carly."

"Then again, Bruno, perhaps it's not," Carlotta cautioned. "Think about it, Bruno. Do you want to spend the rest of your life in prison for an impulsive crime of passion?"

"Stinky stole my woman, Carly. He's got to pay."

"Violence never solves anything," I lied.

"It's fourth down and goal-to-go, Carly babe. Time to punt or go for it."

"Well personally, I recommend a punt."

Bruno brazenly inspected my gown. "Wow, Carly. Is all that back yours? No bra, huh? What's holding up your goodies?"

"Excuse me, Bruno," Carlotta answered, edging away. "I have to get back to my date. He looks lonely."

I lied. Across the room Fuzzy was contentedly nuzzling Heather's lower lip. Four times today and the guy was still horny. Just imagine how I feel after all these years of anguished celibacy.

On the way back Carlotta stopped to chat with the DJ.

"Do you by any chance have 'My One and Only Love' by Frank Sinatra?" I asked.

"Be a miracle if I did," he admitted, taken aback. "But I played a 50th wedding anniversary party last week. So I'll take a look."

"I'd appreciate it," I replied.

And so the evening went on. Carlotta gyrated convulsively through the fast dances, Heather was nuzzled hungrily through the slow ones. Then, when we were all seated back at our table, I heard the first, thrilling chords of Frank's All-time Greatest Ballad.

"God," sneered Fuzzy, "who requested the recliner music?"

"Well, I happen to like it," I replied.

"Carlotta," said Sheeni, "you haven't had an opportunity to dance any slow dances yet. I want you to take this dance with Vijay."

The blood froze in my veins; Vijay appeared to be having a similar circulatory seizure.

"Oh, no," I stammered, "Vijay is your date. I couldn't possibly . . ."

But Sheeni was insistent. When she looked into Vijay's eyes and shifted her charm into overdrive, we both realized protest was futile. Grimly I grasped the repellent hand and walked toward the dance floor of doom. Eyes averted, we faced each other, gingerly linked, and—avoiding actual physical contact as much as possible—began to dance. I cringed as a small, sweaty palm planted itself on my naked back.

"Let me lead," hissed my partner.

"Sorry," replied Carlotta, praying earnestly for an immediate out-of-body experience.

As Frank worked his cross-generational magic, couples began flocking to the dance floor. Heather and Fuzzy, Sonya and Dwayne, Candy and her doomed date drifted by. Then, to my horror, Sheeni swept onto the floor—in the arms of Trent Preston. Across the room, Janice fumed—temblors of hate rippling across her facial strata.

Frank crooned, we lurched, Sheeni and Trent glided along like golden swans.

"Carlotta," whispered Heather, leaning close, "I hate to say this, but don't they look perfect together?"

Vijay heard the comment too. We both looked despairingly toward the woman we love. Then, surprisingly, she and her perfect mate floated toward us.

"May we cut in?" asked Trent.

"Of course," replied the eager Vijay.

As we unclinched, I made an instinctual grab for Sheeni, but was swept up in the arms of Trent.

"You look lovely tonight, Carlotta," he said charmingly, as we orbited away from my usurped love.

"So do you," I replied, distracted. "I mean, so does Janice. How are you and she getting on?"

"I'm cured, Carlotta," he replied. "I've seen the light."

"You've had an aesthetic reawakening?" I guessed.

"Precisely, Carlotta. Beauty is my drug. I am desperate for Apurva."

"I can arrange that, Trent," answered Carlotta, as Frank lovingly caressed the final, sweet words of the song. "But you must promise me you'll dance the next dance with Sonya. I insist."

"Gladly, Carlotta," said Trent, withdrawing his dry, patrician hand from my powdered spine to applaud the end of the song. "Which one is she?"

"Sonya's over there. The lovely thing in lavender."

Trent swallowed, then smiled. "Anything you say, Carlotta."

While Janice fumed, Trent danced with Sonya. Then danced with her again. And again.

"Carlotta, your friend seems to have made a surprising conquest," noted Sheeni somewhat sharply.

"Sonya has a winning personality," I pointed out. "Boys find her vivacity intoxicating."

"Yeah," said Heather, "and she has so much of it too."

A sudden eruption of crepe paper lava from the towering volcano heralded the start of the coronation ceremonies. The DJ put on a Don Ho record, six sophomores in grass skirts and bikini tops danced their interpretation of the hula, and King Kamiwhoever marched about growling and making fierce anti-colonial gestures with his spear. Then Bob Bix, glad-handing president of the senior class, introduced the queen's court in ascending order of beauty, popularity, and personality. As each member of runner-up royalty was announced, she was escorted by her noble date to a place of honor beneath the gold-painted throne. Then it was time to introduce the great Queen herself, chosen democratically by secret ballot.

"Ladies and gentlemen," continued Bob, in his oiliest gameshow-host manner, "let us now pay fealty to our Royal Highness, Ruler of the Islands, Daughter of the Volcano, High Priestess of All Christmas Rites and Celebrations, Redwood High School's Loveliest Monarch, Her Royal Highness, Queen of the Christmas Dance—Candace Jennifer Pringle!"

A tumultuous wave of applause, more amplified Don Ho and streaming lava, three pre-school wahines bearing flowers, then Queen Candy herself, escorted by Royal Consort Stinky, mounted the thrown, smiled through her tears, and waved to her adoring subjects. The three wahinettes presented their bouquets, a fourth placed a rhinestone crown upon the royal head, and—as cameras flashed and Miss Pomdreck's camcorder recorded the scene for posterity—King Kamisutra leaned forward to plant the benedictory kiss. He stumbled, his spear slipped from his grasp, its tip punctured the tender flesh below Stinky's left ankle, he howled, the Queen slapped the King, he slugged the Consort, the Consort replied with a knee to the loincloth, they grappled for the spear, the Queen lost her crown and her composure, ladies in waiting screamed and dived for cover, wahinettes fled, irate chaperons rushed forward, Don Ho warbled on, and behind a crepe paper waterfall a disappointed Malcolm Deslumptner zipped up. His most daring act of public auto-eroticism would have to await another day.

And then it was midnight and we were back in Paul's car. We dropped Fuzzy off in front of his darkened mansion, where he lingered briefly to French-kiss Heather and shake Carlotta's hand. Then on to my house, where Carlotta and Heather—tired but happy—stumbled out of the car and said their farewells.

"Oh, Carlotta," said Paul, rolling down his window, "call your sister. She may have some news of interest."

"Oh, OK," I replied. "Thanks, Paul. Good night all!"

Too tired to write any more. I pray Paul took Vijay directly home and did not permit any underaged, minor hanky-panky. Sometimes I wish Sheeni's brother was a little less hip and a little more rigidly strait-laced.

Tonight, diary, I lost my favorite song. Now "My One and Only Love" will forever be associated in my mind with the repulsive embrace of you know who. I only hope Frank's entire oeuvre has not been tarnished as well. Too bad I hadn't requested a Rudy Vallee ballad instead. Under the circumstances, something like "Donkey Serenade" would have been far more appropriate.

I wonder what's up with my sister? I wonder how you detach glued foam rubber from human skin?

12:30 p.m. Carlotta is back in the library. After lunch Fuzzy came over to my house and requested some emergency privacy. I didn't mind; I wanted to do some research anyway into foam adhesive solvents. None of the common household chemicals seem to work. I was hoping to run into Apurva, but I've seen no sign of her or her handlers. No answer at my sister Joanie's either. Everyone must be out Christmas shopping for their loved ones.

What should I get Sheeni? I just counted my wad and was flabbergasted to discover my net worth had shrunk below $1,000. Cash must run screaming from my wallet when I'm not looking. Once again destitution lurks around the corner. I wonder if I could make some nice handcrafted item for Sheeni? Or perhaps I could swipe her a nice, expensive library book. Maybe one of those glossy picture books of Paris from the oversize shelf. I could get it nicely gift-wrapped and paste a warmly affectionate greeting over the library stamp.

Can't write any more. Carlotta has to make a quick trip to the ladies' room. That recalcitrant adhesive is beginning to itch like crazy.

5:15 p.m. There's been an unfortunate mix-up this afternoon, diary. Fuzzy has suffered a major trauma and is in crisis. Heather is doing her best to comfort him.

I first got wind of the unfolding incident when Carlotta returned from the library to find a large black Mercedes parked in the driveway.

"Holy shit," I muttered, ducking into the bushes and receiving a second frightful shock. I was not alone.

"Hi, Carly," whispered Bruno, crouched in the thorny shadows. "Pull up a chair, babe."

"Bruno!" I hissed, "what are you doing here?"

"Shhhh," he whispered, nodding toward the window overhead. "Carlotta, your uncle's in there boffing some chick."

"You mean Fuzzy?"

"No, Mr. DeFalco, your uncle. You know, mean lookin' dude with the fancy car. I saw him go in about a half-hour ago with Mertice Palmquist."

"Where's Fuzzy and Heather?" I asked, nervously scratching my chest. I had drawn a blank in my solvent research.

"Haven't seen 'em," leered Bruno. "Hey, Carly, need some help there, babe?"

"No, thank you," I said, quickly desisting. "What are you doing here, Bruno? How did you get out of jail?"

"My parents bailed me out last night. It was an accident, Carly. Not my fault the spear slipped. They can't pin a thing on me, babe."

Just then, we were interrupted by the sounds of passionate moaning.

"Wow," whispered Bruno. "I never knew Mertice was a screamer. Wait 'til I tell my brother. He used to have the hots for her."

Carlotta reached up to scratch, then thought better of it.

"Hey, Carly," whispered Bruno, "how about a kiss?"

"Bruno, grow up," I hissed. "And go home!"

"No, Carly. You got it wrong, babe. You grow up and then you *leave* home."

"OK, then do the next thing."

"What's that?" asked Bruno.

"Drop dead."

Twenty-five minutes later, when the big Mercedes pulled out of the drive, Carlotta hurried into the house and firmly shut the door against eavesdropping jocks.

"Fuzzy?" I called. "Heather?"

I heard the door of the bedroom closet swing open. "Are they gone?" asked a frightened voice.

"Fuzzy, is that you?"

It was. Clad only in his undershorts, my hairy friend emerged slowly from the closet, followed by his dramatically underdressed girlfriend. I pretended not to notice.

"I'm going to puke," declared Fuzzy, dazed. "I'm going to throw up."

"I'm going to put some clothes on," said Heather uncharacteristically. "And never take them off again!"

I hurried into the kitchen and returned with a glass of water for my pal. He took several sips, then pushed the glass away.

"God, that was gross," said Fuzzy, absently sitting on the bed, then jumping away. "My dad and Mertice Palmquist, his hired dispatcher. Right here in this room, Carlotta. Right here in this room!"

"I know, Fuzzy," I said consolingly. "It's a tough break, guy."

"Come on, Fuzz," said Heather, putting an arm around him. "Let's go into the living room and sit down."

"I'm going to be sick," repeated Fuzzy, letting her lead him away. "I'm going to barf."

I feel so helpless, diary. What, I wonder, would Freud advise at this point? How does one apply a soothing emollient to a lacerated psyche?

10:38 p.m. Fuzzy just left for home. I think he's feeling better. Carlotta treated him and his girlfriend to a nice dinner at the Golden Carp. I ordered the family-size bowl of won-ton soup for Fuzzy; I have found this to be an effective substitute for the maternal breast in cases of psychological trauma. Working together, I think Heather and Carlotta were able to convince Fuzzy to view today's events as a positive first step toward separating emotionally from his parents.

"It is a normal part of the maturation process," declared Carlotta.

"It's normal to hear your dad ask Mertice Palmquist to swallow the big salami?" asked Fuzzy wonderingly.

"No, honey," said Heather. "It's normal to draw away from our parents. To see them as they are—as real people, faults and all. My parents have done even worst stuff. Believe me."

"Like what, for instance?" asked Carlotta, intrigued.

"I'd rather not say," she replied coldly.

"I think my parents should stop having affairs," said Fuzzy with conviction. "If they want to fool around, they should wait 'til I leave home. Is that asking too much?"

"I don't think so," I said.

"Me neither," agreed Heather.

"Carlotta," said Fuzzy, "can you help?"

"Do what?" I asked.

"Break up my dad and Mertice."

"Well, that's asking a lot," I replied. "But sure, I'll give it a shot."

"Great!" said Fuzzy, brightening.

"God, it was torture," said Heather, biting into her eggroll.

"What was?" I asked.

"Being in that closet, Carlotta. All your shawls and stuff were tickling me. I thought I was going to jump right out of my skin. And Fuzzy kept poking me."

"Well, you kept making noise," he explained.

"What'd you expect? I was going nuts. I just hope I'm not permanently hyper-ticklish now. Fuzz honey, would you still like me if you could never touch me ever again?"

Fuzzy stopped slurping his soup. "Is that actually possible?" he asked in panic.

"I don't know," said Heather. "Honey, why don't you hurry up and finish. We'll go back to Carlotta's and check it out."

"Well, the library is closed," I pointed out.

"That's OK, Carlotta," said Heather magnanimously. "You can stay in the living room and watch TV."

"No way," said Fuzzy. "She can stay in the bedroom. We'll do it on the couch."

They did too, apparently unhindered by epidermal sensitivity, emotional disquietude, or the guidelines promulgated by sexologists for expected frequency and duration of coitus. Nearly two hours (not that I was listening), and after a carbohydrate-laden meal too. Is that normal?

11:45 p.m. I have chiseled off my foam appliances with a dull screwdriver, removing in the process most of my chest hair and a considerable portion of skin. I hope Heather was not disturbed by my groans of agony. At least now I can't feel the itching over the stinging firestorm of gnawing chest torment.

SUNDAY, December 20, 8:15 a.m. I awoke to find a scab had formed on my chest resembling the Golden Gate Bridge. Resisting an impulse to phone the AP, Carlotta dressed and tiptoed toward the back door. From the pronounced periodicity of the sounds emanating from the living room, I deduced my houseguest was already entertaining early morning visitors. My God, thought Carlotta, hurriedly exiting, it's almost as if they were trying to store it up for winter. I wonder how many more quarts of sexual ecstasy they can put up before Heather's bus leaves at two.

Downtown was foggily forlorn and deserted. Carlotta bought the Sunday *New York Times* and dropped in at the Greek greasy spoon for a three-egg lamb, spinach, and feta cheese omelet. They do an interesting version encased in buttered filo pastry. Rather rich, but I needed the caloric fortification. I am due in church at ten.

9:10 a.m. Back in my bedroom. There appears to be a pause in the action in the living room. Perhaps they had to give the sterilizer a rest. What should I wear to church? Black seems so somber. I wonder if my ballgown would be inappropriate? How much bare back can one display on Sunday? May one wear a blouse under one's ball finery? Women know the answers to these sorts of questions, of course; they read *Vogue*. But what's a guy to do?

4:25 p.m. What a spiritually fulfilling day. Sunday makes so much more sense when you take the time to include 90 minutes of ritualistic pageantry.

Carlotta decided to go with black after all. I tried a white blouse under the blue gown, but concluded I looked like a nun out for an evening of casino-hopping in Las Vegas. So black it was, accessorized with a pair of Mrs. DeFalco's amethyst earrings, a nice bead necklace, white gloves, and a small, well-thumbed Bible.

Carlotta arrived at the Saunders' stately Victorian residence punctually at 9:30. Sheeni's mother answered the door, greeted Carlotta with an affectionate hug, and invited me into the living room, where she introduced her out-sized, bushy-browed husband, applying tinsel to a large Scotch pine.

"How do you do?" he bellowed, eyebrows flapping wildly as he squeezed Carlotta's clammy hand.

"Very well, thank you," Carlotta curtsied. I tried not to think about the last time I had received their hospitality, just a few short weeks before.

"Sheeni!" bellowed her mother. "Time to go!"

My Love, a divine vision in saintly white, trooped dispiritedly down the stairs. "Hi, Carlotta," she said. "Mother, I'm only going because you invited Carlotta. I have not altered my principles."

"Then let us pray you receive a revelation soon. I do not want all of my children wallowing in sin."

"Paul is very happy, Mother," said Sheeni.

"His temporal happiness does not interest me," replied Mrs. Saunders. "I am concerned with his eternal soul."

"Carlotta," said Sheeni, sighing. "May I speak with you privately?"

"Yes, of course," I said, startled.

My mind racing, I excused myself and followed My Love into the adjoining study. Sheeni closed the door and turned to face me.

"Carlotta!" she exclaimed. "What on earth are you wearing?"

Instinctively, I reached for my chest. Had a boob slipped? No, all appeared to be in order. "Why, Sheeni?" I asked. "What's wrong?"

"Where did you get that necklace?"

"Oh, it's something I had around. I think Mother gave it to me. She wore it in 'Rocky II.' Why? Does it clash with my earrings?"

"Carlotta, it's a rosary! You can't wear a Catholic rosary into my parents' church. You wouldn't get two feet past the deacons."

"Oh my," I said, hurriedly removing the offending beads, taking care not to disturb my wig. "Sorry, Sheeni. I had no idea."

"Come upstairs," she said. "I'll lend you my amethyst necklace."

"Thank you, Sheeni. Oh, I've got your sapphire earrings in my purse."

"Good, Carlotta. They're my favorites you know. I've asked Santa for a matching necklace, but Father says my dress for the dance cost more than his entire law school education. Of course, the ninny isn't allowing for inflation."

We were a fashionable ten minutes late for the service. Fortunately, the Saunders owned their own prestigiously sited pew, so we did not have to shove in with the rabble of latecomers back by the door.

I think the service on a whole achieved a satisfactory note of theatrical piety. The new minister, however, clearly did not measure up to the high standards set by the departed Rev. Knuddlesdopper. Reverend Miles Glompiphel was a pale, well-fed young man with sandy blond hair combed straight north and a smile borrowed intact from Alfred E. Newman. A dim echo of the double-knit revolution reverberated about his wardrobe, as if he had been ordered by the congregation from an out-of-date Sears catalogue: wide lapels, expansive tie, big collar, sensuously flared pants—all meticulously rendered in coordinated shades of tan polyester.

The season may be a joyous one, but Rev. Glompiphel's themes were sin and damnation. "Some of you have come into this house of worship under false pretenses," he declared perceptively at one point. "There is falseness in your manner, falseness in your dress, yes, and falseness in your heart. You have turned a false face to God and you believe your secret is safe. But, sinner, know that you are mistaken. He sees and knows all."

Carlotta blushed self-consciously and shifted uncomfortably on the hard pew. Sorry God, I thought, I know this looks bad, but it's all for the love of my dear Sheeni. Believe it or not, I'm actually trying to live a good life. It's just that the present circumstances are so difficult.

I felt better after some hearty hymn singing; I only wish I was more familiar with the words. I think I saw Sheeni's mother glance quizzically at Carlotta several times during the more obscure numbers.

After church Mrs. Saunders invited Carlotta to stay for Sunday dinner. As a penance for my sins, I refused seconds on the delicious baked ham and had only two small pieces of her wonderful walnut spice cake. I also participated in an animated theological discussion with the two elder Saunders that dragged on for nearly an hour. I hope God took note of that.

After lunch Sheeni invited Carlotta up to her bedroom to ogle her jewelry collection. We sat on My Love's virginal chenille and passed a pleasant hour trying on earrings, broaches, necklaces, rings, bracelets, anklets, pins, pendants, lockets, and other costly bejeweled ornaments. It occurred to me later that I shall have to have a spectacularly successful writing career if I am to keep Sheeni in the style to which she has become accustomed. I only hope I do not have to sacrifice art entirely in a crass appeal to the fiction-hungry masses.

Needless to say as I sat beside My Love, examining gemstones in the intimate confines of her private bedchamber, my mind soon turned to several semi-precious ornaments of my own. I wished with all my heart I could share them with her, but—through great force of will—stifled the impulse. Self-denial, Carlotta pointed out to God on the walk home. The temptations of flesh successfully resisted once again. Exemplary conduct like this, I feel strongly, surely must be toting me up some points.

Unfortunately, I arrived home too late to say farewell to Heather. I found this hand-written note on the kitchen table:

Dear Carlotta,

Thanks a lot for all your hospitality and helping me get ready for the dance. It was a real blast. Too bad we didn't have time for that massage. Maybe next time. Come on down to Santa Cruz anytime and bring your furry cousin too. You have a real cute little house. I can sense you have a strong need for a home. Be nice to Fuzzy and help him get over his recent shock if you can. Hope you find a guy soon

as neat as mine. How about that fellow Trent? He's cute! Stay in touch . . .
Love,
Heather
P.S. A guy named Bruno was here looking for you. Did you tell him I was your married sister?

Damn, I was looking forward to a few private moments alone as Nick Twisp, but I don't dare change my clothes (or my identity) if that nosy jock is snooping around.

9:45 p.m. Still no answer at Joanie's. Maybe she found out she's expecting quintuplets and has retreated into a catatonic state. I just watched "Holiday Inn" on TV. They must have chosen their camera angles carefully; Fred Astaire did not look all that short. The jury remains out on Bing Crosby. I may never be able to make up my mind if that guy can sing.

MONDAY, December 21 — Two glorious weeks without school. Can anything be more wonderful? Well, I can think of a few things. Still, life is sweet, even if I did spend the first two hours of Christmas vacation cleaning house and laundering my sheets (a fragrant smorgasbord of bodily fluids, none of them mine).

Guess whose ugly puss made it on the front page of the morning newspaper? None other than Dwayne Crampton. He was shown holding a bouquet of daisies and looking on fatuously as his mother married my old radical neighbor, Mr. Ferguson, in his cell at the county jail yesterday. Two guards and a town inebriate served as witnesses. No sign of Dad in the photo. Probably the scab wasn't invited. After the ceremony, reported the article, the groom took a break from his hunger strike for labor justice to drink a glass of champagne. The honeymoon has been postponed and the happy couple expects to make their home apart for the time being.

2:15 p.m. I finally got a Christmas present for Sheeni. Carlotta found a nice, expensive-looking Taiwan pen and pencil set at Flampert's on sale for $6.99. Plated with genuine 12-carat gold. Gift-wrapping was only 50 cents additional. I hope she likes it. A gifted stylist like her should have a prestigious writing instrument at hand for jotting down her ponderous thoughts.

Carlotta ran into Sonya at the make-up counter. My friend was percolating with vivacity and investing heavily in cosmetics of the lilac hues.

"Oh, Carlotta," she bubbled, "I'm in love!"

"Dwayne made a real impression, huh?" I said, surprised.

"Not Dwayne! I must have been out of my mind going out with that boob. On the drive home from the dance he passed such a fart I had to get out and walk the last six blocks—in my tight pumps. Thought I was going to die!"

"Well, I warned him to go easy on the bean dip. So who's the lucky guy, Sonya?"

She motioned me closer and lowered her voice to a conspiratorial whisper. "I got the news last night from a source that knows. Carlotta, Trent dumped

Janice Griffloch!"

"He has?" I exclaimed.

"Dumped her," she confirmed, "zits, stringy hair, bad breath, and all. You know what that means, don't you?"

"No, what, Sonya?"

"Carlotta, Trent danced three dances with me. He was very attentive and complimentary."

"So?" I asked uneasily.

"So the guy likes me."

"Are you sure?" I asked doubtfully. "Has he asked you out?"

"Well, no, not yet. My idiot parents are trying to sabotage my social life by having an unlisted number. I just called the phone company this morning and ordered an emergency listing. They're putting it into the computer as fast as possible. Carlotta, what if Trent already called information? Do you think I should send him my phone number anonymously?"

"Well, that's an idea, Sonya. But maybe you should wait a few days. I mean, Trent might be interested in someone else."

A dark shadow passed over her violet-tinted visage. "He likes me, Carlotta. I know he does."

"Well, if you say so."

"You know what your problem is, Carlotta? You're just jealous. You're pissed because Fuzzy brought another girl to the dance and you only got to dance with Trent once."

"That's not it, Sonya."

"You're jealous, Carlotta. I see it now. You want Trent for yourself."

"No, I don't!"

Startled shoppers began to peer over in our direction.

"Well, you can't have him, Carlotta!" shouted Sonya, her purple tones shifting angrily up spectrum toward red.

"I don't want him!" I insisted.

"We'll just see who he calls first. See if I ever help you again in sewing class you, you Mussolini Revival bag lady!"

Sonya grabbed her purchases from the counter and stomped off.

Notice, God, what happens when I try to live an exemplary life. I do a good deed for a friend and am pilloried in Flampert's for my trouble.

4:40 p.m. Perhaps to expedite her social life, Mertice Palmquist has conveniently listed her phone number in the Ukiah directory. When she answered, I affected the voice of an elderly Italian woman.

"Mertice Palmquist," I whispered ethereally. "Mertice Palmquist."

"Yes," she said, surprised. "Who's this?"

"Mertice Palmquist, I wanta my rest."

"Who is this?"

"Mertice Palmquist," I cackled, "you leeva my son alone."

"I don't know what you're talking about, lady. Is this a crank call?"

"I hearda you. I saw you inna my bed, witha my son."

"All right, who is this?" she demanded nervously.

"Mertice Palmquist, I amma the mother ova Dominic."

"Is this some kind of a joke? Shirley, is that you? I should never have told you about Dom and me."

"I havva come from my cold tomb, Mertice Palmquist. I havva come to avenge your sins againsta the sacrament ova marriage."

"What sins?"

"Inna my bed. Lasta Saturday afternoon."

"Eek! How do you know about that?" she cried. "Who are you?"

"I saw you, Mertice Palmquist. I sawa everything."

"Everything?" she gasped.

"Carnal sins, Mertice Palmquist. Grossa disgusting ones. Inna my own bed. Under the quilt I sewed witha my owna fingers."

"But, but, Dom's mother is dead!"

"You tressapass inna my house. My leetle house, witha the picture ova the Lasta Supper. And the garbanzo beans inna the cupboard thata my Dominic he lovesa so mucha."

"Mrs. DeFalco!" she cried.

"I make-a noise to warn you ova my anger. But you donta listen."

"I, I thought I heard something! Dom said it was squirrels in the attic."

"Itta notta squirrel. Itta outraged mother, coming froma her grave!"

"Oh my God! What have I done?"

"You leeva my boy alone, Mertice Palmquist. He'sa married. You stay outta my house."

"Yes, Mrs. DeFalco. Yes, I will!"

"You promise?"

"Yes, I'm sorry. I didn't know."

"That'sa OK."

"Oh, thank you!"

"Donta mention it."

"Excuse me, Mrs. DeFalco. This is probably rude to ask, but can you do me a small favor?"

"What kinda favor?" I asked, surprised.

"My darling parakeet Hurlbut just died. Can you tell him I love him. And I miss him."

"OK, I guessa so. I'll tella him."

"Thank you. I want you to know I only went out with your son because I was so upset about my bird. I'm not a bad person."

"I forgive-a you. Just donta do it no more. And donta tell Dominic thata we talked. I donta wanta him to worry 'bout hisa poor mama."

"OK," she replied.

"Well, have-a nice-a day."

"'Bye, Mrs. DeFalco. His name is Hurlbut. He's green with a yellow head."

"No problema. I thinka maybe I see hima flyina thisa way now. Ciao."

"'Bye, Mrs. Defalco. Thanks for calling. Have a nice day."

Hanging up, I immediately dialed the DeFalco residence. Fuzzy answered, sounding seasonally dispirited.

"Hi, Nick," he said, "what's up?"

"Frank, I just quashed your dad's auxiliary lovelife. Mertice Palmquist is back on a salami-free diet."

"Great, Nick," he said, brightening. "How did you do it?"

"Never mind that," I replied. "Frank, I need a favor."

"What kind of favor?" he asked suspiciously.

"I need the key to your uncle's house."

"OK, Nick. Should I ask what for?"

"Probably not. But don't worry. I'll give it back soon."

"OK, I'll sneak it off the hook and bring it over tomorrow. Say, Nick, have you been in my dad's gun room?"

"Of course not, Frank. Why do you ask?"

"Somebody broke in. They stole an AK-47 assault rifle. Dad's kind of upset."

"Did he report it to the police?"

"Naw, he can't. The gun wasn't registered. He could get in big trouble. I thought maybe it was you."

"Why me?" I asked indignantly.

"Well, you're always asking me about guns. Remember? You get this wild-eyed look and start talking about disposing of dead bodies."

"Well, I'm no thief, Frank. If I wanted a gun, I'd do what any self-respecting nut case would do and order it by mail. I've got the money."

"Do you, Nick? That reminds me. Uncle Polly's bankroll is still missing. Have you by any chance . . ."

"Oops, have to go, Frank. It's time to add the softener to the rinse cycle. Boy, you guys did a number on my sheets. 'Bye!"

Guns are real targets for thieves. Fuzzy's dad should be more responsible. Now there's one more homicidal maniac walking around out there with a loaded machine gun and a bad attitude.

8:15 p.m. Carlotta just had a nice phone chat with The Woman Who Flocks My Tree. I won't have a totally lonely holiday after all. Sheeni invited me over for dinner on Christmas Eve.

A large bowl of freshly popped popcorn awaits me on the coffee table in the living room. In 15 minutes "White Christmas" comes on the tube. Just me, Bing, and the last vinegary glass of rotgut. I wonder if anyone, anywhere on this planet is planning on remembering Nick Twisp with a small token of his or her affections this Christmas?

That reminds me, what did I get last year? Oh yeah, $10 from Dad and an official Yves "Crotch Jammer" Derbossa hockey stick from Mom. It was all I could do to keep the heart palpitations under control. Oh, and Mom's late boyfriend Jerry gave me a half-empty tube of hair cream that must have been gathering lint in his medicine cabinet since 1956. I used it awhile anyway. I looked like Rudolph Valentino with zits.

9:20 p.m. Bing has started to sing you know what. I like Frank's version better. I wonder what the hip, with-it kids listen to this time of year? Have the Flesheaters recorded an album of Christmas favorites?

TUESDAY, December 22 — I'M RICH! I'm filthy, stinking, obnoxiously rich! I'm wallowing in wealth. I'm green with prosperity. I have received an Official Summons From Manna. Indolence is my destiny; conspicuous consumption is to be my great life's work. Let the news go forth: I'M RICH!

I got the fabulous news this morning when I called my sister. Oh, why hadn't she been home when I phoned before? So many hours suffered needlessly in cruel, soul-shriveling poverty. Stupendous, glorious development: Carlotta's late spiritual mother, Miss Bertha Ulansky, has left me all her money!

"All of it?" I asked Joanie, in stunned disbelief.

"Well, almost all of it, Nick," she said. "Everything except for a $5,000 bequest to the Retired Extras Home and her big color TV. She gave that to me. Phillie dragged it over this morning. The thing is a monster. Would you like to buy it, Nick?"

"Possibly, Joanie. I'll consider it, of course," I said, trying to contain my excitement. "That depends. Just how large a pile am I coming into?"

"Well, the lawyer doesn't know exactly yet. He's still uncovering bank accounts and stuff. She had accounts all over apparently. They found 2,000 shares of IBM behind the refrigerator yesterday."

I'm a shareholder in IBM! I must trade in my clone at once for the real thing.

"Well, give me a ballpark figure, Joanie," I said impatiently. "Is it as much as $10,000?"

"Nick honey, it's almost a half-million. Plus her condo. That's all paid for, and has the upgraded carpets and the double vanities in the baths with the tile counters."

"How much is it worth?" I asked, stunned.

"Well, it's nicer than mine," Joanie replied thoughtfully. "I've only got the single fake-marble vanities. Personally, I wouldn't sell mine for a nickel under two."

"Two what?" I croaked.

"Two-hundred thousand, of course."

"Oh my God!" I gasped, collapsing against the wall. Two-hundred thousand dollars for an apartment with less floor space than the average sharecropper's shack. I must sell it fast before the real estate market loses touch with unreality.

"I don't understand it, Nick," said Joanie. "You only met Miss Ulansky a few times. How come she left you all her money? Her lawyer says she changed her will right after you split."

"Beats me, Joanie. I guess she was captivated by my winning personality."

"It's a good thing I told her that her buddy Frank Dillinger was actually my brother Nick. The lawyer might still be looking for him."

"Thanks, Joanie. You're a lifesaver. Now, when can I get my loot?"

"Well, Nick, it will take a while. It's lucky you called. The lawyer wants you here to sign some papers."

"Can't we do it by mail?"

"I don't think so, Nick. They have to be notarized."

"I can get them notarized here, Joanie."

"Well, I'll ask him. Nick, where are you? We're all so worried."

"I'm, I'm around. I'm OK."

"Well, give me a phone number at least. So I can contact you."

"I can't, Joanie. I'll call you."

"When?" she demanded.

"Every few days or so."

"Nick, have you called Mother yet? She's really worried."

"I'm working up to it, Joanie. I'll call her soon. Well, thanks for the great news."

"Nick, you're rich! Your troubles are over."

Money! It can't buy you happiness, but it can certainly make a generous down payment.

12:17 p.m. Carlotta was frothing with unsuspected vivacity when Fuzzy dropped by with the purloined house key.

"Hey, Nick, you're on vacation," said Fuzzy. "How come you're all dolled up as Carlotta?"

"I have to go out for a bit more light Christmas shopping," replied Carlotta amiably. "Oh, that reminds me, Frank. Here's your present."

"Gee, thanks, Carlotta. Can I open it now?"

"Why not, Frank? Nobody's looking."

Fuzzy opened his gift in an explosion of wrapping paper.

"Gee, a pen and pencil set," he said, somewhat flatly.

"It's genuine gold," I pointed out. "They're modeled on a set once presented to President McKinley by the Despot of Constantinople."

"Wow," he said, slightly more enthusiastically. "You shouldn't have, Carlotta."

"Don't mention it, Frank. How are things at home?"

"Dad's looking a little depressed. I asked him if he felt like going out to buy a Christmas tree, and he gave me a really dirty look."

"He'll cheer up, Frank. How's your mom?"

"She spends most of her time in the room over the garage beating the mattress with the tennis racket and screaming. Carlotta, is your dad named George?"

"Why yes, he is."

"I thought so. She's been hollering the name George a lot."

"Any sign of parental Christmas shopping?"

"Not so far, Carlotta. I'm really worried. This might be my only present this year. Except for Heather's."

"Oh, what is Heather getting you?"

"She gave it to me already," he said. "It was something I'd always wanted to try with a chick."

"How was it?"

"Very nice, Carlotta. I recommend it highly."

7:15 p.m. Carlotta's back. Another exhilarating day spending Uncle Polly's fast-dwindling wad. No need for economizing now; it was time to inject a fiscal stimulant directly into the jugular of Mendocino County commerce. Carlotta began her afternoon spree at a local florist shop, where she ordered a dozen red roses for Fuzzy's mom. I signed the extravagantly poetic forged mash note "Your loving husband, Dom." At the same time, a large masculine potted fern was selected for delivery to Mr. DeFalco, accompanied by a similarly devotional encomium from his ever-constant and adoring wife.

Then on to Main Street's most prestigious jewelers for a suitably upscale replacement gift for playboy Nick Twisp's future Trophy Wife.

"I'd like to see something in blue sapphire," sniffed Carlotta.

The clerk looked at me skeptically. "Well, we have some nice one-sixteenth carat stud earrings."

"I was thinking of something along the lines of a necklace."

The clerk produced a dazzling choker, laden with sparkling blue stones.

"Perfect," said Carlotta. "How much is it?"

"It's $2,800," replied the clerk, keeping the gems firmly within his grasp. "Plus tax."

"Plus tax, hmmm," mused Carlotta. "Yes, it's very nice. Unfortunately I am still awaiting a large dividend check from my attorney. Have you anything less expensive?"

I settled for a nice sapphire pendant and gold chain. Boxed, gift-wrapped, and placed in a prestigious silver foil bag, the flashy little trinket came to $593.12 out the door. It's a good thing I'm rich; adorning your loved one with jewels can run into some money. So Carlotta wouldn't feel left out, I bought her some earrings from the budget display case. A nice pair of dingy brown garnets (quarter-carat size) to match her eyes came to $114.87.

Next, Carlotta strolled to Flampert's, bustling with holiday shoppers, where I was surprised to see three more Mussolini Revival fashion clones. (One woman, though, appeared to be over 90, so she may not count.) After some pleasant browsing, I purchased a box of yellow legal pads for Sheeni's father (lawyers can always use more of these) and, for Sheeni's mother, a set of inspirational dishcloths printed with a full-color map of the Holy Lands. So appropriate and on sale too.

Waiting in a long line at the checkstand, I found myself standing behind a small ambulatory circus tent covered with garish yellow roses. I had seen that faded print before.

"Excuse me," Carlotta said, "aren't you the woman who was in the newspaper?"

"Why yes," replied Mrs. Crampton, flattered to be recognized. "That was . . . little me."

Marriage, I discerned, had not accelerated the pace of her speech.

"Is your new husband still on a hunger strike?" I asked.

"Yes, he is. And I'm . . . so worried. I'm buyin' some . . . peanut brittle . . . to tempt . . . him. I can't . . . resist . . . peanut brittle myself . . . Neither can . . . my boy."

Well, that's two out of three, I thought. "Is there no progress on settling the strike?" I asked.

"No . . . And I think . . . the damn owner . . . ought . . . to be . . . shot."

"You don't really mean that?"

Mrs. Crampton leaned closer. "Right . . . between . . . the eyes . . . *Blam!*"

I wondered if she had recently come into possession of a hot AK-47. "Where are you staying while your husband is in jail?" I asked.

"I got me a job . . . as a domestic," she replied. "But I'm lookin' . . . for a new . . . sit'ation."

"You don't like your present employer?"

"I think . . . he's a bad . . . influence on . . . my boy . . . You see . . . Mr. Twisp is . . . a drinker."

"That's too bad," I said. "You know I might have an opening soon for a housekeeper."

"Really?" she asked, clearly interested.

"Yes, and I'd pay a good salary too. Of course, it wouldn't be live-in."

"That's fine . . . with me . . . I like . . . my privacy . . . So does . . . my boy."

I shuddered. "Yes, I'm sure he does. Well, I'll keep you in mind."

I believe firmly that rich people should not have to cook their own meals and clean their own toilets. That is why humans strive for wealth. These incentives must never be tampered with.

Putting my principles into practice, Carlotta had an early dinner at the Golden Carp. Eschewing economy, I ordered the Supreme Deluxe dinner for one and left Steve a $5 tip. Needless to say, he was flabbergasted.

So was I when I got home and counted my remaining anorexic wad: $63.84. I hope that lawyer gets a check to me soon. I may have temporary cash flow problems. Who can I hit up for a short-term loan? What about Bruno? No, I don't think I'd want to pay his kind of interest.

9:55 p.m. Well, everything's arranged. But it took more than an hour of back-and-forth phone jockeying to work out the details. Operation Thundering Cupid commences tomorrow morning at 9:30. Seems like an odd time of day to experience one's first sexual congress, but when you're blessed with strict

Indian parents you have to be willing to seize the opportunity when it arises, so to speak.

10:20 p.m. I am watching "It's a Wonderful Life" on the tube. I find the story improbable. Clearly, George Bailey should have run away from home at age 14 and never come back.

WEDNESDAY, December 23, 10:05 a.m. — Carlotta is sitting on Apurva's chaste single bed in her neat, maidenly bedroom with the door firmly closed. I am chatting, laughing, and playing tapes (loud). I am also alone. Apurva sneaked out the window 25 minutes ago with the key to Uncle Polly's house. As arranged, Trent was to pick her up around the corner. She is due back no later than 11:30. Subtracting travel time, this gives them nearly 90 minutes for wild, unchaperoned you know what. I'm trying to contain my jealousy.

No, I did not invite the lovers to use my house. All the comings and goings this past week have aroused the suspicions of my neighbors. (The nosy old guy across the street seems especially intrigued.) Besides, I just washed my sheets.

Mr. Joshi is at work, Mrs. Joshi is watching Phil Donahue in the living room (audible through the paper-thin walls), and Vijay the Vile is moping in his bedroom across the hall. Apurva reports he has been "quite morose" since the day after the dance. Naturally, I am interpreting this as a positive development.

11:02 a.m. I just had a bad scare. Apurva's mother knocked on the door and asked if we wanted tea.

"No, thank you, Mrs. Joshi," Carlotta called.

"Apurva, shall I bring you a cup?" she asked.

"No, thanks," I replied, in my best Apurva impersonation.

Thank God she went away.

I have to use the bathroom, but don't dare leave the room in case Mrs. Joshi returns. Why did I have that fourth cup of coffee with my donuts this morning?

I'm trying to distract myself by snooping through Apurva's drawers. I do so enjoy this sort of work. I found some interesting photos of Apurva with her friends in India. They are lounging about in rattan chairs on some sort of exotic-looking veranda. It's hard to believe an entire huge country exists on the other side of the world. As I write this, millions of oddly dressed people are going about in an alien landscape, speaking strange languages, and engaging in foreign activities. Yet one of the girls in the photo is holding a cat that would not be out of place in an American back yard. And another one is having a secret tryst in the California boondocks with an American windsurfing fanatic. We really do live in one world.

11:32 a.m. Where's Apurva? She's two minutes overdue. Couldn't hold out any longer. Carlotta just hiked her skirt and peed out the window. I hope the neighbors weren't watching.

More footsteps outside the door.

"Apurva, turn down the music," bellowed Vijay petulantly. "I'm trying to talk to Sheeni on the telephone."

"OK," I called lyrically, turning the volume UP.

11:47 a.m. No sign of Apurva. Vijay is pounding on the door. Mrs. Joshi will soon be calling us for lunch. How did I ever let myself get talked into this?

12:12 p.m. Apurva is back. She is missing her shoes, has an ugly bruise on her face, a bad abrasion on her thigh, and is babbling incoherently about hot tubs. That Trent is a beast! Apurva also seems to have lost Uncle Polly's house key. Uh-oh, Mrs. Joshi just announced through the door that lunch is served. Time for Carlotta to bail out!

1:30 p.m. Totally panicked, Carlotta exited hastily through Apurva's bed-room window, tearing her dress and losing a critical perfume blotter. Sneaking lopsidedly up the alley toward home, I was obliged to run an unexpected gauntlet of amorous football players.

"Hi, Carly," said Bruno, heaving his garbage can across the asphalt, "how about giving me my Christmas present early, babe?"

"Up yours," I muttered, folding my arms over my chest.

"Hey, Carly, you're showin' a lot of leg today, babe. How'd you rip your dress? Fuzzy get a little too rough for you?"

"None of your business," I snapped. "Get out of my way!"

Bruno stepped back. "I'll be over later, Babe," he cooed. "You know you want it, so why fight it?"

Carlotta paused. "Bruno dear, haven't you heard?"

"Heard what?" he asked.

"Mertice Palmquist broke up with Mr. DeFalco."

"So?"

"So why don't you give her a call?"

"I don't know," he said, scratching his crewcut. "What makes you think Mertice'd be int'rested in me?"

"A friend of hers told me."

"Who?"

"Her ex-roommate. A guy named Hurlbut."

"He did really?"

"Yeah. So ring her up. Tell her Hurlbut asked you to call."

"OK!" said Bruno enthusiastically. "I'll do it!"

When I got inside my house, I immediately called Trent's number. No answer. Two minutes later, the phone rang.

"Carlotta," said Sheeni excitedly, "what's this I hear about you beating up Apurva Joshi?"

"Who told you that?" I demanded.

"Vijay just called me. He said you came over to visit, then his mother found Apurva in her room all bloody and hysterical."

"Did, did Apurva say that I did it?" Carlotta asked, experiencing again that familiar scrotal twinge.

"They haven't been able to get a coherent story from her yet. Carlotta, you didn't . . . didn't attack her did you?"

"Of course not, Sheeni. What sort of person do you think I am? I'm afraid the perpetrator of this outrage was your old friend Trent."

"What!" she cried.

"Apurva invited me over for a game of Mah-jongg," I explained, embroidering the truth only slightly. "Then she sneaked out the window to meet Trent. It turns out she only wanted me there to allay suspicions while she made her illicit assignation. I tried to talk her out of it, of course. But really there's no stopping those two. They are so very much in love. She returned in the state in which her mother found her."

"How peculiar. But why, Carlotta, did you leave so precipitously? So abrupt an exit could only cause suspicion to devolve on you."

"I don't know," I confessed. "I suppose the sight of blood made me panic. And what possible explanation could I have offered her mother?"

"I can't believe Trent would do such a thing," said Sheeni.

"Perhaps, Sheeni, in the end Apurva couldn't go through with it," I said, recalling acutely a prior episode of maidenly hesitation on her part in my trailer. "So Trent forced himself on her."

"You mean . . . "

"Yes, Sheeni. Date rape. What other conclusion is possible?"

"I don't believe it, Carlotta!"

"There may be a side to Trent you have never experienced, Sheeni. A violent side only brought out by extremes of passion and lust."

"That is highly unlikely," replied Sheeni. "I can assure you I have seen Trent at his most passionate and lustful. Many times."

But never again, if I have anything to say about it!

"Well, Sheeni, there's no point in idle speculation. We'll just have to wait for Apurva to regain her reason."

"No, we won't," said Sheeni, "I'm calling Trent now." *Click.*

4:20 p.m. No visits from the police yet. Sheeni just telephoned again.

"Well, Carlotta, I've spoken with Trent."

"Where was he, Sheeni? I've been calling his house all afternoon."

"I found him at the hospital getting his sprained ankle x-rayed."

"Sheeni, what happened? Did they have a car wreck on the way home?"

"No, Carlotta. It was your vivacious friend Sonya Klummplatz."

"Sonya?" I asked, surprised.

"Yes. It seems she followed them. She broke into the house and surprised them in the hot tub."

"She did! Were they naked?"

"I believe they were largely unclothed, yes. They were reading poetry and getting into the mood for, well . . ."

"Yes, I know."

"Sonya apparently became quite abusively belligerent. An altercation ensued. The area was slippery. Sonya fell into the hot tub. Injuries were sustained by all parties. Sonya was scalded slightly. Apparently she is extremely sensitive to temperature. That pale skin of hers, you know. They had to remove her hot clothing."

"Whose clothes?"

"Sonya's."

"They stripped Sonya? Did she mind?"

"Apparently very much. She hit Apurva with the *Oxford Book of English Verse*."

"The paperback edition?"

"No, hardbound."

"That accounts for the bruise on her face. Then what happened?"

"Sonya was threatening to drown Apurva. Apparently she has some sort of bizarre fixation on Trent. She'd been leaving notes with her telephone number all over the Prestons' shrubbery this week. Anyway, it was all Trent could do to keep her from attacking Apurva. They put their clothes on as best they could and left."

"Where's Sonya?"

"Last time Trent saw her she was running down the road after them."

"What was she wearing?"

"Not very much."

"Poor Sonya," I said. "And poor Apurva. All that careful planning and she still comes home empty handed."

"Yes," sighed Sheeni. "I had a long chat with Trent in the emergency room. He's quite all-consumedly in love with her."

"He told you that?"

"Yes, Carlotta. I suppose I must accept it. My childhood sweetheart is gone forever."

"You don't mind?" I asked, thrilled beyond words.

"It hurts. But I can live with it. Carlotta, I think that we should do our best to see that those two finally get together."

"You really mean it, Sheeni?"

"Yes, I do. In some ways, I blame myself for a small portion of their current difficulties."

"Helping them would be most generous of you, Sheeni," Carlotta pointed out.

"I hope I am a generous person," she replied.

"Oh you are," I assured her. "You are!"

After Sheeni rang off, Carlotta performed a dance of wild celebration across the old linoleum. Sonya Klummplatz, my dear misguided friend, I could kiss you!

7:20 p.m. Carlotta just returned from a dinner date with Fuzzy at his restaurant of choice—McDanold's. I was amazed when he actually picked up the tab.

"It's a fucking miracle," he said happily, when we sat down with our trays at the yellow plastic booth. "My parents have never been so lovey-dovey."

"Glad to hear it," exclaimed Carlotta.

"They were going at it for hours," he confided. "I always know when they're doing it 'cause Mom puts on this sappy Frank Sinatra tape. I hadn't heard it in months. Finally, they came out of the bedroom, hanging all over each other, and Dad gave me 20 bucks and said to get my own dinner 'cause they had some Christmas shopping to do."

"Better late than never," commented Carlotta, squeezing ketchup from the tiny packets onto my fries. "I see my plan worked perfectly."

"I'm really grateful, Carlotta. I may have a semi-normal homelife for a while."

"Very likely," I lied. "And since you're so grateful, Frank, I'm sure you won't mind that I misplaced the key to your uncle's house."

"What?"

"Fell out of my purse," I lied. "Sorry."

"What'll I tell my parents?" he demanded.

"Well, suggest a plausible alternative. Tell them perhaps the gun-stealing burglar swiped it."

"Yeah, lie. That's a good idea. Thanks, Carlotta."

"Don't mention it. Say, Frank. Can you keep a secret?"

"Always, Carlotta. You know it. My lips are zipped."

"Frank," I said, whispering, "I'm immensely wealthy."

"Aw, Carlotta, are you going off the deep end again?"

After outlining the events of the past few days in some detail, I managed to convince my friend I was not hallucinating.

"Gee, Carlotta, that's incredible!" he exclaimed. "What are you going to do with all your dough?"

"Well, first I want to secure a permanent living situation. Someplace where I don't have to sneak in and out like a criminal or a homeless person. Frank, do you think your parents would rent me your granny's house?"

"Gee, I don't know," he said doubtfully.

"Well, why not? They won't be needing it any more for entertaining creeps and bimbos."

"That's true," he conceded. "Well, I guess I could ask them. How much can you pay?"

"Whatever they want—within reason, of course. Frank, I'm loaded."

"I wish you'd told me that before I bought your burgers," he remarked sourly. "You want to give me a refund?"

"No thanks, Frank. Rich people never pick up the tab."

"That doesn't seem very fair, Carlotta."

"Frank, you're beginning to understand real life."

9:55 p.m. A police car just drove down the street, but didn't stop. Good to know God is listening to some of my prayers at least. I'm in my jammies and watching "A Christmas Story" on the tube. It's all about this kid back in 1948 who's trying to persuade his reluctant parents to buy him a BB-gun for Christmas. Amusing but dated. Today Junior would be demanding an AK-47 and threatening to have his gang burn down the house or turn little brother into a dope fiend if Santy didn't come across with the weaponry.

Where did all the innocence go? Perhaps it was all those air rifles they sold in the '50s. Kids got a taste for munitions and the arms race was on.

Lacking a fireplace, I have hung Carlotta's pantyhose on the furnace vent with care and placed a can of garbanzo beans in each toe as a festive Christmas offering to myself. When my first check arrives (soon, I hope), I shall be adding a few more carefully selected presents. Santa intends to be very generous this year. I've got 27 items on my list so far, not counting the contract Francois wants to put out on Vijay. He thinks $10,000 should be adequate for this. I hope there's an 800-number somewhere that connects you to the appropriate made-sociopaths in Detroit or Atlantic City. I'd hate to have to put a want ad in the newspaper.

10:42 p.m. The kid in the movie got his BB-gun after all and promptly shot out his glasses. Serves him right. He should have hired a professional.

THURSDAY, December 24 (Christmas Eve) — The ringing telephone jarred me awake at 8:07 a.m.

"Hello?" I said thickly.

"Let me speak to Carlotta," said a familiar voice.

"Is that you, Sonya?" asked Carlotta, now awake.

"It's me, girl. Who's that guy that answered? It wasn't Trent was it?"

"Of course not, Sonya. It was, uh, Mother. She has a frog in her throat. Mother, I told you to gargle."

"Oh, Carlotta, I'm so depressed. I made a terrible fool of myself with Trent."

"Yes, Sonya, I heard all about it."

"Carlotta, Trent has another girlfriend! It's not Sheeni, it's not Janice, and it's not you! Who is she?"

"Her name's Apurva. She's Vijay Joshi's sister."

"God, Carlotta, she's gorgeous. I'm so jealous. You should see her body."

Actually, I'd very much like to.

"I heard you fell in a hot tub, Sonya," said Carlotta. "Are you OK?"

"Yeah, I guess so. I'm a little red, that's all. Trent must have panicked when I started screaming and made me take my clothes off. I sure didn't much feel like it with that goddess Apurva standing there."

"I heard up put up a fight."

"God, Carlotta. I'm so embarrassed. I want to crawl into a hole and die. Trent must really hate me now."

"I'm sure he doesn't, Sonya. He understands the kind of effect he has on women. I'm sure he's used to girls getting carried away."

"Carlotta, I was totally out of control. It was like I was in this fever. I hadn't slept for days. I kept walking past his house, over and over again."

"You were obsessed?"

"Right. I was even nasty to you in Flampert's. Sorry, girl."

"No offense, Sonya. I understand how you felt."

"Then I saw him drive out and pick up that gorgeous dark stranger. Something snapped in my brain, Carlotta."

"Well, no harm done. I'm sure Trent forgives you."

"I have to drop out of school, Carlotta. I could never face him again."

"Don't be silly, Sonya. By the time Christmas vacation is over, Trent will have forgotten all about it. Really, don't worry."

"You think so?" she asked doubtfully.

"I know it. Don't worry."

"I could write him an apology and tell him I'll never bother him again."

"That's a good idea."

"What if he blabs it all over school? Carlotta, I would die."

"He won't. Trent isn't like that. He's excessively honorable."

"Maybe you're right. Thanks, Carlotta. I feel a little better now."

"Good. Now, go take a nice bath and have a large cinnamon bun. That's what I do when I'm upset."

"At least I got to be with him with his clothes off," she added. "That's more than I ever really expected."

"Good, Sonya. You're looking on the bright side now. Keep it up."

"It was up when I got there, Carlotta. But then it shrank down pretty fast. It was just like the rubber mannikin doll in health class, only bigger."

"I've got to go, Sonya. Mother wants me to fix her gargle. 'Bye." *Click.*

What a nut case. I should have known from the way she sewed her seams: too obsessively straight, and such orderly, tiny stitches!

11:20 a.m. I'm in the kitchen listening to Christmas music on the radio and making fudge. Carlotta told Sheeni I'd bring some over today. The recipe on the cocoa can looks pretty easy. I couldn't find any walnuts, so I'm substituting pistachios.

12:40 p.m. No sign of fudge hardening; I've put the pan in the freezer. I should never have trusted a recipe that didn't call for lots of corn starch. What did the morons at the chocolate company suppose would thicken it?

2:28 p.m. Fudge solid as a rock. Too hard to cut with a knife, so I chiseled the icy brown slab out of the pan, wrapped it in foil, and tied a red ribbon around it. Very festive. Carlotta is ready to go. She is wearing her garnet earrings and some red and green eye shadow. I hope Mr. Saunders is not the type to get excessively frisky with guests under the mistletoe.

5:45 p.m. He was. Yuck. Scratchy whiskers and lots of residual pipe tobacco carcinogens. I hope I don't get cancer of the lips.

We've just finished a nice roast beef dinner, and now Carlotta and Sheeni are up in the latter's bedroom catching up on our journals. Sheeni was surprised and delighted that Carlotta keeps a journal too.

"You must let me read it," said Sheeni, eyeing Carlotta's private notebook. "Oh, I couldn't possibly," said Carlotta. "It's much too intimate. I hold nothing back."

"I don't either," confessed Sheeni. "I open my soul and bare my innermost secrets—encrypted, of course. Rather like Mr. Pepys."

"Perhaps, Sheeni, your diaries will be decoded in a few hundred years and cause a literary sensation."

"Not likely, Carlotta. By then I imagine the salacious passages will seem quite tame. And the philosophical insights will have lost their coruscating brilliance."

That reminds me, I must try to be more introspective and contemplative in my journal writing. My diary, I fear, is woefully lacking in philosophical depth.

Meanwhile, back to the juicy gossip of the afternoon. Sheeni has heard from Vijay. Carlotta, I'm happy to report, is off the hook for the assault rap. Veracity-plagued Apurva has spilled the entire story to her parents. As usual, Mr. and Mrs. Joshi are livid and have demanded a powwow with Trent's parents. The meeting is set for tomorrow afternoon.

"But that's Christmas," Carlotta pointed out to Sheeni.

"The Joshis were insistent," she replied. "I just hope Trent's parents don't get railroaded into some extreme action—like sending Trent away to school."

That would be a shame. What a blow to Apurva's philosophical development.

8:30 p.m. My fudge was a great success. Mrs. Saunders chiseled the leaky package off the coffee table and spooned the contents over vanilla ice cream. We all had nice chocolate sundaes topped with whipped cream and shiny holiday sprinkles (made with real gold, a true feast for the affluent). Too bad the pistachios were a little off; I noticed Sheeni picked out all of hers.

9:47 p.m. Pleading holiday fatigue, Sheeni and Carlotta managed to get themselves excused from tonight's church service. Right after her parents left, Sheeni poured two tall glasses of sherry and dragged out the Scrabble board. What a slaughter. My opponent just spelled out 'quatorzain,' a word with a point total rivaling the national debt. She informs me that it's an irregular sonnet (probably the kind Trent writes). Fortunately, the sherry is helping take some of the sting out of defeat. Hard to concentrate too. I'm fighting a nearly overwhelming urge to drag you-know-who under the mistletoe.

11:10 p.m. Carlotta is spending the night! My hosts insist on it. Mrs. Saunders says this way we can all go to church first thing tomorrow morning. Sounds reasonable to me. Carlotta's to sleep in the chaste twin bed that adjoins Sheeni's own virginal pallet. As I write this, I can hear My Beloved in her bathroom flossing her exquisite teeth. Can it be that we shall soon be lying together in the darkness?

FRIDAY, December 25, Christmas Day, 2:15 a.m. — I very much doubt, diary, if I shall ever sleep again. That being the case, I might as well flesh out the details of the past few hours.

While Sheeni proceeded sedately from flossing to brushing, Carlotta took advantage of her absence to change hurriedly into a borrowed undiaphanous flannel nightgown. To my surprise, this was not the sleepwear of choice for My Love, who emerged from the bathroom draped in a few small scraps of filmy black lace, dramatically transparent netting, and satin ribbon tied in provocative bows.

"Goodness," said Carlotta, experiencing a sudden hot flash, "what an attractive negligee."

"Do you like it?" asked Sheeni, sitting on the white chenille and brushing her chestnut locks. "I purchased it in Santa Rosa last fall. I had hoped to wear it for my friend Nick, but things haven't worked out."

"Too bad," I gulped, crawling hastily under my covers. "I'm sure he would have found it most . . . appealing."

Sheeni put down her brush, slipped between the sheets, then looked over toward me and smiled. "Carlotta, must you be so distant? Come warm me up."

I swallowed again, said a secret prayer, and dashed across the carpeted moat. Sheeni snuggled her divine body against my steamy flannel.

"Carlotta, you're so warm," she remarked. "Feel free to take off your nightgown. It's just us girls here."

"That's OK, Sheeni. I'm fine. I always run a little feverish this time of night."

"Oh dear, Carlotta. Our perfumes are clashing dreadfully. I feared this would happen. Perhaps I should put on some of yours to mask mine. Writhe, isn't it?"

"Uh, yes."

"Could you bring me the bottle from your purse?"

"Uh, no, Sheeni. I don't think I'd better at the moment."

"Why not, Carlotta?"

"I'd just prefer not to get up at this time, if you don't mind."

"I don't mind, Carlotta. I like lying here with you."

"You do?"

"Oh, yes. I can't think of anyone I'd rather lie here with."

"Really?"

"Except possibly Nick."

"I'm sure Nick, wherever he is, would also wish to be lying here with you."

"You mean the three of us together?" asked Sheeni innocently.

"No, Sheeni. Under the circumstances, I, of course, would withdraw."

"Why?"

"Well, so you could be alone together."

"And do what?"

"Well, you know, make love."

"Then, why don't we?"

My heart seized.

"Beg your pardon?" I stammered.

"Why don't you take off that silly wig and make love to me?"

"Sheeni, darling! You know!"

"Of course, Nick," she said, tugging off my wig and tossing it across the room. "There, that's better. Now, off with those preposterous glasses."

I blinked with stunned surprise as my companion tugged Carlotta's ornate spectacles from my powdered nose.

"Sheeni, darling! Are you seriously suggesting we do it, right here, in your bedroom?"

"I believe a bedroom is the normal venue for such activities, Nick. But I am open to suggestions. Would you prefer to do it outside on the front lawn?"

"Oh, Sheeni," I swooned, grasping her gauze-glazed nakedness.

"Nickie, darling," she said, returning my feverish kiss, "before we get started, I suggest you go and get the condoms from your purse."

"How do you know I have condoms in my purse?" I asked.

"I peeked earlier this evening when you were looking up 'weazand' in the dictionary. I told you it was a word."

"I should never have doubted you," I said, now indifferent to the prominence of my be-flanneled T.E. as I leaped athletically from the bed and retrieved Carlotta's purse.

Sheeni calmly lay back against her scented pillows. "Nickie dearest, would you like to untie this bow?"

"I'd love to, darling. More than anything in the world!"

And then, diary, Sheeni gave me the best Christmas present a youth ever received.

Fuzzy and Lefty were right. It does come naturally. Clearly, the rhythms were embedded deep in my DNA, almost as if my ancestors had been performing this very act for eons.

Later, as we lay quietly in each other's arms, I asked Sheeni how I'd done.

"Not bad for a fumbling amateur," she replied. "The second time was better. My God, Nick, what's that on your chest?"

"Just a slight injury," I said. "Nothing serious."

"It looks like the Golden Gate Bridge."

"Oh, Sheeni," I sighed. "You were marvelous. It's a wonder humankind has been able to construct any civilization at all with this monumental distraction at hand."

"I'm told the novelty wears off over time."

"I don't see how it could, darling. Shall we do it again?"

"Maybe in the morning, Nick. We don't want to deplete prematurely your limited prophylactic supplies."

"OK," I said, contenting myself with some secondary fondling. "Sheeni, tell me. How long did you know Carlotta was Nick?"

"Since that first day in the donut shop, darling."

"But, but how did you know?"

"Well, Nick, your disguise was masterful, but you neglected one detail."

"What's that?"

"Carlotta's donut selection. I recognized immediately that unique and, if I may say, somewhat peculiar combination of confections."

"Of course! I should have known and ordered apple turnovers. Nick hates apple turnovers. But, Sheeni, why didn't you say anything?"

"What? And miss your performance as Carlotta? Never."

My mind raced. "Sheeni! Your affair with Ed Smith. You didn't, didn't . . ."

"Of course not, darling. It was all tediously platonic. I invented that story to punish you for sabotaging my scholastic career in Santa Cruz. When, in spite of the shocking nature of my confessed infidelity, Carlotta still sought out my company, I realized, Nick, that you really did love me."

"Did you ever doubt it for a moment, Sheeni darling?"

"Only during those many months when you were striving to seduce Apurva Joshi, darling."

"I'm sorry, darling. I think it must have been a temporary hormone imbalance."

"Uh-huh."

"Sheeni! Then you don't love Vijay!"

"I could never love a Republican, Nick. I told Vijay as much after the dance."

"But he's claiming to be a convert to liberal thought," I pointed out.

"I was not deceived, Nick. Indeed, as you should realize by now, I am seldom deceived."

How painfully true.

"Sheeni! When you were trying on those dresses, you knew it was me?"

"Of course, Nick. I confess I rather enjoyed your confusion."

"I wasn't confused, Sheeni. I knew precisely what I wanted to do. It was just that repressing the impulse nearly killed me."

"I did find your response heartening, Nick. I was beginning to fear you seemed rather too comfortable in the role of Carlotta."

"Speaking of which, Sheeni, why did you insist Carlotta get her ears pierced? The torment was beyond excruciating."

"I thought it might help you get in touch with your feminine side, Nick. Did it?"

"I'm not sure. Possibly. That and wearing a brassiere."

Sheeni yawned. "Well, Nick, you may continue pawing my person if you like, but I'm going to sleep."

I leaned over and kissed her sweet lips. "Good night, Sheeni. You have made me very happy. Do you love me?"

"Darling, the hour has passed for existential discussions. Good night. Sleep well. And no snoring!"

I think, diary, she really does love me.

10:15 a.m. Carlotta is jotting a few notes in church, while Rev. Glompiphel excoriates the congregation for wallowing in sin. So far he has condemned all the major ones except premarital sex; I expect he will be getting around to that shortly. Speaking of which, Sheeni and I used up the last of my condoms in our own private holiday celebration early this morning. She reports my performance improves 100% each time we do it. Plotting out the geometrical progression, I calculate I should surpass Casanova in technique sometime late next week. After lingering in bed for as long as we dared, we rose, showered, dressed, and put on our make-up together. I had a run in my pantyhose, so Sheeni loaned me a pair of hers. She also gave me some pointers on styling my wig. This sharing of everyday intimacies is so pleasant—almost as if we were already husband and wife.

Mrs. Saunders just leaned over and asked me what I was doing. I replied I was taking notes on the sermon. She smiled and nodded approvingly. I'm sorry I ever said anything against that noble woman.

I think I should note here to God that I believe a strong case could be made that I have not really sinned in my heart. My intentions are clearly honorable. Were it within my power, I would marry Sheeni immediately, right here in this church, with God as a witness to the purity and steadfastness of my love.

Can't write any more. Time to lip-sync some hymns.

2:10 p.m. Sheeni and I are "resting" in her bedroom. Mrs. Saunders suggested this activity after lunch, remarking that we both looked tired. We agreed a nap might prove beneficial. No condom, alas, so we've had to explore other delightful ways to make nudity fun. Sheeni, for example, has turned my body into her personal canvas, creating an unusual work of art entitled "Four Hickeys Sightseeing on the Golden Gate Bridge."

After church this morning we had a nice country breakfast, then gathered around the tree to open our presents. Sheeni did extremely well, confirming again her wisdom in selecting parents with money. She received two cashmere sweaters, a green wool skirt, an eelskin wallet, a gold charm bracelet, a genuine suede bookbag, four CDs of inspirational religious music, fuzzy slippers, a reading lamp, a rolltop desk, a ping pong table, a mountain bike, and an expensive sapphire pendant.

"Oh, Carlotta!" she gasped, obviously stunned. "It's exquisite!"

"It's real too," I noted for the record.

"Carlotta, such extravagance!" said Sheeni, who leaned close and whispered, "How can you afford it?"

"I'm loaded," I whispered back. "I'll explain later."

"Oh, Carlotta, now nice," expostulated Sheeni's mother, opening her Holy Towels.

"I can certainly use these," added Mr. Saunders, happily displaying his legal pads.

"My gift is so small, Carlotta," apologized Sheeni, placing a delicately wrapped parcel in my hands. "But I hope you like it."

"I'm sure I shall," I replied, savagely ripping the holiday foil.

It was a book. Through suddenly misting eyes, I read the title: *Beginning French for the Linguistically Nongifted.*

"Oh, Sheeni, thank you!" I gasped, my heart overflowing.

"I thought you might need it, Carlotta," she replied smiling. "In Paris."

"I, I know. Thank you. It's the nicest present I've ever received."

"Then I gather, Carlotta, your family exchanges only modest gifts," observed Mrs. Saunders. "How commendable. Sheeni, give your friend our gift."

"Yes, Mother," she replied, handing me an ordinary white envelope.

Instead of the optimistically anticipated fat check, I opened the envelope to find one blurry color snapshot of a short skinny kid in a loincloth. My God, I thought, how barbaric. They're proposing to engage Carlotta in some sort of trans-oceanic matchmaking scheme. Or was this unfortunate youth to be my own personal slave? What an untenable position for a young liberal to find himself in. Yet I dared not risk offending my hosts.

"What a handsome lad," said Carlotta, striving for ethical neutrality.

"That is Omtu," said Mrs. Saunders. "He is a deserving Christian orphan. We have adopted him in your name for this year."

"Oh, thank you!" Carlotta exclaimed, greatly relieved. "What a generous and thoughtful gift. You are too kind to me."

"We are very happy to do it, Carlotta," replied Sheeni's mother. "We want you to feel like part of the family."

"Oh, I do, Mrs. Saunders," I said, squeezing her daughter's warm hand. "Really I do!"

Sheeni has just added another hickey tourist to my chest. This one is despondent from holiday guilt and is depicted in the act of leaping to his death from mid-span.

I have explained to My Love how I came to be a wealthy teen. She finds the story improbable, but has consented to put her ingrained skepticism on hold until such time as I am able to show her a collaborating bank balance. In the meantime, I am showing her other items of an extremely personal nature.

3:30 p.m. While the elder Saunders returned to church (God, they're insatiable!), Sheeni and Carlotta sneaked up the driveway to visit lonely Paul and Lacey in adulterous exile in their tiny apartment over the garage. We arrived to find the happy couple drinking holiday mai-tais and packing their belongings into cardboard cartons.

"Merry Christmas," said Paul, introducing Carlotta to his beautiful roommate.

Lacey smiled tipsily, slurred a friendly greeting, shook Carlotta's clammy hand, then kissed Sheeni affectionately on the lips. What blatant favoritism, I thought.

"Sheeni, how nice," remarked her brother. "You've stopped torturing Carlotta."

"Don't be silly," huffed Sheeni. "I wasn't torturing anyone. And where are you going?"

"We're mooving to Lob Ankeleeze," said Lacey, woozily handing her guests two large mai-tais. "We're gooing to be faaamous."

"Not right away, of course," explained Paul. "I have to get a job first. It may be a week or two before I make the cover of *Downbeat*." He held up his glass. "To young love."

Somewhat self-consciously, Sheeni and Carlotta repeated the toast as we clinked our glasses all around.

"Sheeni," inquired Lacey, "doo you have a new booyfriend?"

"No, Lacey. I still have the same old tiresome one. Carlotta, don't poke me."

"You mean Trent?" asked Lacey. "He's so-o-o cuuute!"

"Yes, he is," confirmed Sheeni. "Carlotta, I'm warning you!"

"Lacey, my sister is in love with Nick Twisp," explained Paul.

"Niick! Is he baack?" asked Lacey thickly.

"In part," replied Sheeni.

"That Nickie's cuuute toooo," said Lacey. "Many a night, I uuused to think 'bout sneaking into his bedrooom. But, Shheeeni, I never did!"

Damn! Why such deplorable restraint?

"Thank you, Lacey," replied Sheeni. "It's probably just as well. I'm certain Nick would not have approved. Don't you agree, Carlotta?"

"Of course, Sheeni. Nick, as we know, is maniacal in his monogamy."

"Yes, maniacal is an appropriate term," agreed Sheeni. "Carlotta, don't touch me!"

Chatting, chuckling, and quaffing strong drink, we sat among the piles of boxes and exchanged presents. Sheeni gave her brother a paperback book (*Poets on Peyote*), and gave Lacey a pair of silver earrings shaped like miniature scissors.

"How cuuute!" exclaimed our hostess, struggling unsuccessfully to put them on.

Paul gave My Love a giant wall-size street map of Paris, and Lacey gave her a battery-operated eyebrow plucker—a recent Taiwanese innovation Carlotta had inspected with interest at Flampert's only a few days before. To my embarrassed surprise, they also had a package for Carlotta.

"But I don't have anything for you," I protested, savaging the gay wrapping. "Goodness, what have we here?"

"It's an answeeering maaachine," replied Lacey, attempting to fish an errant earring out of her mai-tai.

"I'm going away, Carlotta," explained Paul. "So I thought you might need something—to give you the answers."

I inspected my microprocessor-controlled electronic oracle. "Thanks, Paul," I exclaimed. "What a surprise! You shouldn't have!"

7:48 p.m. I'm back home. What a wonderful, fabulous day. I feel so great, I decided not to call Mom after all. Instead, I telephoned my good buddy Fuzzy. He reported a much better than average Christmas haul this year, including— believe it or not—a cherry, low-mileage 1965 Ford Falcon.

"They gave you your granny's car?" I asked in shocked disbelief.

"Yep. Dad signed over the pink slip. 'Course, he says I can't have the keys until I'm 16. But I got me some nice wheels, Nick."

"You do," I said enviously.

"Well, Nick, you'll probably be buying something hot when you turn 16."

"Yes, I'm thinking now of a Porsche. Or maybe a Ferrari."

"Cool, Nick. I wish I had your money."

"Frank, have you talked to your parents about my renting the house?"

"Yeah, Nick. They're into it. That damn strike's hurting bad. Mom wants to rent Uncle Polly's house now too."

"How much for this place?"

"Mom says $800 a month. Can you handle that, Nick?"

"Peanuts, Frank."

"Good. You got to fill out an application. I'll bring it over tomorrow."

"Great. Hey, Frank. Guess who Carlotta slept with last night?"

"Who? Bruno Modjaleski?"

"No, nitwit. Sheeni Saunders!"

"Did she know you were a guy?"

"Of course, she knew I was a guy. Frank, we did it. Three times!"

"How was it?"

"Fabulous, Frank. Totally fabulous."

"Nick, you're rich. You're smart. You've got your own bachelor pad. You got a beautiful chick. Guy, you've got it made!"

He's right, of course. It was a struggle there awhile, but now the tide has turned. No doubt about it, life is definitely looking up.

SATURDAY, December 26 — FRESH HORRIBLE, NIGHTMARISH DISASTERS! I shall discuss them in order of magnitude. According to Joanie, we have a new stepbrother. Mom dropped the fruit of her womb early yesterday morning around the time her elder son was sloughing off a much greater burden. Naturally, they have named the repulsive bundle Noel Lance Wescott (a particularly emasculating appellation, if you ask me). Poor kid: stuck with a neurotic mother, a fascistic cop stepdad, an unwed and possibly pregnant stepsister, and an effete moniker that will make him the particular target of every bully on the playground. Not to mention a lifetime of getting shortchanged on birthday gifts. Still, I might trade places with him.

Joanie's bigger bombshell: Lance Wescott is in Los Angeles! He has spoken with Miss Ulansky's lawyers. He has got his grubby cop hands on my money!

"The man is even worse than I supposed," said Joanie. "Why on earth did Mother marry him?"

"Who cares!" I screamed. "What about my inheritance?"

"Nick, you're still a minor. You have no standing with the law. All property left to you goes to your legal guardians."

"They're robbing me blind!"

"I'm afraid so, Nick. Lance was telling the lawyer you're probably dead. I felt like smacking his fat ugly face."

"Why didn't you?"

"Well, he's a big guy, Nick. And he had his service revolver in his holster. Even Phillie looked a little intimidated. Sorry, Nick."

"You mean I'm not going to get anything?" I asked, dazed.

"Well, you're welcome to the TV if you want it. I decided I don't like looking at Dan Rather with a five-foot face."

"Sell it, Joanie," I said in despair. "And send me the money. Fast."

"Send it where, Nick?"

I gave her my (probably temporary) address, but made her promise to guard it with her life.

"Joanie, you can't let Lance find out where I am. Now he has even more of an incentive to put me behind bars."

"Oh, Nick. This is terrible. I feel awful Mother and that innocent little baby have to live with such a monster. Even Dad was better than him."

Improbable as it sounds, my sister is right.

12:30 p.m. The damn jewelry store wouldn't give me my money back for Carlotta's garnet earrings. The loathsome clerk sneered and pointed officiously to a tiny sign pasted on the cash register: "Returns accepted for exchange or credit only." After a heated discussion, Carlotta announced she would be taking her trade elsewhere, and stomped out. Then a pawn shop refused me a loan on them because Carlotta wasn't 18. So I wound up selling my expensive garnets to Ida, the elderly lunch counter attendant at Flampert's, for a measly $40—a loss on the transaction of $74.87. At least she threw in a free coffee and piece of rhubarb pie. After my application for a bonus grilled-cheese sandwich was denied, I wandered over to the drug department and spent $14 of my profits on two-dozen lubricated, nipple-end condoms. If the choice comes down to food or sex this winter, I can see I shall be cinching in my belt (prior to removing my pants).

1:10 p.m. Fuzzy just dropped by in his new leather bomber jacket (expensive Christmas present) to give me the rental application and moon over his new car. He was alarmed to hear of my cataclysmic impoverishment.

"Nick, this is terrible! Mom said if your application didn't look good, she was putting an ad in the paper tomorrow to rent the place."

"She can't do that, Frank!"

"How am I going to stop her, Nick? They need the money. They just blew $5,000 on Christmas presents!"

"Frank, you got $5,000 worth of stuff?" I asked, appalled at his good fortune.

"I wish. Mostly they bought stuff for each other. Nick, I think you made them too lovey-dovey. That Sinatra tape is going all the time. I'm sick of it."

"Sorry, Frank. God, what'll I do?"

"Why not go live with Sheeni? You say her parents like Carlotta. You'd have a nice house, free eats, and all the pussy you could handle."

"Frank, that's not a bad idea. But I want you to know it's not just physical with Sheeni and me, I care for her deeply."

"I know, Nick," replied Fuzzy, winking. "I say, the deeper the better."

9:45 p.m. To my surprise, Sheeni didn't go for the idea. We were lying together under Granny DeFalco's musty quilt in my bedroom. On the nightstand a knotted latex tube imprisoned 200-million orphaned sperm.

"Nickie, you can't be serious. Live with me?"

"Why not, darling? We could be together day and night."

"That's what I'm worried about. What about my privacy?"

"Sheeni, married people live together without privacy."

"Yes, and that's why so many get divorced. No, I don't think it would work out."

"Sheeni, I'm going to be homeless in two days!"

"I suppose that means you want your pendant back?"

"Of course not, darling. I bought it for you. I want you to have it. I'd rather starve than take it back."

"Well, Nick, they don't give cash refunds at that store anyway."

"Really?" I said, "I didn't know that. Sheeni, I have a great idea! Why couldn't Carlotta live in your garage studio? After all, your brother is moving out. We could be together and you could still have your privacy."

"I don't know, Nick. I'd feel you were spying on me. I know I would come to resent your invasive proximity. I'll talk to Mother," she said, snuggling closer. "Perhaps someone in the church can take you in."

"I'm going to be living in a drainage culvert, Sheeni. I know it. And you don't even care."

"I do care, Nickie. Now is not the hour for despair."

"What is it the hour for then?" I asked.

"Seconds," she replied coyly. "If you are able."

I was.

Later, I popped some popcorn and we indulged in naked bed snacking.

"Nickie," said Sheeni, gobbling two kernels for my every one, "did I tell you I spoke with Trent and Vijay?"

"No, Sheeni," I replied, "you withheld that information. Probably so it would not affect adversely my sexual performance."

"Nickie, I don't know what you mean. The news is grim. Apurva's parents have met with Trent's. They have coerced him into promising never to see or talk to Apurva ever again."

"And if he breaks his word?"

"Apurva gets put on the next plane to India. He wouldn't anyway. You know Trent."

"Only too well."

"I hate to think of poor dear Trent," said Sheeni, masticating sadly. "All miserable and heart-broken and alone."

I didn't like the sound of that. "He doesn't have to be alone, Sheeni. He could always ring up Janice. Or Sonya. I know for a fact he has her phone number."

"Nickie, you really are heartless sometimes."

"OK, Sheeni. I'll see what I can do. Carlotta may have a few more aces up her ravelled sleeve."

"Thank you, Nickie. Now, shall we call up and have a pizza delivered?"

I blanched visibly.

"I'll pay, Nickie!"

We phoned for a pizza, then Sheeni called her parents and asked if she could spend the night at Carlotta's. Of course, being enlightened, they raised no moral objections.

11:30 p.m. Eating pepperoni and mushroom pizza in bed beside the Naked Woman of Your Dreams may be one of life's divine experiences. I have decided to stop worrying and live only in the present.

Presently someone very close to me is doing something extremely erotic with a pepperoni morsel.

SUNDAY, December 27 — There's been a temporary respite in my housing crisis. Fuzzy's mother won't be interviewing prospective tenants this week. She's in jail.

The story was told in gripping photographs on the front page of this morning's paper. There was the hand-cuffed suspect (Irene, holding her jacket over her face); there was the menacing murder weapon (a stolen AK-47 sub-machinegun); there was the bullet-riddled car (a leased BMW); there was the distraught victim of the love-triangle assault (Dad, pointing indignantly at his bandaged temple, where the fatal bullet struck two inches wide of its mark).

"Nickie, your family continues to astonish!" exclaimed Sheeni, sipping her instant coffee. We were having donuts and sausage links (for vital protein) in bed.

"My family? You mean Fuzzy's family! My father was an innocent victim of a heinous assault. Sheeni, you have donut crumbs on your lovely breasts."

"Don't try to change the subject, Nick. You know very well if Fuzzy's mother was driven to take up arms, your father must have committed some unspeakably vile provocation."

"I believe, Sheeni, your breasts are absolutely perfect."

Sheeni pulled up the quilt and swatted me with her newspaper.

"Just as I feared, Nick. These premature experiences have turned you into a sex maniac. I shall never forgive myself."

"Me neither," I said, nuzzling into her musty, crumby chest. My eager lips found a warm nipple. Sheeni fondled my ear and continued to read her newspaper.

"Nick, it says here there was a woman with your father at the time of the shooting. She was injured slightly by flying glass."

"Yeah? Does it say who she was?"

"Nickie, don't talk with your mouth full. It hurts. Let's see, the female companion was identified as Miss Radmilla Sanders, 38, of Oakland, California."

"My old kindergarten teacher! She must have gotten desperate after all."

"Anyone who dates a Twisp is desperate by definition," said Sheeni, kissing me lasciviously. She paused abruptly. "Nickie, you didn't have anything to do with Mrs. DeFalco shooting your father, did you?"

"Of course not, darling."

"Are you sure? Murdering one's father is a natural Oedipal impulse in boys, as you may know."

"Sheeni, I have nothing to do with my father. I only see him on TV. Mrs. DeFalco must have become enraged because Dad dumped her for someone younger and prettier. You know, a woman scorned."

"Don't be sexist, Nick. Most of the violence in this world is committed by men against women."

"Don't I know it. Carlotta was nearly raped by Bruno."

"Really?"

"Very nearly. As it was, I was forced to kiss him good night."

"You mean I've been kissing lips that kissed Bruno Modjaleski?"

"Don't complain, Sheeni. I've been kissing lips that kissed Bruno Preston."

"Yes, but my Bruno is a doll. If only he weren't quite so clumsy in bed. I wonder if your Bruno is any better in that department?"

"With luck, Sheeni, neither of us will ever know."

"Oh dear, Nick. If we don't get out of this bed in two minutes, we'll be late for church."

"Sheeni, I'm not going anywhere that's not clothing optional. Carlotta will phone your mother and make an excuse."

"It'd better be a good one, darling."

It was. Carlotta told Mrs. Saunders we were trying to arrange a phone interview by international long distance with Omtu, my adopted charity ward. The connection was about to come through, I announced excitedly, hanging up.

Sheeni and I dawdled in bed most of the morning, then took a long, leisurely bath together in Mrs. DeFalco's massive tub. Sorry God, it was the greatest Sunday morning of my life.

1:15 p.m. Fuzzy just dropped by in post-maternal-arrest crisis. Carlotta and Sheeni are taking him out for a counseling brunch at the Golden Carp. I pray Sheeni can pick up the tab.

6:42 p.m. I'm babysitting Fuzzy. He doesn't want to go home or be alone. Darling Sheeni kissed Carlotta passionately (and Fuzzy consolingly), then left for home. I'm glad Fuzzy is here. I get disturbingly panicky now whenever I'm apart from Sheeni. The rapture I feel in her presence is like a powerful addicting drug. Withdrawal, even temporary, is scary black torture.

7:18 p.m. Fuzzy and I are watching "60 Minutes." Mike Wallace is putting the thumbscrews to a guy via hidden camera. Fuzzy just expressed a wish that Mike Wallace "do his number" on my father. My pal believes Dad has "permanently wrecked" his homelife "for all time." I continue to counsel guarded optimism.

9:44 p.m. Fuzzy is into his second hour of therapeutic phone chat with Heather in Santa Cruz. I wonder who will be paying the bill? My curiosity is purely academic, since I expect I'll be moving into a nice damp drainage culvert before the bill arrives. I don't care how distraught he is, I wish Fuzzy would hang up soon. Carlotta wants desperately to call Sheeni. I need to hear her sweet voice.

10:28 p.m. Sheeni is well and happy. She has spoken to her parents about Carlotta's housing plight, and they have promised to see what they can do. She was also obliged to give a detailed report on Carlotta's telephone conversation with Omtu.

"I said you had a lively discussion on the role of ritual in the evocation of grace," said Sheeni. "They seemed pleased."

"Thank you, darling," I replied. "What would I do without you?"

"Attend church more frequently, I expect. How is Fuzzy?"

"Better, I think. Heather cheered him up. He's out in the garage polishing his Falcon bumpers. I've invited him to spend the night."

"You're a good friend, Nick."

"How am I as a lover?"

"Not completely incompetent."

"Sheeni, I've added it up. We've done it eight times so far."

"Well, they say boys are more mathematically inclined than girls."

"Sheeni, I wish it was you I was sleeping with tonight."

"I wish I was asleep. I seem to have accumulated a massive sleep debt from your snoring."

"Sorry, Sheeni. I'll see you tomorrow. I love you."

"I sometimes feel not unwarmly toward you, Nickie. Good night."

She loves me. I can tell.

11:07 p.m. We have made up a lumpy, uncomfortable bed for Fuzzy on the sofa. As a precaution, I have clandestinely removed his belt and shoelaces. One can't be too careful when dealing with emotionally disturbed teens. And now to savor one of my precious few remaining nights in a real bed.

This bed is a mess. My sheets look like the site of a three-day Cub Scout encampment.

MONDAY, December 28 — After breakfast Fuzzy irately demanded his belt and shoelaces, then departed for downtown to see if he could visit his mother. He invited Carlotta to tag along, but—citing an allergy to blue wool and authority—she declined. Feeling somewhat morose myself, I decided to reach out for my own mother. She answered on the third ring.

"Nick! Where are you?"

"Oh, I'm around."

"Why did you lie and say you were in India when all the time you were staying with your sister? I was worried sick. We thought you were being held prisoner by gangsters."

"Sorry, Mom. I was keeping a low profile. What's new with you?"

"Nickie, I had a baby! On Christmas Day! We've named him Noel Lance."

"That's nice," I said, feigning surprise. "How is he?"

"Fine. We came home from the hospital yesterday. Easiest labor I ever had. He's a beautiful baby. I only wish he didn't look so much like Jerry. I get a little jolt every time I see the little angel."

I tried to imagine a newborn with a face like Mom's assless, beer-swollen, dead paramour, but my mental screen remained blank. My imagination balked at the tactlessness of the request.

"How does Lance like him?"

"Oh, Lance loves him. He hasn't seen him yet, but he's spoken to Noelly twice over the telephone. Nickie, did you hear? Some woman tried to shoot your father!"

"Yeah, I heard, Mom. She missed."

"Wasn't it terrible? The bullet just grazed him. Talk about lousy luck."

"Mom, where's Lance?"

"He's, he's away, Nick. On business."

"Mom," I said, coming to the point, "what are you guys doing with my money?"

"It's not your money, Nick. You're too young. It's the family's money."

"OK. What is the family doing with my money?"

"We're moving to a nice house in the hills, Nick. Don't worry, real estate is a good investment. And it will be much better for Noelly. I don't want him growing up in this bad neighborhood."

Right, but it was good enough for your first son!

"Mom, can you send me a few thousand?"

"I don't know, Nick. The house we made an offer on is pretty expensive. And I have to buy lots of new things for Noelly. I'll have to ask Lance."

"And what possible say," I asked, trying to remain calm, "does your husband have in a decision to give me a tiny fraction of *my* money?"

"It's not your money, Nick. Besides, we've had to put it all in Lance's name."

"What!"

"It's in case I get sued for all the damages you caused in that fire. They can't touch us if Lance has the money. Nickie, give me your address. I'll talk it over with Lance and send you a little spending money if I can."

"Uh, no, better not. Just mail the check to Joanie. She can forward it to me."

"I'm sorry, Nick. If you can't trust your own mother with your frigging address, I can't help you."

"You're going to let me starve?"

"It's up to you. Give me your address and I'll send you a bus ticket home this afternoon. Nick, don't you want to see your new brother at least?"

Maybe, but only out of ghoulish curiosity.

"Sure I do, Mom. But not while the FBI is on my tail. Well, happy holidays. Have fun with my money. Say hi to Noel for me. I hope he doesn't grow up to look like Jerry."

"Jerry was a very handsome man," she snapped. "Watch your smart mouth!"

I've heard that line before.

12:10 p.m. On the way back from budget grocery shopping, Carlotta dropped into the library to use the rental typewriter. Twenty minutes' labor produced this Letter to the Editor, my first foray into participatory democracy:

To the Editor:

The time for silence is over. Now we must turn the bright light of public scrutiny on the dark stain of corruption, racism, and brutality that is spreading its putrefying stench over this city's law enforcement agency. Mine are not the rantings of some meddlesome, criminal-coddling do-gooder. I have seen the brutality firsthand, I have heard the racial epitaphs and sniggering, I have witnessed the payoffs by drug dealers, pimps, and gambling czars. I am a veteran police officer who believes the time has come to speak up, no, to shout the truth. Fellow citizens, your public trust has been betrayed!

Today, I am demanding an immediate and thorough investigation of this city's police department by the county Grand Jury, the state Attorney General's office, the U.S. Department of Justice, and the FBI. More specifically, I am calling for an inquiry into the unlawful arrest of a truck driver named Wally Rumpkin. The disgraceful treatment afforded this tall, innocent man is just one of innumerable miscarriages of justices I have observed on the job.

Recently, my dear wife gave birth to a charming baby we have named Noel. Even though I am not his biological father, I have pledged to Noel to do all in my power to see that he grows up in a city patrolled by police officers who are decent, honorable, and respectful toward citizens of every race, creed, color, and sexual orientation. Let us unite and pull down the barriers to an egalitarian society. Let us be brothers and sisters together. Come, fellow citizens, join me in this great crusade. The time has come to dial 911 for truth and justice!

Officer Lance Wescott, OPD

To be on the safe side, Carlotta made six copies and mailed them to all the major dailies in the Bay Area. I think Noel will be proud of his daddy's courageous action, don't you?

4:38 p.m. Make than ten times, diary. Ten times I have imposed my living body within the divine sanctuary of Sheeni's innermost temple. At certain moments, I've noticed, the separateness of our physical existences seems to dissolve—almost as if the points of contact, where my flesh ended and Sheeni's began, had blurred. Only one disjuncture mars the perfection of our union: that thin alien barrier of latex. Just once I'd like to feel heat against heat, living cell against living cell, excited nerve ending against excited nerve ending. Just once, I say, let our dammed secretions, our divided lubricities blend (as nature intended) into a common binary soup.

Of course, we don't dare. As Sheeni reminds me when I raise this aesthetic point, I'm not the one at risk for getting pregnant.

We are passing another pleasant afternoon catching up on our naked journal-writing under Granny DeFalco's musty quilt. Every so often I slide my hand along My Love's silken thigh for literary inspiration. I twirl my lazy digits in her chestnut tangle and idly finger that fascinating zone where soft fleshy mound first bifurcates into exotic cleft. She doesn't seem to mind.

In the conversational interval between today's lovemaking, Sheeni informed me that her parents have come up with a solution to Carlotta's housing dilemma.

"Reverend Glompiphel and his wife need an au pair for their twin boys," she announced.

"How old are they?" I asked doubtfully.

"Nearly seven."

"They aren't those fat little monsters who were rioting up in the choir loft on Christmas Eve, are they?"

"They're not usually that unruly, Nickie. Mother said in the excitement of the holiday, Mrs. Glompiphel neglected to give them their Ritalin."

"Two crazed brats. On drugs too. Sounds bad. Your minister doesn't have any other ankle-biters does he?"

"No, Nickie. Just the twins. And the rabbits."

"What rabbits?"

"Mrs. Glompiphel raises rabbits behind the parsonage to supplement her husband's inadequate salary. She has 200 brooding angoras. She would expect some occasional assistance from Carlotta—feeding the animals, cleaning cages, that sort of thing."

"How occasionally?"

"Every day after school. Before you pick up the twins at daycare."

"Sounds like a living nightmare. What's the pay?"

"Room and board and $100 a month."

"Surely, Sheeni, you mean $100 a week!"

"Sorry, Nick. I told you Reverend Glompiphel was underpaid. That's all they can afford. But you'd have your own room."

"Where? In the attic with the bats?"

"No, in the parsonage basement. You'd have your privacy too—except for Tuesdays and Thursdays. That's when the therapy groups meet down there."

"What therapy groups?" I demanded.

"Oh, the usual: the recovering alcoholics, the wife beaters, the newly divorced, the child abusers, the recently unemployed, the depressed seniors, the credit-card bingers, the despondent teens."

"Maybe I could sit in on that last group, Sheeni. I might have a great deal to contribute."

"Carlotta is due at the Glompiphels tomorrow morning at 9:30," continued Sheeni, ignoring my lamentations. "Mother made the appointment. Try to look enthusiastic and make sure your tits are on straight."

I pulled the quilt down from under her chin. "Can you give me a demonstration?"

She did too.

6:18 p.m. Against my expressed wishes, Sheeni donned her clothes (all of them) and went home to dinner. Carlotta is invited to go "dog-walking" with her tomorrow after my slave interview. I can hardly wait.

Is that Fuzzy I hear on the porch?

8:52 p.m. I offered to make my troubled pal a nice garbanzo casserole, but instead he treated Carlotta to dinner at the Golden Carp. We ordered the Deluxe Dinner for two: shrimp chips, potstickers, cashew chicken, Mongolian beef, steamed rice, green tea ice cream, fortune cookies, and tea. A feast for the body (if not the palate) for only $10.95. To broaden Fuzzy's horizons (and take his mind off his troubles), Carlotta goaded her escort into eating with chopsticks.

Over a very leisurely meal, Fuzzy brought me up to date on the criminal proceedings. His mother has been evaluated by the county psychologist (a former high-school boyfriend) and adjudged "in touch with reality, sincerely remorseful, and thoroughly charming." Armed with this adulatory evaluation, Fuzzy's dad and his lawyers are hoping they can get her sprung on bail sometime tonight. After waiting all morning, Fuzzy finally got to see his mother briefly as she was being led down a hallway for arraignment.

"It's very hard seeing your own mother in handcuffs," he said, choking on grief or cashew chicken.

"I'm sure it is," replied Carlotta consolingly.

I tried to imagine Mom and Lance being led off in cuffs and leg irons. Oddly, the image materialized easily with surprisingly light emotional toll. I didn't even have that much trouble slapping the mental cuffs on tiny Noel.

Much later, as we were finally preparing to leave, the door opened and in walked Bruno Modjaleski—arm-in-arm with a radiant Mertice Palmquist.

"Oh Bruno!" called Carlotta, waving coquettishly.

The happy twosome decoupled from Steve the waiter and shunted over toward us.

"Hi, Carly," boomed Bruno. "Makin' the Fuzz buy you some chop suey, huh? Hey, Fuzzy is it worth it, guy? She puttin' out reg'lar?"

"Fairly regular," blushed Fuzzy.

Smiling amiably, Mertice prodded her date.

"Hey, you guys know Mertice?" asked Bruno. "Mertice baby, this is Fuzzy and my neighbor, Carly. She's the one what told me about Hurlbut."

Mertice grasped Carlotta's clammy hand and shook it warmly. "How did you ever know my sweet Hurlbut wanted me to meet dear Bruno?" she asked.

"Uh, I guess I'm psychic," I replied. "A little bird came to me in a dream."

"What did he look like?" she asked eagerly.

"Let me see. He was green with a yellow head."

"Hurlbut!" screamed Mertice, startling the other dinners. "What did he say?"

"He was surprisingly specific for a parakeet. He said he wanted you to have an intense, physical relationship with Bruno Modjaleski."

"Well," said Mertice, squeezing Bruno's massive arm, "we've certainly fulfilled that prophesy!"

"I'm so jealous," lied Carlotta. "But at least I've got my precious Fuzzy." I grasped his hairy hand and held on lovingly as my date struggled to pull away.

"Is your last name by any chance DeFalco?" Mertice asked my companion. Fuzzy paused in his manual effort. "Uh-huh."

"I think I may have met your father once," she said. "And I'm sorry to hear about your poor mother."

"Yeah, what a lousy shot," added Bruno. "You been coachin' her, Fuzz?"

Fuzzy scowled and ripped free his trembling hand. "Time to go, Carlotta," he said.

Gathering up her shawl, purse, umbrella, and doggie bag, Carlotta rose from the red vinyl booth. "Have fun, kids," she said. "Oh, and Mertice, I'll keep you posted if Hurlbut visits with any more messages."

"Oh, could you ask him something?" Mertice leaned close and whispered a question in Carlotta's ear, causing it to turn bright red.

"Well, what did Mertice want to know?" asked Fuzzy later, as we were trudging homeward in the rain.

"Bruno's pushing for a threesome. She wants to know if she should agree."

"Who's the other chick?"

"Who do you think?"

"Boy, Carlotta, you better keep your doors locked."

"I'm not worried, Frank. I think Hurlbut's going to put his little budgie foot down quite firmly on that moral issue."

10:05 p.m. When I got home, I found this message on my new answering machine: "Carlotta, where are you? Mother says you can sleep over tonight, if you like. We can have breakfast tomorrow and all go over to the parsonage together. If you come over, don't forget to bring several of those small utilitarian items. Bye-bye. Hope to see you later."

Thank God for my precious answering machine. What a tragedy if I had missed that message!

TUESDAY, December 29 — I invaded Sheeni's privacy several times early this morning—while the house slumbered in indifferent stillness and anonymous birdlife chirped avian hosannas to the dawn. Curiously, the second time I found my mind wandering from the task at hand. Only my 12th congress with My

One and Only Love, and I spent the middle portion of the act speculating on the breakfast menu. At least my attention was flagged down again at the end by the thunderous crescendo. Perhaps I'm just a quart low from overpumping; I may need to adopt a sensible resource conservation plan. Too bad I can't just put it all back for recycling—I've certainly collected enough of the stuff. Sheeni makes Carlotta take them home in her purse—lest they clog up a toilet or be discovered by her mother in a wastebasket.

Breakfast was fresh-squeezed orange juice, French toast with real maple syrup, crispy bacon, and strong, delicious coffee. Savoring my third cup, Carlotta couldn't help ruminating on her friend's regrettable selfishness. If the tables were turned, I would certainly invite Sheeni to come live with me full-time in my comfortable home.

"Carlotta, my dear," said Mrs. Saunders, "we're very sorry to hear of your mother's sudden passing."

"Her what?" I asked, startled.

"Your mother's death," said Sheeni hastily. "That is why, Carlotta, you are faced with homelessness."

"Oh right," said Carlotta sadly. "Mother went very suddenly. Of course, she was quite elderly."

"And she left you with nothing?" boomed Mr. Saunders indignantly.

"Hardly anything," I sighed. "Just some wonderful memories."

"If you are entirely destitute, young woman," advised the lawyer, "you should become a ward of the state."

"Oh Carlotta is much too independent for that, Father," said Sheeni. "Aren't you, Carlotta?"

"Oh, yes!" I affirmed. "I hate dependency. I'd rather make it on my own."

"How very brave," said Mrs. Saunders. "Elwyn, isn't she brave?"

"Yes, my dear," he rumbled. "Headstrong, foolish, ill-informed, but indis-putably courageous."

"Carlotta," gushed Mrs. Saunders, "you have restored my faith in your generation. I was beginning to despair. I feared everyone your age was as misbegotten as that evil Nick Twisp."

"Nick isn't so bad, Mother," declared Sheeni.

"Carlotta, what do you say to that blasphemy?" demanded Sheeni's mother.

Carlotta nervously adjusted her brassiere. "I believe, I believe there is some good in all of us, Mrs. Saunders. Even, perhaps, in Nick Twisp."

"My husband is correct," she replied severely. "Dear Carlotta, you are ill-informed."

After breakfast, the three ladies motored over to the church in Mrs. Saunders' big green Chrysler. We found my future slave overseer and her twin hoodlums in a dim, odorous shed behind the plain stucco parsonage. Here and there in rusty, makeshift cages, large fluffy mammals were nibbling lettuce leaves and godlessly fornicating. One adolescent rabbit was experiencing a rodent thrill ride as the hoodlums—identical in visage, dress, and juvenile corpulency—tumbled his cage end over end.

"Dusty! Rusty! Don't do that, boys!" called Mrs. Glompiphel, a big-boned, horse-faced, plainly dressed woman about 30. "Mr. Bunny is not enjoying that!"

The twins dropped the cage and began to stare menacingly at Carlotta. Sheeni's mother made the introductions. Everyone except the twins smiled with feigned sincerity and shook hands.

"Carlotta," said Mrs. Glompiphel, "these are my sons Dusty and Rusty. Boys, say hi to your new friend Carlotta."

"How come she's wearin' black?" asked one of them.

"Because, very sadly, her mother just passed away," explained its mother.

"How comes she's so ugly?" asked the other.

Mrs. Glompiphel blushed. "Rusty! Mind your manners!"

After a tour of the rabbit ranch, truck garden (slave weeding next spring!), and orchard (slave fruit-picking next fall!), Mrs. Glompiphel led her guests into the disheveled parsonage.

"Put your things down, ladies," said our hostess, clearing a broken slotcar set from the threadbare sofa over the twins' noisy protests. "I'm sorry this place is such a mess. I could use a little help straightening things up."

Slave housekeeping all year-round!

"Dusty, stop kicking your brother!" hollered its mother. "Sorry, the Reverend was called away on a prayer errand. I expect him back soon. Would you all like some tea?"

"Yuck! I hate tea!" said a twin.

"I want whiskey and soda," declared the other.

"I don't know where he hears such things," apologized its mother. "Probably TV."

"No, Mom," he replied. "That's what Daddy drinks!"

"Uh, tea sounds fine, Mrs. Glompiphel," said Sheeni, pointedly refusing to make eye contact with Carlotta.

As we crowded into the smelly, peanut-butter smeared kitchen, Mrs. Glompiphel brewed some weak off-brand tea and refereed violent pinching and gouging bouts between her combative offspring. She poured the tea, opened a package of generic vanilla sandwich cookies, and watched with relief as the twins declared a truce to stuff in the sugar.

"Now, Carlotta," she said, handing me a greasy cup, "tell me about yourself."

Twenty minutes later, the tea consumed, Carlotta's life an open (but entirely fictional) book, the twins displaying signs of sugar-induced restiveness, we adjourned to the basement to inspect "my room": grim cement-block walls, bare concrete floor, two cobweb-encrusted windows high up the damp walls, a tribe of mismatched stuffed chairs forming a defensive circle under a naked light bulb, exposed floorboards overhead creaking non-stop as the twins wrestled upstairs. At least the mustiness and ubiquitous religious art reminded me of my present cozy home.

"I'm sure one of the parishioners would donate a bed and a dresser," said Mrs. Glompiphel optimistically.

"A desk would be nice too," remarked Sheeni.

Still no eye contact.

"Where's the bathroom?" asked Carlotta uneasily.

"Oh, it's upstairs," replied Mrs. Glompiphel cheerfully. "On the second floor."

"It will be good exercise for you, Carlotta," noted Sheeni's mother.

"Uh-huh," I said.

The inspection completed, the slave mistress switched off the light and we trooped back up the creaky wooden stairs into the ominously silent kitchen.

"I better see what those boys are up to," said their mother.

We followed her into the living room, where we saw our hostess recoil in stunned surprise.

"Dusty! Rusty!" she screamed. "What are you doing?"

"Mommy, look what we found," piped the fat twins in unison, holding aloft their prized discoveries. With a violent shock, I recognized—depending from their fat fingers—the intimate byproducts of this dawn's applied concupiscence.

"Give me those at once!" shouted Mrs Glompiphel, seizing the knotted, engorged rubbers. "Where did you get these?"

The vile monsters pointed accusingly at you know who. "We got them from her purse," they confessed proudly.

The two mothers stared wonderingly at Carlotta, now flushing intense crimson. Was the jig finally up?

"Carlotta," said Sheeni calmly, "where did you find those?"

"I, uh ... " Was my love betraying me as well?

"Carlotta," insisted Sheeni, "I know you have a balloon collection. Now where did you pick those up?"

"Oh, uh, I found them downtown. In the alley behind Flampert's. I usually find several on Saturday mornings. They're most unusual. Don't you think?"

"Carlotta, dear," said Mrs. Saunders, "before your mother died, did she ever, did she ever discuss certain facts with you?"

"What sort of facts?" I asked innocently.

"About ... men and women," ventured Mrs. Glompiphel.

"No, not that I can recall," Carlotta replied pensively. "Why? Is there something I should know?"

"Oh dear," said Mrs. Saunders.

"Oh dear, oh dear," added Mrs. Glompiphel.

12:30 p.m. Back in my snug squatter home. Reverend Glompiphel never showed. We left hastily, after Mrs. Glompiphel promised "to talk matters over" with her husband. I'm not sure she's convinced Carlotta is the right person to guide the moral development of her sons. Personally, I think I'd rather starve to death slowly in a nice drainage culvert.

In the car coming home Sheeni promised her mother that she would divulge the facts of life to Carlotta this afternoon.

"But darling," protested her mother, "are you certain you are competent to discuss these matters?"

"Yes, Mother," replied Sheeni. "I saw several films on the topic in health class."

"Sheeni, you did not have my written permission to attend such films! Why was I not informed?"

"I don't know, Mother," said Sheeni. "Perhaps it's a communist plot."

"Sheeni!" snapped Mrs. Saunders, "watch your smart mouth!"

Sheeni and Carlotta exchanged glances. We'd heard that line before.

4:27 p.m. What a way to spend an afternoon—walking loathsome Albert and Jean Paul while The Woman of My Dreams flirted blatantly with Trent. If I weren't convinced Sheeni's one of the sweetest, most genuine girls who ever lived, I'd almost suppose she exhibits a proclivity toward sadism. Most unsettling, she couched her maddening flirtation in the form of a playful advocacy of the romantic compatibility of Carlotta and Trent.

"Dear Carlotta," teased Sheeni, "have you not admitted openly that Fuzzy leaves you cold?"

"Fuzzy's all right," retorted Carlotta. "He's very good to me."

"Trent, darling," said Sheeni, "does that sound like the sentiments of a woman in love?"

"I have no cause to doubt Carlotta's sincerity," replied the despondent poet.

"Well, I have some cause to doubt yours," said Sheeni. "Did you not confide to me recently in English class that you found Carlotta 'entirely fascinating'?"

"Carlotta," said Trent, blushing under his tan, "I hope you can find it in your heart to forgive my sexist presumption."

"That's OK," I said. "No offense taken."

"I only hope," continued Sheeni, "that you two are not holding back out of any misplaced loyalty to me. I would never stand in the way of your happiness."

"You are too kind," replied Carlotta. "But I know Trent's heart belongs to the lovely person whose dog he is now escorting."

"Yes, and I fear this woven plastic leash may be my only connection to her now," he added lugubriously.

"Then again, perhaps not," said Carlotta.

The procession halted abruptly as my companions gazed expectantly at Carlotta.

"Have you a plan?" they asked eagerly.

"Why yes," I admitted, "I do."

While Albert and Jean Paul nosed through and defaced some of Ukiah's most prestigious landscaping, Carlotta revealed her plan, then successfully rebutted all objections raised by her skeptical friends. In the end, they had to admit it was the only practical solution. Trent agreed to suppress his moral qualms; Sheeni agreed to talk to Vijay to see if the launch date could be scheduled for tomorrow night.

"Are you sure this will work?" asked Trent doubtfully.

"It will if Sheeni can make enough noise," Carlotta replied.

"I shall certainly do my best," answered My Love. "We cannot fail this time!"

I hoped that was the lambent glimmer of sincerity I observed in the cool azure depths of her eyes.

When I returned, I found this depressing message on my answering machine: "Hi, Carlotta. Reverend Glompiphel here. I'd love to speak to you personally about joining our family group. Drop by tomorrow morning at 10:30. I'll be in my study in the church. Let me know if that's not convenient for you. God bless you."

More interviews! More prying interrogations! More insinuating questions! At what point, I wonder, will they be hooking up the polygraph machine?

8:37 p.m. My wad has withered to $24.53. After a meager supper (only three cans of garbanzos remain), I washed the dishes, then Sheeni came over to discuss the facts of life. We took off our clothes and she illustrated her lecture with some extremely attractive visual aids. I have now made love as many times as years I have lived. Four times today! Yet, I believe with the proper stimulus another enlightening demonstration could be undertaken.

Sheeni has talked to Vijay, and everything is arranged. Operation Son of Thundering Cupid commences tomorrow night at eight sharp.

My Love says for a "bookish transvestite" I am becoming remarkably adept at the art and science of lovemaking. The secret of my success? All those hours in lonely confinement spent studying my ex-pal Lefty's illustrated tome on gourmet sex techniques. I am still holding in reserve dozens of the more exotic positions and maneuvers. If, as I expect, Sheeni and I are to be engaged in this activity for the next 70 or 80 years, I mustn't exhaust the vocabulary of love too soon.

9:26 p.m. No news from Fuzzy. I called his home, but received no answer. Sheeni and I ate naked tin roof sundaes in bed and discussed my plight. She agrees the Glompiphel slave position is untenable, but thinks it might be tolerable for a "short interval."

"Until when?" I demanded. "Until I die of rabbit turd fever? Or kill myself in a fit of religious ennui?"

"Don't be morbid, Nickie," she replied, crunching into her last chocolate-drowned peanut. "Something will turn up."

"Most likely my maggot-riddled corpse. I hope they don't call you to come down and identify it, Sheeni."

"I hope not either," she replied, wrinkling her lovely nose. "Maggots make me gag. Nickie, wasn't darling Albert doing cute things this afternoon?"

"Name one."

"Well, how about the time he barked at that policeman in his patrol car and made him spill his coffee?"

I saw through that transparent ploy. The traitorous canine was trying to turn me in to the cops.

10:34 p.m. My spittle on her lips, my heart in her hands, My Dearest One just departed for home. Fifteen times, diary. Sheeni found the right stimulus; she has been reading an old book of Paul's on holistic massage and agreed to try a few beginning relaxation strokes on me. I find it odd that probing softly into a man's ankle can so strategically relocate the tension in his body. How mysterious is the vessel of flesh and bones we walk around in.

And what is the function of the orgasm anyway? I must reread Wilhelm Reich. I wonder if I dare sneak such books into the parsonage?

WEDNESDAY, December 30 — Fuzzy called me this early morning with momentous news. A deal has been struck. Dad is declining to press charges against his erstwhile adulterous flame. In return, Mr. DeFalco has dropped his onerous $3.5 million lawsuit and has agreed to fund Dad's expensive BMW bullet hole cosmetic surgery. Of course, Fuzzy's mom will still face charges of possessing an unregistered assault rifle.

"But that's no big deal," Fuzzy said happily. "The lawyer says she'll probably just get off with a fine. Or maybe a few months' probation at the worst."

"Thank God the judicial authorities refuse to take our gun laws seriously," I observed. "Looks like everything's turning out OK."

"Yeah, Nick. Except Dad's really hurting now that he won't be collecting all those millions from your jerk father. He had to settle the strike."

"He did?"

"Yeah, that commie friend of yours should be happy. Dad caved in totally to those greedy drivers. He's kind of pissed at Mom now. She wants to know where your application is. They got to rent the houses right away."

"Like when, Frank?" I snapped.

"Like tomorrow, Nick."

"Shit!"

"Sorry, Nick. The way I figure it, it's all your dad's fault."

He's right, of course. That drunken carbuncle is still wrecking my life!

Silently I wandered through my little house: pinched dark rooms, impossible traffic flows, ill-proportioned windows, truly dreadful wallpaper, revolting carpets, scarred woodwork, nightmarish drapes, light fixtures from hell. Still it was my first home on my own and I was nearly happy here. Tomorrow someone else may be living here. And me? Where will I be?

Can't obsess any more. Time for Carlotta to dress for her interview.

10:45 a.m. I didn't go. My feet refused to march in the proper direction. So Carlotta wound up instead in the donut shop downtown, where I sit writing this saga of woe while gorging myself on a giant, economical grab bag of day-olds. For once in my life I have decided to take a moral stand against hypocrisy. I don't care what happens, I can't live with that pious deranged family. I just can't!

Should I call up Mom for a bus ticket and take my chances with Lance? I wonder if it's too late to cancel that letter to the editor? Or should I drop in on Dad and surprise him? He might be in a good mood this morning, what with escaping from that oppressive lawsuit and getting his car fixed for free.

Oh, no. That fat moron Dwayne just came in. I hope he doesn't notice me. Damn, he did.

11:15 a.m. Remarkable developments, diary. I am trying to remain calm. Believe it or not, Carlotta's reluctant conversation with Dwayne proved most enlightening.

First, from his "Christmas money" my conscientious friend paid me a welcome $10 installment on his dog-fight entry fee.

"Did you have a nice Christmas?" asked Carlotta, feigning interest as she pocketed the windfall.

With all the grace of Godzilla, Dwayne stuffed a defenseless maple bar into his churning maul. "Nop bud," he chewed. "Did boo?"

"I had an unforgettable Christmas," replied Carlotta. "Truly memorable."

"Wad boo get?" he asked, sacrificing next an innocent cruller.

"A wonderful book on French."

That reminds me, I must start my language lessons. I hope the drainage culvert has good light for reading.

"Sounds borin'," remarked Dwayne, swallowing. "I got better stuff than that. I got a skateboard an' a harm'nica an' a gerbil an' a pogo stick an' three Nint'ndo games an' this zinky watch."

Dwayne stuck out a fat hairless arm. I glanced toward it casually, then felt an electric shock of recognition.

"Where did you get that watch?" Carlotta screamed.

Dwayne hastily withdrew his flabby wrist. "It's mine," he insisted. "Santy brung it for Christmas."

"I know it's yours, Dwayne," Carlotta said placatingly. "It's a very nice watch too. What kind is it?"

"Don't you know? Everybody wants one. Mom had to drive clear to Santy Rosa to find it. It's a Wart Watch."

"Can I see it again?"

Dwayne hesitantly thrust out his left arm. Carlotta leaned forward and examined the unusual timepiece with growing excitement. Yes, there was the crude dial marred by faux rust stains. There was the simulated bullet hole. There was the flesh-colored plastic band distinguished by fake scars and a large, hairy artificial wart.

"It's a very nice watch, Dwayne. Do you mind if I look at the back?"

"What for?" he demanded suspiciously.

"I'd just like to see where it was made. I'll give it right back to you."

Still suspicious, Dwayne undid the strap and handed his precious watch to Carlotta. Molded into the back of the cheap plastic case was this inscription: "American Fashions for Freedom Enterprises, Malibu, CA. World rights reserved. Made in Taiwan."

So, my enterprising friends have moved up the socio-economic ladder to affluent Malibu. How strange they didn't think to notify their partner of their change of address!

"Gimme my watch back," huffed Dwayne.

Carlotta returned his prize. "A most interesting watch, Dwayne. Does it keep good time?"

"It gains 'bout five minutes an hour," he replied. "But I like it anyways."

A satisfied consumer. That is the secret of business success.

11:42 a.m. Carlotta arrived back home in great haste and immediately dialed long-distance information. Miraculously, they had a listing for American Fashions for Freedom Enterprises. It hadn't been a sugar-induced hallucination after all! I dialed the vital number. After three excruciating rings, Kimberly answered, trying to sound like a high-paid English receptionist.

"Hi, Kimberly," I said cheerily, "this is your partner Nick."

"Who?"

"Nick Twisp, Joanie's brother. You know, you're manufacturing the watch I designed."

"Oh, hi, Nick," she said unenthusiastically. "What's up?"

"The watch looks great, Kimberly. How's it selling?"

"Terrible, Nick. We're losing our shirts. It's a disaster. We're really getting our clocks cleaned on this one."

"You're not making any profits?" I asked, spirits plummeting.

"Profits! You're dreaming, Nick. I may have to get a job waitressing to pay my rent this month."

"But, but I know someone who bought one. He loves it!"

"Yeah, well we sold a handful of them. But the development costs were astronomical. Everything was rushed to get it out in time for Christmas."

"That's, that's too bad," I sighed.

"Sorry, Nick. We could send you a complimentary watch if you like."

"Don't bother. I think they're gross."

Another fortune down the drain! Another notch in my Monument to Failure.

11:58 a.m. Or maybe not. I just had this informative phone conversation with Sheeni.

"Nickie, where are you? Reverend Glompiphel just called Mother in a fit. You missed your interview appointment!"

"I'm not going, Sheeni. I've decided not to become a teen domestic slave. I'd rather starve."

"But, Nickie, what will you do?"

"I'm sorry, I can't think at the moment. I just had another sizeable illusionary fortune slip through my fingers."

"Who died this time?" she asked.

Was that sarcasm from The Woman I Love?

I told her about my near miss in the teen novelty market.

"What did you say the name of the watch was, Nickie?"

"Wart Watch."

"Wart Watch! Are you sure?"

"Did Edison recognize the cotton gin after he invented it?" I demanded.

"I believe the cotton gin was invented by Eli Whitney," replied Sheeni. "Nickie, I just read about that watch in *Time* magazine. There was a riot at a mall in St. Louis. Six parents were trampled trying to buy Wart Watches for their kids!"

"You're kidding!"

"No. It's an incredible hit. They're selling them by the millions!"

"Did you say millions?" I asked, flabbergasted.

"Nickie, don't do anything! I'll be right over."

Millions, I think I heard someone mention the word "millions."

3:20 p.m. Sixteen times, diary. But this was my first time as a wealthy person. Sheeni is magnificent. She has taken masterful charge of my affairs (both financial and carnal).

She began by calmly asking to inspect the signed royalty agreement.

"Hmm, do we really need that?" I asked nervously.

"You saved it I hope, Nickie!" she said, not so calmly.

"Certainly. It's around here somewhere. It's got to be!"

Twenty desperate minutes later, I found the precious document in the dust sleeve of my Ravi Shamar album. Sheeni read it over, smiled triumphantly, and dialed the number of American Fashions for Freedom Enterprises. This time Mario answered. I listened in on the answering machine speakerphone.

"Hello, my name is Sheeni Saunders. I'm an attorney representing Mr. Nicholas Twisp."

"Oh," said Mario. I could sense he was blinking rapidly.

"I called to inform you we shall be filing an injunction against your firm tomorrow morning in federal court in San Francisco to halt the distribution and sale of the watch my client designed."

"You can't do that!" gasped Mario. "I just signed a big order with K-Mart."

"Naturally, we would prefer to cooperate for the mutual profit of all parties. But we intend to enforce this contract."

"We, we were trying to find Nick. We didn't have his address!"

"We require an immediate accounting of all inventory, orders, sales, and accounts receivables," continued Sheeni coolly. "We need them in my office in Ukiah by 10 a.m. tomorrow. And we must have in our possession a cashier's check for the first royalty payment."

"OK," capitulated Mario. "No problem. I'll send it all by overnight mail. Is $5,000 enough?"

Five-thousand dollars!

"Certainly not," replied Sheeni. "Make it $25,000. And make the check payable to me."

"OK, OK," said Mario. "By the way. Could you fax us a copy of the alleged contract? Ours seems to be missing from our files."

"Of course," said Sheeni, "we have the signed agreement right here."

"That's, uh, fortunate," said Mario with apparent deep insincerity. "Well, tell Nick I'm sorry Kimberly gave him the runaround. She's a little stressed today. The rabbit died, if you know what I mean. I can't understand it. We were always careful too."

Sheeni said she was sorry to hear of their personal misfortune, then gave him her full name and mailing address.

"Oh Sheeni, I could kiss you!" I exclaimed, when she hung up.

"Well, who's stopping you?"

We kissed passionately, affluently.

"Sheeni," I said, coming up for air, "just one question, darling. Why did you ask to have the check made out to you?"

"For ease of cashing it, darling," she replied. "Don't forget, Nick Twisp is still wanted by the FBI."

"Oh, right. Good thinking, darling."

"Besides, darling, this arrangement will facilitate my collecting my 15 percent."

"Fifteen percent?"

"Yes, Nickie darling. That is my small fee for serving as your legal representative."

"Good thinking, darling."

Suddenly I found myself in love with a wealthy woman. Soon, I was making love to her. To celebrate the occasion, I daringly introduced another sophisticated amatory technique. Sheeni was notably (and audibly) impressed.

4:49 p.m. While Sheeni went to her dad's office to send an important fax, Carlotta hurried over to Fuzzy's house with my completed rental application. I found the hirsute youth home alone, flogging his recalcitrant muscles on his massive weight bench. He was thrilled and naturally envious to hear of my remarkable business success.

"Wow!" he exclaimed, "I'm friends with the guy who invented the Wart Watch! Wait 'til I tell everybody at school."

Alarmed, I cautioned my friend that no one but him must know.

"But why, Carlotta?" he protested.

"I can't afford any publicity," I replied. "The FBI reads the newspapers too."

"Jesus, Carlotta, you're going to end up just like Howard Hughes: a weird secret billionaire. Maybe even weirder. I don't think Howard ran around dressed like a chick."

I'm not worried. Society excuses the eccentricities of the rich. People find them charming.

6:38 p.m. Carlotta grabbed a quick dinner at the Greek diner, then strolled along Main Street to ogle the cornucopia of material wealth now open to me. In the window of a computer store, one particularly powerful laptop smiled wistfully and wagged its tiny modem port.

"Don't despair, little buddy," I whispered. "You will have a good home soon."

Farther down the street, Carlotta noticed a pleasant new sign painted in fluorescent colors on Flampert's main window: "Wart Watches!!!! Shipment expected soon. Put your deposit down now!"

Clearly, demand is far outstripping supply. That being the case, the immutable laws of economics require that we raise our prices immediately. I must make a note of that to my business partners.

7:30 p.m. Carlotta has changed her frock and freshened her make-up. I must be going. We mustn't keep the lovers waiting.

10:05 p.m. Like clockwork, diary. I really should be doing strategic work for the Pentagon. A mind as cogently ratiocinative as mine should be formulating World War III contingency plans.

Precisely at 7:59 Carlotta successfully infiltrated the Joshi backyard. As planned, the amorous poet was crouched, anxious and bookless, in the frigid darkness behind the apple tree.

"Carlotta," he whispered, "I am tormented by doubt."

"Stifle it," I growled. "There's no turning back now."

Carlotta removed her black wool scarf and tied it firmly over the poet's eyes.

"Trent, can you see anything?"

"My vision is obliterated, Carlotta. I am as sightless as Homer."

"Good."

Carlotta removed a roll of duct tape from her purse, cut off a foot-long piece, and applied it to the poet's mouth.

"Trent, can you say anything?"

"Nmnmnmnm," he replied.

"Good. Do you have your condom?"

"Nmnmnmnm."

Interpreting that as an assent, Carlotta grasped the expectant lover's arm and guided him through the shadows toward Apurva's darkened bedroom window. As we approached, the window rose silently and the odor of a seductive perfume enveloped us.

"Right on time," whispered the beautiful teen, leaning forward into the dim moonlight like a fenestral vision. How unfortunate her beloved could not gaze upon the wheatish orbs swelling enticingly above her gauzy bodice. Black mascara outlined her immense dark eyes, and her long dark tresses—brushed until they shone like rare silk—cascaded in alluringly folds over her bare shoulders.

"Has the game started?" I whispered.

"Yes, Carlotta. Can't you hear? My parents, Vijay, and Sheeni are playing in the living room. I never realized Scrabble was such a raucous pastime."

"It is when Sheeni plays," I observed.

Apurva reached down a beautiful hand. "Here, darling. Let me help you."

With Apurva tugging from above and Carlotta pushing from below, we managed to boost the blind poet in through the window.

"Forty-five minutes, Apurva," I whispered. "That's all. Sheeni's a fast winner. I'll wait here."

"Thank you, Carlotta. You're a true friend."

"Nmnmnmnm," added her fortunate consort.

Apurva closed the window, then, uncharitably, drew the drapes. Carlotta leaned against the chilly aluminum siding for the long cold wait. Five minutes later, an icy draft blowing up my pantyhose, I was startled by the sound of the gate creaking open. My heart thumped wildly as a Brobdingnagian caped figure emerged from the shadows and crept toward me. As a scream of terror aborted silently in my paralyzed diaphragm, the figure spoke.

"Carlotta, is that you?"

"Sonya?"

"Hi, Carlotta."

"Sonya! What the hell are you doing here?"

"He's in there, isn't he?"

"Yes, he is. Have you been following him again?"

"Not all the time. I love him, Carlotta. I know he is the only man I will ever love. And I can't have him."

"You're, you're not going to make a scene are you?"

"No, Carlotta. I'll be quiet. We can wait here together. You love him too, don't you?"

"Well, uh, actually . . ."

"That's OK, Carlotta. I know how you feel, girl. And if you are willing to help him be with Apurva, I can be generous too."

"That's right, Sonya. We are performing a noble sacrifice—in the tradition of noble Sidney Carton from *A Tale of Two Cities*."

"Sorry, never read it. But I know what you mean. Is your heart breaking, Carlotta?"

"I suppose so."

She embraced me in her fragrant lilacness. "We can be sisters in sorrow, Carlotta."

"Good idea, Sonya." I appreciated the ample BTUs, if not the sentiment.

"I wonder if they're doing it now?" she whispered.

"More than likely," I replied.

"A knife is stabbing me in the heart, Carlotta."

"Me too," I replied sadly. "Several rusty, blunt ones in fact."

"Shall we end it all together, Carlotta?"

"Of course not, Sonya. We'll get over it. The teen years are full of transient traumas, but people live through them. We'll be happy someday."

"Do you really think so?"

"I know it. Somewhere, some place, perhaps thousands of miles away, is the boy you're going to marry. But you don't know him and he doesn't know you. You have to live, Sonya, so you can find each other."

"I hope he's not bingeing on sweets right now. Or making it with some other girl."

"I'm sure he's not, Sonya. He's probably just as lonely and miserable as you are."

"Don't say that, Carlotta. Who wants to marry some creepy loser?"

She had a point there.

We chatted for another half hour, then, unclinching from our tropical embrace, my friend said farewell and tiptoed off into the gloom of unrequited love. Moments later, the window rose overhead and slowly disgorged two feet, two legs, a manly torso, two strong arms, and a blindfolded, tanned, godlike head.

"Goodbye, darling," called Apurva, now provocatively tousled. "I shall treasure this night always."

"Mnmnmnmn," her Romeo replied.

"Thank you, dear Carlotta," she added. "Same time next week?"

"We'll see," I replied. "It depends on your parents. They may not be anxious for a Scrabble rematch soon."

"I shall try to persuade them that it's educational," she replied, blowing a kiss to her mute, unseeing lover.

Trent waved fondly toward the garage, as I guided him through the gate and down the driveway. When we reached the safety of the street, he tore off his blindfold and gag.

"How was it?" Carlotta asked tactfully.

"Marvelous," he replied, oblivious to the large shadow lurking behind the telephone pole across the street. "Overwhelming, Carlotta. The experience was even more intense with one sense obfuscated. I am a changed man, Carlotta. I have found the meaning of life."

"Oh, really," I said, intrigued. "What's that?"

"Transcendent fusion with our reciprocal otherness."

I think the guy means sex. I could have told him that.

After a post-coital burger and fries at the Burger Hovel (Trent paid), Carlotta arrived home to find two messages on my answering machine. The first was from Fuzzy informing me that his mother would be at the house tomorrow morning at 11:30 to give Carlotta a tour, and I should make sure all my stuff was out of sight.

The second was this message from My One and Only Love: "Hi, Carlotta. I hope you're pleased with yourself. I not only lost my childhood sweetheart, but had to endure a painful Scrabble humiliation as well. Vijay's father cheats by employing many Indianisms and obscure computer terms. How I loathe those heartless machines. Come over tomorrow after breakfast and we'll wait for the express delivery person together. By the way, I told Mother you never received

Reverend Glompiphel's phone message and have been relieved of penury by an unexpected legacy. Oh, did Trent say anything about his little liaison? I am most curious. Tell me all about it tomorrow. 'Bye."

Although intended for my ears only, Trent's shockingly intimate sidewalk and corner-booth confidences will be repeated verbatim to Sheeni tomorrow. For her sake (and mine), she must know exactly where Trent stands with Apurva (and, more importantly) where and how he reclines.

THURSDAY, December 31, New Year's Eve — Consider, if you will, the morning boner. What a metaphor of hope and renewal! How can anyone give way to despair when one's groin greets each new day with such a gala spectacle of physiological optimism? And what an anatomical prod to philosophical contemplation on the final day of the year.

Twelve months ago I was a lonely, forlorn, 13-year-old virgin under the thumb of tyrannical parents. Today I am a independent, enterprising, nearly 15-year-old writer-tycoon committed to an intensely physical relationship with The Woman I Love. And my zits are not looking too horrible either.

9:37 a.m. No check yet. Refusing to panic, Sheeni and Carlotta are waiting in the little den off the entry hall—a cozy room that affords an unobstructed view of the street. In the living room Sheeni's aged mother is humming hymns and taking down the Christmas tree. Mr. Saunders is away at his office planning his first devastating lawsuits of the new year.

I have given Sheeni a full accounting of the Trent-Apurva episode. She is naturally distressed, but is taking it well. She says any feelings of jealousy are outweighed by her sympathy for the couple as victims of harsh oppression. Still, I don't think she was pleased to hear that Trent communicated with his love by tracing amorous messages on her chest.

9:59 a.m. It's here! A big package full of boring financial records, two bonus Wart Watches, and a stupendous check (all those magnificent zeroes!). We're off to the bank with the loot.

11:20 a.m. Nothing like walking in with a check for $25,000 to trigger some obsequious fawning from one's banker. As large depositors, we have been enrolled in the bank's exclusive Prestige Club, entitling us to many elite services normally enjoyed only by prominent Republicans. We have opened a joint account—another significant step, I believe, toward eventual marital union. For walking around money, we each accepted $2,000 in cash from our grateful banker.

On to the donut shop, where Carlotta bought a mixed dozen and two large coffees with a $100 bill. The grizzled regulars, in their lumpy flannel shirts and soiled caps advertising obscure brands of chainsaws, were clearly impressed. One unshaven oaf offered Sheeni $20 cash for her Wart Watch, but she politely refused. Not so sentimental, Carlotta executed the transaction with alacrity.

12:10 p.m. Fuzzy and his mom were waiting on Granny DeFalco's front porch when Carlotta and Sheeni arrived to "inspect" the premises.

"Oh, how cute!" exclaimed Carlotta, following the DeFalcos into the living room. "What lovely wallpaper! Sheeni, isn't it delightful?"

"Mesmerizing," agreed my companion. "It's so post-war."

"No," I corrected her, "surely it's pre-war."

"What war you talking about?" asked Fuzzy. "The Civil War?"

"Miss, how old did you say you were?" asked Mrs. DeFalco suspiciously.

"Twenty-four," replied Carlotta, admiring the sofa's bilious chintz. To increase my apparent age, I had borrowed a pair of Mrs. Saunders' old-lady earrings and a spritz of her obsolete perfume. "Is the lovely furniture included?"

"If you want it," replied Irene. "What did you say you did for a living?"

"It's all on my application, Mrs. DeFalco. I am an independent investor and writer. Is the kitchen that way?"

"Uh-huh. We can paint it, if you want."

The party wandered into the kitchen, where Carlotta peeked into all the cupboards and peered into all the drawers.

"No, this paint is in quite good condition," I lied. "And it coordinates so nicely with the tile and the linoleum."

"Look, Carlotta," said Sheeni, "the oven is spotless."

"Somehow I knew it would be," I replied. "Mrs. DeFalco, are the pots and pans and kitchen items included?"

"If you want them. What is it you write?"

"Literature mostly. Is the bathroom this way?"

"Uh-huh."

The inspection party trooped through the pristine bathroom and then into the bedroom, scene of recent auroral boner contemplation.

"My, what lovely clothes!" exclaimed Carlotta, opening the closet doors. "Are they included too?"

"I suppose so," said Mrs. DeFalco. "Save me the trouble of sending them to Goodwill. And they do kind of look like your style."

"The house is perfect," declared Carlotta. "I would love to rent it."

"Well, I don't know," said Mrs. DeFalco doubtfully. "We were thinking of someone older. Maybe a retired single man who could look after the place and repair a few things."

"Carlotta will pay you the first six months' rent in advance," said Sheeni.

"It's a deal!" agreed Irene.

I like a landlady who can act impulsively. I wrote out a check for $4,800 and gratefully accepted the key. Home sweet ugly home. It's mine!

2:47 p.m. Guess what I'm typing this on, diary? My new IBM-compatible 586 laptop with super-high resolution color LCD screen, 80 megabyte memory, and massive 600-megabyte hard drive. What speed! What raw power! What an imperative to creative expression!

6:14 p.m. Where did the time go? No breaks, no dinner, and here it is dark outside. Sheeni just called to say another package has arrived from Malibu.

She is bringing it right over. Damn, I hope she doesn't stay long. I am right in the middle of setting up my Windows program.

7:28 p.m. Sheeni pitched a fit and made me turn off my machine. We are going out to dinner for "a proper New Year's celebration" (her words). I think she just wants to show off her brand new sapphire necklace. It is quite a dazzler.

The Malibu mystery box contained six pairs of prototype Feetborghinis and a note from Mario explaining that someone else already owned the name Roadsters. He wants us to test-wear the automotive shoes and report on community reaction. I can already report a negative reaction from one sophisticated teen. She says car-shaped sneakers with lighted headlamps and taillamps do not coordinate with a $2,800 jeweled choker. So only Carlotta and Fuzzy will be illuminating new fashion trends this evening. My pal and junior landlord has agreed to sneak the Falcon keys and drive us all to The Spotted Owl, Ukiah's most prestigious (and expensive) luxury feedlot.

11:30 p.m. We're back. Can't write much. Rich butterfat coagulating in all arteries leading to the brain. Sheeni just called home and got permission to spend the night. Damn, no more computing tonight. I hope she's not planning on loitering around here all day tomorrow.

Feetborghinis created a sensation in the restaurant. Could be a bigger hit than Wart Watch. I must consult with Mario on battery placement though. Thin, flesh-colored wires presently run from the back of the shoes, up the legs, and terminate in small plastic battery packs strapped to the thighs with elastic garters. The packs clatter embarrassingly when one walks and tend to bruise the privates while seated. They didn't show under Carlotta's dress, but Fuzzy in trousers appeared to be suffering from a frightening case of severely dislocated and grossly swollen testicles. Perhaps the answer is a flat rechargeable battery molded into the sole.

Must end here. Sheeni just emerged from the bathroom garbed only in $2,800 of sparkling cerulean gems. Happy New Year to me!

JANUARY

FRIDAY, January 1 — Nineteen times, diary. Twice last night, as the sounds of celebratory gunshots reverberated across the valley, and once this morning in a more muted but no less explosive salvo. What a way to begin the year. It's enough to take a guy's mind off his winsome new computer.

Feeling a bit peckish after our horizontal workout, Carlotta dialed Dad's number.

"Mr. Twisp's ... residence," drawled a familiar voice.

"Mrs. Crampton?"

"No ... this is ... Mrs. Ferguson."

"Oh, right, you're married now—to that inspiring labor leader. Mrs. Ferguson, this is Carlotta Ulansky. I'd like to hire you."

"That's nice ... When?"

"Immediately. Mrs. Ferguson, can you bring over breakfast for two?"

"Sure ... thing ... Bacon and eggs ... and home fries ... and biscuits ... and homemade currant jam ... be OK?"

"Fine."

"OK, Miz Ulansky ... be right ... over."

10:30 a.m. Fully satiated, My Love has gone home, but promises to return this afternoon with "a nice surprise." My maid is doing the breakfast dishes; Carlotta is in her room resting up from a monumental caloric assault. By the way, how does one conceal one's used prophylactics from one's servants? I wonder if they have advice lines anywhere to assist the nouveau rich with acclimation queries like this?

Mrs. Ferguson reports she left a brief letter of resignation on Dad's kitchen table. Her erstwhile employer was still sacked out with my kindergarten teacher.

"I won't be ... missin' that ... Miz Sanders," said Mrs. Ferguson. "She was ... always tryin' ... to sneak ... skim milk ... into my kitchen. ... I won't ... have that blue stuff ... Not in my ... kitchen!"

That's what I like—a maid with principles.

11:45 a.m. While Mrs. Ferguson washed down the living room wallpaper, Carlotta called Joanie to wish her, Dr. Dingy, and all potential third parties a happy new year.

"Thanks, Nick," she said. "How come your voice sounds so funny?"

"How do you mean?"

"You sound just like a girl."

"Oh, that's my new voice-disguising phone," I lied. "What's new?"

"Nick, something terrible has happened to Mom's creepy husband. Lance wrote a ridiculous letter to some newspapers and now he's getting death threats. He had to go into hiding!"

"How unfortunate, Joanie. What does Mom say?"

"You know Mom, she's hysterical. Lance blames her. He claims it was really Mom's old boyfriend Wally Rumpkin who wrote the letter."

"That cowardly blackguard. What a calumny!"

"Yeah, and there's something worse too, Nick. Lance isn't being nice to little Noel. He says Noel is the ugliest baby he's ever seen."

"What slander! Of our own blood relative too. Have you seen the kid, Joanie?"

"Not in person, no. Mother sent me a photograph."

"How does he look?"

"Nick, all newborns are a little . . . well, unformed—especially premies like Noel. He's just a tiny baby. Besides, the photo was blurry."

I knew it, my stepbrother is an atrocity of nature. I hope he doesn't grow up to embarrass me when I'm famous. Or worse, expect me to support him just because he's shunned by all normal people.

1:30 p.m. Sheeni dropped by with her "nice" surprise: a small ugly black dog, his food bowl, rubber chew bone, grooming brush, flea salve, and pee-stained bed. Loathsome Albert is back. Not even Francois was pleased by his return.

"But Sheeni," Carlotta protested, "why can't he go on living at Trent's house with his good buddy Jean Paul?"

"Carlotta, you surprise me," she exclaimed. "This is our own precious love child! I should have thought you'd want him with you always. Besides, I know for a fact darling Albert chafes in the presence of that other uncouth canine. I couldn't possibly let him remain in that stressful environment another minute."

"Hi, Albert," said Carlotta grudgingly. "Remember me?"

The vile animal growled and nipped at my ankle, ripping an unsightly run in my expensive new pantyhose. The beast will pay for that transgression.

3:15 p.m. Carlotta generously gave her maid the rest of the holiday off, then accompanied Sheeni and love child on a walking tour of the deserted town. Everyone was inside watching football and gorging on fatty snacks to distract themselves from the imminent resumption of dreaded school or despised work.

As we sauntered along, Carlotta longed to take Sheeni's hand, but resisted the impulse. Ukiah, I knew, was not yet ready for open displays of lesbian regard.

"Carlotta," remarked Sheeni, "I've been going over the books. The figures are most promising. You will soon be a millionaire."

"That's nice."

"You don't sound very enthusiastic."

"I'm grateful for the fortune, Sheeni. It's just, just . . ."

"Just what?"

"Sheeni, do you realize I may have to live out the balance of my teen years as a woman? Do you comprehend what that entails?"

"Certainly, Nick. After all, it is a fate we share."

"Yes, but it's easier for you. You are emotionally and physically equipped for the role. I find it a daunting burden."

"We all have to accept some measure of compromise in our lives, Carlotta," she replied. "Try to show a little more pragmatism. Look what I've had to settle for."

"What do you mean, Sheeni?"

"Life in dreary Ukiah. And a computer-obsessed boyfriend who snores, eschews veracity, and wears a padded bra under his unfashionable dress."

As usual My One and Only Love is right. I must take a cue from Bing and count my blessings. I'm rich, intelligent, healthy, virile, not violently ugly, and enjoy the relatively unequivocal affections of one of the Outstanding Teens of this or any other epoch. I must be thankful for my good fortune. On the whole I am splendidly equipped for this great adventure we call human existence.

4:25 p.m. Thanks an existential pantsfull, Bing. I returned home to find this message on my answering machine: "Carlotta, this is Miss Pomdreck. There's a serious problem with your medical excuse. Miss Arbulash wishes to see you in the girls' locker room first thing Monday morning. Don't be late! And where is your transcript?"

"Damn," I sighed.

Albert growled and hopped up on the sofa.

"Wipe that smirk off your face," I told him.

He curled his upper lip and looked at me with contempt.

"I'll bet Miss Arbulash could use a generous sponsor to assist with her Miss Universe contest expenses," I remarked. "And as for you, Albert, I think I'll purchase a large, pure-bred doberman to keep you company."

Albert uncurled his lip and, grovelling abjectly, attempted to lick my hand.

Great Wealth: it does come in handy at times.

INTERVIEW WITH THE AUTHOR

Q: Why are your Nick Twisp novels so bleak?

CDP: Comic writing is supposed to deal with death and disaster. The trivial and the mundane are the concerns of the serious novelists.

Q: What are you trying to accomplish in your work?

CDP: I write comic novels. My intention is to amuse the reader, not harry him/her with profundities. For me, nothing induces queasiness faster than a comic writer suddenly lurching off into the quagmires of philosophy. Unlike Nick, I am not interested in creating literature with a capital L.

Q: Then your intent is completely frivolous?

CDP: Not entirely. I'm serious about creating something amusing. I'm intent on tweaking a laugh out of the reader on every page.

Q: But don't you deal with serious issues in your work?

CDP: Sure. Personally, I'd prefer to let the reader discover the themes for himself. But, if pressed, I can enumerate a few that I'm aware of. These include: The powerlessness of childhood and its incumbent terrors. The hypocrisies inherent in familial hierarchies. The tenuousness of human connection, friendship, and love. The omnipresence of loneliness. The suppression of feeling and its consequences for self-awareness. The irrelevance of ethics in an amoral world. And, of course, the ever engrossing mysteries of sex.

Q: Aren't your characters too young to be so obsessed with sex?

CDP: Hardly. Consult your own teen diaries or interview a few junior high school teachers. Fourteen is a turbulent age. Nick and his friends are rational (mostly), sexually maturing people with virtually no power to act on their desires. They have almost no control over their lives. At no other age are people in our culture so oppressed by their powerlessness and lack of privacy. Remember, for Nick that ticket to freedom called a driver's license is still two interminable years away.

Q: Why is much of the humor in your novels so juvenile?

CDP: That's called gritty realism. Let's not forget these are, at least ostensibly, the diaries of a 14-year-old boy. Youths of that age are intensely curious about theirs and other people's bodies. They have not yet learned to pretend, as adults do, that they are oblivious to bodily functions. They celebrate their bodies—even as they sometimes despair of them. Much more than adults, they are—as we say in California—*in* their bodies. So, Nick writes matter-of-factly about masturbation, regurgitation, flatulence, etc. The humor may be low, but recall what you were snickering about at that age.

Q: Why doesn't the character of Nick show more growth and change?

CDP: More uncompromising reality. Unlike creative writing teachers, I believe real people change at glacial speed—if at all. These novels cover only a few months in the life of the central character. Cathartic personal transformations in this context would seem contrived. Worse, I think they would be out of place in a comic novel.

Q: So we shouldn't expect to see any change in Nick over the course of your novels?

CDP: I'm not saying that. I think some maturation is evident from the first book to the third. If nothing else, Nick is learning how to cope (or fail to cope) in his first romantic entanglement.

Q: Aren't you just repeating yourself in the second and third books?

CDP: I don't think so. Each book stands on its own, but is part of a larger, continuing story. Each successive book introduces new themes, such as the rewards of work, labor/management relations in '90s America, the disappointments of middle age, drug use, the clash of immigrant cultures, myth making in Hollywood, the supernatural, etc.

Q: Why don't you write books with adult protagonists?

CDP: So I write about the revolts and upheavals of youth. Is that so deplorably childish?

Q: Are your characters to be taken literally as adolescents?

CDP: Well, if you've noticed, a few of them don't talk much like teenagers. It is possible, I suppose, that some of the satire in these novels is targeted at the follies of adults.

Q: Are your books intended then for adult readers?

CDP: That's right. I doubt many teenagers would find much of interest in them.

Q: How do you reply to the criticism that your novels objectify women?

CDP: Even in Berkeley, where I once lived, one would be hard-pressed to discover many 14-year-old male feminists. Nor is this age group celebrated for its freedom from racial bias, ageism, gayism, or fatism. Nick reflects the prejudices and confusions of his times, his class, and his particular circumstances. Readers wearing the blinders of political correctness are apt to find these novels objectionable.

Q: Why do you think some publishers would be reluctant to publish your books?

CDP: Questions of merit aside, I think they tend to fall between the cracks. I'm speaking here of my novels, not the publishers. They are not quite earnestly high-brow enough for the literary guys and suspiciously esoteric for the mass-market folks. There is also the cocktail party factor to consider.

Q: What is that?

CDP: I don't think editors like to go to cocktail parties and admit they have just signed a book that deals with pimples, competitive self-abuse, and Peyronie's disease. No one likes to appear ridiculous before his/her colleagues.

Q: How many more Nick Twisp novels do you intend to write?

CDP: Very likely none.

Q: Do you have anything more to say?

CDP: If you mean in this interview, the answer is no.